Julie Bozza

The Definitive
Albert J. Sterne

Manifold Press

Published by Manifold Press

ISBN: 978–1–908312–99–0

Proof–reading and line editing:
Chapters by Thalia Communications | thaliacomm.net
Stories by PSD and Fiona

Editor: Fiona Pickles

For further details of Manifold Press titles both in print and forthcoming: manifoldpress.co.uk

Other titles by Julie Bozza:
    Homosapien … a fantasy about pro wrestling
    The Valley of the Shadow of Death
    Butterfly Hunter

ACKNOWLEDGEMENTS

Julie wishes to thank Annie,
who had a lot of input
and influence along the way

NOTES

This edition of the novel *The Definitive Albert J. Sterne*
incorporates the stories first published separately in the ebook
Albert J. Sterne: Future Bright, Past Imperfect,
in line with Julie's original intentions

PROLOGUE
NEW ORLEANS
OCTOBER 1971

"No, don't send us Albert!" McIntyre blurted down the phone from New Orleans. "I mean, sir," he continued in a more reasonable protest, "there must be someone else available – anyone else available …"

"Albert Sterne is the best forensics man here at headquarters," Jefferson replied in weary and resentful tones. Perhaps he was tired of defending a subordinate for whom he had no respect. "That makes him the best in the FBI."

"He's only the best because he's incapable of a relationship with anyone still breathing!"

Jefferson appeared rather taken aback by this assertion.

Albert moved around the desk to stand closer to the speaker phone. "You've been listening to scurrilous gossip again, McIntyre. You don't have the imagination to have thought of that yourself."

McIntyre groaned down the phone. "What the hell are you doing there, Albert?"

"I thought that much was obvious: being briefed to join you in New Orleans. It seems you are yet again in need of some expert assistance."

"Then, God love me, pack your knives and drills. We've got a live one here."

"I thought," Albert said deliberately, "you had three dead ones – the latest of which happened since the case was assigned to your superiors."

"You arrogant bastard, you get on the next flight down and help us catch the damned perp."

"Yes." Then Albert added, "You'd best remember that Jefferson is too incompetent to warn people they are on the speaker phone. Next time there might be someone present whose feelings can be hurt."

"Next time it might be someone *with* feelings –" Deadly silence. "You can't possibly have just said that in front of the man." And McIntyre hung up the phone.

"These emotional Irish," Albert commented. "They expend so much energy in the wrong directions."

"Mr. Sterne," Jefferson began in tones of umbrage.

"Yes." Albert was once more facing him across the desk, eyes intent and expression implacable.

"You have a mighty high opinion of yourself for a youngster."

"I'm twenty–four, hardly a youngster. And I simply endeavor to fulfill my potential."

"Is that so?" Jefferson considered the man for a few moments longer. Perhaps anyone else would have exhibited some discomfort, some tension at being the object of such attention, but not Albert. In fact, it was a common story around HQ that, after his last blood pressure test, Jefferson's doctor had warned him off smoking, drinking, and dealing with Albert Sterne. "Don't believe for a moment that I won't report this to the Director. The plane leaves in an hour," Jefferson added, his white mustache quivering with anger. "Dismissed!" And, as Albert reached the door, Jefferson muttered with what sounded like genuine regret, "If we were at war, I could have you shot for insubordination."

Albert snorted. "If I had the time to contradict everything in that rather absurd statement, I'm sure we'd both benefit. But I have a plane to catch."

"You never did," McIntyre said as Albert strode up to him at the New Orleans airport. "Tell me Jefferson left the room before you said he was incompetent."

Albert looked the man over, and turned away with a sneer. McIntyre, a scruffy version of the FBI–clone at the best of times, had become distinctly bedraggled under the influence of the Louisiana humidity. Albert, used to traveling around the States in all seasons, had no trouble adapting to the climate here, even though it was a contrast to the fall weather in Washington DC. "You have some work for me," Albert prompted.

"First you explain why he didn't fire you."

"Jefferson is so ineffectual he couldn't fire a card–carrying communist from the Bureau. He won't talk to the Director about me for fear of highlighting his own inadequacies."

"You son–of–a–bitch," McIntyre said admiringly. It was the first appreciative tone of voice he'd used to or about Albert since they'd met when training at Quantico. "I could almost begin to like you."

"That would obviously be one of your more pointless ventures, as there is no chance of me returning the compliment. You have corpses for me to examine, I believe. Have the locals already done irredeemable damage to the crime scenes, or is it worth my while to investigate them as well?"

"If I were a masochist, I could like you." McIntyre sighed. "Okay, can we do all this with a minimum of garbage?"

"I'm here to do a job, as I trust you are."

"That never stopped you from taking every opportunity to be thoroughly obnoxious, on the job or off. In fact –" and the Irishman unconsciously shifted to a more aggressive stance – "if you weren't so damned good –"

"I don't have time for your inept analysis. Take me to the morgue, and let's see whether you've improved at all. I'm glad I can safely assume the investigation isn't solely in your hands."

It seemed as if McIntyre's temper was about to brim over, but he made the effort to swallow back a variety of retorts. "Baggage?" he asked tersely.

"I have it with me."

"Come on." And McIntyre led the way out through the concourse. Once they were in the car, he said, "You've read the reports I sent."

"Give me a summation. Then tell me what your superiors left off the record."

McIntyre heaved another sigh but as he pulled the car out onto the street he began to provide an overview of the case, and of how the police and the Bureau had each handled it. The victims had all been young women, and all black – and McIntyre added that surely none had deserved such a ghastly death. Albert had a number of detailed questions about the killer's MO, in the midst of which the Irishman protested, "I suppose you've had it all knocked out of you, with what you see every day, but this sort of thing keeps me awake at night."

"Then you don't belong in the FBI."

"Yes, I do," McIntyre insisted. "Or I'm going to, come hell or high water." Shrugging, he added, "So maybe I have to learn how to care a little less – but God save me from caring as little as you do. That isn't the answer."

"But I do, of course, care," Albert said dryly, "or I wouldn't have chosen this field of work."

"The way you behave –"

"Why don't you return to a topic of which you have a slightly better grasp," Albert pointedly interrupted, "and one of far more pressing relevance."

McIntyre cast him a disgruntled stare then took up where he'd left off, with the similarities of MO between the victims, before going on to describe the few differences. "We're here," McIntyre finally said. "The local medical examiner's offices. I'll tell you the rest after."

They left the car in the parking lot of the adjacent hospital, and walked in silence to a low brick building.

"Hey, Albert," McIntyre said as they reached the entrance. He waited until Albert impatiently turned to him. "Not that you owe me, but is there any chance of you doing me one small favor?"

"What would that be?"

The direct sunlight bleached all the color from the larger man, but his discomfort was betrayed in his stance and his tone. "Just be polite for once, would you? For a few lousy hours while we get through this."

"Don't waste my time, McIntyre." Albert walked into the offices, pulling off his dark glasses as the light abruptly dimmed. There was a smell, both cold and spicy, familiar from morgues and hospital basements and medical examiners' labs across the United States. Albert breathed it in, and strode through the foyer.

"Fuck you, too," McIntyre was muttering behind him.

A small neatly dressed woman attempted to shake Albert's hand before he got any further. Her black hair was drawn into a severe chignon at the nape of her neck, her bearing and clothes were precise and contained, but her large violet eyes betrayed her into attractiveness.

"Celia, this is Albert Sterne. Albert, this is Dr. Celia Mortimer. She's in charge here, and has been assisting us until you could arrive."

"Let's get to work," Albert said, ignoring the social niceties. "Where do you have the corpses?"

The woman began, "Mr. Sterne, if you would –"

McIntyre exclaimed, "God preserve me, is it too much to ask –"

"I'm here to do a job, McIntyre, and that is all. Stop making me repeat myself, and stop getting in my way."

"If you'd listen for just one minute, you arrogant bastard, I'll –"

Dr. Mortimer interrupted the Irishman, placing her hand on his arm. "Mac, it's all right. Mr. Sterne, we have an autopsy room ready for you. If you'd come this way." She led them off down a cross–corridor. "Mac, will you be attending the procedure?"

"I suppose I should," the man said glumly, trailing after them.

Albert caught the tail end of a shared smile, and groaned. "McIntyre, you're wasting my time asking me to be polite, for the sake of an infatuation with the doctor?" They had reached the prep room, where Albert and Celia began cleaning up. Albert pulled on a lab coat over his suit. "You must be trying to prove something trite like opposites attract."

"I'm going to kill you, Albert, when we're done here."

Celia was trying not to show her amusement. "Never mind, Mac, he's only the second one to work out your secret." The Irishman's color, still high from the heat outside, brightened. Celia asked, "Have you eaten at Tipitina's yet?"

But there wasn't time for more – Albert had swept into the autopsy room. As Celia trotted after him, there was the crash of steel tools against the tiled floor as Albert made room for his own instruments. McIntyre swallowed convulsively, crossed himself, muttered a brief prayer that he wouldn't either throw up or lose his temper with Albert in front of the lady, and followed them in.

It was Albert's second night in New Orleans and he finally had some time to himself after thirty hours of work, interrupted only by two hours of sleep on a cot in the morgue. The reports were complete, listing all the factual details and briefly explaining the deductions he'd made; the evidence was neatly bagged or bottled and labeled; the last of the photographs were being processed. Dr. Celia Mortimer hadn't done a bad job on her own while waiting for expert assistance, Albert grudgingly admitted to himself. The case was, for now, the province of McIntyre and the special agents. There would be work for Albert tomorrow, or when they found further evidence of the offender, but tonight Albert was free from official responsibilities.

He had time available, in a large city away from Washington. He had plans, and he would put off the necessity of sleep for a few hours until he could see them through.

A certain amount of discretion, if not complete anonymity, seemed wise, so Albert took two different taxis and a circuitous route for the trip to the French Quarter. Then he walked up three blocks, and across two, before choosing a seedy hotel at random, though he signed the register in his own name.

He glanced briefly around the drab little room for which he'd just paid a small fortune and walked over to push at the mattress. The chenille cover was rough, patched and of indeterminate color, and the bed itself rocked from leg to leg, though the mattress seemed surprisingly firm. Albert grimaced, then cast an even more critical eye at the mirror.

For a while he stared at his image, discovering anew all the crude imperfections. It had been years since Albert was prey to the disappointments and self–consciousness that were an inevitable part of struggling through the transition from child to adult. But he could regret that he was driven to this, impatient with the undeniable need in him even as he recognized that it should be one of the more joyous qualities of being human.

Joy was not the prevailing emotion of those he soon walked amongst. It took a careful thirty minutes to find an option he thought even remotely possible.

"You looking to party?" the young man asked.

When Albert drew off his dark glasses, his companion politely followed suit, tucking his own into the back pocket of his jeans. Albert considered the figure before him, stepping to one side for the full effect of the late–setting sun's illumination: male, of primarily Hispanic background; eighteen or perhaps nineteen, which was getting old to be on the game; one–seventy, an inch taller than Albert; light brown and dark brown. Further than that: undernourished, and had been for months if not years; clothes old and torn, though fairly clean and assembled with a harmony of color; eyes too bright; demeanor anxious, assessing. Some might have considered the haunted expression romantic, those who thought fey meant something more whimsical than the tragedy of 'fated to die'. But Albert was instead drawn by the spark of intelligent curiosity.

"If party is a euphemism for having sex," Albert said, "then, yes, I do want to. Frankly, I have no idea why else I'd be approaching you."

"Well, I don't do cops." Though he continued to hold Albert's gaze in what seemed a challenge, rather than turn away.

"I'm not a cop, I'm federal, so the petty crime of prostitution is somewhat beneath my jurisdiction. Apart from which, I'm off–duty."

The young man laughed humorlessly. "So you're the first cop I've met who didn't take the job home with him every night."

"Are you interested in earning your drug money or not?"

The too–bright eyes sharpened. "Is that an accusation?"

Albert heaved a sigh and feigned patience. "The Drug Enforcement Administration has jurisdiction over narcotics violations. I assure you I simply want to … party."

After a long moment of parried stares, the younger man quirked a weary smile. "Then, G–man, I'm your boy."

"Hardly. As opposed to most of your colleagues who would not have reached the age of consent in the most liberal of states."

The smile turned to a frown, more deeply felt. "That a problem for you? Me being older, I mean."

"Quite the opposite."

"Fine. So where are we going?"

"I have a room at the Oberon."

"Obviously a man of style."

"Amazing," Albert commented as he turned to walk beside the youngster. "A two–bit street brat capable of irony."

"You think we're all too stupid?"

"Whoring is hardly the career choice of an intelligent person."

"Yeah, well, that goes both ways – slumming it with the likes of me is hardly the most intelligent way of getting laid. But you enjoy the dirty end of town, huh?"

"Unfortunately, that rather depends on you."

"That so," the kid said flatly. He paced along at Albert's side for a few minutes, silent, arms folded and shoulders huddled. The swift twilight descended, and the city seemed to breathe easier.

Now that he had the briefest chance to reflect, Albert found himself glad this was a man he was about to have sex with. He had considered himself bisexual ever since he was old enough to think the issue through, to realize all the implications of his sometimes wayward urges – but somehow it was reassuring right now that this was someone of his own gender.

When they reached the hotel entrance, the younger man came to an abrupt halt and cast a defiant glance at Albert. "Let's talk money, princess."

Albert let a beat go by. "That endearment at least had the benefit of surprise. How much do you propose charging for further blandishments?"

The kid looked askance at Albert, and said, "Depends what you want to do, and how long it takes."

"Nothing out of the ordinary, and maybe an hour or two."

"Fifty."

"Cheap, aren't you?"

The sullenness grew irritated. "What the hell is your problem, princess?"

Albert didn't break the silence. Instead he indicated the hotel with a nod of his head, and led the way through the foyer. Within moments he was standing just inside the door to the shabby room he'd rented, watching the hooker glance around in much the same way as Albert had when he'd first entered.

It wasn't that he didn't know what he wanted, or that he was unsure of the mechanics of it all, but Albert lacked the experience to know just how to proceed with this boy. Albert's one vanity was a wish never to lose his dignity. That was proving damnably difficult right now – he had an overwhelming need, and was vastly unsure how to go about meeting it. He started by saying, "Tell me your name."

The boy looked at him, giving little away. "Rick. Ricardo."

"Mine is Albert."

"Really?" The laughter did nothing to ease the atmosphere, though it was friendly enough. "I guess you didn't make that up."

"I wouldn't bother lying to you."

"Yeah, yeah, I know, I'm not important enough to lie to. Well, get down to business, or talk for two hours – it still costs fifty."

"I can imagine places more conducive to conversation, if that was my intent."

"So, are you coming over here? Or do you have a kink for doing it against the door?"

Silence again. Albert watched as Rick paced closer. All the biological knowledge in the world, all his experience in analyzing human behavior, couldn't have prepared him for this, Albert knew, though he resented the fact. He absently cataloged the physical effects of Rick's presence: a light sweat; a terrible trembling trying to invade his limbs; helium in the space that his brain used to occupy. Why should this unnerve him, when facing down the FBI's Most Wanted was so easy? There was little sense to it.

Then Rick's hands were sliding up the front of Albert's shirt onto his shoulders, running firmly down Albert's arms, pushing his jacket off as they went. Smooth, Rick caught up the jacket before it fell, casting it across the nearby chair. Then the hands began to slowly but insistently work at the belt and fly of Albert's trousers.

"You're very practiced," Albert said. "How many thousand men has it been?"

"Enough to pay the rent," was the mild reply.

"Women, too?"

"If they have the money, I don't argue. More men than women, though."

The hands reached up to loosen Albert's tie, pull it free. It was tossed to land by the jacket. And then Rick leaned in closer, hands sliding to Albert's waist. Their faces were no more than a breath apart now. As Albert leaned his head back against the door, Rick followed him, his lips ready. But when Albert neglected to seek a kiss, Rick instead offered the caress of skin against skin, gently rubbing his face against Albert's cheek, then his throat, stretching and twisting like a cat. Albert let out a helpless groan.

Still taking his time, the younger man began to ease lower, his face and hands chasing down sensation. Albert found the rates of his heart and his breathing almost alarming. It was all far, far too much.

"No," he said. But his trousers and shorts were already dropped to his thighs, and Rick was kneeling on the floor. "No."

"Hey, you're ready for me." The voice was edged with impatience.

And the mouth engulfed him before Albert could think of any other way to delay this. Wet warmth, hot pressure. The skilled sweep of a tongue. Fingers searching.

Albert reached to fit his hand at the nape of Rick's neck, the sheer sensuality of it all shaking him, the craving in him letting loose. For one moment, he ruthlessly held the boy in place and thrust deeper into his mouth – and then it happened. The white hot gold of orgasm suffused him. Albert cried out, and surrendered.

The sensations were still echoing through him when Albert opened his eyes and frowned down at the boy.

"You certainly were ready for me, huh? That didn't even take a minute."

"You surprised me," Albert said wryly.

"So, you want to pay up for another round?"

"If you think I'm satisfied with that for fifty dollars, you're gravely mistaken."

"I must say, most of my clients manage a little more control."

"I must have been overcome by your manifest charms."

"Sure you were." Rick gave him a sour grin, stood up. Although it was Albert who was half naked, his remaining clothes in disarray, it was Rick who seemed embarrassed. "What next?"

Albert reached to run his knuckles down the boy's cheek. It had been a couple of days since Rick had last shaved, though the re–growth was soft. Judged purely objectively, with the gauntness fleshed out and the eyes no longer betraying his addiction, Rick would be considered handsome. More importantly to Albert, the boy was smart, curious. And, when he forgot to play the obedient little hooker, he was sharp. "You have your charms," Albert said. "You have as many capabilities and possibilities as any other human being."

"You think so," Rick said flatly, uninterested.

"I love you."

Rick eyed him as if Albert had announced he was visiting from Mars. Silence for a few heartbeats. "A few years ago," the boy finally said, "maybe I would have high–tailed it out the door, hearing that."

"But now you're older and somewhat wiser. You don't scare quite so easily. Perhaps you're even listening to me."

"What do you want, Albert?"

"What do I want? To lose my virginity in style. Whatever you cost."

"Are you – ? Shit, no, you're not kidding. You don't kid around at all, do you? Jesus." Rick shook his head as if to settle the knowledge. "I'm honored, or whatever."

"I'm not interested in your sentimentality."

"Then let's talk money again, princess."

"Another fifty," Albert said. "That's more than reasonable."

"All right. Tell me what you want – I bet you've got this all planned."

"Get your clothes off, Ricardo, and come to the bed." Despite the years of speculation, what Albert wanted this first time was simple enough: the feel of a naked body against his, moving in a dance as old as humanity.

He lay over the hooker, concentrating on the touch and push of skin against the length of his own skin, arching up, then down again to undulate in complex rhythmic thrusts. Coaxing the flesh below his to mirror his need, letting the Louisiana heat inspire him. Learning all the while.

At last Rick murmured, "Man, that's sexy."

"You like this?"

The hooker laughed at the naivety inherent in the words, the tone. "Of course, you moron. I'm not immune to getting it on with the right guy." He groaned as Albert bent to meet his mouth with his own, groaned through the inexpert but needy kiss. When they broke apart, Rick panted, "For a hundred, you reckon I should fake it?"

"No. I want you to shut up and bring that limited attention span to bear on this." And Albert kissed him again.

For once, the boy obeyed without question.

Albert lay on the bed, not bothering to untangle the sheet from his waist. He cast a sharp eye over it, observed with distaste, "Perhaps I should have paid extra for clean linen."

Rick, having pulled on his jeans, was sitting in the chair in the corner, smoking a cigarette. The boy lit a fresh one from the butt of the last, unaware that Albert's scrutiny had turned to him. He was lost in his own thoughts. Perhaps he was bored.

It was fully dark now, and the shabby room was lit only by the lamp beside the bed, the light globe of low wattage. It left the shadows so dull that Albert could barely see Rick's face, even when the boy inhaled and the cigarette glowed bright for a moment.

"You're killing yourself," Albert said.

"These things? I'm not going to be around long enough to die from lung cancer."

"Exactly. You have the intelligence, the resources to do something with your life. Yet you choose to do this."

"Hey, it wasn't exactly a choice, princess. But, like I said, it pays the rent."

"You have choices, Ricardo. You make things happen. You should think about why you're doing this to yourself."

"Huh. If it wasn't for guys like you, I wouldn't even have this option."

"That's something I chose to do that I certainly must think about."

Rick stared at him for a long moment. "I've met some weird people, Albert, and some with crazy kinks to them. But you're something else again." He sighed. There was a small bottle of bourbon on the floor beside him that Rick had phoned down for with Albert's permission. Rick broke the cap open and poured a generous nip into the glass from the bathroom. "Look – I never was very interested in school and the one thing I figured I was good at, they told me I was crap. Then I could never be bothered holding a job down for more than a week. I ended up in reform school, graduated with very little effort to prison, picked up a nice little drug habit. There's a million like me out there. So, you tell me the answer."

"You're clever enough to work it out for yourself, Ricardo. It wouldn't mean anything if I simply told you."

"Leave me alone, then, damn you. Jesus, no need to tell *me* hookers have a short half–life."

"What's that? A little graveside humor?"

Rick stood, started gathering up the rest of his clothes. "You owe me a hundred, G–man. For that, you got to use my body, you even got to insult me, but I draw the line at being psychoanalyzed."

"It's hardly psychoanalysis, you sad little idiot, I'm simply trying to help you see the truth. If you want to kill yourself inch by inch, day by day – you have to at least see that it's your choice."

"No way." The boy was fully dressed now. "I've had this too many times – you're taking all your problems out on me, just because you hate being queer. Well, I've put up with more than a C–note's worth of crap already."

Albert hadn't moved during this tirade. He said evenly, "I'm sure you've experienced what you describe a thousand times, but that's not what you're seeing now. You're deliberately misunderstanding me."

"I don't reckon anyone could understand you if they tried."

"Therefore I turn to your cheap charms in desperation."

"You bastard."

"You did say that for a hundred I got to insult you."

"Give me the money, and I'm out of here."

Albert climbed from the bed, at ease with his nudity, and took the wallet from his jacket pocket. "Here," he said, handing over the bills. "I'd give you more, but that wouldn't help you."

Rick let out an exasperated laugh. "Sure it wouldn't."

"Why won't you see the truth? You take responsibility for your life –" Albert grabbed the boy's shoulders, spoke fiercely – "you do that, and I'll help you. But not until then."

"Fine." Rick pulled away, stalked to the door, stuffing the bills into a hip pocket. "Don't call me, and I surely won't call you."

"Goodbye, whore."

"Go to hell, princess." The door slammed. Albert was alone.

McIntyre had insisted on accompanying Albert through check–in, and then all but physically dragged him to the airport bar. Albert, having failed to shake the man off, ignored both him and the offer of a drink.

"I'm in love," the Irishman declared. "So quit glaring."

"If humanity would stop using excuses like that for getting its own way, the world would be much improved."

"What the hell do you care about the world?"

Albert stared at this stupid, sweaty, rumpled man. "If you're referring to humanity as opposed to the planet, it's the only thing I care about."

McIntyre's whisky was swallowed in two gulps – he called for another. "What a load of garbage," he said. "If you care about people so much, why is it your mission in life to make as many of them as miserable as possible?"

"You're incapable of grasping the subtleties and the reasons behind what I am."

"I honestly have no idea why they recruited you, Albert, or how you got through the assessments."

"It was simple: they only had to compare me to mediocrities like you."

"But you're good, that's the problem," McIntyre rambled on, letting the insults slide. Apparently he had a second opinion on his own merits now, after all. "We wouldn't have caught that bastard without the work you did." And he added in a deceptively quiet tone, "Celia was impressed. She said she never would have thought to –"

"I can do without endorsements from people who are so pathetic as to return your affections."

McIntyre grasped his second glass of whiskey, and sat in silence for a while. He laughed as he remembered his hidden agenda for this enforced socializing. "I'm heartily sorry to say I owe you one, Albert. After all, there aren't many people who could make me look good by comparison, but somehow you managed it. Like you said, that's a turnaround from Quantico – though I don't know why it surprises me, now I think about it."

Albert stared at the man. "You can't possibly be suggesting I would change my behavior simply to assist your romantic interests. That's ludicrous."

"I never said you did it deliberately. Celia talked about you all night, you know. She said you were to be pitied, that your anger simply indicates –"

"Dr. Mortimer was the least benighted person I had the misfortune to encounter in New Orleans – despite subjecting me to her pop psychology behind my back. I would hardly have promoted the suggestion that she commence a relationship with you."

"Yeah," McIntyre smiled. "She's one hell of a woman, ain't she?"

"You're impossible," Albert snapped. And he successfully ignored McIntyre until his flight to Washington was called.

THE RENDING OF CLOTH
NEW YORK CITY
OCTOBER 1952

Albert Sterne often examined what little he could remember of his parents, scrupulously reviewing each detail, to guard against idealizing them all these years later. Despite this distrust of the rose–colored tricks his mind could play on him, all his memories of them were good – until just a few days after his fifth birthday, when he recalled them lying pale and beaten and bloody on the living room rug.

Before disaster had befallen them, Rebecca and Miles Sterne had been handsome people. The incontrovertible proof of that was in the two photographs their son had. One was a formal shot, with baby Albert looking solemn, and his parents stiff and uncomfortable in a set pose and their good but somber clothes. Miles and Rebecca had perhaps felt that some record of those early years was needed.

The other photo was a still bought from a newspaper by one of his well–meaning relatives after his parents were dead. A journalist had come down to the soup kitchen during the last month of their lives, wanting to interview this couple who had chosen hard labor over the ease of wealth. Albert remembered the moment captured by the journalist's accompanying photographer, remembered it in great detail, perhaps because of the jolt of this evidence.

The young Albert sat at the table by the window, close to his parents but out of people's way. He was looking through a book of children's tales. If he concentrated, he could read the stories with little trouble, or at least enough of each sentence to guess the rest. He preferred the stories that his parents recounted to him, but far too many of the words in their books were beyond his reading skills, if not his comprehension. Rebecca and Miles, he only appreciated later, had an unusual facility with language – they told wonderful long rambling stories to him, and within their context he learned so much of words and of people.

Unlike these tales he was now supposed to occupy himself with: they were simple and obvious, and Albert suspected the characters were mere fantasy. He certainly couldn't see himself talking and acting like this

Prince Florian, for instance. Even his cousin Howard wasn't quite such an idiot.

There were plenty of distractions today. Albert kept at least half his attention on the reporter, listening to the questions he asked. When it became apparent that Rebecca and Miles were too busy, the man began to interview the people who came there for food, homing in on the regulars. The photo showed him talking to two of the older women, with Albert at the next table, and his parents in the background, serving up the good thick soup and the bread, long plain aprons emphasizing their tall frames.

"And what do you think of these people, the Sternes?" asked the journalist.

Albert considered the question pretty weak, even for an opening, but it touched a chord with one of the women. She pinched her mouth together and sniffed, as if she refused to speak ill of them despite all she thought. It didn't, however, take much badgering to start her off. "If you ask me," she said in a high tone, "they're too big for their boots."

The reporter grinned a little, managing to hide it from everyone but the watchful Albert.

"They come here all humble, saying they want to help us poor souls, but anyone can tell they reckon they're better than us."

"And why shouldn't they?" the other woman broke in. Albert recognized her as one of the twice–a–weekers. "They aren't stuck up, don't listen to her. They just mind their own business – and we'd all be a lot better off if there was more of that." She added, obviously for the benefit of the first woman, "We could do with a little more gratitude, too."

Miles had come over later and advised Albert, "Don't get impatient with the book until you can read it all. Then you can move on to something more suitable." The boy must have cast him a rebellious glare, because his father sat by him and explained, "You have to take these matters in stages, one step after another. There's a logic to it, a reason behind it. You can't read Dostoevsky until you've read everything in between – starting with this."

Overhearing them, the photographer laughed heartily at the thought of little Albert reading the great Russian masters. Albert glared even harder and made a promise to himself: he'd read Dos–toy–whatever–it–was by the time he was twelve, no matter what.

The journalist's article reported on what his parents did – the kitchen, the classes for the street children in the afternoon, the support for people escaping a ruined Europe, the peers they assisted in business and politics – and quoted what people said of the Sternes, but it failed to really grasp who they were. The description of this aloof pair was ambivalent in its praise. Albert imagined Rebecca and Miles at a loss trying to deal with the stranger's prying questions.

With hindsight, it was as if Hitler's death camps and Truman's atomic bombs had seared their nerve endings, and the hurt of it would never heal. Maybe they felt responsible for the whole mess of the world, and needed to atone. Albert sometimes wondered how they'd had the faith to bring a child into such hopelessness, where they'd found the courage to love him so deeply, only two years after Hiroshima and Nagasaki had been devastated by the Sternes' adopted homeland.

Other than the money they kept aside to put Albert through school and college, they used their own wealth, inherited and earned, to do these charitable things, having left their academic and political ambitions behind them in the years before Albert was born. They didn't waste their time or money on traveling; so, except in his imagination, all Albert knew was Brooklyn with its little shops and apartments, its trees struggling out of the sidewalk, and its narrow houses with what Miles called pocket handkerchief gardens.

It seemed Rebecca and Miles had decided they couldn't change the world, but they could at least work to make it less harsh on some. And, while helping the less fortunate seize or regain some control of their lives, while trying to counteract the evil circumstances people found themselves in, Rebecca and Miles took care of themselves and of Albert. The three of them were responsible for themselves and each other – and they needed no one else.

Albert's early childhood was mostly vague impressions. The love between his parents, and their love for Albert, was strong and constant and inviolate. But none of them were ever very demonstrative, there were never any displays of sentiment. The love was simply there as the foundation of everything they did, all the choices they made, the way they kept company only with each other, the scrupulous care taken to ensure that Albert had everything he needed to grow into everything he could be.

There were hazy moments he could remember. Albert, curled up in his father's lap, listening to Rebecca's calm voice tell the story of an old friend, long dead; Miles as rapt as the boy. The three of them being polite at some obscure relative's afternoon tea, then mischievously sharing their boredom with each other through grimaces and raised eyebrows behind the woman's back – they had gone home and read all evening, happy in their shared silence. Both of his parents a little giddy, someone having talked them into a fine restaurant on their twelfth wedding anniversary, dressing in their usual dull clothes – but Miles had bought Rebecca a silk scarf. The dark green of it picked out the reddish tint to her brown hair, which she left loose for once. Her eyes had glowed.

Late that night, she clutched the scarf in her dead hand and wouldn't let it go.

When theorizing, the cops fastened on the poor of the soup kitchen with all the determination of the unimaginative – his parents had, it seemed, raised the resentment of some street bum, with their un–Christian wealth and their patronizing airs. And if not one of the down–and–outs, then it must have been a robber surprised at their unexpected return to the apartment, panicking into violence.

Years later Albert, with studies in forensics and criminal psychology and an FBI career behind him, would find sounder theories. It was more likely that their murderer was a person Rebecca and Miles knew well, or perhaps they had been carefully selected by someone falling into the broad category of psychopath. Few murders were random or motiveless in 1952, and very few surprised robbers or resentful bums had the resources for quite that much blood–spilling. Besides which, he and old Aunt Rose had discovered the bodies an hour or two later, and there had been nothing missing from the apartment, nothing disturbed except by the violence. One of the neighbors had heard a scuffle, a cry of protest – but Miles had been knocked unconscious and Rebecca had her throat slit too quickly for much of a fight.

Albert had never believed in a God he was not even allowed to name. Rebecca and Miles had done all their good works in honor of the Holy One, and for humanity. But Albert had never felt their religious faith, had never seen anything in their hearts but a pure love for him and a saddened love for troubled humanity. The simple rituals of their religion were only dusted off when in company. Perhaps they doubted, in the face of all the world had become, and inadvertently hid their faith as well as their doubts from their son.

There was a gentle joke that Rebecca sometimes shared with Miles and Albert, when they came across someone hopelessly muddled with religion: "He needs his faith and reason reconciled," Rebecca would lament with a mock sigh. "Albert, fetch our *Guide of the Perplexed*."

It had been years before Albert had realized with some disappointment that the title wasn't born of his parents' wry and wistful humor. There was indeed such a book, written in the Middle Ages, purporting to list the thirteen principles of faith of a good Jew.

The wake for Rebecca and Miles was a quiet, understated affair. Albert was expected to sit through hours on a bench, the closed caskets on a dais before him. They were lying there, his dead parents, in wood boxes. Macabre. There was material draped over the coffins; one piece a plain red clashing with the polished maple, the other a muddy green, and a small cluster of cream–colored flowers on each. The room itself was plain; unornamented benches, off–white walls, and glass in the windows that filtered out the warmth of the sunlight. Uninspired organ music drifted through speakers tucked away high in the corners, repeating the same tunes every forty–three minutes.

What must have been hundreds of people filed through over the long hours of the day. There was a handful of the poor and homeless, uncomfortable but determined to show respect. And a host of distant relatives, doing the right thing by their kin. Then there were the immigrants and the children, the businessmen and the politicians. The social workers and the doctors. Tens and hundreds of mourners.

But none of them cried. They signed the book, stood before the coffins for a while, wandered over to speak to their acquaintances in whispers, patted Albert on the head as if he could be dismissed that easily – then left as soon as their consciences set them free. They all wore the little round hat, the yarmulke; most of them, unused to the custom, having been handed one at the door. Some of the Jewish faithful had a torn ribbon pinned to their lapels to symbolize the rending of cloth – but they wore it as if it were a decoration rather than an expression of grief. Most of the people, whatever their beliefs, wore dark clothes.

Albert quickly grew to hate the hushed voices, the muted tone of the whole thing. Except for the somber clothes, this wasn't what his parents were truly about. Yes, they might have appeared to these people as quiet and sober and dispassionate. It may have been assumed they were devoted to the One God and Torah, the One Law. They might be thought to be facing Judgment now, after the death of their earthly bodies. But none of this reflected the Rebecca and Miles he had known.

As the morning stretched into afternoon, Albert wondered which of his parents was in which box. It seemed right, somehow, for his mother to be in the one with the green shroud over it. For a while, as he kicked his feet in small precise arcs, he thought over this instinct. Until he remembered the night they died. He looked up and saw Aunt Rose standing a few feet away with one of the funeral home attendants.

"Does she still have the scarf?" he asked her.

After he'd walked over and repeated the question, all Rose said was, "What scarf, dear?" Looking all gray and tired and befuddled.

Albert sighed, impatient. "The green scarf Miles bought for their anniversary. Rebecca should have it with her."

"I don't know."

"It was in her hand. Did they just put them in the coffins like that, or what?"

Aunt Rose, at last, looked close to tears. "I don't know, Albert," she repeated. She cast an unnerved glance around for help.

The young attendant, who had withdrawn a little, came to her rescue. He said, "Come and sit down here, Mr. Sterne."

For a breathless moment Albert thought he was referring to Miles, but then truth shattered the hope. It was the first time anyone had called Albert that. He shot a steady glare at the man to let him know that, despite being only five, he wasn't easily fooled. "I've been sitting all day," he said ungraciously.

"Maybe you won't mind if I sit, even so." Perched on one of the benches and leaning forward, the young man was at eye level with Albert. More adult games. "My name is Nathan. I helped look after your parents when they were brought here. Maybe I can answer your questions."

Albert said it over, with deliberate patience. "I want to know if my mother still has the scarf my father gave to her. She was holding it, when she was dead. It's important."

The man named Nathan sighed, and glanced up at Aunt Rose, who said, "Please tell him, whatever it is. Anything for some peace." Then she walked away.

"I know the scarf," Nathan said, meeting Albert's gaze again. "It was green silk, very fine. Your mother must have loved it."

"So where is it?" Albert insisted.

"You saw your parents after it happened, you know what it was like. The scarf was ruined." Nathan faltered for a moment, then seemed to measure Albert's resolve and not find him wanting. "It was ruined with the blood. Frankly we usually burn things like that, unless the police want them for evidence."

"Do they?"

"No. It was your mother's blood, so they don't need it."

"I want her to have it. In the coffin."

Nathan thought about this. "Will you trust me to do it after the service?"

Albert said, "No." But it wasn't that he didn't believe this man would do as he promised – it had simply become something he had to see through.

"All right. Wait here." When he returned, Nathan was carrying a brown paper bag as if, incongruously, he had brought his lunch. But Albert knew what it was. He followed Nathan up to the caskets.

Seeing them on the dais, the other people retreated a little. Aunt Rose said faintly, "For the sake of all that's holy, what are you doing?" One of the older men from the funeral home had come in, and seemed angry at what he saw.

"You really want this?" Nathan asked Albert. Then he moved the flowers and the drape of green material, and raised the lid of Rebecca's coffin.

Even on tiptoe Albert couldn't see over the side of the coffin, so Nathan lifted him up onto one hip. Albert said, "Put it in her hands."

The scarf was mostly stained a blurred russet now, stiff and dry and ruined. But the edges still glowed green. Very fine silk. With his free hand, Nathan pushed the scarf under Rebecca's interlaced fingers where they rested on her chest. It was right.

Then Albert looked at his mother's face. Impassive, more so than he'd ever seen her. Not just withdrawn – she simply wasn't there anymore. Her cool living strength had turned to dead marble. Dead painted marble. "But she never wears make–up," he managed to whisper.

When Nathan let him down, Albert turned to face the other people there. They stared back at him, shocked or at least disapproving. None of them cried, none of them cried.

Albert clenched his fists. And he yelled. He yelled so loud that if there was a God who even now sat in Judgment on Miles and Rebecca he might hear their son's grief.

By the time Nathan gathered the boy up, Albert had already ripped his jacket down the front, torn a sleeve off, and was starting on his shirt. The yell sank to a keening that hurt his throat. But it went on and on, the noise, as if Albert was no longer a part of it, could no longer keep it inside of him.

"Let him be," Nathan was saying, though Albert only knew this later, from family stories. "Let him mourn."

"Not here," the young man's boss was insisting. "And not now."

"Then where and when?" But, after a moment, Nathan walked out with Albert in his arms and took him to an anonymous little soundproof room, set aside for this very purpose.

It was dark by the time Albert was fully aware of his surroundings. He felt raw, spent, fragile, and his face was wet. But Nathan, all business now, took him to Aunt Rose's apartment.

"You cost me my job, Mr. Sterne," the young man said.

Albert stared at the stunned and bitter mask of Nathan's face – and Albert's fury returned, as impotent as his grief, though not as fine. He said, "You lost the job yourself." And Nathan turned and left without a word.

Aunt Rose was waiting for him, tired and old and unhappy. "It's done, we buried them, they're at rest now," she said, before sending Albert to his room. *No thanks to you.*

THE VIRTUE OF HONESTY
NEW YORK CITY
OCTOBER 1973

"When they sent you, Washington said you were born and raised here."

Albert stared for a moment, then said, "That's partially incorrect, and it's none of your business."

"You know the people," Special Agent Paula Donnan explained. "You know the people in Brooklyn, and that understanding should help the investigation." The forensics man had walked into her office not two minutes ago, and she'd already decided that conversation with Albert Sterne was like wading in molasses. Uphill.

"I know more about the foibles and failings of the human race than anyone who works here."

"We have some damned good people, Mr. Sterne –"

"The best your benighted recruitment officers could scrape together, I'm sure."

"At least they have manners."

"A set of lies constructed to supposedly assist people. I find them a hindrance."

"Your rudeness is the hindrance."

"Only when you can't accept the truth."

"I don't know how you live with yourself, Mr. Sterne." She shook her head. "For that matter, I don't know how the Bureau lives with you. I'd heard stories, but figured it was all an exaggeration."

"Stories? Idle gossip, you mean. Don't waste my time."

Donnan swallowed a retort. After a moment, she said, "Let's start over. We're short on experienced forensics people right now, so, while I know this isn't your field of expertise –"

"I assure you I am more than capable of handling the case."

"No insult intended," she said impatiently. "I need you to –"

"Investigate the crime scenes, determine the cause or causes of the explosions, discover any evidence that might indicate who the offender or offenders are, and will lead to their arrest and conviction, and write a full report for the Special Agent in Charge within twenty–four hours."

"Yes. And if you could –"

"Hold the hands of your inexperienced forensics people, and walk them through this procedure, you'd appreciate it."

"Thank you, Mr. Sterne. Do you have –"

"Everything I need? Yes."

Donnan paused again, leaned back in her chair, before saying, "I don't know that we can afford to have you here, Mr. Sterne. We have a traditionally difficult relationship with the NYPD, and all the mess since Mr. Hoover died hasn't helped. I think it wise if you have no dealings with them."

"Your relationship with the police is simply another hindrance I can do without."

"So we agree on one thing," Donnan offered with an edge of humor.

"Two – the other is that the work is of the utmost urgency." And Albert stood and left the office.

She was high–class and lovely: milk–pale body too slender, but well–formed even so; hair a long and magnificent mane of red–gold curls, an adequate frame for the kind of face that painters used for angels. She was lowering her standards, letting a mere FBI man pay for her services, but Albert had been blunt enough in his request to interest her. She was the seventeenth prostitute he had used, and the eighth female, in a little over two years. She answered to the name Lily.

After a late supper, Albert took the woman to a hotel befitting her, a warm understated suite overlooking the cool night and Central Park. In all, the night cost him almost a month's salary.

It became a competition between them, to each demonstrate their skills and knowledge on the other's body, to each be the last to surrender to the pleasure they could have given each other.

Albert won, through sheer stubbornness. Her face – which others would have best appreciated in repose, in the removed and inviolate timelessness of a painting or photograph – Albert considered Lily's face to be at its most beautiful when she let orgasm ripple and flow through her. Watching her, Albert at last let his own orgasm unfurl within him in waves of rose–gold.

Afterwards, she made polite, one–sided conversation as she drank champagne.

Albert sat in the bed, still naked, silent. Eventually he said, "I wasn't aware this was a package deal. I only wanted the sex."

"It seems a pity to waste the opportunity to get to know each other," she said, unperturbed by the rudeness.

"You wouldn't want to know me," he replied curtly.

"But I would, and I do." Lily laughed, shook her hair back. Charming, graceful. "You have the virtue of honesty. In fact, you've been refreshingly forthright. And – this isn't news to you, surely – you're a passionate man, Albert. Is that your real name?"

"I am honest, remember. Is Lily yours?"

"It's my middle name, actually, after my grandmother. My first isn't quite so pretty." She poured more champagne. "Albert, this doesn't seem like a bad place to start a friendship."

"Why don't you take your finishing school charms somewhere they'll be appreciated."

He said it in the same tone of voice, so she took a moment to register his serious intent. "All right," she agreed politely. "Thank you, Albert."

"Thank you," he said in turn, laying on the sarcasm, "for condescending to slum it."

"It was a pleasure," she said, icy. By which time she was dressed again, protected by layers of silk, and waiting to be paid.

"You think you're clever, don't you?" Albert asked as he pointedly handed over the hundred–dollar bills one by one. "You used to do it for dinner and a night at the theater – now you do it for cash. You think that's honest."

"Perhaps you believe you hold the monopoly on truth," Lily said, her apparent composure betrayed by a trace of defiance.

"There's more to life than sex and dinner and money."

"What – files and secrets? Criminals and men in bad suits?"

"Far more than that. You have no conception."

"Go take your crusade to the streets. I gave at the office."

"You had nothing worth giving," Albert said, venomous.

She was high class and lovely – and the glow of her fury only heightened the effect.

Albert locked the door after she had gone, drew on the toweling robe provided by the hotel, and sat down at the table to consider his own words.

There's more to life than sex, indeed. Yet he had used these people, taken advantage of their abandoned dignity, their self–hatred. Encouraged their despair, their slow destruction, with his money and his selfish needs. Failed in his attempts to help them; there wasn't one, from Ricardo through Lily, who had truly listened – let alone acted on his advice.

This must not continue.

Albert had long ago realized that there would be no one to love him for who he was, no one to accept him as Miles and Rebecca had accepted each other. And it therefore seemed that he must be celibate from now on.

So be it.

Albert hit out suddenly, randomly, knocking over a vase, a basket of fruit, then deliberately sending the table over as well.

He stood; stared down at the broken glass, the spilled water, the mess of flowers, the oranges rolling to the four corners. Albert despised physical violence and its tawdry results.

Shaking, he at last choked back the anger, the frustration. After long moments, he went to the bathroom, and took a towel to start cleaning up.

FOUND OBJECTS
COLORADO
MARCH 1976

"How long since you found the body?" Albert asked.

"Just after seven this morning. Ran back most of the way, hitched a ride for the rest, got to town by eight, notified the Field Office from the nearest phone I could find – Mrs. Carruthers', just along here. Then I notified the Sheriff in person."

Albert stared at the young man beside him – pale and jittery with shock, but a determined set to his jaw. Eyes focused on something beyond the mere reality of the road, but steering the car with precision. Albert wondered if the man drove this carefully when he had his wits about him, and surmised not.

"That's Mrs. Carruthers on her porch," the youngster said. He returned her small–town nosiness with a wave. "I think she overheard most of my phone call."

With the same horrified tone that others used when expressing the opposite, Albert said, "You're from around here, aren't you?"

"No," he replied, quite seriously. "I'm from Idaho."

"That's all I need – a hick still wet behind the ears. The FBI recruits them young these days."

"The minimum age is still twenty–three." He cast Albert a glance, serious. "I joined up almost a year ago, I've been in the field since I completed the training. You're not much older than me, anyway."

"Only five years older, but possessing a wealth more intelligence and experience."

They had passed the last house now, and the town limits were just ahead. The young man put his foot down as soon as the speed sign was within sight.

"You ran this morning," Albert commented. "Were you scared, revolted or excited?"

The young man swallowed, apparently having to cope with a wave of nausea. "She – The body is lying exposed to the air. It's swollen, and the skin is blistering, falling apart."

"So putrefaction indicates the time of death to be when?"

"That's what you're here to tell us."

"If you don't even know the basics –"

"All right, I guess she died around four to six weeks ago. It's been quite cold, which would have slowed the process down. But we need your expert opinion."

"Of course." Albert left a pause, then, "What were you doing there in the first place?"

"Hiking. Camping." The young man glanced at him again. "I had a rostered day off, a long weekend."

"And – ?" Albert prompted.

"I had a premonition. An intuition. That I would find something up there." He turned the car onto a smaller road that wound up the side of a hill. The trees surrounding them limited any views so that, but for the sun almost directly overhead, it was difficult to keep track of their direction.

Albert was silent, considering his companion. "What's your name?" he eventually asked.

"Fletcher Ash. And I did not kill that girl."

"Did someone accuse you?"

"You implied – I inferred from your manner that you were listing me as the prime suspect."

"I'm here to discover and investigate various facts. One of which is that it's unusual, to say the least, that an overly young FBI agent has such accurate premonitions."

Ash muttered, "I am what I am," and pulled the car over beside another vehicle from the Sheriff's Office. A deputy, apparently loitering with intent to secure the area, looked across as they climbed from the car, but didn't challenge them.

Albert glanced around as he buttoned up his coat. "What is this – the local lovers' lane?" The road looped around the crest of the hill, and turned back on itself. A small paved area looked out to a seemingly endless range of hills and mountains climbing in vain towards the pale noon sun. The dirt amongst the trees was compacted with tire tracks, tawdry with litter.

"The kids come parking here on Friday nights. I'd say the offender brought her here, took her for a walk, then killed her where I found her – just inside the entry to an old mine."

"Planned or opportunistic?"

"Probably –" Ash caught himself, smiled shakily. "I think," he started again, firm now, "that you should see her before I tell you my conclusions."

"It's highly unlikely that you'll cloud my judgment," Albert assured him with heavy sarcasm. When Ash unlocked the trunk, Albert retrieved his case of tools, then stood waiting as the younger man propped himself against the car, apparently unwilling to face the crime scene again. Albert was interested to see to what extent Ash's theories would be proved true. "You're assuming the offender is a man," he prompted.

"Most murderers are, and most victims are women, with sexual offenses like this."

"That tells me little more than that you read the Uniform Crime Reports."

Ash frowned, and absently pulled his cotton sweater into place. The young man had not yet changed from his camping gear to clothes the FBI would approve of: he was in jeans, a T–shirt and the sweater, all of which were stained and crumpled, and an old pair of hiking boots. Nevertheless, Ash's discomfort originated somewhere other than in these externals.

"Was it planned or opportunistic?" Albert asked again.

"To me, the answer's fairly obvious. Which is why I'd rather have your unclouded opinion, in case I've missed something."

"Fine. Did you let the cops beyond this point?"

"I had to get them to cordon off the site."

"And you left them there alone! You moron – they'll have trampled over any evidence, taken souvenirs to show their girlfriends – ignorant hicks, the lot of you."

"My supervisor is there, she drove up from Denver this morning. She has the area secure, and I needed to talk to you, so I borrowed the car and came to collect you."

Silence. "All right." Albert bit off the words.

"I know it's all right," Ash mildly replied.

Albert looked across at the young man. It didn't happen often these days – someone scratching Albert's curiosity through the layers of cynicism. Ash wasn't avoiding him, or his impatient questions. But there was a defensiveness in him, in some way related to the crime under investigation. Something didn't quite fit, and Albert wanted to know what.

"The site's over that way." He indicated vaguely northwards.

Belatedly checking his watch, Albert asked, "You really expect me to believe you ran that in rather less than an hour this morning?"

"I keep fit," the Agent asserted.

"And you were exhilarated."

Ash looked squarely at Albert. "I was scared and revolted: I don't like the sight or smell of a decomposing corpse; I like even less the thought of someone doing such a thing."

"Why make a kid with no stomach for it a special agent? You should have served out your ten years in Records or –"

"But I'm good," Ash asserted, sounding ill. "Too good." He looked away, straightened up from the car. "Let's go, Mr. Sterne."

It was only a ten minute walk, but the way wasn't easy: there were fewer trees, but undergrowth, rocks and fallen branches obscured any direct path, and the ground rose and fell in abrupt, uneven intervals. Added to which, though it didn't bother Albert, the air was noticeably thinner at this altitude. Less than halfway there, Albert concluded, "The girl knew him."

"Trusted him," Ash agreed. Then he muttered to himself, "He said to her, I'll show you a secret, I'll take you to my hiding place, we can be alone there."

"What?"

The younger man cleared his throat. "A loner of a boy, nervous, finally has this wonderful girl with him, she's holding his hand. He's watched her, wanted her for so very long. That's what I feel happened."

"You feel it?" Albert scoffed. "More intuition?"

"Yes." Uncomfortable but determined. "He's surprised her, he's more interesting than she credited, but he wants to have her, all of her, control her. And he doesn't really know how else to achieve that."

"On what do you base this tale you're spinning?"

"A few facts, the crime scene, and what the Sheriff could tell me of the victim."

Albert paused to assess his companion. Two steps later, Ash came to a halt as well, and returned Albert's stare.

Ash's manner still held a little defiance, but otherwise he was serious and intense and focused. Added to which, he was open and he paid attention – Ash didn't seem to hide behind his opinions or habitual behavior.

Physically, the bare facts did little to describe him – white male, twenty–four, one–seventy–five, black and blue. The neat features were regular, framed by a strong jaw, not quite handsome. But there was a presence only hinted at by the hot blue eyes, the dark mess of hair.

"The intuition," Ash was saying; "it's more curse than blessing. But I use it, it serves a purpose."

"Call it what you will. Don't let it pass for fact."

"No," was the abrupt reply, "I don't."

Ash turned away, and led Albert over a rise and down to where yellow plastic tape had been tied haphazardly from tree to tree. Beyond the tape, a crater had been dug at the foot of a small natural cliff, and a gaping mineshaft sloped from the dirt down into the rock. It seemed to have been abandoned decades ago. A woman stood nearby, watching a deputy wrestle a lamp and tripod together.

"Caroline," Ash called. She walked over to meet them, arms crossed in a business–like manner; she was wearing a female version of the FBI–approved suit, with far more style than Albert anticipated ever seeing in her subordinate. "Caroline, this is Albert Sterne. Mr. Sterne, this is my supervisor, Special Agent Caroline Thornton."

"Has anyone been inside the tape?" Albert asked without acknowledging the introduction.

"I have, of course, this morning when I found her. I'll show you where I walked when we go in there. Once I saw her, I didn't move any further. And then I took the Sheriff in, but only as far as I'd already gone."

The Agent was good, Albert had to allow; either that or he was lying: he'd apparently thought to not disturb possible evidence any more than he already had, instead of panicking as so many of them did, and drawing closer as if they didn't believe the evidence of their eyes. "What about the deputy hayseeds?"

"I beg your pardon?" the woman said, though it was obvious from her disapproval that she understood.

"The local uninformed uniforms – give them a badge and they think they're a cross between the Texas Rangers and Perry Mason."

"And who do you think you are, Mr. Sterne?"

"I know who I am, and it's none of your business. Have the hicks been wandering around?"

"No. I sent two of them to fetch a generator and lights – which as you see are being set up now. One of them, who I hope you also saw, is guarding the approach from the road. The others I sent out beyond here to search for clues – with strict instructions to look but don't touch."

"The evidence, if there is any other than the body, is more likely to be amongst the trees around the road, or down there in the mineshaft."

"I'm aware of that, Mr. Sterne. That's why I sent them in the other direction."

Apparently expecting Albert to appreciate Caroline's dry humor, the younger man laughed. He sobered when there was no response, frowned. It seemed he finally minded Albert's attitude.

Thornton asked, "Fletch, why do I feel I have to justify myself to this person?"

Ash shrugged, staring at the forensics man. "You don't."

"Have them photograph the area around the road," Albert said, ignoring the exchange, "then collect all the human debris into bags – one bag for every square yard, labeled accordingly." He waited, with a bland expression, to see if she would carry out the instructions: after all, Ash, and through him Thornton, were ostensibly in charge of this investigation.

"I know the procedure," Thornton said, "and no doubt the Sheriff's people do, as well."

"One can always hope," Albert said coldly as she moved away.

"Be nice to see the place cleaned up," Ash commented irrelevantly.

Oblivious, Albert knelt, took the miniature cassette recorder from his case, and began recording a description of the site.

"Opportunistic," Albert said, finally answering his own question. The body lay neatly arranged, with the face obscured by a pair of underpants, presumably the girl's own. "How did you identify her?"

Ash pointed to the side, where the contents of her purse were tidily displayed: a folded handkerchief, a wallet with coins and a few oddments in a circle around it, a small mirror, two unused tampons, various torn pieces of card and paper, and a bank book. "There's her name and address – and her account number. I didn't disturb anything, I haven't seen her face."

The purse itself was, absurdly, pillowing her head, with the strap bitten deeply into her neck. Her earrings had been removed, and placed to either side. The clothing had been pulled into place, but something bulged the skirt up from between her thighs.

"This is terrible," Ash whispered.

"All those case photographs you pored over in Quantico didn't prepare you?"

"Of course not. How could they?"

Albert took his clipboard from his case and began to draw a diagram of the scene, carefully annotating it with descriptions. "I trust they at least prepared you to use a camera. Here," he said, indicating the Nikon.

The flash went off again and again, as Fletcher took a few shots of the whole scene from different angles, and then a lot of close–ups. Albert noted that Ash's work habits did not seem to be as careless as his personal appearance might indicate. Finally the young man asked, "Will that be enough?"

"Yes. Take a couple of the scene with the Polaroid, as well." Albert made some final notes and returned the clipboard to his case. He handed Ash some plastic evidence bags and said, "Start collecting it up, one item per bag." And then, as the Agent began the task, Albert knelt and carefully lifted the girl's skirt with his pencil, just enough to see what had been left there.

Ash, who'd shifted around to look as well, groaned at the sight. After a moment, he said flatly, "Artist unknown, 1976, found objects."

Albert wasn't fooled by the attempt at irony: the young man was upset. "Not only does he read the Uniform Crime Reports, he visits art galleries," Albert commented. Then he announced, "We'll take her in as she is." There was no point in risking trace evidence from the offender by dismantling all this.

"Did she know that was being done to her?"

"Probably not. From appearances, I'd surmise she was at least rendered unconscious by slow strangulation, and perhaps died of anoxic anoxia before he started any of this. Asphyxia, to the uneducated."

"Good. Well," he amended, "better than it might have been."

Albert slipped a bag over each of her hands, fastened them securely at the wrists, and then a larger bag for her head, over the pants and her hair as well. Neither of them had seen her face yet. It seemed probable that it would be mutilated in some way.

"You know," Ash said quietly, "bagging her like that is almost as depersonalizing as the actual crime."

"It is a necessary procedure."

"I know: preserving evidence. But it's still macabre."

Once the Agent had gathered up the contents of her purse and her earrings, and Albert was free to move around, he began to ease a plastic sheet under the body, disturbing it as little as possible, then enlisted Ash's aid in lifting it into a metal coffin from the local medical examiner's office. Four of the deputies took it for the trip through the forest.

Ash stood in the mouth of the mineshaft, looking distinctly pale. "The smell of it all," he explained. "And the lights made it worse."

"You get used to it."

"I don't know if I want to."

Albert had packed up his case of tools. "Was there anything else? I have an autopsy to perform."

"Yes. If this was the offender's hiding place, then he'll have left things here, private stuff."

"You're making several assumptions."

"But valid ones, don't you think?"

He shrugged, but followed Ash as he walked further into the mine, flashlight searching the walls. And there, in a crevice, were a couple of cheap pornographic magazines, a comic book, a radio with leaked batteries, and a can of Coca-Cola.

"This has been here for a while," Ash said. "He forgot he had these."

"The batteries," Albert agreed.

"And the logo on this can – it's at least two years out of date."

Albert looked at the kid, who grinned back at him. "What a store of arcane knowledge you are," Albert said sarcastically. "Pity it's of little use.

I doubt this would conclusively identify anyone, and there's no reason to believe it belongs to the offender."

"It all helps to build a picture: this was someone's den; and the offender wanted to bring the girl somewhere he felt safe, somewhere he knew he wouldn't be disturbed." Fletcher nodded, looking around the uneven rock walls. "The Sheriff can have a thorough search done."

"I'll go back to town with the hearse."

"No, I'll drive you. I'll come back up here later."

The man's persistence and enthusiasm were tiresome.

They were silent as the car wound back down the hill. Albert considered the man beside him, again driving carefully despite or because of his distraction. Ash was really far too young to be a special agent. What did Quantico, and Assignments at HQ, think they were doing? "Tell me what you made of the fact," Albert said, "that those objects had been inserted in the body's vagina."

The young man was startled by the sudden demand. He cast a glance at Albert, then turned back to the road, thoughtful. "I didn't notice that, this morning," he eventually said.

"What – too busy trying not to vomit?"

"Just missed that particular detail."

Albert nodded. The young man should not be out here. "You didn't have to tell me that," Albert pointed out. "There's no need to broadcast your mistakes."

"I don't mind making mistakes, if no one's hurt, and I learn from them. And I don't lie," he added flatly.

"Are you implying I do?"

"Maybe by omission."

For a moment, Albert found himself immersed in the supremely physical desire to throttle the young man. He rode it out, and swallowed down the bile, loathing the threatened lack of self–control. Wanting to snap, *You're wrong and you know nothing about me* – but fearing Ash would express an interest in knowing more.

"What do I make of it?" he was repeating. "It indicates that the killer had no sexual experience, or no sexual confidence. That he was unwilling or unable to achieve penetrative sexual activity. So he used whatever was at hand – twigs and stones and stuff."

"Is that what your instinct tells you?" Albert asked, sarcasm emphasizing his disbelief.

"A little. It's also what I learned at Quantico. You were right, about the depersonalization – this one couldn't have even done that much if she were conscious, if her face wasn't obscured."

"So what does that do to your theory that he'd been watching her for a long while?"

The kid shot him a glance that held a trace of defiance. "Supports it. She was his symbol of the unattainable."

Silence again. But Albert found he couldn't leave the issue of Fletcher Ash alone. "Why are you out here? Why not stay at HQ in a safe job, do your time while you grow up? In fact, why leave Smalltown, Idaho at all?"

"Idaho? Well ..." Ash mused over this for a moment, then let out an incongruous laugh. "There were bears in the hills. That's why I left. Big hungry angry bears."

The silence of the laboratory had been unbroken for hours, and Albert had achieved a great deal before allowing himself a two–hour rest in the early morning. He was now writing up the results while waiting for a few tests to complete. This was the way he liked to work, alone and undisturbed; but when he heard the echo of the main doors at seven, then footsteps approaching, he was surprised to find he didn't resent the intrusion as much as usual because he guessed who it would be.

"Into it already?" Fletcher Ash asked. "How long have you been here?"

"I thought you wanted a full report as soon as possible," Albert said without shifting his attention away from the files and paperwork.

"Yes, but ..." Ash laughed. "I don't usually get this much cooperation."

"You wouldn't normally get this detailed or thorough a report, either." And Albert glanced at him, sardonic, daring him to argue.

A pause, then Ash said, "I'm afraid your professionalism may be wasted this time. A boy committed suicide last night, hung himself. His landlord found him in the small hours this morning."

"Really."

"I think he might have been the offender." Silence again, as if Ash was waiting for encouragement, or even interest. Then, "The Sheriff disagrees, says he knew the kid, can't imagine him capable of it. He was quiet, kept to himself, didn't have any friends. You should see his rooms, though, it was weird: most of it, the everyday things, a total mess; but some of it arranged so neatly, all set out, just like she was. I've never seen anything quite like it."

"Tell them I'll do the autopsy."

"I was hoping you would – though it's not really our jurisdiction."

"Neither was the girl, but for the fact you found her."

"They don't get too many violent crimes around here, they were happy enough to let the Bureau do the dirty work."

Albert said, "I need samples from the boy, and if they match up with this trace evidence, you'll have your suspect confirmed."

"You're a miracle worker."

"Hardly."

"You don't seem to let the ghastliness affect you – is that a hindrance or a help?"

Albert spared the young man a glance. He had once been asked a simpler question, by McIntyre down in New Orleans, and Albert had answered though he suspected he hadn't been believed. Ash was, however, intelligent enough to work out something so obvious for himself.

"Mr. Sterne," Ash was gravely continuing, "I came here to tell you the news, and to ask if you wanted to see the body before they bring it in."

Trying not to respond to the shift in tone, Albert said, "That won't be necessary, if they handled the situation correctly."

"They did, and Caroline's stayed there to make sure." A pause. Albert didn't bother commenting on Thornton's alleged abilities. Ash said, "I also planned to invite you to breakfast."

"Why?" Albert asked, hating the note of defensiveness that crept into his voice.

"Because I'm hungry, it's that time of day, it's what people do. And because Caroline is unavailable."

"I am not interested in doing what people do," Albert said. "And I am surprised that you are." He ignored the implication that he was only the second choice for companion: judging from the smirk on Ash's face, it was supposed to be a joke.

"Unlike some, I don't do the opposite simply for the sake of rebellion."

"Really."

"Really," Ash agreed. "I'm hungry, and I want to talk with you. Come and eat, Mr. Sterne."

Standing, Albert said in exasperation, "No wonder you never get any work done around here." But Albert followed the man out the door anyway, wondering at himself. It was, after all, highly unlikely they would find a decent breakfast in this hick town.

SUBJECTIVITIES
COLORADO | WASHINGTON DC
MARCH 1976

Fletcher Ash appreciated a breakfast with the works, particularly after such an early and dramatic start to the morning: he ordered eggs and bacon and sausages, two serves of toast, coffee and orange juice. His companion, expression indicating he was resigned to the worst, ordered juice and a cheese omelet, no toast. And, as the waiter reclaimed the menus, Albert Sterne gave a fastidious and apparently unconscious little sniff. Fletch almost laughed, but thought better of it. There was no need to sabotage a potential conversation before it had even started.

The diner Fletch had found was cheerful, crowded and welcoming, and almost too warm. "Caroline would love this place."

Albert cast a look at his surroundings, and seemed to find them lacking. "If you're trying to recommend either Thornton or this diner, you are failing miserably."

Laughing, Fletcher said, "I'll let both speak for themselves. Caroline at least is more than capable."

"For example, she's putting in twenty–four hour days because she has something to prove about female special agents."

"You must have seen for yourself that she's good. The work she does speaks for her, all that she accomplishes."

"Perhaps," was the grudging reply.

"Plenty of people think so." Fletcher didn't often find himself defending his supervisor though, now he thought of it, he was surprised: the FBI had been exclusively lily–white and male for far too long. After their first five minutes in Caroline's company, however, people invariably took her seriously, though her small stature, heart–shaped face, blond hair and blue eyes might have initially prompted them to do otherwise. Fletch said, "She moved very fast once they'd lifted the ban on women in the field."

"They trusted her with you, at least."

Fletch frowned. "What do you mean?"

"You're an unknown quantity, Special Agent. They assume you'll either emulate the Titanic or swim magnificently, so they let you and Thornton do so together – with the smart money on you both hitting the iceberg, preferably without a lot of screaming beforehand."

"Really," Ash said flatly.

"Really. That way they get to not only wash their hands of you, but of the responsibility as well. There aren't enough lifeboats provided."

"What a metaphor." Fletcher was interrupted as breakfast arrived. Once he'd downed a couple of large mouthfuls, he asked, "And if I succeed?"

"They pat themselves on the back, and let everyone know about it. They would hardly give a woman or a youngster the credit. Then they send you off on the next dirty job."

"Next you'll be telling me they sent you to test me. I'm not interested in your paranoia."

"Realism," Albert corrected. "If your instincts were any good, you'd share with me this unfortunate insight into the workings of the human mind: it is capable of so much cunning and self–interest."

"You're a conspiracy theorist, too, I imagine."

Albert appeared to take this suggestion as seriously as anything else. "I believe that people who have interests in common will make or let things happen, things that suit them, without necessarily ever holding a meeting, or acknowledging each other as anything but enemies, or even verbalizing the need. Surely you can see that."

"Maybe," Fletcher allowed, fascinated by this unexpected man. Albert sat there opposite him, cutting his omelet into neat, equal–sized segments, while Fletch wolfed his own food down – but, while hungry, Fletcher was far more interested in the conversation. Few if any people took Fletch this seriously; few treated everything he said as the truth, few expected him to justify his point of view. It made Fletch realize all over again how many lies and half–truths people told in the course of a day: necessary a lot of the time, but the warp of the social fabric was lies.

"We've established that Thornton's punishing but self–imposed schedule is to prove her worth," said Albert. "Is your agenda the same?"

"That's part of it." Ash added, "But I hope there are more noble interpretations. You and I and Caroline have at least one characteristic in common: we like to get the job done as quickly and effectively as possible."

"You're speaking for her after all."

Fletch grinned. "Anyone else would simply take the compliment, Mr. Sterne, instead of insisting on consistency. All right, I'll speak for myself alone: I dragged you here for some sane conversation."

Albert, for the briefest of moments, appeared surprised.

"All this sordid business …" Fletcher said. "I find that it matters too much, and yet it's what I want to do. Perhaps I need a shift in perspective."

"And you're prepared to admit this to a total stranger?"

"It's just the truth, Mr. Sterne. Tell me: what's your agenda? Why are you so hard on yourself?"

Again, Albert seemed thrown, though he recovered quickly enough. "Most people –"

"What? Would ask why you're so hard on everyone else?"

"Most people don't ask at all," was the dry reply.

"You frighten them off, or offend them, before they have the chance."

"Really."

"But your saving grace is that you're hardest of all on yourself."

"I'm sure there are topics more worthy of discussion than my solitary saving grace."

Fletcher almost laughed at the affronted tone, but stopped himself from the cruelty of it. He smiled instead, and leaned a little closer even though Albert instinctively sat back. "You know," Fletch said; "it's just good to talk about something other than the case."

"Then talk about yourself instead of me," Albert snapped at him.

"That's a problem, as well. I'm too caught up in all this, and I want to forget it for half an hour."

Albert seized on the statement. "Why did they put you in the field if you can't maintain your objectivity? How did you even pass Quantico?"

"Because my subjectivity is useful to them." He smiled again, but knew the expression was weak. "I handle it," he added.

"Yes? How do you manage that?"

He let his expression grow droll. "A precarious balance; a tightrope act, juggling madly all the time."

"How colorful. I'm sure the sequins and feathers really suit you."

"Why, thank you."

Albert suddenly asked, "Don't they employ boys who look like you in the Secret Service? As beautiful, stupid cannon fodder, good for the President's photo opportunities, and nobly foiling assassination attempts?"

"No, they don't, Mr. Sterne. The new FBI recruiting and assignment policy is more along the lines of, *It takes a psychopath to catch a psychopath.*"

A disparaging snort. "And you think you qualify?"

"That's not something you want to find out." Having finished his meal, Fletch reached for his wallet, then stood. He had a job to get back to, and the conversation was becoming too uncomfortable. "I'll expect your report by midday."

His first murder case had solved itself, and the offender had carried out his own judgment, leaving little for Fletcher Ash to do but complete the usual series of reports. As Albert Sterne surmised, Fletch had hoped this would be his chance to prove himself, but he was soon back to the routine of updating files, chasing around on behalf of FBI friendlies, and pursuing less brutal crimes.

What he most looked forward to in the immediate future was a refresher training course which marked his twelfth month in the Bureau – though even that had its downsides: Quantico, in Virginia, was pleasant enough, though he wouldn't be given enough spare time to get out into the countryside; but Fletch did not enjoy the city of Washington, and Caroline had told him to stay on for an extra week in order to make use of the files and other records held centrally, to tidy up or at least progress a range of minor cases. There was nothing like squeezing all the use you can out of one airfare. The way this was going, Fletch would miss the best of spring.

At headquarters, Ash cast a daunted glance around the rows of books and files and boxes, the banks of computer terminals. When he had done his original training, the class had been given a tour of this place. At the time, he had considered all this information to be an exciting resource – right now, all he wondered was, "Where do I start?"

"Depends what you're after." A disheveled man with thinning sandy hair, built for comfort rather than speed, stood beside him. "I'm McIntyre, but you can call me Mac. I'm here to help."

Fletch sighed and produced a list.

After a late and rather rushed lunch, Fletcher returned to Mac and the files with a frown. "Who rained on your parade?" the Irishman asked.

"Well …" Fletch supposed it wasn't really breaking a confidence. "I just asked Albert Sterne if he'd have dinner with me tonight."

"Albert Sterne?"

"Yes. From Forensics."

"Yeah, I know him. God love me, what on earth did you want to do that for?"

Fletcher looked at him: Mac seemed almost horrified. "I met him up in Colorado on a case recently. He's an interesting man."

"Maybe he is," Mac allowed, "but let me tell you that's no reason to put yourself through the agony of knowing him socially."

"Attempting to know him socially," Fletch corrected with a reluctant smile.

Mac laughed. "I don't think I want to know just how he turned you down. The bastard can be damned rude when he puts his mind to it."

"Yes, but –" Fletch paused for a moment, then said carefully, "He seems to be very good at what he does."

"That would have to be the nicest thing anyone's ever said about him."

"You know Mr. Sterne well?" Fletch sat down, and began scrolling through a seemingly endless screen of data. He might feel less guilty about gossiping if he attempted to work at the same time.

Mac, on the other hand, seemed to welcome the distraction. He sat back from the files, and stretched lazily, his large frame appearing only precariously balanced on his chair. "Who could know the bastard well?" he asked rhetorically, with no malice in his voice. "We suffered through Quantico together. He was top in every class, which is why they won't fire him despite severe provocation, and I barely scraped through, which is why I spend my time being shunted around the field offices, opening mail and driving people and sorting files. Despite which, we've done some work together. When I was transferred to New Orleans, he came down to help on a couple of cases. There's a lady there who asks after him every time I see her. Wish she wouldn't." He smiled glumly at Fletch. "That's all. It goes without saying he's as rude as possible every time he's within a ten yard radius."

"Why is that?" Ash asked.

"You'd know better than me."

"No, I only worked with him for a couple of days."

"Time doesn't give you much perspective, kid. He's an ugly bastard."

"That's hardly fair. Or relevant."

"You're taking me literally, and with good cause." Mac shook his head. "But he's ugly through and through. What do they say, *The form reflects the function*? Fletch, I used to think Albert Sterne was impossible, but believe it or not he's gotten even worse. Not so long ago, you could at least hold a conversation with him, if you were thick-skinned enough. I came this close to liking him." He held up thumb and forefinger a judicious half-inch apart. "Celia could have liked him."

"She's your friend in New Orleans?"

Mac nodded. "I'm sorry to say I even enjoyed it when he turned that mouth of his on other people. But he's bitter now. It's all destructive."

"He interests me."

"You know what happened to the last person who said that? Went mad and we shot him. No, I'm kidding. There hasn't been anyone, except Celia maybe."

"That doesn't seem right. He has his qualities."

"Most people round here would drop dead of shock to hear you say that. In fact, they send him off on the interstate cases just to be rid of him. You'd think they'd all squabble over who gets to travel, wouldn't you? Most people sitting here talking about the guy would be exchanging horror stories." Mac looked at him for a moment. "Kid, you're smart about people. The rumors say they're watching you, don't know what to make of you. But hanging around with Albert Sterne isn't going to win you any credits, because everyone avoids him like the plague. Sure, he's good at what he does. But no one wants to be there when he does it. What I'm trying to say is that your career is already on the line. Even if you're as brilliant as they suspect, it could still go against you, and they'll use any excuse. You know what The Powers That Be are like."

"Yes," Fletch said slowly. "But I try to maintain my optimism."

"That's nice, kid, but unrealistic. At least Albert doesn't expect anything from anyone, and he's ruthless, though I can't see that it's for the sake of ambition. He'll make it in whatever he chooses to do, no matter what."

"Will he? I think he smacks of disappointment. He's on a dead end, one way street."

Mac truly looked horrified now. "Save yourself while you can, my friend – sounds like he's got you hooked! That much thinking about Albert has got to be dangerous."

"You must be interested in him, too," Fletcher pointed out. "Why else would you be discussing him with me?"

"I have no idea," Mac said flatly, turning back to the files.

"Well, you know the joke about the room full of horse–shit, don't you?"

"Tell me."

"There's a man digging through a whole pile of horse–shit, shoveling it aside. And they ask him why on earth he's doing this. And he says with that much shit around, there has to be a pony in there somewhere."

"A bloody pony!" Mac laughed. "Good luck, kid. I reckon you'll need it, because Albert Sterne surrounds himself with so much shit, I wouldn't know where to begin."

TEMPEST
IDAHO
JUNE 1968

Robert Kennedy had been shot, moments after claiming victory in the California primary. The world was a crazy and forbidding place where youth and vigor, and the determination to put what was right before what was expedient, could be blown away. JFK was gone, shot in the midday sun with his wife beside him; Martin Luther King was gone, only days before Fletcher's sixteenth birthday; and now it seemed Bobby would soon be gone, too.

Fletch hitched the straps of his bag higher onto his shoulder and gazed carefully at the worn path his feet were treading. The numbness wouldn't even let him feel the shock of it yet, never mind the grief and the rage and the sorrow. All the coming years seemed blighted – at least when Jack Kennedy had died, there had been the promise of a grief–stricken Bobby to take up where his brother had left off. Now there would be no one. Fletch's mind trundled uselessly on: how could this happen? How could tragedy after tragedy be allowed to happen?

An announcement had been made over the school's loudspeaker sometime after three o'clock, the principal quoting from a news report: medical tests were inconclusive, and showed no measurable improvement; the Senator's condition remained extremely critical. And Fletch's heart had let the pain of hope go. Until then he had been wrenched up tight inside, trying to influence events hundreds of miles away through sheer willpower: his atheist's version of prayer.

They had been let out of school, most of the kids simply happy to have an early day.

Not knowing quite what to do with himself, Fletch was now heading vaguely into town, as usual. His father would be there at the store; he might have some more news, might find the right words to dispel the numbness.

Over the past couple of years Fletcher had set himself some goals, and was attempting to develop some self–discipline: he always studied for an hour in the library after school, and he always crossed the playing field and took the back path to town through the stretch of woods, on his way to help his father at the hardware store before heading home for dinner and chores and more study. The only variation he allowed to this self–imposed routine was on his walk home: he took a number of different routes, some adding a mile or two, because he loved the trees and hills, the life and secrets of the countryside.

Today he had spent the hour in the library gazing sightlessly at his unopened books, while the librarian sniffled in the bit of lace that had always passed as a handkerchief until she had to use it. The television burbled quietly in the background, news bulletins offering little more than banalities. The librarian hadn't spoken to Fletcher, or offered or asked him for any comfort. When he left, she had locked the door behind him and stayed there on her own.

He always walked through the woods despite the fact that the boys who had nominated themselves the local hoods always hung around under the trees, just out of sight of the school, smoking and wasting time and, if they'd been lucky, drinking. The dirt path was unworthy of Fletch's attention, and presented no obstacles to trip him: staring at it was normally a pretext for ignoring the rabble. This afternoon, Fletch was simply distracted. The rabble, however, were intent on being noticed.

"Hey! Fletcher! You've really gone and done it this time," Curtis called out.

Fletch continued on his way, not really hearing the boy, and certainly not acknowledging him.

Curtis ran after him and bodily blocked the path. "You're deep in it this time."

"Deep in what?" he asked.

Fletch had an economical, slim build, and people tended to assume he was of less than average height. The rather large Curtis seemed surprised to find that Fletch's eyes were level with his own. In more ways than simply the physical. "Deep in shit, of course," he elaborated.

"Why?"

There were groans at this pretense of ignorance from the dozen boys surrounding them. Curtis spat at the ground, just missing Fletch's right shoe. "You know why, you do–good snitch."

"Ah. So, people are beginning to wonder if you aren't behind the current crime wave after all."

"Jesus, Fletch, you've been reading too many damn books."

"And you think I told Sheriff Ryan you might be suspects."

"Yeah," Curtis declared. "I do."

"On what grounds?"

That threw him for a moment. He glanced around at his peers, in need of an idea or two.

Fletch heaved an internal sigh. These boys were so easily seen through: rebelling in the only way they could imagine for a few short years, before the demands of small–town respectability and petty responsibility set in. It was almost noble, this brief fight, in a drab and futile sort of way. But they would grow up to become farmers and shopkeepers, ordinary men. Curtis would end up elected mayor in thirty years, and wonder what to do about the local hoods. And life would continue in the small town just as it always had.

But inspire these boys, encourage them to think a little, install a leader who understood how frustration and alienation could lead to expediency and crime and violence – and who knew what the gang might achieve.

No, Fletch would leave this raw material to safe provincialism. And he would try, as ever, to listen to his own integrity and intelligence and creativity. Sometimes it threatened to become a battle, but Fletch believed the difficult path yielded the best reward.

"Because …" Curtis was at last replying, "it's just the sort of thing you do."

"Well, it might be what I'd do, if I thought you were suspects. But you couldn't be; you couldn't do these crimes."

As Curtis considered this to be an insult, he began to glower.

Fletch risked explaining further. "You think you're rebellious, but you're not. You're too much a part of this place, you hold all the same values. You respect your neighbors, you wouldn't destroy them. And even if you could have stolen from him, you never would have put old man Ferguson in intensive care. You're not the ones sweating on whether he regains his memory."

Curtis was stunned. He seemed about to protest, but Fletch pushed past him and continued on his way.

◆

It was generally agreed that Fletcher David Ash had inherited much from his mother's father. People still recalled the old Irishman with his wild handsomeness and hot temper, determined to make the most of this new land he had emigrated to. The handsomeness and the temper, Fletch didn't think he'd inherited – or, if so, they hadn't been in evidence. To him it was more superficial things like the pale skin, the blue eyes, and the unruly thick black hair. Fletcher's mother had had similar coloring, though she wasn't as strikingly good–looking as her father. As for the determination, Fletch suspected he had that in spades, but he hadn't yet found anything he wanted to focus it on – other than working to get out of Idaho, of course. It had also been rumored, however, that Fletch's grandfather had the second sight. And maybe that had something to do with why people found Fletch so … unnerving.

He was fully aware that he gave people the creeps. Even his father. If his father hadn't loved him so much, with his quiet and generous soul, Fletch was sure that even he would have found his younger son uncomfortably odd.

Most of the time Fletch felt safely nondescript. People often didn't notice he was there. But when they did at last see him, they tended to avoid him. Fletch didn't like it much.

Perhaps it was because Fletch had unusual insight into his fellow human beings, especially for a teenager. It had been a long time since he'd realized that there were infinite shades of gray, that there were too few issues which could be considered as black or white. Perhaps it was as simple and as harmless as that. But people were apparently more inclined to blame the Irish taint in his blood, the Irish nonsense in his grandfather's tales. Because Fletch didn't only understand the good in people, the unselfish and generous and honest. He also understood all the pettiness and deceit and pain. He knew who was doing what with whom, and why. And, even though he never said anything that accused, people assumed that he was forever judging them.

All Fletch could do was wonder why anyone should care so much for the opinion of a boy of sixteen.

He slipped in through the storeroom behind his father's shop, and heard more tears and his father's murmur of comfort. It was Miss Hunt, the latest victim of the recent rash of burglaries. "I don't understand it, Mr. Ash," she was sobbing, "I just don't understand how anyone could do these things. Yesterday was my bridge night, they must have known that, and I arrive home to find everything in the most awful mess, and all my jewelry gone, not that it was worth much, so that just serves them right. And then as I'm trying to set it all to rights again, tidying my poor home, Senator Kennedy is shot, like his brother before him, and heaven help all his children! Ten children, and I've heard there's another on the way … None of this is right, Mr. Ash, the world is all going wrong somewhere, and who knows what to do about it?"

"I certainly don't, Miss Hunt," Fletch's father replied. "I wish I did." He was a quiet man, with light brown hair and hazel eyes. If feeling uncharitable, Fletch might have called him mousy, but there was really nothing of the mouse in Peter Ash's manner.

"So I came by today to buy some new locks and bolts for my little house, if you please, because I'd never even tried to lock the doors before last night, and wouldn't you know they've all rusted away inside; the locks, that is. I had to go and spend the night at Deirdre's, in case they came back while I was there, like with poor old Mr. Ferguson, but I didn't get a moment's peace, worrying over it all and poor Bobby Kennedy lying in hospital, too … Why, he's only about your age, Mr. Ash."

"Yes, it's a tragedy, that's for sure, and all we can do is hope for good news from California. Well, Miss Hunt, we've had a lot of people buying locks recently – we ran out at first! But we ordered plenty of new stock in. If you'd like to come and have a look at the range … Was it just for the doors, or for the windows as well?"

"Everything: the doors, the windows, everything!"

Fletcher hung back and then, seeing his father might be a while, took up the broom and began sweeping the floor.

At last Peter Ash was ringing Miss Hunt's purchases up on the cash register, and she was fumbling with her purse. He asked, "Do you have someone to help you with these? Perhaps Fletcher can walk you home, and start installing them."

"No, thank you, Deirdre's boys are coming after school –" She suddenly swung around, suspicious, and saw Fletch. "There's your son now. He does turn up unexpectedly, doesn't he? Did school finish early?"

"Yes, Miss Hunt," he replied. And she gathered up her bags, and was gone. Fletch felt like he'd frightened her off.

Peter Ash joined him. "Terrible news," Fletch offered.

"Terrible that someone felt they had to resort to such violence, terrible that a young man who could have made a difference might die, terrible that his wife and children are in danger of losing him. So terrible, in fact," and his father cocked an ironic eyebrow, "even the die–hard Republicans around here are shocked."

Fletch nodded, unable to raise a grin right now. "Don't you wish you were out there? Able to do something?"

"I'm happy here," his father said mildly, as he always did when Fletcher brought this up.

"You could have been working as a journalist on one of the big papers, you could be covering all this. Or, if not, you could be writing books, novels that mean something."

"What's a novel against this? It's no answer. No, you won't make me regret staying here in Idaho, son." Peter Ash smiled a little. "You've tried often enough, since your mother died."

"A young man who could have made a difference," Fletch quoted. "Is that what we'll have to say about you, too?"

"You say what you see, Fletcher. Isn't that what I taught you?"

Fletch had reached his father's height a year ago: he straightened to meet Peter's gaze directly, and said, "Well, I see that you could have been a writer, a good writer, and it's all gone to waste. And Harley should go and study to be a chef, but he's just going to marry Beth and stay here, too."

"It's not a waste, is it, for me to have been a good husband, to bring up two fine boys? And your brother won't be wasted, either, Beth will see to that. Come on, I know you like her."

"Of course I like her, that's not the point." An old but vivid memory: Beth in pale winter sunshine, her bobbed blond hair flying around her laughing face, breath steaming as she played tag with her boyfriend's little brother in the backyard. Beth and Fletch had been evenly matched back then, before he'd really begun growing, while Harley could always run rings around them both without even trying.

"They'll make each other happy. Besides which, I hate to think what you and I would have ended up eating without Harley to take care of us, these last years. We're each entitled to make our own decisions."

Fletch sighed, kicked disconsolately at a convenient pile of boxes. His burst of frustrated anger seemed a little ridiculous, from this side of it. "Yes, all right. Sorry."

"Never mind, Fletcher. It's an overwrought sort of day, that's all. I don't want the man to die, but this waiting is a difficult thing to bear."

"Go on – do it with overwrought."

Peter put his head back, considering for a moment. He listed, "Overwrought, overwhelming, overpowering. Excitable, emotional, explosive. Turbulent, tumultuous, tempestuous."

Fletch did laugh a little, then. "Yeah, it's a tempestuous sort of day."

"See, son? This amazing talent isn't wasted. Amazing, astonishing … awesome."

"All right, all right," Fletch allowed, still smiling. But when the bell announced a new customer, and his father asked him to stay around, he just shrugged. And, as soon as he was alone, Fletch snuck out through the back again.

They were strangers: that was what made Fletch's mind up.

He'd been dragging his feet, walking down the main street, watching the townsfolk. The suspense was wearing their shock down into grim grief. Surely by now no one was expecting to hear Bobby would survive. They stood in knots of three or four, talking in hushed tones, nodding a greeting to him as he wandered past. The café and the shops with televisions had clusters of customers, though trade was slow.

Off to one side of all this quiet dismay a couple sat in the front seat of their nondescript car, drinking spirits from a bottle. In contrast to the rest of the people, they appeared almost excited.

So, there were strangers in town who, even though they apparently found the upheaval of an assassination to be stimulating, still felt swayed by some herd instinct to share the experience. Or maybe they got a kick out of watching all this. Grief voyeurs. Anarchists. Interesting, anyway.

Fletch strolled along casually, carefully not drawing anyone's attention, until he was level with the pair – then he swiftly opened the back door of their car and slid onto the seat. "Hello," he said.

The man and woman were startled. The woman continued to stare at Fletch, her expression resembling a disapproving maiden aunt more than anything. The man turned away to face the windshield, and said, "Beat it, kid."

"You must be the only people around who aren't crying."

The woman relaxed, and said with weary sarcasm, "I don't see the tracks of your tears either, honey."

"Don't encourage the brat," the man snapped. He caught Fletch's eye in the rear vision mirror. "I told you to get lost."

"Where are you from?" Fletch asked. "Not from around here."

"We're from Disneyland, kid. Happy now? So, beat it."

"Where were you last night between the hours of nine and midnight?"

"What is this? Twenty questions?"

"Do yourself a favor," the woman said at the same time, "and scram."

"What, you think we shot Kennedy, then drove up here to hide out?" the man asked.

"You were at Miss Hunt's, weren't you? She said the jewelry wasn't worth much."

"I don't know what the hell you're talking about," the man insisted. But he looked distinctly uncomfortable. The woman was staring fixedly ahead as if she didn't want to give anything away.

Fletch smiled, having suddenly been inspired. A local deputy, in plain clothes, was strolling down the far side of the road with his daughter. "You want to do over a place that has the real goods? A new television, diamond earrings and necklace from his grandmother, probably a bit of cash if you knew where to look."

"How likely is that?" the man asked.

"His mother was a Kansas City debutante, married an Idaho farmer. She had plenty of money, so he's got lots of valuables, portable ones. Isn't that what you're after?"

"A society dame and a farmer … this is about as believable as a soap opera. Look, kid, I don't know what you're getting at –"

"He's always out drinking on Wednesday and Saturday nights, with the men at the roadhouse. It's a town tradition."

"Tonight, who knows what people will be doing? Look at them! He was only a politician."

Fletch swallowed a few loyal retorts. "Yeah," he agreed softly. "Just another politician. Used to be his brother's pet bureaucrat."

The man laughed as something occurred to him. "Hey, you'd think they'd be used to this by now, all these politicians being gunned down." But when neither the woman nor Fletcher responded to the black humor, the man sobered. "Kid, I don't know what your idea is –"

"Let me come with you. I owe him."

"And how do we know we can trust you?"

"You don't. But how far are you going to get? I mean, if you just pick them at random. You need a little local advice."

The man was silent for what Fletch's watch timed as eleven minutes and thirty–five seconds, while the woman cast uneasy glances at all and sundry. Fletch patiently waited him out. Maybe it was a test of sorts.

"All right," the man finally agreed. "But if you rat on us, kid, you have no idea what sort of trouble you'll be buying into."

The essence of the dream was always the same: he was going to fall, and he didn't have the willpower or the strength to save himself. Sometimes he clung to the ledge of a building, with a busy street twenty stories below; sometimes it was a cliff and rocks and the pounding sea; or he was supposed to climb this rope ladder he dangled from, climb up into the safety of the helicopter, though mountains and gorges swung dizzyingly beyond his feet.

There was always help, and there was always some way he could scramble up. His father was reaching a hand out, or there were footholds, or it was a simple matter of exerting himself.

But he could never make the necessary effort, never had the guts to live through the agony of suspense. It wasn't that he lacked the physical strength – it was more like strength of character that he needed. "Hang on, Fletcher, just one minute more," his father would promise. But he couldn't bear it any longer, he always gave in, took the easy way out, decided to end the wait.

"Sorry, Dad," and he'd stretch out his cramped fingers with relief, and slip away. At first the air would welcome him, cushion him in its expanse. Freedom, floating. But then he'd twist and see the hard uncompromising ground rushing at him. And terror would wash through him. He didn't even have the courage to accept the result of his own decision. He'd scream out a protest, claw at the air as if he could clamber back up to where Peter waited aghast.

Small mercy – he would wake himself with his cry, or Harley would throw something at him from across the room, and Fletch would lie awake, sweating out the rest of the night. He didn't want to know what would happen when he hit ground.

The sound of a key in the front door. The thieves were so busy hefting the television to the pile they were collecting in the front room, they didn't hear. Fletch, standing on nervous watch by the door to the hall, froze, then leaned back against the wall in dramatic relief. He'd been expecting Sheriff Ryan to return home at least quarter of an hour ago.

"Peter?" A woman's voice in the dark.

Fletch almost said, *Mom?* but remembered just in time: his mother was dead; the Sheriff and his father shared a name. His heartbeat didn't slow as he realized this was Marissa Ryan, the Sheriff's wife.

She must have heard a noise, but all was quiet now. A breathless pause, then she turned on the light.

Another long moment as she stared at Fletch. She almost seemed relieved, until she caught sight of the other two straightening from their burden. Time for an accusing glare back at Fletcher, and then the man stepped towards her.

Marissa dropped the paper bag of groceries she was carrying, let them plummet to the floor without a second thought, which was smart, but then she began running down the hall towards the back of the house. The man gave chase.

Not so clever, Fletch was reasoning, even as he sprinted after them, the woman on his heels squealing in excitement. Why hadn't Marissa slipped out through the front door? It was only three steps away, and she'd left it open.

They were still in the corridor when the man tackled her, and the two of them went down, Marissa's cry choked off. Fletch skidded to a halt, and the woman ran into the back of him, loudly encouraging her partner in his tussle.

Dragging Marissa to her feet, the man hauled her into the kitchen, pushed her up against a bench. Her dark hair was loose now, and her blouse in disarray. The man was laughing, enjoying this. Fletcher followed in a daze, having fifty ideas of what to do, and none of them any use.

"Fletcher!" Marissa appealed. How could he be a part of this? The man slapped her, and when she tried to cry out again, he smothered her mouth with his own. Her eyes rolled as if she would faint, her struggles intensified.

"Come on, kid," the man said to Fletcher, before kissing her again. The woman shoved Fletch forward, laughing.

Fletch took a dazed step, then another. He surely wasn't capable of doing this. But he couldn't tell if he was more revolted or excited by the power of it, by the realization of all that this man was experiencing. Too tempting, too easy, to give in to the urge, the imperative, to allow the riot of sensation, to experience all that life had to offer at this very moment.

But, no – not at Marissa Ryan's expense.

He stepped forward, grabbed the man by the shoulders and threw him down, away. The man's hands, bereft of Marissa, grappled with Fletch instead. They rolled across the floor in fits and starts, Fletch wondering whether the man was trying to hang on or wrestle free.

He was dimly aware of Marissa running, fumbling at the back door, the woman too slow to stop her – Marissa calling out, "Peter!" So, he thought: smart after all, if the Sheriff was out there, and Marissa had been trying to reach him.

There was never an opportunity to take a swing at the man, so Fletcher kept clinging on, desperate for Ryan to show up and take charge. The woman had first run to escape through the front door, but now returned to try and tear Fletch off her partner. She had long fingernails, a wiry strength, and a piercing shriek.

But then at last Marissa and the Sheriff pelted in.

Confusion all round, and embarrassment, and frayed nerves. Fletch told his story each time he was asked, in a different order, with a different emphasis, examining each detail. They seemed to guess he was hiding his personal reactions and reasons. Peter Ash spent the night justifying him.

"It's not so much what he did, as how he did it," Ryan said for the hundredth time. "He could have told one of us when he spotted the pair in the street. He even admitted Doug was walking by at the time."

"And what could you or Doug have done? Arrested them for illegal parking? This way you caught them red–handed. There's no chance the charge won't stick."

"Don't go advising me on how to apply the law. We caught your son red–handed, too, remember. He was aiding and abetting a crime."

"His only intention was to get the pair in a position for you to do something about them. You should be calling him a hero, not treating him like a villain."

"Maybe. Those two have a record a mile long, all petty thieving and minor assault and what have you. I'm just glad they didn't get to add rape to the list."

"We're all glad of that, of course."

Silence for a moment, then: "It's almost two in the morning, Ash, and it's been one hell of a day. Take the boy home."

"Not until you make a decision, Ryan. Tell us where we stand. Though I have to warn you that if you decide to press charges, you'll have a fight on your hands. This boy just gave you the biggest collar you could hope for around here."

Ryan sighed wearily. "All right, all right, we won't press charges. Just get him out of my sight. And don't let him near Marissa for a while, or I won't be held responsible."

"He's already apologized to her, explained what happened."

"Don't tempt me, Ash – his story lacks a certain something."

"He stopped the worst of it."

"Marissa's in no mood to listen to reason, and I can't say as I blame her. Let her simmer down. There's no real harm done."

"Does she want to press charges?"

"No. No, to be fair, she told me not to. She wasn't against me scaring him a bit, though."

Peter stood, put his arm around Fletcher's shoulders. "He's scared enough."

"Yeah. Go on, take him home."

Fletch said again, "I'm sorry."

For a long moment Ryan just stared at him, then at last he held out his hand, and they shook on it. "You'll probably give yourself enough hell," Ryan commented. "In fact, I'm counting on it."

It was only too true. Fletch felt he would be re–living that afternoon and evening for years.

"Sheriff," one of the deputies murmured from the doorway, "there's news coming in from Los Angeles."

"Bad news?" Ryan asked even as he reached for the radio, and the man nodded.

Bobby Kennedy had died a few minutes ago. Fletch slipped his arms around his father's waist and held on tight, wishing he could cry, dully amazed that he had been hoping for good news after all.

Peter drove them home in silence. They found Harley asleep at the kitchen table, with fresh–baked cookies and a brew of coffee waiting. He listened to the outcome of Fletcher's escapade, and gave his brother a hug, before stumbling off to their bedroom. Fletcher sat down opposite his father, nibbled at a cookie. It was ridiculous that it should taste so good, despite the circumstances and his lack of appetite.

At last he said, "I'm going, I'm leaving Idaho."

"I know," Peter said quietly.

Fletch groaned, a little amused. "Of course you do."

"The last couple of years, you've been working hard. Had yourself moved up a grade, tested out of that and into the next. You've been applying to colleges. It was hardly a secret, was it?"

"I'm sorry." Fletch was sick with how sorry he was. "I should have talked it over with you."

"I trust you. You're young, very young, and you'll find it rough out there – but you set yourself a worthy goal, and you'll reach it through your own efforts. I'm not going to stand in your way. Just remember we'll be here for you."

"Even after tonight?"

Silence for a few beats of Fletcher's heart. Then Peter said, "There's more to tonight than is readily apparent. You'll have to think it all through. I certainly will. But, yes, I still trust you."

"There are bridging courses available next semester."

"All right. Harley and I will be all right."

"What about me?" Fletch asked, choking off a surprised laugh.

"You'll be fine. You're vulnerable, but you have strengths, too. There's more to you than any of us know."

Too difficult, to be placed so firmly out from under his family's wing like that. A terrible responsibility. But Fletcher could acknowledge, over the hurt and the fear, that Peter had just done as much as he could for his younger child.

Fletch stood, and said, "We found some strange ways to mourn for Bobby Kennedy today."

"Chaos begets chaos."

"Goodnight, Dad." Fletch hugged him, left Peter alone at the table.

For a long while, Fletch lay awake in his bed, restless but trying not to disturb Harley. Eventually his brother asked, "Are you going to have nightmares again?"

"I suppose so," Fletcher said.

"Come over here, then. You need your beauty sleep, little brother."

He crept through the darkness into Harley's bed, and cuddled up close in the reassuring arms. Though Harley was over six feet tall, with a football player's build, he had inherited Peter's unassuming manner and warm brown eyes: Fletch felt forever comfortable with his big brother. He smiled to himself as Harley began gently snoring, and let himself pretend to be a child one last precious time.

CHAPTER ONE
COLORADO
MARCH 1981

"Doesn't this feel like déjà vu?" Special Agent Fletcher Ash asked, the uneasy laugh in his voice betraying the fact he was shaken. Not that Ash ever tried to hide such vulnerabilities.

Albert Sterne forced himself to turn away from his companion and instead stared out the side window of the four–wheel–drive as trees shrouded in cloud sped by. Ahead, the asphalt road rushed at them, winding out of nowhere, oddly hypnotic. Yet the man's image remained clear in his mind's eye. The bare facts did little to describe Fletcher Ash: white male, of Irish descent though born and raised in Idaho; twenty–nine; one–seventy–five; black and blue. The neat features were regular, framed by a strong jaw, not quite handsome. But despite Ash being invariably unkempt, there was a very real presence hinted at by the hot blue eyes, the thick dark mess of hair.

"Or don't you ever get déjà vu, Albert?"

"No, Idaho Joe, I do not. And it is only a form of paramnesia; the result of a misfiring in the temporal lobe. It has no real meaning." But eventually Albert sighed and said with what he hoped was a pointed lack of interest, "What is it that I am supposed to be reminded of?"

"Our first case together, five years ago almost to the day. Don't you remember? I found that body out here in the mountains, too."

"I trust you can't tell me exactly how many of your cases I've worked on since then."

The uneasiness yielded to a genuine chuckle, though Ash's face remained even paler than usual. "Thirteen, unlucky for some. Not counting my various visits to Washington, of course."

"Of course," Albert echoed, hoping he didn't sound as alarmed as he felt.

But Fletcher was laughing outright, which was somewhat reassuring even though Albert suspected he was the butt of the joke. "Had you worried there, didn't I?" the younger man said. "Thirteen is a guess, I don't know how many it's been – probably more, don't you think? I just wish we could stop meeting like this."

"And I wish your conversation wasn't so littered with clichés."

Fletcher cast him an amused glance. "Do you mind people associating you with death? I hardly ever see you except when we have a murder case up here – or when I stumble across another corpse."

"It's a wonder the local murderers haven't realized you spend half your life tramping around these forests. They could find more secure places to leave their refuse."

"I don't have much luck, do I? I'll have to find some other way of spending my weekends. Hiking has produced too many nasty surprises." Silence for a while, then Fletcher said very low, "There are three graves. They're shallow, maybe only two feet deep, in a patch of dirt by a river. One of them –" He paused for a moment before continuing, "The spring thaw has washed one of the graves partly open."

"You're trying to tell me that one of the bodies is exposed."

"Yes." Ash abruptly slowed the vehicle for no reason that was immediately evident, then turned onto a dirt track that appeared to their left. He frowned in concentration, as the track quickly became steep and burdened with rocks and potholes.

"Whoever buried the bodies either brought them hiking – alive – or killed them and drove them here," Albert postulated.

"Yes. He's likely to have camping equipment or a four–wheel–drive vehicle or both. Perhaps someone who fishes, or traps, or hikes. Mind you," Fletcher added, "that doesn't narrow it down. In Colorado every man, woman and dog owns a four–wheel–drive."

"Does he know this particular area?"

"Well enough to have found the site – there wouldn't be many suitable places to bury three bodies around here, it's very rocky – and to return to it at least twice over a period of weeks. The snow would have hidden the graves in winter, though perhaps he didn't foresee the river flooding in spring."

"Or perhaps he didn't care."

"Yes. He may have figured that by the time the bodies were discovered or washed downstream they wouldn't be any use to us."

"Naïve."

"He's gotten away with murder three times at least. He probably thinks he's too clever to be caught. Actually," Ash continued, "I'm working on the assumption that he wanted the bodies to be found – because if he didn't, the easiest thing to do is just drop them down an old mineshaft. There are plenty around here, and the bodies would never be seen again." Ash pulled over to park behind a line of cars on the side of the track. "We're here."

"Obviously."

"Once again, we have to walk the rest of the way. Told you this feels like déjà vu."

"Fine," Albert said, all the more impatiently because the memories were indeed vivid. After five years he still found Ash as compelling as he was annoying. And Fletcher Ash was inevitably *very* annoying.

Albert climbed down, hefted his metal case from the floor of the cabin to the ground, then paused to button his coat. Fletcher, already bundled up in a shabby–looking quilted jacket, headed off into the trees, glancing back once to ensure Albert was following. "If the bodies were carried in," Albert concluded after a couple of minutes, "he's strong – or there's more than one offender."

"Strong as a bear," Ash muttered.

"What?"

"I feel that it's just one man. Built large, strong."

"I see." And then there was the familiar bright yellow tape strung between the trees. Albert ducked under it to see the swollen river, which had retreated from the bare dirt surrounding an arm and shoulder. There was torn black plastic around the limb, and the usual flood–debris of leaves and twigs. The flesh was bruised and tainted. If that was the most recent body, then the two bare mounds further from the river would contain little more than skeletons.

Albert could see why Ash had assumed there were weeks–long intervals between the graves. The one closest to the rock wall that sheltered them was only just visible – the dirt was old, the mound sunken. The site itself was well–chosen, tucked away underneath a cliff, with no reason for anyone to visit or even notice it. The other bank was only a few feet away, but the combination of rocks and the spring thaw made it virtually inaccessible. The river had washed mud and silt into the corner formed by the rock wall, so the dirt was damp and easy to dig. The river would also wash away any indication of who'd been there –

though if the murderer had realized that, he'd have known the bodies might be uncovered at some stage.

"He's smart," Albert said. "Other than the shallowness of the graves."

"Too smart," a woman agreed from behind him.

It was Agent Caroline Thornton, Ash's supervisor at the Denver field office. Albert nodded a perfunctory greeting.

"I'm afraid he won't have left anything useful," Thornton continued, "especially with the weather recently. Fletch and I have been over the area with no luck."

Shrugging this off, Albert began a quick examination of the site himself, dictating notes to a miniature cassette recorder.

It was a painstaking business, unearthing the bodies. Albert, as patient and thorough as ever, worked with a small trowel and tray. He let Ash and Thornton sift through the dirt for anything that could provide a clue to the offender, but kept an eye on their progress. The local cops clustered around, watching, but for once kept out of the way.

After an hour's work, Albert had uncovered the rest of the corpse closest to the river. It was encased in black plastic, the sort that might be used in gardens to control weeds, and was bound about the neck, waist and ankles with tape, in what originally would have been a careful parcel.

"He took his time over this," Thornton observed. "He's a cool one."

"Cool, smart, strong, confident," Ash listed.

Albert had stepped back outside the crime scene tape to collect his camera from the case. "I assure you I'm smarter," he said flatly.

"You can include arrogant on both sides of the equation," Thornton muttered, loud enough for them all to hear. The locals nervously chuckled.

Several photos were added to those Albert had already taken of the undisturbed site. And then he carefully cut the bindings and pulled the plastic open.

"First corpse is male," Albert told the cassette recorder. "Apparently naked – no clothes, no watch, no jewelry. Face down in the grave. State of the flesh indicates he's been dead at least three months, though probably longer due to the cold conditions." He turned to add to Thornton, "Have the coffins arrived yet? We'll have to box this one up now or he'll fall apart."

"Half an hour ago," she informed him. The only signs of discomfort that betrayed her were a tightly pursed mouth and her position up–wind of the grave.

By contrast, Ash looked a little green. But he also bore the determination that Albert had come to expect from him.

"Tell them to bring a coffin over – but you and Idaho Joe carry it in." No point in letting anyone other than the three of them invade the crime site.

It was dusk by the time Albert was satisfied. The three had lifted the body from the grave, grasping only the plastic, laid it carefully on a clean sheet, wrapped it loosely, and placed the whole bundle into the metal coffin. Albert stuck FBI seals across where the lid met the box. "No one touches the stiff until I get there tomorrow," he said, glaring around at his colleagues and the locals. "Put it on ice."

The cops looked annoyed but carried the box away without argument. Thornton went with them, soothing ruffled feathers.

"You're staying up here tonight?" Ash asked.

"Unless you think there's some urgent need to dig up the other corpses in the dark, or examine that one in town." Albert waited with a sardonically raised eyebrow, though Fletcher Ash never argued with him about forensic procedure.

"There seems little point in risking evidence, given the age of the bodies. The offender is long gone."

"Exactly. I intend to wait here and discourage the curious."

"It'll get colder," Ash warned, "once this fog clears."

Albert shrugged.

"I'll stay with you."

"I don't want you here."

The young man looked at him. "I'm staying. We can take it in turns to catch some sleep in the truck." Silence, which Ash ended up filling: "It's not wise for you to stay up all night. We need your skills unimpaired over the next few days."

"Very tactful. Is everyone in Idaho as willful as you?"

"No one. Not even close."

"Just what I thought. Well, if you can possibly avoid getting scared, you can stay." He bit off those last words, unwilling to sound grateful.

The early darkness closed in, the world still muffled by cloud. Albert stood, leaning back against a tree, with his arms crossed. To his right, maybe ten feet away, Ash was hunkered down on the ground, staring fixedly up at the gravesites.

"What did you make of the fact," Albert eventually asked, "that the stiff was planted face down?"

Ash was quick to answer, as if he'd been mulling over the same thing. Or perhaps he'd been expecting Albert's interrogation. "If the killer was alone, then perhaps he rolled the body into the grave rather than lift it again, and didn't bother trying to move it when it landed face down. Or perhaps it shows a complete depersonalization of the victim, which would fit the standard profile of a disorganized killer. Or there is something else significant about it, especially if the others are also face down – perhaps something sexual."

"And what does your infamous instinct tell you?" Albert prompted.

"You don't believe in that," Ash reminded him. But when Albert just shrugged he continued, "Not the depersonalization – this one is organized. Mainly the sexual. Powerfully sexual."

"Powerful – as in overwhelming to you, or referring to his dominant behavior?"

"Yes. Both."

"You get a kick out of this sort of thing, don't you?"

"No," the young man said in a quiet little voice. Albert could read something of a lie in that; perhaps it was denial of a truth he disliked. Ash added, "I think you'll find he raped them."

"Really. And you sound so unhappy about it, when I expected you'd be glad of this chance."

"Glad of this? What on earth do you mean?"

"You're ambitious, Special Agent."

Ash was glaring, but after a moment he turned back to his consideration of the graves and sourly agreed, "Yeah, ambitious and unhappy."

Silence again, until a tediously polite argument over who would sleep first on the front seat of the four–wheel–drive. Ash gave in, and left strict instructions to be woken in three hours. Albert agreed solely for the sake of avoiding another argument.

CHAPTER TWO
COLORADO | WASHINGTON DC
MARCH – SEPTEMBER 1981

A tap on the window, and Fletcher sat up too fast – still half asleep, it took him a moment to recognize Caroline Thornton. "Slowing up, Fletch," she said, shaking her head in mock despair.

He swung open the door of the four–wheel–drive. "Good morning."

"Rough night?"

"Not so bad, considering I spent the small hours watching over three graves."

"I brought you some breakfast." She forestalled his immediate question: "And coffee. Plentiful, hot, black and strong …"

" … like I like my men," he completed their old joke. "Yeah, yeah."

She laughed. "You'll do, Fletch, and I don't care who says otherwise."

"Do for what, though?" he asked rhetorically. He stretched. "Come on." And, first collecting the precious thermos of coffee, Fletch led the way to the river.

Albert was already working on uncovering the second grave. "It's about time you showed up," he said, impatient. "The morning is already half over."

Thornton sighed, and cast a glance at Fletcher. "Damn. I thought he was just a bad dream I had last night."

"No such luck," Fletcher muttered. "Albert, Caroline brought us some breakfast, if you'd care to join us."

"Preferably before you open that one up, Mr. Sterne, if yesterday's stench is anything to go by," Thornton added.

It seemed for a moment as if Albert was going to subject them to another retort but he appeared to find the inner resources necessary to swallow the insult. And surely it was logical to eat right now, just as it had been logical to accept Fletcher's company overnight. "That would be fine," he eventually said as if the words tasted bitter.

It was a familiar sight that Fletcher found both reassuring and ghoulish: Albert working alone in a morgue, surrounded by corpses. He had all three of the bodies out on the tables, rather than his usual procedure of dealing with them one at a time. Fletcher closed the door behind him, and asked, "Have you determined the cause of death yet?"

"You'll have my report tomorrow morning."

Ash stared at the man for a moment. "If you know now, I'd appreciate you telling me."

"The second one," Albert said with exaggerated patience, indicating the corpse on the table he stood beside, "the offender hit too hard. Cause of death was coma due to this head injury."

"Compression of the brain," Fletch interpreted as he walked over, remembering the grisly textbooks that had haunted him, "resulting from a depressed fracture of the skull." Casting a quick look at the evidence, Fletch asked, "Are you implying he didn't intend the boy to die like that?"

"He didn't want to kill the boy that quickly. The other injuries – the few on this stiff, and all of them on the first and third – were inflicted before the victims died."

"So he takes sadistic pleasure in hurting them."

"In slowly and systematically killing them," Albert corrected. "Cause of death for the other two was anoxic anoxia."

"Asphyxia? What – he suffocated or strangled them?"

"If you look at the X–rays, you'll see the hyoid bone in each throat is fractured."

Fletch nodded. "Classic sign of manual strangulation."

"And, in this case, the evidence is not misleading. But the offender only killed them once he was finished. You'll be pleased to know there is evidence that, as you suspected, at least those two were sodomized. I suspect this one wasn't – the offender is not a necrophiliac. Now, if you'll let me continue before they decay any further ..."

But Fletcher asked, "Any identification yet?"

"No. I plan to search the dental records of local missing persons. The earliest one, for instance, used to have braces."

"Used to, sometime before he was killed? Or did the offender remove them to hinder identification? I guess he could have really hurt the boy, doing that, if pain was his main intent."

Albert cast him a surprised look. "You have a nasty imagination, Special Agent. The boy still has a correctional plate – I conclude that a qualified orthodontist removed the braces and replaced them with the plate."

"All right." Refusing to react to the pedantic delivery of this information, Fletcher sat down in a chair over by the wall, and watched Albert return to work. "They aren't as decayed as you anticipated."

"The bodies were securely wrapped, so the first two were well preserved, and they would have been kept very cold throughout the winter months. You might consider whether preservation was his intention or whether the plastic was simply to minimize the exchange of trace evidence. It was only the latest that was decaying badly because the wrapping was breached in the flooding."

After a while, Fletch said, "I thought I might go to HQ, start examining the files for similar crimes. I can't find anything here, none of the police can recall anything similar. Caroline said she'd stay on and look into the identifications."

"You won't find anything in Washington."

"He must have killed before. He was too cool about this."

"But he's too smart to leave a trail."

"I assure you I'm smarter," Ash said, quoting Albert's words of the previous day. "I'm going to find this man."

"Really," Albert said, with a patent lack of interest.

"And you're going to help me."

"That's not for you to decide."

"Really." Fletcher held the cold gaze easily. "You know, it's fifteen. I worked it out. Fifteen cases you've helped me with, over five years."

But Albert turned away.

Fletch deliberately changed the subject. "It's not that I want to go away right now. If I break one more date with this woman I'm seeing … It's getting complicated, and I'm afraid she'll think it's simpler to –"

Albert said, "I have work to do, Ash." He leaned over the table, reaching for one of his steel tools.

"That's fine, Albert. I'll see you when I get back." He didn't get a response, so Fletch left the room, quietly pulling the heavy door shut behind him.

When in Washington, it had become Fletcher's habit to meet with McIntyre, who'd been transferred to Records at HQ some years ago.

They always went out together for lunch and gossip, and Fletch found Mac very useful when he needed to search the Bureau's files for a case. This visit was no different. Fletcher headed down to Records as soon as he arrived, called Mac to the counter and told him that he'd left Albert behind conducting autopsies.

Before Fletch could explain any further, Mac drew away and gazed at him in wonder. "You voluntarily asked Albert Sterne up to Colorado again? You must be a masochist or something. Most people are smart enough to avoid him and there you are encouraging him at every opportunity. You're gonna learn this one the hard way."

Fletcher chuckled, though he couldn't help but reflect that, while Albert was not the easiest person to know, he surely didn't deserve this continual antipathy. "Come off it. You like him, too."

"Don't tell him that. Anyway, it's more a case of I used to like him, but I wised up. Celia always asks after him," Mac commented wistfully, "but at least she's not always inviting him down there. You should wise up, too."

"Caroline would agree with you."

"Hey, did you hear the latest?" Mac cast a glance around Records to ensure there was no one within hearing distance, then leaned closer over the counter. "Albert walks in one day, and there's this photo on his desk, in a nice frame so it looks like it's a girlfriend. But it's not a photo, it's an X–ray of a stiff, one of the Jane Does from the cold room. Someone had done its hair up, given it earrings and one of those cheap metal necklaces, you know the ones with a name – the name being *Albert*, of course – and posed it. Everyone was expecting him to hit the roof, but he just looked at it, and got on with his work. Then the next day the whole forensics staff, and anyone else even remotely connected, find themselves sitting through this mandatory three–hour lecture on ethics and professionalism in forensic pathology, by the driest professor on earth."

Fletch listened to this with a raised eyebrow. "Serves them right."

"Nothing fazes that guy. A couple of weeks ago, someone slipped a paper clip under a body when it was being X–rayed. They must have taken a proper X–ray for Albert to work with, then slipped this fake one into the report to Jefferson. You could hear Jefferson yelling a mile away, wanting to know why Albert hadn't included in his report that the stomach contents included a damn paper clip – it was a poison case, you see. I don't think Albert deigned to react that time."

"That's going a bit far."

"True enough," Mac agreed. "But you have to admit it was kind of funny."

"Yeah. So, did they get a laugh out of the lecture?"

"Laugh? Don't be ridiculous. They were bored out of their brains, they hated him for it."

"But that's just Albert's sense of humor. I know it's dry, but …"

"Sense of humor," Mac was musing. "*Albert* with a sense of humor. What a crazy concept."

Fletch stood straight again, frowning. "Doesn't anyone know him at all? He'd have been thoroughly amused, putting them through that."

"You think? Apparently he just sat up the front, totally bland. You know that standard expression of his."

"I know there's a lot going on behind it."

Mac mirrored Fletch's frown. "I guess they appreciated him not turning in the people responsible. On the other hand, no one thought it was fair to punish them all."

"I can't believe they find him that difficult to understand. He must have *some* sort of relationship with his colleagues – even if it's only playing horrible jokes on each other. You know, Mac," Fletcher continued, "I thought at least you understood him. We hardly ever gossip about anyone else, and you're always right when you bother analyzing him."

"You're the one who does most of the analysis."

"This is mad." Frustrating. Fletch didn't know if he was more annoyed at Albert for his stubbornness, or at the rest of the world for being so easily fooled.

"It's revolting, that's what it is. Her skeleton hands over her heart, and that ghastly necklace. I think – I *hope* he shredded the thing."

"Why does he make his life so impossible?"

"Don't tell me he's finally losing your sympathy after all these years."

"No … He interests me, and I can still see that pony in there – but I want to know why there has to be so much shit. Anyway," Fletch continued with a conspiratorial smile, "I suspect the interest is mutual, and what more does one person need to like another other than to be liked in return?"

Mac shrugged, and drew back. "Just don't tell him it's me that passes on the gossip."

"You value his good opinion, don't you? I'll tell you the truth, though – that's only one on a long list of reasons I don't want to broach all this with him."

"So what are you doing here, Fletch? Other than catching up with the gossip on Albert, of course. What's this case you have him working on?"

"I found three bodies," Ash said quietly after a moment, "and I need to trace the offender. He's done this before, he has to be somewhere in your files."

"What have you got on him?"

"White male, probably in his late twenties or early thirties; victims all white males, between eighteen and twenty–five; sadistic sexual homicide; fits the organized profile."

Mac stared for a moment. "What else have you got? That's very broad. There's too many of the bastards out there. Though I suppose most of them prey on women, don't they?"

"Yes, they do." Fletch said, "Let's find a spare desk – there's plenty of detail."

"How was the flight?" Caroline Thornton asked on Fletcher's return to Denver.

"Scary."

"Bad weather?"

"No," Fletch told her, "this ghastly stuff they tried to convince me was coffee."

"You poor boy."

They eyed each other and laughed, and then grew serious. "You've identified two of the victims," Ash prompted. The high cold wind and the weak sunshine made the airport parking lot an uncomfortable place to loiter. But it seemed better to talk about these things in the clean open air.

"The first was through the orthodontic plate – his dentist matched it up. Andrew Harmer, an eighteen–year–old college student, lived on campus here in Denver. Went missing in September, six months ago, with no warning."

"Family?"

"Parents and two younger sisters. They live out of town." She exchanged another glance with Fletch. "And they're taking it about as badly as you'd expect. The father insisted on identifying the body, you know what state it was in."

"Do they know all the gruesomes?"

"The broad story, not the detail. I did the hard stuff last night, you missed out on that – but we're going to interview them now, before the papers take hold and shake it up."

"We, as in … ?"

"You and me, Fletch. That's where we're heading."

Ash sighed. "All right. Is there someone local?"

"No one who knows them well. The police lent us someone to leave with them for twenty–four hours."

"I don't suppose this ever gets any easier."

"We need the information, you know that. And I don't trust anyone else to do it."

Fletcher suddenly smiled a little, wry. "Like Albert Sterne, for instance?"

Thornton groaned. "Don't even joke about it. This is the last time you invite him onto our cases, I swear. The bastard has finally succeeded in annoying everyone in Colorado. It'll be a wonder if he isn't the next corpse we find two feet under a river bank."

"We'll have to try to prevent that – we're going to need him. What about the other ID?"

"The third body was Brett Jones, twenty–four, worked in a restaurant outside Grand Junction."

"So the offender traveled a lot, at least within Colorado."

"Yes …" Thornton frowned thoughtfully. "I was going to assume that he might be a truck driver, a salesman, something like that. But it seems to me that a fair proportion of the serial killers we know about covered a lot of miles, looking for victims. Perhaps that's how they operate."

"Maybe one of the things we look for is a four–wheel–drive with a relatively high odometer reading. And someone who's away from home a lot. But does he live out in the country where the bodies were found, or around Grand Junction, or in Denver –"

"– or somewhere else entirely?"

"And how did he meet the young men? He must have brought them home, somewhere he felt safe and could take his time, but how did he get them there?"

"Invited them," Caroline suggested.

"That would make him very plausible."

"Many of these serial killers have been."

"Yeah, you're right. Maybe he has a cabin up in the mountains."

"You want to start narrowing this down, Fletch?"

"Not yet. Tell me about Brett Jones."

"He lived alone, only a father – they weren't close. Brett didn't turn up for work one day back in November but his father didn't report him missing for two weeks."

"How did you identify him?"

"Matched the photo from Missing Persons and confirmed it with medical records. The father seemed to think his only son was heading for a nasty end and got what he deserved."

"I hope you're kidding."

Thornton shrugged. "Maybe he's just trying to cope. Anyway, we're due to go talk to the Harmers. All right?"

"All right." Fletch slid into the passenger seat of Caroline's car. "So, getting to the mundane side of this business, who are we answering to on this one?"

"The Special Agent in Charge himself," Thornton declared with a tiny smile.

"You mean they're letting you and me run with it?"

"Cut our teeth on the thing, was how the SAC put it. This is it at last, I figured. A chance to prove ourselves, clamber up a rung or two. There's only one problem – you'll need to cancel that leave you wanted at the end of the month, or postpone it at least."

"Doesn't matter," Fletch said absently, puzzled by this unexpected opportunity.

"Wasn't it some family shindig up in Idaho?"

"Harley and Beth's tenth anniversary. And she's expecting their first child soon. Any excuse for a party, that lot."

"You're going to be an uncle? Congratulations! You going to mind missing the party?"

Fletch shrugged. "They won't miss me." He continued, "The thing is, why are they giving this case to us?"

"You found the bodies. That counts for something."

Not necessarily, Fletcher thought. He and Caroline were both relatively raw when it came to murder, especially a case like this which would surely prove to be complicated and high profile. Mac had said that he thought Fletch was being watched, that the Bureau still didn't know what to make of Fletcher Ash – and that hanging around with Albert Sterne wasn't going to win him any credits. Meanwhile, Caroline was in much the same boat because it wouldn't take many mistakes or misadventures for women to be edged out of the field and back to the typing pool. "Caroline," he said, "we're going to have to be careful."

"Yeah, why?" she asked absently, more interested in the traffic as she turned onto a busy road.

"Our careers are on the line. I've been working towards this since I was a kid, you're heading for special agent in charge if you play your cards right …"

"Cut the flattery, Fletch. I know all that, I know how important this job is to you." She spared him a glance. "Don't you think we're up to this?"

"We're good, we've been ready for this for years. But we've got to be careful, too."

"Sounds like perfectly normal paranoia to me."

"I'm serious."

"Okay, I figure I've been dealt a pretty damned good hand of cards. And you just happen to be one of them. So my advice to you is to view this case as an opportunity."

"But so many of these serial murders aren't solved."

"I know, Fletch. But you're as sick as I am with all the paperwork and shit–shoveling. Let's make this happen."

Ash said, "All right." Silence for a few minutes. They turned off the highway and into a town that seemed set to resist the urban sprawl. "Albert's in that good hand of cards."

Thornton let out a laugh. "A wild card, maybe. Or a joker – and who's the joke on?"

"He's very good, you know that as well as I do. And he has a lot more direct experience than both of us put together."

"God," she groaned, "if we must. I suppose we must. I'll talk to Washington again, see if he's assigned to anything else right now. If not, we'll ask him to hang around here for a few more days."

"Great," said Ash. "Thanks."

"Well, if he doesn't make you sorry for it, I surely will."

Andrew Harmer's sisters were only eight and eleven years old. The youngest, sensing the mood of the adults, swung between silent sulks and tearful stubbornness. After a few minutes of this chaos, Caroline asked the police officer to take the children off to play somewhere.

But the older sister turned back at the door, gazed directly at Fletch. "I thought you were bringing Drew home."

"I'm sorry, I'm afraid Drew won't be coming home," Fletch said evenly.

"So where is he?" she persisted.

"He's in heaven, child," her mother said, impatient and upset in equal measure. "I told you he's in heaven now."

The girl kept her eyes fixed on the young FBI man as if she expected a better answer from him. Fletch shrugged mentally. There were too many other toes he'd be stepping on. "Drew is in heaven," he repeated, willing himself and the girl to believe it. "He's happy there."

Then the children were gone. The five adults remaining waited in silence for a long moment, no one willing to begin this. Caroline and Fletch were on a two–seater, facing Mr. and Mrs. Harmer on a matching sofa. A tray of coffee makings sat neglected on the table between them. Albert was behind Fletch, sitting at the dining table, with strict instructions from Caroline to be seen and not heard unless he had some particularly useful question. The bereaved parents ignored his stony face.

Caroline at last moved to pour them each coffee. In the bustle of milk and sugar it seemed easier for her to say, "I know this has been truly terrible for you but we have to ask you some more questions."

The mother said, "I thought it would be a relief, to finally know one way or the other. But to think of the things you told us last night ..." She trailed off, and seemed to be waiting for someone to deny what had happened.

"I know," Caroline said as gently as she could, "it's the worst news we could bring you. But it's better coming from us than the lies they'll put in the papers."

"To think of the pain Drew went through, the shame of it." Her gaze was direct but Mrs. Harmer seemed unaware that she was wringing her hands as she spoke, wringing them over and over each other. "It's worse than not knowing, it's worse, and I thought it would be better. I'd rather imagine he ran away, though that would be – I shouldn't be thinking of my own feelings, but I can't help wishing, if he had to die, it could have been cleaner. For his sake, of course, for his own sake."

"The first thing I have to ask you," Caroline said, "is whether you have any idea who might have done this thing."

It seemed that this was the final outrage. Her hands tightened into fists. "Are you saying this monster could have been someone we *knew*? That Drew knew? That he endured all that at the hands of a *friend*?"

"An acquaintance, perhaps," Fletcher said. "Someone he'd met, even felt comfortable with."

"I have no idea how we can help you. We don't know any perverts like that."

"You often don't know with these people," Caroline said softly. "You often can't see it until you have the benefit of hindsight."

"His eyes on Drew," the mother was saying distractedly, "my poor boy suffering under the eyes of this inhuman monster. The shame he must have felt."

Caroline said, "It's over now. No more pain, and Drew had nothing to be ashamed of. We need to talk to you, to his friends, try to work out who did this. Try to stop him before he does it again. Can we ask you some questions, Mrs. Harmer? Mr. Harmer?"

"But we went through everything with the cops when Drew disappeared."

"I know, and I've read the paperwork. But maybe we can jog a memory that might not have seemed relevant at the time."

The father said with a frail calm, "The cops didn't care back then – you know how many people go missing each year? It's a wonder there's anyone in the State who's *not* missing from somewhere."

The questions took almost an hour. Had Drew been planning on meeting up with a man for the evening? Going away for the weekend?

Going on a trip, or camping, or hiking? Had he mentioned any new friends or acquaintances? Someone he was afraid of, didn't trust, felt uneasy with? A man who might have made sexual advances? Who'd made offers of work or money? Who owned a four–wheel–drive vehicle? An outdoors man? Someone who was built large and strong? But neither of Drew's parents could think of anything new.

"We saw a great deal of him, he was always bringing his laundry, expecting to be fed," Mr. Harmer said. "He'd catch the bus down, then want to be driven back to town. But he didn't talk much about his friends. There was a boy he roomed with at college, Scott. You should give him the third degree. They were close as thieves."

Albert spoke up. "What happened to his belongings?"

"It's all here. We'd hoped – of course, we wanted him to walk in that door again one day."

Caroline asked, "Would you mind if Agent Ash and Mr. Sterne had a look? There may be something useful."

Drew's remaining possessions were in boxes at the back of the garage. Fletch thanked Mr. Harmer, who lingered, perhaps mulling over the hopes that had now been thwarted. Eventually, Harmer said, "It might be six months ago for you, and for Drew. But it was yesterday for us."

"And it will take time," Fletch agreed. The FBI men waited in silence. When Drew's father finally left, Fletch opened the nearest carton.

There wasn't much to show for a life. As he and Albert worked through the record albums and the school books, Ash wondered if his own possessions would betray as little to an observer. Surely not. Drew's records were a range of Top 40 disposable pop, the subjects he studied a basic mix of math and accounting and economics, the notebooks and lecture pads carefully devoid of doodles, the three magazines all cars and hot rods, the few pieces of fiction dog–eared student issues of Austen, Melville and Shakespeare.

"Do you get the feeling," Fletch asked Albert, "this is all a little too bland? Very safe."

"Not everyone has such wide–ranging interests as you," Albert said sarcastically, flipping through another lecture pad. "Did you expect this place," and he tipped his chin towards the house, "to produce anything more flamboyant?"

"Maybe young Drew hadn't found himself yet."

"If you must use clichés. It's more likely he was simply as bland as these things indicate – after all, he was studying to become an accountant."

"I have an accounting degree." Fletcher faced the sardonic lift of an eyebrow, and smiled. "It used to be a requirement to become a special agent."

"I suppose you had to fill in the time until you turned twenty–three somehow."

"Yes. I went on to an arts degree in English, American and Russian literature."

"Spare me the banal details of your life, Ash." He turned away to the next box. "Pity the child was too boring to keep a journal or diary. Learned all about double entry bookkeeping today, he'd write. Drank my first cup of tea this evening – what would mother think?"

"Now who's descending into clichés and stereotypes? If you must insult a dead boy, you might as well say something original or witty."

Albert stared at him, furious. Fletch returned the gaze easily. But apparently it was not worth Albert's time and trouble to brawl with him – the forensics man turned away, adjusting the cloak of his dignity, and began working through the last carton.

For a few minutes, while Albert Sterne was absorbed in the task, Fletcher watched him. The man and his manner could be really ugly. And of course there was nothing to be done about the features of his face, which were each too bold, and didn't quite belong together, as if Albert were a botched Photo–FIT picture. The habitual expression of passionate indifference didn't suit him – but surprise or provoke him, and the dark brown eyes kindled into a beautiful intensity. The man had sensibilities, certainly, though they were heavily guarded from all, including himself.

As for the things more directly under Albert's control, they were a strange mixture of style and quality and severity. His hair was a very practical crew cut, which wasn't attractive, but Fletch couldn't imagine him wearing a longer style. His suits were understated and perfectly fitted and, Fletch suspected, not bought off the rack; while they were in strict accordance with Hoover's old dictates, they were of good material and pleasing color. The shirts and shoes were functional, the ties were subtle; though they were fine percale, leather and silk respectively. Albert appeared to appreciate comfort, but Fletch could read little vanity in him.

"I always suspected you couldn't perform more than one task at a time, Ash. Perhaps you should sit down while you have a little think. It might be safer."

Fletcher smiled. "Do you want to take any of Drew's things?"

"There's no point. But you can tell them not to dispose of them yet."

"Okay, that's sensible."

Albert looked a tad offended. "I'm so glad it occurred to you that I do make sense occasionally."

"I suppose we should go in." But Fletch didn't move, though he knew Caroline would be expecting him.

"All this tawdry grief makes you feel fragile, does it?"

"I … empathize too much. My mother died. I suppose that every time I witness someone else's grief, I feel my own."

"How self–indulgent. It's a wonder you can even function."

Fletcher stared at him. "I hope you're speaking from personal experience."

"My parents were murdered when I was five. I was the one who found them."

"And if you can survive it –"

"Anyone can. Yes."

"You're a hard man, Albert Sterne. Did you never let yourself grieve?"

For the briefest of moments, Albert flinched away from him, a potent flash of loss and rage in his eyes. But it was over so quickly, the mask was back so perfectly in place, that Fletcher wondered if he hadn't imagined the reaction, the sudden excess of a child's need.

Albert said, "You're wasting time with this trivial chatter."

Caroline had joined them, looking weary. "They wanted me to go over it again. It's hard to know where to draw the line, how to tell them about Drew without burdening them with the ghastly details."

"You poor thing. How are they doing?"

"How do you think? But his mother said that if she's going to have nightmares, they may as well be about what really happened. I think she thought she was capable of imagining something worse."

Albert snorted. "Imagination is the last thing these people suffer from."

Thornton looked at him, eyes narrow, but she addressed Ash. "Doesn't it seem awful to you that we build our careers on all this death?"

"We're making a career of catching criminals, Caroline." He looked away from his two companions. This was something he had to regularly remind himself of, and something guaranteed to provoke Albert's impatience.

"I know – really, I know intellectually that it's the offender alone who's responsible for the deaths. Emotionally is another matter."

"Are we trapped in a soap opera," Albert Sterne asked, "or can we get on with the job without the histrionics?"

"Have you finished out here?" Caroline asked Fletch.

"Yes, for now."

"Then let's say our farewells. I've invited the two of us along to the funeral – I'm sure Mr. Sterne will be far too busy to attend."

"If I can trust you to keep an eye on who else is attending, I won't need to go."

"You can trust us," Fletch said, before Thornton could retort. "Come on, let's get out of here."

"You drew the short straw again," Albert observed as Fletcher walked up to him in the foyer of the Bureau offices.

"No, I simply volunteered to take you with me to visit Drew's roommate. Caroline was so glad to be rid of us both, she said we could use her car."

"What overwhelming generosity," Albert muttered.

Once he had pulled out of the parking lot, Fletch said, "Meanwhile, Caroline is phoning HQ to see how long we can borrow you for."

"You didn't see fit to ask me first?"

"I figured this is the sort of case you joined the Bureau to solve, and you're loving every minute of it."

"Let's get two rules straight, Idaho Joe: you don't make asinine assumptions about me; and you minimize your morbid interest in my life and my career."

"You're an interesting person, Albert. Surely you'd be the last person to disagree with me on that score."

"Your lack of control is alarming."

"Yeah," Fletch agreed. "But, persistent as I am, a person can only take so much rejection. The woman I was seeing dumped me *in absentia*. Said she had her own life to lead, which is fair enough –"

Albert asked, "Am I supposed to care?"

"She was so pretty, had a beautiful smile. I loved making her smile."

"You think all women are pretty," Albert informed him. "You lack discrimination."

Fletcher grinned. "Yeah, I do, don't I? Guess I just adore women." Then he heaved a sigh. "It would be nice if they adored me back, mind you." He received no reply. "Rejection," Fletch repeated, looking across at his companion. "You're not much better, you know. I figure I'm going to stop asking you out to dinner one day."

"I can but live in hope."

"I'm harmless, you know. My only motive is friendship." Fletch laughed. "The anticipation of a friendship, to be more precise."

Albert cast him a dry glance. "I hardly suspected anything else."

"Well, you're not going to frighten me away like you do everyone else."

"Two rules only. Do I have to repeat myself?"

Fletch laughed again. "All right. A truce is declared."

"Don't flatter yourself," the man bit back.

"Are you Scott? Drew Harmer's friend?"

The boy looked from Fletch to Albert and back again. He was abruptly scared, as if he guessed at the news they brought. "Yes."

"I'm Special Agent Fletcher Ash, this is Mr. Albert Sterne, from the FBI. Can we come in? We need to talk."

"You've found him, haven't you? Drew. Is he – ?"

"Let us come in," Fletch said gently.

The boy suddenly sobbed, backed away, and the men followed him into the room he'd once shared with Drew. Albert shut the door, stayed there while Fletch went to sit by Scott on one of the beds.

"I thought it wasn't that, all this time I was hoping Drew was happy, he found what he wanted."

"What did he want?" Ash asked.

The storm had already passed, though Scott still shook in reaction. He was silent for a while, catching his breath, then he stood up and walked to stare out of the tiny window. "The usual things, I suppose," he said distantly.

Fletcher remained seated, studied the boy's profile. He prompted, "Tell me."

"You see, I didn't think he was dead."

"You've been keeping something secret for him, haven't you?"

Scott whispered, "Yes." He might have cried again, but perhaps decided to save it for later. "Drew went to meet a man that night. I was hoping he'd moved in with him. He didn't come to get his records and things, his family did, but I thought this man might have given him –"

"Why didn't you tell the police that at the time?" Albert snapped.

"It was Drew's business!" Scott protested. "His family were so horribly straight, he made me promise not to tell them *ever*. He thought they'd fuck it all up, drag him back home. I mean, he thought this was it, this was what he'd wanted – Did he, I mean was he – ?"

"He was tortured, raped and murdered," Fletcher said. "Maybe that night, and maybe by this man you say he went to meet."

"Oh hell," the boy moaned.

"It wasn't just Andrew Harmer's business, you little moron," Albert said, "it was Brett Jones' business, too. He died, and another boy we don't have a name for yet, who's lying in the morgue waiting to be claimed. And if you'd told anyone at the time, the man might have been stopped before he reached them."

"Oh fuckin' hell …" The sobs began again.

Fletcher moved to stand close to the boy. "Just tell us what happened," he said quietly.

"Drew met this man that afternoon. Drew was gay, you see. And this was his big chance, he'd never been with anyone before. He was so … high."

"Where did they meet?"

"I don't know. On a street somewhere. Drew was walking, and this guy drives up, and they talked."

"What sort of car did he have?"

"I don't know, honestly, I don't know. Black, it was – but Drew really didn't say any of that. He thought the guy was rich, thought he'd set Drew up sweet."

"If Drew thought the man was rich, could that be because of the car? Drew knew about cars, didn't he?"

"Yes, he did. Maybe that was why, or maybe the clothes he was wearing."

"All right." Fletcher cast a glance at Albert. "Now, what did the man look like? Drew must have told you whether he was handsome."

"Just that – big, he said, and handsome. Big, and good for …" The boy went to rummage through the drawers for a handkerchief.

"Good for what?" Fletch asked after a moment.

"For cuddling." Scott groaned. "Hell, this is terrible."

"Yes, it is. What were they going to do? Dinner, or a club, or a movie, or what?"

"They were just going back to his place. Watch the baseball or something, and – you know."

"What else did Drew say?"

"I don't know anything more. Except the man knew what he was doing. Suave. Drew was all a–flutter, he wasn't in any state to tell me much."

Albert commented sourly, "Some first date."

Scott pleaded, "I thought all this time Drew was happy."

"Did you really?" Albert asked.

The boy shuddered, and Fletch dropped an arm around his shoulders. "All right, that will do for now. Scott, I want you to come down to the Bureau offices tomorrow morning, in the Federal Building – do you know it? We'll get this down on paper. And think hard in the meantime, try to remember if Drew said anything else, a comment or a joke or any little detail."

"Okay," the boy said.

"Now, is there anything of Drew's that you kept? Anything he didn't want his parents knowing about?"

Scott went to the wardrobe, dug into a pile of clothes. "We had a couple of books – you know, gay books. Are you going to tell his parents?"

"We'll probably have to."

"Here. *Maurice* was his favorite." The boy cast a sad lingering glance over the novels. "They'll hate it, his folks – him being gay, I mean. Serves them right. Anyway," he continued, "there wasn't anything else. With

Drew, it was all in here." And he indicated his chest, his heart, with a clenched fist.

Albert rolled his eyes at this display.

Fletch gave the boy a business card. "Come and see me tomorrow, around ten."

"All right. Can I have the books back sometime? And do you think they'd let me have Drew's records?"

"I don't know," Fletch said distantly, and walked to the door.

Albert broke the silence. "You're here to get an education. Take responsibility for that, and quit wasting your life with day–dreams and pop music. Prince Charmings are as extinct as the dodo bird. Your friend Drew should have known that."

Scott seemed stunned. Fletch asked, "Is there anyone we can ask over, someone you can be with?"

"Adam, in the next room," the boy whispered, and he walked with them, slipped in through his neighbor's door when it opened.

Outside the building, Fletch said, "That was severe. He's just a kid."

"It was the most sense that butterfly's heard for years."

"You have a rather self–defeating way of helping people, Albert." But, Fletch reflected, at least the man tried.

After a moment, Albert asked, "How did it make you feel? Lying to the child this morning about her brother being in heaven."

"It was a white lie. Necessary."

"Most of society's interactions are white lies. But not therefore necessary."

"The rules don't go both ways? I have no problem with you showing a morbid interest in why I think what I think, Albert, and I'd like us to get to know each other better – but fair's fair."

There was a silence. Fletch added it up: Albert valued honesty, but when that conflicted with his precious privacy, the truth lost.

"Why don't we continue this over an early dinner?" Fletch suggested.

"I thought you were going to stop asking me."

"Give it a rest, Albert – I'm hungry, and I could do with a drink right now, that's all. Then we can head back to the office and get some more reports started."

Albert said, "That would be fine." The venom in him soured the words.

Perhaps the rules did apply both ways. They sat in silence over dinner, Fletch more interested in the wine, and Albert apparently not hungry. Fletch was mulling over all they'd learned that day.

"So," he said at last, after the waiter had cleared away their plates, "this man sees a boy walking, a good–looking boy, and pulls over to talk. The man is confident, attractive. The boy's suspicions are quickly put to rest, even though the man's built large and strong, even though he's picking Drew up off the street as if he were a prostitute. The man appears rich, drives a nice black car – is that a classy four–wheel–drive, or is it his town car? He probably has good clothes, a good haircut, maybe wears jewelry. He asks Drew home for the evening, they're going to watch the baseball on the television – we'll have to check the programming for that night. He's very plausible, persuasive. And Drew thinks all his dreams have come true. They agree to meet later."

"Why didn't the offender take him home right away?"

Fletcher shrugged. "He didn't want to frighten Drew until he had him safe. Or he had to prepare for what he wanted to do. Or Drew wanted to go and change his clothes, or tell Scott his good luck, and the man didn't risk insisting."

"If either of the brats had any sense, this never would have happened."

"True enough. And if Scott wasn't so loyal, or if Drew had thought his parents a little more tolerant, we might at least have been on the trail right away."

"Both too naïve for their own good."

"Do you think the offender liked that?"

"Speculation," Albert reminded him.

"Yes. Perhaps he liked that Drew was expecting romance, perhaps he liked devastating a virginal bright–eyed kid. The fear in the kid's face when he realized that Prince Charming had betrayed him."

"There's no need to sound like you relish the idea."

"It's not that I relish it – but I can empathize with the man who did."

"A distinction so small as to be meaningless."

"It's not something I'm comfortable with, but my instincts and intuition enable me to do this job. I use it."

"We've had this conversation before, Ash."

"And you didn't believe me. Do you now?"

"It's probably nothing more than an overactive imagination."

"Albert, I'll avoid making unjustified assumptions about you but that's the only rule, okay? And you can do me the same favor."

Silence again. Perhaps Albert wasn't used to being challenged, or to anyone showing such a persistent interest. After a while, Albert began talking about the case, going over ground already covered, but that tacit agreement was enough. Fletch smiled.

"It's been six months since you found the bodies," Caroline said. Her tone of voice was overly reasonable, gently insistent, as if she were trying to make a willful child see logic for the first time. She was sitting beside Fletcher, rather than behind her desk. "Two months since the bulk of the task force was stood down. A year since the first boy died."

"Drew Harmer," Ash murmured.

Caroline sighed and repeated, "A year since Andrew Harmer died."

Fletch wouldn't look at her. "You said we could hold them off, keep the case open." A willful child betrayed.

"Only for so long. We've taken all the leads, such as they were, as far as we could. There's been nothing on the car, no common acquaintances, no one who fits the profile, the few clues were all dead ends. We've been getting absolutely nowhere."

"That's not true – I'm sure those four victims in Wyoming were the same man. I only found that case in the files seven weeks ago. And there was something the previous year in Montana but I'm not sure yet whether that fits in."

"But no one else has been convinced that the Wyoming case and this one are linked. If the Behavioral Science Unit was more supportive of the idea, that would be a different matter. Face it, Fletcher, the link is a hunch."

"Do you believe me?"

Caroline sighed, watching him carefully. "There's never been any point in lying to you, has there?" she observed with an amused smile. She sobered again when he didn't respond. "Yes, I believe you, Fletch. I think you see this a little clearer than the rest of us. But the boss is calling us off. There are other cases, other crimes we need to devote resources to. It's important that we solve the ones we can, that we get some results."

"I understand all that. But this man has murdered at least seven young men, and he was so cool about it that he must have killed before – and he'll keep on doing it. That's the important thing."

"I know you've got Albert Sterne and that Irish guy helping you on this in Washington, and I fully expect you'll keep looking out for this man. If you find something, bring it to me, I promise I'll get the case re–opened – otherwise it will have to be on your own time from now on. That goes for all three of you."

Fletcher let himself smile a little. That was a better arrangement than he'd hoped for. "All right. As long as if we make progress –"

Thornton nodded, apparently pleased that Ash had seen reason at last.

"So, how are we doing? They gave us a case to cut our teeth on, and we still haven't solved it."

"We're doing fine. I don't think they expected us to get as far as we did."

"That's hardly reassuring."

"These cases – serial killers, random murders with no link between the offender and the victim – it's usually luck that solves it. Or the killer begins acting suicidally."

"Luck …" Fletch mused. "It's his bad luck that I'm on to him." And he offered Caroline a grin before heading out of her office.

CHAPTER THREE
WASHINGTON DC
DECEMBER 1981

Fletcher looked up as Albert entered the room. "This is a ghastly building," he said by way of a greeting, instead of the usual polite 'Good morning' he offered everyone else. "I hate headquarters. I don't know how you work here."

Albert shrugged off his coat, hung it up, and took the files out of his briefcase. "It's functional."

"I could debate that and win. Doesn't it seem typical to you that Hoover spent half the gross domestic product on a building that's more like a mausoleum than offices?"

"It never occurred to me, no." Albert sat and logged on to the computer, already used to these irrelevant tirades. They rarely lasted long, and Ash never indulged in his dissatisfactions with anyone else. Albert supposed he should consider it an honor rather than a burden.

"He haunts the place, you know ..." Fletcher said in what was presumably supposed to be a provocatively mysterious tone.

Albert merely raised a cynical eyebrow.

"Mac was telling me –"

"If you're going to listen to McIntyre's whisky–sodden tales, you'll get nothing but banal speculation and unjustified complaints. You should know better."

But Fletcher was in a restless relentless mood. "The staff on the night shift say they hear him every now and then, walking the corridors. He had these little feet, and he trots along as if there's something important going on. Then they hear Assistant Director Tolson dragging along behind, with his bad leg, trying to keep up with Hoover."

"Amazing what an abundance of caffeine will do to your imagination."

"Mac swears it's true. Now he's petrified he's going to end up working nights. He's more superstitious than my grandfather." Fletcher laughed. "You'll have to be more careful of what you say, Albert. Hoover's beyond just bugging the telephones and restrooms now – *way* beyond ..."

"That last story is not unfounded," Albert said. "I've seen proof that he used to bug the restrooms in the old HQ building. He was paranoid and assumed everyone was as unscrupulous as himself."

Silence for a moment, then Ash asked hesitantly, "Do you think it was true, about Hoover and Tolson?"

"I have neither seen nor heard any evidence to prove the existence of ghosts."

"Don't be obtuse. I mean the rumor that they were gay."

"We have work to do, Ash. And gossip does not become you."

"It's a fair question."

Albert said impatiently, "Then my considered opinion is that, if they were homosexual, they had even less justification for discriminating against and blackmailing people who shared their inclinations, though they had no real justification in the first place. But as it's unlikely we'll ever know the detail of their personal lives – the irony of which I'm sure does not escape you – there is no point in speculating."

"All right," Fletcher said, betraying a little annoyance.

What was next? The boy would declare, *Mac thinks you're gay, too.* To deflect the possibility, Albert asked pointedly, "Happy now?"

"No."

"Then what is the problem?"

"I'm tired of this place."

"After Thornton went to a great deal of trouble to get you two months' temporary assignment to Washington?"

"Just at the wrong time, too. I met this woman who travels around selling software, games and things, and she was only in Colorado for –"

"I believe you were complaining about the building," Albert reminded him.

Fletcher sighed. "We're here seven days a week. I've had enough."

"As I recall, you wanted the assignment so that you could work through these case files in your own time."

"I know, I know, and what fascinating reading they are ..." Fletcher sighed defeat, and sat down next to Albert, pulled a pile of files over. "What are we up to?"

"Looking for similar misdeeds in North Dakota." At the momentary confusion on the younger man's face, Albert said, "I finished Montana last night. Other than that pair of murders we'd already dismissed, there was nothing."

"Nothing, or hundreds. And they're hardly misdeeds. If I have to read one more description of –"

"You two here again?" It was one of the security guards on his regular patrol.

Fletcher dredged up a smile for the man. "Hello, Luther. Yes, we're on the same old wild goose chase."

"Chasing a promotion," he suggested.

Laughing, Fletcher disagreed. "The opposite – once they're convinced we've no idea what we're doing, and the goose couldn't possibly have done it, we'll be busted down so far you'll have orders to open fire if we approach within thirty feet."

"Sure, Mr. Ash. Good luck," Luther offered, and went on his way.

"Come on, then, Albert," Fletcher said as he opened a file. "Once more with feeling."

"I've got an idea," Fletcher declared.

Albert sighed at this interruption. "Is it an original, or another of Mac's stories?"

"It's almost noon, and I really do hate it here. Let's take the files to your place, have lunch, and work there for the afternoon."

"No," Albert managed faintly. He stared at the boy, mind inconveniently dazed. Fletcher surely knew this was trespass.

But Ash was continuing, determined. "I've got to get out of here, or I'll go stir crazy. The hotel's no good, there's no place to work, and they've turned the heating way up since the weather got cold. It's hot and stuffy and uncomfortable, and I hate the place." He was already gathering up the files. "Come on, it'll be fine. We'll grab a takeaway pizza on the way."

"We're not eating that garbage," Albert interrupted him. "If you want a pizza, I'll cook one."

Fletcher grinned at him. "Okay."

Silence for a long moment, resounding with Ash's mischievous victory. Albert made a last attempt: "That wasn't an offer or an agreement. You won't manipulate me into this."

"I didn't mean to –"

"Yes, you did. You use your knowledge of people to get what you want, just like anyone else. The trouble is that you see far more than most do of other people's motivations."

The boy's mutable face was all chagrined anger. Ash stood, wandered over to where a window should be. Let his fists come to rest against the wall. "You're right, of course," he said in an overly reasonable voice. "But I'd really appreciate it if you'd invite me home for the afternoon, despite how badly I've behaved."

"Emotional blackmail isn't going to help your case."

"Albert –" Fletcher turned to face him. "I wouldn't ask if it wasn't important – I know it's a big deal."

"Really," Albert said. "Don't flatter yourself." He sent some of the computer files to the printer, and as it chattered angrily away in the corner, started packing up his briefcase again.

Fletcher said, "Thank you," very quietly, but Albert wouldn't respond.

It was an alarmingly big deal, and he didn't appreciate Ash realizing that, and he certainly didn't want to talk it over. He might as well accept the inevitable, even though it must seem that Fletcher had gotten his own way after all.

They walked down the stairwells to the underground garage, checked the files and themselves out through security, and headed for Albert's car. Fletcher had been in the Saab a number of times, but no one had ever visited Albert's home before. There had been three deliveries of furniture he couldn't handle himself, and once he had needed some electrical work done by someone with a license – which added up to five people other than himself who had been inside since the necessary evil commonly known as a real estate agent had cringed and crawled his way through the sales routine.

It was ludicrous to be nervous. Really.

When Albert unlocked the back door and walked in through the laundry, he almost headed left to his study, but thought better of it. The dining table would be adequate for this intruder to work on.

"You'll have to wait on the pizza. I'll make it for dinner."

Fletcher said, "Whatever you like. Whenever's convenient." He was looking around, trying not to gawk. Curious, always curious, but unwilling to offend now that he had what he wanted. Albert hated this.

There was nothing for Ash to see, and there was everything – this was Albert's home. And Fletcher was too perceptive.

"You set up in here," Albert abruptly ordered. "I'll get lunch."

It seemed that the quality of the sandwiches Albert soon produced surprised Fletcher. He ate enthusiastically, drank the blended fresh fruit juices as if they were ambrosia, all the while babbling on about Harley, and how Fletcher had never met anyone who could make food taste as good as his brother did, until now at least, about how he missed that one thing. And he missed his father. But not Idaho.

Albert sat through the rambling reminiscence, face stony. He didn't eat more than a bite or two, unable to stomach it. It occurred to him that the boy was offering a confidence in return for being here. That wasn't nearly enough. But Albert found himself planning the magnificent pizza he would make, and the right salad to complement the tastes, a combination to impress. It was strange to cook for someone after all these years of eating alone. Strange but undeniably challenging.

CHAPTER FOUR
GEORGIA
SEPTEMBER 1982

John Garrett put on his best smile as he opened the front door, the winning smile that somehow reached his ice blue eyes. He was an attractive man and he knew it, used it. Trustworthy, that broad friendly mouth. Compelling, the spark of light in eyes that could be severe at work, frightening in play. Handsome, the perfectly even features. Irresistible, though he so loved resistance.

"Philip," Garrett greeted his guest. "Welcome." Then, with an effort not to let the smile fade, "Who's this?"

"My girlfriend, Stacey. Hope you don't mind."

"Mind?" Garrett looked from one to the other. All–American youngsters – the boy, who worked for a firm Garrett's company was about to contract to do a construction job, and the girl, who appeared from her clothes and her flushed skin to have just come from the gym. Stacey wasn't exactly pretty but her serious expression fit well with the long waves of dark hair and the firm small body. Philip wasn't much bigger than the girl – both together wouldn't add up to Garrett's bulk – and the boy's demeanor was altogether more frivolous, his blond hair unruly and his expression usually mischievous. Garrett had followed him one evening, watched him chugging beers with his friends, degenerating into raucous ribald tales. Not something Garrett could see Stacey taking part in. "Why should I mind?" Garrett asked rhetorically, though there were a hundred reasons. "Does she follow the football?"

"No, sir," the girl said. "But I can learn."

"I'm sure she can." Garrett stood back to let them in. Stacey slipped by first, then, as Philip passed close by him, Garrett murmured, "What, scared I might jump you? Needed her to hold your hand?"

"No." But the boy threw him an embarrassed stare before speeding up to follow the girl, who was heading for the kitchen – that was exactly what Philip had feared. That was, after all, exactly the impression Garrett had wanted to convey.

Garrett smiled, this time from the heart. He wasn't losing it, no, not in the slightest. He pushed the door closed, and turned the lock. It made a satisfyingly melodramatic sound, the bolt of metal shooting home into the doorjamb. From down the corridor, Philip cast him another glance, obviously unnerved all over again. That was exactly the way Garrett liked them at this early stage.

Stacey was raiding the fridge in a flurry of organization, handing Philip the makings for sandwiches. "You guys want a beer?" she asked.

"We most certainly do," Garrett replied. He walked over to take the bottle from her, twisted the cap off with his bare hand, and grabbed two glasses. "Come on, Phil, the game's about to start."

"But I'll help –"

"No, you won't help her, you'll come and watch the game." And, getting between the two of them, Garrett shepherded the boy out of the kitchen. It was laughably easy, really – the boy didn't want to let Garrett within reach of him, so kept backing away every time the bigger man advanced.

They settled on the old sofa in the billiards room, Philip sitting a wary four feet away. Garrett dug the remote out from behind the cushions, turned on the television, poured the beer, then let the boy be. No point in scaring him too much just yet. They had all night to work around to that, if they could get rid of the girl. Though she would know who Philip had been with.

Stacey appeared with a tray full of sandwiches, an extra bottle of beer and a glass. She seemed about to sit between the two men – but Philip had a crisis of conscience, and decided he was marginally safer next to Garrett than she was. Perhaps he was playing the gentleman. Or perhaps it was an admission that he had turned on to this, that he was already halfway roused.

"Did you tell anyone?" Garrett asked.

"No. You said not to, with the contract and all."

Garrett smiled. The kid had bought the story that an evening watching the football together might be seen as compromising the contract negotiations, though Philip himself had nothing to do with the financial wheelings and dealings. "Good. And Stacey?"

"I picked her up straight from her dance class."

"He surprised me," the girl said. "I wasn't expecting him."

"No one knows I brought her here, Mr. Garrett. It's all right."

"All right," Garrett agreed. They made it so damned easy for him. He settled back, content to wait for now.

Half time and the Atlanta Falcons were behind by ten points. Philip was incensed enough with the score and the beer to be making some noise. Stacey was curled up beside him, listening to the boy's explanations of the finer points of football.

Garrett was smiling. It had been far too long since he'd indulged in this pleasure, far too long since he'd heard and smelled and touched a boy's fear, seen and tasted his resistance, lived his pain and humiliation. An evening's worth of anticipation, of creeping up on the tension until all at once the boy would know just how much terror there was in the world.

The girl, he'd deal with. She wouldn't get in the way of this. If anything, she'd help make it happen.

He stood, and the kids both turned to look up at him, startled by the movement. Time for something stronger than beer. Garrett headed for the bar in the far corner, caught up the vodka and three shot glasses, brought them back over and poured generous nips. He toasted the kids silently, grinned, and swallowed down the liquid fire in one mouthful. Waited expectantly until they did the same. Poured them another round, then left the room.

Perfectly choreographed, though he'd never had to factor a girlfriend in before. As he returned a few minutes later, silent, the couple were kissing. Garrett stalked across the thick carpet, was sitting beside them on the sofa before they noticed him. "Don't stop," he murmured.

But they did, abashed and confused. The football was about to resume, and Philip was turning towards it.

"No," Garrett said. He moved in close behind the boy, his body echoing Philip's, though remaining a few careful inches away. And Garrett took the boy's hand in his own, placed it flat on the girl's hip, rubbed his palm and fingers across the back of the hand in encouragement.

After a brief hesitation, the boy copied his moves, caressing the girl's waist and then her shoulder and arm. She was startled but seemed focused more on her need for the boy than her uncertainty of the man.

"Kiss her," Garrett whispered.

Again a pause, the boy trying to work out what was going on and whether to protest. But he'd been a little high on the sexual undertones of Garrett's invitation ever since he'd walked through the front door, and was too far in now. He leaned to meet the girl's mouth, hand still following Garrett's lead back down to her hip.

Garrett moved up against the boy, buried his face in the blond hair, inhaled the scent of him. Philip flinched away from the contact but Garrett soothed him with a murmured repeating of, "It's all right, it's all right." He gathered the girl in tight, she put her arms around them both, and the boy began kissing her in earnest.

"The game …" Philip said once, as the crowd cheered a Falcons touchdown. The camera zoomed in on the players dancing around the end zone, embracing.

"I've an even better game," Garrett murmured, "upstairs."

"No."

Laughing, Garrett stood, hauled the pair of them up from the sofa. "Come on."

"Stace?" the boy asked.

"If you want to," she whispered.

Philip looked uncertainly from one to the other, and all the time Garrett held them trapped in his arms, waltzing them towards the stairwell. Then they were on the first steps, and it was too late. Garrett let them go and closed the door at the foot of the stairs. It locked.

But, while their fear eased up a notch, their excitement was still running fire. So deliciously easy. "Go on," Garrett said gruffly, not wanting to touch them again just yet. It had been a long two years, so the need in him was an imperative. And he'd had an idea, a glorious idea, about the girl …

"Mr. Garrett?" she whispered, at the top of the stairs.

There wasn't much up there. He supposed they'd been expecting to find his bedroom. Instead there was the attic space, an old single bed and some odds and ends. No windows. The boy had turned, was staring at him, beginning to draw a few conclusions. But Garrett walked up the stairs, calm and controlled, and the kid lost the one slim advantage of higher ground.

"Go on," Garrett said.

They backed away, the girl hanging on to the boy's arm, peering over his shoulder.

Garrett strode up to them, grabbed the boy around the waist, lifted him up tight, and kissed him – a savage driven kiss that left blood on the boy's mouth.

He was struggling, the girl was hitting out ineffectually, but Garrett just laughed.

"Run for it, Stace," the boy said once his mouth was free. "Run for it!" She stayed there, trying to pull the boy out of Garrett's embrace. "Go!"

Keeping her gaze on Garrett as if expecting him to try to stop her, she edged away back to the stairs. Garrett ignored her, dragged the boy along with him.

"Let her go, Mr. Garrett, just let her go, I swear I'll do anything, I swear I'll –" And the boy was crying. "I swear, Mr. Garrett, I swear …"

Garrett dumped the boy on the bed, and cuffed one of his ankles to the bars at the foot.

There was an angry, frightened scream from the stairwell. "Phil, he's locked it!"

"Let her go," the kid was pleading. "You don't want her."

The boy was secure now. Garrett turned away to fetch the girl.

Philip was further beyond misery, further beyond despair than he'd ever imagined was possible. Apparently, in essence, he was nothing more than a mess of tattered pain and shame. So reduced by so little. His flesh no longer held in all the pain. At first the sensation had been sharp and focused and intense – but now it welled beyond the simply unendurable, to cascade out and up to fill the room, to suffocate him with its metallic taste.

Garrett had left him alone for a while, so Philip closed his eyes and went under. He was beyond caring for his own sake that Stace was seeing him like this, was even further beyond caring for her sake that she had to witness such a thing.

But of course John Garrett didn't want him beyond caring. No, Garrett wanted them both to be fully and terribly aware of every little thing.

When Philip was jolted back to the nightmare, he was on his back, wrists cuffed to the bed posts at either side. Chains ran from leather straps around his ankles to his upper arms: short chains, so that his legs were spread, and bent almost to his chest. He didn't struggle, not like he had at first. Three of his fingers were now little more than bone; his skin was raw and broken; he had been hit so often he figured most everything inside of him was smashed. There was something in his chest that felt like fire.

Garrett hadn't hurt Stacey, barely even touched her. Her hands were cuffed to a rafter over her head, and she was just out of reach but close enough to see it all. She was weeping, head fallen forward so she didn't have to look at Philip.

But for splatters of Philip's blood, Garrett was naked. He was moving to kneel on the bed.

Philip knew what would happen next. It shouldn't have mattered anymore. But it did. He said again, through torn lips, "Let her go. Got what you want."

"Tell her to watch!"

"Let her go," Philip repeated weakly.

Garrett grabbed up the baton he'd been using, brought it down across the back of the boy's thighs. Hard. "Tell the bitch to watch!"

"Damn you," Philip muttered, "damn you damn you …"

"Yeah," Garrett breathed. "Don't give up the fight yet."

" … damn you damn you …"

"Make it good, boy, and I'll let her go. If I wanted to fuck a corpse, you'd be dead already, wouldn't you?"

" … damn you …"

"You listening to me?" Then Garrett was explaining in the most reasonable of tones, "You liven up a little, kid, make it good, and she watches – then she goes."

" … don't trust you …"

Garrett laughed. "There's no one else to trust. No one else in the world except for me. And her."

"Just do it, damn you to hell," Philip said. It shouldn't have mattered anymore. He tensed as Garrett knelt between his legs. The tension brought its own pain – his body hurt all the more, and he dimly realized Garrett enjoyed that he wasn't yet beyond humiliation.

"Tell her."

"Stace. Look at me, Stace. Come on, damn you. Stace –"

Garrett was running a hand across Philip's belly, wiping up the blood, then rubbing it on his own penis. He laughed, then moved again.

Philip cried out as Garrett pushed into him. There shouldn't have been anymore pain, anymore shame.

Stacey choked out, "Phil –" and he opened his eyes. She was staring at him, and he stared back. "I'm with you, Phil. We'll get through this. We'll get through it together."

Her words shouldn't have helped, but they did. The shame didn't matter so much, when Stacey could look at him, when she could meet his gaze, when she could promise that they'd survive this and still be together. Maybe Philip could let this happen and stay sane.

Garrett cried out, full of rage. He pulled away, took two steps, was lifting something from behind a loose board. Philip looked around to see what he was doing just as there was a deafening blast. Garrett had a pistol in his hands.

Stacey slumped, weight suspended only by the handcuffs, body shaking in unnatural spasm. There was a little blood, though Philip couldn't make out where she'd been hit. But then she was quiet, and then she was gone.

Philip sobbed his despair. "Damn you – Damn you – Damn you!"

Garrett dropped the pistol, went back to the boy, fucked the bloody flesh, pumping hard. It was good. The boy screamed, beyond petty curses.

Afterwards, Garrett chain–smoked almost a whole pack, standing in the shadows out of sight. He left the boy on the bed, let him lie there all twisted up while he died. The kid was merely whimpering by then, utterly pathetic. Garrett liked the depths he'd brought the boy to. It was very good.

At last the shakes caught the kid up, something internal rupturing, bleeding, convulsing him. It was over.

No – this time was over. This was over, though it could have been better. Next time – Garrett would wait out the month, find another boy, and he'd get it right, make it perfect. Next time.

CHAPTER FIVE
WASHINGTON DC
MARCH 1983

Albert stood in his backyard, considering the latest outbreak of a groundcover. The parent of this plant belonged to some neighbor of common tastes. Its misbegotten siblings had been weeded and cut back any number of times, yet it persisted, and he didn't want to resort to chemicals to be rid of the thing. It wasn't that the plant was unattractive – it had variegated leaves, of cream and apple–green, and a five–petaled flower of a blue somewhat lighter than delphiniums – but it did not belong here in Albert's garden.

A single flower was staring back at him now, pert in its stubborn survival.

Sighing, Albert returned to the mowing. It took him a while, usually at least two hours, not because he owned a large block of land, but because he used a hand–driven mower. The noise and the stink of motorized mowers offended him, and this way he exercised and could enjoy the fresh smell of the cut grass.

"Hello!"

Albert turned, having recognized the voice. Fletcher Ash had come to Washington to speak at a conference being held during the following week, and had arrived early in order to see another of his women friends. It wasn't as if the neighbors greeted Albert, anyway – they had long since gotten the message that he wasn't interested. "Ash," he said as he walked up to meet the man by the house. Then, bluntly, "What do you want?"

Sitting on one of the wickerwork chairs on the veranda, Fletcher stretched his long legs out before him. He seemed perfectly at home. "It's a beautiful day. What else could I want?"

"If you like that sort of thing."

"Well, you obviously do."

"Really."

"It's self–evident, Sherlock. Here you are, outside, enjoying the sunshine."

Albert squinted up at the sky. It was, indeed, blue and free of clouds. And the sun was gently shining, the air was full of spring's sweetness, a breeze was soughing the trees that shaded them, and a myriad flowers dotted the burgeoning green. There was laughter every now and then from the neighbors. He said flatly, "I am merely tending the garden."

"If that's all you're doing, then why don't you have someone tend it for you?" It was a rhetorical question, and Fletcher was smiling, that mischievous glint in his eye.

Albert wouldn't have brooked anyone else laughing at him. And he wouldn't have told anyone but Ash the truth. "I don't expect others to take on my responsibilities."

"And you don't want to have to owe them, even so much as a few polite words."

"Perhaps."

"And you don't like relying on other people, it makes you uncomfortable."

"It's true that I strive for self–sufficiency." His parents had paid a woman in an adjoining apartment to help them with the housework but Albert thought this had been just another way for Miles and Rebecca to redistribute their wealth. They had rarely let anyone intrude on their family, or in their home, for any reason.

Ash was continuing, "Even when it comes to the gardening."

"But I do, in fact, rely on the Doyle brat next door to keep an eye on the garden, if I'm absent on a case."

"Which is only the exception that proves the rule: you have the watering set up on an elaborate timer, you have a decent security system for the house, your mail is held at the post office. You rely on the minimum number of people possible."

"Are you quite finished?"

"I think so," Ash said easily. "For now."

"If you're trying to encourage me not to trust or rely on you, there's no need."

Fletcher looked away. "No, that's not what I'm trying to do."

"Fine." Albert considered him for a moment. "Is this a social call, or was there something you wanted to discuss?"

Ash's face brightened again, then slowly began to outshine the spring sun. "Purely a social call." He shook his head. "I can't believe you made me forget why I came."

"I can't believe I reminded you," Albert said dryly.

"Too late now."

"You came to tell me that you've fallen for her, though I have told you a number of times that I am not interested in such matters."

"I'm in love, Albert. I'm completely, three–hundred percent in love." The grin supported this extravagant claim, but there was a note of despair along with the joy.

Albert grimaced. "You're worse than a cheap romance novel."

"You know, deep down inside, we all just want to be loved."

"Speak for yourself," Albert advised. "And, if you really believed that was true, you'd break this tedious habit of falling for the most impossible women you can find."

"It's not the women who are impossible," Fletcher protested.

"Tell me about this latest star–crossed tragedy, then."

"Her name's Tyler – Ty. And she's a remarkable woman. It's not my taste that's at fault, or Ty herself. It's the fact she's still married to a fellow she broke up with some two years ago. She sees him at least once a week, and she's nuts about him, they act as if they're dating. We went to a movie last night, and she wouldn't stop talking about him." He added, with a wry twist to his smile, "Nevertheless, I fell in love."

"Well done, Ash," Albert said sarcastically. "You deserve some kind of award."

"I have terrible luck with women," Ash agreed. "She's having lunch with him today," he continued, "but she's meeting me afterwards to show me the cherry blossom. Washington's renowned for cherry blossom in spring, isn't it?"

"Haven't you ever asked yourself why you have this terrible luck?" To Albert, Ash seemed even more self–destructive when it came to these matters than Albert himself. The tawdry transactions of flesh and currency that Albert had once indulged in were honest and uncomplicated when compared to Fletcher's tangled, emotional, and usually short–lived affairs.

"But I obviously don't know the answer yet."

Albert turned away, began mowing the last quarter of lawn. Fletcher Ash was one of the few people who rarely disappointed him, and the only one of those few whom he knew personally. But this was the issue on which Ash failed to live up to even his own standards, let alone Albert's. And it was growing worse. What disaster would it take before the man quit wasting all his love on these increasingly farcical relationships?

I'm impossible.

He kept mowing, but it hit him then – all the dizzying blue of the spring firmament tumbling, cascading down upon him in slow motion. Surely he was supposed to be happy about this. Instead, Albert felt sick, crushed by the weight of it all. Was he supposed to be the disaster or the solution? No doubt the former – was there anything more ludicrous than an FBI employee falling in love with a colleague of the same gender? Perhaps he should be glad that Fletcher was so determined to find a woman, any woman, no matter the consequences.

But, while it was certainly ridiculous, Albert soon began to realize that this was virtually inevitable. He considered Fletcher Ash to be the one person closest to fulfillment of all humanity's potential. That was an objective opinion formed over the years of their acquaintance. So perhaps Albert should have anticipated the danger of this sudden and overwhelming subjectivity, perhaps he should have been prepared, even though at thirty–five he should have known better.

In any case, the whole idea was completely out of the question. He would simply have to bury it deep, and let it wither.

He walked slowly back to the house to fetch the rake. When he was closer, he looked at Fletcher, and met his gaze. There wasn't anything in Albert's expression to betray him but Ash's smile faded, and he grew serious.

Albert picked up the rake and went back to work.

CHAPTER SIX
OREGON
MARCH 1983

John Garrett had spent the afternoon helping a pair of muscular young men move him into his new house. The moving company he'd used seemed to recruit with Garrett's taste as the main criterion. So, he was almost twice their age, but he hefted and lifted and carried along with them; as strong, as tireless, as ready with a joke and a laugh. There was cold beer in the car and he had pizzas delivered for lunch. It surprised them, to have that much fun on the job with a client. He suggested they drop by the construction site, to see if he could offer them something more.

Once he was settled, he drove into town and watched the five o'clock crowds. It seemed there were young men everywhere he turned. There were the college students, of course. And the boys earning a living, with their brawn or their brains, the former ones fit and the latter weight–trained under the well–cut suits. Then there were the sailors who docked and the whores who serviced them. Portland had been a wonderful idea.

He liked them straight best. John Garrett liked the college quarterbacks and the tough tender young construction workers. The ones with spunk and maybe a little ambition. The ones with a string of girlfriends. So naïvely provocative.

Sometimes, Garrett thought that was the most perverse part of it. They were hardly the smartest choice for victims, after all, even if they rarely confessed to anyone where they were heading, who they were drinking with that night. He intrigued them yet embarrassed them, with his invitations for a beer and the football, his eyes promising more, daring them to accept. But because it wasn't smart to even seduce, let alone kill, too many of society's Most Likely To, Garrett often made do with the strays and runaways, the hookers – the ones who wouldn't be missed, the ones who society had already discarded.

Perhaps he would make do with one of the whores tonight, just for sex. Which would be fine; he was still riding high on the memories of last fall. Wandering the streets, letting the crowds jostle him, Garrett thought of them: Philip, with his mess of blond hair, and his nervous but mischievous response to Garrett's barely veiled sexuality; then a college boy from the gym, with a dash of Latino blood to add a little spice – they had talked half the night away before Garrett took him, though Garrett couldn't recall his name now; and Mitch, picked up while hitching a lift, who'd given Garrett a black eye and bruised ribs in the scuffle to get upstairs to the attic, infuriated that Garrett had only enjoyed it all the more. Yes, Garrett had loved his righteous fury. All three of them left behind in Georgia, given to the ground until some meddlesome cop dug them up.

Let them, Garrett thought. Let them disturb the boys if they wanted. Who cared? It was over. It was over, and no one knew who the hell he was. Rather than immediately move here from Georgia, he'd traveled, taking odd jobs when he'd felt like it, spending time in the country when he didn't. It had been good, like taking a holiday, and it had also been smart, drifting under a variety of assumed names.

As dusk drew in, Garrett walked towards a guy bouncing around by the last set of traffic lights before the docks. It seemed too absorbed a dance to be a display but Garrett nevertheless stood waiting to be noticed. Finally, the guy's arms threw wide, his head fell back, his legs spread with knees bent – which only drew attention to the crotch of his jeans – the pose miming a dramatic chord before collapsing back into the cool of self–consciousness. The eyes opened, the fingers pulled the headphones away from the ears. "The lights have changed, mister."

"Why did the man cross the road?"

"Is that a joke?"

Freckles – the guy still had freckles, and even a chipped tooth. Garrett almost laughed at the apple pie cuteness. He said, "Are you looking for a little pocket money? A place to spend the night?"

"Maybe."

"How old are you?"

"Sixteen." Defiance.

Garrett looked skeptical.

"All right, seventeen, and that's the truth."

"That's too bad," Garrett said. "Kids aren't my thing."

"I'm eighteen, I swear. Not my fault if I look young for my age."

"I'm sure it's good for business."

The guy – too cute to be called a man, though he was of age – The guy laughed, and asked with a pretence of wariness, "Just what sort of business are we talking about here?"

"You know what we're talking about," Garrett said easily, appreciating the smart humor. He walked forward, ruffled the guy's thick mop of hair, gathered him up with a strong arm around his shoulders. "Why don't you come home with me?"

"Yeah? Okay."

"You can help me unpack."

It was the guy's turn to look skeptical.

"What's your name?" Garrett asked.

"Rusty. Russell, if you really don't like me."

"John. I just moved here today, Rusty. Everything's in boxes."

"Everything?"

"So we have to find the sheets and blankets somewhere. What, you're going to charge me extra for a little honest labor?"

"Depends ..." The guy eyed him: Garrett's bulk, his strength. "Depends how hard you work me afterwards."

Garrett laughed, loud and happy. The few other people wandering the street or hanging around the intersections cast him world–weary glances, or ignored him. They didn't care, he didn't care for them. That was just as it should be.

He did work Rusty hard. But the guy seemed to expect it, found pleasure where he could and submitted cheerfully enough when Garrett wanted other things. Rough and tumble sex was fine; if he couldn't do what he dearly wanted to do with this boy, then he would take it only a little further than permissible.

Garrett pulled the young man to him again, hands hard. Maybe he would bruise but Garrett didn't slap him or hit him. He kissed and bit at the guy's shoulders, but didn't draw blood. Rusty, the guy's name was Rusty. Rolling onto his back, Garrett hauled the guy with him, sat him up, impaled the boy. Too tired to protest, Rusty let him do it, helped Garrett fuck him, even though it hurt both of them without lubrication. Garrett grabbed the guy firmly around his ribs, lifted him, set the rhythm.

"Jerk yourself off," Garrett ordered. And the guy did, though he'd had more than enough already. The face scrunched up as he concentrated on getting this over with, as he found a thread of pleasure despite the painful penetration, the sore abused genitals. Finding that thread, Rusty chased it, determined – spurted semen across Garrett's belly with a pathetic cry.

Letting out a breathless laugh, Garrett dug deeper into the boy's flesh with his fingers and his penis, orgasm tearing through him. It was good.

A small whimper as he lay the boy down beside him. Rusty. He seemed worried, fretting, curling up like a child. Garrett said, "Sleep now. Stay the night. It's over."

"Take me back home."

"No, stay. It's over, I won't hurt you again. I'll pay you."

"Yes," the guy said. And, after a time, he settled and fell into sleep.

Garrett lay awake. Maybe he'd been too rough. After all, he didn't need the violence, not all the time; he could function without it, have sex like any other man. More than that. One of the boys back in Colorado had pleaded, "Make love to me,' and Garrett had been so very careful with him. Even those sensations had been an excess of a sort – though betrayal of the starry–eyed virgin had been sweeter still.

What was the naïve one's name? Andrew. Drew had had no idea of how much trouble there was in the world. This young scamp Rusty had seen more, but still didn't seem to really fear Garrett. He had regained his cheerfulness by morning.

"So, you're new to town. D'you want some company, help with the unpacking, someone to show you around?"

"And how much do you charge for these services?"

"Nothing you can't afford."

It was tempting. A better offer than Drew's. Garrett liked living alone, but he'd sometimes shared his home with a stray for a week or so, in return for sex. Sometimes those strays moved on. Or, if it was time again, they might find the truth of what Garrett was, and then be given to the earth. But Rusty would be safe. Garrett was proud of his restraint: he didn't kill needlessly. "A few days," he agreed.

Rusty grinned, went back to his makeshift breakfast of toast and fruit.

Garrett laughed, heartily delighted. Even street–smart Rusty didn't realize how close he was to hell.

"So what are you doing here?" the young man asked. "Did you come for work or something?"

"You know that big hole in the ground, on the main street up from the court house? I'm putting a building in it."

"Yeah?" He sounded mildly impressed.

"A beautiful tall glass monstrosity that everyone will hate." Garrett added, with satisfaction, "I'm the project manager."

Garrett had never reached college and though he figured himself smarter than a lot of those who did, he still envied them, bitter at what he could never be. He'd had to drop out of school early to support his mother, use his brains and ingenuity in ways that most college boys seemed incapable of. He was proud that he'd made his own way, gotten so far from so many miles behind. Money to burn, these days, and prestige. He knew all the right people, wherever he was, held the right jobs, bought the right influence, donated to the right charities and political campaigns. A rags–to–riches story in which he had both directed and starred.

For so long he had carefully tried to do the right thing, always the right and proper and smart thing, because he wanted to succeed in the world and he was hungry for success. He had married the right girl, when he was twenty and his mother had died, married the boss's only grandchild, though she was awful, useless, more of a non–entity than his mother. The wedding had earned him what he needed at the time but if the choice were his to make again, he would find another way.

Sex with her had shamed and then bored him. He had been the virgin, not she, despite the white lace and the blushes she wore and the conspiratorial jokes all the men made that he'd smiled at. He had hated being cheated and fooled like that, loathed being at a disadvantage. But it didn't matter anymore, she didn't matter. He'd left her behind years ago, and only regretted that he'd had to leave the job behind, too.

At twenty–three he'd discovered young men, discovered the power of rough and tumble with something that struggled, something that wouldn't break or even complain much. That had been enough for a long while – doing things he could pay a guy to forget, things a whore expected in any case, things that became rape even if they started out as seduction. A couple of times he'd had to dump them at a hospital: drive them as far away as possible, and leave them for someone else to care for.

There were so many dull frigid years to make up for, though he had to be careful. He had a business to run, a growing reputation to protect. There were some situations, after all, that you couldn't buy or charm your way out of; some foibles that would not be overlooked.

Though back then people had been willing to accept him despite knowing, hearing somehow, or figuring out that he was queer. There had been more comfort about the issue in the seventies than the eighties now offered. It had been forgivable, ignorable.

One night he'd taken the sex too far; been so caught up in the young man's humiliation that sheer sensation had carried him beyond where he'd dreamed possible. It had sickened him afterwards – not the injuries he'd caused, but the surrender of control and the intolerable situation it had put him in. It had infuriated him.

He'd stood over the guy, impatient with his repetitive pleas, trying to assess the damage. Yes, this time it was fatal. "No hospitals," he'd said.

But the guy hadn't shut up. "Help me, get me some help, please ..."

And then reckless sensation seized hold of him again, the nauseous panic swamped by delight, as he'd realized this was what it had all been about, right from the beginning. He sat in a chair, a short distance away, and watched. Sometimes he'd crept closer to kiss the guy, run a hand over the shuddering flesh, feel the fever heat come and go. Once he'd masturbated sitting back in the shadows, laughing at the crazy excess.

It took the guy three glorious, scary, divine hours to die.

Garrett was left with a body to deal with. The dreary denouement, the anticlimax of aftermath. Trying to think it all carefully through, despite the panic returning to jolt him.

No one had known he'd picked this guy up, that was all right. Perhaps someone would have missed the young man by now but it was a Sunday, so Garrett himself wouldn't be looked for until the next day.

He'd driven up into the mountains, with the body wrapped in a blanket in the trunk. Having already done without sleep for thirty–six hours, another six wouldn't matter. The body was already naked but Garrett also took the two rings from his hands and the chain from his neck, slipped them into his hip pocket. Kissed him, kissed the unresponsive mouth, held him for a long while, sitting on the cold ground with the weight of the young man in his arms. It was hard to let this one go. But he had eventually dumped the body in the river, watched the rapids take him.

Home again, he'd packed the guy's few possessions carefully into a box, sealed it up, and stashed it in the back of a cupboard, anonymous amongst all his junk. Perhaps it would have been smarter to have dumped the jewelry and wallet as well but Garrett couldn't bear to leave them behind. It had been enough to sacrifice the guy's clothes to the incinerator's fire.

And then, for no reason he could now fathom, he'd walked to the kitchen, picked up the sharp vegetable knife, and slit open the veins from the inside of his left elbow to his wrist and on into his palm, cut again across the meat of his forearm. Quickly dizzy as the blood pounded out of him, as the darkness approached. Was this how the young man had felt? Garrett cried out loud, roared out defiance and grim joy and completion, let his heartbeat fill the world.

A sorry coincidence had been his undoing, his savior. One of the few neighbors had been passing this isolated house of his, heard the painful noise, came in through the door that had stupidly been left unlocked, tied a kitchen towel tight around the biceps, called an ambulance. Lucky that she hadn't passed by the previous night, when it hadn't been Garrett screaming.

Garrett could have lost the arm, almost lost his life, almost followed the young man into the darkness. But he survived, pleaded lonely despair, promised to get help. Moved interstate with the scar of a cross on his arm, a cross bound with stitches. The stitches reminded him of thorns.

It had been five weeks and three days before the papers announced they'd found the body washed up against a bridge.

Rusty touched the raised lines of skin on Garrett's forearm, traced the defiant cross, walked his fingers along the puckered dots left by the irregular stitches. The scar was white now, refusing to tan, but that was better than the unhealthy grey that had lingered just beneath the surface for months. "Bad times, huh?" Rusty asked, all light sympathy. Then, with the enthusiasm expected from a child, "I bet there was lots of blood."

I could show you, Garrett thought. What an interesting idea, to mark a boy in the same way. Maybe when it was time, in a little less than two years, when the monstrous building rose into the sky. Or maybe right now. No one would miss this tramp. There was a cellar to the house, small and dark and sound–proof. He could strap Rusty to the shelving on the wall: one lash at his right wrist, and one at his left elbow, perhaps one around his ankles to prevent him from kicking out; that's all he'd need. And then he could hold Rusty's hand as he carved an identical cross deep into the boy's flesh. Watch as the blood pulsed out, spattered them both; watch as Rusty resisted the fearful darkness drawing near. He imagined the young man crying and begging, the big childish eyes afraid, his breathing harsh and ragged; then Rusty's head wilting as he went under, the heavy mop of hair listing forward. *Yes, I could show you, my friend.*

"Don't you always just die if you lose more than a pint of blood?" Rusty was asking. "You only have eight or nine pints or something, and you go into shock, and just die."

Let's find out, shall we?

But that wouldn't be sensible. Garrett rationed himself, only so many deaths, only so many attempts at that ultimate satisfaction. And it would not be wise to link himself so obviously to the victims.

"It takes more than a pint," Garrett said. This cool control was fine. In fact, control was the whole point, it all had to mean something, life was too precious to take with anything less than finesse. Screams should be conducted like music. Garrett was creating poetry, just like a football team executing a classic play, like the beauty of smoothly slotting each piece of a glass tower into place. Perfection.

Sacrificing Rusty right now would not be poetic: it would be an uncontrolled indulgence. Even if the idea of how he would die was beautiful, irresistible. For two years at a stretch, Garrett obeyed the signs. *Don't walk on the grass.* But then he'd leave the path behind, net the right young man, and chase sensation with him, through him. Taste the power of it. Live life with a shit–eating grin.

It was good. And the joy of it lasted for months. Rusty was safe.

He pulled the guy to him; took care to make Rusty groan at his own ecstasy rather than scream at Garrett's; reached climax with the memory of that first, accidental, beautiful death hovering just behind his eyes. Was Rusty so blind he really couldn't see that potent image?

Mark. The first boy's name had been Mark. Someone else had taken him from the river, and given him to the ground.

Garrett looked stunning in a tuxedo. He smiled at the mirror's image as he adjusted the bow–tie, just so. His hair was white–blond, and had been since his mother died, which made him look older than his thirty–three years – but combine that with his flawless skin and regular features, and the result was sophistication. His ice blue eyes were pleased right now – he added the sparkle to them, expression smooth, then the tiny self–deprecating smile that undermined any interpretation of smugness. Perfect.

"Cool," Rusty exclaimed appreciatively, bouncing around on the bed. "Didn't take you long to get invited to the classy parties."

"Of course not," Garrett agreed urbanely. He began searching for the silver ring he wore on his left hand at these occasions. He liked to think it distracted from the tail end of the scar. But what with Rusty's help and hindrance, his belongings were in greater disarray than ever.

"I found some jewelry and stuff here. Is that what you want?"

Garrett turned, wary. The boy was pushing a box across the floor, the box of all the watches and chains and earrings and other oddments he had taken from naked bloody bodies. "Leave that alone," he said, soft and cold as velvet.

"Lots of it. Not classy like you're dressed now, though. Where did you get it all?"

"I told you to leave it alone."

"All right." Rusty glanced at him, looked away, uncomfortable. "Sorry."

Garrett's smile, his sparkle, even his smugness were gone. But it wouldn't be sensible to frighten the boy, after all these hours and days of hints and clues that might add up. Rusty had an imagination, after all. What to say? Start with the truth – every good lie needs a core of truth. "They're mementoes," Garrett said. "Fond memories."

"Oh," Rusty drew out the vowel in dawning comprehension. "A boyfriend?" he hazarded.

"Yes. He died."

Rusty nodded, respectful of this grief.

"I'm going to take you home now," Garrett said. "What do I owe you?"

Surprise, disappointment. "I didn't mean to, you know, upset you like that."

"It's all right. I was planning on taking you home anyway. Perhaps I should have discussed it with you first." Those last words held such an elegant sarcasm.

Rusty lifted his head, shrugged. "No." Of course not. "A hundred."

"Don't be silly," Garrett said coolly. "We agreed on more than that."

"You already gave me two."

"Here." Garrett reached for his wallet, counted out four fifty–dollar bills. "Take it. Take care of yourself."

The guy accepted it, wouldn't touch him. That was fine. Garrett didn't want Rusty scared, but he didn't want the guy to come looking for him again, either.

He drove the boy down to the docks in silence.

CHAPTER SEVEN
WASHINGTON DC
MARCH 1983

These days, it was the most peace Fletcher knew. Strange to find peace in Washington DC – a place he associated with politics and HQ and the highest murder rate in the States – when he'd only found it in the country before, with his own complications for company, and no one else's crowding for attention. But Washington now meant Albert, and Albert's home; and Fletch found himself coming down here on the slightest pretext, often just for the weekend, even though Albert was inevitably unwelcoming. Perhaps it was stranger still to find peace in the den of a creature so determined to show a bitter and objectionable face to the world.

Fletcher sprawled in the wickerwork chair on the back veranda at Albert's, let his head fall back, a stray breeze teasing his hair, caressing his throat. Last night, it had been Ty's fingers instead.

So Washington DC now meant Tyler Reece as well.

She was gorgeous, so alive, with a unique energy. Fletcher had never met anyone who quite deserved the description vivacious until now, and Tyler was vivacious every minute of every day.

They had talked; both scrambling to say it all, listening to each other, fascinated, and then talking some more. She taught literature at high school, and worked with a lobby group dealing with women's issues. He thought of her vitalizing the children, bringing Shakespeare alive, of her swaying the old men in Congress with her sharp intelligence and snappy eyes and wide generous mouth. And she was still nuts about a particular actor, who was based in New York, and who Ty had happened to be married to for fifteen tumultuous months.

She had come up to Fletcher's hotel room, blew the drab walls away with her bright laughter, lay on the lumpy old bed and made it a magical place.

And every grain of time, every ounce of energy, every spark of creativity in Fletcher had all been dedicated to surprising Tyler into thinking of him rather than her husband. Perhaps he had succeeded.

A little. At least she had been polite enough to quit talking about the man. Verbally. And Fletch had fallen for her in the middle of it all, as she shared the pleasure with him, as with a delighted gasp she had …

Fletch shook himself. This was fruitless, let alone unwise. He opened his eyes, dazed as if he'd been asleep, and he looked for Albert.

Albert, who was standing close by, where the paving ended and the grass began, gazing at Fletcher as if the answer was at last, unexpectedly, within his reach. Albert, who seemed a little taken aback, but speculative as if he were already analyzing available facts and finding some kind of coherence. But mostly there was need, an age–old need, that few would fail to recognize. Anyone else might have thought it sat oddly on Albert's face, but Fletcher had the privilege of seeing passion there before – if only in relation to Albert's work until now.

Fletch wished Tyler had looked at him like that.

A child ran out into the garden next door, laughing, intruding albeit unknowingly. Albert turned away and the moment, the answer, was lost, put behind him. He began methodically raking up the grass clippings.

So, Fletcher thought, as the dazed numbness faded to an ache. Albert loved him. Why hadn't he seen it before? In a Sartre play, this was high art. In real life, it was tawdry tragedy, undeserved.

He stood, escaped into the coolness of Albert's home, leaving ignoble thoughts of Tyler behind. She wouldn't, couldn't, belong in this place – but Albert surely did.

When Fletch first came here, he thought the place bland. Now he thought it provocative, richly evocative of Albert, though it still posed mysteries, cast tantalizing glimpses of the man who would perhaps remain forever hidden.

From the outside, it was simply one more house in streets of clones – all wood painted white and a handful of minor variations in design. Maybe it was better proportioned, certainly better taken care of. But it was anonymous, and screened by a row of trees.

His first impression of the interior had been of cool greens and subtle harmonies, of impeccable style, everything neat and clean. But even though it could have graced the pages of any glossy magazine, it was comfortable, accessible. An antidote to the hot Washington summers, a haven in the cold of winter.

It had been a few hours before he'd realized what was bothering him.

There was no clutter, no memorabilia. No photos loved more for their subject than their quality; no ornaments or oddments significant to the owner but ugly to anyone else.

Fletcher remembered his great–aunt Kit, a plain–speaking nurse, gesturing with cigarette in hand at an object she loved only for the sake of who gave it to her: "As for this abortion of a lamp ..." Despite the appropriate description, Kit kept the thing, even used it rather than buy something new and tasteful. But Fletcher was certainly not going to find any garish orange–tiled pedestals and crocheted shades here at Albert's – the man protected himself too well and could not be considered sentimental by even the most generous observer.

There were paintings on the walls, though they were little help. Again, they proved the owner had impeccable taste – each was an original, the colors a summary of, or perhaps the inspiration for, each room. But none of them were of people; they were all landscapes or still life, with one subdued and elegant abstract in the front hall.

Fletcher hadn't expected Albert to care so much for where he lived; he had assumed the man would brush the necessity of shelter off as he did so much else. It had been surprising to discover the place to be nice, if bland, and then to slowly realize how intimate and revealing it was, to see Albert taking an unconsciously sensual satisfaction in the trappings of his lair.

Here was the living room, large and well–proportioned with a high ceiling, walls a pale sage, the furniture a range of darker greens and fine polished walnut, with every here and there a warm red that reminded Fletcher of the robes and ribbons in old European paintings. Then the dining room, even cooler and lighter, with splashes of blues amidst the sage and the walnut.

The blues deepened to that of Van Gogh's irises in the kitchen, with the greens paling on the cupboards and benches. All that a serious cook needed was out of sight but easily to hand.

Everything was coordinated. Even the Saab parked in the garage fitted into the scheme, painted a deep forest green, and reflecting the choice of quality and function and style, the lack of ostentation and uselessness and decoration for its own sake.

This was the home of the most interesting person Fletch had ever met, someone he dearly wanted to know better, who hid his secrets away so well, though revealing much that he didn't intend to. Someone worthy of all that life had to give, uniquely able to make the most of opportunity, who had so much to contribute – and yet someone who had won so little, who had so few friends, who was thwarted at every turn whether he admitted it or not. Someone who loved Fletcher with a generous heart, just as Fletch loved – no, to be fair, Albert wasn't one to fall in love lightly. It had to mean more to Albert than Tyler meant to Ash, supported by years of friendship rather than days of infatuation. It was a staggering notion. But what was there to do? Sartre had stacked this play too well.

There was the clatter of the garage and then the back door being shut, the splash of Albert cleaning up in the laundry. Fletcher wandered closer, stood hesitant at the doorway to the dining room. Albert appeared, drying his hands on a towel. He came to a halt, and they stared at each other across the expanse of the kitchen.

Albert's face was close to his usual expression – shielded, impatient, a touch of arrogance. Gone was the intensity and honesty that had betrayed so much. But the man still seemed to be off–kilter with the shock of it all; he must surely have been more rocked by the realization than Ash.

Fletch had the feeling that if he led the way to Albert's bed, to the one room he had not yet set foot in, then it all might happen without a word, the last of those defenses would be tumbled, the love Fletch had witnessed would find an answer of sorts, there would be some kind of satisfaction. Fletcher could make it happen, yes, Fletch could become the focus of all Albert's passion. Incredible.

But Fletch's memories of Tyler were too sharp. She had made love to Fletcher only hours ago, bestowing a favor because it didn't really matter to her.

Fletcher couldn't do that to Albert. On reflection, considering that Albert wouldn't let him under any other circumstances, perhaps this was the one chance Fletch would ever have.

He turned, headed back to the living room, made himself sit. Heard Albert begin to gather the makings for dinner. Sighed in frustration. What else to do for the man?

CHAPTER EIGHT
WASHINGTON DC | COLORADO | GEORGIA
APRIL 1983

"Are you busy?"

"Of course I'm busy, Ash, as you should be. What – Wait a moment." Albert put the phone down, reached to close the door of his office cubicle, and sat down behind the desk before continuing. "What do you want?"

"I was wondering if you can come up here and do an autopsy for us."

"Why not the medical examiner?"

"You know the Bureau – once we decide it's our jurisdiction, we don't let anyone else poke their nose in. So I suggested to Caroline that we invite you up to dispense some expert advice."

Albert glanced through the glass walls at the laboratory. The three staff out there were going about their business, paying him no mind as usual. But these days he was uncomfortable taking calls from Fletcher at work. His unwelcome nervousness sharpened his impatience. "What's the case?"

"A woman from Salt Lake City, dumped by the roadside on our side of the border. She's cut up pretty bad, looks like she's been raped. Anyway, she's someone's friend's niece, so we've been told to take it on the grounds of kidnapping across state lines and get it solved yesterday."

"You have a problem with that," Albert observed.

Ash let out a hollow laugh. "We should solve them all yesterday, shouldn't we? Not just the ones who happen to have a relation who fancies himself important."

"I'll remember your attitude when you're in a position to call in favors."

"Trying to keep me honest, Albert?"

"I don't know why you alone should escape humanity's hypocrisy."

Fletcher groaned. "It's too early in the morning for insults. Look, we need the best up here. It's not just an excuse to have the pleasure of your company, you know."

"I'm sure it isn't," Albert said, then wondered if he sounded affronted rather than irritated.

"Not from Caroline's point of view, anyway."

Albert ignored both the comment and the teasing tone of Fletcher's voice. "I have something to finish up here –"

"What's that?" Ash interrupted, always keen to hear the latest.

Aware that he shouldn't be passing on restricted information, Albert said, "The lab has received a pair of severed hands from Texas." It was humiliating to be reduced to gossiping.

"They're trying to tell you something?"

"Spare me the pathetic attempts at humor. The hands were sent to the Dallas police by mail but the flesh is too decomposed for them to print easily."

"I'm glad I already had breakfast."

"The interesting thing is ..."

Silence for a moment. "Well, don't leave me hanging," Fletcher said.

"The police assumed both hands belonged to one corpse."

"You mean there's two corpses somewhere, one missing a right hand, and the other ... ?"

"A left hand. Yes."

"That's grotesque. I don't know how you cope with this sort of thing."

"Unlike you, I don't have a hyperactive imagination."

"So, can you come up to Denver or not?"

"Book me on a flight; give me three hours to finish up and get to the airport. Tell Thornton to clear it with Jefferson."

"Thanks, Albert."

"Did you hear about the body they found in the Georgia Pine Belt?"

"This isn't a joke, is it?"

"Don't be ridiculous. Young man, eighteen to twenty, buried face–down in a forest, naked, beaten and sexually assaulted. Sound familiar?"

Silence. Finally, flatly, "He's killed again."

"Maybe not."

"He's killed again and it's my fault."

"How can it be your fault, Ash?"

"I gave up on him, I almost forgot about him after all this time."

"Melodrama will not help. It may not be the same man. This was more haphazard than the cases in Colorado: the grave was dug barely six inches deep, with dirt and debris heaped over the body; the location was near a busy lumberyard; and there was no shroud or wrapping, plastic or otherwise. Cause of death was anemic anoxia."

"Insufficient supply of oxygen to the tissues," Fletcher said, "which means loss of blood."

"Yes. Apparently the markings indicate use of restraints on wrists, arms and ankles. I would like to check on that, however; it has been some months since the time of death, and I doubt much can be clearly determined."

"Except by you," Ash commented.

Albert ignored this. "Perhaps it was a sexual liaison that went too far, and the offender panicked. This certainly doesn't seem as clever or as organized as the Colorado cases."

"I don't know. I don't like the feel of it. Have you seen the body?"

"It's not FBI jurisdiction."

"He wasn't someone's relative," Fletcher observed.

"They haven't identified him yet," Albert replied, deliberately taking the comment on face value. He wanted to continue the conversation, prolong the contact with Ash, even though to do so might delay seeing him in Colorado that afternoon. He hated these irrational, often self–defeating urges, not least because such impulses might become apparent to other people. And Ash was presumably in the best position to perceive them. Abruptly, Albert said, "We'll discuss it when I've finished your autopsy. I told McIntyre to push for full copies of all the Georgia reports. Let me know the flight details when you have them."

"All right. And I'll pick you up at the airport."

"Yes." Albert hung up, and then stared at the phone, pictured the lines that had connected them across hundreds of miles. Imagined Ash sitting by the phone as well, maybe already calling the airline, having gone out of his way to ensure it was Albert who attended to conduct the autopsy. Albert knew he was the best when it came to human remains, the results of human violence, and that the case therefore wouldn't suffer because of this whim of Ash's – but what was the man's motivation?

Too easy to distrust the only person in years who'd tried to be a friend; too easy when that person was unusually perceptive, and Albert had inadvertently become all too attached to him. And too difficult the effort to act as if nothing had changed, to maintain the carefully built facade.

But Ash was in no mood to notice anything untoward. As Albert walked towards him in the airport, amongst the first rush of arrivals, Fletcher gestured impatiently; he barely waited until Albert was within a yard to say, "Mac called. They've found another one," even as he turned to hurriedly lead the way through the lounge.

"Another one of what?" Albert snapped as he followed Ash, annoyed with himself for having expected and wanted some kind of greeting from the man.

"In Georgia, ten miles from the first, four or five months since time of ..."

Apparently Fletcher was unwilling to say the word amid the swirl of people. Albert pointedly clarified, "Time of death?"

"Yes." Ash cast a distracted look around, perhaps wondering if that had drawn unwanted attention, then came to a sudden halt. "Do you have bags?"

"I have them with me."

Fletcher grabbed the small suitcase, left Albert with the metal case that contained his tools.

"A second body doesn't mean anything, Ash. You're making assumptions."

They were at the car within moments. Once inside, Fletcher turned and furiously spat out, "That sort of sexual thing doesn't *go wrong* twice, does it? We have a serial killer on the loose and chances are it's the same one we dealt with up here."

"No, the chances are that it is not the same one." Albert hung onto the dashboard as Fletcher pulled out into the traffic a little faster than necessary.

"Same *modus operandi*."

"Different cause of death and differences in MO, too. This one wasn't as clever."

"Maybe he's losing control."

"You're clutching at straws."

"Or maybe he planned it to look that way. It's the same man. I feel it."

"Nice for you. But what's the basis for that? You don't even know anything about the case that isn't second– or third–hand."

"It's enough. I'm taking you to the medical examiner's labs, you do what you can with this woman, we leave it with Caroline, then we head to Georgia tonight."

"They should put you back on your medication."

"Don't give me any of your garbage, Albert."

"Progressing from passive, straight through assertive to strident, are you?"

"You know as well as I do – if we'd caught the sadistic bastard two years ago, he wouldn't have got to these boys and God knows who else in the meantime."

"And if you don't slow this car down he'll soon be indirectly claiming another two victims."

Silence, as Fletcher stared straight ahead. But, after a moment, his hands loosened their white–knuckled grip on the steering wheel, and his foot eased off the gas. "All right," he said. "But I hate this, that I didn't stop him. You can't reason that away."

"You never will stop him if you don't calm down. You'll need your wits about you for this one."

Fletcher looked at him, those intense blue eyes insisting on the truth. "You think it's the same man." He looked almost handsome, Albert noted. The mutable, quite pedestrian features were all fired up into … beauty. "Don't you?"

Albert turned away. "I'm prepared to consider the possibility."

"Then why give me such a hard time about it?"

"No one deserves unqualified support, least of all you."

"So much for friendship."

"If you can't justify this feeling of yours to me, you won't convince anyone else."

"You would have to be the most difficult person –" The younger man was smiling poignantly. Yes, he was beautiful. "I'm sorry. I wish I could live up to what you expect of me."

Albert wanted to suggest, as directly as possible, that he had no expectations of Ash, and that Ash shouldn't bother making doomed and misguided efforts to live up to the nonexistent, but Albert realized that might sound like disappointment. He stayed silent.

"How long will the autopsy take?"

"Some hours."

"We need to get to Georgia."

"Book us on the first plane tomorrow."

"Not tonight? I thought you could do it quicker than that."

"You can't possibly be asking me to rush through a vital procedure in a murder investigation – one, I hasten to add, that you insisted I perform – simply because you're hot to chase down another case."

"No," was the small, resentful reply.

"Then rest assured I'll work as quickly and thoroughly as usual. And I'll accompany you to Georgia in the morning."

"All right, all right. The lab's just around the corner here." Fletcher pulled the car into one of the emergency spaces directly in front of the building. "Come on. I'll introduce you, then I'm heading back to the office for the afternoon."

"Spare me the introductions. Just get me to the procedure room."

It was a relatively straightforward autopsy. There was evidence – particles of skin and dirt under the woman's fingernails, fibers on her back and legs, loose pubic hair, and semen – that would serve to identify any suspects. The cause of death was clearly coma as a result of bludgeoning, following repeated sexual attack. There were numerous cuts and bruises, all of them fairly superficial, indicative of a struggle and of someone's naïve conception of torture. Nevertheless, Albert meticulously conducted a full examination and dissection, took photos to supplement his documentation, and collected the necessary samples of organs and fluids, all the while recording his report. The only unexpected discovery was that the woman wore a diaphragm, complete with an application of spermicide. She obviously had been prepared to have or had had sex with someone voluntarily – what had happened next was a matter for others to determine. By the end of the procedure, Albert was prepared to broadly describe two offenders, their coloring, and the type of carpet on which the woman had been attacked.

It was five in the evening before he'd reassembled all the organs and sewn the corpse back together. Albert washed, then opened the door to the corridor. As he'd expected, Fletcher was loitering.

Albert held out two cassettes. "Get someone to type a transcript. I'll do what tests I can, and send the rest to Washington."

"All right." The younger man seemed uncomfortable.

"Anything more from Georgia?"

"Nothing significant."

"Did you book me a hotel room?"

Fletcher looked at him. "No, I forgot all about it. And the suite the Bureau usually uses is taken." He considered for a moment, expression speculative. "Stay with me."

"I don't think so."

"Come on … It's only an apartment, but there's plenty of room for two of us. The sofa pulls out into a bed – I slept on it myself for years." But something about the tone indicated Fletcher expected to have his offer refused.

Albert obliged by saying, "No," and turned to head back inside.

"Wait." As Albert paused, Ash continued, "I'm sorry about before. I shouldn't have taken it out on you – it wasn't you I was angry with."

"Everyone gets frustrated, Ash. You know how counterproductive it is to react emotionally, yet you allow yourself to do exactly that."

"Yeah, I know."

The man seemed more amused than chagrined. Albert suspected he'd sounded prissily moralistic. Why did Ash of all people always have him at such a disadvantage?

"So, stay with me? It will be more convenient to get to the airport tomorrow – the plane leaves at quarter past six. Apart from which, you've already had a long day, what with the time difference."

"It's only a difference of two hours," Albert snapped, while trying to balance the conflicting urges to be with Ash as often and as closely as possible – and to save himself from situations with such intimate possibilities. Impossibilities, he corrected himself. Even so, it would be too easy to make a complete fool of himself over this. "If you insist," he told Fletcher, and was rewarded by a relieved grin.

"Okay. I am sorry, you know. Even Caroline doesn't suffer through my self–indulgent moments quite as often as you do."

"Am I supposed to feel honored?"

"How much longer will you be? I'll take you out to dinner when you're done."

"Something to look forward to."

"You'd agree any of the restaurants would be preferable to my cooking."

Albert nodded. "I'll be ninety minutes." He turned away, and closed the door between them.

Under the circumstances, it was inevitable that Albert wouldn't sleep well. As it happened, he didn't sleep at all. At first, as he lay awake in the darkness of Ash's apartment, Albert went over the autopsy and tests he'd just performed, re–considering each detail. He'd been thorough at the time but with the benefit of hindsight, he jotted a few extra notes on the pad he kept in his case.

After that, he thought through the little he knew about the first Georgia case, and compared it to the three bodies Ash had found in Colorado. There were enough similarities to make investigation worthwhile, if the few early items of information were facts. It was amazing how many errors and assumptions and embellishments were passed on as fact, especially this early in a case, with everyone taking an interest and expressing an opinion, with the community crying for quick and easy answers, and the press baying for sensation.

Then Albert considered Fletcher's apartment, which was everything he had expected: adequate but not well–designed. It consisted of one large room, with an inconvenient kitchen tucked away up one end, and only the bedroom and bathroom separate to the main living area. Fletcher wouldn't be comfortable without plenty of space around him, such as this large, open–plan room. In fact, Albert suspected he'd find a view of the mountains from the main windows once the sun rose. The few possessions Fletcher had collected over time were scattered randomly throughout the place, as if Fletcher forever had his mind on higher matters. No doubt he'd slept on the sofa bed for years because he'd simply not wanted the bother of buying himself a proper bed. The overall impression was messy, though not unclean and hardly cluttered; certainly as shabby, though not as disarmingly charming, as Fletcher himself.

That brought Albert to the other current vital issue. Fletcher Ash was a room away, lying asleep and vulnerable in his own bed, no doubt untidily sprawled in rumpled sheets, just as he'd used to sleep where Albert now lay. Ridiculous, how provocative that image was, when

Albert had accepted from the start that Ash was not and would never be available to him.

He had decided on restraint almost ten years ago, in a New York hotel room, following an unexpectedly honest and tawdry encounter with a beautiful woman. But that resolve was being sorely tested by this unexpected turn of events. Albert hadn't thought he would fall in love, as witless teenagers were prone to do, and suffer all the mundane and petty defeats it brought. Hadn't thought there would be someone who could have such a glorious, frightening effect on him both physically and emotionally, who could threaten the order of his life. Who could so easily read him, and yet who must remain oblivious to this disaster. Surely it wouldn't be long before the intensity of his reactions faded and this problem resolved itself. It couldn't be much longer; he'd already survived the first weeks of it.

The phone rang at two–thirty in the morning, interrupting the pointless speculation. Albert let it ring a second time, heard Ash groan from the other room. The rustle of bed clothes, uncoordinated footsteps, the door being opened. A third and fourth ring, while Fletcher blearily muttered, "Where is the damned thing? Hello." Then, "Caroline. What's the time?"

Albert sat up, swung his legs off the bed, stared fixedly at the opposite wall.

"All right … Yeah?" Silence for a while. "Yeah, that's good … Do we have to? Okay, okay, I'll see you soon." Fletcher groaned again as he hung up. "You awake, Albert?"

"I could hardly have slept through that."

"The police have made the arrests already."

"What arrests?"

Ash was stumbling into the kitchen. "I need coffee. Caroline wants me at the office – you, too. We'll have to go straight to the airport from there."

Albert repeated impatiently, "What arrests, Ash?"

"The woman's ex–boyfriend, and a mate of his."

"Based on what?" Albert stood, reached for his clothes. On second thoughts, he put them aside, and began folding up the bed linen instead.

"Your transcript. Seems a cop had questioned the ex and your description fitted perfectly. Uncanny, he called it. So the cop goes down and sees the carpet you'd identified in the back of the guy's van, and tells him an expert from Washington has fingered him long distance, and it was all over bar the sobbing confessions." Ash was busy rubbing his temples, but spared Albert a humorless grin. "He and the mate are each saying it was the other's idea, mind you."

"You needed me to solve this common little crime?"

"I guess so. Let's have some light in here."

As the darkness fled, Albert looked across at the man before he could stop himself. He'd never seen Fletcher in less than his weekend uniform of a baggy T–shirt, jeans and sneakers before – now he was bare–chested and bare–footed. The torso was slim but with well–defined muscles and broad across the shoulders. Pale creamy skin. A dusting of dark hair, with a concentration of it above his breastbone shaped like a stylized flame. And below all that was a pair of old, washed–out, poorly–darned flannel pajama bottoms.

"What elegant night attire," Albert commented.

"These terrible things." Fletcher peered down as if he hadn't examined them closely for years. "Sort of like a security blanket. I can't throw them away."

"You're pathetic, Ash."

"I know." But the grin this time was far brighter than the dazzling kitchen lights. "And you haven't even seen my teddy bear yet."

Albert shook his head, overtly in despair of Fletcher, but privately at the craziness of his situation. Surely there was someone else in the world with whom it would have been sensible to fall in love.

"You don't want coffee, I suppose. Wouldn't want to waste a good brew on you."

"Quite. But if you've been organized enough to buy some eggs and butter, I'll cook breakfast while you shower."

"Great. It's all in the fridge." Ash headed for the bathroom, turned back with his hand on the doorknob, about to say something.

Albert was caught taking in the sight of a fine pair of shoulder-blades. He stared at Fletcher, stony.

"Sorry," Ash murmured.

"For what?" Albert bit.

But Fletcher slipped behind the door, shut it firmly.

Albert pushed the whole awful thing aside, angry at too many things to even begin to name, and started preparing the food. But even that, a formerly simple and enjoyable process, was now tainted and complex – because Albert could only be aware that soon Ash would eat this food, would derive comfort and satisfaction from it. He whisked the eggs, furious.

"You get credits for this one," Caroline Thornton said. Ash, with Albert in tow, had finally tracked Thornton down in the corridor outside the office of the Special Agent in Charge, so they were speaking in whispers, hurried because they were running late for the plane.

"Why?" Ash returned. "Albert did the hard work, pointed them in the right direction."

Albert shrugged as Fletcher glanced back at him. What did he care?

"You got him here," Thornton was saying. "I never said any of this was fair. Now, go to Georgia, if that's what you want – but you remember those credits get used up damn quickly in the Bureau. You've got two days, and the weekend's all yours, but you've got no jurisdiction, all right?"

"It's not all right, Caroline. That man is getting away with –"

"I know. But you know you're out on a limb with this. I'll do what I can, but it won't be much."

Ash appeared unable to decide whether to rage or cry. His hands bunched into useless fists, then were shoved into his trouser pockets.

"Come on, Ash," Albert said, not bothering to lower his voice. "Either prove them wrong, or quit sulking about it."

Thornton grimaced. "You go do what you can with what you've got."

"I tell you, I've never been so angry."

"I know, okay? Now, get going or you'll miss your plane."

"Yeah." He walked off.

Albert slid on his dark glasses and followed him. He was spending far too much time chasing after this man; literally, if not figuratively. "I'll drive," he said once he'd caught up.

Fletcher was striding through the foyer. "Whatever. You realize you were just insulted?"

"Kind of you to notice," Albert replied. He didn't care for other people's opinions, hadn't for years. With one exception that he made every effort to minimize.

The air outside was bitterly cold and the sky, paling towards dawn, looked dirty.

"I don't suppose you'd want an apology. I could shame it out of her easily enough, especially after all the help you just gave us."

"Forget it."

Sitting back in the passenger seat, resting his head and closing his eyes, Ash directed, "First right, second left, it's all signposted from there."

"Yes." Silence. Then Albert said, "Get a grip on yourself before we reach Georgia. You're behaving like a child."

"Oh, don't you start in on me again."

"You've got one chance at this, Ash, and you're set to ruin it. To use a particularly picturesque expression, you're going off half–cocked. You don't know enough yet, neither of us do, to be sure this is the same man. If it isn't, you've put yourself back in the red when it comes to credits."

"When I was a kid, I thought the FBI would be, I don't know, nobler and braver than this."

"So Hoover was good at public relations. But it was a well–constructed lie. The Bureau isn't like the movies and agents aren't all James Stewart."

"If it's such a persuasive lie, it has to have some basis in truth."

"He had good people working for him, and he accomplished good things amongst all the dross. But he wouldn't have recruited you."

"No, my suits don't fit well enough." Fletcher offered him a smile, then, "Thanks for getting this other case solved so quickly."

"Any half decent medical examiner could have done the same."

"Modesty, Albert?" Ash laughed. "How unexpected."

"If I valued the currency I'd take credits for the difficult cases."

"Look, I'm sorry. Again. I hate feeling so … impotent."

"This is getting tiresome, Ash."

"Okay." The man sighed. "You know, you're the last person I can afford to alienate."

Albert stared ahead at the road, hoping the pre–dawn light and the dark glasses hid enough of his reaction. He used to admire Fletcher's perceptions. Now he was inclined to hate them.

"And I'm not just talking about the case."

No further declarations, no explanations. Fletcher turned away to the side window, appeared to drop off into a doze. But Albert didn't want to know what the man had meant, didn't want any of it to have been said. He especially didn't want to love this man. It was a pity that he seemed to have little choice in the matter.

There was a high wind tattering the clouds and soughing the highest branches of the pine trees, but it was quiet on the ground, a contrast that created a pregnant atmosphere. Ash was crouched down by the gravesite, completely still, as if lost in thought. Albert had seen him like this before – the man was paying far more attention than you would assume from his appearance, taking in details that others often missed. And then there were the less exact matters Fletcher was drawing on. A lot of law enforcement people liked to visit a crime site to get a feel for it but Ash seemed to take that one step further, somehow gathering up the offender's feel for the place instead. Albert wasn't sure that he believed in this ability but he had seen too many of Fletcher's predictions proven true to be able to dismiss it entirely. And he would be the first to assert that humanity usually wasted the bulk of its potential.

Rather than continue to stare at Ash, Albert gazed around the site. It seemed to have been chosen at random, with short term convenience rather than long term safety in mind, being only a few yards from a dirt track and within hailing distance of a lumberyard. The trees hid it to some extent: even though they were widely spaced and the branches began at least six feet up the trunks, the undulating ground limited the possible range of vision. There were few other plants; just bare dirt and years of dead pine needles.

The cop who was escorting them at last broke the silence. "This one wasn't planned," Alanna Roberts said. "Not like your lot in Colorado."

Ash stirred and looked up at the woman. "He's clever enough to try to throw us off like that," he said.

"But these types stick to the same MO, get themselves fixated on a particular way of doing the job. That's the whole point."

"Young white male, tortured, slowly killed, sexually assaulted, anal penetration. Body left naked, no jewelry or clothes. Buried face–down, in a forest." Fletcher listed these facts as if they were a litany he had repeated a hundred times. "You tell me, Alanna."

"Your lot were killed differently, which is a very significant point. These bled to death and yours were strangled. I won't deny there are similarities but there're too many differences."

"The differences are more superficial than the similarities."

"You can't call the cause of death superficial. And it's been a long while," Roberts said, "maybe two years between your case and this one. What's your man been doing in the meantime?"

"I don't know. But two years before the Colorado case, there were four murders in Wyoming, still unsolved, that also bear similarities."

"You're seriously suggesting a cycle of two years? That's too long. Now, every full moon, I'd believe, or every Christmas …"

Ash didn't smile.

"And the body count is going down, rather than escalating."

"It's not that I don't trust you to do everything you can to solve this, Alanna. But I'm afraid there are clues we'll miss if we treat each case separately."

"Or, if you're wrong, it will all get confused, jumbled in together, and we'll never sort it out."

"Yes, I see that." But he obviously didn't like it or agree with it.

"What about the missing girlfriend? Stacey Dixon. You don't have a parallel for that."

"No, we don't." Ash looked up at Albert. His expression was relatively bland, but Albert could read the defeat.

"I'll keep you appraised of any developments," Roberts said.

"Thank you. And if you need FBI resources, call me."

"Of course."

"One favor – your list of suspects. Once it's compiled, why don't you let me compare it to mine?"

The woman grimaced. "Look, we've had police in from all over the country, angling for a piece of the pie, trying to get a solution to whatever's outstanding on their own books. You're as convincing as any of them, Fletch, but that's a big ask. I can't let the world know names of men who are most likely innocent."

"I know what I'm asking. I could give you my list, perhaps, and you could see if there are any matches."

"How many did you have?"

"Fifteen–hundred. And nothing to tie any of them with more than one of the victims, if that. You know how it is – some were included just because of the cars they drove."

"Send me the ones who have moved out of Colorado, perhaps."

"Thanks, Alanna."

"I have to tell you, we're going to do this one alone for now, keep it within Georgia. You understand, Fletch."

Albert waited out the silence. True to his word, Ash had been entirely more reasonable than in Colorado, if quietly persistent. Albert wondered which was preferable: Ash trusting Albert enough to indulge himself, to be open and vulnerable; or Ash behaving like a responsible adult? It seemed strange to Albert to have fallen for a man who could exhibit so little restraint. And yet wasn't it a sign of Ash's friendship that he wouldn't bother controlling his impulses in Albert's company?

Frowning, Albert looked around, saw Roberts walking back to her car. He hated this: how his thoughts rambled, how consideration of Fletcher Ash could distract him at the most inopportune moments. A complete waste of energy. But he realized there was no way to undo the damage. He could only hope to minimize its effects, give it the necessary time to wear off.

Ash was circling the area, wandering, casting his glance over everything in the vicinity.

"Still convinced?" Albert asked.

"Even more so. Though I can't justify it enough to satisfy anyone but you." Then he stopped and asked, "Unless Alanna's talked you out of believing in me? It's so frustrating: I agree with every word she says, I'd think exactly the same thing if I were in her shoes, but she's wrong."

Albert shrugged this off. "We'll monitor their progress."

"Good. Thanks." He walked closer, casting one last glance around the area. Then he focused on Albert. "Come on, then, this is the fun bit. Alanna's taking us to the morgue."

"Are you attempting to worry me, Ash?"

The younger man just grinned.

◆

"Mitchell Brown," Roberts said as the morgue attendant pulled one of the drawers out. "I knew this boy. Mitch would have gone down fighting."

"He might have injured the offender in a struggle?" Ash asked.

"Hell, yeah. He gave me a black eye once." Then she sighed and added, "I don't know. The bastard must have tied him up fairly quickly, or cuffed him. But I bet Mitch left his mark."

"When did you win the black eye?"

"Mitch had been drinking, under age. He was quite special, you know the sort – they're full of possibilities, but could go either way. You have to watch them through the teenage years, minimize the trouble they cause, but you step on them too hard and you send them off in the wrong direction."

"I know the type," Ash said.

"I think Mitch was beginning to write, poetry and what–have–you. Pity we'll never know what he might have achieved."

Albert said, "From the reports, the other victim is beaten just as badly. You're not suggesting Brown sustained more injuries because it's likely he fought back?"

Roberts shook her head, expression troubled. "On balance, no. That was the offender's MO."

Shutting them out, Albert concentrated on a visual examination of the corpse. There was nothing he could see under these conditions that hadn't been in the report. And, given the obvious extent of the injuries and the advanced state of decay, he could understand the difficulties the medical examiner had in handling the internal organs. He would have far preferred to have dealt with this one himself.

"No traces of the offender except his semen," Albert said.

"Nothing," Roberts confirmed.

"There has to be something."

Fletcher said, "That's what we need, of course. Something to match him up with ours."

"They were careful, sifted the soil around the body. But there wasn't anything to find. And you would have read that the offender's a non–secretor."

"So was ours," Ash said. "Which limits the search to twenty or thirty percent of the population."

"That's not proof the cases are connected, Fletch," said Roberts. "And we need a suspect first, before we can try to eliminate him on those grounds."

"Agreed. But doesn't it strike you as odd, in a case that otherwise seems disorganized, superficially at least, that the offender took such great care not to leave trace evidence?"

"A combination of luck and the time that's passed could have the same result."

Albert said, "Show me the other body."

While the attendant pushed Mitchell Brown back into cold storage, Ash muttered, "Offender. There has to be a better description." He was staring sightlessly at the rows and rows of steel drawers. "This doesn't *offend* me – it outrages me, horrifies me."

Roberts was nodding, saying, "I know." She shared a sympathetic smile with him.

Turning to the second body, Albert rolled his eyes in exasperation. But he couldn't prevent a stab of jealousy at the easy understanding between Fletcher and this woman. He hated being reduced to begrudging Ash a new friend.

Outside, Ash seemed revitalized by the crisp, pale sunlight. "We drew a blank," he said, though he had apparently accepted that.

"No, we didn't," Albert disagreed.

"I suppose time will catch up with this man, even if we don't. But what does he get away with meanwhile?"

"If you're right, we have sixteen or seventeen months."

"And if I'm wrong? I might have missed some cases for the intervening years."

"You've done what you could."

"Not quite." And Fletcher grinned at him. "Sorry, but I'm coming to Washington with you."

CHAPTER NINE
WASHINGTON DC
APRIL 1983

Perhaps he shouldn't have pushed his luck and invited himself to Albert's for dinner. It wasn't, strictly speaking, fair: they were both tired after too little sleep and too much tragedy; and they were both used to living alone. Albert had withdrawn, even further than required by his usual policy of non–involvement, and no doubt that was because he'd had enough of Fletcher's company for now. Usually they talked when they were together over a meal like this: discussions and disagreements about cases and the Bureau, about Fletcher specifically and people in general. Fletcher enjoyed being challenged by and learning from this man's conversation.

But even Albert's silence was preferable to Fletcher's own thoughts tonight. Albert's undemanding company and his cooking always made Fletch feel at home because they echoed his memories of Harley. The echoes were indirect, perhaps, for where Albert was precise, Harley was slapdash, but they both knew how to make the best of food.

Fletcher took another long swallow of the white wine he'd bought on the way here. It was going down all too easily, and of course Albert didn't drink alcohol, so Fletch had the whole bottle to himself.

It helped take his mind off the case, at any rate. Instead, he considered Albert. Because Fletch wanted to put the guilt behind him – not forget it, but get beyond it – the guilt at the results of his failure. More immediately, he wished the images of Mitch, with his dark gold curls, and young Philip would quit haunting him. He sighed. Alanna was looking for someone who liked his young men strong and blond but Fletch knew his offender had broader tastes than that.

Albert sat across from him, distracted and yet purposeful. Albert never did anything, wore any expression, that wasn't wholly focused and deliberate. There was a grace to him because of it, that might otherwise never have developed because the man was normally devoid of self–consciousness. Even now, with his thoughts miles away, Albert looked intent.

It seemed the only thing in the world that Albert found disconcerting was his partiality for Fletcher. Of course, Fletch couldn't deny he was extremely flattered by such an unanticipated turn of events but he was sorry Albert was so perturbed by it. In fact, the man seemed to be unhappier and more ill–at–ease each time Fletch saw him. And still there was nothing Fletcher could, in all conscience, do for him.

It was tempting to try to include the sexual in their friendship, to broaden the relationship beyond the subliminal sensuality that blessed any close friends. Ash couldn't deny a few speculative day dreams along those lines. He'd long been curious about what sex would be like between two men, figured everyone at least *wondered*. And here was Albert, dependable and surprising, and in love with Fletcher. It was tempting to experiment with this damned interesting idea, with this attractive and available man, even though it was guaranteed to do far more harm than good.

Albert probably wouldn't let it happen, even if Fletch did try. He had the stubbornness to deny himself. And the passion to hate Fletcher if the younger man forced the issue. That would be a disaster, even compared to muddling along as they were now.

Finding his glass empty, Fletcher poured himself more wine. It wasn't an answer, but it would do.

And it got him out of the drying up. One near–slip with a wet plate and Albert relieved him of further duties. "Pathetic, Ash," was the comment. "But I suppose a harmless drunk is preferable to a ranting child."

"Who are you calling harmless?" Fletch retorted. He swallowed the rest of the wine, managed to safely return the glass to the kitchen, then tottered back to stretch out on the sofa.

Home. Or a more than reasonable substitute for it.

Fletch was dimly aware that it was late when he woke. His more immediate concerns were an insistent bladder, a skull protesting at what it contained, and a tortured spine. Then there was the distraction of the smell of brewing coffee. Which to deal with first?

After some consideration, logic dictated that he stand and stretch. Fletcher did so, momentarily tangled in an unexpected blanket. He'd been lying on Albert's sofa, and now he was standing on Albert's cropped sage green carpet, therefore it seemed reasonable that this was Albert's blanket. He tried to cope with the image of Albert Sterne bothering to bring the blanket and tucking Fletch in, then put it aside. It was too early in the morning for these mind–bending ideas. Instead, he slunk into the kitchen.

The next matter that caught his attention was the full pot of hot coffee. It belatedly dawned on him that Albert didn't drink coffee and certainly hadn't owned a coffee–maker before now. Fletch stared at it for a moment.

And then quickly reassessed his priorities and headed for the bathroom.

A few minutes later, feeling a little more human, Fletch poured a mug of coffee and started wondering where Albert was. But that was a mystery soon solved. One of Albert's business cards had been placed neatly on the kitchen bench beside the coffee. On the back, in Albert's neat printing that was usually found only on forensic reports, it read, *I am at headquarters.* Fletcher groaned.

Albert was in his tiny office, typing away at the computer as if his fingers were trying to beat the speed of light. Fletcher smiled. One of the things he loved about Albert was his serious, energetic, determined dedication, although he was easily distracted today. Fletcher tapped quietly at the glass wall and Albert's head whipped around to see him. His gestured invitation to enter was brusque, which was nothing new, but to the practiced eye, his expression was darker than usual. He snapped, "Good of you to put in an appearance."

"Sorry it's so late," Fletcher replied. He closed the door behind him, dumped the bag he'd brought and sat down in the solitary visitor's chair. He idly wondered how many other people had sat here; he suspected it was only a few and none by choice.

"It is just as well some of us are prepared to put in a full day's work."

"Actually, I was hoping that you could spare me an hour for a game of squash. Wouldn't mind sweating copiously right now, do me the world of good."

"What a revolting idea."

Fletch chuckled, though he felt uneasy, and hefted the bag up to the desk. "I went through your wardrobe, I was trying to find the track pants and sweater you wear when you ride your bike, but I've never *seen* so many suits. I mean, if I didn't know better I'd suspect you do the garden in them as well." The words and then the smile faltered as Fletch looked across at Albert. Though the man was temporarily speechless, his expression seemed to demand, *You did what?*

"Sorry," Fletch tried. "That was the wrong thing to do."

"You can manage better than that, Ash. I've never heard such a weak and insincere apology."

"I *am* sorry. I didn't think."

"And what are you sorry for? Invading my privacy? Abusing my trust? I should never have left you alone there."

"All of that," Fletch agreed, nodding. His head still hurt, and he really didn't want to listen to this, but he should have anticipated it and not put himself or Albert in the situation. Albert must indeed be angry to talk in such clichés.

"That's my home, Ash. Have you no respect? If it wasn't for your physical violence this morning –"

Fletcher stared at him. "What?"

"You should have been in here, anyway. Friday is a workday in Washington, even if it isn't in the backwoods. And didn't you come here to progress the case you were so wound up about only yesterday?"

It was bizarre, Fletcher thought. Albert was simply sitting there, across the desk, barely raising his voice, and yet spitting out pure malice. No one out in the lab would be aware Albert was anymore furious than usual. And Fletch was just sitting there, too, taking it, because it wouldn't be fair to give all this anger back to the man. Albert was feeling vulnerable right now. It was a compliment, really, that Albert should be so defenseless before Fletcher.

When he had the chance to interrupt, Fletch repeated, "What violence?"

"You hit me, Ash."

"No …" Such an assertion was impossible to credit. He'd never have done such a thing. Surely not … "What do you mean?"

Silence for a moment. It was difficult to tell whether Albert looked more offended than bitter, but Fletch hoped so. "I tried to wake you from your drunken stupor this morning, and you hit me."

"Really?" Poor Albert must have run a mile, being confronted like that. It would almost be amusing if it hadn't hurt the man. "I'm sorry, it was completely unintentional. Maybe I was dreaming. I have bad dreams, you know."

Either the apology was acceptable or Albert had got everything off his chest now. In any case, the man's expression gradually settled into merely grumpy.

"I'm going for a run, if squash is out of the question, then a shower and then to work."

"What work?"

"Records for Georgia over the past two years, anything that might be our man showing his hand. If you're too busy, I'll ask Mac to help."

"Don't be anymore ridiculous than you have to be, Ash. You need expert assistance."

"Mac's doing all right," Fletch said mildly – but he meant it.

Albert rolled his eyes, turned back to his computer.

"Any chance of you working late with me tonight? I know it's been a long couple of days, but I'd really appreciate it."

"Of course I will," the man snapped.

Fletch smiled at him. "Thanks."

"Get out of here, Ash."

Not prepared to push his luck any further, Fletcher got.

The phone rang at ten–fifteen, startling Fletch. HQ had been deathly quiet for hours. Albert reached out, barely pausing in his search of the computer records. "Sterne." He listened for a moment, said, "Yes," and then handed the receiver to Fletch. "It's Roberts."

Ash smiled. "Hello, Alanna."

"I thought I'd find you working, Fletch."

"And I expect you are, too."

"Yes."

He pictured her in her uniform, with the checked woolen jacket she wore over it, her blond hair in a long braid, her expression thoughtful. Then he thought to ask, "Is this good news, bad news, or just an excuse to chat?"

"Good and bad. We found the missing girlfriend, Stacey Dixon."

"I suppose the bad news is she's dead."

"Yes. We concentrated a search around where Philip Rohan was found, along the roads in and out of the area, you know the routine. She was downstream in the river, would have been found weeks ago but she was caught in a submerged fallen tree."

"How did she die?"

"Shot in the chest. She was fully clothed, no sign of any assault, but the similarities are that it seems her wrists were restrained for a while before she died, and it appears she and Philip were killed around the same time. Does that sound like your man?"

"You know, I think it has to be. But, whoever it is, it sounds like she got in the way, she wasn't to his taste."

"Yes, that's the way I saw it. In the wrong place at the wrong time, poor kid."

"Did you find the bullet? What sort of gun?"

"The cold–blooded bastard dug it out before dumping her."

"But he didn't strip her." So he could overcome his distaste only so far. Or perhaps he wanted keepsakes from the boys, but not from Stacey. "Has anyone else shown an interest in this?"

"I haven't called anyone else outside Georgia and no one's come forward."

"Then I doubly appreciate you letting me know, Alanna. Does this mean I've convinced you?"

"No, it means you're crazy, but I'm willing – against all my better instincts – to give you a chance."

Fletcher laughed. "That's the second nicest thing anyone's ever done for me."

"I'll keep you posted."

"Thanks. You can leave a message for me if I'm not here." Fletch said goodbye, hung up, then turned to fill Albert in. He went on to say, "If she wasn't weighted down, he can't have cared whether she'd be found right away, and he certainly didn't care that her clothing would help identify her. With the boys, he at least gave himself some time."

"And what did he do with the time?" Albert asked.

Fletch mentally reeled for a moment, already knowing the answer but not having considered the implications before. "He moves on to another state before the bodies are found." Standing, Fletch began to distractedly pace around the table and back again. "I'm sure he wants them found at some stage, though. This man is so in control, so cool about it. It's a waste of effort looking for traces of him. He's not going to betray himself."

"Why shouldn't he? People do, in various ways, and this man is more compulsive and obsessive than most."

"All right, all right," Fletch said impatiently, though he welcomed Albert's challenges. "So he wouldn't survive two years at a time without surrendering in some way to these urges. He's sensible, but he can't be totally controlled. What are we looking for? Reports or cases involving sodomy or assault, with Caucasian boys between eighteen and twenty-five years old. None of the murder victims have been prostitutes but they're easy prey for abuse or violence, so he might use them in between times. Complaints from boys on the street or their pimps, and from college kids and their families. How's that?"

"I'm glad you're finally able to keep up, Ash."

He smiled. This sort of insult from Albert was tantamount to an expression of affection, especially when compared to his fury that afternoon. Then Fletcher's back twinged again. Stretching, grimacing, he said, "No offence, but your sofa was not made for sleeping on."

"I never intended it to be slept on," Albert replied curtly.

"I'll go to the hotel tonight."

"There's no need."

Fletch looked at the man, as Albert studiously avoided meeting his gaze. He'd always known it was a big deal to visit Albert's house. No one else had, not Mac, not ... Fletch couldn't even think of any other candidates. And here was Albert as good as asking him to sleep over for last night, tonight, at least Saturday night as well. Who cared about the spine–crunching sofa?

"We're working tomorrow?" Fletch asked.

"Yes." Of course.

"Then let's get out of here. We both need our beauty sleep."

Fletch caught the tail end of a sardonic glance and managed to choke back a surprised laugh. How absurdly flattering.

Albert pulled the Saab up to his garage, let it idle for the prescribed thirty seconds to allow the turbo to settle while Fletch clambered out, then Albert turned the ignition off. Usually he would grudgingly let

Fletcher unlock and open the garage's main door. Tonight, he did it himself, then impatiently beckoned Fletch over. "Help me with this."

A double mattress and box springs, still swathed in plastic, was propped up against one wall. "You didn't," Fletch said.

Albert was silent. They lifted the mattress between them.

"Okay, so you did," Fletch continued as Albert led the way outside and up the front steps. There was a pause as the man dealt with the two locks on the door. "How?"

"It took three simple phone calls, Ash. It would not qualify as a miracle."

"You let someone have a key to the garage?"

"I told you, the child next door does the gardening when I'm called away."

They were maneuvering down the hallway now. "Where? The spare room?" Fletch asked.

"Yes."

It was empty in there but for the darkly forbidding wallpaper; the only room Albert hadn't decorated and furnished. They left the mattress and returned for the box springs, working together in silence.

It was difficult to find the right words to express Fletch's appreciation of all this, words that wouldn't betray his knowledge of Albert's secret agenda – which in itself was the wrong term, for Albert wasn't scheming to win Fletch over, he wasn't trying to bribe him; far from it. So – a few simple and heartfelt words. Fletch, the son of a writer, felt woefully inadequate. And then he realized such words would only further embarrass Albert. Perhaps a quiet acceptance, a lack of fuss, was all that was required. This atmosphere of friendship, ease, that was the important thing.

Fletch caught Albert's eye, and simply smiled. Happy, in this at least.

Albert, impervious mask firmly in place, fetched sheets, pillows, and a quilt. But, as Fletch imagined the crazy dangerous intimacy of them making up a bed together, Albert said good night, and walked out. The door to Albert's bedroom was shut, quietly but firmly.

Just as well, really. Fletch agreed wholeheartedly that humanity in general could resist anything but temptation, and Fletch himself was no exception.

◆

It was Sunday. He really should be heading back to Colorado, once he'd sorted through these files spread across the dining table. Or catching up with old friends, like Tyler Reece. He'd only seen Tyler once since their brief affair ended, though he'd spoken to her on the phone a number of times. He wanted to stay in touch, because she was an incredible woman, lover or not.

But Albert apparently had something else planned for the day. After a couple of undisturbed hours, Fletcher pushed aside the last of the files and wandered off to find him.

He was in the spare room. "Help me move the bed out," Albert said. They leaned it up against the wall in the foyer, Albert neatly folding the bedding and placing it on top. And then, back in the room, Albert gestured at a steamer. "Strip the wallpaper," he ordered.

Fletcher smiled. "It will be a pleasure. The pattern gave me nightmares."

They worked in silence for a while, Fletch steaming and peeling off the paper with Albert following him, washing the last of the glue off the wall, and plastering over the few cracks.

"So, what's this room going to be?" Fletcher asked, though he hoped he'd guessed the answer.

"Guest bedroom," Albert replied absently.

The man was frowning in concentration, Fletch was amused to note, a perfectionist in this as in all else. It must have taken him a damned long time to work through the rest of the house alone – or maybe not. Whatever Albert decided was worthwhile doing, he did well, and he put in far longer hours than most would. Intense, that's what he was. Fletcher liked it, especially as he was the man's only guest.

"And the color scheme?" Fletch asked. Albert was silent, though Fletch knew he'd heard the question. He persisted, "Darker greens maybe, or peaches and reds like in your room?"

That provoked a defensive response. Fletch was all too aware that the main bedroom was Albert's one remaining sanctuary now Fletch had invaded his home. "Blues," Albert said. "A dash of purple. An iron bed."

It was Fletcher's turn to be surprised. "What? That doesn't fit, does it?" Silence. "The house, it's all so coordinated. This won't go."

"A progression from the blues in the kitchen."

Fletch considered this, and frowned. There was something wrong here. "No … that doesn't link in. Everything else is linked. It's all a harmony."

Albert snapped, "Since when were you an expert in interior decoration?"

"Since I saw this place," Fletch retorted.

"I expected you to have stripped that wallpaper by now."

"Well," Fletch drawled, "I wanted to prolong the agony." He cast a glance over the few remaining feet. "I could never have imagined this stuff, not in my worst dreams, not in the depths of my paranoia."

Albert let out a breath, a quiet snort. It was the closest he ever came to a laugh. "You should have seen the paper in the dining room."

"Can't imagine them able to eat in there?"

"No."

"If it were me, I wouldn't have bought the place."

"But it had obvious advantages, it was in the right location, and the rooms are a good size."

"And you could work on the problems, one by one."

"Yes."

So intellectual, so unswayed by emotional reaction, and of course Albert had been completely right – the house itself was lovely, and Albert's work had perfected it. Fletch wanted to say, *Albert, you're amazing*. But he didn't. "So, have you bought the paint? Can we make a start on that?"

"The walls have to dry, and the filler needs to be sanded back. I'll do it tomorrow evening."

Fletcher stuck out his lower lip. "Only if I get to stay and help you."

"So easily distracted, aren't you?" But the voice was mild, wondering rather than critical. "There's a case to devote your time to, and Thornton is expecting your return."

"Let me see the paint, at least."

"When you've finished stripping the paper."

"All right, all right," Fletch laughed.

Once they were done, Albert led him out to the garage. He opened up one of the paint cans, then stirred it for a couple of minutes before he would let Fletcher look.

The paint was a startling and beautiful color: a medium blue, with more than a hint of lilac. Fletcher stared, and gravely said, "I wish you'd tell me why."

'Do you not like it?' The tone weary, but not defensive.

"I love it, of course I love it. But there's something wrong, something doesn't fit. Your house shouldn't be mucked up just for me."

Albert said, "You don't know what you're talking about."

"Don't I?" Fletcher looked up. Albert rarely let him meet his gaze, not when they were discussing something as personal as this – and Fletch couldn't help but wonder why the color of Albert's guest room should have turned out to be such a sensitive issue – but Albert wasn't looking into him in that intense way of his. It was more that he was looking *at* Fletch, seeing only the surface, the face that the man was far gone enough to think didn't need any beauty sleep, the blue Irish eyes for which Fletch blamed his grandfather.

It would be churlish to refuse all this, Fletcher thought: the coffee–maker, the bed, the room; the attention and thoughtfulness and generosity. Churlish and ungrateful, when all that seemed to be expected in return was friendship, companionship. But it also seemed unfair to accept, as if he were letting Albert be taken advantage of. Surely he should at least offer a warning. Fletch said, "You should know that I'm as selfish as the next man."

Silence. Then, with timing so bad it was almost comic, the phone in the house rang. Albert handed Fletch the can of paint, and walked out of the garage, unhurried. Fletcher picked up the lid, pressed and then hammered it into place. By which time Albert had returned.

"That was headquarters. Your father left a message. He wants you to ring him, but apparently it isn't urgent."

"No, I always talk to him on Sundays. He's probably just wondering where I am."

"You could have left him this number, Ash."

"I didn't like to." Fletch asked, "May I call him now?"

"Of course." He was clearly annoyed at even being asked.

Fletch smiled at the man, but Albert was once again avoiding him. "Thanks."

◆

Peter Ash usually had no particular news but that never stopped him and Fletcher from spending an hour or more talking each week. The Idaho people joked that the Ash family must have shares in the phone company.

Today, however, Peter had plenty to update his younger son with. Fletcher was to become an uncle for the second time and the local diner was up for sale – Peter, Harley and Beth were going to buy it, with a view to running it themselves and eventually converting the empty shop next door into a more up–market restaurant. "We figured that for once our week was almost as exciting as yours."

"Congratulations," Fletch said wryly.

"So, what's happening with you? You're not sounding very happy."

"I'm all right."

"Come on, what is it? A case? If you finally solve an interesting one, maybe I can write a book about it."

Fletch laughed. His father had been threatening that for years. "I'll tell you all about it when I have the guy in jail for at least ten lifetimes."

"And don't spare me the sordid drama or the juicy bits."

"Fine, Dad. Look, I'm staying with Albert Sterne for a few days – remember I've mentioned him?"

"How could I forget? He's the forensics specialist."

"Yes. I'll give you his number here in Washington, for next time."

"No more of that terrible hotel the Bureau uses?"

"Of course that's the only reason he's a friend."

"A good enough reason, from all reports."

"You won't believe this, Dad, but he's doing up his spare bedroom for me, painting the walls this beautiful shade of blue. I've never seen anything like it."

"That's good, Fletcher." Silence for a moment. "He's the one you described as *vastly bitter and rude*, isn't he? Do I have the phrase right?"

"That's Albert. But he's not really – People make the mistake of dismissing him because of his manner."

"You have a generous heart, Fletcher."

"You're sentimental and biased, Dad."

"And now we have the insults out of the way …" Peter chuckled. "Well, I suppose we'd better save your friend's phone bill while we can or his bitterness with his new lodger will reach epic proportions. Bitter, baleful, belligerent."

"More like passionately disappointed," Fletch said.

Silence again. Then, "Who calls whom next week?"

"I'll call you, probably from Colorado."

"My son, the traveling Special Agent," Peter said with mock pride.

"My father, the Idaho hardware man," Fletch replied fondly.

Peter wasn't going to let him get away with it this time. "And restaurateur!"

Fletch hung up, laughing. Within moments, the phone rang again. Albert was still outside, so Fletcher answered it. "Hello."

"It's Mac – McIntyre. I was hoping I'd catch you, Fletch. You're not heading off home again are you?"

"No, but I should be. Why?"

"I was reading some of the old newspaper clippings, and there was a missing person case back in 1976 that rang a bell. This youngster was seen talking to a man in a flash car the afternoon he disappeared, and I remembered you describing –" Mac got to the point: "I should just read it out and let you decide."

"Okay. You're thinking of Andrew Harmer in Colorado."

"Yes. This one was … let's see, Darren Maxwell in Seattle. I can go through the files for any related material in the morning, if you think it's worth it."

"Read it out, Mac." And Fletch listened with that odd feeling in his heart that was both despair and elation. "Sounds like it might be our man," he said when Mac finished. "I'll be in to help you tomorrow."

"Good. And tell Albert I ate the bit of paper with his phone number. It's not my fault the duty officer didn't want to make the call for me. Said she'd disturbed him once already today, and didn't want to risk twice."

Fletch laughed. "Okay, okay. See you bright and early."

"Early, anyway," Mac offered before cutting the connection.

The phone rang yet again while Albert was cooking dinner. He picked it up and held it to his ear with a hunched up shoulder so he could continue to chop a green pepper. "Sterne." He listened for a long moment, said, "All right," then hung up. "Headquarters," he said.

Fletcher, sitting on the other side of the counter watching Albert work, almost laughed at the thought of the duty officer having to risk calling Albert again despite all her efforts. But he sobered when he saw Albert's rather pointed expression. This was going to be bad news. "What?"

"Roberts left a message for you. They've found a fourth body, another boy."

CHAPTER TEN
WASHINGTON DC
APRIL 1983

Fletcher was taking the news of this fourth death hard. He looked thoroughly miserable for a moment, and then opened his mouth to ask a question.

"Yes," Albert said.

A confused frown. "Yes, what?"

"Yes, you may call Roberts. You've had the gall to make yourself at home in most other respects, Ash, I don't know why you have this problem with using my telephone."

The young man had a wry twist to his mouth. "Allow me a few scruples. Inconsistent though they are."

Albert turned back to the cutting board, swept the diced pepper into the pot simmering away on the back burner. Fletcher liked spicy food so Albert was making him a Mexican dish based on beans and rice, with an avocado and lettuce salad. An unwelcome surprise, that all this trivial domesticity should have become satisfying in its own right. Had he really overlooked the entire point during all these years of dismissing such ordinary comforts? Could he possibly have forgotten that his own parents' quietly joyous contentment had been drawn partly from such moments?

But he was in no way entitled to compare his problematical friendship with Ash to the marriage of Rebecca and Miles.

The phone call was brief, and Albert learned little from Fletcher's few words. Once he'd hung up, Fletcher sat in silence for a moment. Then he said, "The victim was young, maybe seventeen or eighteen. Looks like a Latino background, but they haven't identified him yet. Been dead for months." Ash smiled unhappily. "Alanna is closer to believing me, but she's not all the way there yet."

"Same MO as the two other boys in Georgia?"

"Exactly the same, which has to tell us something. Does he go through phases? For a while he likes it in a particular way, but then he gets tired or bored with it. Or he's experimenting with different methods, maybe, finding the best or most effective for him. Or he's acting out a whole range of fantasies, one by one. Whatever it is, he's very neat and tidy about it."

The man fell silent, and remained subdued over dinner, not paying much attention to the food. Albert studied him, realizing that Fletcher was disturbed at some deep level. Impatient with the tantrums that had greeted the first news from Georgia, Albert had made the mistake of assuming Fletcher's reactions to this were shallow, easily expended and forgotten. But it seemed all that extravagance had obscured this more weighty concern.

"You're doing everything you can with what you've got, to paraphrase Thornton," Albert offered. "That's all you can ask of yourself."

"It's not enough."

Albert said as patiently as he could, "Then nothing will ever be enough."

"No, nothing ever will."

If this had been moroseness, Albert could have dismissed it but instead it was a simple, profound sadness of which Albert was almost envious. The purity of it would fade, tainted by self–pity, and Ash would regain his determination. For now, Albert simply watched the man. Was it possible to love Fletcher more, all of a sudden, and only because of witnessing this emotion?

Albert had wondered at himself, in Colorado, doubting the suitability of this man he had chosen to love. Of course, there was all the glory and inconvenience of the physical reaction, which was perhaps inevitable – Albert defied anyone not to find Fletcher Ash attractive. But beyond that, what sense did it make for Albert to love a man who seemed to lack qualities, such as self–control, that Albert particularly valued? Looking back on it, though, Albert could understand Ash's frustration and guilt, the horror of not stopping this murderer. Fletcher had willingly taken on the responsibility of solving this case when no one else would, which was commendable. Perhaps his manner of expressing his frustration at the lack of results left a lot to be desired, but Ash felt things deeply, and that again was not a bad trait even if he took it too far – he was no doubt ready to have himself arrested for aiding and abetting the man they were after. Albert had to conclude that, despite all these justifications he had to make to himself, Fletcher Ash was worth loving.

As predicted, Fletcher's fine sadness seemed at last to dwindle into depression. After a while Albert advised, "Snap out of it, Ash."

Rising from his thoughts, Fletcher was slow to respond. "Let me grieve."

"What use is grieving? This hopelessness won't get you anywhere."

"There's nothing to be done this evening. And I can't be working twenty–four hours a day."

"Instead of wallowing, you could keep a clear mind, and be in a position to let yourself work this through."

"I would love to work it through, but I can't right now."

"Can't or won't?"

"To be brutally honest, I'm grieving for Philip and Stacey and Mitch and this other young man – and also for me. I'm not who I thought I was, who I wanted to be, if I can let this happen." Fletcher looked up, smiled humorlessly. "See, I'm so selfish that I mourn my self–image at a time like this."

Albert was careful not to react. Fletcher had called himself selfish only that afternoon, presumably in an attempt to warn Albert off providing a friend with the most basic hospitality. But Albert could both admire Ash's scruples, and dismiss them as unnecessary. He said, "Selfishness is the last attribute I would accuse you of, Ash."

The man seemed genuinely surprised, and protested, "I'm the most selfish person I know."

"That's ridiculous." Yet another matter on which Fletcher would not see reason.

"You won't allow me my guilt, either, will you? But I hate feeling that there's nothing I can do, that I'm a step – no, I'm twenty steps behind this man and he's on a roll. Everything's proceeding so perfectly for him, life couldn't be better, and I'm stumbling along and running into walls and I can't even keep up."

"You're taking this out of proportion."

"How can I possibly take any murder out of proportion, let alone a string of them? It's horrific, no matter how you look at it."

"Don't pretend to misunderstand me. You need a cool head to be of any use, rather than overreacting like this." Albert added, "Tell me rationally, what's so important about this case in particular?"

Fletcher took a long breath, but the answer came easily enough. "He's why I joined the FBI. People like him."

"Yes?"

"To stop them, of course." Ash shrugged. "It's as simple as that."

Albert frowned at him. "There's more to it, you've said so yourself."

"Okay. I also joined up in order to use this imagination of mine, this intuition you don't believe in."

"I believe you have intuition, that you reconstruct crimes through your imagination," Albert said. "But I don't believe the conclusions you reach can always be true."

Fletcher insisted, "I can imagine what happened between this man and Mitch, I can feel how it would be to murder the boy."

"But the flaw in your argument is that you couldn't actually do it."

"You think not?" Fletcher bit out.

This still made no sense to Albert. "Of course you couldn't, you would never seek that situation or go through with it if you did have the opportunity. You don't have the personality or the background."

"Is that so?"

"No need to sound so affronted, Ash," Albert said dryly, "when someone accuses you of being incapable of murder."

"I'm only affronted that you don't take me seriously. You should have met my grandfather, the one I look like – *he* was capable of murder. He could be the most cold–blooded, vindictive man. When I was just a kid, he said to me that if a man is cuckolded, it's all right for him to kill his wife or her lover or both. He honestly thought the law should allow that: 'A man can't be expected to let that sort of thing be.' And I inherited other things from him, apart from my looks. *He'd* understand my determination to do my job well and bring this killer to justice. And he was supposed to have the second sight, I don't know if that has anything to do with my intuition. Frankly, I don't really know what the second sight is meant to be."

"Perhaps you have inherited some of his traits. Your grandfather gave you more than his genes, however; he was someone you learned from, even as an example of what you didn't want to become."

Fletcher shrugged.

Growing impatient, Albert asked, "What exactly would you do with him if you took Mitchell Brown home? Or Stacey Dixon, if she's more to your taste," he quickly added, not wanting an answer to the first. "You wouldn't cuff her and shoot her as this man did. You wouldn't torture, rape or murder anyone. It's ridiculous to dwell on such an idea."

"It's not ridiculous when understanding the power of it, the rush and surge of it, gives me a feel for what this person is."

"As long as you don't treat that – what is it? Instinct or fantasy? As long as you don't treat it as knowledge."

"It's hardly fantasy," Fletcher said, weary now. One hand cut short an exasperated gesture. "We always run around the same circles when we have this conversation."

Albert considered this whole thing such a waste of Fletcher's energy. They were both quiet for a while. Fletcher seemed safely deflated.

But then he asked, "Why did you join the Bureau, Albert? And why forensics?"

"To find the person or persons unknown who killed my parents." *No trespassing.*

It stopped Ash for a moment. And then, the gears in his mind visibly beginning to turn again, Fletcher protested, "No. It's not that simple for you, either. You can't – you definitely do not mean that literally. It was all too long ago. And figuratively, it's not enough. You're not seeking revenge, it's nothing obvious like that."

Silence. Albert loathed feeling foolish. It hadn't been such a smart thing to blurt out after all.

Fletcher was continuing, "The forensics, it's something you're incredibly good at. People would call you a genius if they liked you better. I have no idea what makes one person a genius at something like that. I mean, why forensics and not … astrophysics, or music? You specialize in everything, anything to do with people inflicting violence on each other: pathology, biochemistry, toxicology, dentistry –"

"Odontology," Albert corrected.

"Psychology," Ash said, "ballistics, hairs and fibers, fingerprints, weapons and poisons, crime scenes; more things than I can even think of right now. Most people specialize in only one or two of those fields. You're unique, Albert. So why the FBI?"

"You think you have the answer," Albert said, frowning at this impertinence.

"I suppose an organization with national jurisdiction gives you the chance to use the best facilities, work on the most important cases, do the most good. But you must hate the bureaucracy of it, the politics."

"Must I."

"Worse than I do. Though I suppose none of that weighs very heavily against the chance to bring murderers and rapists to justice."

"To what passes for justice in this society."

Fletcher stared at him, startled at the sourness.

Albert shrugged. "Forensics is a worthier endeavor than tapping Noam Chomsky's phone."

Choking back a laugh, Ash said, "You're right."

"Don't you do sordid, trivial little things like that, Special Agent? All in the name of lies, corruption, and the American way."

Apparently Fletcher had a hundred replies to that, and none. He kept opening his mouth to say something, then changing his mind.

"You're comfortable with all the duties the Bureau has required you to perform?"

"Albert –"

"What?"

"Sometimes you are the most difficult person to talk with." The younger man gestured helplessly. "So many things I can't say to you."

"We were only talking about work."

"No, we're talking about our personal reasons for what we do, our reactions, our compromises. And it isn't *just work* for either of us." Ash looked around the dining room, apparently searching for a change of topic. "This is a wonderful meal. I appreciate that you go to the trouble of indulging my tastes."

"That's the best you can manage?"

"All right," he said impatiently. A moment of thought, then a very direct stare. "For friends, we sure bicker a lot."

Albert looked down at his plate as he neatly gathered together a last mouthful of food. "It would be ludicrous to expect our opinions to always coincide."

"Well, I certainly agree to disagree with you on some things."

"Such as?"

"You've spent half the evening telling me what I am – or what I'm not, to be more exact. And, yes, you're often right about people, even if you always underestimate them. But it would be nice if you'd respect my judgment."

"I don't see why. You're hardly in the best position to make judgments about yourself. And I'm not going to lie to you if I think you're wrong."

"There's a line beyond which honesty becomes sheer nastiness, and tact or understanding are called for." Ash grimaced and added, "Besides which, you seem to think no one's in a better position than you to judge Albert Sterne. Why can't that principle apply to us lesser mortals?"

"Is that an example of nastiness?" Albert asked scathingly. "Thank you for the demonstration."

A turbulent silence.

Albert stood, reached for Fletcher's plate that had, at last, been emptied, and carried it through to the kitchen. The last few days had been horribly tiring – Albert was used to long hours, tragic cases, little sleep – but he wasn't used to dealing with a friend as well, not someone who meant so much, invading his home so there was no retreat.

"Never mind, Albert," said Fletcher Ash, in the quiet, reassuring voice he used with frightened children. He was leaning in the doorway, at ease.

Does this mean so little to you? Albert flared at him.

"I'll be heading back to Colorado soon. Or Georgia, if Caroline will let me. Out of your way, in any case, let you have some peace and quiet."

A strange sensation, akin to the shock of Ash striking out at him two mornings ago. Which was worse: Ash threatening to leave, or the thought of this domestic chaos continuing? Albert felt at a loss for a moment, his anger dying, and not even this unfamiliar disorientation rekindling it. He plugged in the coffee–maker, filled the jug with filtered water, measured out the required amount of ground beans, added an extra spoonful because Ash preferred his coffee strong.

The man was just standing there, watching him. Albert didn't like it, but he had nothing to push Fletcher away with right now. If Ash started again with those declarations – the ones impossible to interpret because they left so much unsaid, the half–explanations that assumed there was some kind of understanding between them – if Ash started with those, in that pitying tone of voice, Albert had no idea what he'd say. The tension of all the unshouted words churned in his gut.

But when Ash moved at last, he simply walked over to the sink and ran a tubful of water to wash up in – water as hot as Albert insisted on for proper sterilization, so he couldn't even take the man to task for that. Silence, as Fletcher washed, and Albert dried, and the coffee brewed.

A silence that slowly became companionable. Albert knew that now he had truly let the man into his home, a large part of him didn't want Fletcher to leave; and yet the rest of him couldn't bear anymore of this. And Ash knew that, too, of course. One of the things Albert loved him for was his instinct for how people were feeling and what they were thinking, even though that was so dangerous right now, with Albert's unwanted yearnings and confusions all too evident.

But there was always the good and the bad when it came to Fletcher. For instance, the man was still optimistic enough to see the best in people, to expect and therefore to find quality, despite all the years of what Albert considered must be disappointments. But when that ability extended to seeing something worthy in mediocrities like McIntyre, Albert had a difficult time remembering that it was a desirable attribute.

And then there was this strange idea of Fletcher's, that he had the potential for evil. The man was not a killer, he did not fit any of the profiles. Rather the opposite. He no doubt had problems with carrying a gun, and being expected to use it within certain situations, even though that was a requirement of being a special agent in the field. And yet Ash insisted there were impulses within him that had to be fought and contained. Albert couldn't accept that as possible – but even this mistaken and melodramatic notion of his was reason to love Ash. Humanity was capable of so much evil and Ash was all the more valuable for choosing to make a career of fighting it, and for wrestling the bad within himself as well.

Contradictions, paradoxes. Could that be love? Surely it had been simpler for his parents. Miles and Rebecca were different sorts of people from Albert, and they had each found someone who embodied all of the best qualities. Yet wasn't that exactly what Albert had found in Fletcher? Humanity's drive and complexity and passion and idealism, all in a package that, to add insult to injury, was so obviously attractive.

Fletcher seemed to realize that Albert should be left alone, and once the kitchen was set to rights again said a quiet, "Goodnight," then retreated to the guest room with a mug of coffee.

Albert took his time doing the rounds of the house, ensuring the locks were set, the windows closed and fastened. Exhausted, and yet too troubled to even contemplate sleep.

At last, safe in his room, with two doors closed between him and the intruder, Albert undressed; carefully aligning his shoes with the others, hanging his suit and tie, folding his shirt and shorts and socks and placing them in the laundry hamper. Then he headed for the bathroom, stepped into the shower, and turned the taps round to full. At first the blast of water was icy hostility, but the temperature soon raced up the scale to hot, perhaps unhealthily so. Albert braced himself with palms against the cold tiles, and let the water pummel his face and skull, his shoulders and back and torso.

He was aware of a tension that wouldn't go away, a dull and distant ache, an irritable hunger. His penis was stubbornly engorged despite his efforts to ignore it. Images filled his mind of Ash's bare chest, his ribs and musculature, the dark flame of hair that Albert wanted to cool with the flat of his tongue. Then less prosaic memories of the man's smile, the blue eyes merrily sharing some irony. The wistful seriousness of, *I wish you'd tell me why.*

Albert had reached down before he was aware of the decision to masturbate. Seeking a release, no matter how fleeting the satisfaction would be, despite the terrible loneliness of the act. The despair was flavored, this time, with illogical excitement at Ash being a few feet away rather than a thousand miles. Excitement and, to be honest, fear – though what difference did it really make? The man was just as unavailable, inaccessible. And there was no danger of Ash walking unannounced into the bedroom, let alone opening a third door and breaching the privacy of the bathroom. Even so, the potential humiliation of being caught going at it like some schoolboy was awful. His penis lost some of its enthusiasm. What if Ash's instincts led him to realize what Albert was doing right now, and he came to investigate … ?

But no. The idea of Ash barging in was ridiculous. Every now and then the pressure built and must be answered, so it might as well be now. The memories of Ash in those worn flannel pajama pants flooded back. And Albert decided to get the deed over with.

He unwittingly let out a groan at the end of it, frustration and relief and need claiming him – but surely it wouldn't have been heard over the water's thunder, through the three doors. He was disappointed with the results, as always – there wasn't any depth to an orgasm when he was alone. During all those years since the beautiful Lily, his satisfaction had been bleak and cold, grey and tasteless. He hated that it must be that way.

Albert let the shower run, wanting all this discontent to be washed away, but eventually he cared more about the waste of electricity and water than he did about his frustrations, and he turned the taps off. More tired than he could remember ever being, he forced himself through the motions of toweling off, then settled for his old pajamas rather than a fresh pair, and fell heavily into the haven of the bed.

Nothing had changed the next day except that somehow, from somewhere, Albert's equilibrium had returned. He even felt like smiling when he took freshly brewed coffee in to Fletcher, who was always slow in the mornings. The mess of hair, the hands eagerly grasping the steaming mug, and the wry gratitude were appealing in a pathetic sort of way. Albert wondered at himself all over again but there was little criticism to it this time.

At the office, he lost himself in the work that had backlogged in his absence, prioritized it and quickly cleared through what he could. Then, as he was expected to, he took an updated report of current tasks to Jefferson, who supposedly oversaw the allocation of work and resources in the forensics area. What actually happened was that Albert allocated his own efforts as he saw fit, unless the bureaucracy needed a signature on a travel request or a supplies order or some other such form. As Jefferson apparently knew little about either priority–setting or forensics, this suited Albert and dealt effectively with a large workload, but played havoc with Jefferson's peace of mind. It had been years since Jefferson had tried to defend Albert to anyone but as he had only ever produced ineffectual excuses on Albert's behalf, Albert wasn't sorry for the change.

The older man seemed particularly stressed today, Albert noted, like a pressure cooker about to burst. While Albert had long ago accepted that he was required to answer to the worst manager in the Bureau, Jefferson still fought his fate.

Albert rarely reflected on it but he knew there was no career path for him in the FBI. It didn't matter to him because he was doing exactly what he wanted to do, and had no desire to be promoted from a position dealing with crime scenes and corpses to one handling forms, memoranda, budgets, and troublesome subordinates. And even if he had wanted promotions, no one would have given them to him. Fletcher had been right about one thing last night: all the merit in the world couldn't save Albert from the fact that no one liked him. That made him impatient because while he couldn't care less whether people liked him or not, he considered that there were a number of far more important qualities to judge someone by. At least Ash obviously agreed on that.

As for Jefferson, having quickly risen to a level of management that he simply couldn't cope with, and having then been shuffled sideways time and again until they found an area he would do least harm in – Jefferson was trapped here, too, though not by choice. Albert pondered for a moment on whether having to supervise him was Jefferson's punishment, or whether someone had been bright enough to realize that Albert was the last person to be adversely affected by Jefferson's uselessness. Albert was always going to function to the best of his abilities, no matter what the Bureau threw in his way. Or perhaps the higher level managers were testing Albert as well, waiting to see which one of them would hand in his resignation first.

Fletcher would accuse him of being a conspiracy theorist at this point.

Albert might not be affected by Jefferson, but he obviously had been by Ash. This was Fletcher's forte, mulling over the whys, speculating on the wherefores. Albert was far more inclined to reach a conclusion whenever necessary, and then get on with the job.

It didn't occur to him to ask what Jefferson was so uptight about, but at least part of it was soon made clear. As Albert turned to leave, Jefferson spluttered, "Aren't you going to ask me if you can swan off to Georgia again at Bureau expense?"

"No."

"Why not?"

"I wouldn't want to give you the pleasure of refusing me."

It seemed as if Jefferson was going to blow a gasket right then and there. Albert looked at him, considered whether to leave, and postponed the decision until he had further information. Much as he despised the man, Albert didn't want to be the sole cause of the inevitable coronary.

He continued, "I'm sure Special Agent Ash is capable of investigating the situation, at least as far as our lack of jurisdiction allows us."

"And that's another thing," Jefferson said.

Albert closed the door and waited out the tirade. It seemed that relations between the Bureau and the police were at a low again, and it would not be appreciated if he or Ash trod on any toes in Georgia. And it was Jefferson's opinion that if someone were to be sent out there to heal the relationship, Albert was the last person he would consider for the honor. And Jefferson couldn't see anything in the whole mess anyway; the young man from Colorado ought to be careful he didn't throw away the last of his credibility.

"Yes," Albert said, before taking his leave. None of this mattered to him personally – even if he'd had any respect for Jefferson, he doubted it would really matter – but when Fletcher needed him for this case, it would obviously have to be an unofficial use of Albert's own time. So be it.

Fletcher knocked on his office door at two in the afternoon. "My flight leaves in an hour. I thought I'd give you the chance to say good riddance."

"Don't tempt me," Albert advised, standing up behind his desk.

"I'll call you when I get in tomorrow. Caroline agreed to me staying overnight in Georgia, then back to Colorado in the morning."

"I prepared this for Roberts." It was a report Albert had written over lunch, summarizing the forensic evidence in the Colorado case. Roberts didn't want to be lost in extraneous detail but it was in their interests to ensure she had the salient facts.

Fletcher leafed through the pages. "That's great, I appreciate it."

Now that it came to the crunch, Albert was mostly inclined to be sorry the man was going. He surprised himself by asking, "Do you need a lift to the airport?"

"No, I –" Fletcher was staring at him, quizzical. "Mac's driving me, actually. But thanks for offering." A pause. "I'll miss helping with the painting."

Albert snorted. "If you time it right, I'll have all the hard work done by your next visit."

"And it will look magnificent."

Silence. They had had some disjointed conversations in the past but this would have to be among the most pointless. "You should go."

"Yes. Thanks for everything."

Fletcher held out his right hand, and after a moment Albert shook it. A good firm grip, maybe a little extra pressure, which Albert assumed was supposed to be reassurance. Long fingers, cool fine skin. But surely they had dispensed with these formal gestures some while ago.

"Good riddance," Albert said.

"Yeah, until next time." And, with a smile, Fletcher was gone.

Albert reached out to close the office door, and sat down again. It was a few minutes before he regained the momentum of that morning.

He stood alone in the twilight, staring back at the blue flowers of the rogue groundcover that had infiltrated his garden. He'd fought it long enough. It was time to accept an inevitability. Albert muttered, "Let the damned thing grow."

FAITH
NEW YORK CITY
SEPTEMBER 1957

"I can't cope with him anymore," said Aunt Rose, apparently close to tears yet again.

Albert listened to the conversation with less than half his attention. The Meyers' library held more interest for him than Rose's words – he hauled out a volume of their encyclopedia at random, and began skimming.

"He always seemed so good when Rebecca and Miles were alive, so quiet and clever. They loved him, adored him." She said this wonderingly, as if her memory might be deceiving her. "But ever since that scene at the wake …"

"Don't remind me," Barbara Meyer said. "Throwing a tantrum like that in front of everyone, disrupting the whole thing, and he's been a terror ever since –"

"The boy will hear you," her husband interrupted softly.

She retorted, "Don't try to tell me he doesn't know it, Elliott. Rose is right, he's smart. Smart enough to know better."

"And we can't make allowances for all he's been through?"

"That was five years ago, he probably doesn't even remember."

Rose's tears returned. "We found them, lying there on the floor, how can you say that …"

Elliott hushed her. Albert knew Elliott Meyer was a kind man, and also knew that Elliott never seemed to achieve anything, especially with Barb pitted against him. "The mind is wonderful," the man was saying, "it will block out terrible things like that, especially for a child. I hope he's forgotten."

"Don't count on it," Barbara said.

Of course Albert hadn't forgotten, though everyone avoided the topic in his company, and no one asked him for details despite the fact they'd like to. Even the police at the time had been reluctant to have him fully describe what he'd seen. If he closed his eyes now it all came back, the colors and smells, the contradictory image of this violence within the safety of his home. Rebecca and Miles, such gentle people, left discarded like unwanted toys, tossed into twisted unnatural poses.

"And he's too much for you, Rose," Elliott was saying.

"I don't know, it breaks my heart. It's not his fault, really."

Barbara snorted in disbelief.

"No one's good enough for him since his parents died, you can't blame him for that. And he's such a well-behaved child mostly, he helps with the housework without even being asked, he takes care of himself, half the time I wouldn't even know he was there, except –"

"Except," Barbara interrupted, "he's trouble. He certainly manages to annoy me every time I see him."

Albert flipped through the encyclopedia, scanning for something interesting. There was a footstep, the shuffle of someone sliding along the far wall. Without turning, Albert said, "I thought they told you to go to your room, Howard."

"What are you doing?"

"Reading."

"You can't read that, you're not old enough."

"*The Attorney General Harlan Fiske Stone,*" Albert began quoting from the page in front of him, "*appointed the twenty-nine-year-old J. Edgar Hoover as Director of the Federal Bureau of Investigation in 1924. Hoover immediately began making major changes, starting with a reorganization of the Bureau at every level. The entry requirements and qualification levels for special agents were increased, and –*"

"You don't know what them words mean."

"*– all employees were retrained in a series of newly-devised specialist programs.*"

"He's scrupulously honest," Rose said, out there in the living room; "honest to a fault."

"That is his fault," Barb replied; "one of the many. He should learn a little tact."

Howard suddenly blurted out, "What's going on?" He sounded suspicious and frightened.

"Rose wants me to come and live here," Albert said coolly. "With you."

"No!"

"I'm more upset about it than you are."

"Dad!" Howard ran out, apparently forgetting that his parents had banished him from this particular discussion.

Albert continued, murmuring under his breath though he hadn't needed to read aloud for years. *"The Bureau's scientific laboratory was established in 1932 to undertake the examination of a wide variety of crime scene evidence from around the country. This has included bloodstains, bullet markings, clothes and footwear, explosives, fibers, glass particles, hairs, handwriting, paint flecks, and weapons."*

Now both Howard and Rose were crying out there. Elliott was apparently trying to comfort them, while occasionally protesting the things they said about Albert.

"The scientific laboratory has been useful in not only establishing guilt but – vitally for all concerned – innocence." Albert thought that last comment must be an understatement: it seemed so dry, just as Miles would have said it. *"The laboratory deals in cases of murder, safe–cracking, bank burglaries, kidnapping, hit–and–run vehicles, fraud, and bad checks."*

For a moment that scene of five years ago threatened to overwhelm him, despite the seeming inconsequence of bounced checks: Rebecca lay on the rug, her hair fanned out behind her, clutching the bloodstained scarf, even though he tried to tug it out of her cold hand. Her eyes were wide open, watching him. Aunt Rose came back from the phone and said, horrified, "Leave it alone, Albert! Leave her alone." Miles was curled up at Rebecca's feet, as if holding in something precious. The police arrived and swarmed all over the place, looking at and into everything, either ignoring or gawking at the bodies, while Rose and Albert sat at the kitchen table and Rose was questioned as if she were the murderer. Then Rebecca in that coffin, looking like she was made of marble, the make–up only adding to the weirdness. Had they used make–up on Miles as well? And what sort of examinations would the FBI laboratory have run on that scarf, if they'd had it? Whose hair did they examine, and why?

"Why can't the Bryants take him?" Barbara Meyer demanded in a loud voice.

"They said they never wanted to see him again, they had him for four months and said that was it, not even for Rebecca and Miles would they do this. The child has lived with three other families now, it's not right, but I can't keep him any longer."

"They kept themselves to themselves," Elliott said, "but Rebecca and Miles were good people, they helped Jennifer through college, remember? It's only fair, Barb, we have to take our turn. He'll be company for Howard, they're about the same age."

The boy started crying in earnest.

But Barbara muttered, "Oh, grow up, Howie," so Albert figured the worst had come to pass. He sighed, and returned to the bookshelves, pulled out the last volume of the encyclopedia.

"*Zoology (biology): pertaining to animal life. For detailed entries see: anatomy, ecology, ethology, genetics, morphology, physiology, and taxonomy.*"

"Money?" Elliott asked. "No, we have plenty, we don't need more."

"The Sternes had plenty, too," Barb said. "Thank you, Rose." And she muttered, "If we drew the short straw, and we're taking the brat on, we may as well not have to worry about the extra expense."

"There's enough to see him through, until he can work?"

Rose said quietly, "He'll be able to go to any college he wants, they always made sure of that. He could probably take a graduate degree, then take a year off to tour Europe as well."

"So they didn't give it all away," Barb whispered. "That was the rumor, that they were always sharing it with any bum on the street."

"And our niece Jennifer, and getting the mayor re–elected, and helping the charities, and feeding the poor. Don't gossip, Barbara."

"You were going out, weren't you, Elliott? Why don't you take Albert with you? Rose and I have things to discuss."

"*Time,*" Albert read. "*A notion attempting to explain how we experience events in an unfolding sequence; a practical idea relied upon by everyone every day; and yet the keenest minds in a range of related disciplines have remained unable to define or even really understand it.*"

Elliott was standing there behind him. "Come on, Albert, we've been told to make ourselves scarce."

Silence. "*We regard hours and days and years as, more or less, equivalent units of time; yet this is a matter of faith.*"

"I like to wander down to the synagogue in the early evening," Elliott was saying, "just to be alone, and to think, and to pray. Perhaps today you'll join me."

Albert said, "I don't believe in all that."

"Well, now," the man replied softly. "That's a pity." Silence again.

"Timmermans, Felix: Flemish writer and artist; 1886–1947. Well known in his time, but remembered now for his novel Palletier *(1916), a remarkable celebration of life."*

"Let's at least take a walk."

Reluctantly, Albert left the books behind, and followed Elliott down the hall and through the front door.

"Now, tell me what this is about. Didn't your parents bring you up in their faith?"

"No." *And it's none of your business.*

"They did so much good in this world, for so many people, but they failed in this?"

Albert glared at him. Rebecca and Miles never failed at anything. He said, "Just because you believe, doesn't mean I have to as well."

"But, you see, because I believe, I consider it a tragedy that you don't."

"I don't care," Albert said. He stuck his hands in his pockets and looked around him. He knew all these streets, had been here with Rebecca and Miles so many times for so many reasons. This would just have to do for another year or so, until he decided which school to board at, and was accepted. Surely Rose and Elliott and Barbara would be happy to let him go by then.

The man beside him was quiet, withdrawn. And he could stay that way, as far as Albert was concerned; if only he would stay that way.

As usual Albert's report cards were mixed, full of inconsistencies. He always scored perfectly, or nearly so, for 'achievement' in all his subjects. Science in particular was his forte, though he took classes intended for twelve–year–olds because the topic wasn't normally available at his age. But in 'effort' his marks varied wildly. The more honest and objective teachers would rate him highly because he did indeed put more time and thought and energy into his school work than any three of the other children put together. The teachers he'd insulted, however, or those who resented him, or those who had no idea what to make of him, would grudgingly give him a marginal pass. The written comments ranged from 'Albert has performed brilliantly this term, despite various and numerous difficulties', to 'Albert would do well if he was less disruptive and rude; though his project work was still the best in the class, he suffers from a lack of the social graces', to a flat 'He would do better if he acknowledged that I do have something to teach him'.

This was virtually the opposite of Howard's report cards, which invariably commended him on 'effort', but were ambivalent on 'achievement'. Elliott would take Howard on his knee and say, "As long as you try your best, son, that's what we want, that's all we expect, and we'll love you whatever happens." But the boy would still be envious of Albert, on top of his fear and hate.

Albert didn't care. At the moment he was pointedly working his way through *The Brothers Karamazov*, and though he suspected there was far more to it than he could understand now, he thought it a fine book, worthy of Miles' recommendation. And he would finish it almost eighteen months before the deadline he had set himself.

"Bet you don't really know all those words," Howard kept saying. At least his grammar was improving.

"I know ten times more words than you do. By the time I'm fifteen, I'll know a hundred times more."

"You're just pretending."

"And you can't understand anything over three syllables long." Albert smiled coldly. "I bet you don't even know what *syllable* means."

Howie's lower lip trembled. "My mom says you're wicked and Godless."

"Do you know what that means? Lucky she uses small words."

"She said you'll be sorry when you grow up."

"She's wrong, I'll never be sorry." Albert put the book down for a moment, looked at the boy. "You really believe in God?" he asked.

"Yes."

"That's strange, because I bet God has a hard time believing in you."

Howard stared at him, perhaps trying to figure out the full implications of this alarming idea. Then, "Dad!" he cried, and ran off.

Barbara was furious. "What gives you the right, young man, to frighten my child? Or to question his faith?"

Albert's usual policy was unrelenting silence but, by the time of this confrontation, he had months' worth of anger smoldering inside him. The sooner he was old enough to go to a high school that took boarders and specialized in science, the better. Perhaps he would choose a Catholic school, just to annoy Barbara. But, no; he had to make a better decision than that, prove to these motley relatives that he was capable of taking care of himself, that he didn't need them.

He said now to Barb, "Why are you always bugging me about religion? Elliott's the one who really believes in all that bunk. For you, it's just duty."

She was furious, but she had always tried to give Albert good and honest answers, even when it was some truth that other people thought would hurt him. She was the only one since his parents who respected the fact he was intelligent, though it obviously didn't lessen her dislike of him. "There are reasons for duty, for a society based on cooperation and restraint, for rules to bind and guide people's actions. Good reasons."

"If the reasons are good," he replied, consciously thinking this through for the first time, "then I'll figure them out myself, won't I?"

"Will you, Albert?" she asked.

"And then I can figure out the rules, too."

She sighed, weary. "I wouldn't put it past you. But be careful, young man: pride can lead you far astray."

Elliott had appeared by then, a wet–faced Howie hovering behind him. "And then you're going to judge God by your own rules, are you?"

Albert had no answer, or nothing he could put into words. Yet.

"You poor boy," said Elliott. And he looked at his wife with the same sorrow, before turning away. He said distantly, "I think I'll take Howie for a walk."

CHAPTER ELEVEN
OREGON
SEPTEMBER 1984

Only seven days to go, and John Garrett was running high on anticipation. Two years since the last deaths, two years of exhilaration sliding to patience descending to terrible frustration. But he never questioned the few rules he'd imposed on himself and one of those was that he had to wait, he had to space the beats of his heart.

This coming Saturday, the game between the Seahawks and the Denver Broncos was being broadcast and Garrett couldn't decide who to invite over to watch it. There was Tony, one of the construction workers, who had a strong tanned body and long dark hair that fell over his face if he didn't wear it in a ponytail. Garrett suspected he had more than a drop of native blood pumping through his heart. He'd caught Garrett watching him months ago, as he worked in frayed jeans and leather boots and little else. At first, Tony had been annoyed but now he thought it was funny and he treated Garrett as slightly ridiculous, harmless, even someone he could be fond of.

The alternative to Tony was a hooker Garrett had had sex with a fortnight before. A latecomer to the streets, the young man hadn't had the spunk kicked out of him yet – but if Garrett left him for next time, over a month away, it might be too late, the boy might have already lost his attractions. A tough decision.

If he were honest with himself, what Garrett really wanted to do was take Tony but that brought risks as well as joy. There was the link of employment between them, and the chance that the young man had joked with someone about the queer at work who couldn't keep his eyes off him.

All these temptations every day. It wasn't so long ago that Garrett had to drive halfway round the state to find someone suitable. The miles he'd covered in Colorado, for instance, had been incredible. This place was too convenient. It almost seemed a pity to move on.

But, no, that was another rule he wouldn't break – create a plausible if vague reason to move to another state once the two years were done, and mislead anyone who asked where he was heading. It was by far the smartest thing to do. As for his reason this time, the glass facade was going up on the beautiful monstrosity he was building, he was about to hand the interior over to the decorators, his job would soon be finished, and of course he would be off looking for other work, despite a few offers to manage other construction projects in Portland.

There was a knock at the door, and Garrett frowned. He wasn't expecting anyone and the football was about to start. Beer in hand, he walked through to the hall, opened the door.

"Hello, Mr. Garrett," said the young guy standing on the step.

He had to think for a moment but once he'd mentally added overalls, grease in the light brown hair and an engaging grin, the guy fell into context. "Sam. What are you doing here?"

"You said – don't you remember? Last time you filled the car up, you said I should come watch the game with you."

"So I did." What had he been thinking of, for God's sake? Garrett hesitated, wondering whether this was really as bad an idea as he suspected it was. But then the guy smiled, and Garrett immediately itched to wipe the expression off the impertinent face. "Come on in," he invited, stepping back to allow Sam through. "You've missed the first few minutes."

"Sorry. Mom *still* won't let me out of the house until I tell her where I'll be. Ridiculous. Think I'll have to move out. Big argument like you wouldn't believe."

"Yes, I would believe." Garrett paused. "And you told her?"

Sam turned back to face him, shrugged. "I lied to her."

"Good. Mothers are suspicious creatures. And you're a man now."

"Hey, tell me something I don't know."

They shared a laugh as Garrett locked the door. He ushered Sam through to the living room where the television cast its flickering light into the darkness. "Do you want a beer?" Garrett asked.

This was what he should have been doing years ago, Garrett figured, back when he was a teenager: necking on the sofa with some guy as eager as he was, the football mostly forgotten, a few beers warming him. Maybe his whole life would have been different, maybe he could have found someone who'd treat him better than his parents had, maybe he could have done the normal thing and gone to college, maybe there wouldn't be this terrible resentment burning within him –

Was this how it should have been? Crazy kissing until his lips were numb but still aching with hunger, hands blindly roving over every part of this body beneath his, Sam's arms around Garrett's back rarely venturing below his waist, sensation oddly unfocused and hazy, chasing something he didn't even know the shape of – that's what prompted Garrett to make believe they were both teenagers. It seemed this confused pleasure would just go on and on, with no thought of resolution, until Sam maybe decided he'd better go home to stop his mother worrying, and they drew reluctantly apart as if it weren't even possible to go to Garrett's bed or make each other come.

"Hey," Sam was murmuring, but Garrett kept kissing him because the easiest thing to do right now was feed this vague but insistent need, and he really didn't want the boy to go home yet. When Sam turned his head away, Garrett simply began mouthing his neck. It was nice, these dull sensations, in an innocent sort of way. "Hey!"

"What?" Garrett mumbled, not wanting to be bothered.

"You're squashing me."

He murmured an agreement, sought the boy's mouth.

Sam allowed the endless kiss to begin again but brought his hands to Garrett's shoulders, began pushing ineffectually. Eventually he turned his face away, whispered on a breath, "You're too big for me."

Garrett lifted his head, blearily looked down at the guy. The eyes were hooded, from embarrassment or need, and the lips were as swollen as Garrett's felt. He was panting.

"Sorry," Sam offered. "Too heavy. Can we move – ?"

They were both panting after breath. Garrett's heart flared, and he bent to meet the boy's open mouth, the dazed lust abruptly focusing into beauty. Within moments Sam was struggling, though he had no chance against Garrett's strong and generous frame. For a while, Garrett simply let the boy feel his weight, gently rocking so his penis pushed hard into the boy's softening genitals, sensation sharp even though they were both fully clothed. Kissing him as if Garrett would eat him alive, one hand holding the boy's head still, Sam breathing through his nose in panicked rushes, clearly not getting enough air.

The kid's hands beat at Garrett's back, then his head, grabbed at his hair, but Sam wasn't desperate enough, or thinking clearly enough, to really hurt Garrett. Or maybe he was incapable. Couldn't hurt a fly, couldn't even hurt his murderer.

God, so close to climax, and so easy, so childishly easy to take his pleasure this way. Garrett shuddered, moaned into the kid's mouth – and finally Sam was smart enough to go for Garrett's eyes. But even then it was simply a matter of gathering both the boy's hands in one of his, forcing them over the kid's head and painfully down against the wooden arm of the sofa. Garrett suddenly raised up, and the kid tried for a lungful of air, but Garrett's other hand was on his face, palm over his mouth, thumb and fingers pinching the nostrils closed. Sam's eyes widened in an essential terror, he tried to twist away his head or his body, but Garrett had him secure. Thrusting as the kid heaved uselessly, bearing down on him as he fought, coming as the darkness took the child away. It was so incredibly good.

Good, yes, but uncontrolled and very unwise. Garrett sat in the armchair, gazing at the body stretched along his sofa, the arms dangling back as if broken. He smoked, one cigarette after another, trying to find the reason why he hadn't been able to wait for another seven days. And this wasn't even how he'd planned it to happen this time around: this was greedy and meaningless and opportunistic, and Garrett knew better than that. Inviting the kid over in the first place had been unwise enough, let alone taking his life with no malice aforethought. And it had all been so … intimate, the sex and the dying so personal and simple, with no props and no planning. Sweet. Damned sweet, but that was no excuse for something so dangerously self–indulgent. What in hell was the matter with him?

He lit a fresh cigarette, and noticed his hands were shaking. Unbelievable. Well, he figured, he was in no fit state to deal with the disposal of a body right now. He couldn't afford to make this many mistakes as it was, let alone compounding the problem. Tomorrow, when he was thinking clearly, he'd decide on the safest thing to do. Tomorrow.

For now, he'd have to hide the body in the cellar, just in case. Yes, that was smart. Get it out of the way. You never knew what might happen, who might knock on the door.

Garrett stubbed out the last half of a cigarette, and stood to haul the body up over one shoulder. Walked unsteadily through to the kitchen, then bent to unlatch the half–sized door at the end of one of the benches. The damp musty smell hit him at once and he frowned.

Unable to deal with this in any sort of sensible way, Garrett hit the light switch then let the body tumble down the concrete stairs, watched it land in an ungainly sprawl.

He was going to shut the door and leave it all until the morning, but something made him decide to check the place. To get down there, it was easiest to sit on the top step, and start walking from where his legs reached, one hand on the ceiling to steady himself and avoid hitting his head.

The sight that greeted him as he stepped over the fresh body was old blood, dark dry stains everywhere. He looked around in disbelief: caught the dull glint of a knife abandoned in a corner, saw leather straps hooked on the shelving.

That was what prompted the memory. A fantasy, that's what he thought it'd been, to slash a cross into a boy's arm and wrist in the same way he'd misguidedly cut himself all those years ago, to watch what might have happened to him. A fantasy, surely. But it seemed he'd acted it out. Had it been that tramp with the apple pie freckles and the thick mop of hair? Garrett couldn't even remember the boy's name. This was crazy.

And what in God's name had he done with the body?

Garrett groaned a protest, let the groan become a sickened growl – the noise grew out of his chest, opened his throat in a yell of bewildered rage. What in hell was happening to him?

CHAPTER TWELVE
WASHINGTON DC | CONNECTICUT
SEPTEMBER 1984

"Albert. Let me in."

It was Fletcher David Ash on the doorstep of Albert's home, dark and rain–laden storm–clouds massing behind him, obliterating the stars. "Do you have any idea what time it is?" Albert snapped, having been woken from precious sleep.

"Late," Fletcher replied. "Let me in, Albert."

"I gave you the keys months ago, Ash, so I trust there's a good reason for you waking me up. Your few polite habits seem to be the most inconvenient." Despite having the keys to Albert's home, the man never would let himself in if Albert was there to answer the door. Such deference was usually acceptable, as Fletcher kept civilized hours, or at least more civilized hours than Albert did. Until tonight.

"We need to talk."

"What about?"

"Something urgent."

"The case?"

"Something urgent," Fletcher repeated. "And personal."

"At this time of the morning? Can't you have your crises over dinner like other people?"

"I drove right here from Scranton to see you," Ash said. He'd remained focused on Albert throughout this ridiculous conversation, frowning in concentration, but now he seemed to take in something of the situation. "We need to talk, Albert. Trust me, you don't want to do that on your front step."

Then the wry awareness was gone and Fletcher was staring at him again, all of him honing in on Albert as if trying to influence him through sheer willpower. But there was something forced about the intensity, there was a false note to it. Albert could guess at the cause of this display. It had been exactly two years since three young men and one young woman had died in Georgia; four years since the deaths in Colorado. He'd anticipated Fletcher finding this a difficult time to live through, but there was an unexpected factor in Ash's approach. Something didn't ring as true as Ash's tantrums when those bodies were found in Georgia, or as true as his sadness and dejection and sense of failure. The histrionics and the increased consumption of alcohol had been annoying, but they had at least been direct and honest reactions.

"I wound up the Scranton case earlier than I thought," Fletcher was saying into the silence, deliberate. "I drove right here to talk to you."

"You're presuming a lot, Ash. I have to work tomorrow, and I don't have the time or the inclination to talk. If it can't wait until tomorrow – this evening," Albert amended, glancing back at the clock in the hall, "then I can't help you."

"Let me in, Albert."

Now it was a demand, not a request. Albert's hackles rose and he briefly contemplated the satisfaction of shutting the door in Fletcher's face. But Ash seemed in no mood to leave, despite the discouragement Albert had already thrown his way. It might result in less aggravation if he humored the man. Every now and then, Albert would ungraciously allow Ash to be more stubborn than himself.

After a pause amply illustrating his reluctance, Albert stood aside, then locked the door once Ash was through, and followed the man to the kitchen. Ash had seated himself at the table. "You want coffee, I suppose," Albert said, already filling the jug with filtered water.

"Yes. Thank you."

Silence as the coffee brewed and Albert communicated his impatience of this ill–timed melodrama. Communicated it for anyone to see, if they'd bother showing any interest. Fletcher was turned away, apparently gazing at the floor, and only straightened to face Albert once he'd placed a mug of coffee on the table. Albert prompted, in cool tones, "Talk, then, if that's what you're here for."

And Fletcher looked across at him, the wildness in his eyes betraying the taut calm of his expression.

Letting out a breath, Albert glanced away. He should have expected Ash to come undone at some stage. That was, in itself, a pity. But why did it have to be at moments like this – when the younger man was troubled, even slightly crazed – why did his normally ignorable features then intensify into such dangerous beauty? Did it require a focus for his energy for him to look this way? Was it a matter of concentrating some essential core of him? And, Albert unwillingly extrapolated, did sex provide that focus in the same way that this obsession with the serial killer did?

"Yes," Fletcher said.

For a terrible moment Albert feared Ash was answering his mental speculations rather than his verbal prompt. Wanting only to end this situation as soon as possible, Albert sat at the table across from Ash. "This has to do with the serial killer, I assume. It is now fall, two years since the last deaths."

Ash lifted his eyebrows in a show of surprise. "If you realize that, then I'm right to come to you."

"That remains to be seen."

The briefest grimace, as if attempting to offer a smile. Fletcher often seemed to treat Albert's remarks as if they were intended to be humorous; a strange quirk in the young man's perceptions. "I've lost my balance, Albert."

"That much is obvious."

"I understand what this man does when he tortures and kills these boys."

"We've been through all that," Albert told him. "Cut to the chase, Ash."

"You're hardly the easiest confidant."

"But you're going to tell me anyway," Albert said.

"There's no one else I can ask for help."

Silence again for a long moment, which Albert at last broke in exasperation. "You're the one who chose to come here, if you recall. Just get this over with, Ash, so I can get back to sleep."

"I understand this man; I understand the thrill it gives him," Ash finally said in a low voice. "I feel the thrill and the need, the insatiable need for more, the power of it all." He met Albert's gaze. "And I hate that I understand this."

"Then you hate yourself," Albert observed.

Ash nodded in agreement. "I'm walking a tightrope, madly juggling all these parts of me, and one of them is darkness. It's the heaviest. When that falls into my hand, I falter, I might fall. There's no safety net down there. Or I might turn away and walk on air, holding only the darkness –" Fletcher lifted his right hand, palm up, cradling this part of him – "letting it give me strength, leaving the rest of me to fall where it may. I could let the darkness become the whole of me."

"I see." Albert couldn't help but sound slightly disapproving of this overblown metaphor, though it did not bode well that Fletcher had taken his familiar tightrope image and developed it far further than ever before.

"Do you?"

"Yes."

"You're right. It's been two years since the murders in Georgia. He's out there now, maybe tonight, torturing some poor young man. And, in my imagination, in my nightmares, it's like I'm there, looking over his shoulder. Or worse, sometimes – I'm him."

"I see," Albert said again.

Fletcher leaned forward, intense. "And do you see what I need? Something to counter–balance the darkness, Albert, something to think of that has nothing of this terror." He lifted his left hand, bounced it as if to compare the weights of what he held. Still contemplating his upturned hands, he continued, "This man brutalizes boys, rapes and destroys and discards them. I need to love a man, make love with him, grow with him. Something creative to counteract the destructive." He looked up. "I need your help, Albert."

"Yes? What for?" His face was the one he turned to the rest of the world – stony, uncommunicative, bitter, offended. He was aware that this mask hadn't been directed at Fletcher for months, years now, but he was powerless without the defense it gave him.

"I'm asking for your indulgence, Albert. A little of your loving."

No point in pretending to misunderstand the proposition, no matter how unexpected. "Surely there are many more suitable candidates."

"None. Your friendship – I trust you. I need something special, something worthwhile. And I've never – I've only loved women before." Fletcher directed a wry but happy smile at him. "Who else but you?"

"Maybe I can recommend someone," Albert offered, urbane, refusing to be touched by the unexpected happiness. "A young man I met once in New Orleans springs to mind."

Ash was not to be distracted. "I assure you there's no other option."

"You're assuming I'll agree."

"I'm hoping you won't ignore a plea for help." He took a moment to sip at the coffee, thoughtful. "You've never let me down before. Not when it really mattered."

So Fletcher knew, had probably known all along. And was not above manipulation in this as in all else.

The storm broke at last, rain a percussion sweeping across the roof. Albert was released from his cool politeness. He stood, pushing his chair back, asking angrily, "How dare you expect me to do this for you? What do you think I am? More to the point, who do you think you are?"

"Someone who needs you," Ash said quietly.

"And you presume I'll fill that need, whatever it happens to be?"

"I didn't think you'd find the idea abhorrent."

"You know I don't, damn you – and it's only now that it suits you to acknowledge the fact. I thought I was beyond being surprised by the depths to which humanity will descend, but your effrontery amazes me."

"I'm proposing to use your love, I know, and that's unfair of me. But I wouldn't have come here if I wasn't clutching at straws."

"Unfair is the least of it, and there's no need to remind me that I'm your last choice."

"You're my first choice," Fletcher protested, managing to look both angry and chagrined. "I meant that I'm in a desperate situation."

But Albert continued his tirade. "You're not the only one who has to cope with fears and nightmares. What a pity you have no internal resources to fall back on."

"You have bad dreams, too, Albert?" Ash asked quietly. "Maybe we can help each other."

Albert glared at his companion, lately considered a friend. "The trouble with you, Ash, is that you're an intelligent man too often driven by your hormones."

"They drove me to think of you," Fletcher offered. "All I could think of was you – not just because I thought you'd be amenable, but because of who you are and what you mean to me. You're my first choice," he repeated. "My only choice, Albert, because I love you, too."

"Not in the way I want you to," Albert said sourly. But that would be a ridiculous situation if ever there was one. He'd long since concluded he wasn't capable anymore of responding to that sort of love even if it was offered. Maybe he never had been capable. Perhaps he should simply take the little that was available.

Silence, until Ash pushed his chair back, stood, and turned away. "I'm sorry. For all of it."

"Where do you think you're going?"

"I'll leave you be. I hope you get some sleep. Call me sometime, Albert?"

"Don't you dare walk out on me," Albert said furiously. "We'll do this, but we'll do it on *my* terms." Ash was staring at him with those hot blue eyes, confused perhaps, but so full of trust and need. It was enough. "Come here," Albert ordered.

The man walked nearer, doubts now visibly warring with the deliberate return of that intense focus. It could have been frightening, having all five of Ash's senses locked in on him, but Albert was well practiced in mastering difficult situations. And Ash made it so easy for him: the younger man stood close now, close enough to kiss, and whispered, "It's really going to happen, isn't it?" Wondering, and scared, and in awe. "I've wanted this so bad. You pushed my curiosity up to overdrive."

"Don't give me dialogue from your soft porn romance novels," Albert said. But he lifted a hand, snaked his fingers through the dark tangle of Fletcher's rebellious hair, and drew the man near so that their mouths met and meshed.

Ash seemed to enjoy that. When he lifted his head, he was smiling broadly, his eyes afire. Then, without drawing away, he whispered, "I'm safe."

Albert perhaps betrayed surprise, and perhaps suppressed the distaste at this inelegant but necessary topic of conversation.

"I mean, I'm safe from AIDS," Fletcher was continuing as if Albert might not have understood. "I've used a condom every time, even before AIDS became an issue. I figured I was the sort who'd have to do the right thing and marry the girl if I –"

"Spare me the sordid explanations," Albert interrupted dryly.

The smile grew wry again, and Ash insisted on continuing, "Which would be a disaster, because you know how impossible all my women are. And I had the test done, too, about six months ago, just in case. It was negative." A delicate pause. "What about you?"

Albert grimaced. He was not about to tell this man that he hadn't had sex since 1973. Fletcher, who judging by his behavior did not consider chastity a viable option, would think Albert was asking for pity. "There hasn't been an opportunity for me to catch AIDS," Albert said instead, hoping that would suffice.

"All right, I trust you," Fletcher said. "You don't have to explain, either."

That was an attitude that Albert would consider sentimental and dangerous, except that Albert did not intend to do anything that would be classified as unsafe, anyway. He dismissed the topic by kissing the man again, and once Fletcher was suitably eager, which really didn't require much effort or skill, Albert led him down to the main bedroom.

He found he could play Fletcher Ash like he imagined a musician played an instrument – every touch, just so, precise and controlled, creating the most beautiful music Albert had ever heard. Fletcher sighed and groaned and cried out, sometimes inarticulate, sometimes voicing words both sacred and profane. He had climaxed twice under Albert's expert guidance.

"Must be your turn, Albert," Ash panted at last, sprawled back in beautiful abandonment, overly pale on the peach–colored sheets. "When I've regained a little energy," he qualified, "and equilibrium … then let me at you!"

Albert was sitting cross–legged on the bed. While he wasn't touching this unexpected partner lying beside him, his gaze ate Ash alive. Even so, he snorted disparagingly at the younger man's enthusiastic words and everything that belied them. "I would have thought you had more stamina," he commented. When Ash opened his eyes, Albert's impassive mask was in place. The younger man didn't seem to expect anything else; he smiled fondly.

"You're obviously not taking enough credit for this current state of affairs," Ash said lazily, expression as content and honest as Albert's was not. "*Quantity* of orgasms isn't the issue here; we're talking *quality*."

"That sounds suspiciously like flattery."

"Truth. In fact, truth and beauty – this has been amazing. And it only gets better from here on in."

"And that sounds like misguided and romantic optimism."

A hand reached to shape itself around Albert's knee, then to slowly progress up his inner thigh as if intent on learning him by touch. "Let me at you, Albert," Ash asked again.

"I told you, we do this on my terms."

"And that precludes me making love to you?"

"It's not making love," Albert snapped. He covered Ash's exploring hand with his own, halting it mere inches away from his genitals. "I can do without the verbal embellishments."

"Come on," Fletcher murmured, "it's obvious you're interested. There's some weighty evidence here to prove it."

"Don't. Just stop it right now."

The cold words finally broke through Ash's preoccupation. He took his hand away from Albert's thigh, though the gesture lacked the umbrage and embarrassment that Albert would have anticipated from anyone else. "Then tell me your terms," Fletcher said softly, "because I'll meet them, whatever they are." And, at last, there was the faintest hint of rebuke: "You should know that."

Albert stared at the younger man, totally disarmed all over again and wholly unwilling to show it. "Is everyone in Idaho as contrary as you?"

"No one. Not even close."

After a moment, he realized Ash was obediently waiting, though patently hungry for more, so Albert leaned over him to work on playing a new symphony on this most perfect of instruments.

It was only when Albert kissed the sensitive and willing mouth that he remembered exactly how many months it had been since he'd last had an orgasm. The eleven years since he'd had sex abruptly added an urgent impulse to that knowledge. The need and the music combined to inundate him, to sweep through him and the man he was touching. *Tsunami*. The power of it overwhelmed all thought, all responsibility, so that when his body urged possession the only voice Albert listened to was Fletcher's: "Do it, Albert. You said you were safe. Just do it, damn you!"

Even the clumsy hectic painful confusion of two novices didn't cause Albert doubt. The confusion resolved to a hard hot haven – and Fletcher's moans somehow conveying both his own difficulty in accepting Albert as well as his insistence that Albert continue – and Albert's own sense of victorious joy in having this beautiful man.

The tumultuous wave reached its apex, there was a taut still moment, then it came crashing down upon him, dragging Albert below to pressured completion, buffeted by the darkest of blues.

Eventually he surfaced, groggy and terribly unsure. The din of the storm had settled to a monotonous, insistent drumming. Their joining had become an uncomfortable tangle of heavy limbs. "Fletcher?" Albert asked, afraid to move or to look at the man.

"Oh damn," Fletcher murmured, dazed but heartfelt.

Albert grimaced. He'd rarely known this man to swear before today. "Are you all right?"

There was a sound somewhere between laughter and a groan, which coalesced into a chuckle. "I hate it when people ask things like that." And he quoted in a mock passionate tone, "Was it good for you, too, darling?" Fletcher laughed again. "Well, you were there – if you were paying any kind of attention, you should know!"

"I'm sorry."

"Don't worry. I'm a little too overwhelmed right now to make any kind of sense. Let alone be polite."

Albert considered this for a moment, then at last opened his eyes and turned to his companion. For some reason, Fletcher seemed happy. His smile, while shaky, was genuine. "I meant," Albert clarified, "I'm sorry for …" How embarrassing, to find your vocabulary so limited, in such a ghastly situation – all the words that sprang to mind were too clinical or too cruel. He couldn't quite say the word *rape*, though it was true. And he wouldn't resort to –

"… fucking me?" Fletcher supplied.

"If you must. Yes."

"Don't be. Sorry, that is."

Albert frowned. "It wasn't my intention to do that. I lost control. It was wrong."

"Are you serious?" Fletcher's expression became overcast when he ascertained that was indeed the case. He continued, "It would not qualify as a felony and you should damned well know that. I wanted it, too, Albert. You were there, you heard me, you felt me. Was I struggling? Did I once tell you no?"

Shrugging, Albert tried to turn away from the bright gaze, but Fletcher grabbed him, forced him to face the issue.

"If I had, you would have found another way."

"Would I?" Albert asked bleakly.

"Yes. I have complete faith in you. And it is not unfounded nor is it misplaced." Ash let him go, but settled them both into what was presumably supposed to be a comfortable embrace. "You want proof I enjoyed that?" Ash murmured after a while. "Proof that is refusing to go away?"

Albert remained silent, but Fletcher took one hand in his, and guided it to Fletcher's engorged genitals. The poignant regret of it all was close to bringing Albert to tears, but he had cried himself out for good or ill when he was five. For a while, he simply let himself caress the younger man.

"Gently, this time, Albert." Fletcher chuckled again, breathless. "You are so damned good at this."

"I have to know something first." Albert leaned up on an elbow.

"What, love?"

He flinched at the endearment, but continued, "You wanted me to provide you with a counter–balance to the darkness. And I do that to you."

"It's all right," Ash said in a whisper.

"But I ..." There was no way to say it without descending into Fletcher's melodrama. Anger roiled through him again. Damn this man and what he brought Albert to. "I rejoiced in possessing you!"

"How terrible," Fletcher agreed, but ironically. "No, Albert, it's fine. I was rejoicing in being possessed. If only you'd paid as much attention – " Fletcher ran a hand down Albert's arm. "I didn't think you were listening to all my nonsense about juggling the darkness." Before Albert could reply, he added, "Come on. I think you should rectify this rather more immediate problem you've left me with."

No one else had ever known quite how to disarm him. For that matter, there had never been anyone else Albert would suffer to try. Reflecting on this alarming thought, Albert leaned in to kiss the man and deftly brought him to a bright, soaring orgasm.

"This is the truth!" Fletcher Ash said. Then he called it out loud: "The truth!"

Albert had never been so frightened by the truth before. He said, "Go to sleep now. I have to work tomorrow."

"Sweet dreams, love," was the happy murmur.

"That would be a first." But he settled in beside Fletcher, and to his later surprise promptly fell deeply asleep.

Albert sat in the passenger seat of the Saab, waiting for Fletcher to turn the ignition, to drive them back to civilization. They were in their FBI suits again, after four days of casual clothes – which for Ash meant torn jeans and tatty cotton sweaters, and for Albert meant shirts and knitted woolen sweaters and slacks. Ash had taken extra leave to coincide with the weekend and Albert's rostered time off – though, as Albert usually chose to work through the majority of these imposed breaks, the younger man had to insist on them spending the days together. "You're prepared to take a day off to look after the garden – do the same, but look after me instead."

Reluctantly acceding to Ash's wishes, Albert had followed him on a whirlwind sightseeing spree through New England, providing a sardonic counterpoint to Fletcher's enthusiasm and admiration for all things natural. They had returned to a hotel room at intervals, in a different town each day, where Albert further indulged them both. It had been, he admitted to himself, a richly pleasurable experience – but also a comparatively insignificant one. There were other things in life. It would have been wiser to keep working, and spend their free nights together at his house.

Ash had been staring blindly through the windshield for a while now, apparently lost in some internal dialogue. Suspecting that Fletcher might be entertaining similarly regretful thoughts, Albert didn't break the silence. But eventually Ash turned to him and said in his blunt and honest way, "I don't love you the way you deserve to be loved, Albert. The way you want me to."

Albert scowled, and snapped, "I don't want you to."

"If you give me a little time, if we're together, surely …" But the younger man wasn't comfortable holding out hope that he couldn't guarantee. It was a measure of how much he cared for Albert that he'd even consider a promise of possible future love, let alone voice it.

"I don't want to be another of your romance novel adventures, Ash."

Focusing now on his companion's annoyed denials, Fletcher's expression was at first disappointed, then patient. "You told me you did want me to love you that way," he said in quiet but firm reminder, "nine days ago, the first night we spent together. Don't start lying to me, Albert. That would be the cruelest part of this."

"I'm not lying," Albert retorted impatiently. "I said that, yes, without fully considering the implications. But it would never work, so I don't want it."

Ash frowned at him. After several beats, he asked, "So, what do you want that I can give? Would you like to have sex with me sometimes? Do you want to be friends?" And again he offered, "Just tell me your terms."

"All of that," Albert said, ungracious at this understanding and generosity. "While you're willing. If you're prepared to take second priority."

"I was prepared for fourth or fifth." Ash chuckled for a moment. Then the seriousness returned, and he murmured, "You dislike yourself about as much as I hate myself, don't you, Albert?" But the silence stretched easily enough between them now. Ash smiled sadly, reached a hand to hold fast to Albert's, even lifted it to his lips for a moment.

And then Ash drove them back to Washington.

CHAPTER THIRTEEN
WASHINGTON DC
OCTOBER 1984

The phone rang and Albert sighed before answering. "Sterne."

"You can drop the formal tone – it's me."

"Ash," he acknowledged, having guessed as much. The only other calls he received at home were from headquarters – although there had been three from Peter Ash over the last eighteen months, as he rang around the country trying to find his son for their Sunday conversations. Albert added dryly, "What a surprise."

"I don't know how I'm supposed to take you seriously when you drip that much sarcasm." Then, with no pause, "What are you doing?"

Albert had suffered this interrogation most evenings over the past seven weeks. "Eating dinner, reading an article, listening to Mozart." Anticipating the next question, Albert continued, "Dinner is a vegetable roulade, made from corn, leeks and ricotta cheese."

Fletcher groaned. "That's so unfair. I just fried up some eggs and toast. The former was tough and the latter was burnt."

"Even you should be able to learn how to cook properly. Eggs and toast is hardly a nutritious meal."

"But how can I ever aspire to the standards you and Harley set?"

"I should apologize for being a good example?"

"And what's the article?" Fletcher asked. He rarely seemed to have qualms about diverting the course of a conversation, or ignoring Albert's barbs.

"Some student's suggestion that hypostasis can be used to give an accurate time of death, a theory that no one has taken seriously for decades. There are too many variables, though someone with a great deal of experience can draw a fairly accurate conclusion if the surrounding temperature is known, and the corpse's –"

"You're not kidding, are you?" Fletcher interrupted. "How can you read that stuff over dinner? I'm in danger of losing my appetite just thinking about it."

"Perhaps I should discuss the Mozart instead," Albert said, laying the urbanity on thickly. "*Serenade for Winds*, K 361. A beautiful piece."

"Yes, I can hear it. Sort of slow, isn't it?"

"It is exquisite and you are a philistine."

"Why, thank you. Remember that vegetable gumbo you made me? Next time we eat Creole, we're going to listen to something more appropriate. I just bought an album of zydeco music."

"I'm sure it would be safer for all concerned if you left it in Colorado."

"You don't scare me."

"What a pity."

A full-bodied pause, then the younger man said, "I miss your ... cooking."

"I'm sure you can survive on eggs and toast," Albert replied, annoyed at both the innuendo and his body's warm reaction to it. "If you're visiting on the weekend, I'll make a roulade for you then."

"Great – and what else is on the menu?"

How best to quash this conversation without overtly acknowledging what Fletcher was implying? "Don't you have better things to do than badger me?" Albert eventually asked. "I have a report to write. I told Jefferson it would be ready first thing in the morning."

"Since when did you care about Jefferson?" But, even as he protested, Fletcher had caught on. "You're still paranoid about our phones being tapped, aren't you? Why would they do that?"

"Because they can."

"That sort of thing went out with Hoover."

"I think not."

"You're implying our conversations are open to misinterpretation."

Albert took a moment to swallow his anger at this man, even though Fletcher was more or less playing along with the word game. "Don't push it, Ash," Albert advised in what he hoped was a reasonable tone of voice. "You know they will hear exactly what they want to hear."

"Maybe they're not imaginative enough to make the assumption."

"It's so unlikely an assumption to make, is it?" Albert bitterly retorted. But, yes, who could possibly leap to the conclusion that anyone loved Albert Sterne? That anyone would be prepared to have sex with him, without generous recompense? Fletcher Ash was, for example, using him as a distraction, a way of keeping his sanity from unraveling. Albert had resigned from hope years ago – he was surprised to find that these disappointments still rankled.

"Yeah," Fletcher was saying. "No one with an ounce of intelligence or common sense puts up with me for any length of time, just look at the trail of failed relationships I leave behind me. Yet we've been friends for years. Whatever else they think of you, no one denies you're smart. The question therefore becomes: what do you see in me?"

Silence. Then, "I have to write that report," Albert said. "I assume you haven't any news about your pet serial killer."

"No, nothing happening today, as far as I know. But it's only a matter of time."

"Call me when you hear something." And Albert hung up the phone, alarmed to find his hands shaking, annoyed that thoughts of Fletcher refused to beat a dignified retreat. Albert should have known better than to surrender himself to this curious, demanding, ebullient man. The costs of transitory sexual satisfaction were high; Albert trusted that Fletcher's interest in him would prove just as transitory.

The previous weekend amply demonstrated some of those costs. Despite Albert having made it perfectly clear in the early years of their friendship that he was the last person to acknowledge his own or anyone else's birthday, and despite the fact Fletcher had until now tactfully pretended ignorance of the date, Ash apparently felt that a sexual partner was expected to help celebrate such mundane occasions, even though a friend wasn't.

To make it all worse, Albert could hardly complain about the gift he was presented with on the Saturday morning after his birthday: a Blaupunkt CD player for the car. In reply to Fletcher's inquiries, Albert had expressed something about it being quite satisfactory, and then he'd spent ninety minutes installing the machine in the Saab. He'd taken Ash for a drive through the neighboring countryside, an indulgence with no purpose other than to listen to Mozart's *Mass in C Minor* and *Requiem* – or, as Ash insisted, Mozart's *Great Mass* and *Terrific Requiem*. Although Albert didn't expect Fletcher to appreciate the somber music, the younger man had slowly begun to enjoy himself. They had eaten a late lunch together at an adequate restaurant, over which they'd conducted a moderately intelligent conversation. In all, a pleasant if frivolous day.

Though nothing could compensate for Fletcher asking, "Who's Elliott Meyer?"

The words, innocent enough on Fletcher's part, were cold numbing fear to Albert. Fletcher had loitered over coffee on the Friday evening, apparently minding his own business – but of course he was observant enough to notice the unusual occurrence of Albert receiving a personal letter, of Albert skimming through six pages of close handwriting. Forever irrepressibly curious, Fletcher had picked up the envelope in order to read the return address, and asked the inevitable.

It was a pity that some of the qualities Albert most admired in the man – those very qualities that made Fletcher a useful special agent – could be the most inconvenient.

Somehow, though Albert couldn't now remember the words he'd used, he'd indicated that Fletcher's interest was not welcome, that the whole topic was off limits. But even though Ash had let the matter go, his curiosity was aroused, and Albert knew exactly how persistent that curiosity could be. Added to which, it was hardly a difficult conclusion for Fletcher to reach, that Elliott was family, indeed the only family member with whom Albert had any contact anymore. And Albert knew very well, without Fletcher saying much, that the younger man would be fascinated to learn more of Albert's background.

Elliott's annual letter contained family news and gossip, in which Albert had no interest. As usual, however, Elliott recounted a few stories and images of his long–dead cousin, Albert's father Miles, and of his mother Rebecca, some of his own and some from other people. Albert knew Elliott only did this to ensure Albert would read the letters; nevertheless, he couldn't find it in him to resist the man's manipulation.

Under Fletcher's gaze, which was watchful though the man pretended nonchalance, Albert committed to memory those few scraps of information about his parents, then returned the letter to its envelope, intending to throw the lot out. But then he was seized with fear that Fletcher would go so far as retrieving it from the trash and reading it without permission. *Standard operating procedure under Hoover*, the man might say, providing a justification that was no justification at all.

Albert had taken the damned thing into his study and locked it away. Then, on the following Monday once Fletcher was safely gone, he'd finally been able to throw the letter away.

Damn Fletcher Ash. And damn Elliott Meyer! Albert had insisted on going his own way when he was accepted at college just before his sixteenth birthday. Elliott, who'd been his guardian for five years, had only agreed on the condition that they exchange letters every October. Twenty–one letters later, and Elliott still hadn't given up. Why was Albert cursed with such persistent presences in his life?

He put the impossible, unpalatable question aside and, after reading another column of the puerile article on hypostasis, he managed to focus on work again rather than Fletcher Ash or his own dissatisfactions. The rest of his dinner, however, he wrapped securely and placed in the fridge for the next day.

The phone rang on cue the following evening and Albert briefly considered not answering it. That would, however, be an evasion and, as such, should be beneath him. He took a moment to reflect that Fletcher obviously wanted more from this relationship than Albert was in any position to give. Would he have been capable of meeting the man's expectations if he'd fallen for Ash ten years ago? Fifteen or twenty?

He took a breath and picked up the handset. "Sterne."

"It's me. I think I found one."

"Found one what?" Though Albert knew perfectly well, from Fletcher's urgency if nothing else. He picked up the pen by the phone, ready to jot down any notes.

"A possible victim," Fletcher was explaining, exasperated. It seemed he was too focused to even notice this opportunity for the meaningless repartee and teasing that often passed for personal conversation between them. "In the latest bundle from Mac – you know he sends me newspaper clippings and police reports once a week. He received this one yesterday, sent it up with all the latest in the overnight bag. I only just had a chance to read it."

"Tell me." Sometimes, if in Mac's limited judgment a case was particularly significant, the Irishman even braved the probability of cadavers and insults in the forensic labs to bring Albert a copy as well. For whatever reason, that hadn't happened this time.

"Young unidentified teenage male, found buried face–down in the forests outside Portland, Oregon, died maybe six weeks ago. They're not quite sure on the cause of death – it's definitely asphyxia, though the injuries aren't related, so it doesn't look like manual strangulation."

"Ligature strangulation," Albert suggested, "with something soft, a scarf for instance, or with padding, so it wouldn't leave external marks. Or suffocation with a pillow. There are other options, but if this is the man you're after, those seem most likely."

"That's good," Fletcher said, distractedly. He was apparently writing this down.

For the sake of his professionalism, Albert had to add, "Maybe I should remind you I'm simply suggesting what you might look for that's consistent with your pet murderer. It doesn't seem likely, for instance, that he would suffocate the boy by confining him in an airless compartment, such as a cupboard."

"Couldn't rape the boy as he died if he did that, could he?"

"Exactly."

"Speaking of which, it appears there was penetrative sexual activity, and there's a lot of severe bruising, though the injuries aren't as comprehensive as the victims in Georgia."

"But in Georgia, the offender intended that the boys die as a direct result of their injuries. The Colorado victims, and this one if it's his, he tortured and raped first, before killing them."

"You think it's the same man?"

"I hardly have enough information to draw that conclusion yet. You certainly seem to believe so."

"It feels right, and it's the right timing. It's just over two years since Mitchell Brown, Philip Rohan and Stacey Dixon died in Georgia. This man has to have been killing again. I think the Oregon police are going to find another couple of bodies with similar MO."

"Given the timing, your expectations might be leading you astray. Your basic assumption is that he's been killing again, but anything could have happened in the intervening period."

"Like what?"

"He could be incarcerated for, or under suspicion of, another offence; he could have died by accident, murder, suicide or natural causes; he might be ill or incapacitated; he might have finished whatever it was he thought he was doing, or simply lost his taste for it. Ninety–nine percent of law enforcement officers would assume that one of those things had happened over that length of time, and close the case."

"I almost did, too, after the Colorado cases. But that's what makes our guy so damned clever."

"Wasn't there a serial killer about ten years ago who turned himself in because he felt it had become a waste of time?"

"You're thinking of the one who surrendered in 1973. He said his original purpose was gone once he'd worked around to killing his mother." Fletcher added more forcefully, "But this one won't ever lose the taste for it."

"Once again, you're projecting your warped intuition onto this man's behavior."

A pause before Fletcher continued, enthusiasm only slightly abated, "You're right, I have to be careful not to make assumptions. It just feels so right sometimes, it fits so well – but I must always trace that back to whether it's based in fact or feeling."

"Yes," Albert said. He'd forgotten how devastatingly honest Ash could be about himself. But that wasn't a reason, in itself, to believe everything the man said.

"This guy, with his handful of killings in each state every two years – he's not finished yet, he could keep doing this for a long time. He's still in control of it. We have to worry about when it escalates, gets beyond him. Once he breaks out of his pattern, anything goes."

"But surely he won't break out of the pattern very far. Which is why no one believes your theories, when something as central as the cause of death is different in each case."

"I know, I know." The younger man sighed. "Okay, I guess we have to treat Oregon as just another option for now."

They briefly ran through the other options, which were looking less and less likely. There had been a body found in Texas that broadly fitted the MO Fletcher was looking for, but the boy had been killed almost four months before the two years was up, with no other bodies found since then. Another one had been found in Georgia. Fletcher wouldn't rule it out, on the grounds that the man was more than capable of that sort of double–think, but again there were no related cases during that time. There had also been a possibility in Arizona but an arrest had been made within the last few days. Ash was apparently sickened that the alleged offender had been the victim's best friend.

"It happens," was Albert's offhanded comment.

"Is that a threat?"

"Don't be revolting. There is, far more often than not, a close link between the murderer and the victim."

"No need to lecture me, Albert, that's partly how I'm ruling most of these cases out."

Fletcher rarely took Albert's barbs that seriously these days. Albert let a beat go by before asking, "Are you going to Oregon?"

"Not yet. Caroline said she'll approve the travel if they find a second body with the same MO." Fletcher laughed. "She probably only agreed in order to shut me up."

"No doubt. Let me know, and I'll accompany you."

"I was hoping you would. Any chance of Jefferson considering it official business?"

"Highly improbable. I'll use some of my rostered days off."

"Thanks, Albert." A pause. "Let me pay the airfare."

"That won't be necessary."

Silence again. Fletcher, who had finally begun to suspect that Albert was not solely dependent on his salary, seemed to be on the brink of asking something that would no doubt be difficult to answer. But all he ended up saying was, "If nothing more happens in Oregon, is it still okay for me to visit for the weekend?"

"Of course."

"Don't forget the roulade." Then Fletcher said goodbye and hung up the phone.

After a moment, Albert put the handset down. He hated lame and drawn–out farewells, as Fletcher knew. But this one felt lame and abrupt, and Fletcher was obviously unhappy, probably disturbed at this new evidence of what he perceived to be his failure. And Albert couldn't offer anything to help, especially over the phone. He sighed and went to his study, where he tried to lose himself in the latest British research on the possibility of DNA profiling, which was of course exactly what Fletcher needed to prove that the same offender had committed all these crimes. But it appeared that the technique wouldn't be available for months, if not years.

CHAPTER FOURTEEN
WASHINGTON DC
OCTOBER 1984

The drive from the airport was accompanied by a CD, loudly played, of something called *Carmina Burana*. Fletch listened to it with more than a little surprise. The first part was suitably dark and ominously dramatic. But then, "What's this next bit about?"

"It is called *Primo vere*, or *Spring*."

It was light and joyous and sexy, and didn't seem to suit Albert's dour demeanor at all. "This is lovely."

"Sublime," Albert informed him, though he seemed totally unaffected by the burgeoning music.

For a few minutes, within the car at least, fall was banished and spring was celebrated. Fletch thought of fresh green leaves and soft warm air, of infinitely clear blue skies and the urge to share all that joy with another human being. His hand itched to slide over to rest on Albert's thigh – which Albert would be furious at, even though no one could possibly see them.

To distract himself, Fletcher concentrated again on the music. Spring's joy had ended, and the dark had returned. This part was grim and boisterous, deep male voices at times turning sharp and discordant. "Tell me about this," Fletch asked. "I've never heard anything like it."

And for the rest of the journey, Albert did so, though he fell silent again as soon as they reached home. Albert headed directly to the kitchen.

Fletch trailed after him, a wry twist to his smile. "When I said I missed your cooking," he murmured, "it *is* true that I missed your cooking as well."

Albert just stared at him for a moment, before saying sardonically, "Don't feel shy, Ash, and don't let taste or discretion restrain you – just come right out of your shell and ask for sex if that's what you want."

Fletcher's smile grew. "You could come help me unpack," he suggested.

"You need assistance with the contents of one rather small overnight bag?"

But Albert was already approaching him, taking Fletch by the hand to lead him to Albert's bedroom.

The air was so crisp and clear that Fletch felt like he was floating in champagne. It had been easy to let go, exhilarating to leave the struggle behind. He grinned now, spread his arms wide and arched to lean back into the careless freedom of it.

A sheer wall of rock sped away to the sky, and the first doubt chilled him. Below, far away but noticeably closer every second, water foamed over rocks in a narrow gorge. He'd known it was there and yet he hadn't wanted to bother hanging on or climbing those last few feet to safety, hadn't wanted to make the effort. A growl shaped his mouth into something savage. Why did he always do this to himself?

There were arms snaring him, suddenly, from close behind; one round his shoulders and the other round his waist. His name urgently spoken. "Ash."

Fletch twisted, trying to escape this person weighing him down. Plummeting out of the sunlight and into the cold shadows, the sound of rapids echoing, destroying the last illusion of peace. *"No!"*

"Ash. Wake up."

It was completely dark. Fletch lay, wary and still, breath heaving. He was in a bed. Some internal voice was telling him it was okay now, it had just been another dream, but his sense of danger was having trouble catching up with his intellect.

"Are you all right?" The tone was of enforced patience.

Albert. Fletch was in Albert's bed, lying in Albert's embrace. They had only been lovers for a couple of months and had spent far less than half of those nights together, but already they fell naturally into this position for sleep: Fletch lying back against Albert, who held him loosely. On the few occasions Fletch had woken first, he'd found Albert had buried his face in Fletch's hair, mouth at the nape of Fletcher's neck.

"Ash?"

"Yeah," Fletch muttered, "I'm all right."

"This is usual for you, is it? Nightmares every time you fall asleep."

"Not every time."

"You don't always wake up," Albert informed him. "You don't remember them all."

"Really?" Fletch brought his hands to Albert's, so he was held in a double embrace as he considered this troubling thought. He had no reason to doubt Albert's observations, though he knew he wasn't supposed to have realized that Albert rarely slept a full night. "It's this waiting that's getting to me," he said at last, "this waiting for another boy to die. Ever since the two years were up, I've known that he's out there killing and that I didn't stop him. All I can do is wait for another death and hope to all I believe in that I get him this time."

"Blaming yourself is pointless and counterproductive. Not to mention self–indulgent."

"You're right, absolutely right."

"Well?"

"I can see your logic, I know intellectually that you're right. But that doesn't mean that my heart or my conscience know it." Fletch sighed. "We've been over this a thousand times, Albert, and we never agree. Can't you just accept how I feel?"

"Obviously you can't accept it, or you wouldn't wake up yelling so frequently."

"Why won't you understand how ghoulish this feels? To know that some poor boy's being tortured and murdered, and we're waiting for someone to find his body?"

Albert was silent.

"Okay, fine – give me a hard time about it in the morning. But, right now, how about you just pretend you sympathize?"

"I am definitely sorry for you," Albert said dryly.

"Not half as sorry for me as I am. You get impatient with the whole issue, Caroline's more than half convinced I'm making it all up – whose shoulder am I supposed to cry on?" It had been even more difficult and frustrating when Caroline had begun to give him nothing but routine duties, which were unlikely to cause a problem if he made mistakes or wanted to fly off to Oregon with no notice, but that couldn't serve to distract him from the days sliding past.

"I don't suppose you discuss this with your father."

"No," Fletch said flatly. He was under oath to keep any Bureau case confidential. Though he suspected he'd happily break that oath if he didn't feel Peter Ash would be as uncomfortable with Fletcher's empathic understanding of this murderer as Albert was unsympathetic.

"Perhaps you should see someone who's qualified to deal with this."

"What?" Fletch was flabbergasted. He twisted around to see Albert's face, which was closed tight. "You don't believe in shrinks and things."

"I don't need a therapist," Albert amended. "But I am beginning to suspect you might."

"No way. Where do you get off suggesting I do something that you never would?"

"You enjoy this unbalanced state of mind?"

"I hate to break it to you but I've always relied on myself and a few select friends to maintain that balance. And you are my best and closest friend."

"You're being ridiculous. A qualified practitioner would simply aim to help you cope with reality."

"If you want to spend the night trying to agree on a definition of reality," Fletch snapped, "that's fine by me."

"Now you're being infantile as well. Perhaps I should have been clearer – the realities of your life and your situation."

Silence, though Fletch didn't move out of Albert's arms. He'd been unfair, he admitted to himself; Albert had Fletch's best interests at heart, even if he had a rather abrupt bedside manner. Ash suddenly laughed, having realized something he should have thought of years ago. "You're qualified, aren't you?"

A moment's pause, as if Albert was surprised. "You're not yet a suitable subject for forensic psychology."

"I mean, you're a doctor. Though no one calls you Dr. Sterne."

Albert shrugged. "I began working at the Bureau forensics lab while I was still studying."

"And you never made a fuss when you qualified and neither, of course, did they."

"It enabled me to earn promotion to the position I occupy now. I started as a lab assistant."

Ash almost laughed again: Albert would indeed be difficult to work for, with his high and exacting standards. What could be worse for some people than working for a boss who knew how their job should most perfectly be done because he'd done it himself? Under the circumstances, they couldn't even justifiably complain about the situation. Fletch said, "That's quite an achievement, working full time and finishing your studies, especially in such a demanding area. And I'll bet you became a doctor at a younger age than usual, too."

Albert shrugged, acceding to this speculation.

Of course he had, Fletch figured, and no doubt at the same time he'd also pursued knowledge throughout the myriad topics crucial to forensics. "Why don't you insist on being called Dr. Sterne? People should show you more respect."

"I'm not interested in their respect. And I don't believe in titles."

"What, you only believe in results, and you let them speak for themselves? That would be right."

Albert lifted a hand, as if to say, *Assume what you like.*

Fletch knew Albert would have vehemently denied it if Fletcher were wrong. He chuckled at his mischievous success. "Did you always plan on working in forensics? It's a thankless sort of job, isn't it?"

"It seemed a better option than becoming a general practitioner," Albert said, casting a dry glance at Fletcher when he laughed. It was an impossible sort of image, Albert Sterne coping with diverse living patients each day, with all their needs and ailments and complaints. "Feeling happy again, are you?"

"Must be talking about you that does it."

"I sincerely hope not."

Fletch turned fully, pushed closer to kiss him, and was quickly caught up in the subtle mysteries and the simple intimacies of sex. This man did it to him every time. But Albert was apparently, as ever, unwilling to lose himself in sensation – Fletch could feel him holding back, remaining in control, even as he responded to Fletch's need by initiating something more intense.

Offering a smile, Fletch drew away, hands roaming for a last precious moment, then settled back in Albert's arms to go to sleep. "Good night, love," he whispered, though he didn't expect or receive a reply.

The muffled clatter of the garage door vibrated through the house, and Fletch groaned from under the quilt. Had Albert never heard of the civilized practice of sleeping in on the weekend? Apparently not, for whenever Fletch was in Washington, Albert got out of bed every morning at six, changed into his tracksuit, and rode his bike for half an hour, no matter what the day or weather. Fletch suspected that, given the precise timing of each trip, Albert had mapped out a route years ago and still stuck to it. He probably allowed for an adequate warm up, then twenty minutes of aerobic exercise, and then a warm down as he pedaled home. Always the same. In fact, as he heard the back door open, Fletch bet to himself that it was now twenty–five to seven – he groaned again when he saw the bedside clock confirmed his surmise.

Albert had come in and was undressing, placing his neatly folded sweater and pants in the laundry basket. He nodded a greeting when he noticed Fletch was awake, and Fletch smiled. Albert looked nice naked: compact and firm and balanced. "Come back to bed," Fletch suggested.

"I have work to do." Albert headed for the bathroom and ran the shower.

Fletch retreated under the quilt. His own exercise regime was far more random. He and Caroline would play squash every other day, or Fletch would go for a run. There were sociable football and baseball games held between the various federal and state public servants in Denver during the lunch hour. And, on the weekends before he began visiting Albert so regularly, Fletch tried to get away from town, up into the mountains, and hike for miles.

But the only exercise he got in Washington these days was in Albert's bed; a situation he would have to remedy.

"Isn't this early for you, Ash?"

Fletch was inclined to agree: the sun was barely over the horizon. Nevertheless, he struggled into a spare pair of Albert's track pants.

"You do realize it's Sunday today," Albert said rather pointedly.

"It's not my fault you have these uncivilized habits."

"I had no intention of waking you."

Fletch sat down on the bed to tie his sneakers. He frowned at a sudden recollection. "I don't know what's wrong with me lately; if I were out hiking I'd be two miles away by now; if I had work to do I'd be halfway through it."

"Don't delude yourself, Ash, you're always slow in the mornings."

"I don't know, it feels worse these days."

The man said, "I have to go."

Yeah, Albert, don't want to ruin your schedule. Fletch broke the news: "I'm coming with you. You ride, I'll run."

Silence. "You won't keep up."

"Try me," Fletch retorted, though he backed down in the next breath. "All right. You'll just have to slow down a bit." Albert was looking dubious. "Oh come on," Fletch said, "this is bonding or something, me sharing the things you do and all that."

"Indeed." Albert glanced at the clock. "If you insist, then let's go."

Fletch's smile didn't last long. He soon discovered that Albert took his exercise even more seriously than Fletch had anticipated. "I've got a better idea," he panted out at last, "I'll ride, you run."

By the time they returned home, Albert's schedule was forty minutes behind.

"I'll make it up to you," Fletch promised, collapsed across the bed. And, when Albert had the shower running hot, Fletch joined him there and tried to do just that. Which only delayed Albert's precious schedule even further.

CHAPTER FIFTEEN
OREGON
NOVEMBER 1984

Fletch stilled for a moment and cast a careful glance at the ground surrounding him: it looked undisturbed, innocent of secrets. He was distracted by his surroundings, then, loving the dark and abundantly green forests, forever damp and fertile where Colorado tended to be dry. He didn't even mind the cold, though he kept his hands in his coat pockets as much as possible. One day, when he had some time to himself, Fletch decided, he'd come hiking up here.

But right now, he wasn't here for enjoyment. There had been a second body found and Fletch had volunteered to find the third victim that no one, but for Albert, quite believed in. Welcoming the chance, Fletch suspected, to keep him quiet and out of their way, the local police had given him detailed maps of the areas surrounding Portland, marked with the locations of the first two bodies. Fletch had a few ideas on likely locations for the third and was now searching around six to ten feet from the roads and trails in those areas. He had, however, been out here since early morning and the light was beginning to fail him, so it seemed today's search would be in vain.

"You find something?" It was Owen Ross, the officer who'd been assigned to help Fletch – and, more to the point, shadow him. No matter how misguided the locals thought Fletch was, they didn't want to risk any potential evidence that he stumbled across. It was also their case and they were resentful of his intrusion, suspecting that Fletch would find it easy enough to make this federal business. Fletch, on the other hand, knew how hard he'd have to push the issue with Caroline and the local Bureau field office if he really wanted jurisdiction. Nevertheless, he trod carefully in his dealings with the Oregon people, as he desperately needed their cooperation. "Hey, Fletch. You find something?" The man was leaving the road to join him amongst the trees and undergrowth.

"No, I'm just wool–gathering," Fletch replied.

"All right," Ross said easily, returning to his amble along the road as Fletch began his search again. "You say he always buries them," Ross called out. "He never leaves them lying around?"

"There's something significant about burial for him," Fletch replied. "Up in the mountains in Colorado, the sensible thing to do with a body is dump it down an old mineshaft. It's an easy method of disposal, and no one would ever find the thing. But this guy went to all the bother of digging graves two–foot deep that would eventually be discovered. It must mean something – some sort of ritual, or some gesture of respect for the victim. Or it's a part of how tidy and careful he is, and he simply considers burial is the proper way to dispose of them. Or it's because burial slows down putrefaction – but that increases the risk of us identifying the victim, and it preserves evidence. Actually, I've been working on the assumption that he wants us to find them. But, in short, Owen, I don't know exactly why."

"Sounds like you have it as figured as anyone. You'll get him."

If there was one word that summed up Owen Ross, Fletcher thought, it would be sincere. Fletch continued, "The thing that gives me hope is that, this time, we're only weeks behind him. The previous cases, we didn't find the bodies for months." He sighed. "Even so, I've been after this guy for years, and I don't really feel I'm any closer."

"Still reckon you'll get him."

"Thanks," Fletch said, grimacing to himself. This was the first vote of confidence he'd had for far too long, but it didn't help. There were things Ross didn't know, and Fletch in no way deserved his faith.

Albert's hotel room was as neatly ordered as Fletch anticipated. They'd only checked in the day before, and Fletch's room already looked like tornadoes hit it on a regular basis. He grinned to himself at the disparity and closed the door behind him, as Albert returned to the reports spread in neat piles on the table. "I didn't find anything," Fletch said.

"I assumed as much."

"So little faith," Fletch joked uneasily. He continued, "Well, if I don't find something tomorrow, either the locals will throw me out or Caroline will insist I return."

"You should be able to charm both into allowing you a little more leeway." The tone of voice was totally bland and uninterested, without even the dryness that Fletch interpreted as humor.

There was a silence, which Fletch stood through. Albert seemed less and less approachable these days, but Fletch couldn't doubt that he would always be welcome; he knew he was unique in Albert's affections. Eventually, Fletch said, "You want to know the truth?" And then he evaded the issue by slipping off his jacket, discarding it on a handy chair, and pouring himself a double nip of whisky from the mini–bar. He hadn't really faced up to this himself.

When Fletch didn't continue, Albert prompted, "Yes," though he didn't look up from the report he was scanning.

"I didn't go to the most likely places. In fact, after I visited the other two sites yesterday and got a feel for the general lay of the land, I reckon I could have walked right to the other gravesite. But I didn't. I spent the day wandering around all my third and fourth and fifth choices."

That caught Albert's attention. He was staring, furious, but Fletch knew him well enough to read disbelief underneath it. "I trust there's a good reason," Albert bit out.

Fletch was impressed, having expected insults. Perhaps they would come later. "You know who the first suspect always is," he started.

"The person who finds the body and reports it."

"Always, even if you can clear them within moments, you always check them out. There's so many cases where the offender, even if they're not immediate family or a close friend, has been one of the on–lookers, part of the search team, or simply the first to come forward."

"Are you suffering from a guilty conscience of some kind? Is there some reason you want to avoid the questions?"

"Yes, I –"

Albert was standing. Here it came. "That is the most foolish and self–indulgent thing you've ever done – and that's saying something, Ash." The voice was low, presumably to avoid sharing this with their neighbors. "Deliberately delaying part of a murder investigation – there are laws against it. I used to admire the professionalism and dedication you exhibited, despite the haphazard and slovenly way you conduct other areas of your life. Now you confess to obstructing the pursuit of justice."

Fletcher managed to hold Albert's angry gaze throughout, for it was only what he deserved. Albert might be better at verbalizing such chastisements, but Fletch felt them with greater strength in his heart. "It hardly matters at this stage," Fletch tried, though he knew he sounded sheepish.

"Of course it matters and you know that very well. The offender, who is more likely to have been alerted to the investigation, has another twenty–four hours to destroy evidence, prepare his alibi, leave the vicinity. The body and the trace evidence will decay further or be lost –"

"All right, all right, it was the wrong thing to do."

"Every hour is significant; particularly in this case, when we are closer behind the offender than before. Why do you think the initial stages of these investigations are carried on around the clock? Why do you suppose that in ninety percent of cases, an autopsy will be conducted immediately, whatever the hour, rather than wait until morning?"

"Albert, please. I made a mistake, a serious mistake – but I admitted it. Show me a little mercy."

"It makes no sense, you exhibit no consistency. You want people to believe in these instincts of yours, the intuition, the empathy you have with this murderer – yet you fail to prove this capacity when you have the perfect chance."

Fletch poured himself another nip of whisky, drank it down in little more than a gulp. "I consider myself suitably reproved. If you're done?"

"Yes."

As Albert sat down again, Fletch wandered closer. "You're a hard man, Albert," he commented.

"But thankfully I'm hardest of all on myself," the man said flatly, completing one of Fletcher's oft–spoken observations.

"No, what I was going to say was …" Fletch leaned in to slide his arms around Albert's shoulders, to whisper in his ear, "A hard man is good to find."

Albert shrugged him off, more annoyed than Fletch had seen him in a long while.

"You may interpret that in at least two ways." Fletch sat in the closest chair, felt something akin to physical collapse – it had been a fraught few days. He propped his elbows on his knees, and hung his head. "You know, sometimes I just want to be normal. Not often, not very often at all. Sometimes, however, I'm nothing but doubt and fear, and I wish I was – I wish with a vengeance I was anyone else. Harley, maybe. A good old–fashioned country boy who's barely different enough to be interesting." On consideration, Fletch smiled bleakly. "But I wouldn't have you, then, would I?"

Albert was silent.

"Beth is nice, one of the nicest people I know. I had an enormous crush on her when I was a kid and never quite got over it, if you must know. But she isn't you, not by a long shot."

Turning another page of the report, Albert seemed oblivious.

"It's too late now," Fletch said.

"Yes," Albert said distantly. "Please don't consider yourself permanently encumbered with me, but I seem to recall that Beth and Harley are married."

Fletch laughed, with some genuine amusement. "I meant it's too late to go find that body. They'd just love that, wouldn't they? You and me showing up at midnight having traipsed around the crime site alone."

"The watch dog who's been at your heels all day should be available."

"Now, there's an idea. I have Owen's home phone number here somewhere."

"Call him, then." Albert tidily bundled the reports up, and slid them into his briefcase. "And don't forget you owe me six dollars for the whisky."

Fletch grinned. "Love you anyway," he said, fishing in his wallet for Ross's card. Scraps of paper, receipts, assorted business cards, dollar bills and a few photos ended up scattered across the bed. "Here it is." He gathered the rest up, leaving some of the money behind, and stuffed it all back into his wallet wherever it would fit.

Albert was staring at him rather pointedly, but Fletcher barely noticed. A woman answered the phone, and yelled for Ross, who agreed to meet Fletch in ten minutes.

"I don't know." Ross's troubled voice drifted clearly down the slope to where Fletch waited in the night's darkness. "He said he was looking at the maps, and inspiration struck." Radio static obscured the reply. "Yeah, well, I reckon he's okay. You'd better all get up here, though, soon as possible. No, they're down there, but I told them not to touch anything.

Yeah, I'll be sure, but you gotta agree these guys know what they're doing. Okay, Ross out."

Fletch tracked Ross's circuitous approach as the man crashed through the undergrowth off to one side of the site – what they'd quickly decided was the least likely path for the offender to have taken – the beam of his flashlight bouncing crazily. "They're on their way," Ross announced when he reached the tiny clearing.

"I heard," Fletch said. "And don't worry, we haven't disturbed a thing."

Albert was methodically but quickly searching the ground surrounding the site with the second flashlight, while Fletch crouched near the mound of dirt and rocks. He was impatient to unearth the body, despite the part of him that dreaded what he would find – his inclination was to forget cold procedure, to get in there now and shovel the dirt aside with his bare hands, lost in some mad grieving frenzy. Instead, he helped Ross tape off the area. *Do not cross this line.*

"Nothing?" Fletch asked when Albert joined them outside the tape. Albert shook his head. Fletch observed, "He's far too clever. As smart and as tidy as you."

"I hope I'm not supposed to be flattered by the comparison."

Ross was watching them with a sharp eye.

Albert was continuing, "It's necessary for us to remain thorough. One day this man will make a mistake."

"Just like me – is that your point?" Fletch grinned a little, humorless. "But when does his control run out? When do the edges start fraying?"

"You said yourself he might keep doing this for years."

Fletcher widened his eyes, mostly in jest, and whispered, "I'll go mad."

Turning to consider him, Albert said seriously, "Judging by the last two months, you might be right."

After a moment, Fletch shook himself, cast an apology at their companion. "Never mind us, Owen. I've been on this guy's trail for too long. It's getting to me. As for Albert, he has no excuse – he's always like this."

Albert's stare turned up a couple of notches to furious, but Fletch was saved from an insult by the arrival of the local police and deputies.

◆

"Strange," Fletcher said, frowning down at the body. It was dawn, though the lights they had set up were still providing necessary illumination, and it was bitterly cold. "Right location, wrong MO."

There was plastic wrapped loosely around the body – not in a neat parcel like in Colorado, and unlike the other two Oregon victims who'd had no shroud – and the boy was fully clothed, though his sneakers were untied. He had been buried face up.

Fletch said, "That T–shirt is distinctive. Does anyone remember a missing person report mentioning a logo like that? It must be a rock band or something."

A few of the surrounding officers indicated that they didn't recall. One said gruffly, "I'll check on it." *Don't tell us how to do our job, G–man.*

"What do you make of it, Albert?"

The forensics man, who'd helped unearth the body, walked over to stand next to Fletch. "Do you recall the corpse in Colorado who died as a result of a head injury?"

"Before the offender had a chance to torture and rape him. Sure. But he disposed of the body in the same way as the other two, in that instance; we found all three in exactly the same conditions and circumstances." Fletch frowned, considering. "And this was the right location. Maybe he's losing it, he's letting the consistency go. Maybe this one didn't count, the kid was extraneous like Stacey Dixon – he just dumped her in a river, remember. Or he wanted it to look unrelated for some reason –" Fletcher folded his arms, and hunched towards Albert for emphasis rather than grab the man in public – "Perhaps this one is too close to home, and he wants us to concentrate on the other two because they fit his MO."

Albert agreed. "Maybe," he said, doing Fletch the favor of not backing off from the sudden intensity.

"Maybe –" Fletch groaned. "Albert, what if this one didn't satisfy him because he didn't get to play his damned games and there's still another victim to find."

"Possible, though that wasn't the case in Colorado."

"I know, but he's going to escalate, he's going to need it more and more before he's done. Maybe he could still control it back then, despite disappointments." Fletcher turned to find the officer in charge. "Would you let Dr. Sterne at least observe the autopsy? Or use him to conduct or assist, if you like; he's the best in the Bureau."

"He can observe," the man agreed.

"All right." Fletcher ran both hands back through his hair, trying to keep track of his thoughts: the new knowledge and the old cases, the assumptions and connections, the conclusions and theories; all these had to be kept separate and clearly identified. Sometimes his mind seemed like a box of cards, all cross–referenced and tabbed, an image he thought far more appropriate for Albert to deal with. "I need to keep Owen," he continued. "I have a horrible feeling there's another body out here."

It was only later that Fletcher remembered he'd reached a hand to grip Albert's shoulder, seeking reassurance, before heading off up the trail with a tired Ross in tow. But Albert hadn't complained or made a fuss, which would only have drawn attention. And such a gesture surely wasn't open to misinterpretation.

But such musings were banished within the hour by the discovery of another gravesite close to where Fletch had predicted. Fletcher knelt at the edge of the road, gazing down at the disturbed earth, while Ross ran back to the car to call it in. Alone, the Special Agent found he was blinking back tears.

"Ash. Wake up."

Albert. Fletch sought consciousness, confused by the awkward position he was cramped into, by the unnatural cold, by the artificial light. Then he remembered he was in the basement labs of the Oregon medical examiner's building, and Albert had been assisting in the autopsy of the fourth body. "All done?" Fletch asked, slowly prying himself out of the plastic bucket seat he'd been sitting in.

"Yes. You could have returned to the hotel, Ash."

"Didn't want to be alone."

Albert raised an eyebrow at him, conveying surprise and disdain and warning. *Don't be obvious.*

Fletcher said, "I also wanted to hear the results." He tried to stretch but didn't get very far.

"Same MO as the first two bodies. Time of death for all four was within a period of four weeks, perhaps during September. Cause of death in this instance was anoxic anoxia, due to ligature strangulation with something soft that left no external markings. Numerous bruises and minor injuries, sexual penetration. I believe the boy was also gagged."

"Was the offender a non–secretor?"

"The tests won't be ready until morning."

"What about the third body?"

"Cause of death was anoxic anoxia, too, but due to suffocation. Both arms were severely fractured – the radius, to be precise," Albert indicated the top of his forearm with a chopping motion. "There are no other injuries, and no evidence of sexual activity. I understand, however, there was a partial fingerprint on the boy's shoe."

"What? One that didn't match the boy's prints?"

"I would hardly have mentioned it if it did."

"That's great!"

"Don't get carried away, Ash: it could easily belong to a parent, friend or sibling and, if not, is little use at present unless the offender's prints are on file."

"Come on, Albert, that's the first print we've got on this guy. Possible print," he amended at Albert's impatient expression.

"I wasn't in attendance for the full procedure, so we'll have to wait on the reports for more detail."

"Let's get them now."

"Ash, you're still dreaming. The reports won't be transcribed until tomorrow. Apparently the typists here are all two–fingered."

"Damn it, I –"

"It is after one in the morning, neither of us have slept since the night before last. Put the obsession aside. We've done all we can for now."

Mutinous, Fletch glared, but Albert refused to back down.

"It would have been nice to see this dedication yesterday, before you lost us twelve hours."

"All right," Fletch said ungraciously. "Let's go." But he could be stubborn, too. Once they were back at the hotel, Fletch followed Albert into his room, and sat on the bed before Albert could draw breath to protest. "Don't want to be alone," he repeated.

"Exactly what are you suggesting? It's hardly wise to –"

"Oh just come here and hold me, will you?"

After a moment, Albert did so, sitting beside Fletch and taking him into a firm embrace. No matter how mad he was with Fletch, the younger man noted, Albert rarely stinted on providing what Fletcher needed if it was at all possible.

"Felt like crying out there, finding I was right and he's killed another four boys. Four more lives, Albert, four young lives. Felt like bawling my eyes out, but I didn't."

"If you must, my shoulder seems convenient at present."

"Don't think I can. Don't know that I want to, actually."

"It might prove a better option than the nightmares."

"True. But, you know, I haven't cried since I was twelve. It was 1964. I remember –" And he was lost for a moment, swamped all over again.

One of Albert's hands settled for a moment on Fletcher's head. "Your mother dying?"

"She'd died two years before, though I guess that was part of it. Is that the last time you cried? When your parents were killed?"

"It's late, Ash. Go get some sleep."

The embrace, however, was not withdrawn, so Fletch assumed that was a *yes*. He wound his arms tighter around Albert's neat waist, lodged his head comfortably in the crook of Albert's neck, and told the story. "I remember it was 1964, because we were watching the TV coverage of the Democratic convention and Bobby Kennedy was there. He stood up at the podium, and they applauded him for fifteen, twenty minutes. Do you remember that? When they finally let him speak, he said that when he thought of President Kennedy, he thought of what Shakespeare wrote in *Romeo and Juliet* – of all the plays to choose for your brother! – and he quoted from it. *When he shall die, take him and cut him out in little stars, and he will make the face of heaven so fine, that all the world will be in love with night, and pay no worship to the garish sun.* And I was sitting there in Harley's arms, sort of like this, bawling my eyes out, partly for JFK and partly because I idolized Harley like that, too."

It had been a rough couple of years for young Fletcher David Ash, so all that wailing on Harley's shoulder must have been some kind of necessary catharsis. It was true that he'd never cried since, though tears had often threatened. It wasn't that he was ashamed to cry, or thought it improper or unbecoming for a man – Fletch simply suspected that if he wept every time life did something terrible to him, there would be no other possible reaction. It would be like giving in to an indulgence that he could not afford, being governed by an emotion that would get him nowhere.

He had a brief but vivid image of himself old and grey at Albert's funeral: he was wearing one of Albert's suits because none of his own were good enough; and he wanted to bawl his eyes out like a child, but couldn't. No one knew they'd been lovers, no one could guess at Fletcher's grief. Except maybe Fletch would at last meet the mysterious Elliott Meyer, and maybe he could tell the man that Albert had had a share of contentment in his life, though Albert kept his love such a complete secret ...

Fletcher brought his thoughts back to the present, noticing that Albert had remained silent. It appeared that, where Albert had previously provided a sharp retort or an insult, now he would sometimes say nothing. Because he didn't want to hurt Fletcher? Because he didn't want to hurt himself? Because he wanted their relationship to be different from what it had started as? It certainly wasn't because Fletch never disappointed him, the younger man knew that much.

Fletcher asked, "Can I impose on you and sleep here tonight?"

"No, you may not."

"Why?"

"Don't be childish, you know very well why. All it would take would be Ross trying to call you and our discretion so far would have been in vain."

"You being there and holding me helps the nightmares, Albert." Fletcher lifted his head to meet Albert's gaze.

"Resorting to emotional blackmail?" the man noted coldly. Then, warming with sarcasm, "I'm so glad to be of use to you as a security blanket. Nevertheless, we can't spend every night together."

"What if you come stay in my room? They're more likely to call me than you."

"No."

Fletcher sighed. This was something he wanted badly, but he'd anticipated defeat before he even tried. "How did I end up with a lover so stubborn?"

"By being so stubborn yourself, as I recall."

"I guess you get what you ask for," Fletcher observed with a smile, "or what you deserve."

"How trite. Perhaps you should look for a job composing the messages in greeting cards, or the sayings on cheap desk calendars."

Fletcher chuckled a little – that was the Albert he knew and loved. "I'll be sure to consult you when I need a change in career."

Albert lifted his hands, wove his fingers through Fletcher's hair, pressed his cheek and lips against Fletcher's forehead. It wasn't a kiss, and it was too brief, but it was very nice. Then, in a tone that did not betray any affection, Albert said, "Go to bed. You need sleep."

Accepting the inevitable, Fletcher hugged the man, then went to his room alone.

The FBI men had been allocated a desk in a small and dingy disused room that opened directly onto the police station's briefing room – which was fine in one way, because they got to hear everything that went on in every case in the Portland area, but inconvenient in many others, beginning with the distraction and the lack of privacy.

Fletcher was in the cubby–hole now, poring over the transcript of an interview with the mother of the third victim they'd found – and the first to have died – Sam Doherty. He had wanted to attend the interview itself, partly because the disposal of Sam's body had been inconsistent with the other three and Fletcher had found that the exceptions to the rules often provided the most telling evidence. However, four of the locals had insisted on conducting or observing the interview for various reasons, and a fifth member of the party wasn't welcome on the grounds that the numbers would be too intimidating. Fletch was left with planning a separate interview, perhaps after the funeral, when he could ask about the men Sam had known, and whether any of them fitted his offender's profile.

Albert was supposed to be meeting him here, otherwise Fletch would have taken the reports outside into the fresh air despite the cold weather. There wasn't even a window in sight. He hated not being able to at least see the sky. But, Fletch reminded himself, he should be grateful he was part of this investigation at all, despite the headache he could feel looming. He dug his fingers into his temples, and waited, re–reading the transcribed words for the tenth time, guessing at the meanings revealed only by tone and gesture. He'd read certain phrases so often that his imagination began suggesting ludicrous interpretations on what had no doubt been completely straightforward.

"What kept you?" Fletch asked when Albert turned up.

"The tests took longer than anticipated. One of the samples had been contaminated. Not by me, I hasten to add."

"But you got it all sorted out?" Of course he had. Fletcher grimaced in reply to Albert's raised eyebrow, and continued, "I've just been going over the interview with Sam Doherty's mother. It's very interesting. Sam worked as an apprentice mechanic but he still lived at home. The night he disappeared he told his mother he was meeting a particular friend. The friend, however, says they hadn't agreed to meet, though he says there was a football game on the television and Sam often turned up to watch it with him; the friend adds that Sam never missed a game. Does this sound familiar to you?"

"Go on," Albert prompted.

"The only information we have so far on how this guy operates is from Andrew Harmer's friend, Scott, in Colorado. And Sam fits in with that. I think this man identifies his victim, then asks the boy home to watch football on television, maybe offering or at least hinting at sex as well, depending on how receptive the boy is."

"Wasn't it baseball in Harmer's case?"

"That's what Scott said, but he didn't know anything about sport and Drew wasn't much better. And, remember, when we checked the programming, the only sport being televised the night Drew disappeared was football. *His* motivation for accepting the invitation was romance. Sam's might be more related to watching the game. No one's asked the mother or friend whether Sam was gay, by the way."

Albert considered all this, then said, "The scenario is possible. Are you going to start looking into the case files of every young man in the country who disappeared, was assaulted or died on the night of a televised football game?"

Fletch groaned. "If Caroline would let me have the resources, perhaps I would. But I can't even begin to do all this properly on my own."

"You have my help, and McIntyre's hindrance."

"And I'm grateful for both, of course, though what we need is a full–blown, nationwide task force. At least he operates within certain parameters, particular timeframes, which narrows the search down – for his victims, at least."

He, Fletch had said, and *his*, and they both knew who he was referring to, though Fletcher never gave him a name or a nickname, or used one of the codes that the police and newspaper reporters in each state allotted for the sake of convenience and sensation. The most Albert did was call him Fletch's pet serial killer.

The Oregon people were unimaginatively calling the offender they were after the Portland Strangler, even after Sam Doherty was discovered – though they weren't convinced, as Fletch was, that there weren't two killers on the loose, given the differences in MO. The Georgia reporters, faced with three brutal and bloody deaths, had called their offender the Mauler, which had led to a few cartoons and jokes about the Shopping Maller. Fletch found his sense of humor didn't extend that far. The Georgia police, knowing more about how the victims were restrained and bound, called him the Killer de Sade when they weren't in public. And the Colorado people, four years ago, had opted for the simple Boy Killer – except in certain circles, whose prejudice was alarmingly callous, where he was known as Just Another Queer Basher.

"I have been considering the results from the Doherty autopsy," Albert was saying.

Fletch found he had sunk his head to his arms, which were folded on the desk, and couldn't remember collapsing like that. He was exhausted. "And?"

"The radius in each arm was badly fractured, almost broken, about two–thirds along from the wrist. Due to the symmetry, I suspect that Doherty's hands were close together, though there is no evidence that he was bound or handcuffed. Perhaps the offender held the hands together, placed the arms against something strong but fairly slim, like a metal pipe or even the edge of a heavy table, then exerted enough force to cause the injury. The result being a boy in pain who couldn't use his arms effectively, and who was therefore easy to control."

"But what did he want to control the boy *for*?" Fletch pondered. "There's no sign of sexual activity and it doesn't seem like our man to put clothes back onto a naked corpse. So all he ended up doing was suffocating the boy."

"Perhaps he needed to shut Doherty up in a hurry, perhaps they were in danger of being found or heard." Albert, who was still standing, put his hands on the table and leaned forward. "I believe the other three bodies had been gagged at some stage. None of the victims in the other states have been, and we were therefore looking for an isolated location, or one that was secure and soundproof. But perhaps he didn't have that luxury here in Oregon."

"You mean he couldn't afford the noise this time, so perhaps we can assume that he lived in town or whatever." The box of cards in Fletch's head seemed about to topple into massive disorder. He clutched at his temples again, willing the headache and the chaos away. "I can't keep all this straight."

"You have to, no excuses. Or I won't listen to anymore of your theories."

Fletch looked up at Albert. "A hard, hard man," he commented. Which was exactly what he needed. "Okay with you if I pass that on to Owen Ross? About that he couldn't afford the noise, I mean. I'll tell him it was your idea."

"Of course you may, but there's no need to attribute it to me."

"Credit where credit's due."

"There's been no match on the fingerprint."

Disappointment sank hopes Fletcher thought he'd already given up on. "No?"

"It didn't match the mother's prints, and there was no match at HQ."

"So that means the man has never worked with the military or the government, and doesn't have a criminal record."

"If it is the offender's print," Albert reminded him.

"Yeah," Fletcher agreed dispiritedly. "So, what are you doing next?"

"Assisting them in identifying the fourth body and finalizing various tests."

"You're a wonder and a marvel, and I have no idea what I'd do without you."

Impassively returning Fletch's gaze, Albert said, "How gratifying. There must be very few people who could fully appreciate having a pet forensics expert at their beck and call."

Fletch, surprised at this, let a beat go past. Then he said, "I definitely appreciate it," with all the sincerity he could muster, for that was about the closest Albert had ever come to declaring a need for Fletcher's friendship or approval. He watched as Albert turned and left, and then he considered the man's statement again, less interested in the compliment than in the vulnerability it betrayed.

The fourth victim, a twenty–year–old man named Tony Shields, was identified by chance – a friend, working in a temporary clerical job at the medical examiner's offices, glimpsed photos of the body – rather than as a result of the forty–eight hours of solid work put in by the police and the FBI men.

Fletcher attended the funeral, a simple graveside service. He stood just out of hearing distance, with Ross beside him identifying as many as he could of the people attending. One of the local police also took photos as unobtrusively as possible.

It was a cold and colorless day, and everyone appeared grateful to return to the family home for lunch and a beer. Fletcher and Ross sat at the kitchen table and made a detailed list of who'd sent letters and cards and wreaths, while Jane Shields, Tony's older sister, helped them and kept Fletch supplied with coffee.

"With love and sympathy from the Colby family," Fletch read from a card that had accompanied flowers.

"Paul Colby was Tony's friend all through high school. He got on well with Paul's parents, too, though they're very strict. Anyway, they're all here, I think, except Paul had to go back to work."

"I met Paul at the medical examiner's, when he told us who Tony was."

"That's right," the young woman said. "I know it sounds awful but somehow it makes it even worse that Tony was lying there in a refrigerator, and we didn't claim him for days. Thank heavens for Paul."

"You couldn't have known," Fletch offered. He checked that Ross had noted the relevant details, then picked up the next card. "*In memoriam*, John Garrett."

"Don't know, actually. Robert –" Jane called to a brother nearby. When she had his attention, she beckoned him closer and handed him the card. "Do you know who this is?"

Robert thought for a moment. "Oh right, yeah, I'm guessing that's his boss from the construction site. I never met him or anything, but Tone mentioned him a couple of times, reckoned he was good to work for, like he was one of the boys."

"I thought Tony was unemployed when he went missing," Fletch said.

"Well, yeah, but only for a week or so. They'd just finished the new building in town, and Tone was taking a break before he looked for more work. I think he got a good reference from this guy."

"Can I see it?"

"Sure, if I can find it. Why?"

"We're just making sure there are no loose ends," Fletch said calmly, not wanting anyone's imagination running wild. "Once we tidy everything up and get a feel for who Tony was and who his friends and acquaintances were, then we'll know where else to look."

The young man seemed satisfied with that. He shrugged and meandered off.

Fletcher read from the next card. "In sympathy, Liz Barnes."

Jane Shields looked very sad. "She's the girl in the armchair over there, the one with the red hair. Liz was Tony's girlfriend."

Having only just quit work, Fletcher lay back on the bed in Albert's room, arms pillowing his head. Albert had the radio on quietly, tuned to a station playing classical music, which was nice enough. Relaxing, even. The forensics man was working on yet another report – Fletch often wondered how many forests were lost in any one murder investigation, what with all the reports and copies and bulletins, and then all the newspapers, too.

"What a ghastly day," Fletch murmured, mind wandering.

"Don't get too comfortable. I expect you to leave by midnight. You have ten minutes."

"Or what? I'll turn into a pumpkin?" Fletch chuckled, then subsided again, too tired for laughter. "Everyone's in the same condition but for you, apparently. Absolute exhaustion, running on nerves alone. You should have been there this afternoon. Everything tense and sort of glum because of Sam's funeral and we haven't made an arrest yet, and Owen tells this joke, this real simple thing – Two peanuts walking in a park. One was a salted. You see? Assaulted." Fletch giggled for a moment. "I mean, it isn't that funny –" But, helpless, he giggled again. "Or maybe it is, I'm not fit to judge right now. Anyway, this room full of grown men and women just crack up like you wouldn't believe. Complete hysteria. That's the state we're all in. What about you?"

"I'm tired," Albert allowed.

"Yeah. You should have been there, love, I mean it, a laugh would have done you good. Laughing at us, if not the stupid joke."

A pause. "You have two minutes."

"A hard, hard, hard man." Fletch glanced over at Albert, and was abruptly struck by an alarming thought. "In all the time we've known each other," he said slowly, thinking back over eight years, "in all that time," he continued, sitting up on the side of the bed, "I can't recall you ever laughing. Not once."

"That's entirely possible," Albert conceded.

"That's entirely terrible!"

"Why?"

"Why?" Fletch repeated, horrified. "Well, I don't know – it's not like you don't have a sense of humor. But I guess I can't imagine someone never laughing – it sounds so …" He'd been going to say *unhappy*, but thought better of it in time. What if that were the truth?

"It's midnight, go get some sleep. I'm sure tomorrow will prove as demanding as today."

"No, I – I'd really like to hear you laugh. What does it sound like, Albert?"

"This whole issue is of no interest to me."

"But I feel like I've failed you."

"Maybe you have."

Fletch stared for a moment – but Albert was just trying to scare him off. He grinned, humorless. "You're as good at emotional blackmail as I am, aren't you?"

"Go away, Ash."

"No." He walked over to the man where he sat beside the table, knelt before him, ran his arms around Albert's waist. "I love you."

"You have told me so on a number of occasions." Albert impatiently put the paperwork down.

"I want to do you good."

"I don't imagine we'd be friends otherwise." As if it was self–evident and easily dismissed. But Albert seemed sad underneath the annoyance, which was alarming if only because the man was usually too good at concealing his emotions.

Fletcher stretched up, kissed Albert as thoroughly as he knew how. When he broke away, he said, "At least I do this for you."

"Yes."

For a moment, Fletch thought he'd be dismissed again but Albert gathered him up closely and made careful love to him, right there. Because Fletch needed to be needed, right then.

Even though Fletcher was on his knees on the floor, even though he was only being jerked off and kissed, even though he was exhausted, Albert made the sex feel so damned sweet. Why was something this simple so good? Fletch wasn't one to wish he were a teenager again, so it wasn't the return to the basics that did it – and Albert was too precise and knowledgeable for Fletch to pretend this was a fumbling first time, even if he'd wanted to. They were both in their FBI suits and ties, Fletch's trousers unzipped but still hugging his hips, which added a jolt of the forbidden, but that was only part of the answer.

Albert loved him, Albert made him feel perfect, that was all. Even with only a mouth on his own, and a hand at his genitals.

Fletch groaned, so close to orgasm so quickly. Albert would often hold back at this stage, and let Fletch calm down before bringing him to the brink again and again, but Fletch was in no condition for that tonight. "Please," he whispered. The hand withdrew, and he began a protest, but then he was being forcibly lifted to his feet, Albert's hands on his hips. The man bent forward to take Fletch's penis into his mouth, sucked hard. Fletch came almost immediately, crying out before he could stop himself, leaning over to prop himself on the chair's arms. Then he fell to his knees again, and they held each other.

"What about you?" Fletch whispered when he could.

"You're going to your room and I'm going to get some sleep."

"All right, love."

"I'd prefer you kept the endearments to a minimum."

Fletch grinned. "That is the minimum."

"Really. If good taste doesn't restrain you, what about the thought we might be bugged?"

"I can't take that seriously, Albert. Anyway, it's too late now, isn't it? You've just been caught with your hand in the cookie jar."

Albert appeared to despair. "What an interesting image," he said. Then he admitted, "I think it probable they'd simply tap our home telephones. It's less likely they'd have the field office conducting surveillance on us here in Oregon, especially as we're spending the majority of our time working and therefore presumably behaving appropriately. Or, if they have gone that far, then we're already in a great deal of trouble."

"Your job means even more to you than mine does to me, doesn't it?" Fletch said, considering this man.

"I imagine we're equally committed."

"But then, we're committed to each other as well, aren't we? So what do you want us to do?"

"To use your own metaphor, for now we juggle."

Fletcher smiled a little, falling for the man yet again. "You're wonderful."

"And tired."

"All right, all right, I'll go." He kissed the man. "Sleep well, love."

Fletcher felt downright cheerful the next day. When his breakfast was delivered, he took the tray next door to join Albert. "Morning!" Fletch said brightly when Albert opened the door. He walked over to the table and began making room for his loaded tray of coffee and juice, bacon and eggs, toast and jam. As usual, Albert's breakfast was fruit and bottled water and the *Washington Post*.

Albert sighed and moved quickly to shift his precious reports and newspaper out of harm's way. "Good morning," he replied.

"I've got a joke for you."

"That's really not necessary."

"You're going to like this one. All right – these three bits of string walk into a bar."

"I beg your pardon?"

Fletch groaned. "It's a joke, Albert, give me a break. Okay. These three bits of string –"

"You're talking to me about animate pieces of string?" Albert asked. His tone implied that Fletcher must have lost his mind.

"Yes. Stay with me here, I promise you're going to like this. They sit in a corner booth, and one of them goes to the bartender and says, 'Three beers, please, for me and my friends.' The bartender takes one look at him and says, 'We don't serve your kind here.'" Albert was looking highly dubious, but Fletch took a breath and plunged ahead regardless. "So the bit of string goes back to his friends and explains why he doesn't have the beers, and the second piece of string says, 'We'll see about that,' and heads for the bar. He says, very assertively, 'Three beers, please, for me and my friends.' But the bartender says, 'I told your pal, we don't serve bits of string here.'"

"Is there a point to this?" Albert asked.

"The third piece of string is pretty angry about this. But he has a think about it and comes up with a solution. He ties a knot in himself, about a foot of the way down, and unravels the top bit, so it looks like hair, arranges it nicely, then heads for the bar. 'Three beers, please, for me and my friends.' The bartender is very suspicious. He looks him up and down and says, 'Aren't you a piece of string?' And the bit of string replies, 'No, I'm afraid not.'"

Dead silence for a few beats. An uninterested Albert prompted, "Yes, and then what happened?"

"That's it," Fletch said, exasperated enough to throw his hands in the air. "Don't you get it? 'No, I'm a frayed knot.'"

"Your taste obviously encompasses jokes that rely on puns."

"Even Shakespeare wrote puns."

"That's hardly a recommendation for your juvenile sense of humor."

Fletcher stared at the man, and shook his head. "Okay, be impossible." Frowning, he added, "For lovers, we sure as hell bicker a lot. But I can live with it."

"What a pity," Albert commented. The only topic they touched on during the rest of their breakfast was the current murder case.

Fletcher and Ross were allocated the task of looking into everyone who showed an interest in Sam Doherty's funeral. They still had to chase up the last of the names identified following Tony Shields' funeral; one of whom was Tony's old boss, who had apparently moved interstate. Fletch began with the secretary of the head of the company that owned the new building, an efficient, gum–chewing girl named Trish.

"Maybe I have it wrong," she said, clearly believing she couldn't have, "but I thought Mr. Garrett said he was moving to Wyoming. On the other hand, Mr. Connolly swears he said it was Maine."

"That's quite a discrepancy."

"Uh huh. Other side of the country entirely." She sighed and snapped her gum. "I have some mail for him but I can't forward it, can I? Why do you want to know, anyway?"

"I'd like to talk to him, that's all. Did you know Tony Shields? He was a construction worker on the building site."

"One of the boys who were killed. Yeah, I didn't know him personally but I read about it in the papers. The Portland Strangler, huh?"

Fletch grimaced. "Yes."

"We sent a wreath from the company, you know."

"I do know, actually."

She looked at him, perhaps surprised that the FBI would bother with that level of detail. "You want to give me the third degree? I organized it, on Mr. Connolly's orders. A big flash one to make us look good. Poor kid."

"John Garrett sent a wreath, too. But if he's in Maine or even Wyoming, how did he know about Tony dying? The case hasn't received much in the way of national coverage."

"Well, if he'd contacted me, I'd be able to forward his mail," Trish said flatly. "I guess it's just junk mail, from the look of it, but I don't like having it hanging around."

"Who would he have kept in touch with?"

The girl frowned. "I don't know. He was a nice enough guy, though I don't reckon he liked women much, if you know what I mean, but I can't think of anyone around here being such good friends with him that they'd stay in touch."

"No, I don't know what you mean about him not liking women."

Shrugging and snapping her gum, she said, "You just get a feel with some guys, you know, that they'd never even consider being interested in you. Not like they're straight but married, or they don't sleep around, or whatever, just that they wouldn't even think of it."

Fletcher put on his best smile to hide his amusement. Trish seemed a nice enough girl but she wasn't necessarily everyone's type. "I see. Well, if I could also talk to Mr. Connolly, I'd appreciate it."

"He's a busy man," Trish warned, but then she relented and returned Fletch's smile. "You are, however, in luck. I'll go check with him now."

But no matter who Fletcher spoke to, only one thing was clear: even though John Garrett had socialized with the mayor and the other local elite, and worked directly with a hundred or more people at one time or another, he had completely slipped out of these people's lives.

Trish wasn't the only one who'd received the distinct impression that Garrett was gay, so Fletch had to revise his initial private estimate of her, having assumed she'd simply been disgruntled at a rejection. Men remembered Garrett as a friendly and approachable guy, but no one knew him well; women remembered him as distant and unremarkable, though handsome. And everyone had vague and wildly different recollections of where Garrett had said he'd moved to.

"He had a whole heap of job offers," one of his colleagues from the site explained. "First he'd be talking about tendering for a job in Wyoming, then it would be a refit of an office building in New Jersey, or a contract to build a new movie lot in California. Each time it was like he'd made up his mind, then he'd see something else in the newspapers. No wonder people are confused. I don't have any idea which one he ended up taking."

Another colleague was able to clear up the mystery of the wreath. "John Garrett called me out of the blue, said he'd seen a two–line thing in the *New York Times* about some murders in Portland and he hoped it wasn't anyone he knew. I told him one of the boys was Tony Shields from the site and he said he was sorry about that, he remembered Tony well. Then he asked me to arrange the wreath for him, said he'd send the money on."

"And did he?" Fletch asked.

"Yeah, he sent me a fifty–dollar bill in the mail, which was too much, but there was no return address to send him the change. I guess I'll hang onto it, he might call me again or something."

"If he does, would you let me or Owen Ross know?"

"Sure."

"You didn't notice the postmark, did you?"

"Yeah, because there was also this note saying thanks for helping out, and he was on an airplane, and he'd be in touch, and the postmark was New York City. I remember thinking he must have a good life."

Of course the man had thrown the note and the envelope out a few days ago. Following another line, Fletch asked, "Do you think there was any specific reason that John Garrett remembered Tony Shields well?"

The man cast him a look. "I know what you're getting at, no need to beat around the bush. People figured Garrett was queer, right?"

"Maybe."

"Well, they might have figured right." The man laughed. "I've never worked a site with so many good–looking guys on it, mostly young ones, too, and he had the say on hiring. He was always friendly, kept everyone happy, was willing to get his hands dirty, liked hanging around with the guys. Don't know that he had a thing for any of them in particular, though. And he'd have been too smart to try it on. Construction sites are dangerous places, you know. Accidents happen."

Fletch raised an eyebrow. "I'll keep that in mind. Thank you for your time." And he left the man a business card, just in case, though he thought John Garrett must be long gone.

When Fletcher filled Ross in on all of this, Ross asked the big question. "So, is Garrett a suspect or not?"

"Yes, he's a suspect. All these stories make sense, and sound perfectly innocent, except for the fact that he disappeared so thoroughly. Not many people can do that. There's not enough here to push it further for now, but there's nothing to eliminate him, either."

"There doesn't seem to be any connection between John Garrett and the other victims," Ross commented.

"Very true." Fletcher sighed. "But leave him on the list." As with the other cases, the list of suspects was long, and many of the connections between the suspects and the victims were tenuous. "You know, there's something that keeps bothering me," Fletch said after a long silence. "One of the victims in Georgia, a boy named Philip Rohan – he was a construction worker, too."

"Could easily be a coincidence," Ross said. "But you're still convinced this was the same man, aren't you? Where were the other cases – Georgia and Colorado?"

"Yes, and I think Wyoming before that. There are differences but there are also too many significant similarities."

"I can't see it, if you want the truth. I can't see this guy waiting for two years, or whatever you said it was, before killing again."

"Maybe he won't be waiting so long next time, maybe he's losing control."

"Why do you say that?"

"The differences between Sam Doherty and the other three bodies. The fact that all four were from within Portland itself, whereas in the other cases the victims were from all over the state. He's not being as careful as he was." Fletcher mused over this for a while. "I have to catch this guy," he said at last, "and this time I don't think I have two years to do it in."

CHAPTER SIXTEEN
COLORADO
NOVEMBER 1984

Albert lay awake, systematically taking note of all of this though he already knew it by heart; from Fletcher's sparsely furnished though untidy bedroom, to the feel and sight and sound of him lying in Albert's arms, to the lingering smell and taste of him. The younger man was deeply asleep, exhausted by the ten days they'd spent in Oregon and by the manic way he'd survived through the couple of months before that – and also thoroughly sated by the recent hours of sex.

Fletcher had seemed surprised when Albert accepted his invitation to stay the night in Colorado on the way home to Washington, and was apparently still wondering why. Albert, however, hadn't explained. Instead, ignoring Fletcher's suggestion that they postpone sex until the morning, Albert had worked hard over the man, alternating from exquisite gentleness to spectacular energy. That was another thing that Fletcher must be surprised about – Albert was acutely aware this was the first time he'd initiated sex without Ash having asked for it in one way or another. Fletcher had soon been caught up in Albert's urgency, protests forgotten; had been so touchingly open to Albert, so trusting and eager. Albert often wondered whether Fletcher was this responsive to his other lovers but thought he – Albert – might have the edge, being both willing and able to learn this man as well as he knew himself. He noted again that his speculations had been proven correct: Fletcher, whether his focus was turned inward on sheer sensation or outward on Albert's attentions, did indeed intensify into beauty, free of the trouble brought by his obsession with the serial killer.

But this would end tomorrow morning, once Albert left for the airport. Albert had found that he wasn't above taking a few vivid memories with him and endeavoring to also leave a few unforgettable ones behind. He'd been dismayed to discover that he wanted Fletcher to regret letting him go. It seemed so petty, yet so persuasive, an idea.

As if aware of Albert's disturbed thoughts, Fletcher stirred, his sleep becoming shallower. Albert remained still, hoping the man would drift away into unconsciousness again, but his efforts were in vain. Fletcher stretched, then settled himself more comfortably back into Albert's embrace. He whispered, "Are you awake?"

There was no point in denying it. "Yes."

Silence lengthening as Fletcher's sleep–slowed thoughts apparently caught up. "Why did you do this?" Fletcher murmured at last. "Come here to Colorado with me to start with. I wasn't expecting that. And then the sex. The sex was incredible. And I thought it had been incredible before." He laughed a little, under his breath. "I feel wrung out."

Albert said, "You know why."

"No, I don't."

"You're a bright boy, Ash. Figure it out."

Fletcher sighed. "Just tell me, love, it's way too late for word games. I want to know what this was for."

Sometimes Albert found himself hating Fletcher's patience. He considered the easiest way to prompt the younger man. "You have something to tell me."

"Do I? What do you want me to tell you?"

"You know very well. You're the one playing word games."

"I'm not," Fletcher insisted. He twisted around, propped himself up on his elbows to look down at Albert, then dropped his head to rub at his temples. "I don't know what you want right now. Something's wrong, isn't it? And I'm too damned tired to work it out. So just tell me." There was a pause, while Fletcher's face remained hidden, which Albert was presumably supposed to fill. Eventually Fletcher looked across and gave him a wan smile. "Just tell me your terms, I said once. That's all you ever have to do."

Perhaps Ash hadn't planned on saying anything. Perhaps he would simply stop visiting Washington on the weekends, stop inviting Albert up to Colorado every time there was the slightest need for forensic work, stop asking for sex. Albert said, "You're going to end this."

"End this. End what?"

"*This.*"

Fletcher stared at him. "You're mad. You mean our relationship?" He seemed bemused, though it was difficult to read him precisely in the dim light. "Why would I do that?"

"Because it was an antidote to the deaths you knew were happening. And they're over now."

"No, that was a reason to begin this, but it's not a reason to end it." He leaned closer. "We have more than that, far more than that between us now, I don't understand how you can think I'd end it. I love you." He added flatly, "I tell you that all the damned time."

Albert shrugged. "I accept that you care for me as a friend."

Fletcher was angry at last. "And I just use you for sex? Is that what you think?"

"Perhaps."

"All right, all right, leaving aside how this started. I know you want to continue this –" Fletcher demanded, "Don't you?"

Albert didn't reply. Fletcher seemed to interpret that as an affirmative.

"Well, I want to continue, too. So it's settled."

On the contrary, Albert felt like telling him. *Nothing is, can be, or will be settled.*

"Sometimes you amaze me," Fletcher was saying. "You honestly thought this was goodbye? Yet you barely touched me back in Oregon. I sort of assumed that's why you made it so incredible tonight. Where do you find the strength for that sort of restraint?"

"You don't want to know."

Fletcher watched him then, for a long moment. "I have no idea what to say to you."

"Then go to sleep."

He seemed reluctant. "Well, all right." Settling back into their usual position, Fletcher said, "As long as you're still here in the morning."

"My flight doesn't leave until eleven, as I recall."

"You're perfectly aware that's not what I meant."

Albert took a deep breath. "I'll still be here in the morning."

CHAPTER SEVENTEEN
COLORADO
NOVEMBER 1984

And I just use you for sex? Is that what you think? The angry words kept echoing through Fletcher's mind. He had pushed the issue aside the previous night, selfish in his need for sleep, but it returned to haunt him in the morning.

There was every reason for his defensiveness – he knew he had taken advantage of Albert. In fact, Fletch had long been fascinated by the idea of having sex with Albert, and was now beginning to suspect that he'd simply found the one excuse to proposition the man that Albert couldn't refuse. And it was an excuse, not a reason, because sex obviously wasn't even a short term answer to the craziness and the nightmares. Fletch had, however, thought they'd quickly left that behind, that they'd moved from an inauspicious beginning to something worthwhile – but evidently that wasn't the case. Albert had answered Fletch's plea for help and assumed that once the immediate need was past, Fletch would turn away from him again.

Fletcher had been able to avoid too much self–recrimination as he showered and shaved and dressed, the routine distracting him somewhat – but now he sat at the table down one end of the long room of his apartment, with only a cup of coffee to occupy him, while Albert cooked breakfast at the other end. Fletch had his back turned to the kitchen, unwilling to look at the man too closely. He hadn't met Albert's gaze since they'd woken. Another thing to feel bad about. Instead, he stared sightlessly out of the window, ostensibly at the view of the mountains.

Eventually, of course, they'd have to talk. Fletch put it off until they'd eaten, the silence only broken by Fletch's compliments on the food. Albert was facing away as well, now that Fletch nerved himself to look at the man. They were both in their FBI suits, as they would each be returning to work that afternoon, which lent the atmosphere a formality Fletch could have done without. Once breakfast was over, Albert brewed another pot of coffee while he washed the dishes, and then came back to the table as if he agreed they should talk. Fletch suspected the man would rather do anything but.

"I'm sorry," Fletcher said at last, holding the fresh coffee in both hands as if the warmth would give him courage. "We've misunderstood each other from the first."

"I don't think so," Albert said distantly.

"All right. You knew what was going on when this started – I needed you and you agreed to help. But I'm the one who knows what's happening now – we have a relationship that we both want to continue with." Silence. It seemed Fletch would have to do all the hard work on this one. But that was fine, because he needed to do whatever it took to be fair to this man. Fletch said, "I know you love me."

"Don't rely on that," Albert replied in a harsh tone.

But Fletch did rely on it – in fact, it was the only thing he was sure of in the whole mess. Albert Sterne was capable of one fierce and all–consuming loyalty in his life and for some reason, he had chosen Fletcher Ash as its object. "Your love is very precious to me. If I could, I'd – Well, I'm still on that tightrope, you see, probably always will be, madly juggling everything I have. One of those things is your love for me. It's a mystery I want to hold onto and get to know but I can't, I have to keep it circulating with all the other things in my life. You deserve better than that, but you also understand that there's something else that has to take priority – I have to find this serial killer and bring him to justice. And I need you to help me."

"Another reason to humor me."

"You insist on seeing this in the worst possible light, don't you? Can you really think I'm sleeping with you just so you'll believe in this man when no one else does, or so I'll have your expertise available whenever I damned please?"

"Your conversation is becoming littered with swear words."

Fletcher stared at the man. "What does that have to do with anything?"

"I assumed that would be another thing you'd leave behind after you'd done all you could in Oregon."

"Offends your delicate sensibilities, does it?"

"No. I find it unimaginative but inoffensive. Swearing doesn't, however, sit easily on you."

"Don't try and change the damned subject, Albert."

The man said distantly, "I wasn't." And he took his dark glasses out of his suit pocket and slid them on. It was done with a trace of belligerence, as if daring Fletch to see it as a defensive gesture. "Your latest theory is that your pet serial killer is beginning to lose control, isn't it?"

Fletcher frowned. "Yes. Maybe. There's some indication –"

"I suggest you keep a firmer grip on your own sanity. There are unfortunate parallels between the two of you."

Predictable reactions coursed through him: shock, resentment, denial, anger. And then Fletcher forced himself to begin considering this, because it would have been a difficult thing for Albert to say and therefore merited particular attention. There was some truth to it, enough for Albert to be worried for him. And Albert had seen the beginning of their relationship as a plea for help from a man fearful for his sanity. So what did Albert see the continuation of their relationship as? A need for security that hadn't yet been answered? A need so strong for Albert's faith that Fletch would pay for it with sex?

"It would not be wise to continue this relationship," Albert was saying. "In fact, it would be extremely dangerous."

Fletcher sighed, shook his head. There was already too much going on in this conversation. Trust Albert to make him feel he couldn't possibly be across all the issues. "You're paranoid about the Bureau."

"You know they fire anyone they suspect is homosexual or who engages in homosexual activity."

"So how did you get away with it before now?" Fletch retorted – challenging on more than one front, as neither of them had ever dared the issue of Albert's previous sexual experience.

The man turned to consider him, his expression as much a mask as the dark glasses. "By keeping the encounters anonymous and minimal, and ending them some years ago."

Fletcher's curiosity, already interested in this topic, moved into overdrive. But it wasn't the time to ask for details. Instead he said, "With Hoover gone –"

"Neither policy nor practice has changed on that particular issue. Unlike you, I am directly affected by these matters because of my sexual preferences and my Jewish background, so rest assured I know exactly what I'm talking about."

"All right, I accept that. But why would they be interested in us? Why would they even look at us? We're just two flunkies doing our jobs."

"You have no idea, obviously." Albert took a breath, apparently beginning to run out of patience. "On these issues, they are interested in everyone. Anything outside certain parameters – our recent excessive telephone calls, for instance, or the fact that I stay here in your apartment rather than in the Bureau's hotel room, or your regular visits to my home in Washington – anything of that nature attracts attention. Caroline Thornton might not give it a second thought and may even be sympathetic. Jefferson is too dim to notice. However, someone will pick up on these things at some stage, and the Bureau has the means to investigate and discover the truth."

"You make it sound so oppressive."

"Good. You're seeing sense at last. Add all that to the fact that, as I've warned you before, they've always been interested in you. When they recruited you, I believe they thought you were either perfect for the job of special agent or one of their bigger mistakes. For a number of years, your performance was safely acceptable, neither unsatisfactory nor excellent, and you caused no problems, but your obsession with this serial killer is drawing their attention again."

"Damn it, that's simply me trying to do my job," Fletcher protested.

"It proves my case – if against all the odds you're right, then you're perfect. If on the other hand you're wrong, then you're a liability they don't need."

Fletch fumed over this for a moment. "Well, I'll stake my career on this man, I have no problem with that. I guess I always knew that was the bottom line. But I'm willing to risk continuing with you, as well."

"You said yourself that bringing the killer to justice has to take priority over your relationship with me. It doesn't seem logical to continue this until you've met your first priority."

"I'll risk it," was all Fletcher would say. Though he suspected Albert would not want to cope with a lover guilt–ridden over losing his job and therefore his only legal way to catch this man; Albert would not approve of the vigilante Fletcher knew he'd have to become. The last two months of craziness had been bad enough.

"I have seen evidence of covert surveillance on other employees. Staff who were fired, with no possibility of finding other work with the federal government, or transferred to the field office in Alaska, or quietly resigning for personal reasons."

Fletch let out a breath. "You've made your point. Besides," he said whimsically, "I'd love to live in Alaska."

"I wouldn't. In any case, we would be further separated and you couldn't continue your crusade."

"Albert, I understand what you're saying. I agree I need to keep this job, definitely while I'm working on this specific case, and hopefully after that until I retire. I need to catch this man and I want to remain a special agent. But I also want to continue with you and I can't decide to call the relationship off simply because of the chance I'll lose my job. I'm willing to be careful, but it's not a fear I can know in my heart. I'm not cold-blooded enough to end it with you for what feels like a remote possibility."

"You're being illogical and foolish."

"And so are you, because you won't end it with me, either."

Albert glared at him. "Don't rely on that."

"But I do rely on it, Albert. I'll be careful, but not unreasonable. If we can't make love in the privacy of our own homes, then there's a lot wrong in the world, and I don't want to play along with it."

"Now you're being willfully blind to the reality of the situation. You know the sort of technology they have access to, you've no doubt used it yourself. There is no longer such a thing as the privacy of our own homes."

"We've been staying with each other for well over a year now and in all that time before we became lovers, you never once worried about this. What's different now?"

"We now have something to hide."

"But they don't know that! Maybe they've already bugged us, seen there was nothing to worry about, and moved on. Maybe they accept that two of their more unusual employees, two outsiders like us, can be *friends*."

"They would know there's something to hide just by looking at your phone records over the past eleven weeks."

"The calls can be explained by my paranoia about the serial killer."

"You're ambitious, remember?"

"Yes – to be a special agent, to handle the important cases, to do some good in the world. And to spend some quality time with you."

Albert took a moment to swallow something back. "Thank you so much for tacking that on the end," he said eventually, too cold for the sarcasm to hurt.

"Look, you're right about the level of technology they can use – we're not safe sitting here talking, we wouldn't be safe talking even moving around outside. So as long as we try to avoid drawing their attention, there's little else to do except live every moment of our lives as if the Director of the FBI was standing right beside us. And I'm not prepared to do that and I don't think you are, either." There was a silence, which seemed to indicate Albert had run out of arguments. "Can I visit next weekend?" Fletch asked.

"No," Albert said heavily, "you can't. I will need to catch up with a great deal of work. And I believe we should limit our time together."

"Reasonable limits," Fletch countered. "The weekend after?"

Albert seemed defeated, utterly weary. "Is this so easy for you?" he asked in a quiet tone of voice Fletcher had never heard before. But, without waiting for an answer, he agreed, "The following weekend."

They sat in silence for a while, not looking at each other. "I'm sorry," Fletch said again. "For all of this."

"Are you? Do you think I'd change it if I could?"

"Actually, I think you would," Fletch said as flatly as he felt. "You're obstinate enough." He stood, walked behind Albert, put his arms around him. The embrace was not welcome. "But, since you can't, I'll continue to take advantage."

"That's supposed to be amusing, is it?"

"Not really." They were both too raw, even for this mild bickering. Fletch eased around, sat in the man's lap, as insistent as a child. Albert, with a great show of reluctance, lifted his arms to encircle Fletch's waist. They held on, faces hidden from each other. "I do love you. More than as a friend."

"You expect too much."

"No more than you're capable of."

"Far more," Albert corrected him.

"Then I'll suffer for it." Fletch needed to offer this man something, but neither of them seemed to want to make promises or plans beyond the fact they would be lovers at least until the weekend after next. A confidence had usually sufficed in the past, or a declaration of vulnerability that Albert could choose whether to be rude about. "I was thinking about the sex," Fletcher said.

"No."

"I don't mean now." Fletch tried for a chuckle. "You expect far too much of me, if you think I'd be capable after last night. It's just that I had this idea for a bit of fun and figured there's no one better qualified to play with."

"I'm sure you could find someone who's more willing."

"You're perfect for it," Fletch assured him, and he whispered the details in Albert's ear. This way, there might be no promises, but there would at least be short term plans made, and Albert would be sure Fletch was interested. As a strategy, it would do. Fletch lifted his head. Their faces were maybe six inches apart.

Albert looked at him, unfazed behind his dark glasses, expression betraying nothing. "And what would be the point of the exercise?"

Fletch laughed at that. Surely it was self-evident. "Come on," he teased, "wouldn't you like to tie me up and have your wicked way with me?"

"For some weeks now, I have had my way with you every time we've been in the same town, Ash, and I haven't had to capture you yet. Our conversation had led me to believe you were willing to continue on the same basis."

"Oh, don't be so damned obtuse."

"Isn't the point more that I tie you up and do all the things that I know *you* enjoy?"

"I guess so," Fletch said grudgingly.

"I have no problem with you choosing to take a fairly passive role in sex but it does mean that I shoulder most of the associated responsibility. In fact, it seems as if I would be more at your beck and call than ever."

"All right, all right. Forget it." So this hadn't been such a great idea. It was more than time to call it quits for the day – they had gone through too much already. He dropped his head onto Albert's shoulder, and said, "You really know how to take me to pieces, don't you?"

"It's all part of the service," Albert said.

"What – embarrassing me?"

"Perhaps *mortifying* is more accurate in this context."

Fletcher frowned. The dry humor rang true, but something about the wording didn't. "Albert –"

"It appears that you've progressed from empathizing with your pet murderer, to identifying with his victims."

Albert was rarely that nasty to him. "How can you damned well say that?" Fletch asked, stung despite himself. "I tell you this nice little fantasy of mine and you ruin it."

"What did you expect?"

"I didn't expect to – Now, if I ever find someone to play that with, I'll be thinking of this killer instead. Fear isn't an aphrodisiac; not your own fear."

"But you would expect to feel a *soupçon* of fear while playing the game, wouldn't you? Just so much, and no more, because you trust the person you're playing it with."

"Leave it alone, Albert. Forget it."

"If you trust him –"

Fletch pushed away from the man, put some distance between them. "Leave it alone, damn you."

Albert stood as well. "Perhaps I'll phone for a taxi to take me to the airport."

"That won't be necessary," Fletcher snapped.

They were silent throughout the drive and didn't even speak at the airport. Albert did, however, allow Fletch to shake his hand in farewell.

CHAPTER EIGHTEEN
NEW ORLEANS
DECEMBER 1984

John Garrett strolled down the sidewalk, hands in the pockets of his Saints jacket, newspapers under one arm. He knew the walk by instinct now, knew where to step to avoid the haphazard gutters and the bags of garbage, the abrupt bumps and depressions caused by tree roots and the high water table. While the summer weather lasted, he'd learned where to dodge the drips from air conditioning units, too, but the oppressive humidity had finally broken three weeks ago. There had been no fall: this city had only two seasons. Though today was officially the third day of winter, the bitterly cold weather had immediately followed the end of the heat. And Garrett, for one, welcomed it.

This city he found himself in was not only hot, it was flatter than a pancake and five feet below sea level – all of which seemed bizarre to a man used to cool climates and mountains. Who on earth had the idea to build a city in this swampland, fed by the omnipotent river and encroached on by the hungry ocean? There must have been desperate need for a trading port or defense of the river mouth, or some such thing.

Strolling, Garrett took it slow and easy, which tended to be the New Orleans pace at this time of day. No one had hurried in the heat and no one sped up now winter had arrived. The walk to buy the newspapers, with the humidity a physical presence bearing down on him even this early, had been all the exercise a man of Garrett's build had needed. In fact, he wondered if he'd even survive the height of summer in this place.

He reached the cafe where he regularly took breakfast and sat in his usual seat. They brought him coffee and a pastry, and he opened up the first paper. He had to order it in from Oregon, which was irritatingly obvious, so he used the name Smith and walked a half mile out of his way to a newsstand that specialized in papers and magazines from across the States and from Canada and overseas. He could buy the *Weekend Australian* off the rack, for God's sake, but he had to have a special standing order for the Oregon paper.

But he was prepared to do all that, and take the risk, in order to follow his case. Annoying, that three murders were barely enough to make the national papers and the television news. Murder was just background noise these days. What would he have to do, hit double digits within one state to get decent press coverage? But that was part of the whole idea – keep it within limits, keep it local, don't give the feds an excuse to sniff around. Acceptable risks, minimal danger, just slide past the trouble with an irresistible smile. One day, too far in the future for him to picture clearly, Garrett would let everyone know what he'd achieved, and how many deaths, how many unsolved murders could be attributed to his charm and wits. Perhaps a posthumous confession of some sort, or he'd write a best seller once he was too old for them to send him to jail.

There was nothing in the paper today, so no progress had been made. Not that the police didn't lie to reporters, either directly or by omission, in misguided attempts to manipulate the case. But Oregon had been quiet for over ten days now, and there was no sign of the FBI renewing its early, low key interest – though there had been mention of Bureau help from interstate. Garrett hoped that had simply been forensics or some other technical assistance, but whatever it was, nothing seemed to have come of it.

He was beginning to breathe easier at last. For too long a while, Garrett had feared he'd blundered, and badly. Finding a fresh body and old blood stains in the cellar, neither of which he could explain. Giving in to the temptation of taking Tony from the construction site. None of that had been sensible. But he'd disposed of the stranger's body out in the forest, in such a way that the police suspected there was a second murderer; he'd bricked over the entrance to the cellar, laminating the end of the cupboard so smoothly no one would guess it had ever been a door; and he'd left Tony until last, once the construction job was over, ambushing the boy on his way out for the evening, seducing the unseducable. Sure, Garrett had been clever – but after the fact rather than before. It worried him, that there might be something else, some forgotten detail, that he hadn't dealt with.

Nothing in the paper, nothing for his scrapbook. He would toss the thing into one of the trash cans on the walk to work – a different one each day, which was as anonymous a method of disposal as he bothered with.

He reached for the local *Times–Picayune*, mouth already quirking into a smile. They took crime seriously in New Orleans and with good reason – the city gave Washington DC competition in the race for the highest murder rate each year. It had amused Garrett to find the local paper kept a running tally. There it was: a box on the front page headed *MORE VIOLENT DEATHS*, and *327* underneath in large black numerals, which meant another five deaths since yesterday. So melodramatic! Garrett scanned the surrounding article. The latest murders had been shootings, three deaths in one incident, with a mugging that had gone too far providing the only variety. Garrett thought happily of the day when the paper's murder toll would increase, with far more macabre details than this commonplace violence, and Garrett alone would know who had been responsible. *Fall 1986*, he promised them. *If you find the bodies quickly enough, I might even beat the Christmas rush.*

They took their football seriously here, too. Garrett turned to the sports pages. On his arrival, Garrett had immediately bought the camouflage of a New Orleans Saints jacket. It was classy, in black and gold, and he was better pleased with it than most he'd worn. He could not, however, say the same for the team itself, who were so bad and lost so often, it was almost funny. This time, his new loyalty was definitely nothing more than convenience.

Garrett stood, dropped the correct money plus a two dollar tip by his cup and walked out. He hadn't said a word to anyone in the cafe for weeks now – he was just a regular, always turned up at the same time Monday to Saturday, always had coffee with cream and one refill and a pastry, always tipped generously. Besides which the cafe only ever had female staff for some god–forsaken reason, and Garrett generally ignored anyone of that gender and mostly they ignored him. Garrett enjoyed making influential friends in the right places, took pleasure in supervising young men and developing camaraderie in the workplace – like in the hardware store he was managing now – but there were plenty of situations he liked to slip quietly through. He was sensible, he had it all figured. Though these days anytime there was a young man around who met his tastes, Garrett found it hard to resist flirting a little, trying his luck.

These weeks in New Orleans, he reflected as he resumed his stroll down the sidewalk, had been happy ones from that point of view at least – there were lovely young men in abundance here, in all shapes and sizes and colors. But, despite that, he hadn't yet taken up any of the multitude of opportunities. He'd been too worried over Oregon, his faith in himself too shaken.

Garrett always followed his cases. He loved getting away with this, misleading the police, leaving the state before they'd even found the bodies let alone cast their investigative net. At home, he kept all the newspaper clippings, the missing person notices, the funeral announcements, along with the boys' jewelry and wallets. In his imagination, he relived those deaths again and again as he held the silver chains and crucifix earrings in his hands, as he gazed at the photos reproduced in the newspapers' grainy black and white, as he had rough and tumble sex with some unsuspecting young man.

He walked into the hardware store with a smile on his face.

"Hey … you got lucky last night, Mr. Garrett?" Kenny murmured through a grin, in that charmingly insinuating manner of his.

"No, just day dreaming," Garrett replied. As he headed for the office, Garrett looked back to cock an eyebrow at his employee. At twenty–seven, Kenny was older than Garrett usually liked them, but he appreciated the man's attitude. It was sweet to contemplate the lips that were so full it seemed they'd already swollen from savage biting kisses; it was sweet to wonder whether the dark skin would show bruises.

But taking Kenny would not be sensible. Tony had been enough of a risk, one worker amongst a hundred. Here, Garrett supervised three full time staff, and another three casuals. The odds were definitely against him.

Though who knew what he'd be doing by fall 1986? Garrett had taken on this job because he'd arrived in the craziness of the Big Easy, unusually restless, unable to settle, unsure of what he wanted to do. And the contracted manager of this place suffered a heart attack and needed eight to ten weeks off work. Available in the right place at the right time, Garrett was offered generous payment by a desperate and grateful owner. It was fun, in many ways, to be carrying something this simple, and it filled in the time until he figured out exactly what he wanted to do. Meanwhile, the owner was a rich businessman, someone useful to know, to be able to call on for favors. No matter how curiously reluctant Garrett felt, he had to start the process of fitting in, of being respectable. He did not mean to end up on a list of suspects as an itinerant store manager, with a black shop assistant his only friend.

But Garrett grinned. He'd kept the local paper so he could begin looking for a long term contract or a business for sale. This would work out. The Oregon police had missed him, just as law enforcement had missed him every time before. Garrett was too clever for them. Life was good.

"A dollar for a cup of coffee, mister," a clear voice said, as if no reasonable man could refuse such a request.

After a couple more paces, the tone registered with Garrett and he came to a halt, turned back to the group of street kids sitting on the sidewalk. He wasn't disappointed in what he saw.

"My name is Zac, and I'm a caffeine addict," the guy confessed, straight–faced.

Garrett laughed and Zac's companions all quietly chimed in, playing along. He asked, "That's more urgent than your addiction to food, is it?"

"Yeah, mister. Wouldn't miss a dollar or five, would you?"

"Five? What's that – inflation?"

"No – a refill for half price and tax and a gratuity." The guy finally lost his poker face and smiled, then stood as if too polite to continue the conversation on such an unequal basis.

Garrett definitely liked what he saw. There were five kids, three of them boys, all in their mid to late teens, all in torn black and ragged denim, just the wrong side of dirty. Their hair provided as much variety in cut and color as you could get within the range of punk styles. The guy talking to him, perhaps the oldest of the lot, was handsome despite all that; his features were regular, his skin good and his expression unguarded. As for his hair, it was bright red with no attempt to look natural, generous curls on top and tumbling down the back, and closely shorn over each temple. The other four kids sat there, lined up against an empty ruined shop, huddled against the cold, watching warily. Garrett was used to being accosted by strays of all age groups on his walk home from work. Most of the time he ignored them but if they met certain criteria ...

"You're a man of style," the guy was saying easily, either comfortable with or oblivious to Garrett's silent appraisal. "Surely you understand these things."

"What – that coffee and hair dye are higher priorities than food?"

Zac shrugged, offered a smile. "I try for the lot. Want to help me reach the third?"

"Sure. Walk home with me. Bed for the night, whatever food you can find in the fridge, we'll have some pizza delivered, and as much coffee as you can drink."

"I only asked for a dollar," the kid said in mild, unthinking protest as if he had some residual scruples.

"Did I leave that out? Bed, food, pizza, coffee, money for you and your friends."

"In return for what?" Forget scruples – he was suspicious now.

Laughing again, Garrett didn't even bother looking around for people who shouldn't overhear. "Sex, of course. Nothing you can't handle."

Zac looked down at the other kids, and they stared back at him, waiting for his reaction.

Garrett couldn't read their faces, didn't know whether they were supportive or not. He said, "Come on – your friends will think you're crazy if you turn down easy money. I'll walk away and they'll call you ten kinds of fool."

The guy turned back to him. "I have my pride, mister."

Putting on his most irresistible smile, Garrett promised, "You're going to enjoy every minute of it. Trust me on that. We won't do anything you don't want to." When Zac still didn't agree, Garrett pulled his wallet out, offered a fifty–dollar bill. "Down payment."

Zac reached for it, pure instinctive need, wavered; then made the decision and took it. "All right." He cast a look at his young friends, worried but defiant, and stepped away.

"I'll bring him back tomorrow morning," Garrett reassured the kids, who remained blank and wary. One of the girls was standing, as if unsure whether to interfere. Garrett smiled again before she could say anything, and turned to walk up the street beside the guy, his heart singing. He still had it: the charm and the nerve; the ability to entrance and entrap. He had it in spades.

◆

Having taken exactly what he wanted from the young man, Garrett felt expansively magnanimous. He could afford to be generous now. In fact, he liked to be.

It was dawn, and neither of them had slept. Garrett ran a warm bath, eased the guy into it and soaped him up. He'd only broken the skin in two places, which was quite good considering. The guy's real hurt was from being fucked raw. And despite all they'd been through, Zac let Garrett kneel here by the bath, so drained he simply accepted the thorough and careful washing, apparently too dazed to consider how easy it would be for Garrett to push him below the surface, hold him down while he tried to breathe water.

But what would be the point? Sure it would be interesting to watch, good to feel the guy struggling under his palms, wonderful to dig his fingers in as panic widened Zac's eyes. Garrett's hands itched, and he even took hold of the boy's shoulders.

No: it was more important right now to retain the control. He needed the control, to savor the power rather than let it devour him.

Difficult, once he'd had such a nice idea, to let it go.

"Stand up," he said, gruff. The boy did so, weary and beaten beyond protest. Garrett pulled the plug, fetched a towel and dried the kid off. And then he took a lovely long time examining the bruises that were already beginning to show, tending to the two patches of roughened, bloodied skin.

By the time he'd done, the guy had regained a little awareness, and was looking at him as if this was the weirdest experience of the whole night. Garrett grinned at him, letting his eyes sparkle. "Coffee before you go? I guess you'll want to skip breakfast."

Zac nodded, dumb. When Garrett let him be, the guy struggled awkwardly into his clothes, then trailed after him into the kitchen and obediently swallowed the two cups of coffee Garrett poured for him, though he seemed to have a hard time stomaching it.

The streets were just beginning to come alive when Garrett drove Zac to the old shopfront where he'd found him. There was no sign of the other kids amongst the few passers-by. "Where are your friends?"

It took a moment for the boy to speak his first words through swollen lips. "Here's fine."

"No, I want to make sure you're all right. Where do they hang out?"

The kid, slumped in the passenger seat, turned further to look out the side window so that Garrett couldn't see his face.

"You don't have to worry about me coming to find you again, Zac," Garrett said. "I had what I wanted. Now it's over and I'll take you to your friends. They can look after you."

"Here's fine," the guy repeated. And he added a dull, "Thank you."

"Don't be a fool." Reason touched with amused impatience. "Just tell me where they are."

The boy sighed, surrendering the last of his streetwise instincts to a more persuasive force. Garrett grinned, loving this thorough defeat. Turning stiffly to the front again, Zac let his head fall back, eyes closed. "Next left," he whispered, "middle of the block, there's an old wooden house."

Garrett quickly found the ramshackle place down a narrow street little better than an alley, then helped the guy out of the car. The girl came out, the one who'd wanted to interfere, took one look at Zac and glared at Garrett.

"He's going to be fine," Garrett said placatingly, his hands refusing to let the guy go. "Don't make this into something it's not."

"Zac?" she asked. "What's he done to you?"

The guy shook his head, docile in Garrett's grasp.

"Just let him get some sleep today, he'll be fine," Garrett continued.

"Will you?" she asked Zac. He nodded, and the girl turned, angry. "There are laws against this, mister."

"Oh come on, there's no need to start all that. I gave the kid the best meal he's had in months last night, gave him a bath this morning. He's not really hurt."

"Not really hurt?" she repeated, incredulous. "Look at him!"

The other kids were there now, including two Garrett hadn't seen yesterday, listening from the doorway, hovering in consternation.

Zac whispered, "It's okay, Patrice."

"Yeah, it's okay," Garrett said, finally handing him over to the girl's support. He reached for his wallet, slipped a fifty–dollar bill into the guy's hip pocket, pressed another into the girl's hand, held one more out to the nearest kid, who reluctantly drew forward to take it. "It's okay," Garrett said again in his most reassuring voice.

"It's not okay," the girl said, though her anger had been disarmed and resentment seemed to prevail. Perhaps she wished she could afford to not accept the money. "It's assault, it's … rape."

The kid winced at the word and she took him deep into an embrace.

"You don't want to get into all that. The kid will be fine, no real harm done. And if you're talking law, then Zac consented to have sex with me, as you witnessed yesterday – and sex between men is illegal down here, so your friend will be in as much trouble as me. And it's the word of a street kid against a man with friends and money in all the right places. Just let him sleep today and be sensible about this."

The girl was still glaring at him, but she was almost beat. Garrett knew his arguments were mostly a bluff but it all rang true in her ears.

"Trust me. You don't want to see me again," Garrett said. He reached to grasp the kid's elbow, dug his fingers in. "Tell her."

"We don't want to see him again," Zac said quickly, weakly.

"Good. And you won't. It's over. Just calm down and let it go." And, after she'd finally nodded, Garrett pushed another fifty dollars into the kid's pocket, more than willing to pay for his pleasures, to grease his way through potential difficulty.

Taking the young man had been good, Garrett reflected, unable to stop himself grinning at the memories: Zac crawling away from him, blindly trying to get free; clawing at the sheets until he ripped them, hissing and growling like a wild thing with its leg caught in a trap. Garrett laughed. He'd had a great time and he'd gotten away with it yet again – stopped himself from killing the kid, ensured the whole thing would remain a secret, bribed Zac's friends so they felt like guilty accomplices. He laughed and declared, "That was great, kid," and he took Zac's head in both hands, kissed the unhappy lips, bit at them, bruising them one last time.

There was someone walking past the alley mouth but Garrett didn't care. He loved the disgust on the kids' faces, Zac looking ill with it all.

He waved a farewell, climbed into the car and drove to work, picking up the newspapers on the way.

"Good morning, Mr. Garrett," Kenny murmured in that soft full voice of his.

"Morning, Kenny." Garrett paused, waited expectantly. "Today of all days you're not going to ask me?"

The young man eased into a wide smile. "You got lucky last night, sir?"

"Yes, Kenny, I damn well did." And he couldn't stop grinning about it. So many weeks since the deaths in Oregon, and no sex in the meantime. He'd almost been too worried to even think about it much. He'd spent hours sitting in his living room, hands full of jewelry from dead boys, clutching at it in a state of mild panic. Ridiculous way to live his life. He'd just have to be more careful from now on, that was all. He'd lost the threads of it, let a few stitches slip. There were some things he still wasn't clear on, like the who and when and how of the blood and the body in the cellar, but he'd gotten away with it all, and it was time now to live again.

He spread the Oregon paper across his desk, skimmed the front page. And there, with headlines blaring, was an article about the murder of a school boy. His body had been found dumped in the river, he'd been sexually molested and beaten to death about six weeks ago. The police stated they felt there was no connection to the four bodies found early last month, though the previous case or cases remained unsolved. This new victim had been identified as Jack Brooks.

Garrett frowned. Surely he'd known a Jack Brooks, the kid had lived nearby, delivered the papers on his bike each morning. Could it have been the same boy? A serious kid, only about thirteen years old, poor thing; studious with dark hair and wire–rimmed glasses, and a smile that needed coaxing. Who would have killed him? Six weeks ago Garrett had just arrived in Louisiana, after a meandering trip through the States.

The frown deepened. Today was the fourth day of winter, and he'd already been in Louisiana for six weeks? That couldn't be possible. He'd killed the first boy during the early days of fall, during the second game of the football season. The second one should have been four weeks after that, and the third one after another four weeks, which left most of November – yet he'd been here since late in October.

Panic gnawing his stomach, confusion growing. All right, work it backwards and see if a different answer could be reached. He'd been sensible enough to leave Tony until a week after the construction job finished, but he'd formally handed the keys over on September twenty–

seventh. And Tony had definitely been the third death, which meant he'd killed all three boys within a matter of four or five weeks, instead of spacing them over eight, which was one of his rules, and he hadn't even realized he'd broken it until now.

He sat at the desk, breathing hard, eyes wide and unseeing. What the hell was going on in his head? What other rules had he broken, what blunders had he made? Yes, the longer his crimes went unsolved, the less and less likely it became that he'd ever be caught – but what if he'd left evidence behind somewhere, in the house, at the gravesites? It might only be a matter of time before they pieced it together. What if he hadn't been clever enough about the wreath for Tony? What if – God, he'd been too scared to have sex for all these weeks and then he hit on this smart guy with an even smarter friend, and he didn't bother denying anything to them. That Patrice bitch might simmer over this, no matter that his cocksure bluffing and his money had silenced her at the time. And he hadn't even started setting himself up as the respectable citizen beyond reproach and above suspicion. He was getting lazy, crazy …

God save him.

Garrett sat at his desk, drenched with sweat despite the cold, gripping the edge of the desk as if it were his sanity.

"You want lunch, Mr. Garrett?"

He'd lost his confidence, he'd lost the shit–eating attitude that ensured nothing could go wrong because he was functioning at two–hundred percent, thirty hours a day, and he had every play and every move figured out all the way to the Super Bowl.

"You want me to fetch you some lunch, Mr. Garrett?"

Kenny. Midday. And he'd spent the morning sitting here doing nothing but sweat, the front page of the Oregon newspaper still spread before him. "I'm not hungry," he managed to say through a dry throat.

The man wandered back over to the door. "Must have had a good time last night, some good times," he murmured, slyly amused.

"Get out of here, Kenny," Garrett said, with a hint of the banter the man was used to.

"Yes, sir." And he left, shutting the office door behind him.

He'd lost his confidence. Maybe he should do it, get away with murder once more, satisfy the hunger, feel the return of the control. Just to prove to himself he still could.

Maybe he'd be feeling better now if he'd taken it all the way with Zac. But the kid's friends would be able to identify the man Zac had left with, so killing him would have been a mistake.

Garrett dropped his head to his hands, growled his frustration and confusion. Everything had been so clear, so obvious before Oregon. But he'd lost the clarity and the ability to plan somewhere along the way, and didn't even know when. No telling what he'd done, what he might do. What he might risk.

The mistakes had begun so long ago. Even back in Georgia, for God's sake. Going through with his plans for Philip despite the fact the kid had brought his girlfriend along. Foolish.

Then, moving to Oregon, he'd chosen a house with a cellar, thinking it an ideal way to avoid surrounding suburbia hearing bumps and screams in the night. In reality, the cellar was cold and damp and hardly conducive to perfect satisfaction. After all, it would be a trifle undignified to orchestrate a boy's death while wearing socks to keep his feet warm. Ridiculous.

But then, of course, he must have suffered the cold cellar at least once, if not twice.

To start with, a boy had lost his blood down there some months before. What had the strong pulse of blood spattering his own naked skin felt like? Garrett shook his head – he still had no memory of it, and his imaginings rang false. And where was the body? Had it already been found and written off as unsolved, or was it lying in wait, ready to tell Garrett's secrets? Who the hell had it been?

And lying amidst the old blood stains had been a fresh body, a boy he seemed to recognize, who'd only died within the previous couple of days. A complete puzzle – Garrett hadn't even been able to see how the boy had died. The blood wasn't his, because there were no corresponding injuries and, as far as Garrett could tell, no blood loss. But there was some vague familiarity, something to do with a high school day dream, lying kissing on the sofa – which made no sense at all. He hadn't even begun to suspect he was queer back in school.

Two troubling mysteries. Dangerous.

His plans for the three deaths that really counted had seemed full of finesse. In the event, ligature strangulation seemed tame. He'd thought to control the boys by slow deprivation of oxygen, but all he'd ended up with were breathing corpses. He'd revived the first one, used the scarf to gag him instead until he was ready to let the kid die, and he'd followed the same pattern, doggedly, with little joy. Stupid and wasteful.

Except for Tony – he'd been a lively enough victim. So damned good, yet so crazy to have preyed on someone that close to him. It had been all Garrett had ever wanted, this strong young man completely his, and fighting the fact every inch of the way. Even as he'd died, Tony's eyes had held his, cursing him. Glorious. But insanely misjudged.

So he moved to this passionate, murderous city and lived in fear, continuing to break his rules, only compounding his mistakes.

All right – what to do next? How to get this back on track, how to reach the Super Bowl from this defensive position, so low on the ladder? He couldn't afford to lose one more game, one more point.

Garrett stood, began pacing the office, five steps from wall to wall, forcing himself to think.

But no matter how he considered the outcomes, weighed the odds, he couldn't work out whether it would be sensible, or if it would be yet another mindless error, to go back to that alley tonight and charm Zac and Patrice into talking to him alone, and then kill them.

CHAPTER NINETEEN
COLORADO
JANUARY 1985

Fletcher Ash was beginning to feel himself grow old and tired and grim, which wasn't fair: he was only thirty–two, an age he'd anticipated heralding the prime of his life. Until lately, he'd been an energetic and optimistic person. If he'd lost those qualities, Fletcher asked himself, then why couldn't he have also lost the darker qualities, like the vulnerability and the doubt? Why couldn't he lose the drive and the empathy, so he simply wouldn't care where he was right now?

He knew what it was – this case was ageing him, this man who Albert called his pet serial killer was taking Fletcher's youth along with the lives of young men across the country.

It was quiet in his apartment, a quiet that previously had seemed like peace but now resembled isolation. Reaching to turn out the lamp on the coffee table, Fletcher added darkness to the quiet, then sat back in his comfortably sagging armchair and gazed through the window to where he knew the mountains to be. It was too overcast a night to be able to see them, though he knew the horizon's silhouette so well he almost convinced himself he could pick it out.

That was a fairly inefficient distraction from the unmarked folder lying at his feet. Guiltily, he'd collected extra photos of all the killer's victims they could identify, the school photos and the family snaps; and every now and then he leafed through them. A shot of Drew Harmer dreaming of Prince Charming, taken by his friend, Scott. Mitch Brown, standing slightly apart from his family with his arms crossed, the poet who could have been merely trouble. Philip Rohan and Stacey Dixon, a badly focused shot of them embracing, as if the photographer had seized the chance too quickly. Sam Doherty, looking heartbreakingly young, freshly scrubbed but with his shirt collar askew, in the latest shot from school. Fletch had never let Caroline or Albert know of this collection, only looking through it late at night, alone and unsure.

What he really should be doing was working on the next name on his list of suspects. It was difficult, tracking down and checking out suspects for a crime that had happened over four years ago, but Fletcher didn't have any jurisdiction in the Georgia or Oregon cases. At least Caroline had let him unofficially keep the case open on the three bodies he'd found here in Colorado, and he had access to the full range of information they'd collected at the time. That was what he should be doing, not sitting here staring at photos of men he'd only known as corpses.

These were attractive boys, in body and heart. Their family and friends, anyone who knew them well, described the young men as full of life, brimming with emotion, young and happy. That only added to the simple tragedy of it because the murderer inevitably chose victims who had a future; ones with talents, plans, promise. So, Fletcher wondered, could his own guilt be partly due to the suspicion that he himself found these boys attractive in the same ways that the killer did? That he would, for instance, find the unsubtle strength of Tony Shields sensually stimulating?

Fletch grimaced and continued to interrogate himself. Could his discomfort be a result of him identifying with some of the boys because, for example, he felt Mitch had the same potential as Fletcher himself did for either creativity or destruction? Or was his guilt simpler than that? Was it because eight young people from Georgia and Oregon would not be dead if only Fletcher had done better here in Colorado?

He sighed, acknowledging to himself there must be something of all three of these questions in the truth and probably more, too.

It should help that the man he was chasing had consistent, if broad, tastes. And that Fletcher shared those tastes to some extent, though he didn't want to empathize with this murderer, even in his choice of victim, let alone feel the old understanding of what the man did to these boys.

Too often when he was this tired and the files were spread before him with Albert's clinical descriptions of the results of brutal rape, augmented with glossy black and white photos of torture and decay – too often Fletcher's imagination ran away with him and built up the story of how all this happened, what it felt like to have a young man's life in your hands, to choose whether to inflict pain and fear or healing and joy. The killer chose pain and fear every time. Or did he? It was only those results that the police discovered, after all, and the man was controlled enough to wait two years before killing again. What did he do in the meantime?

Fletcher sighed and gazed around his apartment, not wanting to let his imagination run wild again. As usual, the only thing that held any hope of distracting him was the telephone.

Albert never exactly welcomed Fletcher's calls but the younger man had no other straws to clutch at. And Albert would be there for him whenever Fletcher asked. It helped. Somehow, Albert even at his dourest and most disparaging inevitably cheered Fletch up.

It was eleven o'clock. Fletcher dialed Albert's home phone number.

"Sterne," was the blunt greeting after only two rings.

Fletcher laughed under his breath. "You know it's me. You could just say *Hello* or *Albert* or something."

Silence.

"Caroline's got me busy on this money laundering case," Fletch reported. "Not very exciting. Not exactly why I joined the FBI."

"The Bureau has traditionally focused on property crime."

"Yeah, I'd just prefer to deal with violent crime. And I'm –"

"Obsessed with your pet serial killer."

"Must you call him that?" Fletch protested, but mildly because he had little hope of changing much about Albert.

"You should have studied psychology and related sciences. Perhaps the Behavioral Science Unit would have offered you placement."

"But even they think this man exists only in my imagination, they're worse than the bureaucrats at HQ. So if I worked with them, I probably wouldn't have seen the connections, either."

Another silence stretched, which was something Fletch liked about Albert – he was one of the few people Fletch knew who didn't mind lengthy pauses in a conversation, or hours spent together without a word exchanged. In fact, he was the only person other than Peter Ash who remained completely comfortable in those situations. Unlike Peter, though, Albert probably preferred them.

"I decided about that boy in Oregon," Fletcher eventually said.

"The Brooks murder. What did you decide?"

"It wasn't our man. It doesn't feel right. The victim was too young, there was no sexual penetration –"

Albert said, "There wasn't with Sam Doherty, either."

"But Sam's method of disposal was the obvious link there, the forest burial. Brooks had bite marks – our man hasn't left bite marks before. And the only body he's thrown in a river was Stacey Dixon, and she's the exception that proves the rule."

"All right."

"You agree?"

"Yes."

Fletch almost chuckled. "I guess I can still rely on you challenging me if you don't. Agree with me, that is." The abortive chuckle turned into a yawn. "I'd better go. Wish me a good night's sleep, no nightmares. I'm a desperate man."

"Indeed," Albert said flatly.

Fletch did chuckle then, happy for that moment. His imagination would run wild with innuendo and Albert always knew it – and disapproved of it, on the surface at least. But Fletch suspected that Albert enjoyed the innuendo, too, despite the impatience with which he greeted it. Albert, who was forever trying to keep the strength of his sensuality a secret, perhaps even from himself.

"Good night," Fletch said on that provocative thought, rather than risk getting himself in trouble with the man, and they both hung up.

The unmarked folder was sitting there at his feet. Fletch leaned forward, hand straying, wanting to flip through the photographs one last time. But there was no excuse for it – there was no more to learn from the appearance of the victims, they surely held no more clues. It would merely be self–indulgence.

Too tired to halt the speculation, Fletch wondered whether he would have found the young men attractive if Albert hadn't re–awakened his curiosity about sex with people of his own gender.

It was an impossible question to answer. Fletcher sighed again, and forced himself to head for the bedroom.

TRUTHS
WASHINGTON DC
JANUARY 1985

Fletch stood on the sidewalk with his briefcase and his overnight bag, quiet amid the airport's Friday night bustle, ignoring the importunate taxi drivers. It wasn't like Albert to be late to collect him, but Fletch knew Albert wouldn't have forgotten, and assumed that something unavoidable had happened, so was content to wait. No one working in the FBI could call their time or priorities their own. It was cold now that the sun had set, but that had never bothered Fletcher much and Denver had been far colder. He hunched into his coat, hands stuffed into his pockets, watched his breath fog, and reminded himself for the hundredth time that he should either get the coat's lining fixed before it fell out completely or buy a new coat for next winter.

This was the third weekend he and Albert had spent together in the seven weeks since the case in Oregon, since that ghastly discussion in Colorado resulting from Albert's assumption that Fletch wanted to break off their affair – and, when Fletch hadn't, Albert had done his level best to make Fletch realize it would be the only reasonable thing to do. Despite which, they had continued to be lovers. It was the only thing in his life Fletch was even remotely happy about right now.

Albert had his way on one thing, though – the majority of their time outside normal work demands had been devoted to the murder case rather than their relationship. Fletcher was only permitted the luxury of flying to Washington if there was some lead they could usefully pursue together, or Fletcher needed something only headquarters could provide. Priorities, damned priorities. When Caroline had said the word to him that morning Fletch had laughed harshly, startling her.

To be honest, though, the thing he resented most was that he couldn't even argue with Albert about this. The man was right and yet, of course, it made so many things wrong. Nevertheless, during their time together – minimal though it was – they had found some peace and some small ease of companionship.

It wasn't as if Fletcher couldn't afford to visit Albert more frequently. Fletch had always considered a special agent's salary to be rather generous, and he'd always lived well within his means because there was rarely anything or anyone for him to spend money on. The balance every month accumulated in his savings account, and his bank manager would periodically suggest he invest it, but Fletch couldn't be bothered. He liked to live simply, and a single bank account he could ignore, rather than varied investments he would have to manage, seemed easiest to him.

He was in the unusual situation of having been continuously posted to Colorado since the beginning of his career. Most special agents, especially in their early years, were transferred around the field offices with little reason or warning. Fletch had always held himself ready for such a move, though nothing had ever come of it. He supposed Albert would say that Denver was safe for the potential renegade and his female supervisor, with little excitement to provoke him.

Albert. Returning to the topic of money, Fletch had received the distinct impression that Albert was rather well off in his own right. There had been no stinting when it came to his home, for instance, or his car or clothes, though none of it was overly extravagant or unnecessary. If Albert chose to, he could surely indulge Fletcher when it came to airfares.

But that was a churlish thought. Albert had, for instance, paid for his own travel to Oregon, and his hotel room there, because his supervisor refused to consider the serial killer as official business. That was more than enough.

And there had been a lovely and thoughtful Christmas present, though the unsentimental Albert, a lapsed Jew, was surely disinclined to celebrate the holiday. The parcel had been sent up to Idaho by courier to ensure it would arrive on Christmas Eve. Peter, Harley and Beth had been a little surprised, and very impressed. It had been difficult not to confess then and there to what he hoped for him and Albert.

The Saab pulled up to the curb at that moment, and Fletcher's smile was perhaps a little warmer than necessary. Albert got out and lifted the heavy hatchback, offering no apology or explanation for his late arrival. Fletcher swung his bag and briefcase in beside a box of groceries.

"It's good to see you, love," Fletch said, earning a glare. He sighed, before observing, "You know, no one can hear us."

Nevertheless, Albert remained silent. As they drove off, Fletch began telling him where he and Caroline were with the money laundering scheme. Working in conjunction with the Utah Field Office, and police in both states, they were slowly but surely building a good case, which looked like broadening into corruption within the Salt Lake City public service. Albert provided no response to any of this – in fact, he acted as if he thought himself alone.

When they reached Albert's home, Fletch went to drop his bags in the spare room, which he still lived out of for the sake of appearances, though that seemed ridiculous to him because no one else ever came here and he slept in Albert's bed anyway. Without bothering to unpack, Fletch went to find Albert.

"What's the occasion?" Fletcher surveyed the dining room, quirking an eyebrow in inquiry.

Albert barely acknowledged him.

"Have I missed something? Birthday? Anniversary? Promotion?" Though he knew very well it was none of those things.

"No." Which was the first word Albert had said. Having apparently arranged the table to his satisfaction, Albert disappeared into the kitchen.

Fletch lingered a moment, eyeing the slender silver candlesticks and cutlery, the blue linen cloth and napkins. It all looked new – so had Albert bought it particularly for whatever this was about, or had it been waiting unused in the buffet? He followed the man, and was immediately assailed by the spicy smell of dinner. "You're making me something Creole? You know that's my favorite."

"Eggplant Creole."

"What's going on?"

Albert was still avoiding him, even the sight of him – until a withering glance at Fletch's third–rate suit, rumpled after a difficult day and a mad dash to catch his plane. "Get changed, Ash, or you'll ruin my appetite."

"You're not going to tell me, are you?"

"So perceptive. One day you might learn patience as well."

"If you want to teach me patience, you shouldn't tantalize me like this."

Albert leveled a glare at him. Fletch grinned in response.

"Go get changed," Albert repeated. "Dinner will be ready in ten minutes."

"All right." Fletch ambled closer, ran his hands around Albert's hips: trim, and encased in smooth linen. "I like you in these trousers," Fletch said. "You're almost as tasty as eggplant Creole." He received a disbelieving snort in reply, which was fine. But there was definitely something afoot.

The slacks were an olive green that complemented Albert's complexion. They were also well cut, which complemented other features ... Mac and the rest of the world might honestly find Albert ugly, but if an observer could remain objective enough to fairly describe Albert from the neck down, it would have to be along the lines of damn nicely built. And Fletch knew he was beyond objective these days, couldn't resist the man at the worst of times. He nuzzled a kiss at the nape of Albert's neck, reached around his waist to steal a piece of tomato from under the blade of the knife.

"A shower might be in order," Albert said sourly.

"Just give me a hint –"

"Nine minutes."

"I'm going, I'm going," Fletch said, laughing. He headed for the main bathroom.

Whatever was going on, he supposed he should follow orders. He had a brisk shower, then went to search the few belongings he kept here and the essentials he'd brought with him. The Christmas present from Albert was hanging in the wardrobe: a shirt, finer than Fletcher had ever considered paying for. Perhaps this was the right time to wear it, maybe that would call Albert's bluff. Fletch slipped it on, pulled on his most comfortable jeans, and returned to the kitchen.

Albert was serving up the meal. His impatient glance returned, lingered, became an expressionless stare. Fletch shrugged, self–conscious but unable to help smiling at the reaction, enjoying the feel of the heavy raw silk against his shoulders. It was incredibly flattering to have someone care so much for how you looked, how you felt. Who could be so floored by the shirt he had chosen for you. Blue – of course the shirt was blue.

However: "Pity about the jeans," was the only comment.

Fletcher laughed again. It wasn't as if he hadn't caught Albert eyeing the snug fit of the worn denim, caught him at it a hundred times. And he knew the silk looked good with the faded jeans – the shirt had, after all, been an astute balance between his own liking for casual clothes and Albert's more up–market tastes.

It was as Albert lifted the plates that Fletch noticed: the man had rolled his shirtsleeves back, in two neat folds; had loosened his tie and undone the button at his collar. It was Fletch's turn to be floored. Preposterous, that such a simple thing could be so erotic: Albert's wrists bare, a hint of the strong forearms; the throat exposed. So simple, yet so deliciously unexpected, like a Victorian gentleman catching sight of a lady's ankle under her skirts and petticoats.

Fletcher whispered, "Albert –" Found his voice and tried again. "Albert, what mischief are you up to?"

No reply. The tail end of a glance, and then the man took the plates into the dining room.

When Fletch followed, he found Albert pouring a glass of white wine, setting it in Fletcher's place. They were seated across the table from each other; intimately close and yet divided by solid walnut.

"This is sweet of you," Fletch said, and immediately regretted it. Too lame and trite. But he didn't know how he was expected to respond to all this. Poignant classical music in the background. The candle flame brighter than the dimmed lights; the dull subtle gold of Albert's tie changing pattern with every move. The spicy food, the crisp wine. And Albert staring at him, intense. Fletcher offered, "I love you," and was rewarded by the briefest of pauses.

Albert began eating, and Fletch followed his example. After a time he began to give in to sensation. Trust Albert to assault all five of his senses at once: from the rough cool texture of the shirt against his nipples, through the music and the food, to the sight of Albert himself. The man was focused solely on Fletcher. There were so many clues Fletch could read, that perhaps no one else would have even noticed. Albert was very ... *on* tonight.

Which must explain this seduction. It was so unlike this man to use traditional props as a means to an end. So what was the desired result? What did Albert want from Fletcher that he didn't already have? They had never promised each other anything, never even talked about the future, although Fletch had been assuming for a long time now, from way before they'd become lovers, that Albert would be there with him for all the foreseeable years. Perhaps that was it, after all the turmoil and misunderstanding of their first months together; perhaps Albert was seeking some surety. Fletch tried to imagine Albert proposing, promising, vowing – tried, and failed miserably.

Albert poured him another glass of wine, asked, "Are you still hungry?"

"Yes." It had only been a small serving, when Albert knew what Fletcher's appetite was like.

Silence again, but for the music, as Albert cleared the plates away, returned with two glass bowls. Sorbet – tangy and cold. Another stimulation on top of all the rest.

Fletch said again, "I love you."

And Albert, all of him still focused on Fletcher, replied, "I know." Which wasn't quite the reassurance that Fletch had been asking for.

They finished the sorbet, then Albert stood, walked around the length of the table to Fletch, took one hand in his.

"What are you –"

He was hushed. Albert blew the candle out, tugged at Fletch's hand and led him off, through the kitchen and down the corridor.

"Are you –?"

"Shut up," was the terse order.

"What?" Fletch was too surprised to be hurt. This wasn't his Albert at all – his lover could be abrupt, blunt, but was never rude – and his colleague relied more on biting wit than on brute force.

They reached Albert's room. Fletch walked in alone and glanced around at the familiarity. He'd always felt safe here, this haven of peaches and deep warm reds, this last best hiding place of a fiercely private man. But he didn't feel safe now, with Albert running hot, and no clues to what he wanted.

"Take your clothes off."

Fletcher wheeled, and stared at Albert, who stood against the door, arms crossed. Blocking the exit. "Why?"

"Why do you think? Shut up, and take your clothes off."

"Albert, this is ridiculous."

"You're wasting time."

Fletcher considered the man for a long moment. He trusted Albert, trusted him implicitly. Perhaps there was no one else in the world Fletch would have obeyed without question. But he couldn't look at the man without noticing that every line of Albert's body betrayed the fact that he was incredibly turned on. Tonight, that was threatening. Fletcher closed his eyes, sank within himself. He was excited, too, what with Albert's intensity and the uncertainty of the evening. Despite which, it took a fair amount of mental energy to let the trust overcome the fear.

Slowly, Fletch began to unbutton the shirt that Albert had given him, let the heavy fabric slip to the floor. Even that didn't distract the man, or provoke a reaction – at any other time Albert would have found a hanger, smoothed the shirt out, made some barbed remark and called him Idaho Joe. Instead, Albert was feeding on him from ten feet away, feeding on his bared chest, drinking him in through those dark liquid eyes. Fletch shivered, suddenly goose–flesh in the warmth.

"Go on," Albert ordered.

"What about you?"

"Get on with it, Ash." The voice was impatient, as usual, but there was a hoarseness, a roughness in the tone.

Fletch heeled off his shoes, unzipped his jeans and pushed the denim down along with his shorts, stepped out of them. Naked now, before this lover of his who was never so demanding. He stood, his need apparent in more ways than the obvious.

"Sit down on the bed."

Fletcher was unwilling to do more than perch on the side, up by the pillows. He looked at Albert again, uneasily awaiting the next instruction.

And Albert began pacing towards him, deliberate and unstoppable and unnerving as a train bearing down. As he moved, Albert loosened his tie further, pulled it slowly through his collar, let the knot fall away, held it loosely dangling.

He walked up to Fletch, captured his chin, and took a kiss. Fletcher tried to reach up, to embrace the man, but found his right hand grasped firmly. Then, too quickly for the implications to register, Albert's mouth left his, silk brushed and encircled his wrist, and his arm was lifted wide, held against wood.

Incomprehension, a suspicion of absurdity, as Fletch stared at his hand neatly tied to the post of the bed–head with Albert's tie. He could undo it, even slip out of the loop of silk, he noted, but for now he stayed put, puzzled. "Albert, what are you doing?"

"Shut up," the man overrode him. "I'm having – What is that quaint expression you used? I'm having my wicked way with you." He was at the foot of the bed now. "There's one simple rule –"

"You took me seriously?"

"Pay attention, Ash: there's two parts to the rule. You have no say in this, and I can do whatever I want. The only way you can stop me is to say the code word."

"I changed my mind," Fletch said, more than half afraid. He'd had no idea Albert hadn't dismissed that conversation the moment it was over.

"Lie back on the bed."

Fletcher groaned. He had wanted this so much that he'd nerved himself up to ask Albert for it – but being thrown in the deep end like this was terrible … "I can't," he said, though he wished he were brave enough to simply surrender.

"The code word you can use to stop me," Albert said, "is McIntyre."

"You have got to be kidding," Fletch exclaimed. When Albert blandly returned his stare, Fletch believed him, and started laughing. The humor was blessed relief. "I guess," he offered, "that's about the last thing I'm likely to cry out in the throes of passion."

"If you say McIntyre, I'll stop. Otherwise, any pleas or protests will have no effect. Are you clear on that?"

The man was relentless, so damned serious. It was difficult to remember that this was simply what the role called for. Fletcher found himself goose–flesh again. "Yes, I'm clear on that," he said.

"Lie back on the bed." And Albert retreated to the wardrobe, came back with a handful of ties.

"You can't use them, they'll get all creased."

A hand on his shoulder, pressing him back, then a hand wrapped firm round his right ankle, lifting it, placing it so he had to shuffle further onto the bed, tying his ankle to the bed post. Walking around the foot of the bed, reaching for Fletch's left ankle.

There was still time while his left hand was free – he could twist his right, slip out of the first tie, sit up to undo his feet. "Albert –" But what to say? Again, he had no idea how he was supposed to respond. Perhaps the truth. "You scare me," Fletch said.

A sardonic glance. "Isn't that a necessary part of the proceedings?"

The man had paused, again giving Fletch a chance to call a halt to this. After a still moment, Albert moved to tie Fletch's left wrist, and he was spread–eagled on his back. The nakedness of it was terrible; fear overcame the slight foolishness. Fletch whispered, "McIntyre."

And Albert immediately loosed his wrist, lifted an eyebrow in civilized inquiry.

"Just testing," Fletcher said. But he couldn't keep his voice steady.

Dropping the formality of the game, Albert gifted him with the tiniest quirk of a smile, knelt on the bed, leaned over to kiss him. This time the kiss was deep, loving, giving. Fletch let his fears free, let the kiss intoxicate him again, let his doubts recede.

When Albert drew away, Fletch said, "All right." Lifted his hand to where Albert had tied it.

It might have been wiser to do this with a stranger, Fletch figured in a quiet moment. He was so wrung out, had been on the threshold of orgasm for what felt like days – and Albert knew him well enough to keep him there indefinitely. The pressure of this need was painful. "Please," Fletcher said.

Of course Albert ignored him. That was part of this game, after all. He was sitting at the end of the bed, having loosed Fletch's left foot, and was concentrating on massaging it. Under any other circumstances it would have been relaxing. The hands progressed to his calf, kneaded the tense muscle, caressed the skin, smoothed the hair neatly. Fletch was beyond appreciating the humor of the last fastidious gesture.

He tried to read Albert's expression, though it was difficult with the man's face down–turned. Perhaps the hands betrayed more: each time Albert had slowed the pace like this, his hands took the opportunity to explore every nuance of Fletcher, to adore him. And then it would begin again, the arrogant use of this plaything strapped to the bed.

"Let me come," Fletch asked. The man was oblivious, apparently didn't even hear him. Fletch let out an ironic laugh. "You're too good at this." He was still panting – despite Albert's ministrations, Fletch hadn't been able to calm down at all this time. Still, he wasn't quite prepared to end this exquisite torture by saying the code word. Another laugh, more a giggle, at the thought of Mac being so intimately albeit unknowingly involved in this. "Please."

Albert moved at last, neglected to tie the foot again. He knelt, straddling Fletch's chest, slipped a hand below Fletch's neck. And Fletcher obediently took Albert's penis into his mouth, was rewarded by a groan. It seemed that Albert was almost as strung out as Fletch was. The needs of the moment drove Fletch to rely more on enthusiasm than skill as a way of chasing resolution. But, too soon, Albert pulled away.

He began backing down Fletch's body, bending to graze at his nipples, tease at his waist with soft kisses and hungry teeth. Then a savoring of Fletcher's genitals with the flat of Albert's tongue.

Crying out, Fletcher grasped a wooden slat of the bed–head in each hand, tried to heave up into haven – but the sensation was gone before the promise of an orgasm could coalesce into satisfaction. He cried out again, bereft, never having imagined such frustrated, mad urgency. It made him abruptly angry. "Albert, you bastard, when I get to have my wicked way with you, I'll make you damned well suffer."

Hands arranged him, twisted him so his lower body was propped up on his right hip, though his shoulders were still held flat against the bed. His left leg was curled almost to his chest, his exposed buttocks were caressed. Then he was being bitten and kissed again, the tongue sweeping closer to his anus, until at last it rasped over the sensitive pucker of skin. The delicious shock of the intimacy jolted through Fletcher, almost enough on its own to push him over the edge. He turned his face away. Albert hadn't so much as touched him there since that first night together. Wonderful, that he'd realized all that Fletch had intended for this game. "I've been wanting this," Fletch mumbled the admission into the pillow, "for so damned long."

Cool moisture soothed across the opening, the pad of a finger tip pressing within him. Fletch groaned, unable to find words, trying to stop himself keening in need.

"Look at me," Albert ordered. "Watch me."

"Please, no," Fletch said brokenly, but he turned his head. His whole body felt flushed; the shame of his own imperative to yield shouldn't make any difference, surely.

Then something was pushing into him – not Albert, he wasn't close enough – not even a finger. A dildo of some sort. Fletch whimpered, caught between the urgent swirl of sensation and the aching disappointment. Of course Albert wasn't going to fuck him. That was something Albert had forbidden himself, forbidden both of them, for whatever damned reasons he had.

But soon the regret ebbed away, the piquancy of it only adding to sensation, as Albert gently worked the thing inside him, began a slow and rhythmic devastation.

Perhaps hours later, with the dildo fully inside him, Fletch was being moved, spread–eagled again. Hands pushed, kneaded up the inside of his thighs. Stirring, Fletcher yelled. If he thrust up, his genitals the focus of need, then his ass clenched on the intruder and completion threatened. "Albert – now – please, now."

For once he was listened to, or perhaps their needs coincided. Fingers gentled his balls, a mouth hungrily sucked at his penis, then a hand slipped down to twist at the dildo.

Throat raw, Fletcher Ash told the world how good it was.

"Albert, please," Fletch said, still trembling. Albert was lapping at his genitals, soothing them, carefully drawing the dildo out. "Please, just hold me." Fletcher had never in his life felt so reduced. He felt like curling up and sobbing in Albert's arms, though that seemed such an absurd image. And then Fletch remembered, tried saying, "McIntyre."

"What?"

The word lacked the snap Fletch was expecting. He lifted his head, saw Albert had withdrawn to the foot of the bed. "Hold me," he asked.

"In a minute."

Albert was loosening the ties, that was the delay. As each limb was freed Fletch withdrew, so he ended up huddled. And then, at last, Albert lay beside him, pulled him into a close embrace.

"All right?" Albert asked, hoarse.

Fletch let out a breath, not having the energy to chuckle. "As in, was that all right? Or, are you all right?"

Albert touched Fletcher's temple, raked the hair out of Fletcher's eyes. "Are you," he said, "all right?"

"Yes, I'm fine. Despite the fact you're too damned good at overwhelming me."

"I did in fact notice that the sex was all right," Albert continued with a touch of irony. "I was paying attention, as required."

"Yes," Fletch said again, touched at the reference to their first night, and at what he assumed was an expression of doubt. "The sex was perfect."

Albert pressed a kiss to his forehead, an unusual enough occurrence in itself. "I'll run you a bath."

"Great." Fletch clung on to him for another moment. "I thought you'd forgotten all about this silly idea of mine."

"Of course not."

"Thank you," Fletch said.

"You're welcome." Flat, but not sarcastic.

Fletch let him go, feeling Albert's discomfort. Thoroughly sated, exhausted by one solitary orgasm, Fletch lay still for a while. Then, lonely, he wandered through to the main bathroom. Albert was there, in his robe, measuring out a precise amount of crystals, letting them foam under the steaming running water. Absently amused, Fletch noted that even the color of the crystals harmonized with the bathroom's decor.

"This is perfect, too," Fletch said. "You had all this planned, didn't you?" No reply or acknowledgment, but he hadn't expected one. "I love you."

"I should think so," Albert said.

"You'll get sick of me saying that tonight."

"Perhaps."

Fletch gave himself over to Albert's ministrations again, lay in the hot water, let Albert soap him, rinse him. The man was businesslike, thorough, yet gentle. "Don't ever stop loving me," Fletch murmured.

There was no response, but for the care of the hands. And, every now and then, hidden by so much else, a tremble, an uncertainty in Albert's touch.

Fletcher frowned. As Albert reached Fletch's legs, the soapy hands echoing the massage of a time ago, he again tried to read Albert's expression. Unsurprisingly, so much was masked, so much of the good in him was hidden. But there were hints – the mouth was pinched, the eyes unfocused though fixed. To the initiated, Albert seemed quite shaken.

Had it been selfish of Fletch to ask for something that Albert wouldn't ordinarily have done? Even though, at the time, he'd assumed Albert, always in control, would have enjoyed the experience as much as Fletch anticipated enjoying it himself? And yet Albert had done this voluntarily, with no further hints or requests from Fletch; had put so much thought and trouble into what Fletch might want, how to do this as perfectly as possible. That was maybe the nicest thing anyone had ever done for him.

"Albert," Fletch tentatively began. The man was turned away, massaging Fletcher's foot. "I'm sorry."

Not even a pause. "What for?"

Of course – specifics were called for, general apologies were never accepted. "For doing that to you."

"I seem to recall that it was me doing that to you." So brisk.

"Come here, Albert."

He stood, walked the few steps, towered over Fletch. "What?"

How to judge best, how to read this difficult man? "Kiss me," Fletch asked, sitting up, leaning his folded arms on the edge of the bath.

Albert knelt, leaned in willingly enough. But the kiss was strange, both restrained and betraying excitement. Fletcher broke away, and placed his hands on Albert's shoulders, not letting him draw back. He remembered the sex, without the selfish perspective of his own needs.

"Yes, you did all that to me," Fletch said slowly, "but you did damn all for yourself, didn't you?"

Too close to the mark, apparently: Albert turned his face away, radiating resentment. But he didn't snap out a retort, didn't hide behind aggression. The whole evening had been strange, but perhaps this was strangest.

Fletch said, "Get in here with me."

When Albert didn't move, Fletcher instead reached into the robe, pushed it off. Albert's penis was revealed: dusky wine red, unbearably hard.

"Get in the bath," Fletch repeated, impatient.

Albert seemed ashamed. What was it about the game that had so shaken him, when it wasn't that different to their regular sex anyway?

"Come on." Fletch moved back, made room for Albert to lie in the water beside him, drew the man into his arms when he finally climbed in.

It was sweet to be taking care of Albert for once. Fletch held him, caressed him, tried to soothe him – while Albert linked his arms around Fletch's waist, buried his face in Fletcher's neck, and remained tense. It seemed only the limited space within the bathtub provided any sense of intimacy.

What to talk about, to give Albert time to unwind? Something unrelated to sex and relationships. Not work, either, in this situation. Fletcher began talking about Albert's garden, how he'd always loved it best in the spring, with everything freshly green and burgeoning. He liked the simple elegance of the white and yellow theme for the flowers, the restraint in color contrasting with the informal arrangements. Then, amongst the elegance, a few scatterings of blue flowers adding variety and cheer, echoing the spring sky. During his trips to Washington in September and October Fletch had however begun to consider Fall as a serious contender for the prettiest season. He'd missed the aspens turning gold back in the Rockies because of his new love affair, but Albert's garden had made up for that. The crisp air of Fall was as perfect in its own way as Spring's softness; the fiery reds and golds were beautiful; Fall was symbolic of maturity and harvest and plenty, brought images of fire and cleansing.

"All right," Albert at last interrupted him with; "you can stop now. And the blue flowers were unintended."

The voice was quietly ironic, if firm, and the body Fletch held had relaxed, if only marginally. He said, "A happy mistake. Serendipity or something."

"Or something," Albert agreed dryly.

Fletcher risked lifting Albert's chin up. Those beautiful dark eyes were luminous, mysterious. Leaning in, Fletch met the lips with his own, initiated the softest kiss he knew how.

Simple and quick and painless, that's what this had to be. Bestowing relief. Nevertheless, Fletch found it delicious to show Albert this small mercy. Too rare, for them to be like this. "Is this the truth?" Fletch murmured between kisses. "Is this the truth, love?"

Of course there was no answer. Albert shuddered under Fletch's hands, climaxed with a soft muffled cry. Fletcher would have given anything to see Albert's face right then. They held each other, quiet and complete and peaceful now.

But then Albert was standing, unplugging the tub so the water began to drain away. Fletch, who'd had to quickly sit up to get out of the way, felt bereft. Over his shoulder, Albert said, "I'll rinse off now," though he grabbed the soap once he had the shower running.

Fletch said, "All right," to this abrupt dismissal, and clambered out of the tub. So Albert needed some room right now, needed to reassemble his dignity. Fletch could let him do that, figured he owed Albert that much after creating this difficult situation.

He toweled off quickly, then went to find his pajama pants, the old flannel ones that Albert found so disgraceful and Fletch found so comfortable in more ways than the physical. Thirsty, he wandered to the kitchen and helped himself to the jug of fresh fruit juice. He was surprised to find he wasn't hungry, despite the fact he hadn't eaten much dinner. Unsure, he lingered in the darkness.

When Fletch returned to the main bedroom, Albert was dressed in his cotton pajamas, the peach colored ones that made Fletch want to cuddle the man. The look Albert threw him was anything but inviting, however – it was full of dislike and resentment. Every move, as Albert tidied the bedroom, broadcast anger. Finally he scooped Fletcher's pile of clothes up from the floor, brought them over, dropped them into Fletcher's waiting arms. Close up, the body language was pure venom.

Fletch swallowed, suspecting he shouldn't let this happen, but not quite brave enough to face Albert down. His self–doubt undermined any resolve. He said weakly, "Perhaps you'd prefer it if I slept in the guest room tonight." What else to do for the man?

"Fine."

"All right." And Fletch turned, walked out – the door was shut behind him before he was barely over the threshold. *Be careful of what you offer*, Fletch thought, *because you might just get it.*

There were a lot of things very wrong right now, that was patently obvious, but what could he do about it? Albert wouldn't suffer him to approach, let alone try to talk about it. So he'd just let Albert calm down, regain a little equilibrium, and if the worst came to the worst they would just continue tomorrow as they'd always been.

"Morning, Albert," Fletch said, wandering over to press a kiss to the man's forehead before heading for the coffee machine.

"Good morning," was the cool acknowledgment.

"Thanks for putting a brew on."

Silence.

All right, so Albert always had a fresh pot of coffee brewing whenever Fletch was there. A thank you, at this stage, was superfluous. Fletcher sat at the kitchen table across from Albert. "Are we going in to work today?"

The man turned a page of the newspaper, not lifting his gaze from the print. "As soon as you're dressed."

That was a blunt suggestion that Fletcher should hurry up, but Fletcher chose to ignore it. Instead, he considered his companion. Despite the fact they were heading for work, Albert was only in shirt and trousers and shoes and he'd let Fletch sleep in. It seemed promising, these slight relaxations. But then Fletcher caught sight through the doorway of the dining room – there was no sign of the silver candlestick or the blue crockery or the other lovely props of the previous evening. Albert must have gotten up even earlier than usual this morning to clean away the remnants of dinner. Was it supposed to have never happened? The delicious food, the sweetly poignant music, everything so special that Fletcher almost anticipated a proposal – all gone.

"Albert," Fletch started, "do you think –"

"Do you want breakfast?" Albert interrupted him with.

"No. I want to know if –"

"Then go and get ready. I have a lot to work through today."

Fletcher sighed. "All right." He swallowed the last of his coffee and headed for the shower.

If Albert now wanted to pretend the whole thing had never happened, he was doomed and by his own actions. Distracted, puzzling over Albert's current state of mind, Fletch didn't pay much attention to externals until they were checking into headquarters through security. And then he caught himself staring at Albert's tie.

Fletch laughed before he could stop himself; an undignified giggle. He wondered if he was blushing. Had that been deliberate? Using something that symbolized work, that was part of Albert's careful and elegant appearance, as part of the sexual game? A reassurance at the time, if a subtle one, and a blatant reminder from then on, so that even the FBI dress code was subverted by their relationship. Who could claim Albert didn't have a sense of humor?

Except that the idea had backfired. Albert seemed to bitterly regret the sex, and was now glaring at Fletch as if to defy him to see the tie as anything more than an article of clothing. Everything Albert did was deliberate and fully considered – but this had evidently turned out to be a mistake. The ties became a reminder of troubled resentment rather than a loving game, of serious discord instead of the nicest thing anyone had ever done for Fletcher. But Albert couldn't quit wearing ties – so did that mean the four he'd used, including that beautiful gold one, would never be worn again?

"Ash, have you at last taken leave of your senses?" Albert was saying from over by the elevators. There was an angry bite to the words, if you knew how to listen to the man.

Fletcher realized he'd been cast adrift by his thoughts, and the security guard was beginning to look askance at him. "I took leave of my senses some months ago," Fletcher said, lifting an eyebrow. *It was Fall, the beginning of football season, and crazy I came to you for help.*

Albert turned away impatiently.

Figuring he should offer some explanation to the guard for at least the incongruous giggle, Fletch said, "Sorry. I have to laugh at my own jokes, because no one else does." And he smiled the smile that charmed almost everyone.

"And some people never will," the guard muttered, indicating Albert with a nod of her head.

"Exactly. I've given up even trying to tell him jokes. Did you hear the one about the grasshopper who walks into a bar?"

"Everyone's heard that one, Fletcher." It was Mac, with a woman following him, bustling up with his arms full of cluttered newspapers and files. "Albert said you'd be here. I'm glad we caught you."

"How are you, Mac?"

"Can't complain. And yourself?" The woman was already signing in as a visitor; Mac began checking all his clutter through the guard's x–ray machine.

Fletcher turned to see Albert holding the elevator. "Won't be a minute, Albert," he called. The man, obviously reluctant to wait, might disappear down to his office at any moment. Fletch didn't want to let him out of his sight right now, and was annoyed Albert wouldn't even stay to greet Mac – but he decided to take pity. "All right, you go on. I'll help Mac with all this, and see you down there."

Without even an acknowledgment, Albert stepped into the elevator, and the doors closed.

"I want you to meet someone," Mac was saying, as if he attached no significance to Albert's retreat.

Fletcher looked at the woman, and added it up. "You must be Celia from New Orleans."

"And you're Fletch from Denver."

She reached out her hand, and Fletcher shook it. "Dr. Mortimer," Fletch said.

"Agent Ash," she replied, echoing his chivalrous tone of respect, adding a touch of humor.

Fletch grinned. "You might know who I am, but I bet Mac doesn't talk about me half as much as he talks about you." The woman was pretty, despite the severity of her clothes. There was an elegance and a preciseness about her that reminded Fletcher of Albert, though it seemed she presented herself in ways calculated to undermine her attractiveness, whereas Albert appeared completely unconscious of whether he was attractive or not – unaware, perhaps, that such a question might even be asked.

For good measure Fletch hung onto Celia's hand for a little longer than strictly necessary, beaming away happily. It was no hardship, after all, to flirt with this lovely lady. And he thought to the security guard, *There – put that on my file, if you're so suspicious about me and Albert.*

Fletcher asked, "Why haven't we met before?"

Groaning, Mac said, "Why do you think?" He turned to Celia. "You watch him – he's too gallant to be safe."

"I see exactly what you mean," Celia said, smiling encouragingly. The three of them, laden with Mac's paperwork, began heading for the elevators. "Would you be available for dinner tonight, Fletch?" Celia asked. "Of course, we'll take Mac and Albert along as chaperons."

"I'd love to."

"And Albert, do you think –?"

"I'm sure he'd be happy to join us." Fletcher laughed at the dubious expressions. "You know him pretty well, don't you?"

The elevator arrived, and they piled in. Mac said, "We thought it was a nice idea, seeing you and Celia are actually in town on the same weekend – a nice idea, but impossible. Albert doesn't go in for socializing much, does he?"

Fletch said thoughtfully, "Not like that, anyway." But it would do them both good, bring them out of themselves. Surely it was better to spend a pleasant evening with friends than to brood – or argue – alone together. Maybe it would give the immediate anger time to settle so they could then discuss whatever the real problems were in a more rational manner. "I'll bring him along. This will be fun." He was determined to make it so.

"Any thoughts on a restaurant?" Celia asked as the three of them reached Records and headed for Mac's desk.

Fletch shrugged. "I'll leave that to you two – you probably have a better idea than me. Somewhere nice, with good food. A place that caters for vegetarians."

"You're not –" said Mac, frowning. They had shared a few steaks for lunch over the years.

"No, but Albert is."

"The things you find out about people," Mac reflected.

"There used to be an Ethiopian restaurant around Dupont Circle somewhere," Fletch offered after a moment. "Tyler took me there a couple of times. Delicious food, so many spicy flavors." He was inundated for a moment by the memory of it: her long fingers tearing a strip of the soft bread, folding it up, dipping it in the sauce of her meal, and popping it into her wide mouth. When he had kissed her, she'd smelled and tasted hot and exotic.

"Ethiopian?" Celia asked. "That's unusual."

"It couldn't be any stranger than some of your Cajun dishes," Mac said.

Maybe the sexual trend of his recollections prompted him, but Fletch suddenly said, "McIntyre," and burst out laughing, a long aching rolling belly laugh.

Mac and Celia stared at first in wonder and then in shared amusement, though Fletch couldn't possibly tell them what was so funny. Memories led to a mad image of Celia tying Mac to a bed, and telling him the code word was Albert.

It was only when he heard the note of hysteria in his own voice that Fletch attempted to pull himself together.

"We could try for an American cuisine," Celia offered, deadpan; "if the Ethiopian place causes that sort of reaction. Unless you were actually laughing at poor Mac?"

"No, really," Fletch demurred, before dissolving again into helpless chuckles.

The labs were quiet and all in darkness, but for the one Albert was using. He was standing at a bench with his back to the door, so Fletch called, "It's only me," as he advanced, wondering all the while whether he really wanted to see whatever it was Albert was working on. It turned out to only be a shirt.

Fletcher sat up on the next bench along to watch from a high vantage point. Albert had already drawn a diagram of the front and back of the shirt, including the stains and cuts, each of which had been allocated a number. The drawing, as usual with Albert, was a precise and detailed rendition of the shirt – as opposed to what Fletch managed, when he had to do this sort of thing, which was more the equivalent of a stick figure.

Now, hands deft in latex gloves, Albert cut three precise strips of cloth from each of the stains, placing the pieces in small test–tubes lined up in a rack, and labeling each tube with the stain's number. Fletch found it almost mesmerizing, watching Albert working through this careful and thorough procedure.

When he was done, Albert folded the remains of the shirt and returned it to its evidence bag. Still ignoring Fletcher's presence, he reached for a bottle of clear liquid.

Fletch racked his brains, trying to remember what the liquid was, but his Bureau forensics courses were too long ago. If Albert had been in a better mood, Fletch would have asked – Albert was never more communicative than when passing on knowledge to the less well–informed. In fact, it used to be a good–natured game between them – Albert would describe something like a cause of death in technical terms, and Fletcher would be expected to interpret that in plain English and draw relevant conclusions. Nothing was ever said, but Fletch knew that Albert liked this particular special agent passing the tests he set.

"Albert," Fletch said at last, "you and I are meeting Celia and Mac for dinner tonight."

There was no pause as Albert used a pipette to fill each test–tube with the liquid. "I don't think so," he said smoothly.

"Don't be antisocial. Mac's been a good friend, and it would be horribly impolite to refuse. Anyway, I'd like to get to know Celia."

Albert cast him a withering glance that Fletch didn't have time to interpret, and said, "I apologize if I offend your sense of etiquette, but I have no interest in such dinner companions."

"I do."

"Then the solution is obvious," Albert returned, the urbanity turning cold: "you meet them for dinner, and I'll get some work done."

"Albert, listen to me –"

"Unlike many people, I am capable of doing two things at once. I am unfortunately listening to you at present." He began to methodically seal each of the test–tubes, working down each row of the rack.

Fletcher grimaced. He'd known this would be difficult, and should have been better prepared not to give in to the temptation to raise his voice. He said, "I am far more determined than you are. So just this once you may as well save your breath and give in gracefully. I owe these people; they specifically requested your company as well as mine; that is what I intend to give them."

Albert turned a silent glare in Fletcher's direction.

Perhaps it had been wise to confront this at work, where there were so many things they couldn't say. "All right," Fletch said, "giving in sullenly will do."

"Save your feeble witticisms for tonight's glittering conversation," Albert bit back.

"Thank you," Fletcher said, taking that as reluctant agreement. "Mac has a couple of new reports from Oregon, and some newspaper clippings, so I'll be up with him and Celia for a while, okay?"

"Good riddance," Albert muttered.

Fletcher walked out of the lab, neglecting to say a farewell. He usually said something, even though Albert rarely responded, and it felt childish not to. But Fletcher told himself that if Albert was going to insist on being childish, Fletch may as well give him a taste of his own medicine.

CHAPTER TWENTY
WASHINGTON DC
JANUARY 1985

Albert was bitter. He'd prefer to be blazingly angry, furiously righteous, but all he had was this cold and familiar lump of lead in his chest – just below his sternum, wedged between the right ventricle of his heart and his diaphragm. It was a physical sensation, though he knew even the most skilled of autopsies would never find the poisonous thing.

He sat there at the circular table covered with fine white linen, opposite Ash, amidst the muted activity of this popular restaurant. The mediocre McIntyre was at Albert's left and the willfully misguided Dr. Celia Mortimer at his right. The bitterness tainted everything so that even the food, which might otherwise provide an interesting distraction from the surrounding mundanity, was all but inedible.

Bitter resentment, because this whole intolerable situation was Fletcher's fault.

It began with the pervasive self–disgust. Albert had at first tried to put behind him the events of the previous night and the related mess of emotion; when that had proved impossible, he'd endeavored to work out the reasons for his reaction; when that failed, he tried again to ignore it. He had given in to Ash's whim, and staged a sexual bondage game for him not twenty–four hours ago, and now – now Albert was nothing but self–disgust. It was as if the game had shown Albert a caricature of himself, and he loathed the image with all the immediacy that a continuing sexual arousal could provide. Fletcher's fault.

Then, for the briefest of moments, while sharing a bathtub of all indignities, Ash had actually *given* to Albert rather than, as was usual between them, taken from him. And by doing so, Fletcher had shown Albert Sterne the tiniest part of how devastatingly vulnerable he could be. Albert had always worked on the assumption that he would never need anyone even a hundredth as much as this. Fletcher couldn't have done better if he'd planned it. Had it been revenge, subconscious or not, for the man's observation: *You really know how to take me to pieces, don't you?* It was too cruel of the man to demonstrate that the knowledge was mutual. Fletcher's fault.

And after breezing through the day as if nothing significant had occurred, Fletcher now forced this inane company on Albert for the evening. Destroying the modicum of respect Albert held for Mortimer, because she was taking great delight in teasing Fletcher about that woman he'd been in love with, Tyler Reece. Fletcher's fault.

Fletcher himself was being charming, in that disarmingly honest and unaffected way of his that was all the more effective for being so; apparently undaunted by the stony gaze opposite. It was Fletcher's fault, too, that the righteous fury Albert should have felt had been demoralized into this ineffectual bitterness.

Ineffectual, because it could not stop him reacting in ways he hated. Ineffectual, but not impotent. The urge was so strong to drag Fletcher Ash home, to unleash this aggressive sexual need on him. It didn't help that he knew Fletcher would welcome such an act. Albert lost the last of his minimal appetite, loathing this part of himself he did not want to be. Fletcher's fault, for awakening it.

All this, surely *this* was why Albert had kept himself strictly to himself over the years, avoiding the entanglements of family, friends, lovers. Why were human beings so prey to relationships that only served to pull them down into the petty, sordid mire of emotion?

Melodrama. Fletcher's fault.

Yes, there was Ash, being unutterably charming, as if oblivious to all the trouble he had caused. McIntyre was responding to the convivial atmosphere, more relaxed and confident than Albert had ever seen him. Mortimer was allowing herself to look prettier and prettier, and was contributing as much wit and substance to the conversation as Fletcher.

Of course Ash set out to deliberately charm people, to establish a rapport with those who could help him. Charm was such an effective form of manipulation, after all, and one suited to Fletcher's instincts for who people were, where their weaknesses lay. And he carried it all off with such an open and vulnerable manner that almost everyone was willing to be fooled. Including Albert.

Yes, Albert had been charmed by Fletcher David Ash long ago and was still being rudely awakened to the ramifications of it. Fletcher's fault. And his own, for having that one weakness, that one blind spot.

His own fault, of course, not Fletcher's.

This whole thing was his own fault for allowing Ash into his life, and Albert must remember that. In fact, that would have to be the worst of it, that Albert could sit here and blame everything on another person when his life was his own responsibility.

What on earth had he wanted, Albert wondered; what had he wanted years ago, when he'd slowly developed such an alarming partiality to this man? What had been his goal then? Because surely this miserable farce of a relationship wasn't it.

And what, Albert had to ask himself, did Fletcher want? What was the attraction? Ash had few long term relationships and all were sustained by external factors: ties of blood and marriage to the minimal family in Idaho; a working partnership with his supervisor, Caroline Thornton; use of Mac for research and support; use of Albert for forensics expertise and sex. Fletcher's other relationships tended to be friendly but short term, pleasant and superficial, despite his charm and the traits most people found likeable. The women, lovers or friends, were all impossible and doomed. The men Ash knew were acquaintances rather than anything more.

Although Albert had been interested in Fletcher Ash from the start, it had been years before he'd decided the man was worthwhile, before he'd acknowledged Ash's persistent claims of friendship. So, did Celia Mortimer blindly accept Mac's poor judgment and dogged loyalty as indicating value? Or could she, on so short an acquaintance, already see something valuable or interesting in Fletcher?

On immediate display were Ash's frankness, directness, sincerity; the honesty that often appeared naïve but at times seemed alarmingly sophisticated; the vulnerabilities that seemed to cry, *Show me yours, here are mine for all to see,* all of which was made bearable by the respect and humor, the fresh intelligence and enduring enthusiasm. Only Albert and, at times, Caroline Thornton were inflicted with the occasional bouts of despondency and self–recrimination.

This was, naturally enough, an attractive package, especially when Fletcher was focusing it all in a genuine show of interest in the acquiescent subject. Of course Celia and McIntyre were enjoying the man's company.

Albert abruptly turned his gaze elsewhere. He wasn't in the habit of eulogizing when someone died, let alone when they were sitting there, flesh and blood, very much alive. Fletcher's mitigating good points were the last thing he wanted to think about right now.

He forced his thoughts to follow his gaze. Despite the fact Albert was still in the clothes he'd worn to work that day, having refused to get changed for the sake of this evening's imposed venture, he was better dressed than most of the people in the restaurant, and certainly outshone his three companions. He noted that Fletcher had *not* worn the blue silk shirt Albert had given him. So be it. If it wouldn't be a melodramatic, futile and wasteful gesture, Albert would throw the thing out. Albert rarely regretted his actions but sending Ash a Christmas present now seemed stupidly romantic. And the sex last night – only last night, though Albert's time sense declared it an eon ago – he surely regretted that.

And here he sat, with no distraction from his reflections other than this inane dinner party. He should have brought those test results from the lab – he could have reviewed and summarized them by now, and drafted a report in long hand.

Even the music the restaurant was playing was an irritant. It sounded as if some popular music star had sought the influence of Africa's native music. The impulse was sound, as rock music's rhythms originated there, but the results were an unsatisfactory mishmash. A theme was needed, some central idea beyond the simple exploration of origin, to unite and guide the whole.

"No, no," Ash was protesting, "I've already bored you to tears this afternoon with the story of my wild goose chase." Albert heaved an internal sigh, wishing this man, his illicit lover, was better at keeping secrets.

"But I'm fascinated," Mortimer replied, leaning forward a little. Her voice deepened, as if what she would say was important or confidential or both. "I suppose any puzzle, any unsolved crime or mystery, any hint of a conspiracy, the more macabre the better, is bound to fascinate. Who was Jack the Ripper? Did Lee Harvey Oswald act alone? Who is Fletch's serial killer?"

"See, Albert, I'm going to form a task force with or without the Bureau's cooperation."

He did not deign to respond, though he considered this more a mutual admiration society than a law enforcement task force. Why didn't he say something scathing along those lines? But Fletcher's presence had gagged him.

After a beat, Celia said, "I'd love to help, of course, but you have Mr. Sterne. He's far more qualified for this type of investigation than I am."

Fletcher laughed. "Speaking of qualifications, it's *Dr.* Sterne, actually."

She turned a concerned expression on Albert. "I do apologize, I didn't realize."

"Me, neither," Mac added.

Wonderful – all three of them were now staring at him. Albert began to glare indiscriminately around the table.

But Fletcher was drawing their attention back to himself. "Simply having another true believer on the team is fine. For a start, it's good to talk about it. Keeps me sane."

"We'll definitely try to help there."

"The downside for you being that I have no other conversation these days. Every waking hour is either the Bureau's official cases or this."

"You're doing fine tonight," Celia assured him. "And, of course, if there's anything I can do to help –"

"Great. The more people there are across the country, keeping an eye out for anything that might be our man, the better. We need to be onto him as soon as he shows his hand. It's becoming crucial, not that it wasn't before."

"Of course. Mac's told me what he does for you."

McIntyre had the grace to shrug. "So much for my vow of silence," he murmured.

Smiling, Ash said, "Perhaps it shouldn't go any further, but damn the rules – the Bureau isn't playing fair by us."

"At least I have a full security clearance," Celia offered. "The field office often uses our facilities, so they've cleared our core personnel."

"Not good enough. You obviously haven't read our rule book – it's thicker than the Bible, and has a hell of a lot more than ten commandments."

"Yeah," Mac agreed, "enough Thou Shalt Nots to drown in. But at least now Hoover's gone we don't have to take a vow of chastity."

"Cheers to that," Fletcher declared, so fervently that the other two laughed in surprised delight. The man cast a mischievous glance at Albert, who maintained his stony composure.

The table's conversation, still dominated by Ash and Mortimer, rambled on and then quieted as one of the restaurant's lackeys cleared away the plates and debris. "Did you enjoy your meal?" the lackey asked; a standard formula rather than a genuine request for information. Nevertheless, the other three all provided enthusiastic words and gestures to indicate an answer in the affirmative. The lackey smiled graciously and withdrew, smoothly bearing his precarious load.

"It *is* incredible here," Fletcher repeated for the benefit of their own party. "But," he added, "nothing compares to Albert's cooking."

Albert repaid this impudence with a furious glare – for now. No doubt there would be a chance for suitable remonstrance later tonight.

McIntyre was looking surprised, flummoxed by this disparate information. Mortimer was interested. "You cook, Dr. Sterne? Do you specialize in a particular cuisine?"

Silence. And then Ash belatedly attempted to remedy the situation. "Actually, Celia, I really like the Cajun and Creole styles. Tell me about the restaurants in New Orleans."

After a shaky start, Mortimer took up the conversation easily enough, answering Fletcher's queries, with some input from McIntyre on how strange everything was down south, particularly the food.

To the practiced eye, Ash was by turns annoyed with Albert and chagrined with himself, but he apparently felt he owed it to McIntyre and Mortimer to continue to charm them.

After describing one of the Cajun dishes, Celia said, "The cuisine doesn't exactly cater for vegetarians, though. Dr. Sterne would have trouble finding any authentic food to eat."

"Doesn't it?" Ash was wholly surprised. He looked quizzically across at Albert. "Would he?"

"Yes, everything includes seafood or meat. Even the red beans and rice dish comes with sausage."

But thankfully Ash let Celia continue rather than ask Albert about his eggplant Creole and other variations on the cuisine's themes. Ash had betrayed more than enough confidences for one night, and perhaps he had at last realized it.

♦

A terrible cold silence blanketed the drive over the Potomac, past the Arlington Cemetery, and all the way home. Fletcher unlocked and opened the garage doors; then waited for Albert to park the Saab inside, let it idle for a precise thirty seconds, and join him outside. After securing the garage again, Fletcher led the way into the house, to the kitchen – and proceeded to brew himself a pot of coffee rather than, as was usual, wait for Albert to do it.

It was only then, with a mug of coffee steaming on the table and the two men standing either side of it, that Fletcher spoke. "That was pretty damned childish, Albert." Unmistakably angry, if unexpectedly restrained. Perhaps a hint of the same bitterness that Albert himself was feeling. "Sulking through dinner and not saying a word. I can understand you not particularly wanting to be there but you could have made some sort of effort."

"You're the expert on childish behavior, so I'll take your word for it."

"So you haven't lost your voice," Fletcher said – then, under Albert's withering stare, he apparently realized what a pointless observation that had been. He continued, with renewed feeling, "What would you call it? Maintaining a quiet dignity? Well, it wasn't dignified at all – it was just plain rude."

"Really," Albert said.

"Really," Fletcher confirmed.

"If that's all you wanted to say, I'll retire for the evening."

"Oh, no you don't. Those people are willing to be our friends when we have damned few, and none in common except Mac. They're entitled to be treated with respect and maybe even gratitude."

"I don't have a reason to make an effort. You think you need something from them, but I don't."

"Yes? What do I need?"

"The same as from me – assistance in chasing your pet murderer."

Fletcher grinned humorlessly. "And it really burns you up that I value their help as well as yours, doesn't it? Your pride is your most unattractive trait, Albert."

"Why don't you drop this petty argument about official and social dealings with the mundane and the gullible – and shout about the real issues?"

The grin grew wider, encompassing some mad sense of satisfaction. "I'd love to, Albert – if I knew what they were. Tell me. You're the one who's been in a foul mood all day. You tell me what the real issues are."

Albert glared. "What makes you think –"

"It's so easy, really, to goad you into blurting out the truth. Yes, there're real issues behind all this garbage. But you're the one who knows what they are."

Silence for a while, then Albert said as evenly as he could, "You don't understand me as well as you thought, otherwise you'd know the answers already."

"But I know some of your secret places all too well, don't I? Places you won't look at, let alone admit to."

"That's enough."

Fletcher nodded knowingly. "Finally abused the privilege of your friendship, have I? Stepped well and truly over the line?"

"Many times," Albert coldly informed him.

"But we're both still here, aren't we? I'll tell you something, Albert, anyone else would have called it quits by now – the argument, the relationship. It just wouldn't be worth all the aggravation."

Albert looked elsewhere. "Perhaps you want a medal for endurance."

"Both of us endure. Why? Because there's something between that us we both want."

"Indeed." These last twenty–four hours of bitterness had left Albert weary, weary beyond all sense. But he wouldn't sit down now, that would be too much a gesture of conciliation and weakness.

Never worried about such things, Fletcher sat, and sipped at his coffee, staring at the table and avoiding Albert. Quietly, Ash said, "Tell me about the real issues, Albert. Shout about them if you want."

"So much for your famous instincts," Albert taunted. "If they won't serve you now, how can they ever be of any use? How can you rely on them?"

"I never said I was omnipotent!" Fletcher was definitely feeling defensive, glancing his resentment, then hiding his face. "But maybe," he added, "maybe I'm too subjective about you. Maybe I've lost my judgment."

"Don't you think your subjectivity should help your insight? No wonder you waste most of your time in self–doubt."

Silence, as if Ash was too wounded to reply. But then he said, "Tell me why the sex last night scared you." Calm, level, on the offensive. Maybe he had only pretended ignorance and defensiveness in order to draw Albert out. Albert wished he could despise this man and his manipulations. Fletcher was continuing, "Why did it mean so much? And when we made love afterwards, in the bathtub, why did that scare you even more?"

Anyone else would call it quits, Albert reminded himself. *Why don't I?* He ground out, "I wasn't the one who ran away to sleep in the guest room."

"I wasn't running away. I was giving you space."

"Then give me some space now, Ash."

The man frowned up at him as if Albert was a tricky case that needed to be solved. "No," Fletcher said. "And I shouldn't have last night, either. You weren't rebuilding your dignity – it was your defenses against me."

"Wrong again, Ash."

"Sorry, but I don't think I am."

The fury, which Albert had sorely missed that evening, abruptly returned, hot and potent. *If you think I'm well-defended right now, you're a bigger fool than I took you for.*

"I've handled this badly." Fletcher was musing. "All of it, from asking for the sex in the first place, through every reaction since. What would have happened, do you think, where would we be now, if I'd done the right thing last night, and not given you any space?" He gazed up at Albert, thoughtful. "What would we have between us today? The truth, I imagine, and I bet it would be pretty wonderful."

A number of sarcastic observations occurred to Albert, but he couldn't find the voice for them. Fletcher's hot blue eyes were too busy taking him apart and re-making him in some petty *pretty wonderful* image. Albert dearly wanted to halt any such speculation.

"As it is, what do we have between us but space?"

"Then why don't you do the expected thing," Albert said, "and call it quits?"

"Why don't you? Because you still wouldn't change it even if you could."

"I told you before you shouldn't rely on that."

"But I do, I continue to rely on it."

Why? Albert wanted to ask both Fletcher and himself. *Why can't I finish this?* For a disorienting moment, he thought of that photo of Miles and Rebecca hidden away in his study. He even turned as if he'd go to it and ask, because surely they had an answer if anyone did. But then he was overwhelmed by the foolishness of such a gesture. There could be no answer from a photograph, from two people who had been dead for decades, or from the child he had once been. How futile and sentimental. Nevertheless, the urge remained, and he had to force himself to face Ash again. "This discussion is pointless," he said, suspecting his voice betrayed his weakness. "I suggest we retire for the night."

"Albert, if you'd –"

"Perhaps you would like to sleep in the guest room again," he suggested with forced urbanity.

Fletcher stood. "All I want right now –"

"If you find it unsatisfactory –"

"Stop it! Just *stop* it, Albert. I want you to listen to me."

The very air threatened with all the truths and ultimatums that had been spoken, and all the many more that had, until now at least, been left unsaid. The air was so thick with them, Albert found it difficult to breathe.

"If you can leave me," Fletcher said quietly, "after all that's happened – I mean, if you can go to your bed alone right now without some kind of reassurance from me – then you're far stronger than me."

"You said you relied on me not changing this."

"Give me a break, Albert. Pretend I deserve it."

"I don't see –" Albert started. Why verbalize what was so disastrously evident? "I will not be fair to you," he said, surprising himself. "I will not."

Fletcher was frowning. "All right," he said quickly, offering reassurance to someone who would give none. "It's all right."

But Rebecca and Miles had expected a lot from Albert, and they always expected him to be fair. He raised a hand to stop Ash from moving, either closer or away. And, at last, Albert said, "You'll visit for the weekend, in a fortnight's time?"

"Yes," was the immediate and relieved reply. Then Fletcher was saying, "Goodnight, Albert. How about I lock the place up for you?"

No.

"Trust me." Fletcher essayed a smile. "You go on to bed. I'll see you in the morning."

After a moment Albert nodded, then walked to his bedroom. With the door safely closed behind him, he forced himself through the night's routine: hang and fold his clothes; dress in a clean pair of pajamas; brush and floss his teeth. All the while reminding himself that he *hadn't* forgotten to check the house, Fletcher was doing that. Briefly, he listened to the footsteps from one room to another, Fletcher testing each window, each door. Then Albert turned his bedroom lights out, arranged himself in the bed, and waited for sleep to grant him oblivion.

CHAPTER TWENTY–ONE
WASHINGTON DC
JANUARY 1985

Arms sliding on treacherous white marble, hands grasping for holds that weren't there, legs wildly swinging over empty space: Fletcher clung to the ledge of some damned stupid Washington monument, trying not to think of the stone pavement far below. Albert was standing above him, mere inches outside his arms' reach, mocking Fletch for his weakness, taunting him.

It was all very well attempting to goad Fletcher into scrambling up. The angry desire to save himself, if only to throttle Albert, might give Fletch the necessary adrenalin, the strength and determination. But that wasn't what he needed from Albert. And Fletch had rarely responded to or even cared about Albert's scathing insults. Instead, Albert was supposed to help him, supposed to reach for him, lift him up off the edge of the abyss. That was why they'd become lovers, wasn't it?

"You love me, Albert," Fletcher reminded him, gasping for breath. Albert poured more abuse on him. Didn't Fletcher have the imagination to want something different, better? Would he never break free of his disastrous, middle class notions of romance? Couldn't he make his own mold, his own pattern, rather than forever trying to conform to society's discards? "Help me, give me your hand," Fletcher tried again. "If you love me, do it."

"No. Climb up here yourself. Forget your weakness, and find your fortitude. You're as bad as Drew Harmer. Throw out all the Prince Charming garbage – you don't need anyone else to save you. Rescue yourself."

"You're hardly my idea of Prince Charming," Fletch found the breath to mutter.

"Exactly," Albert said.

Fletcher couldn't take this. His fingers were cramping and bruising from trying to dig into solid marble, the muscles of his back and shoulders were a–fire. Might as well get it over with – there was nothing for him, no reason not to. "If you love me," he said to Albert.

And he fell.

Albert didn't even care. Sneered down at Fletch falling as if this was only what he'd expected. The bastard.

Fletcher screamed in defiance and outrage, and then in fear. The stone pavement loomed below and behind him. He cried a protest against waiting for the sickening crunch and splatter of his blood and bones and brain against that cruel surface. "No!" His imagination of it was worse than any reality could be.

"No!" Darkness instead of harsh sunlight stabbing off polished white marble; a bed and quilt rather than stone. A bedroom that should have been familiar. He was alone, and that in itself was something wrong.

Fletcher rolled onto his back, drew the covers up to his chin, then lay still, breathing hard, trying to sort some sense out of all this fear.

The details soon coalesced out of the darkness: Albert's guest bedroom. Fletcher should feel safe here. In fact, after that troubling variation on his old nightmare – *Yes, it was only a dream, Fletcher,* he reminded himself – he probably felt safer here alone than in the haven of Albert's room, Albert's arms.

Wonderful, he thought with dry despair, *even that safety is gone now.* If Albert showed up, having heard Fletcher cry out, Fletch suspected it would take a conscious effort of faith on his part to welcome the man. That was ridiculous. *Do I even have that much faith left?*

It was some hours before Fletcher fell asleep again.

Breakfast was a silent meal. Fletcher watched Albert warily, trying to shake the last feelings of uneasiness from the night's restlessness. There were more important things to deal with than his latest dream, despite the memory of the expression in Albert's cruel, cold, hard eyes.

For instance, how were they to survive the Sunday of this ghastly weekend when Albert appeared so fragile that one wrong word might shatter him, when the man seemed completely unaware that he was at all vulnerable? And when Fletcher himself required reassurance, someone to tell him his doubts were unfounded, even someone to provide simple distraction?

Fletcher began to talk, one of the monologues that he usually used over the phone, intending to chat about anything impersonal. But he soon found himself saying, "Everything's pretty damned grim at the moment." Surely it wouldn't hurt to talk about work. "Caroline's money laundering thing is proceeding according to plan but I can't stay interested. I'm getting nowhere with this serial killer. It's ludicrous, trying to solve it on my own. There are hundreds of possible leads to chase up, thousands, though none of them were promising enough for the Bureau to keep the case open, all the real ones were dead ends. If I'm very lucky, one of these unlikely ones might give me a hint of the answer. So I fritter my time away, turning from lead to lead, suspect to suspect, trying to guess the right one, letting my instincts choose for me – and not really following up on any of them. I exhaust myself and all for nothing. This would have to be the most unproductive time of my life. And now you, love," Fletcher said, looking at Albert. "Everything feels so wrong between us. What we have, under all the trouble, is precious." And he said, worried that his tone sounded irresolute, "I won't give up on it."

Albert looked away, as if bored at going over old ground.

"I won't give up on the serial killer, either. I just have to – in both cases – find a way to the heart of the matter."

Well, he'd had an effect: Albert was distant now, instead of hurt and immediate. That wasn't good but if Albert needed his defenses, then perhaps he should have them.

There was one message to get across while he could. Fletcher said, very gently, "I don't want you to feel you've let me down, Albert."

The man stared at him as if Fletcher had gone crazy. "And how have I done that?" he demanded.

Fletch shook his head, and lied. "You haven't. I misinterpreted what you're feeling."

The stare grew suspicious and then slowly became uninterested.

All right. Albert had expected Fletcher to end this relationship some weeks ago, which was perhaps a reflection of what Albert really wanted. Maybe, if Albert couldn't end it, he trusted Fletcher to do so. *Be brave*, Fletcher admonished both Albert and himself, *have mercy.* When Albert had first consciously realized he was in love with Fletcher – it had been a beautiful spring day, out in the garden, Fletch remembered – Fletcher had seen Albert as forever asking a question to which Fletcher was the answer. It had been so tempting to meet the problem with its solution. But now he figured he wasn't really the right answer and maybe Albert was no longer asking. Despite all of which, this was still the most successful love affair Fletcher had ever had, which wasn't saying much, but he was grateful nonetheless. "We don't make each other very happy, do we?" Fletcher observed quietly.

Albert immediately retorted, "Happiness was never my goal in life."

That surprised Fletcher enough to threaten a smile, but he quashed the impulse. It seemed, yet again, he had goaded Albert into revealing something of the truth.

And, even more surprisingly, Albert actually continued the thought. "Only people like McIntyre are mundane enough to set happiness as their goal."

Fletcher nodded, thoughtful. All right, he would take that as license to continue the relationship rather than break it up. So be it. So help them both.

ISLAND
MASSACHUSETTS
AUGUST 1963

The summer course in analytical chemistry was being held at a college three buses away, but Albert had judged attendance worthwhile and fought to be admitted despite his age. He got so impatient with people who didn't realize ability counted for more than age. It had made a battle of learning for at least the last five or six years: teachers were inclined to decide Albert was difficult rather than realize he was intelligent.

Often, on days like today when his mind teemed with questions to which he couldn't find the answers in biology or psychology or philosophy – often he would walk home from the college, and gain two hours' exercise and fresh air while losing valuable study time. He'd reluctantly accepted that, every now and then, his powers of concentration were subject to internal disruption.

One of the distractions today was the thought of a college football jock who was also studying over the summer, though Albert suspected it was remedial mathematics and English rather than the heady heights of chemistry. There was something undeniably attractive about the big, dumb, good–natured idiot. Though how a mess of blond hair continually falling across blue eyes and an easy warm smile could make up for a deplorable lack of intelligence, Albert couldn't figure. It made no sense for Albert's heart rate to increase whenever he saw the guy loafing around the deserted corridors, offering a smile to the misfit from high school. They'd barely spoken, but the jock was surprisingly friendly for one of the in crowd.

Intelligence wasn't the trouble with the other current distraction – the girlfriend of Albert's physics tutor. The class had been taken to a planetarium on the other side of town for a demonstration. The woman who was their guide for the afternoon was tall and ungainly, but the rumor soon spread through the class: there was romance here, and the tutor was the guilty party. Everyone was impressed, even those who'd been rude about her. Albert had found himself interested despite knowing plenty of astronomy already; he was caught up by the woman's enthusiasm, by her ability to communicate with everyone in the class, to teach all of them something – even the dullest and even the smartest. In that way, she reminded Albert of a history tutor from the previous year who'd made the past come alive, teaching the class about people and motivations rather than names and dates. The planetarium guide and the history tutor shared the knack of putting any fact into context, of describing both the detail and the big picture.

Albert sighed. His recent day–dreams usually featured these two disparate people together – because, no matter how impossible it was that this football player and this scientist should like each other, it was even less likely that either of them could like Albert Sterne. To one he was the ugly geek from high school; to the other he was a difficult if gifted student to encourage.

No one liked Albert, that was simply one of the many facts of life. For that matter, Albert didn't like anyone either. He'd learned some hard lessons. Everyone on the chemistry course resented him because he was doing far better than all these people who were three, four or five years older. He could hardly admire them for such pettiness. One day soon the jock would demonstrate his lack of intelligence, or an example of his conformist racist sexist homophobic attitudes would make a lie of his friendly nature, and Albert would no longer be able to forgive all for the sake of a friendly smile. Or – if he lasted that long – the jock's fashionable and popular friends would return next term, and Albert would again be less than dirt. The teacher at the planetarium would betray her intelligence and bow to society's demands, content to marry the physics tutor who was surely beneath her, and become merely a suburban housewife and mother, thinking she was lucky that her mousy looks had gotten her that far. She could make a difference to thousands, but instead she'd settle for cooking and cleaning for four. Everyone had potential, and so far everyone in Albert's life had disappointed that potential, let themselves be less than half of what they could have become. Why?

He reached his school, and the dormitory building, with seventy–five minutes to spare before the evening meal would be provided in the dining hall. Good – he would have time to sketch out the main points he'd make in his human biology summer project. He'd helped the lecturer in setting the project, and had spent days in research already, so had a good idea of the content and layout of the finished paper. The only points he still needed to work through were the result of an unexpected trail his research had led him down, giving him a bonus conclusion to present.

In the midst of day–dreams of explaining this important finding to the woman at the planetarium, of exciting her with his own succinct, brilliant insight into the sciences – in the midst of such pathetic mental meanderings, he noticed his door was ajar. Which meant an intruder.

There were three options, in Albert's experience: someone was snooping, a teacher or a student; or someone was stealing from the rich Jewish kid; or someone was setting up a practical joke. Impotent fury swept him, left him physically shaking. He, Albert, was none of anyone's business, that was first. And second, his property and his person and his dignity deserved respect. If respect wasn't available, then distance would be a very satisfactory substitute. He wanted to yell out loud, *Leave me alone!* He had cause to cry it out silently every hour of every day.

Well, things might be different if he had a blond jock here holding his hand, some dumb ox twice as big as him, whom no one would ever pick on. Things might be very different – but Albert had never had anyone to rely on, to call a friend, so he would once again deal with this himself. And even though none of this victimization was his fault, he would feel the familiar humiliating guilty shame. *Leave me alone!*

He pushed open the door, quickly just in case he could surprise the intruder. And it seemed the name of the game today was snooping, for it was Elliott Meyer, self–elected family representative from New York, who stood up from Albert's chair.

Startled silence for a taut moment, then Elliott offered a sheepish smile. "Albert. How are you?"

"What are you doing here?" The fear and resentment wouldn't leave him, the adrenaline rush that urged fight or flight. Albert put his bag down and walked over to the desk. The man quickly shuffled out of Albert's way in the cramped quarters, and Albert checked over the desk to see if Elliott had been prying amongst the books and papers. He'd left no evidence if he had.

"If I'd told you I was coming, you'd have disappeared, wouldn't you?" Elliott said, reasonable but a little apologetic. "Like last time. I waited six hours, Albert."

"So? I didn't ask you to visit."

"This time, I really need to talk with you."

"I don't know what about," Albert said, as if he couldn't imagine they had anything in common. He busied himself tidying an already neatly and logically arranged room. "Two months and seven days until I turn sixteen," he said, "and then I won't even need to ask your opinion about anything." The terms of his parents' will and the extent of his fiscal inheritance had in effect emancipated Albert, although everything was arranged through a law firm, and there was a stipulation that he have the advice of a guardian – though at least that was only until the age of sixteen and not the usual eighteen. Needing to be worthy of his parents' faith in him, Albert had soon learned about investments and shares, the basics of the contradictory world of economics. He'd found it quite easy. "You know I only ever asked because of the legal obligation. It's not as if you manage your investments any better than I manage mine." *Worse, in fact.*

"Am I supposed to infer you don't need a guardian for any other reason?" Elliott had sunk down to the chair again. Albert glared at him. "There's no point in me asking you whether I may sit here, Albert, you'd only tell me no. But we need to talk, and I'm staying here until we do."

To his credit, Elliott seemed uncomfortable with these aggressive tactics. His wife would have no scruples about barging in like this. Elliott, though, was fidgeting, and had gone a silly shade of pink around the ears and cheeks.

Albert, still busy at nothing, said, "So start talking and get it over with."

"Where do you get your stubbornness?" Elliott asked gently, wonderingly. "Miles and Rebecca could be determined, but they had none of this belligerence."

"Leave them out of this!" the boy flared.

Elliott sighed. "I can't very well do that – I'm sorry to state the obvious, but they were your parents. They're partly why I'm here."

"You're being stubborn, too," Albert pointed out.

"Because I believe I'm doing the right thing."

"So do I."

"What's the right thing you're doing by trying to drive me away?" Elliott asked, putting on a convincing show of interest in the answer.

Silence for a moment while Albert marshaled his thoughts. He had to break his ties to these people, that was an imperative. He'd tried so many times before, throwing trouble and insults at them, insisting on speaking blunt truths, yet they persevered in considering him family. But if Elliott was going to listen today, then maybe it was worth trying the truth once more. He said, "Making my own way in the world. Without a bunch of people who think they can take the place of my parents."

"Now, be fair, Albert. I never tried to take their place."

Albert shrugged, not bothering to debate such semantic niceties.

After a thoughtful pause, Elliott asked, "Do you have friends, a best friend?"

"No."

"A girlfriend?"

Albert almost laughed. Couldn't the man see how impossible that idea was? "No." *And I don't have a boyfriend, either.* He came so close to saying it. What if he had walked in with the blond jock holding his hand? *Elliott, you wanted me to have a special friend, didn't you?*

"One of the teachers here, surely someone's taken you under their wing?"

"They make sure I take care of myself, if that's what you're asking. Like you did."

"I'm glad, but I wondered if one of them had become a friend? Surely you're someone's star pupil at least?"

"No." *Can't you see? I'm too ugly and too intelligent and too difficult. And I don't care, anyhow.*

"If you weren't so alone, this would be easier for me," Elliott said quietly.

A silence again – but Albert was abruptly interested. Okay, he'd bite. "What would be easier?"

"One more question, and I'll explain. All right?"

Shrugging in lieu of agreement, Albert sat on the edge of his bed, at the furthest corner from Elliott.

"Have you found God yet, Albert? Have you stopped denying Him?"

"No! I told you before I don't believe in that stuff."

"It's important, Albert."

"Well, carrying on about it all the time isn't going to help your case. Or your god's case," he added sarcastically.

"Then, what will help?" the man persisted.

"Nothing." Honestly, he was fed up with this bunk, and had been for years.

"Are you an atheist? Or an agnostic?" Elliott offered, "I could accept agnosticism, with your love of science. Or is it that you've found some other religion? Become a Christian?"

"Of course not," the boy snapped.

"Do you believe that we all have a soul?"

Albert frowned. "No. But … did you know when you die, your body becomes lighter? Something has left, I mean not just the expulsion of waste products. It's a scientific fact, at least I've heard that, I haven't had a chance to research it yet. I was thinking, nothing's ever lost in the universe, no matter or energy is ever destroyed, it transforms into something else – so what happens to the life force?"

"You consider science a substitute for religion? You think it will explain these mysteries?"

"No." Albert kicked himself for getting carried away. He didn't want to encourage this conversation. "You said one question."

"Answer it, then."

Albert declared, "I'm an atheist."

Elliott seemed saddened. "Rebecca and Miles lost their faith during the war, which I can understand to a certain extent. It was the sorest trial we have put ourselves through yet. Nevertheless, they did so much good, all their work, in an effort to be worthy of God. But they had no right to bring you up this way, Albert."

"They did it for people, not for your god."

"Why do you say that?"

Albert looked away, annoyed at being tricked into participation. "I told you to leave them out of this."

"How can I?"

Suddenly the boy was trying to explain it to Elliott, trying to provide something the man would consider justification. "I'm doing the best I can, and I can achieve a lot with my life, if you'd let me get on with it. Why can't your god be satisfied with that, if he exists?"

Elliott shook his head. "You are so arrogant, Albert."

"Arrogant and stubborn. Fine."

"You're setting yourself in His place, saying that you can judge what to do with your life better than He can. What if you're wrong?"

"I'm doing my best, no one can expect more than that. I don't tell other people how to live their lives, or what's important, or what to believe – and I expect the same consideration. That's fair. And at least I try. For every Einstein or Gandhi or Lacassagne there's a million rednecks out there."

"Gandhi and Einstein," Elliott repeated thoughtfully, apparently considering the boy's choice of heroes. "Who's Lacassagne?"

"The founder of modern forensic science. His main principle was, *One must know how to doubt.*"

Turning from this information with a bemused shake of his head, Elliott said, "Which brings us to my main purpose."

Silence, until Albert impatiently prompted, "Yes?"

"I don't like this. In fact, it feels all wrong, but I've thought for a long time about what's best for you. You're not giving us much choice – you made that perfectly clear yet again, refusing to join the family during the summer vacation. It's become a rather pointless charade, us inviting you every holiday and you always turning us down. Anyway, I don't suppose you'd agree, but we do have your interests at heart, Albert, for your sake as well as for Miles and Rebecca. Your father was a cousin of mine, you know, though I can never remember how many times removed."

The boy stared, sullen, waiting for Elliott to continue.

The man leaned forward, hands out as if to plead his seriousness. "Tell me what you're going to do with your life, Albert. Tell me these things you plan to achieve. Convince me you'll be all right, that you won't need us. I warn you, it will take a lot of convincing. But if you succeed, and you really want us to leave you alone, then I promise we will."

"Why?" Albert asked, suspicious of this adult promising things he surely didn't mean. "Why should you be reasonable all of a sudden?"

Elliott let out a laugh. "You're not giving us much choice, as I said. You're almost sixteen. And if that's what you really want – to be alone – then it's getting to the point where we're tired of trying to force you to be otherwise." There was a long pause. "We've failed you," Elliott continued, "and we've failed your parents, because you shouldn't be like this. But if that's the case, then we should admit the failure and let you make the most of what you are. For the record, I don't see this as being reasonable: I think it's wrong. I think being alone would be terrible for you. But it also seems like the best we can do right now. Well, not the best, but the lesser evil."

"What happens if I can't convince you?"

"Then you acknowledge the family's claims on your time and affection, and you at least listen to our guidance."

"But you're not going to let me convince you, and you're not going to convince me," said Albert. "And whoever loses isn't going to keep his side of the bargain."

"Trust me, Albert. I'm serious, as I thought you would be. We both always stand by our word."

"What if you thought you'd won the argument, but I still didn't feel convinced? You couldn't expect me to be part of the family then."

"In that case, I wouldn't have really won. We both have to agree that one or other of us has won. That's what it's all about, both sides becoming convinced of one point of view."

"This isn't just words?"

"Words are powerful things, Albert, as we're about to prove. But, no, these words are not just empty promises." Elliott paused, then said, "I know you find some things hard to talk about, but just try, and I'll listen as clearly as I can. I've given you every incentive to do well, haven't I? Tell me the words that occur to you, even if they're imperfect."

The presumption of the man. Albert was so annoyed that he almost walked away from the whole thing. But this was too important to abandon at this early stage. He finally ground out, "You don't know me. Don't think you do."

"No," Elliott said easily. "But allow me to know some things. Allow me a little wisdom."

When he could swallow back the bulk of the anger, Albert finally nodded agreement. "All right." While he didn't *want* to explain himself to this man, if that was the price of a future policy of non–interference, then Albert would try his hardest. The war of independence. He began, "I want to be a forensic pathologist."

"What?" Elliott seemed to be expressing both ignorance and surprise.

"Conducting autopsies, discovering identity, determining the cause and time of death. Investigating suspicious deaths, deciding whether violent deaths were murder, accident or suicide. Examining evidence, bullets and bloodstains and things. The clues are all there, if you know how to look. Locard – he was Lacassagne's assistant – developed the theory of the exchange of trace evidence: *Every contact leaves a trace*."

Elliott hadn't recovered from the surprise yet. He held up a hand to halt the bombardment of information. "Why on earth that particular field? And where would you work? It must be a very specialized area to get into."

"The obvious places are the medical examiners' offices in each state, but I'd prefer the Federal Bureau of Investigation: they're national, and they're very well–funded."

"Why that field?"

"Because all my skills and interests are leading me in that direction. I don't want to do medical research all my life, and I don't want to be a general practitioner."

"Isn't it rather a … macabre choice of career?"

Albert rolled his eyes, bored with this inevitable response. His fellow students were mostly squeamish about or uninterested in the class exercises that involved such things as the dissection of rats, while Albert was granted permission to conduct autopsies on the rats in his own time. The children thought he was weird. He'd heard that, in college, students actually dealt with human cadavers. No, it wasn't weird or macabre – it was fascinating, exploring this incredibly complicated and functional machine, and all that could go wrong with it.

"But why not help the living?" Elliott was continuing. "You can't help the dead."

"I can do both. If it was murder, then I can help catch the offender before he or she kills again. If it was an accident, we can learn from it and prevent other accidents. From a biology point of view, any autopsy is research. And the first thing you always try to determine is the identity of the corpse – that at least helps surviving relatives, doesn't it?"

Elliott was staring at the boy. "Is this – is this about your parents? The way they died?"

"No!" He should have known Elliott wouldn't understand. Trying to batten down the excess annoyance, Albert stood and began rearranging the bookshelf at the foot of the bed.

"I'm sorry, you must have some terrible memories. I'm just trying to fathom all this. I knew you were studying sciences, though I pictured you in – yes, in research, like you said. But you want more immediate results, do you, a more visible effect? More drama? I thought of you in a physics laboratory or something, not on the medical side, not dealing with people."

"You were wrong," Albert said, resentful. His most passionate needs were to be uniquely, completely himself and to be alone. But there was also the tiniest niggle: like most people, he wanted to be known well enough that no one would misjudge him so badly, he wanted to make sense to others. Well, from now on he'd have to forget about that. Certainly no one but his parents had ever understood him. And, if Elliott didn't know him, then no one would ever know him. On consideration, that was fine.

"All right," Elliott was saying. "But it is very specialized, isn't it? Forensic pathology. How do you know you'll get a job in the right field? Maybe you're heading up a dead end street."

"I know because I've got what I wanted so far."

"That's naive, Albert."

"No, it isn't. Remember I told you I'm studying a special course in analytical chemistry at college this summer? It was only open to advanced students there – but I was accepted because I'm good, I'm very good, and now I'm doing better than any of them. I'm already two years ahead here – and college will be the same, if not better. Later on, I might work as a lab assistant while I finish my studies, to get more practical experience."

"So it's all down to hard work and determination?"

"Yes," said Albert, letting a hint of irony creep in. "Isn't that the nicest thing any of my teachers say? *Albert applies himself.*"

"They also say you achieve the results you aim for," Elliott said, conceding a point. "But life is rarely that straightforward, or that fair. You can try and try, and still have nothing but bad luck."

"If I can't get a job dealing with forensics," Albert bit out, not really believing he wouldn't, "I'll be more than qualified for a whole range of things in the medical field – hospitals, laboratories, morgues. Broadly speaking, there's a lot I could do in most scientific fields. I can always learn the detail quickly enough. And I don't believe in luck, anyway. All right?"

"All right," Elliott allowed.

But the man wasn't sounding convinced yet. Albert turned away for a moment, figuring there were two other points to make, only two, and then he might be free of them all. This conversation must have taken longer than he'd thought for it was now dusk outside, the sun having set without him noticing. Only the desk lamp was on, so Elliott, sitting just outside the pool of light, was little more than a dimly detailed shadow. Being on the far side of the room, Albert himself would be almost invisible. That made this slightly easier.

Into the silence, and fiercely enough to startle the man, Albert said, "I'll be everything I can be, I'll work hard, and I'll do a lot with my life. That's what Miles and Rebecca expected of me, that's what they wanted for me. And that will have to be enough for you and the rest of the family." Then, haltingly, but still fierce because that was one way of forcing this out: "I'm grateful that you took care of me. I know I was ... a sore trial for everyone. You could have just put me in a home or something. But I have to be on my own now. If I can be everything my parents expected of me, and if I can do even half as much as they did, in my own way, then I've succeeded. Then you've done what you can for me, and I've done what I can, too; for their sake, and for your sake, and for me."

Silence stretched again as Elliott considered this. Then he said slowly, "I can't fault you intellectually. In fact, I'm impressed. You have goals, you have plans to meet them, and it all seems realistic, as far as I can judge, though perhaps you'll let me talk that through with your teachers. Anyway, that's all to the good. But, Albert, while you are bearing your share of a very adult conversation with me, you're still subject to so much confusion and emotion. You're older than your years in intelligence – but, emotionally and spiritually, you're still a fifteen–year–old boy."

Albert sent a steady glare of denial through the twilight, which no doubt wasn't the smartest thing to do. The trouble – one of the troubles – was he couldn't be honest with these people about some things, and he wasn't prepared to be honest with them about so much else: he wasn't prepared to give them that much of himself. And yet they were in a position to know too much about him. They'd known Miles and Rebecca, and they'd known Albert as a child, when he was too naive to keep himself to himself. Here was Elliott, clumsily blundering through this conversation – he made mistakes, but when he got it right, he really hit dead center. And it hurt.

"Maybe that's why you still need family, Albert, and religion and society. Our community is based on faith, yes, which you say you don't share, but it provides more than that. Don't turn your back on us simply because you can't believe in God."

"That's not the only reason. I never fitted in there. I only ever fitted in with my parents."

"Albert –"

There was pity in Elliott's voice; and the boy was torn with fury, undermined by the need to be understood. He really had to banish that yearning. "I'm not asking for sympathy," Albert said, betrayed by a tremble in his voice. "No one wants me back there, no one likes me, not even you, Elliott. It's the truth. So what's the point in going back? I don't like them, either. We'd all just make each other miserable. So why don't you let me go?"

Yet another silence stretched between them. Perhaps that was why this conversation had taken so long: there were so many pauses while one or other of them thought things through, worked out how to say the next thing. How few conversations involved people actually listening to each other, and changing their views accordingly.

Elliott at last murmured, "Your honesty shames me, Albert."

"You won't deny all that?" He'd cried that out, surprised and hopeful, and perhaps wanting some sort of reassurance despite everything.

"You wouldn't believe me if I did," Elliott replied sadly, "and I must try to reward your honesty with mine." After a moment, he continued, "You're an unusual person, Albert, we've always seen that. Difficult, but unusual. And we've obviously failed you. I wonder what you'd be like now if Miles and Rebecca had lived. They wouldn't have been as lost as I feel, they would have known how to guide you. What would you be? Just as smart, if not smarter, but maybe not quite as driven. You'd be happier, wouldn't you? Happier, in that quiet way of theirs. We all looked in enviously from the outside, because inside your little family you were all very contented, weren't you?"

Albert said stiffly, "If you're trying to upset me, you won't succeed."

"No, I'm not trying to do that. To be truthful, I can't see you being happy on your own, without fitting in somewhere, without having a context. Family and community and religion can provide that context. I've found that work or even a career seldom do."

"I don't care."

"I need a better answer than that."

What would the rest of his life be like, with no more of these conversations, no family dragging on him? He assumed the college teachers would be less willing, and have less cause, to take an interest in anything but his academic life, too, especially without Elliott forever peering over their shoulders like he did here. Which would be wonderful. But to make that happen, he needed to find some words now. Albert said, "If I do my best with everything I have, I might not be happy, but I will have succeeded. I think a career is more important to me than to you. And I think happiness isn't as important as other things. It's not something I give much thought to."

After a while, Elliott nodded, barely discernible in the dimness. "And fitting in?" he prompted.

"I fit in up here," Albert said, gesturing at his own head. He'd blurted that out in reaction, but now he thought of it, he found it true. "I fit in fine, just the way I am. I like to be alone. I like to have no one else to answer to, or to hold me back. I like to work things out for myself. I fit in perfectly, Elliott, and I don't want to always be adjusting that in order to accommodate other people." He took a breath. "That's the best I can say it for you."

"You're more eloquent than you suspect," the man said. "But can you understand why I find it hard to accept –"

"Yes, I can," Albert interrupted quickly. "You're applying your way of thinking to me, you're making assumptions about me based on your own thoughts and experience, but that's not valid. You like to be part of a group; I want to be alone. You believe in God; I don't. We think differently, Elliott, we value different things. We're seeing this from opposing points of view."

"That's right," the man said. "So can you explain to me why you place such a high value on solitude?"

Albert opened his mouth to begin, and then thought better of it. "You won't like it."

"Give me credit for a little objectivity, Albert. Tell me some home truths if you must."

How to word it so that Elliott didn't think Albert was being irredeemably childish? Unsocialized to the point of neurosis. Maybe he couldn't, but he had to try. "Being with people confines me," Albert started: "it feels like claustrophobia. Politeness isn't the truth. I hate having to either keep my mouth shut or tell white lies. I can only be honest when I'm alone. I want to be in a position to make my own decisions without taking anyone else into account. Other people are distracting and demanding and disrupting. They impose on me, they irritate me. They say the stupidest things, just asking to be contradicted and corrected, and then they turn on me when I do. All I want is my own peace, my own thoughts, my own place."

Elliott didn't respond.

Albert took a breath and continued, "You probably think I haven't grown up yet, that I need to accept other people will have an effect on my life, that I need to be socialized. You're probably feeling sorry for me, and guilty at not preventing this, because it's too late for me to change now. But I've just told you the truth about me, however it happened, and whoever you blame for it. And I want you to let me be that way, because that's what I choose. If I'm not what you would call happy – then I'm happiest alone and working."

A long silence, which Albert was wise enough not to fill.

And at last Elliott said, "That's all right, Albert. It's very sad, but that's all right." After a moment, "Turn the main light on."

Albert did so, and they looked at each other through clearer eyes; Albert wary, Elliott worried and mournful but with a spark of interest.

"You know," said Elliott, "I didn't think you'd win."

"It's not really about winning," Albert offered.

Elliott sat a little straighter. "You're right again."

"So you'll leave me alone?" Still not prepared to believe. Albert had long ago given up on other people, especially the New York family, doing anything outside the norm. "Now I've told you the truth about me, can you leave me alone?"

"Yes, Albert, if that's what you truly want, it seems that's the only way. It's in no one's interests to continue the battle of wills."

"It's what I want."

"I wish I could do something to help, to change this –"

"But you can't. It's all right."

"Perhaps," Elliott said, "it's time for me to learn to be as tolerant as Miles and Rebecca always were. A difficult lesson, but a necessary one. You're right: it's hard to walk away from that much pain when one feels a responsibility. But they would have had the strength to do so." After a moment, the man continued, "One thing gives me hope, Albert: forensic pathology is about the results of people's interactions. You're not as disconnected as you might think."

Albert refrained from arguing about that. He and Elliott both stood, but then didn't move either together or away. Inclined to simply say goodbye and show Elliott the door, Albert suspected the farewell wouldn't be that easy.

"Do me a favor," Elliott said.

How unexpected, Albert thought. "What?"

"Such suspicion in your voice! One small favor, so I don't feel we've completely let you down. Every September, drop me a postcard to let me know your address. You don't even have to say Dear Elliott or anything. Just an address, in your handwriting, so I'll know you're still alive. And every October, for your birthday, I'll write you a letter, to keep you up to date with the family."

"That wasn't part of the deal."

"You might want family one day, Albert. Admit it."

Privately, Albert thought not; but he shrugged.

"If you do need us, we'll be there. Let me stay in touch, at a distance."

"No more visits? Just the one letter each year?"

"And you don't even have to reply."

Or read them. Albert sighed. It was probably the best he could hope for. And who knew? Over the years, when it became obvious he was no longer part of their lives, maybe the letters would dwindle away to nothing. "All right."

Finally Elliott was heading for the door. "I've made you miss your dinner," he observed apologetically.

"I'm not hungry." How could he be, after all that turmoil? In fact, now he had time to think about it, he felt rather nauseous, and far too exposed to deal with even the few people who still ate at school. Anyhow, he could eat a larger breakfast tomorrow, if necessary. *Can we do this with a minimum of sentiment and trivia?*

Apparently not. Elliott was saying, "You know, I still miss your help in the garden."

Albert shrugged again. *Big deal, Elliott.* Sure, Albert had helped with the housework and the garden, which was fair, and which also served to cancel at least part of his debt of gratitude. He'd actually enjoyed the gardening, though that was his secret.

"Goodbye, Albert," the man said. He was almost weeping. "I wish you luck – you won't need luck, though, will you? But if there's anything else you need –"

"Yes," Albert said, partly as a gift for his father's cousin, mostly to get rid of him. "If there's anything I need, I'll let you know."

Elliott abruptly leaned down to press a kiss to Albert's forehead. Crazily, Albert almost wished he'd raised his head at the last moment so Elliott's mouth met his. That was something he often wondered at – the magic that was supposed to occur when people put their mouths together. He knew about the nerve endings there, that explained some of it. Elliott drew him into a brief hug. And just what caused that chemical reaction in the brain that meant you were in love? Strange. Apparently chocolate stimulated the same chemical reaction, which Albert supposed was the reason why it was the standard gift from hopeful lovers. He'd tried eating the stuff, but it really didn't do anything for him. He far preferred healthy food. And his chance to experiment on the too–shockable Elliott passed. The man was out the door, then was nothing more than receding footsteps.

One worry remained. Would Barb accept Elliott's decision, or would her infernal sense of duty drive her to put Albert through more trials? Albert dreaded the thought of being dissected by that woman: she was too intelligent and sharp. But, no, surely she would take this chance of at last washing her hands of the boy she called the brat. Albert sighed, locked the door, and sat at his desk. That, hopefully, was that.

Exhausted, he cast his thoughts back over the afternoon and evening.

And was struck by his own weakness. It was pathetic that his emotional life was wildly swayed by a friendly smile from a dumb jock, by an embrace from an old cousin many times removed. Was he so desperate for human contact that he fixated on such meaningless gestures? He couldn't afford that kind of vulnerability, that kind of distraction. Yet another yearning to be rigorously suppressed.

It was too early for bed, but Albert undressed and got into his pajamas, and spent another night restlessly tossing and turning. What was the secret of a good night's sleep? And why, he wondered, couldn't he find the answer somewhere in his biology texts? Why couldn't life treat him as fairly as he tried to treat it? And why were there so many impossible and unanswerable questions in the world?

CHAPTER TWENTY–TWO
COLORADO
MARCH 1985

"What do you know about Xavier Lachance?" Caroline Thornton asked.

Fletcher essayed a boneless shrug. When it was just the two of them in the relative privacy of Caroline's office, and work wasn't a burning urgency, then they would both sprawl back in their chairs – Caroline's was a high–backed executive model, Fletch in a lowly visitor's chair – and talk lazily at the ceiling. This would often occur first thing in the day, as both were slow starters by preference, or after lunch. Or, in this instance, around eleven o'clock on a Monday morning.

It wasn't that Fletcher felt lazy today, though. Instead, he was restless with the first stirrings of spring and he knew that Caroline would indulge his lack of focus to a certain extent, whether she condoned it or not.

On consideration, Fletcher thought that *friends* was too warm a description of their relationship, but he and Caroline knew each other passably well and had successfully worked together for more years than he cared to remember right now. They shared a random but enthusiastic exercise regime and were able to – this was the best part – relax with each other. They didn't socialize much, though, simply having a drink together if necessary or sharing a meal if convenient. Fletch had never met any of her family or friends or boyfriends. He smiled a little, wryly – on the other hand, Caroline had certainly met Albert, though how could she ever suspect that he was Fletcher's boyfriend? What an expression. It suggested a levity, a lightness of heart, that was certainly not present in the relationship.

"Just how long are you going to ignore me, Agent Ash?"

"Sorry." He pushed himself up to shrug properly this time, his smile turning sheepish. "Mind's wandering."

"What's new? Fletcher –" and she frowned. Something serious was forthcoming. "You've been more distracted than ever lately. And unhappy, which is not like you. Usually you're the one we all rely on to cheer us up. What is it – the money laundering case? I know it's not exactly exciting, though we did arrest twenty–two people on ninety–eight charges …"

"Yeah, you'll be quoting those statistics at every damned opportunity, won't you?" The teasing was fond, but then Fletcher asked seriously, "Is that my supervisor asking about my morale?"

"No," Caroline said slowly. "I can't fault your work. Your heart hasn't been in it but you haven't let your work suffer. I'd always wondered if that would be a problem, frankly, whether you'd let your mood or your motivation adversely affect your work. But I'm pleased to say it hasn't."

"Good," said Fletch, without much enthusiasm.

"So tell me as a friend. What's the problem? Is it your serial killer theory? Or are you having doubts about that?"

"Sorry, but there's still no doubt in my mind. Other than the fear I won't find him soon enough."

A silence threatened to stretch between them. "Why am I doing all the talking here?" Caroline asked.

"All right, yes, it's the serial killer. You know how I feel about that. And it's everything else as well. I'm at a low ebb right now. But there will be a sea change sometime soon, I promise. And, no, I don't want to talk about it."

Caroline nodded. "If you ever do, I'll be here, okay?" She smiled at his acknowledgment. "Now, returning to the business at hand … Francis Xavier Lachance. What do you know about him?"

"Not much." Fletch sat up straighter, pulling his thoughts together. "Councilor campaigning for mayor; African–American; seems rather popular. You know I don't take much interest in politics."

"You vote, though, don't you? Would you vote for Lachance?"

"Yeah," Fletch said, not having given much consideration to his decision before. "He's a Democrat, he's black, and I don't like his opposition."

"He's got my vote, too. Okay, all that aside, I guess you didn't hear the news this morning. There was a fire at Lachance's campaign headquarters in the small hours, and it looks like it was deliberately lit."

"Much damage?"

"Most of the contents of his offices are gone. The rooms to either side mainly suffered water damage. The roof had caught, but it didn't get the chance to spread. The building itself is fine."

"Is the Bureau taking an interest?"

"Yes …" Caroline seemed ambivalent about it, though. "You've assumed the good news and the bad news by now, haven't you?"

"Tell me anyway."

"The good news is that you're temporarily excused from the money laundering business."

Fletcher let out a quiet cheer.

Caroline continued, "It's going to be even duller from here on in, helping the state attorneys prepare the case. But don't celebrate too soon – the bad news is that you're going to go hold Xavier Lachance's hand for a while."

"That's fine," Fletch said, frowning. "Why is it bad news? And what makes it Bureau business?"

"Bad news because it could be a load of political garbage. It's not FBI jurisdiction, but Lachance wants to make it a civil rights issue."

"The idea being that some right–wing whites are casting their votes early?"

"Something like that. Meanwhile, he garners sympathy from the African–Americans and other minorities, and righteous outrage from the left–wingers. It's a real vote–getting stance. This guy's good. If you haven't been following the campaign, you'll find he can be very persuasive."

"I've gathered he's not short on charisma."

"There might be another reason for crying civil rights. Calling the feds in could backfire, after all – he can't let the local police think he's lost his faith in them. If he wins, he'll need a close working relationship with local law and order. But I'm wondering if he's trying to distract attention from something. A cover–up of some sort."

'Did I ever tell you you're a devious and suspicious person, Caroline?"

"Why, no," she responded cheerily. "Thank you, Fletcher."

"My pleasure."

"Anyway, you know the Bureau likes to have its fingers in as many pies as possible. We're not going to turn down a chance to make Xavier Lachance our business."

"Am I going in alone, or as part of a team?"

"Alone. But you're more than a token presence, Fletch, I assure you. I'll take your advice on this but I envisage you keeping an eye on the police investigation rather than taking it over. You'll have to handle Lachance on that if he sees it differently. The official line is that we're busy people, we have trouble sparing even one valuable agent. Unofficially, we don't want everyone thinking we're at the beck and call of any politician. Though, unofficially, it doesn't hurt to establish a relationship with future mayors ..."

"Wait a minute. Are you saying my reports should be broader than the fire itself?"

"No," Caroline said. "Unless there's more to it, as I suspect –"

"You know," Fletch interrupted, "if you were a man, you'd have got on well with Hoover."

A defiant flash of the eyes, but also a quirk to the lips and no heat to the reply. "That's a foul thing to say."

"Yes, it is. You're supposed to be mortally offended."

"I'm talking realities here, Fletcher. If Lachance is trying to muddy the waters by crossing jurisdictions and making this something it's not, then you need to be very careful to cut through all the emotive camouflage. That's something you're good at, seeing to the core of a person."

"Really," Fletcher said flatly.

"Yes. And if he tries to charm you, you can charm him right back, which is something else you're good at. You strike some people as gullible and naïve, believe it or not, and I think we can use that to our advantage. There aren't many people who can fool you for very long." And she made a peace offering: "With one notable exception, of course."

Fletch smiled, as he was supposed to, though he immediately began wondering whether Caroline suspected more than he'd assumed. "Albert," he murmured in acknowledgment. "You're so clever, Caroline, I figure one day you'll realize he has *you* fooled, not me."

"Sure, Fletcher." She continued, "One last thing on Lachance – did you know he's openly gay? Always has been, so it's old news, not an issue. Which is probably as it should be."

"You really believe that, Caroline?" Fletch asked before he could reconsider.

"Yes," she said very deliberately. "In principle. Why? Do you have something to tell me?"

Surely she was only kidding him. Fletch quirked a smile in reply to hers, and said, "No, Agent Thornton, I have nothing to declare."

"I don't know about that," she continued in the same vein. "It's been quite a while since you were in here moaning about your latest bad luck with a girlfriend. And I can barely remember the last time you wandered in wearing that inane grin that means you got lucky last night."

"You know how it is," Fletcher said casually. "A person can only embark on so many impossible relationships in one lifetime. I've sort of given up for now."

Caroline seemed taken aback. Eyebrows raised, she said, "Get outta here. I'm a few years older than you and I've had my share of impossible men. Damned if I'm giving up yet, though."

"Good for you," Fletch murmured. Then he thought he'd better offer something more, though he hated lying, especially to and about people he liked. "I took this really pretty woman out to dinner not so long ago, one weekend in Washington, but she lives in New Orleans, and she's sort of friends with McIntyre, anyway. You know, Mac from headquarters. I think she liked me but it's not an option right now. Then there's Tyler – remember I told you about Ty? She's as nuts about her ex–husband as ever. It's all impossible, believe me."

"Poor Fletcher," Caroline said with mock sympathy.

"But we were talking about Xavier Lachance, weren't we?"

"Sorry, didn't mean to pry. All right, Lachance's platform is strong on minority rights, including blacks, of course, and gays. You've seen his bumper stickers?"

"'Unity through diversity'," Fletch quoted. "'The politics of inclusion.'"

"Yeah, the guy should appeal to you," Caroline said in a tone of voice that indicated it wasn't necessarily a compliment. "I mention the councilor's sexual inclinations so that you realize –"

"What? That the Bureau can't blackmail him, on that issue at least."

"I'll make a cynic of you yet."

Fletcher grimaced, mourning his optimism, though he said, "Over my dead body."

"I've pulled the background material on him. Go introduce yourself – he's doing a meet–the–people at the mall at one o'clock – shadow him anywhere you feel is relevant, learn all you can from the police, follow that investigative nose of yours. And don't blow our expense account."

"What about forensics?"

Caroline grinned. "Too late to call *Dr.* Albert Sterne in, I'm afraid. The police and the fire department have it in hand."

Weakly returning her grin, Fletcher scooped up the file she indicated, and stood. "Thanks," he said, and headed out to his desk. As he slumped in his chair, he saw Caroline's worried gaze was still on him, through the slats on her office windows. He sat up and waved, mock cheerful, and she waved back then turned her attention to something on her desk.

Fletch sighed and quickly flipped through the file: newspaper clippings, two police reports of incidents relating to Lachance, a security clearance, copies of his birth certificate, passport and educational qualifications, and transcripts of three speeches. It shouldn't take Fletcher more than half an hour to get a broad idea of Francis Xavier Lachance.

The mall was busy with the lunchtime crowd: office workers with sandwiches and steaming polystyrene cups; women with strollers overbalancing with shopping bags and restless babies; school kids hanging out, their clothes in various stages of disarray if not disrepair. Nevertheless, it wasn't difficult to find the campaigning politician. A steadily growing knot of people wound its way through the three open squares, the people all following one man as if mesmerized. Fletcher easily picked out the man's retinue from the public: four men and women in suits, hovering but not getting in the way.

Fletcher bought himself a coffee and trailed along behind at first, but he soon became curious and eased around the crowd to watch from the front, wandering backwards when he had to.

Xavier Lachance definitely merited a second look and once anyone gave him that, it seemed he had them hooked. He had dark, warm brown skin, and traditional African–American features, all of which Fletcher recognized from the photos. But Fletch hadn't anticipated Lachance's effect when seen in the flesh, talking and smiling and moving. The energy that was somehow both dynamic and graceful obviously couldn't translate into a paper image, but even the handsomeness – or was it beauty? – couldn't be captured through a camera lens. In photos, even in the campaign shots on the posters, Xavier Lachance looked ordinary. In person, Fletcher thought, in the flesh the man was gorgeous.

It was partly the fault of the nose, perhaps. From the front, Lachance's nose was too broad, and too up-turned, though fairly short – very unflattering. But once Fletcher caught sight of the man's profile, he kept seeking the angle again and again. The man's profile, snub nose and all, was exquisite.

His hair was worn in a businesslike cut, closely slicked back, which enhanced the delicate shape of his skull. He was tall, with a quarterback's build – Fletch remembered the files noted he'd played football in college – and his every move was supple. His suit was as good and as subtle as any of Albert's, though worn with an outrageously colorful silk vest over the white button-down shirt, and a matching silk bow-tie. Fletcher grinned in appreciation. Xavier Lachance had style.

Everyone who came up to him had their hand shaken with an untiringly sincere grip. Lachance had words for them all, he listened if they had a question or a message, he replied, looking them in the eye, he smiled – and, having been thoroughly charmed, they inevitably joined the knot of people following along behind.

"Now that's an important question." A strong but melodious voice, carrying over the general bustle. And of course it was Xavier Lachance. "In fact, I'd like everyone to hear it, and I'd like to give everyone my answer."

More people drifted over to the throng, others paused in their conversations or their wanderings: so many willing to give him this chance at being heard.

"I promised no speeches today," Lachance was continuing. "And, although I'm a politician, I want you to know I don't make a habit of breaking my promises."

The crowd liked this; there was a sprinkle of laughter and a lot of smiles.

Lachance smiled, too, sharing his humor. For a second his gaze met Fletcher's, and the Special Agent found himself focusing even closer on the man, while telling himself not to be taken in simply because Lachance was willing to look him in the eye and ask for his attention. But, for a ploy, it was an honest and up-front one. Other ploys were more covert – such as, for example, the fact that the mall's usual muzak was silent today, presumably because it would have interfered with this impromptu speech.

The white teenager who'd asked Lachance this apparently vital question was still beside him, her hand captured in his. She seemed both bashful and coolly amused at being dragged into the centre of attention. And, with long red hair and a green cotton dress that showed off her figure, she was also very attractive. Who wouldn't want to hold her hand?

"Now, what was the question, Amy?"

The girl spoke, though not loud enough for Fletcher to hear.

"Amy wants to know if I'm pro–choice," Lachance said. He had a resonant voice that easily carried to the scattered crowd. "And the answer is yes, Amy, I am pro–choice. I certainly want to work towards the smallest possible number of unplanned and unwanted pregnancies, through education and the availability of effective contraception. Let as few women as possible face that difficult situation." He nodded, considering. "Personally, I admit I have some ambivalent feelings about abortion – but my personal feelings are irrelevant."

All the while, Lachance was speaking to the teenager beside him and to the crowd, still seeking gazes to meet, presenting himself as firm and fair.

"Irrelevant," he repeated, "because what matters is that the woman involved has the right to decide for herself, and for the unborn child, what the best course of action is. No one else has the right to force her either way. That's what I solemnly believe."

He looked around. Light applause scampered from hand to hand. Amy nodded happily and most people seemed supportive, or at least willing to accept that and hear the next bit.

"Pro–choice," Xavier Lachance mused in his warm strong voice – and everyone waited in near silence for a beat or two. "Yes, I'm pro–choice regarding abortion, I'm pro–choice regarding just about everything, in fact. My definition of freedom is having the opportunity and the ability to make your own decisions. *You* have the choice when to have children, which religion you place your faith in, what your sexuality is, where and how you want to live your life. And I respect that choice. It's my job, if you'll kindly choose me as mayor, to help you make the best choices for you, and to help you work together to make those choices happen."

A pause. People still waited, expectant.

"Yet freedom of choice is a heavy responsibility. It must not be abused. We must not reach the situation where one person's choices take away other people's rights and liberties. Freedom of choice must be available to all. If people haven't had the chance for a good education, if they're too poor to care about anything more than their baby's next meal, then those people have too few choices. Maybe no choices. And that's not good enough."

The crowd was mostly nodding, everyone listening.

"We all agree our community is in trouble – our town, our state, our country, our world is in trouble. Together, we need to address the causes of the problems, as well as the symptoms. We need some long term thinking as well as short term action –"

Lachance stopped, and there was dead silence. He grinned, shook his head.

"Listen to all that rhetoric," he scoffed. The crowed shifted uneasily – they had been caught up regardless. Fletcher was surprised at the use of a word with such negative connotations. "I promised no speeches. But I got carried away because I care so much about these issues. And so, I think, do you."

General agreement.

"I shouldn't call it rhetoric. I've just been talking about my approach, my broad goals. This isn't the right time or place to get into the detail of how we can make this work. But let me just say again, this is about *you*, I want to help *you*. How many of you are below the poverty line? How many of your children are receiving an unsatisfactory education? How many of you are unemployed, or have no career? How many of you suffer from prejudice, or have been treated unfairly? How many of you have been victims of crime, or even been driven to bend a law just to try to make ends meet? Our community's problems affect all of us directly. It didn't used to be that way. It used to be that these problems were always someone else's, that these problems affected most people only indirectly, if at all. That's not the case now. We are all together in the same boat these days."

There was definite agreement now.

"You've heard the call to 'think globally, act locally'. Good words to live by. But I want to do more than that. I want us all to think of the future, and act *now*."

There was a fair amount of applause, which was good for these self–conscious times. Most people were nodding and smiling, some shrugging as if to shake off the spell and regain their cynical outlook. Fletcher, supposedly an apolitical FBI agent, contented himself with smiling, then swallowed the last of his coffee and threw the paper cup in the nearest bin.

Lachance looked around, acknowledging the crowd's goodwill, again meeting Fletch's gaze among others. This time, Xavier Lachance returned Fletcher's smile with a grin.

"I have to go take care of business," Lachance said, his voice still pitched to carry. He squeezed Amy's hand and let her go with a kind look. "Someone took my words seriously and acted now – they set fire to my office last night. Any help anyone can give us in setting up again would be appreciated. Thank you all for your time today, thank you all for listening."

And, with that, Lachance led the way towards the parking lot, his retinue and a few last well–wishers tagging along behind.

Fletcher followed quickly, and caught up with the party by the curb just as their minibus pulled up. "Mr. Lachance, I'm Special Agent Fletcher Ash, Federal Bureau of Investigation." He offered his credentials, which the nearest member of the retinue peered at.

Lachance grinned. "Yes, Agent Ash, we were expecting you. In fact, I wondered if that was you."

A pause, while the other people piled into the bus. Only one woman stayed on the pavement, eyes roving. In contrast, Fletcher and Lachance were still and their gazes remained on each other. Fletch was happy enough to let the moment last, comfortable under the scrutiny, but he figured Lachance no doubt had places to be.

Before Fletch could speak, however, Lachance said, "I'm off to inspect the temporary offices my people have set up – incredibly quick work, don't you think? I'll have to thank them accordingly. You're welcome to come along, if you like, but I probably won't have time to talk to you at any length until this evening."

"Then I'll inspect the old offices this afternoon," Fletch suggested, "and talk to the police."

"Are you busy tonight? Come and have dinner with us at my place and we can discuss this sad business. Will that be convenient for you?"

"Sure."

"Sorry about the odd hours but no doubt you often find yourself in a similar predicament – there's not enough hours in the day for everything that needs to be done. You have my home address on file, yes?" That was said with an impudent smile Fletcher couldn't help but respond to with a smile of his own. "Good. I'll see you around seven."

"All right. Thank you, Mr. Lachance." Fletch nodded a farewell as Lachance slid into the bus, watched as the woman followed suit, and then the entourage drove away. He shook his head, waiting to resume normal transmission. If it were possible for someone to overwhelm his or her way into public office, then Francis Xavier Lachance was set for a very successful political career.

Xavier Lachance's old rooms were at the end of a long, one storey string of offices hired by service professionals: architects and graphic designers, solicitors, doctors and accountants were all represented. The overall look was upwardly mobile, classy in a modern pastel–and–palms way, though if Fletcher remembered correctly, the building's structure had originally housed a warehouse of some sort. The whole looked onto a paved walkway, made pleasant with wooden seats, budding trees and early flowering plants. Lachance had chosen an attractive but businesslike location.

The pastels were interrupted by water and smoke stains, then gaping broken windows exposing nothing but charred and blackened ruin. A handful of fire fighters and police officers were peeling the steel roof back from the adjoining offices, and taking photos of where the flames had reached. Most members of the public who walked past lingered to stare; workers from the other offices brought their coffee and cigarettes outside into the weak spring sunshine to participate in whatever gossip there was to be had.

A man in police uniform knelt just inside where the doors hung askew, conferring with another man in a suit and tie, who used his pen to indicate something along the skirting boards. "Hey, Hogan," Fletch called from outside the crime scene tape. "Permission to come aboard?"

The police officer looked up, then beckoned him across. "Permission granted."

Fletcher ducked under the tape and walked over to join them. "Did a thorough job, didn't they?" he observed, casting a look around the shell of the offices.

Hogan stood and said, "You G–men stick your noses into everything, don't you?"

"This time we were invited," Fletch replied with a smile and a shrug.

"So you figured you'd come down and tell me how to do my job."

"No way, Hogan, you're far better at this than me. I'm nothing but a glorified accountant, remember?" That earned him a chuckle. "I do a nice little sideline in serial killers," Fletch continued, looking around curiously, "but fires aren't my specialty."

"So why did they send you?"

"To keep Mr. Lachance happy. And I can help you with interviews, Hogan. I'll talk to his people, if you like –"

"We've done the preliminary interviews."

"– or I can do the follow–up with them. I'll try to sort out if there's anything to the theory that there's all these right wing, heterosexual, Caucasian pyromaniacs who don't want this guy elected, or whether Lachance is crying wolf. That's the boring work, right? Meanwhile, I'd appreciate you letting me know what's going on, that's all."

Hogan was nodding in a way that indicated he would suffer this arrangement, though under protest. "Well, at least they sent you," he said grudgingly. "I wouldn't let most of your people audit my taxes, let alone investigate a real crime."

"Yeah, but you only like me because I buy you a beer at the end of a case."

"And don't you forget it." Hogan grimaced in his equivalent of a grin, then beckoned Fletcher further inside. "This is our working hypothesis, right? Nothing to get excited about yet but we should have it sorted by tomorrow evening once we get the chemical tests done. The fire spread from here," and he indicated a spot low on an internal wall. "That mess of plastic used to be an electrical outlet. These walls are treated with fire retardant, so it probably wouldn't have caused much damage by itself before setting the smoke detectors off. The problem being a stack of cardboard boxes full of mail–outs right by the outlet – his people told us that's what this pile of ashes used to be – and these shelves beside that, which were full of pamphlets and posters and some stationery. There doesn't appear to be any surprises in how it spread, so we aren't anticipating finding any flammable liquids tossed around, but we'll check of course."

"So what caused it? Faulty wiring?"

"Could be," Hogan allowed. "This place used to be a warehouse, with a shopfront up by the street. When they renovated it into separate offices, it looks like there were a few corners cut, especially with the interior fittings, though nothing major. You know how it is."

"If they think they can get away with it –"

"– they will."

"You're a cynic, Hogan."

"Aren't you?" The man cast Fletcher a long look. "You're getting there at last," he observed.

"Thanks a lot. Any other theories?"

"Being a cynic, I'm not ruling out the possibility that the wiring was tampered with. We haven't dismantled this part of the wall yet, though. I'll let you know if we find anything that shouldn't be there."

"Being a cynic in embryo, I might reflect on the fact all that paper was rather *conveniently* close to the source of the flames."

Hogan almost smiled. "It was, wasn't it?"

"All right," Fletcher said, "so what was destroyed?"

"That's a smart question for a glorified accountant. And the answer is pretty much everything. The only room in the suite that didn't suffer much damage is through here." Hogan led the way, stepping carefully around all the debris, any of which may yield vital evidence.

There was a large table and a few chairs located in the next room. The wall adjoining the rest of the office was burnt almost to the point of collapse, though the other damage here was mainly smoke and water. "What's this – a conference room?"

"Yeah, meetings and press conferences and coping with groups of visitors. Nothing of value, except the furniture and fittings."

"So what was of value in the other rooms?"

"Furniture and fittings, of course; office equipment, including state of the art computers and a photocopier; glossy publicity stuff, which costs a small fortune to print; and most of his records, financial and otherwise."

"Financial records," Fletch repeated, considering. "What about the building and contents? Were they insured?"

"Yes, but for fairly conservative amounts. And, between you and me, this guy is rolling in campaign donations. You can probably find out more detail on that through your lot. Anyway, I don't figure he needs the insurance money."

"And he's popular, too."

"So he doesn't need the publicity," Hogan concluded.

Fletcher nodded absent acknowledgment, deep in thought. "Hang onto copies of the preliminary reports for me, would you? I'll come collect them tomorrow morning. Meanwhile, I'm spending the evening with Lachance and his people. I'll let you know what we talk about, all right?"

"Fine with me," Hogan said before leading the way out again. "And you'll give me copies of your reports?"

"Heavily edited, maybe," Fletcher said, smiling. "You know how it is."

"Yeah, I know how it is." But the police officer sent Fletch on his way with a friendly wave.

Dinner was a casual, chaotic affair. There were nine or ten people at Lachance's home, all scurrying around answering phones and making calls, drafting speeches and letters and press releases, seeking his approval of various papers and issues, catching up with the TV news and current affairs shows, and scattering the day's newspapers across any available space. A hive of industry, bearable because they all seemed to be having an intent kind of fun. The food was available on the kitchen table: bowls and platters of salads and breads and meats that everyone helped themselves to before returning with laden plates to whatever they'd been doing.

Somewhere in the middle of this whirlwind, Fletcher sat on a chair near Xavier Lachance, and ate a hearty meal, while trying to make sense of the group's conversations, most of which seemed to be in their own verbal shorthand. He followed the talk of points and polls easily enough and guessed that *demogs* were demographics and *ops* were photo opportunities, but when the group began talking in acronyms like DSG and RMs, Fletch lost track, though he guessed what BS was. Lachance was apparently referred to as XL, and *Excel!* seemed to be the unofficial group motto: Fletcher only sorted that out when both terms were used within one quick sentence.

"I'm sorry for all this," Lachance said as they finished eating. He collected Fletch's plate and cutlery, and led the way out to the kitchen. "It must seem like utter confusion."

Fletcher laughed. "Yes, but it's fascinating."

"We're not usually this crazy, the fire has thrown us out of kilter. But it's good to do this at home sometimes, rather than down the office, we can pretend to relax a little. And I wouldn't see home otherwise, let alone a homemade meal. Now, would you like a cup of coffee before we get started?"

"You just said the magic word."

Lachance filled a jug and plugged it in, then turned around with his arms crossed. "I shouldn't waste any more of your time, Agent Ash. You want to talk about the fire."

"Yes," Fletcher said, and hesitated a moment. "Perhaps my first interest is why you asked for FBI involvement."

"I spoke to the special agent in charge about this."

"As the agent assigned, I'd like to hear it from you. I'm sure you've already found that investigations like this inevitably involve everyone repeating themselves twenty times."

Smiling, Xavier acquiesced. "My campaign headquarters is destroyed by fire. It's located in a fairly new office building, there are no obvious fire hazards, my staff aren't careless people. I therefore suspect the fire was deliberate rather than accidental. Being a high profile and popular candidate for mayor, I am automatically a target. As I am also black and gay, I am even more of a target for certain groups of people who would not want to see me elected. I therefore suspect a crime against me that could become an important civil rights issue. I therefore invite your early participation."

Fletcher nodded thoughtfully. "If people try to hurt you, whether it's politically or personally, do you always tend to see that as a reaction against you being black and gay?"

Acknowledging this with a lift of his chin, Lachance said, "How do you have your coffee?"

"Black, no sugar." Then Fletch wondered if he should have said *no milk* instead.

Lachance laughed at his expression. "Don't be afraid of the word," he advised. A few moments passed while Lachance made two cups of coffee, then he continued, "I'm not paranoid about being forever victimized, Special Agent. But these two issues of race and sexuality are something I identify with very publicly, and they are issues guaranteed to generate reactions, both positive and negative. No, not everything comes down to me being black and gay – people also dislike me because I'm a Democrat and a feminist, for instance – but those are the issues that have aggravated people most in the past, and I see few signs of growing acceptance from some groups."

"Yet other groups are, of course, sympathetic to your honesty on these matters."

"Yes." Lachance frowned at him. "If you're suggesting this might win me a few votes of sympathy, I won't argue. But I could also easily lose people who are scared by this violence and don't want me to provoke any other incidents; I could lose people who see me as making political mileage out of this; and once the papers begin exploring the notion that this incident was staged by my own people, then I could lose the whole game because mud sticks whether it's deserved or not."

"Isn't that overreacting?"

"No, Agent Ash. I can't and won't tell you how to do your job, but you might keep these things in mind when the media come begging you for dramatic sound bites."

"I won't be making any comments to the press," Fletcher said. "Can you tell me what you've lost as a result of the fire? What was in those offices?"

"My records, on paper and computer – they'll probably be the greatest loss. Office equipment and furniture. Publicity posters and hand–outs. My staff's time and energy. They'd just put together a mail–out package for every household in Denver, and now it's all destroyed. There's no way we'll be able to replace that in time to be effective."

Fletcher was pleased to note that tallied with Hogan's estimates. He asked, "If it was deliberate, are there specific people you suspect? Individuals or groups?"

Lachance considered this for a long moment. "I'll tell you something I didn't tell the police – I wouldn't name names to them. There's no one I have any evidence against, no one I have any good hard reason for you to investigate. But I have a couple of hunches, I have my suspicions of who might be involved, or at least who might know better than I do. They might be people you're aware of yourself, people who've been militant in promoting their beliefs, which don't accord with mine. I don't tell you this lightly because I don't want any false accusations made or repeated to others. But if you could quietly look around in those directions, I'd appreciate it."

"No promises, but name me some names."

"Come back to the living room. My people will be dispersing soon – except for Lucy, she's nominated herself security after last night – but we'll talk about this in peace. This should be as confidential as possible."

"All right," Fletcher said, and followed the man. Was this where it would all get sordid and difficult? He hoped not, because he found himself liking Xavier Lachance, perhaps liking him a lot more than he should.

Almost midnight, and the house was quiet, though it still looked chaotic. Lucy, concerned with Lachance's security, had retired to a bedroom on the first floor. Names had been given, and Fletcher was relieved: there were well–reasoned arguments for Lachance's few suspicions, and there appeared to be logic and insight, rather than vindictiveness, in his approach. "These are just ideas of mine," Xavier said again in conclusion. "I hope nothing comes of it, I hope it was all an accident, but if not ..."

"I still won't make any promises," Fletcher replied, "but I may be able to look around."

"That's fine." The man smiled, for the first time in an hour or so. "Another coffee?"

They stood silent in the kitchen as the jug heated, Fletch contemplating this man he was with. Francis Xavier Lachance had proved himself intelligent and sharp and a fair judge of character throughout the day, whether he was talking to his people or his potential voters or Fletcher. He was manipulative, yes, and took advantage of opportunity, but so far at least, it seemed all for the sake of a political agenda Fletcher couldn't help but sympathize with. No doubt Lachance would make a clever and successful and stylish mayor, no doubt he would achieve a great deal in office. Added to which he was, as Caroline had warned, very persuasive. His sincerity and humor, his openness and energy were almost as seductive as his beauty.

Caught staring at the man, as Xavier was recalled from his own contemplations by the jug boiling, Fletcher smiled. "I was thinking your campaign shots should be taken from this angle."

"I'm supposed to look them directly in the eye, be honest and bold and unafraid. Staring off to the side would appear haughty at best."

"But you have the most exquisite profile." He said it matter–of–factly, then continued with more enthusiasm when Lachance merely raised an inquisitive eyebrow. "Such a finely shaped skull and that lovely up–turned nose."

Xavier suddenly turned foreboding. "No one mentions my nose and lives."

"It's gorgeous," Fletch protested, taking the proffered cup of coffee. "Thank you."

"It doesn't look gorgeous in the mirror, and certainly not in the photos."

"All right, maybe it isn't the greatest from the front, maybe you don't photograph well, but from this perspective –" He grinned, rather than provide another superlative. "Anyway, it's part of your racial heritage."

"I can be proud of my heritage without liking every little detail. How do you feel about the pale skin that's part of your heritage? What is it – British? Proud, but you just hate looking like a lobster when you catch too much sun."

"Irish–American, and I take your point, though I won't change my mind."

Lachance looked at him, musing. "Are you in the habit of paying compliments to other men on their appearance?"

"Not really." *Only Albert, and he doesn't care.*

"You know I'm gay."

"Yeah, I know," Fletcher said softly. "It's on your file, along with your home address. I know your birthday, and your mother's maiden name, and where you went last time you were out of the country."

Lachance grinned. "How fascinating for you."

"Well, you've piqued my curiosity."

"Oh yes?" The voice that had reached every corner of the mall that afternoon was now quiet, and as rich as brocade, laced with unmistakable sensuality. "How did I do that? Politically?"

"You know FBI agents can't show an interest in politics," Fletch murmured.

"Sexually?"

Fletch laughed, surprised at the man's boldness. Delighted, too, if he were honest. He said, "You know FBI agents are all straight. We're not even promiscuous."

"How, then?"

"What was the fire intended to hide, Xavier?"

This time it was Lachance who was taken unawares by Ash's boldness, though his expression was quickly schooled into mild amusement. "I knew you'd get around to accusing me of setting fire to my own offices. Sure, you have to explore every avenue but you obviously have no idea what trouble it will be to reconstruct those records, replace the furniture, virtually start over with the publicity campaign ... You think my records showed something incriminating?"

"I have to consider every possibility."

Lachance smiled, his mood returning to the playful sensuality already. It seemed that either his conscience was easy or he was a very smooth and skilful actor. "Agent Ash, you know what I think?"

"No, what do you think?" Difficult not to respond warmly to this man who hadn't taken offence at being accused, whether it was true or not.

"I think the Bureau sent me the right person for the job. We need a suspicious and creative and open mind like yours."

"I suppose I should feel flattered."

"Oh yes. But I am definitely in the habit of paying compliments to other men. Especially ones I find attractive."

For the moment, Fletcher couldn't think of how to respond. He was too busy becoming conscious of an arousal he'd been ignoring all evening.

"Especially," Xavier continued, "when I suspect the attraction is mutual."

Oh yes, Fletch silently cried in triumph. But he said, very formally, "Mr. Lachance, perhaps you've misread me."

"I don't think so." Manner still easy and unoffended.

"Then perhaps you'd do me the courtesy of taking the hint and pretending you've misread me."

"I don't think you really want either of us to pretend."

"This relationship must remain strictly business."

"But it hasn't been strictly business, has it? From the first, you liked me, you liked what I was saying in the mall, you're curious about me, and I like you, too."

"I should leave now. I'll meet with you tomorrow. Lucy gave me your schedule."

"I'm only interested in seducing your body, Agent Ash, not your objectivity. I'm perfectly happy for you to remain as suspicious of me as you feel necessary. This is sex, or I hope it will be, and the fire is business and never the twain shall meet."

Fletcher grinned weakly. "I thought I was naïve …"

"Do you always run away when another man propositions you?"

"That's an impossible question for me to answer under the circumstances."

"We both have an interest in keeping this secret. You can afford to be honest with me."

"You're openly gay," Fletch protested. "You have nothing to hide."

"But it's still not politically expedient for me to have an active sex life. And definitely not a casual one, especially with a fine upstanding FBI agent. The scandal would hurt both of us. This is just between you and me, I promise."

"And you don't break your promises." Fletch sighed. "All right. I admit I'm attracted to you. But it would be the most impossible relationship. There are so many reasons not to do it."

"But let's do it anyway. Stay the night here, and then we'll see what happens next."

Impossible. The Bureau's Thou Shalt Nots; Albert's love and trust; this case in which Lachance was suspected of at least a hidden agenda; Fletcher's serial killer case that deserved all his spare attention. But Fletcher began laughing helplessly. "I make it a rule to only get involved with the most impossible people. And you are that."

"I am that," Lachance murmured. He walked over to stand in front of Fletcher, placed a hand on the kitchen bench either side of Fletcher's hips so that he was trapped, kissed Fletch before he could draw breath to protest. The kiss was passionate, full of promise. And when Lachance raised his head, he laughed happily. "This is going to be so good," he said.

Albert never laughed, let alone joyously like that. Fletcher's heart soared, leaving the doubt behind. Yes, this was going to be damned good.

Getting to the bedroom was a haphazard dance, a maddened kiss interrupted for nothing but the necessities of shedding their own and each other's clothes. Fletcher's only moments of sense were while safely disposing of his holster and gun, wallet and credentials within sight by the bed, rather than letting Xavier dump them in the hallway. This was glorious. Being undressed by Albert was more like having a personal valet.

Xavier hauled Fletch into a close embrace, tumbled them onto the bed. Perhaps Fletch would have preferred to pause for a moment or two, drink in the sight of this new lover now that he was naked; but they were moving, Xavier over him, encouraging him to match and better Xavier's thrusts. Fletch had done this with Albert so many times: frottage, fire generating fire, skin against silken skin, so direct and simple. Yet Albert choreographed it beautifully, with endless subtle and mysterious variations on a lovely theme. Xavier was careless and joyful energy, often imperfect, but wonderful nevertheless.

Reaching their mutual goal required effort. There was none of Albert's expertise which would inspire Fletcher's nerve endings to delirium with or without Fletch's own input. From the first, Albert had seemed to know by instinct exactly how to make Fletcher feel better than he'd ever thought possible. A combination of exact biological knowledge and Albert's brand of driven perfection, and maybe some small proof that they had something unique between them …

This orgasm, while incited by beauty and boundless enthusiasm, needed effort and cooperation – but it was an orgasm, after all, as nice as orgasms always were. Nothing to be ungrateful for. And, judging by Xavier's cries, he seemed to enjoy his just as much.

As they calmed, Fletch lay still in the heavy embrace, mouth on the verge of smiling, uncomfortable in the simple physical ways that Albert ensured he was never subjected to.

Once he had his breath back, Xavier leaned up on an elbow. "First times are never really spectacular, are they, lover man?"

"Oh, I don't know," Fletch demurred.

"So let's work on it, shall we?"

Fletcher smiled fully now. "Yes, let's work on it." And soon he put away thoughts of Albert and comparisons, favorable and not. Xavier deserved – and demanded – Fletcher's full participation.

◆

The cool gray light of dawn. Fletcher woke abruptly from an uneasy sleep, troubled dreams scattering away from him even as he chased those last images. Then he shook his head, and opened his eyes wide to let the morning in, realizing he probably wouldn't want to confront the nightmares even if he could remember.

Xavier lay close behind him, providing welcome warmth and a generous embrace. The man provoked even while asleep: Xavier's early morning erection was digging into Fletcher's buttocks.

There had been a few precious times when Fletcher had woken before Albert, found himself being held as intimately as this, Albert's mouth pressed to the nape of Fletcher's neck, Albert's penis as hungry as Xavier's was. But upon waking, Albert had never done the obvious thing from that position, though he must surely have known all along that Fletcher would have welcomed it.

Fletch barely knew himself why being fucked so appealed to him. That first time with Albert, the only time the older man had ever given himself over to all the passion he felt, the act had been strange and painful. But it had also been necessary and compelling, and Fletcher had desperately wanted to get used to it, to learn to appreciate the pleasure to be gained from it. Why did Albert refuse them both something that must surely be even more pleasurable for Albert than for Fletcher? Was he too fastidious, perhaps? Did he find the idea of it distasteful or crude?

Albert must have known Fletch wanted it. He could always read Fletcher when it came to sex, read him better than Fletch knew himself and too many of Fletcher's groans were of frustration. It got to the point where Albert's hands on his buttocks mere inches away from where Fletch wanted them, while Albert sucked him, were enough to send Fletcher over the edge and beyond. Sometimes Fletcher lay back as Albert's tongue invaded his mouth, dazed with all the imagined effects of surrendering to complete passion.

Perhaps Fletcher had moaned then, at the memory of being devastated by his other lover, at the thought of what Fletcher needed. Xavier stirred beside him, stretching and incoherently mumbling and, as he moved, rubbing his penis against Fletcher as if by sleepy instinct. Fletcher answered the pressure with his own, reaching an arm back to prevent the man from drawing away.

"Sweet man," Xavier murmured, already finding a rhythm of thrusts, no matter that he hadn't yet fully woken.

Fletcher chuckled breathlessly, delightedly. How absurdly invigorating to have a lover this eager. A hand, spread–eagled against his skin, explored the back of his thigh, then encouraged it higher and forward. Fletcher moaned again, wishing with all his might, turning to lie face–down, his arm keeping Xavier with him. The hand moved from his thigh up to his buttocks, then swept along the cleft between them to cup Fletcher's balls. Fletch couldn't stifle a pleading cry. Discarding his careful lack of reaction with Albert, his policy of polite but disappointed silence, Fletcher begged, "Fuck me, Xavier. Fuck me."

The man's answer was a needy groan, a surge of warm strength against his back. "Done this before?" Xavier asked, even as his fingers ran back along the ridge behind Fletch's genitals to caress the pucker of flesh.

"Yes." Fletcher cried out the word as a finger pressed inside him.

"Not often," was the verdict. "So tight, lover man."

They were both panting after air, needing this urgent ultimate act. Xavier moved away, kneeling above him, despite Fletch's bereaved protest. Surely Xavier wouldn't abandon him, too? "Just once," Fletcher admitted. "A dildo once. And a finger, sometimes, when I masturbate." Telling all these secrets with his face in the pillow. "I want it, Xavier, so damned bad. Don't care if it hurts."

"Patience," was the reply, exhibiting more control than only moments before. "Need some stuff."

Then the miracle of those fingers returning, soothing cool lube into him. A strip of condoms dropped onto the sheet beside him. It was going to happen. Fletcher almost whimpered with relief and crazy need.

"First I'm going to ease you up a little," Xavier said in that rich brocade voice of his. "Make you come, let you relax. Then I'll fuck you all you like, lover man. It'll be so damned good."

Xavier never breaks a promise. Stripped of wry humor, it was the only coherent thought later, amidst the feverish hot and cold of being possessed. "So damned good," Fletcher repeated again and again, even when the pain fought for supremacy.

"Sweet man," Xavier murmured in reply, "my sweet lover man."

"Are you all right, Fletcher?"

He didn't bother opening his eyes. "Overwhelmed," Fletch said, before thinking about it. "No, thoroughly annihilated."

"That doesn't sound so great."

"It's damned wonderful, actually." The feel of this warm strength lying against him, after all they'd just done, was devastation in itself.

"Lover man …" The voice hesitant, the body shifting uncomfortably. "I'm on a schedule, you understand."

"Ah, yes." Fletcher looked up at Lachance, moving now to kneel above him, and couldn't help but smile at what he saw: Xavier was so damned beautiful. "I excuse you from further duties," Fletch intoned. Then, at the other man's fleeting exasperation, "Sorry, you've got me feeling all whimsical. Whoever created the phrase *fucked silly* must have known me in a previous incarnation. I'll start making sense again soon."

"Good. You take first shower, if you're up to it, and I'll make the coffee, all right?"

"That would be fine," Fletch said lightly, and then frowned at himself. Why did that sound wrong?

"What is it, Fletcher? I know I was pushy last night. And then this morning." Xavier groaned in what sounded like confusion and disbelief. "One hell of a first date, but I have to take the opportunity when it comes these days."

That would be fine. It sounded wrong because it was one of Albert's phrases. Fletch sighed, and looked up to where Xavier hovered over him, concerned but running late. "I'm all right, really, you haven't hurt me. There might be a million reasons we shouldn't have, but don't ask me to regret it, okay? I would have done the same even if I did have time to think. And I expect you not to regret it, either. There's a difference between force and passion, isn't there? And I like your passion, very much." Having settled that to his satisfaction, and received a nod of assent from Xavier, Fletcher began the arduous task of sitting up. "You go have first shower, I'll make the coffee," he suggested. "I'll only hold you up otherwise."

"Are you sure?"

Fletcher smiled at him. "Yes. Now, go!" He was rewarded with a kiss on the nearest available piece of skin – his shoulder – and then he was alone.

CHAPTER TWENTY–THREE
COLORADO
MARCH 1985

By rights, he should be exhausted, what with a lack of sleep and an abundance of sex. Instead, Fletcher was all euphoric energy as he rushed around his apartment, showering, shaving and dressing. Beyond this brief reflection, he didn't even bother worrying about fatigue catching up with him. He just wanted to get ready and out on the case again. He just wanted to see Xavier, in any context, and talk to him and make it clear he'd enjoy more than the one night together.

But first he should check in with Caroline. He scooped up the phone from where he'd last left it, hunched his shoulder to hold the receiver, then tried to dial Caroline's number while walking over to the kitchen and simultaneously untangling the phone cord. Sure, it was convenient to have the cord so long he could use the phone anywhere in the apartment – he'd often pace restlessly when talking to Albert, or sprawl on the sofa, or make endless cups of coffee, or lie on his bed – but it was damned inconvenient when the thing tied up his few pieces of furniture. "Caroline, it's Fletcher. I'm probably not going to get to the office today."

"Lucky you. How's it going?"

"Fine." Having reached his goal without mishap, Fletch poured himself a cup of coffee. "The fire could go either way: arson or accident. Hogan's in charge of the police investigation and cooperating under token protest. Lachance has some theories about who might have done it, which aren't as crazy as I was expecting but I'm going to step very carefully there. Frankly, if the fire turns out to be accidental, it won't do anyone any good to make loud accusations and Xavier sees that as well as anyone. It's his political career, after all. I'll probably be running around all day doing follow–up interviews and checking alibis, and Hogan's initial reports should be ready."

"Fletcher," Caroline said slowly, as she always did when thinking out loud or considering ramifications, "you sound like you're having fun."

An alarmed pause, then he quickly replied, "Actually, it seems like a pretty fruitless exercise."

"So why do you sound a lot happier than you did yesterday morning?"

Damn. He'd assumed the inundation of information would mask any evidence of the inane grin he knew he was wearing. "Change of scene, I guess," Fletch offered.

"Well, stay happy, and stay in touch, okay?"

"Sure. Look –" How to word this? "You might find it hard to get hold of me. Xavier and his people keep long hours, so I'm fitting in interviews whenever I can. You could call his office number, that's the same as before the fire, or his home number, or call Hogan, and if none of them know where I am, just leave a message with one of them. All right?"

"All right. As long as you stick to the usual routine."

"Nice of you to care, Caroline." The rules demanded that he phone in or physically check in at least once a day, and advise his location at any time if there were even the slightest chance of danger. He should also be contactable so that he could be assigned to a new case, or take care of developments in an old one, within two hours.

But Fletch didn't want to tell Caroline he hadn't gotten home until an hour ago. Not yet, anyway, not unless it became a habit. He'd already figured he could imply he'd slept with Lucy in the guest room, rather than with Xavier. And he loathed himself for thinking of such a self-serving lie, even more than he loathed the FBI for forcing him to consider telling it.

Hogan was at his desk in the middle of the chaos of the police station, typing with two fingers and great concentration.

"Is that a report on the fire?" Fletcher asked, sitting down beside him and casting a curious eye over the cluttered desk. No knowing what fascinating information lay here.

"No, it's real work," Hogan growled in reply. Then he said with mock politeness, "Good morning, Agent Ash. I was expecting your interruption this morning."

"I wouldn't want to disappoint you."

"Why don't you make yourself useful and fetch me a coffee? Then I can get this finished before wasting my time with you."

"All right." To give the cop a few extra minutes, and to save himself from this precinct's sad idea of coffee, Fletch headed over the road to a cafe he knew was decent. He returned laden with two cardboard cups and a half dozen bagels.

"The day is looking up," Hogan observed, eyes lighting as they saw this offering. "I don't usually get bribed until lunch at the earliest."

Fletcher contented himself with munching a bagel and sipping his coffee, while Hogan did the same and finished his report. When the police officer could spare him his attention, Fletcher's first question was, "Why do you say it's a waste of time?"

"I'll bet you any money you like the fire was accidental."

"So why does Lachance see it as more than that?"

Hogan shrugged. "He's overly sensitive. Inclined to see life's misfortunes as political commentary."

It was hardly a new notion but Fletcher considered it with a frown and offered, "Lachance doesn't strike me as likely to overreact." But Fletch respected this cop's hunches: if Hogan felt this wasn't arson, he was probably right. "I was wondering," Fletcher said, "about the front doors of the office – they were hanging open. Were they like that when the fire department got there?"

"Another good question from the glorified accountant. No, they weren't. The glass in the windows and doors had been blown outwards by the heat. There was very little broken glass inside the office, and the door frames appeared to be intact and securely locked, which indicates there was no forced entry. We busted the doors open yesterday morning, once we'd examined them, to get better access."

"Was there any evidence of forced entry through the other offices? Holes in the walls or whatever?"

"Nothing yet, though we're still looking just in case. There's a back door with access to shared facilities – kitchen and restrooms. If someone had access to that area, or to the adjoining offices, he would still have to break into Lachance's office. But it looks like there's no forced entry anywhere, so we need to look at the people who had a key. Who could get in there, and do any of them know about fire?"

"What, they'd have to know something about how to hide evidence of arson?"

"Yeah. This was either very clever, or an accident, or maybe carelessness. There was cloth trapped in amongst the wiring inside the internal wall. We're talking to the electricians who helped with the renovation but they're protesting their professionalism. There's still no evidence of flammable liquids, on the cloth or the box of mail–outs or anywhere else, though there's turpentine available in the common kitchen, among the cleaning stuff. And there's no timer, so if it were arson, the guy would have to let himself in, get the thing started, then neatly lock up again and leave. I can't quite see it."

But Hogan appeared to have some remaining doubt. "Not quite?" Fletcher prompted. "What doesn't add up?"

"The sprinkler system came on, activated by the smoke, but it was fairly ineffective. Still, there's no evidence of anyone tampering with it. The building owners are having it replaced once we're done."

"You're not closing the case?"

"No, we're not closing it," Hogan said, "but let's say we're scaling it down. There are a number of things we'll still check out as thoroughly as possible but there're a few more urgent cases we need to work on, too – some definite cases of arson."

Fletcher sighed. "Lack of resources, right? We're the same. If your instincts tell you it's a hopeless case, you tend to devote your energy elsewhere."

With a trace of defensiveness, Hogan said, "I've been dealing with fires a long time, Special Agent."

"I know. I'd trust your hunches about fires any day of the week." Fletcher let out a laugh. "Anyway, I'm the last person to criticize another for acting on their instincts – I do it all the time and then spend days trying to justify it to my supervisor."

Hogan accepted this with a nod, and reached for another bagel.

"This is where I come in handy," Fletcher continued. "I'll keep looking out for suspects and working with Lachance, and if I come across anything useful either way, I'll let you know." He pulled out his notebook, and tried to interpret his scribbled thoughts. "One last question. You would have got the staff to describe everything that was in the office, right? So, was it all where it should have been?"

"You'll want my job next, won't you?"

"No way. I've just been doing a little research." Some while ago, Fletch had borrowed a basic forensics text from Albert, with the sworn intention of brushing up on a few technical matters relating to the serial killer case. As it happened, the first time he'd opened it was this morning, after he'd called Caroline. A quick skim of the section on arson had been the source of the questions that Hogan was so impressed with.

"Yes, there are burnt remains of the right substances in all the right locations. If anything were moved or stolen beforehand, it was replaced with something similar enough to fool us."

"All right." Fletch stood. "Thanks for your time."

Hogan demanded, "You're going to leave those last bagels here, aren't you?"

"In return for copies of your reports so far."

"You drive a hard bargain," the police officer said, but he handed over an envelope already marked with Fletcher's name. "No doubt I'll be hearing from you."

"No doubt at all."

Late that morning, Fletcher tracked Xavier Lachance to a new childcare centre he'd just opened and watched from the sidelines as the politician did the rounds of the gathered crowd, glass of champagne in hand. It seemed only Lucy was accompanying him today; she nodded a greeting to Fletcher, and tapped Xavier on the shoulder, drawing his attention to the waiting FBI agent. As soon as Xavier's gaze found Fletcher, he smiled so unreservedly Fletcher couldn't help but respond.

Careful of the inane grins, Fletcher reminded himself, too late. Xavier held up a spread hand: *Five minutes?* Fletcher nodded, and sat by the door, content to watch.

Again, Xavier seemed friendly and sincere, interested in everyone he approached, willing to listen and be concerned and respond in whatever way he could. If it were an act – and Fletcher had to force himself to assume it was, to some extent at least – it was a very convincing one.

True to his word, Xavier and Lucy joined Fletcher five minutes later and they walked outside, Xavier waving a few last farewells. "You've found me at my main occupation of late – kissing hands and shaking babies."

Lucy rolled her eyes as if she'd heard this a million times already, but Fletcher laughed.

"How's the investigation going, Agent Ash?"

Fletcher smiled at the formality, which was surely unnecessary in front of the one person who knew where and how he'd spent the previous night. "I saw that you had a free hour on your schedule, so I was hoping we could discuss a few ideas I've had."

"Of course. Let me take you to lunch. Lucy, will you let Fletcher be my shadow for an hour? I think you can trust him."

She let out a chuckle. "It's all right, I know when I'm not wanted. Shall I pick you up in an hour? Or, Agent Ash, could you drop Xavier off at the new offices?"

"I can do that," Fletch said. And, minutes later, he and Xavier were seated in a booth at a nearby Chinese restaurant, ordering a feast.

Once they'd been served their drinks and there was no one in earshot, Xavier leaned closer and asked, "Are you all right, Fletcher?"

Smiling at this concerned echo of Xavier's question that morning, Fletcher said, "No harm done." He felt used and abused, rather than hurt, and it was delicious. "I'm still damned wonderful."

"You are that, sweet man." A moment of silent communication, then Xavier withdrew a little, and said, "We'd better talk about the fire."

Fletcher refused to let himself acknowledge a tiny smack of disappointment. "It's beginning to look more like an accident than arson," he said, then waited for a reaction.

Lachance nodded slowly. "I'd be glad if it were. But indulge my paranoia for a while longer, will you? I don't want to take any chances."

"I haven't been given any time limits but I'm gonna have to get back to other work by next week if we don't uncover anything surprising."

"What have you found so far?"

But Fletcher hadn't thrown all caution to the winds. "We have less than an hour and I need to talk to you about possible suspects. Besides, the police haven't finalized their reports yet and I don't want to mislead you. All right?"

"All right." The food arrived, and they each piled their plates high and took a few hungry mouthfuls before Xavier prompted, "Which possible suspects?"

"When you're investigating cases of arson, the motivation behind the crime is the most important thing to consider. There are as many possible motives behind arson as there are behind murder. For instance, it could be vandalism just for the thrill of it, or a pyromaniac fulfilling a need."

"Is that a possibility with this case?"

"There's a chance it could have been a pyromaniac, but we haven't had any other similar incidents for some while. A factor in favor of that theory is that you're in the public eye, so there was guaranteed publicity. Another motive could be your political opposition wanting you out of the election."

"The other candidates personally? No." Xavier shook his head decisively. "And I don't want people speculating along those lines. My colleagues and adversaries could retaliate by throwing far more effective weapons at me than that."

Fletcher frowned. "Like what?"

"Nothing justifiable, lover man," Xavier said with a smile. "Don't you know how dirty politics can be? There's always a lot of innuendo flying around during a campaign but if the opposition pick the right rumor, I could spend all my useful time in denying it, and still the mud would stick. I am very careful, for instance, not to spend any time with children unless there are a great many adults there, too. The average person on the street still seems to equate gays with pedophiles, which is not only insulting and prejudiced, but has also been proven statistically untrue."

"I see," said Fletcher, taking a moment to consider the implications of this.

"If it's political, it's more likely to be a maverick acting alone, or a local Klan type of group, as we discussed the other night." Lachance punctuated this thought with a stab of his chopsticks. "Have you been looking into those names I gave you?"

"You'll have to trust me on that for now. I'm handling it."

The man turned a small, intimate smile on Fletcher. "Of course I trust you," he murmured. "I wouldn't have talked to you about my suspicions otherwise."

Fletcher let a beat go past. They had to trust each other in this situation, that was all there was to it; Fletch had to work on the assumption that their mutual respect was robust rather than fragile. "Okay, another motive is revenge. How about jealous or spurned lovers?"

"What, all of them?" Xavier cried in mock protest. The smile turned to a deep laugh. "No, I haven't had a lover for far too long, Fletcher. There's no one who's jealous of my time or attention right now, except maybe you."

Ignoring this, though unable to repress a smile, Fletcher continued, "Revenge by a disgruntled employee or ex–employee?"

"No. I am blessed with a happy team of people, you've seen that for yourself. Most of them are volunteers, of course, and a few of them have dropped out along the way, but not with any bad feelings on either side. I could be deluding myself about all this, but I honestly make a big effort to be fair and to let my staff know that I appreciate them."

"Revenge by a dissatisfied voter?"

Xavier shrugged. "Unlikely, though I can't answer for everyone out there. The problem with that theory is, as a councilor, I don't think I've been individually involved in anything that's caused anyone to feel that sort of grievance. Once I'm mayor, that might be a different matter."

"The fire could be camouflage for another crime, such as burglary or embezzlement."

"There was nothing there to burgle other than the furniture and office equipment, and the police tell me my photocopier and computer are puddles of plastic."

"There's nothing missing from the lists your people gave us," Fletch acknowledged. He helped himself to the honey beef, and began chewing happily.

"As for embezzlement, I don't think so. I trust my people and there're a few of us who keep an eye on the finances. There haven't been any untoward losses. But I suppose I'll have to leave that to you – seeing as you suspect me of destroying my financial records on purpose."

Fletcher shrugged an apology. "You know how it is. Who's trying to sort through those records? I'll need to look at your bank statements and maybe I can help them with the reconstruction at the same time – it's in my interests to work all that through as quickly as possible."

"I'll introduce you when you take me back to the office."

"Have any of your people worked for the fire department?"

"What?" Xavier frowned. "No, not that I'm aware of. I don't know enough about all the volunteers to say, mind you. Does that make them more likely to be suspects?"

Grinning, Fletcher said, "No comment, Mr. Lachance."

"All right, have you maligned everyone possible yet?"

"One last motive – insurance fraud."

"Me or the owner of the building? Either, I suppose, though you can count me out. We had the contents insured, so I'll be able to replace that fancy photocopier, but that's hardly a reason to go to all this bother, is it?"

"Not really," Fletch agreed. They each leaned back against the walls of the booth, having eaten their fill. "That was delicious," Fletcher said after a contemplative moment. "Let me take the check. I'll claim it as expenses, seeing as we mostly talked business."

"Or I could take it," Xavier offered. "Campaign expenses. Have to woo the voters, you know."

"You won my vote this morning." And Fletch laughed, a little surprised at his own boldness.

Xavier murmured, "So, what are you doing tonight, lover man?"

"Putting a few hours in on this case."

"I'm attending a dinner function but you could come over later on – midnight, perhaps? – and stay the night."

"Yes." All the reasons not to do this crowded round him again, but Fletcher was too focused on the man across the table to pay them much heed.

Breaking the moment of silence, Xavier said, "You know, Agent Ash, I've often wondered something."

"What?" Fletch asked.

"I've often wondered whether the FBI bugs my house."

Great – another lover paranoid about eavesdroppers. But Fletcher grinned, and said, "We'll soon find out because if they do, I'll get fired."

"If that happens, you could work for me instead," Xavier suggested.

Fletch said, "Sure I could," as if it were a joke. But the idea was appealing in a silly kind of way, which he put down to being under the influence of a mammoth crush.

❖

It was so damned good to seek satisfaction with this man, the shared journey as rewarding as reaching their goal. The intense, unbounded sensuality of Xavier Lachance in this intimate situation was … something far beyond the persuasiveness with which he swayed voters, and that was overwhelming enough. Fletcher responded to it with passion welling within him, answering every move with joy. He was aware of the moment when Xavier abandoned rationality and surrendered to the need driving him – Fletcher let himself enjoy that for a while before the urge to also give in became irresistible.

He didn't remember himself for a long while afterwards, then swam up to consciousness as if he'd been deeply asleep. Cool thoughts intruded.

His lover caressed his face. "Regrets, sweet man? You look sad."

"How could I be sad?" Fletcher asked.

"Sex is best when it's unwise," Xavier asserted in that lazy rich voice of his.

Laughing, Fletcher said, "You think so?" He turned, edged a little closer to increase the reassuring physical contact between them. "This is about as unwise as it gets."

A long and easy silence as, so very slowly, they grew from exhausted, through considering it possible that they might have sex again this lifetime, to knowing it would happen again and very soon. Xavier's hands began to gently skim Fletcher's skin, explorations at first soothing, becoming stimulating. "Tell me about this other man of yours."

The unexpected request left Fletcher afloat in poignancy. "There is someone," Fletch acknowledged.

"But you're mine for now."

"Yes." The poignancy sharpened to regret, stabbed him through, but the pain died away. Xavier's lips were sweet at his throat. For a myriad complex, tangled reasons, most of which he didn't really comprehend, Fletcher couldn't have this with Albert. "Love me again," Fletcher demanded.

Xavier did not immediately obey. "If you're sad for him, you could ask him to join us."

A surprised laugh strangled Fletcher for a moment. The idea was so preposterous it was almost funny. "I don't think so …" And then he remembered Albert had conscientiously performed that bondage game merely because Fletcher had asked for it. He wondered if Albert would agree to this request, too, and voluntarily hurt himself that much. It was a bitter, sickening thought.

"As you wish."

The lips moved lower, fastened on a nipple, but Fletcher batted him away. Doubt opened a chasm beneath him. This all seemed so wildly inappropriate. Fletch said, "He loves me, you know."

"Then he'll forgive you for this, for me. He'll do what you want, if you change your mind about a threesome."

"No, you don't understand; it will hurt him just knowing about this. Don't make light of him. He really loves me. He deserves respect, if nothing else."

"But you don't love him," Xavier said. "Is that why you're sad?"

"I do love him. But not as much as he deserves. Not in as many ways as I want to. There are things … missing between us." And it did make Fletcher sad, indeed. He wanted to forget about the whole damned heartbreaking mess. "Love me," he demanded again, voice tainted with desperation.

"I am going to love you," was the murmur as Xavier at last moved over him, "I am going to fuck you, sweet man, I am going to make you mine."

Fletcher lifted his arms in welcome.

Despite utter exhaustion, Fletcher lay awake, troubled and restless with thoughts of Albert. Beside him, Xavier snored, obliviously taking up two-thirds of the bed. He was not so polite a sleeping partner as Albert.

Fletch grimaced. This was simply the worst timing because, some while ago, he had finally talked Albert into taking a weekend off to visit him in Colorado, rather than Fletcher forever going to Washington, and here he was in the first passionate throes of an affair with Xavier … It had taken a lot of work to talk Albert into spending a few days up here without the pretext or distraction of work, but Fletcher had needed the man's loving attention.

Well, he had gained more loving attention than he'd bargained for. And, to be fair, Albert would have to be told.

It would hurt him, Fletch knew it. Albert's barriers and defenses would never have been built so strong unless there were some precious, tender, deep feelings in there to protect. And Fletcher was the one person to be allowed to broach the fortress, even to the small extent he had. This was betrayal, despite that he and Albert had never promised each other anything, never vowed fidelity, never planned further ahead than the next weekend they would meet.

But Fletcher needed the sort of passion he'd found with Xavier. The sort of passion Albert may well feel but that couldn't breach the defenses from inside. And, *Oh damn it*, Fletch groaned, he'd long ago warned Albert that Fletch was as selfish as the next man.

Albert Sterne was the most interesting and valuable person Fletch had ever met. Albert's regard for Fletcher was the highest compliment he'd ever been paid, and should be rewarded with continuing loyalty. But Fletcher figured that, from this perspective, Albert was also the most frustrating and sad person he'd met. It was tragic that such incredible potential should be so flawed.

Take the sex with Xavier, for instance, Fletcher thought. Only once had he been caught up by Albert like that, carried away by a partner who had already let himself be carried away by passion. Only the first time, when Albert had shed the care and the caution, provoked by whatever need into possessing his new lover. It wasn't even the prosaic act of fucking, it wasn't simply that. There was so much that Albert would not let himself, and therefore Fletcher, feel.

But Fletch didn't want to justify this to himself or reason it away, and he didn't want to blame this on Albert, or on Albert's acts and omissions. He owed more than that to the man.

Well, Fletcher figured this affair with Xavier would soon be over. The passion was glorious but there was nothing substantial enough to sustain it, no friendship or love. Just a crush, a sense of being overwhelmed, merely lust. Beautiful and intense but short–lived, like a desert cactus that brought forth the most luscious and delicate of blooms on but one day a year.

Though maybe they could build on that lust, just as he and Albert had built on friendship. After all, Fletcher and Xavier believed in many of the same things. Xavier was going to do so much good in the world, work on achieving his broad goals of equality and acting together to solve the world's problems. *Think of the future and act now.*

Fletcher turned to look at the man beside him, his arm casually embracing Fletcher's waist even as he murmured something in his sleep with evident satisfaction. Fletcher would watch Xavier's career with interest, with joy. But wouldn't it be even better if Fletcher could be part of it, could follow not only his career but his thought processes, his decision–making? Wouldn't it be wonderful if they could be not only lovers, but partners? Xavier's joking offer, *You could work for me instead*, might be possible, might be serious. A way to do good, to give something back to the world, without having to empathize with a serial killer or spend weeks mired in laundered bank records. What a seductive idea.

"All we do is talk and have sex," Fletcher observed, standing propped against the kitchen bench.

"Is that a complaint, lover man?"

"No." Fletch grinned. "I'm partial to both activities."

"There's no time for anything except sex," Lachance explained, "and what can we do in between times but talk?"

"Talk and drink coffee," Fletch said, lifting his mug for a welcome mouthful.

Thursday night – or, to be precise, very early on Friday morning – and another post–midnight rendezvous at Xavier's house. They were both running on nervous energy by this time but, being a politician and an FBI agent, this was nothing new. And the rewards, in this instance, were both immediate and obvious.

As soon as Fletcher had walked in the front door half an hour ago, he'd found himself wrestled to the carpet. Xavier had only paused long enough to inform him Lucy had returned to her own home, before going down on Fletch and encouraging him to return the favor. Fletcher feared he'd never again see the front foyer without an attack of self–consciousness.

"Actually, I do need to talk to you," Fletcher added at last.

"What about, sweet man?"

"I'll spend the day tomorrow wrapping this case up – I'll talk to you about that in a minute – but then I have a visitor for the weekend, so I can't see you again, until next week at least." He paused, unsure of Lachance's intentions. "I would like to see you again, lover."

"I'd like that, too, Fletcher," was the easy response, but then a silence stretched before Xavier asked, "This visitor is your man, right?"

Fletcher nodded.

"And you'll tell him about me because you're more honest than smart, and he'll be jealous. And maybe you'll change your mind about seeing me again."

This deserved some consideration, but Fletch soon shook his head. "I'm afraid I won't change my mind."

"Hey, I'm amenable if you are, but let's see how you feel after the weekend."

"You're more fair than smart."

Xavier smiled. "Call it fair if you like, sweet man. Now, tell me about the fire."

"They're closing the case, calling it an accident."

"*Calling* it – Do they have doubts? Do you?"

Leaving a long silence, Fletch again considered how much he should say. "There was cloth amongst the wiring. It shouldn't have been there. The wiring was faulty but that in itself might not have caused much damage. The sprinkler system wasn't as effective as it should have been. If it was an accident, it was unlucky. If it was arson, it was clever, almost too clever as if they wanted to taunt us with doubts but no evidence."

"I'll accept your judgment in this, Fletcher. Do I push it further, or do I let them close the books?"

"Let them close it, Xavier."

After a moment, the man nodded. "You have no doubts, then?"

Fletcher laughed. "There aren't many things in this world I *don't* doubt, actually."

Xavier seemed interested. "What are those few things?" When Fletcher refused to answer, Xavier laughed, too. "The fact your man loves you, right?"

"And the fact the sun will rise tomorrow. I can't afford to doubt that." He hadn't yet told Xavier about the serial killer – that could wait.

"But you doubt me," Lachance continued.

"Yes. Because you didn't have to call the FBI in. You're not inclined to overreact and you're not naïve about what the Bureau's agenda is. So what was the real reason, Xavier?"

"If you haven't figured it out, lover man, you're not as clever as I suspect you are."

Fletcher frowned at him, and took another fortifying swallow of coffee. "I think you knew I'd find something in that story of a Klan group. You knew they weren't behind the fire, but it was an excuse to point the Bureau in the right direction, without making any public accusations that could easily rebound on you."

"You have a devious mind, Fletcher. I knew you were right for this job."

"You're admitting it?"

"Certainly not, sweet man. So are you doing something about the bastards?"

"You'll have to trust me on that. I'm not allowed to give you any detail except whatever directly relates to the fire." Caroline's explicit orders were to ensure Xavier would leave the other matter alone. "I really can't talk to you about it."

"Just promise me the FBI will do what they can, and I'll trust your word."

"Yes, they'll do what they can." Fletcher took one look at Xavier's eager face, and his instinct to honesty won. He knew it could be a problem in an FBI agent but if Fletch couldn't see a good reason for keeping a secret, or if there were better reasons to tell it, he found it hard to keep his mouth shut. "As soon as I told the people who handle that sort of thing, their eyes lit up. You should have seen them, you'd love their enthusiasm. But you'll have to patient, Xavier. To do this properly, to net as many of the right people as possible, it could take a couple of years to infiltrate and investigate the organization."

"That's fine, as long as it gets done."

"You know, I should be angry with you for wasting my time and lying to me."

"But it was worth it, right?" Xavier smiled, disarming. "The result justifies the tactics."

Fletcher almost wished he could resist returning the smile.

"Your people wouldn't have taken me seriously without the pretext of the fire because I had no evidence. There were a lot of rumors, though, if you knew where and how to listen." Xavier put his coffee mug down and began stalking around the kitchen bench towards Fletcher. "I appreciate your honesty, lover man," he murmured. "Tell me truthfully this hasn't been worth it. Apart from business, we were obviously both in need of –" each word now punctuated by a step nearer – "some raw, uninhibited, hot –" until he was close enough to kiss – "fucking."

"Yeah," Fletcher breathed, letting the spell fall over him again. "Slowly this time, Xavier," he whispered. "Let's savor this."

"Sweet lover man …" as Lachance led him to the bedroom.

Soon Fletcher was exploring skin with hands and eyes and mouth. "You're rich dark chocolate, just as sweet and addictive."

Xavier laughed. "That's an obvious image. Almost crude in its lack of imagination."

"Maybe," Fletch retorted, "but some of my most erotic fancies involve chocolate."

"So what else are you being obvious about? You think I'm a tireless black stud with an enormous hungry cock?"

Fletch smiled up at Xavier from the man's nether regions. "Well," he demurred, "you're a tireless black stud."

Lachance's laughter grew broader. "Hell, I'm looking forward to being excused from further duties this weekend – I don't claim to be tireless. And, as for my hungry cock, admit the fact that your lily white ass loves it. I know exactly what to do with it."

"Yeah, you know what to do with it." Though Fletch couldn't help remembering Albert, whose knowledge about exactly what to do with Fletcher exceeded Xavier's in both quantity and quality. Except for the fucking, of course, and Albert was probably aware of that, too, even if he never acted on the knowledge.

"Hey, sweet man, concentrate. What are you day dreaming about? Or who. That man of yours, right?"

Fletcher smiled self–consciously, offered, "Sorry," and bent to his task. In between kisses, he asked, "You're rich sweet chocolate, but what am I? Pale and uninteresting. *Vanilla* means boring, doesn't it? What does a beautiful black man like you want to sleep with a boring white man for?"

Laughter a rumble now, that Fletch could feel through his hands and lips. "You're rich cream from the dairy; sweet ice cream on a summer day, cool on the flat of my tongue. And then your eyes are fire, white boy.

How did Baraka put it? *Those silk blue faggot eyes.* I like those hot silk blue faggot eyes of yours, sweet lover man."

"Xavier, you're a poet."

"*That's* poetry," the man murmured, "what you're doing now – yes, that."

Fletch chuckled, and continued, but then his thoughts distracted him again. "I shouldn't call you black. I should say African–American."

"That's a mouthful," Lachance said absently.

"*You're* a mouthful."

"Flattery, now, sugar man? You can call me black, you can call me anything you want. You don't need all that white liberal shit with me, that's strictly for the public."

"Then I'll call you … lover."

"Oh Christ," Xavier exclaimed. "A white liberal *romantic*. How do I get into these situations?"

"You were so pushy," Fletcher reminded him. "You didn't let me refuse."

"That's true." Xavier stretched, disrupting Fletch's ministrations, then sat up. He hauled Fletch up the bed, and began to respond in kind. "I wanted you," Lachance murmured. "Sure, I like my brothers best but I like anything male. And I hate being sensible, though I've tried to be since I started college, and I have to be sensible now. It's like I said before, there're some liberals, white or black doesn't matter; they'll vote for the other guy if they think I actually *do* have sex with men. The church's attitude is the same. It's okay if you're gay, as long as you're chaste as well."

"Maybe you should outrage them with the truth."

"Maybe I'll take you along to lunch tomorrow with the Colorado Catholic Ladies' Association. I'm sure they'd be as bewitched by you as I am, sweet lover man, with your fresh dairy skin and your silk blue eyes. If we kissed over the champagne and strawberries, we'd probably make the front page of Saturday's papers. Great photo op."

It was a funny and absurdly charming idea, but Fletch soon considered the serious thoughts behind it. "How do you live like that, Xavier? Constantly presenting different facets of yourself to different people, acting so many different roles."

"We all do that to some extent, sugar man, even you. You don't act like this at work, do you?"

Fletcher insisted, "I'm not *acting* now. I try to minimize the pretence, wherever I am. Mind you, the Bureau doesn't make that easy."

"Neither do the voters." Xavier smiled, almost wistful. "You try so hard to be honest, don't you, Fletcher? Honest and true."

"Don't you?" Fletch said.

The smile was suddenly a grin. "You know what? Not only do I fuck white boys like you, Agent Ash, I've even slept with a couple of women."

Fletcher laughed at this confession. "Is that so dreadful?"

"Oh yes. If you're gay, you're not supposed to be sexually interested in women."

"That's ridiculous," Fletcher observed, encouraging Xavier to continue rambling.

"Brothers loving brothers," Xavier intoned, "sisters loving sisters, sure that's sweet. But some would call me a snow queen, sleeping with you. And it's not intended as a compliment."

"And me?"

"A dirge queen. Or they might accuse you, being a decadent dominant white, of tainting me, seducing me, using me. They'd tell me, Brother, cast off your chains, you're being abused."

Fletcher reached for a pillow and stuffed it under his shoulders. It was tempting to joke about Xavier being the dominant one in their love–play and perhaps to thereby provoke a more physical interaction, but this conversation was too interesting. Fletcher liked talking with this man and he was forever curious. He said, "Subcultures within subcultures … We can't all keep to our separate little factions like that."

Xavier lay between Fletch's legs, leaning up on his elbows to answer him seriously. "A minority people wants to maintain solidarity, to create a home or an identity without internal divisions, so that it can face the rest of the world. They want to present a positive image. So dissidents, like gays within that minority, are silenced twice over because they're disruptive and they're seen as negative. You find that with blacks, with Jews, with Chinese–Americans, whatever."

Jews, Fletcher thought. That was Albert's distant background. Fletch knew so little about the man. Did Albert have any family other than those long–dead parents? What about the mysterious Elliott Meyer? Had

349

Albert's isolation been partly because his community wouldn't accept his … Fletcher found he didn't even know that much. Did Albert consider himself gay or bisexual? He couldn't think of anyone, male or female, whom Albert had seemed to relate to sexually, other than Fletch himself.

Belatedly returning his attention to this lover, Fletcher said, "They lose in conformity whatever they gain in solidarity."

"You're right," Xavier said, smiling his approval. "We need to mingle to successfully co–habit this small world of ours, but mingle without imposing templates on everyone. We need to appreciate the individual, celebrate differences rather than persecute them. On the other hand, in our society today, a minority within a minority, like gay black men, needs to first find pride and dignity in its own identity, on its own terms. If you leave us gay blacks as scattered parts within the whole, we have nothing, we are nothing. Because we don't yet celebrate differences. A small group needs to develop authentic self–determination and *then* they can choose to become part of mainstream society – a part of the wonderful diverse whole that deserves and demands as much respect as any other part. Your hero, Robert Kennedy, realized all that when he was working on poverty, and with blacks."

Fletch laughed. "Are you telling me you're a modern day Bobby Kennedy? Do you want me to fall in love with you?"

The smile that greeted this was broad. "I'll tell you anything you like, sweet man, and I want everyone in Colorado to fall in love with me."

"All of Colorado? Tell me your ambitions."

"I'm going all the way to the White House, Fletcher. I'll be the first black President."

"Yeah, I bet you will." Fletch reached to caress the man's hair. "I'll vote for you, lover." After a moment he added, "I'd wondered why you weren't running as an independent. Surely you don't always see eye to eye with the Democrats?"

"No, but the party system works, and it will work for me. I toe the party line on most things and I try to persuade them on others. The party can be, and should be, shaped by its members, especially influential ones. I could be mayor of Denver as an independent, I might even be sent to the Senate from Colorado, but I couldn't be President as an independent."

"So you take a ride on their established power –"

"Of course. You have to take the power before you can change things. What's the point of me running here and losing, and never being in a position to *do* anything about what I believe in?"

"You're telling me there has to be compromise."

"It's not a dirty word, you know. Compromise can be a good thing. It's the meeting in the middle of disparate views."

Fletch nodded, but said, "As long as you don't compromise on the basic issues, like human rights."

A reassuring smile. "Sure, lover man." He began to ease up Fletcher's body, pressing kisses along the way.

"You're not quite as callously ambitious as you pretend," Fletch said.

"You think not?" Mildly surprised.

"Running for office from Colorado – it's not the easiest place to promote gay rights, is it? You'd have a better time of it somewhere a little more open–minded, like California."

"This is my home state, sweet man, these are my people."

"Loyalty," Fletcher observed, "even if it doesn't suit your best interests. I like that."

"Good," Xavier murmured absently. And then he effectively silenced any further conversation.

"You look like you need this," Caroline said, handing Fletcher a mug of coffee.

He accepted it gratefully, then dragged over a visitor's chair for her to sit on and even made room on his desk for her own mug. "Do I look that bad?" he asked.

"Put it this way," she replied, "I bet you're glad the case is closed and it's Friday."

"Yeah, I'm glad." Though he was left with the thought that his relationship with Xavier would inevitably be scaled down, if not closed as well. "I'm just writing the conclusion of my report for you."

She grimaced. "Monday is fine. Unless there's anything unexpected to add?"

"No. The last couple of days I've mainly been clearing Lachance himself, now Tanya's working on that Klan thing. I don't think any of his people had the ability to start the fire, if it were arson, which I don't think it was, and I couldn't find any evidence of money changing hands illegitimately."

"Bit of a waste of your time," Caroline observed.

"From the point of view of the fire. I'm glad Lachance gave us that lead, though, even if he went about it the wrong way."

Nodding, she asked, "You squared him on that? He won't make any trouble for us?"

"Yeah, he'll keep quiet and let us get on with it, that's fine."

"Good."

Fletcher lifted the coffee to take a sip, then ground to a halt and stared at it. "Hot, black and strong," he murmured under his breath, "like I like my men." And he began giggling helplessly.

Caroline eyed him warily. "Sounds like it's been a long week."

"Just an old joke, boss," Fletch offered when he could. "You started it, actually."

"I can't believe that only last Monday I was asking why you were so unhappy. Then you were high as a kite all week – and now you're glum again. That's quite a roller–coaster ride, Fletcher."

"You should sympathize, Caroline, I'm currently looking forward to spending a weekend with Albert. That would make even you glum, wouldn't it?"

Caroline frowned. "Which case? Not the arson, surely?"

"No, don't worry, it's not an official visit, it's more the case of friendship and sightseeing. We're heading up into the Rockies – which reminds me, I'd better give you the phone number at the hotel, just in case."

"Better you than me," was Caroline's comment. "But I'm the fool who can't imagine *Dr.* Sterne progressing the case of friendship, aren't I?" They drank their coffee in companionable silence, then she asked, "Are you about ready to head off?"

"I am," said Fletcher. "Especially if the report can wait until Monday."

"Give me five minutes, and I'll walk you to the parking lot."

"All right." He smiled as she bustled off, then turned to reshuffle the clutter of his desk prior to leaving.

Once they were outside the building, jackets and briefcases in hand, Caroline slowed their pace to a stroll. "I've been considering the conversation we had Monday morning," she said. "I told you that if you needed to talk, I'd be here for you."

"Yes, and I appreciate it, Caroline, but really –"

"No, let me finish." A long pause, then she said very carefully, "You know the Bureau's rules. They're very prescriptive and they begin with, *Don't embarrass the Bureau.* Strictly between you and me, I can't agree with all of them. On the other hand, I'll follow the rules for the sake of furthering my career. You know I'm ambitious and you know how difficult the FBI can be for women."

Fletcher nodded. "Yes, I know."

She held up a hand to halt him. They were on the edge of the parking lot now, and there was no one within hearing distance. "I don't want you to say anything, Fletcher, I just want you to listen. All right?" She looked up at him, direct and determined, and said, "If there is anything that I should know about as your supervisor, then as long as it doesn't affect your work, *I don't want to know.* You've been on an emotional roller–coaster lately, which isn't good for you or your work, but I want you to think very carefully before you take up my offer of talking about it, okay?"

"Okay," Fletcher said, frowning.

"If there is anyone else you can talk to, who can help you, then do what you can, because I don't want you throwing your career away either."

"I'm fine, really," he said. "But if I need to, I can talk to Albert, and my father."

She looked dubious. "Try your father," was the advice.

Fletcher almost smiled, then opened his mouth to speak.

Again, Caroline held her hand up. "You're an honest person, Fletcher, and that's good. So don't pretend you don't know what I'm talking about, for your sake. And, for my sake, don't go saying anything I don't want to hear. You might think I'm being supportive but you should act on the assumption that I'm simply playing to win." A pause, and then a smile. "Have a good weekend." And she turned away, and was gone.

So Caroline had figured it out about him and Albert, or at least had enough of the facts to suspect something. Had he even handed her a clue or two about him and Xavier? Fletcher knew he had to be far more careful, though he hated the lies that involved. Still, there wasn't simply his career at stake, or Caroline's, or Albert's – it was a matter of life and death. Because he'd have even less of a chance at catching the serial killer if he were out of the Bureau.

And, anyway, Albert would dissect him very slowly if he knew Fletcher had given them away. Fletch definitely didn't want to be the first live subject of an autopsy.

CHAPTER TWENTY-FOUR
COLORADO
MARCH 1985

Albert was approaching amidst the crowd of arrivals, luggage in hand. Fletcher waited impatiently. Jittery at facing this difficult and unpleasant problem that required a solution, however inadequate, by the end of the weekend. Nerves and exhaustion affecting his sense of time so it seemed that Albert stepped in ponderous slow motion, when all Fletch wanted was for this trouble to speed by and for Monday to dawn bright and simple.

It occurred to him during the long wait that he hadn't really put any thought into this, or at least no more than necessary. The first imperative was to get Albert away from the danger of Denver, because Denver was Xavier and passion and joy. The second was to unload the truth on Albert, make his apologies as gracefully as possible, and then to suffer through the consequences, get Albert safely on a plane back to Washington, and trust that something of the friendship – which seemed a very remote, intangible thing right now – would remain to be claimed and possibly healed in the future.

At last Albert was there, and events began rushing by Fletcher too fast. Nodding a greeting, Fletch asked, "Baggage?"

"No." Of course not. Albert packed logically and lightly, and rarely had to suffer through baggage retrieval.

"The car's this way." Fletch led the man off, mentally kicking himself. The plan, such as it was, was to act normally until they had driven up into the mountains, and were settled in at the hotel. Then, late tonight or first thing tomorrow, Fletch would talk to Albert. At whatever length was necessary. Then listen to whatever abuse Albert felt was required.

Silence, until they were in the car and Fletcher was driving along the freeway heading out of town. Until he remembered that he hadn't told Albert about even this much. "We're going to drive up into the mountains," Fletcher said. "I've made reservations at a hotel for two nights."

The silence continued. Fletcher risked a glance at the man, who was looking over at him. Surprised, but apparently unwilling to ask. Fletch felt annoyance flood through him and then defeatedly ebb away. This was the trouble. Albert asking a question, even a relatively harmless one like this, would be too much like Albert expressing a need, a vulnerability. How had the man ever satisfied his intellectual curiosity? How had the man, or the boy he'd once been, ever learned about anything at all?

"I need a break," Fletcher offered as a reason for this trip. It was true enough – he was so tired right now, though his mind was far too busy to let him relax even if he did have the opportunity. He belatedly asked, "Do you want anything from town?"

"No," Albert replied, and turned to face the front again.

All right, Fletcher reflected, he knew Albert wouldn't appreciate a bout of enforced sightseeing, like those few days in New England they'd spent together when they first became lovers. That was only last September but it felt like an age ago. And of course Albert knew Fletcher knew Albert wouldn't appreciate it, but would acquiesce if Fletcher insisted.

Maybe that was part of why Albert was so unhappy these days – realizing how much power Fletcher held over him and realizing that Fletch knew it, too. Though Fletcher tried not to abuse the privilege, he really tried hard.

Except he was just about to hurt Albert, hurt him a lot.

Fletcher pushed the thought away. It simply had to be done, that was all there was to it. And, frankly, he didn't want to feel that hurt, to empathize with what Albert was suffering, until he actually had to.

They traveled in silence, climbing into the mountains that began abruptly just beyond the town limits. There wasn't much traffic and the moon was full, so Fletcher didn't devote much effort to keeping his attention focused. He always maintained he'd be able to follow this road blindfolded, he knew it so well.

Continuing silence. Albert certainly made it easy for Fletch to keep a secret from him – and the younger man hated that. It was easy because Albert invited no confidences, extended no friendship, initiated no conversation. If he noticed Fletcher was unusually quiet and undemonstrative, he didn't comment. He didn't even mention the fact

Fletcher hadn't phoned him more than once in the previous week. Surely any other lover would demand an explanation of such gross dereliction.

It was amazing how few words Fletch and Albert could subsist on. Most of the time, that spoke eloquently, if silently, of a profound ease with each other's company. Right now, it appeared sinister, especially compared with Xavier's friendly, fascinating outpourings.

By habit, Fletcher turned the radio on for the news, then instantly regretted it. Too late to turn it off again, as Albert would consider that strange, though perhaps he wouldn't comment on that either. Within moments, Fletcher's fears were realized – Xavier's voice, rich brocade even over the airwaves, laughing warmly and agreeing with the newsreader that, yes, he'd had an eventful week. A brief mention of the fire, and that it had been accidental, a thanks to all the law enforcement people involved – Fletcher almost blushed in the darkness, wondering whether that had been for him – then a run–down of his more successful schedule, all of which Fletcher knew by heart, finishing with a confident prediction of victory.

Fletcher's hopes that Albert hadn't paid attention were now dashed. "You've closed the investigation?" he asked once the news was over, distantly polite.

"Yes," Fletch said quickly. "Seemed like a combination of accident and carelessness."

"You're not sure? If we return to Denver tomorrow, I'll examine the evidence for you."

"No."

Albert was obviously surprised at such a blunt refusal – usually Fletcher used Albert's expertise, involved him in every case whether the older man liked it or not, welcomed a second opinion Fletcher could trust.

"I mean," Fletch continued, trying to recover lost ground, "the police had jurisdiction, and they closed the case. There's no need to go back over it, they knew what they were doing. Anyway, it's not your field, is it?" He couldn't help spitefully adding, "No one died, Albert."

Apparently offended at this lack of faith, or maybe stung, Albert turned away. "I assure you I'm capable," he said dryly. "In fact, I often investigated arson and bombings during my first years with the Bureau."

"No, Albert, it's over. And I need the weekend off."

A return of the silence. It seemed heavier now, though Fletcher tried to tell himself that was only his imagination.

Of course there was one advantage in their need for secrecy. Fletcher had booked them two single rooms, rather than a double – though, now he came to think of it, he supposed that a twin room would be the best compromise between discretion and enthusiasm. The advantage was that once they'd eaten their room service meals, with Albert stoically not complaining about the standard of the food, Fletcher could retire to his own room and not have to worry about the fact he wasn't going to ask for sex.

Usually, on the Friday night of a weekend together, Fletcher was ready, willing and able. It would normally have been two weeks or more since the last time, after all. Well, tonight he'd plead exhaustion, which was true, but attribute it to the case. He stood, and wandered over to the door. "I'm going to turn in early, all right?" Fletch waited, uneasy, but Albert did nothing more than nod curtly. Eventually Fletcher murmured, "Not tonight, is that okay? I'm really tired."

"Of course," was the reply, the phrase bitten off hard. The man didn't even look up from the print–out of test results he was neatly annotating.

Another mistake. Normally they either had sex, on Fletcher's initiative, or they didn't, and no comment was made, no excuses given. Fletcher wondered whether Albert would add all this up. There had surely been enough discomfort and thoughtlessness this evening. Unless it merely seemed to be business as usual. He sighed.

And was thoroughly surprised when Albert asked, "Any progress on your pet serial killer?" There was Albert asking for information for the second time that night, making what might be considered small talk, expressing an interest. Amazing.

"No progress," Fletcher said.

"I'd assumed you'd have more time for that while working on the arson case. Didn't you anticipate your involvement would be minimal?"

But I devoted all my spare time to fucking with Xavier, Fletcher thought, looking away. He schooled his features into something approaching neutrality. "The case generated a lot of work I didn't expect," Fletch said. "I basically had to recreate their financial records because I wanted to check whether Lachance had paid someone to set the fire."

"But you didn't find any evidence?"

"No. That's not to say there's not some doubt but I don't think he was behind it."

Albert nodded, accepting this. No doubt he thought Fletcher's assessment was objective rather than subjective. Fletcher hoped it was, too.

He lingered a moment longer, dissatisfied and uneasy. It had been nine years since he first met Albert. There had always been, at least until the last few miserable months, a connection between them of some sort, a mutual respect and interest, though Fletcher had had to do all the work in creating a friendship, making them lovers. And now, just as Fletch was about to risk severing that connection entirely, Albert seemed to be making an effort, no matter how negligible, to maintain it. Strange.

Still, there was rarely any way of resolving this familiar feeling of dissatisfaction without holding the man in his arms and establishing at least a physical connection. And Fletcher's conscience had deemed such approaches to be completely out of the question. "Goodnight," Fletcher murmured instead, pleased when he received a nod of acknowledgment.

Passing the room service trolley that they had left in the corridor with the debris of dinner, Fletch thought of Albert's barely discernible expression of displeasure when he first tasted the food. Once, during those whirlwind days in New England, Fletcher had caught that very expression and asked about the food. Albert had immediately given a succinct and detailed description of all its faults and shortcomings. But the man never complained otherwise. That might surprise most people, that such a fastidious man would not voice a complaint. He seemed to accept that, especially as a vegetarian, he was unlikely to find a great deal of food in hotels and restaurants that was up to the standards he set with his own cooking. And given the amount of time Albert spent traveling around the country on cases, he must have encountered a high number of unacceptable meals.

Well, there was no point in worrying over Albert. Tomorrow's trouble would come soon enough. Fletch undressed and slid between the cold sheets. Odd not to be in Xavier's king size bed, in Xavier's overwhelming embrace. Wondering vaguely whether Xavier missed him, too, Fletcher slipped into sleep.

◆

The bedside clock read 11:07, which must be wrong because it was light outside and surely he'd only gone to bed half an hour ago. Fletcher rubbed at his eyes, then tried again. It was light, it was morning and when he reached for his watch, discarded on the floor by the bed with his shirt, it confirmed that it was indeed almost lunchtime. That meant he'd slept for over twelve hours. "Oh damn it to hell," he whispered hoarsely.

He had enough presence of mind to order coffee from room service before taking a quick shower, so could gulp down two cups of it while dressing. Then he headed for Albert's room.

The man was sitting there at the table, reading a medical journal.

"I'm sorry," Fletcher said. "I didn't mean to sleep in late."

"You said you were tired," Albert pointed out, "so it wasn't unexpected."

"But I meant us to –"

"What?" Albert prompted with a small show of interest when the silence stretched. He turned a page and scanned it.

"Talk. Spend time together. See the mountains."

"You obviously needed to sleep instead, and that allowed me to catch up on some work."

"Damn it," Fletch started, then subsided again immediately. No point in getting angry at the mess this weekend would be. He just had to get through it, that's all. "Are you hungry? Could we grab an early lunch, or a late breakfast or whatever the hell it is, then go out for a drive?"

"That would be fine," Albert replied mildly. He stood, put the journal neatly away in his briefcase, then pulled on his suit jacket. "In fact, I took a walk this morning, for exercise. The surroundings are attractive, and the air is fresh."

Fletch frowned in consternation. There was something very wrong with this scenario but he was in no condition to figure it out right now. "Let's go," he suggested, and led the way out of the room.

South Park stretched before them, an enormous flat valley high up in the mountains, the surrounding peaks creating a jagged horizon, a pale blue sky arching infinite above them. Fletch stared at the view, trying to appreciate it, attempting to put off the necessary conversation a few minutes more.

He'd parked the car to one side of the look–out, hoping the few tourists would stay out of hearing distance. Albert sat beside him in the passenger seat, silent, and apparently also contemplating the scenery, though Fletcher presumed the man's thoughts were elsewhere. How to start this horrible thing?

"This is more dramatic than attractive," Albert said. "The massive scale of the mountains impresses all the more because of the distance."

"What?" Fletch had said that aloud, astounded at this commentary from a man who never voluntarily went sightseeing, whose pleasure in nature seemed to extend no further than his carefully tended garden boundaries. "I mean, I'm glad you like it."

"Perhaps *appreciate* is more accurate than *like*. This view provides an interesting perspective on the size of the mountain range."

"Yes." What else to say? He wasn't used to having this sort of conversation with the man. Odd and amusing, how formal Albert's language was, as if he were writing an autopsy report.

Of course, Fletcher reminded himself, Albert wasn't used to having this sort of conversation with anyone. That meant that Albert was making an effort at communication right now, maybe at not only maintaining but enhancing that connection between them. That meant that maybe Fletcher had had some sort of positive influence on the man, that Albert was now considering the things that Fletcher liked, and was trying them on for size. Perhaps he was even beginning to enjoy nature in general or the Rockies in particular. Incredible.

And incredibly bad timing.

"I have to tell you something," Fletcher blurted out before any further progress could be made.

"Yes, I know," Albert said. When Fletcher turned to stare at him in surprise, he continued dryly, "I did realize that something is troubling you."

Fletcher suddenly felt like crying. Albert was about to be hurt as deeply as he'd ever been, at least in his adult life, and Fletcher hadn't even properly considered the consequences before now. Sure, he'd thought about it on an intellectual level, but not on a gut–wrenchingly emotional one – Fletcher was swamped by how he imagined Albert was about to feel. Hurt, betrayed, jealous, in epic proportions. He'd doggedly remain friends, or so Fletcher hoped, but their relationship might never really recover from this. And if it didn't, Fletch thought, that would be suitable punishment for his own selfish if necessary desertion.

"I didn't mean to keep this secret," Fletcher finally said, talking more in the direction of the dashboard than to Albert. "But I thought I should tell you in person, which is why I haven't been phoning you as much. Well, that was one of the reasons, anyway." He sighed, searching for words, not having planned this in any detail. "This is hard to say. And you probably won't credit *how* damned hard, which makes it worse. I really don't want to hurt you."

A silence grew. No further encouragement was offered.

He would just have to say it straight out. Like that doctor when his mother was ill, walking up to the huddle of Ash males in the corridor and saying, "I'm sorry, she's died." No preliminaries, no preparation. But Fletcher, for one, had preferred it, rather than waiting through the social niceties all the while knowing the worst and screaming inside, *Just damned well tell us!*

"All right. I'm having an affair. With a man. He's ... part of the arson case. Which makes it stupid, as well as unfair on you. Damn it –" Fletcher broke off, considering. There was no possible point in hiding anything. "You know his name, at least. Xavier Lachance. You've even heard his voice, on the radio last night."

"I see," was the distant comment.

"He's black." Fletcher laughed humorlessly. "I'm a real equal opportunity fuck. Any race, any color, any religion, any gender –" *Shut up, Fletcher, he already knows you're a slut.*

Silence.

"Say something, Albert. Anything. Lacerate me with that damned tongue of yours. It's years since you last insulted me."

And the man said very calmly, "There is no need for histrionics." Then, with a slight tightening of the voice, "I didn't exact or expect any vows of fidelity from you."

"Didn't you?" Fletcher risked a glance, surprise more urgent than the guilt. His lover was stony–faced and remote, but that was nothing out of the ordinary. "The vows are implicit, aren't they, in a relationship like ours? Even if they're not spoken?"

"No."

"I don't understand."

Silence.

All right, obviously Fletcher had made a false assumption or two along the way, but that didn't mean Albert wasn't hurt by this. "Look," Fletch continued, "I want to be your friend still, but I want to continue with him. He's – worthwhile. More than worthwhile. I know this is selfish of me but that's as honest as I can be."

Albert was indeed hurt. He had retreated behind his dark glasses. He remained silent.

"Would you *please* say something?"

"Why are you telling me this?" was the distant question.

"Damn it, why do you *think* I'm telling you this? I'm being unfaithful to you. Partners usually confess such things to each other, don't they?"

"You've never confessed such things to me before now."

"Well, it only began on Monday," Fletch said, frustrated and annoyed. "I haven't had the chance." It was as if they were taking part in two disparate conversations. And then Albert's meaning dawned on him. "Do you mean – Oh *damn* it all, Albert! You think I've done this before? Who the hell with?"

"I'd assumed –" Albert's jaw visibly set. He forced out, "With women. Tyler Reece. Whomever."

"No." All this time, Albert had lived with the assumption … "How could you even *think* that?" Fletch demanded. "I couldn't have done that to you."

The man turned to stare at him, expression sardonic and bitter. *Obviously you can be and are unfaithful.*

Angry at being caught in an apparent contradiction, and unable to immediately explain himself, Fletch bit back. "Where's your logic, Albert? You never left me the time or energy to see anyone else, especially when I was in Washington. I've hardly even spoken to Ty for months." And he cried out, "Damn you for thinking that of me!"

"But my assumption was justified, even if the details were incorrect."

"No. This, with Xavier, it's important to me, don't you see? It's not some meaningless fling."

A pause. Then, surprisingly light, as if it really didn't matter, "Are you telling me that you love him?"

Fletcher didn't answer.

"Are you?"

"No," Fletch said at last, "I couldn't tell you that." The man was waiting, as if he wanted to hear all the details. *Then he shall damned well have them.* "It's more lust than love, it's more a crush than being in love, it's more convenience than anything. But it's important."

The curtest of nods. Albert was facing forward, arms crossed, expression masked.

"Is that it?" Fletcher asked, feeling betrayed.

"Unless you have anything more to confess," Albert replied coolly.

"Nothing more."

"Then, once you're feeling recovered enough to drive, I suggest we return to the hotel."

Fletcher stared at his companion, wondering what the hell was going through Albert's mind, wondering how he ever could have thought he knew the man. He should have realized Albert wouldn't react in predictable ways, he should have anticipated this ghastly confusion. Everything felt so damned wrong. "All right," he said. After a few moments of trying to gather his thoughts, Fletcher turned the ignition and headed back to the road.

Casting a last glance at the view, Fletcher figured he'd never visit South Park again without reliving this sour, sickening, guilty frustration.

Fletcher was proved wrong again. He'd assumed Albert would want to pack up and check out, return to Denver, take the next flight to Washington. He'd thought Albert would walk past him, carry on alone to his own room without a word. But, no – Albert followed Fletcher into his room, closed the door behind them and took Fletcher into his arms.

Fletcher had assumed that, in the improbable event of being offered such an embrace, he'd respectfully decline it, as was only right and proper. No – he almost whimpered in relief, and held on tightly around Albert's waist.

"I'm sorry," the younger man whispered with his face buried in Albert's neck. As Fletcher was slightly taller than Albert, this was an uncomfortable but necessary posture. "I mean, I'm sorry for hurting you."

A hand settled on Fletcher's head, began stroking through his hair, the fingers tangling in the unruly thick waves and then patiently extricating themselves. It felt like forgiveness. A timeless while later,

Albert placed a hand either side of Fletcher's head, and raised it for a kiss. The kiss felt as sweet as love.

Moaning into the man's mouth, Fletcher indulged himself for a moment, but then tried to pull away. "I want to be fair to you," he said, finding the courage to look directly at Albert. The dark eyes were mysterious, unreadable. The expression, however, was almost grim in its determination.

Another kiss, brisk this time, then the hands dropped to tug the T-shirt out of Fletcher's jeans, to draw it up and off over his head. The mouth targeted Fletcher's right nipple and began a teasing game with teeth and tongue, while an arm wound firmly around his waist just in time to save Fletcher from losing his balance as he arched back, the lips following him effortlessly. The free hand caressed his buttocks and the back of his thighs through the denim.

"No," which was really only a token protest. *He knows I'm a slut, he's always known.* How could Fletcher have forgotten this precise, knowing, generous loving? "You're too good at this," he said. "It shouldn't be this perfect."

No reply, of course, other than the demonstration of intimate knowledge. Though there was something remote about Albert when he did this, something so in control. Fletcher responded to it with yearning loneliness. So it was both a wish for greater connection with Albert, and a need to hurt him more, when Fletcher tried to explain, "He's imperfect, but he's passionate. You choreograph it all, you work on my pleasure. He dances beautifully, though he steps on my toes, and he takes his pleasure, too."

Apparently refusing to be put off, Albert withdrew a little but only to untie and pull off Fletcher's sneakers, slide off the jeans and shorts and socks. In turn, Fletch tried to undress Albert as well, but only got as far as unbuttoning the suit jacket before he was stopped. Albert, it seemed, intended to remain fully dressed. He led Fletcher over to the bed, and sat him down.

"I want you to understand," Fletcher said, with a tone of desperation. It seemed he wasn't even being listened to, let alone having any effect. "With you, it's like art. With Xavier, it's like flashfire."

Albert knelt between Fletcher's legs, hands stroking in tantalizing patterns up the inside of his thighs, encouraging them wider. "Is that what you want?" Albert asked, mocking, though continuing the caress. "A natural disaster?"

Almost laughing at this retort, Fletcher said, "Yes. Won't we ever share that kind of passion, Albert?" No reply. It seemed hopeless. "Why are you doing this?" He recalled Xavier moving over him, relentless, promising, powerful. Possessing. Fletcher asked, "Are you trying to make me yours?"

"Don't be ridiculous, Ash," Albert replied, his gaze direct. "I have no interest in owning you."

"So what the hell are you doing?" But, again, no reply.

The continuing confusion had robbed Fletcher of an enthusiastic response, so Albert bent to nuzzle at the quiescent genitals. The tongue lapping at his penis, or the mouth gently sucking by turn at each of his balls, while the fingers busied themselves between his thighs, soon provoked the required erection.

"I trust you practice safe sex with Lachance."

Fletcher let out a breath, winded by this sardonic comment, so cold and blunt. And actually saying Xavier's name for the first time in such a context. Fletcher almost bit back, *Yes, he uses a condom every time he fucks my ass.* But perhaps he could measure how much Albert had been hurt, by how badly Albert now tried to hurt him. Instead, Fletcher gently said, "Yes, I do. You're safe."

Albert returned to his task, mouth providing a haven for Fletcher's penis, one hand reaching up to tease a nipple and push Fletcher onto his back.

"I love you, Albert," Fletcher offered as he lay down, letting the man continue. His body was too attuned to Albert's skills for further protest. Yes, this might be choreographed, but the dance was precious and beautiful, the variations in each stanza intriguing, every move elegant and stimulating. Fletcher groaned as Albert brought him to exquisite completion. "That was perfect," he whispered.

"You prefer imperfection."

"No," Fletch demurred, reaching to draw Albert up beside him. "But a little honest passion wouldn't hurt us."

"This is what I provide. If you require something else, then do what you will."

"That's what you want, me continuing with both of you? How can we make that work?"

Albert sighed, impatient with him. "If you could avoid seeing our relationship as a bourgeois marriage, we might well make it work."

"It sounds so tawdry and difficult."

No reply. Albert stood, rearranged his suit, briefly brushed it down. Fletcher longed for one of his pubic hairs to cling there, somewhere socially unacceptable. Albert said, "Shall we meet for dinner in the hotel restaurant or would you prefer room service?"

An evening alone with this cold and remote being? "The restaurant," Fletch said.

"Then I'll meet you there in an hour." And Albert left.

Fletcher curled up on the bed, wanting to cry with disappointment. None of this was right, none of this was good. He wished for Xavier's wholehearted loving, no matter that outside of the bedroom the man was more manipulative than Fletcher and Albert put together.

But then, as Fletcher considered exactly what had transpired out at South Park, and here in the hotel, he began to realize something of the truth. Albert had been hurt; Albert had been made to see Fletcher's betrayal as a serious defection rather than as something casual that could be safely ignored; Albert nevertheless wanted to continue with Fletcher if at all possible; but, to do so, the relationship needed to be redefined as merely convenient sex rather than as a marriage, and Albert's barriers needed to be rebuilt stronger than ever. What a ghastly mess. Something inside of Fletcher was weeping with frustration, but it wouldn't surface or give him any relief.

CHAPTER TWENTY–FIVE
COLORADO
MARCH 1985

"Welcome back, lover man," Lachance greeted Fletcher as he opened the front door.

"Thanks," Fletcher said, dredging up a smile without too much difficulty.

Xavier led him into the kitchen. "The coffee's on. You're a few minutes early, so you ruined my plans. You were going to find me exactly where you want me …"

The smile became more spontaneous as a few provocative ideas flitted through Fletch's mind. "And where exactly is that?"

"In bed, naked, with a mug of black coffee in one hand and a whole box of condoms in the other."

"It's certainly an attractive idea, Xavier." Instead of leaning against the kitchen bench, as he usually did, Fletcher hauled over one of the stools to sit on.

"What's the matter, sweet man? All this finally caught up with you and you're tired, right? After I gave you last night off, as well."

"I'm damned tired, sorry. There's a lot going on at the moment. And I missed you last night, I'm not used to sleeping in my own bed anymore. What was so important on a Monday night that you couldn't see me?"

Xavier shook his head, and tried for what was presumably a resolute expression. "Interrogate me all you like, Agent Ash, but I will not say a word."

Fletcher almost laughed. "We'll see about that. I learned some pretty interesting interrogation techniques at Quantico, you know." They shared a speculative grin before Fletch admitted, "I'm only kidding."

Pouring Fletcher a mug of coffee, Xavier asked sympathetically, "Was the weekend with your man really terrible?"

Silence for a while as Fletcher reconsidered the whole mess yet again. "You know what I thought the worst thing would be?" he mused, more to himself than his companion. "I assumed we'd be finished as lovers but we might salvage something of our friendship. Because I suspect we're the only best friends either of us have ever had. Pathetic, isn't it?"

"You're important to each other." Xavier shrugged. "Nothing wrong with that. In fact, it's a good thing – how many grown men in this society can say they have a best friend?"

"Well, I don't think I can anymore. That was my worst case scenario, but it's turned out the other way around. I can't see that we're still friends but he insists we remain lovers. If *lovers* is the right word." Fletcher looked across at Xavier. "I wanted to tell you, so there'd be a minimum of misunderstandings. I know you don't expect me to be faithful or anything, but that's the way it is."

"You look miserable, sweet man. Want to talk about it?"

"No, thanks all the same." Fletcher shrugged. "I mean, I'd like to, you might even make sense of it for me – but it doesn't feel right telling you anything about him, because he's such a private person. Talking about him with you is betraying him more than having sex with you is. So for once I'll shut my big mouth. Or at least put it to better uses."

"You do that," Xavier murmured encouragingly.

Nevertheless, Fletcher didn't make a move towards this lover. "I'm beginning to think I'm the only one around here who values honesty. I must be a good old–fashioned country boy after all. I have my boss counseling me, in so many convoluted words, to maintain discretion –"

"Why? Did you tell me too much about those Klan bastards?"

"Well, I did, a bit, but she doesn't know that. The problem is that I think she's added up a few clues and has her suspicions about me and –" It didn't even seem right to use Albert's name. "Me and my man. But she told me she'd turn a blind eye as long as I keep it sane. Or I assume that's what she was telling me. You know, I'd rather she and I just said it all out in the open and then got on with whatever we have to do."

"Lover man, you're skating on thin ice. Be careful."

"I'm trying to be. It's just that my boss and I have worked closely together for years. We're not friends as such, but she knows me well enough to see things that others don't. And that's meant to be our second most important characteristic, isn't it? An FBI agent has to be untouchable first and incredibly observant second. That's about the only thing the movies do get right."

"She doesn't suspect you and me as well, does she?"

"I don't think so. I really doubt it." Fletcher frowned at the man. "That bothers you, doesn't it?"

"Yes, and it should bother you even more." Xavier suddenly grinned. "Unless you're willing to chuck the job, and work on becoming First Lady to a black President."

It was such a crazy and delightful idea that Fletcher laughed. "Actually, there are times when I wish that was a serious proposal."

"Patience, lover man."

Fletcher sighed. "Patience, you say, when you're the only thing I have any enthusiasm for." He took another mouthful of coffee. "You couldn't mind my boss possibly knowing about us half as much as my man would mind her definitely knowing about me and him. I didn't tell him on the weekend, for the simple fear he'd kill me. And I thought he'd call it quits anyway."

"Surely he's more forgiving than you make him out to be."

"You haven't met him … He's perfectly capable of insulting me to death."

Xavier laughed, richly amused. "No wonder you love him so much."

"Do I?" Fletcher asked, wanting it to be either true or false. Anything but this confusing in–between sort of love, where he could hurt the man so badly but then share his pain, where he could love the man so much but need more than Albert would give.

"I think he matters to you a great deal."

"Well, of course he does. It's just so impossible to make the relationship work." Fletcher said bitterly, "You know, he'd assumed I was still seeing women, having casual sex, and lying to him about it. It seems he'd prefer that to me seeing you and being honest with him."

"Of course he would. Casual sex would be less meaningful, less painful, less threatening. And, if you don't mind me saying so, if it's casual sex with women, it would provide you with a very good cover. Your boss would be far less likely to figure out the truth if you were still fucking anything in a skirt."

"I couldn't live like that. It wouldn't be fair to him or me or the women. I mean, how could he have thought I'm cold–hearted enough to systematically betray him?"

Xavier at last walked over, slid a companionable arm around Fletcher's shoulders. "And me, sweet man? I'm adding to your woes by talking of compromise and the realities of politics."

"You can't deny you prefer the indirect route, and the devious approach, every time. I bet your mind is busy all your waking hours planning cunning conspiracies; plots forever simmering on the back burner."

Richly appreciative laughter. "You make it sound so exciting."

"I suppose it is, really. By comparison, my other lover reads medical texts, listens to Mozart, and verbally takes me to pieces to exercise his mind."

"You're dangerous, Agent Ash. It's too easy to dismiss an honest man as naïve and simple. But you're as subtle and seductive as anyone I've met. You interest me, you know that?"

Fletcher smiled. "I'll take your interest as the highest compliment. The rest I'm not so sure about." It was a warm feeling, knowing that what he felt for Xavier was mutual. Curiosity and attraction and shared ideals weren't a bad place to start.

The friendly arm became a more intimate embrace, and Xavier leaned in to murmur, "Sometimes, lover man, I prefer the direct route." He eased around to stand behind Fletcher, fitting his chest and hips to Fletcher's back and buttocks, bending closer over him and wrapping his arms around Fletch's waist, so Fletcher was engulfed. Xavier confessed, "I've missed this tight lily white ass of yours."

"I've missed your enormous hungry black cock," Fletcher replied. He loved this all–encompassing, protective, possessive hug. And then the familiar clothes–shedding tumble down the corridor to reach the bedroom. They were both hot and eager, as was usual between them – though Fletcher took a moment to regret Albert at his best, with his endless, gentle, beautiful foreplay.

In bed, naked, exactly where Fletcher wanted them. Xavier murmuring, "Feels so sweet, sugar man, ice cream skin on a hot summer night." A finger, cool with lube, exploring, insinuating itself into Fletcher's ass. "And your hot blue eyes catch fire when I do that. Why doesn't your man ever do this for you?"

"I don't know." Fletcher moaned, trying to capture the teasing finger. "Don't talk about him. Not like this." He turned to watch as Xavier rolled a condom onto his penis, moved close to begin pushing into Fletcher. Already this didn't hurt, the smell of rubber familiar, the welcome fullness easing inside and hinting at future pleasures. Fletcher sprawled ungainly, letting Xavier take his time. Surely this was almost everything that he'd ever wanted.

Stairs: dizzy endless flights of stairs, a double helix twisting in empty blue sky; Fletcher clinging on desperately to the smooth angles, hands slippery with terror, equilibrium shot to hell. If he let go he'd spin off into nothingness, the blue fading to vacuum, the cold inaccessible stars oblivious to his slow torment. *I've lost my balance, Albert.*

Footsteps echoing, vibration felt through his entire body. Fear at who might approach, what they might do – dislodge him and let him float away, grasping desperate, gasping thin?

Feet, bare dark chocolate brown, caught the corner of his eye. Carefully lifting his head, Fletcher saw Xavier standing on the steps – not above, because up and down had no meaning, there was only the treacherous stairs and the slow horrible nothingness – Xavier superbly naked, smiling confident.

The man crouched, offered a hand, within reach if Fletcher would loosen his tenuous hold. "Come on, Agent Ash," Xavier chided. "Stand and walk. There's nothing to it."

"Can't," Fletch muttered, though his gaze never left the other man's, beseeching. *Can you save me?*

"Look –" and Xavier pointed to somewhere beyond Fletcher's sight, dizzying – "we can reach the White House from here."

"No." A drop of blood squeezed from beneath one of his painful digging fingernails, slid spiraling across the smooth surface as the stairs twisted. Fletcher closed his eyes, but that lost him even the illusion of up which was surely where Xavier was.

"Come on, sweet man." Cajoling. Loving?

When Fletch looked again, almost unbalancing as he tilted his head, Xavier was offering both strong arms. Fletch unlocked his right hand from the stairs, stretched out his talon fingers, reached across the inches – Xavier's hand met and held it, sure and firm. Fletcher's second hand, and then his body lifting also naked, his feet walking up the stairs, so he stood just below Xavier, confidence flowering.

"I knew you could do it, sugar man. Now, get that lily white ass up here." And, dropping one of Fletcher's hands, Xavier turned to lead him – into the blue nothingness.

"No!" But it was already too late. His other hand slipped from Xavier's and Fletcher felt himself float away, the stairs receding into distance, and his lover there standing, hands on hips frustrated, feet planted solidly on blue sky. Vision dimming, oxygen thinning. *"No!"*

"For Christ's sake," Xavier said, annoyed.

Darkness, and hands shaking him, a shadow man looming. Xavier's white sheets twisted around his hips, the expanse of bed bearing him. Fletcher sat up abruptly, forced away the last sensation of falling, pushed away the hands. *Just a dream.*

"The neighbors will think I'm a sadist at this rate," the man was complaining.

"Sorry," Fletcher muttered.

"What the hell was that about?"

Xavier reached out again, and Fletcher shied away by instinct. "Bad dream. I get them sometimes. Sorry I woke you."

"Christ, you scared me." Matter–of–factly, but shaken. "And you wouldn't come out of it."

Fletcher wished for Albert's no–nonsense comfort, wondering whether his other lover had also tried and failed to wake him during a nightmare. He'd never mentioned it, perhaps showing a little mercy. "Sorry," he said again, lying down, hoping Xavier would settle.

Silence for a few tense moments, before Lachance lay beside him, carefully not touching. "Can you get back to sleep?"

"Yes," Fletcher lied. "How about you?"

"Yeah, I'm fine." No endearments. "Goodnight." Xavier rolled away, his back to Fletcher, and was soon snoring.

Left alone, Fletcher waited grimly for dawn. He really shouldn't be scared by a dream, he really shouldn't give it any thought at all. These nightmares had never taught him anything.

The phone rang, and Fletcher panicked for a moment, eyes following the tangled cord through his apartment until he located where he'd last left the receiver. "Hello," he said once he'd picked it up, "Fletch here."

"This is Albert."

Fletcher let out a laugh. It had been years of, *This is Albert Sterne,* so the abbreviated greeting was an improvement, though Albert still maintained an uncomfortable formality that Fletch found comical. "Hello." But Fletcher's laugh had also been born of relief, which required vocalizing. Fletch said, "It is so good to hear you."

A deadly silence.

Perhaps Fletch had surprised them both with that. He offered, "I've missed you."

The silence continued, until Fletcher thought Albert might decide to hang up, although it seemed unlikely he would be quite that rude. At last the man said in a tight voice, "I am calling from Seattle in Washington State. I'll be working on a case here for the next day or two."

"What's the case?"

"I'm not at liberty to discuss that with you."

"Since when did that stop you, love?" Fletcher asked.

A moment, and then Albert said, "I thought you'd agreed to be more circumspect. There's no reason for you to use a blandishment that is open to gross misinterpretation." And then unwisely betraying resentment: "It is inaccurate."

"Really," Fletcher said, a flash of annoyance destroying the brief moment of happiness. *As if you know all about love, Albert.*

"Really."

"Why did you call?"

"Simply to let you know where I am."

Fletcher took a breath, and began pacing slowly around the apartment. He couldn't bear it if they were reduced to nothing but this meaningless bickering. "Look – I'm glad you called. I'd really like to talk with you."

"Then talk," was the only encouragement provided.

"All right." Every topic was, of course, fraught with danger. Work would ordinarily be the safest, especially now that Xavier's arson case was closed, except that Caroline's convoluted warnings still echoed in his ears. She'd treated Fletcher no different from normal since then, but he'd trod warily, no longer relaxed in her company. But of course she hadn't been convoluted at all – Fletcher was retreating behind his guilt and resentment, blaming her for the situation rather than himself, indulging unrealistic wishes of how things should be. He sighed, still wholly unwilling to confess his blunders to Albert.

"Perhaps you should call back when you've thought of something to say to me." So urbane, so sarcastic.

It would have to be work. "I'm catching up on federal security clearances at the moment, running around tidying up all sorts of odds and ends. It's pretty tiresome. I don't think Caroline's going to put me back on the money laundering thing. The trial date's been postponed, so it's not as urgent."

"That should allow you plenty of time to work on your pet serial killer."

"No," Fletcher said with a frown, fearing where this was heading. "No progress."

"Are you working on the case at all?"

"What exactly are you asking me, Albert? How I spend my evenings? Is this the first night I've been home to answer the phone?" Silence seemed to confirm Fletcher's suspicions. Easily finding it in him to match Albert's sarcasm, he said, "I have laundry to do. Why don't you call me back when I'm in a better mood?" And he slammed down the phone.

Within five minutes, Fletch was in the basement of his apartment building, throwing shirts and shorts and socks into the washing machine, waiting for the phone there to ring. He and Albert had only done this a couple of times, when they needed to talk long distance with the surety of privacy and Albert wasn't at home. Fletch waited impatiently, unable to make an out–going call on this line – no one in the building had been able to agree on how to pay the resulting bill. Surely Albert had taken the hint. Surely he had the number with him.

The phone finally rang during the second wash cycle. Fletcher picked it up and said, "What took you so damned long?" A silence greeted him, but he didn't for one moment doubt who the caller was. "Just say what you wanted to say, Albert."

"You're frittering your time away with your pet politician."

Fletch swallowed various angry responses, amazed that Albert would voluntarily raise such a contentious issue. Finally he said, "You don't really want to hear the truth."

"I assume that's a reply in the affirmative," the man said immediately, as if that was only what he'd expected. "You should reassess your priorities, Ash. How will you feel when your pet murderer tortures, rapes and kills yet another young man, and you remember what you were doing instead of catching him?"

Gripping the phone so hard he might break it, Fletcher said, "That was totally uncalled for. You can't force me away from Xavier like that."

"If I'm attempting to force you to do anything, it's to remain focused on your goals and to consider the ramifications of not working towards them."

"Admit what your real agenda is, Albert. I'd prefer your honesty, no matter how brutal, instead of these heavy–handed tactics."

"I explained my purpose a moment ago."

"Don't lie to me, Albert. It's only been ten days since I met him. The serial killer case won't suffer because I've ignored it for ten days."

"Perhaps not, but when are you planning to return to it? Another ten days? Or ten weeks?"

"And may I remind you that it also got ignored last weekend while I spent time with you?"

"When will you start working on it again?"

Fletcher took a deep breath, trying not to give in to the temptation to yell. "There was plenty of time for recriminations on the weekend. Why didn't you get all this off your chest then?"

"I'm not interested in recriminating you for breaking a promise I never required you to make."

"Don't give me that garbage again, Albert. This whole conversation has been about you trying to stop me seeing Xavier. Admit the truth." And he did yell – "Tell me the truth!"

Another silence, and then Albert said very deliberately, "Listen to me, Ash. You react as if everything is centered on Xavier Lachance. But, in this instance, you're wrong. I am talking about you."

After a while, during which he began to suspect he'd been a little foolish, Fletcher said in a small voice, "What about me?"

"It used to be that the most important thing in your life was catching your pet serial killer. That now seems to have changed. If I'm the only one who's thought about these issues during the last few days, then you're no longer who you wanted to be."

"Damn it –" Fletch cried out. He wanted to hang up. He wanted to burst into frustrated tears. He wanted to ignore the whole horrible thing. But Albert was waiting on the line, patient despite all that Fletcher had just said to him. Fletcher didn't want to confront this, but he had to.

He lifted himself up onto the sorting table, to sit cross–legged by the phone. And then he said in as reasonable a tone as he could manage, "Look, I wasn't achieving anything, I wasn't making any progress in catching the man."

Albert didn't reply immediately, and when he did, it was obvious this was difficult for him. "I realize you weren't progressing the case but you were working on it. You were concerned about your priorities, and how you might best devote your time and energy."

"I was so tired of it, Albert." Fletcher sighed. "Anyway, it's another eighteen months before he's due to kill again. That feels like a lifetime away."

"Three lifetimes, Fletcher."

A startled pause – Albert spoke his first name so rarely – and then Fletch thought about what the man was saying. "There are three unsuspecting boys out there," he extrapolated in a murmur, "whose lifetimes are only another eighteen months long."

"But you can't rely on it being only three deaths, and you can't rely on him waiting that long."

"I know, I know."

"You still have hundreds of suspects to work through on your own."

"Albert –" A deep breath. "What if I don't want to do that anymore?"

Silence.

Fletcher hadn't really faced this himself, hadn't really taken his flirtation with the idea seriously. "At long last, I've fallen out of love with the Bureau."

"That's hardly surprising. I suggest, however, that we discuss the serial killer case separately from your feelings for the FBI. From this perspective, the serial killer is the priority."

"Why?"

"Because if you decide to devote your time to the case again, then you will need to remain with the Bureau."

"And if I don't?"

A pause. Then: "I don't like to consider the consequences for you. I suggest that I come to Denver for a few days, *en route* from Seattle to Washington DC. We can review the current status of the case and devise a strategy to which both of us can work over the next few months."

"No," Fletcher protested quietly. "Give me a little time, Albert." He sighed and leaned back against the cold of the wall. "I know we're supposed to be talking about the serial killer and the Bureau, rather than Xavier specifically, or my personal life in general, or our relationship – but the whole lot is tangled up together. I'm only just realizing that. I can't talk about the Bureau without talking about Xavier, I can't talk about the serial killer without talking about you. It's all linked. Maybe I wouldn't be having an affair with him if I weren't so unhappy in other areas of my life."

"I see."

"That's not news to you, Albert. We've been making each other miserable, and I for one have been unhappy about everything else as well." There was no response, so Fletcher continued, "You surprised me last weekend, love. I thought you'd finally give up on me and call it quits, but you didn't. Now you're surprising me again. I was afraid we couldn't be friends anymore but we wouldn't be having this conversation if we weren't."

"Don't rely on that, Ash."

Fletcher almost smiled at the routine protest. "I continue to rely on it, Albert. But don't come here for a while, don't visit me. It wouldn't be fair. I've done something horrible to you, to us, and I don't want to rub salt in your wounds. Or mine."

"We need to progress this case. No one else will."

The washing machine had finally spun into silence. Fletcher whispered, "Are you bargaining for my body, or my soul, or both?"

An audible sigh. "If you insist on using such melodramatic language, I assure you I'm only interested in your soul at present. It seems your body is freely available."

Fletcher did smile then. It had been far too many years since Albert was that nasty to him. And of course he had the ideal retort: "Yeah, I told Xavier you're perfectly capable of insulting me to death."

No reply. Perhaps that had been a bit much – Albert was far more vulnerable than Fletcher when it came to trading insults, after all.

Fletcher continued, "Well, maybe I just can't handle this serial killer case anymore. There are better ways of spending my life. This way hurts, Albert."

"Really." As if the hurt should be easily bearable.

"You never did believe in me and my instincts, did you? So you can't understand how tempting it is to never again think of murder and torture and rape, to never put myself in this man's place and feel how it would be, to never again imagine how that bruise was dealt, or why that skin was torn, or how long before death that bone was broken. To never speak to the parents, being calm and in control for their sake, all the while seeing in my mind everything that had been done to their child. Never again fear that I have more in common with this vicious and cunning killer than I have with my colleagues."

But Albert asked, "Why do you find it tempting to never bring this man to justice? To never save the lives he would otherwise take? To never use your abilities for the greatest good? To never again respect yourself?"

Fletcher unwound himself from the table and began transferring his washing to the drier. "I've done my time in hell, Albert."

"You're being incredibly selfish."

"Just once in my life," Fletch pleaded, "can't I be incredibly selfish? Maybe I'm bargaining for my soul, too."

"If you give up on the serial killer, you won't want to live with the results."

A long silence, before Fletcher set the drier going. "What is this?" he asked. "You're practicing forensic psychology on me? I'm not dead yet, Albert."

"Obviously you have no reasonable arguments to reply with."

"So I'm using your favorite tactic," Fletcher said spitefully, "and being nasty instead."

Again, Albert had difficulty saying the words: "Admit that, in this instance, resorting to my tactics is an admission of defeat."

Fletcher thought some more while he threw another load of clothes into the washing machine. "One of the reasons I love you," he finally said slowly, "is that you always insist on me doing my best. We both know how often I fall short of the mark but on the important things, you insist and I try."

"Then try now."

"Is that why you love me? Because I do try to do my best, I mean. Is that one of the reasons?"

Silence again. Then, in a painfully tight voice, "I do not love you, Ash."

"Have it your way," Fletch said easily, not believing it for a minute. "It's just that I think your expectations of me are unrealistically high. Flattering but impossible."

"Whether they are my expectations or your own, they should be high. The effort to live up to them is as important as setting the right goals in the first place."

"But I get so tired of failing, Albert, so tired that I don't want to try anymore. And now I've told you that, you won't love me."

Albert said dryly, "Whether I love you or not is surely the least of your worries."

"I wish you didn't believe that." Fletcher hauled himself up onto the sorting table again. "All right, I'll tell you one of my most urgent worries. I'm doing these security clearances on federal employees right now. What if I find out one of them is gay or lesbian? If I report the fact, they'll lose their jobs for no good reason. But if I don't report it, I'll lose my job somewhere down the line and all for nothing because they'll lose theirs as well. I don't want to sort my way through that dilemma."

"You're missing the point, Ash," Albert informed him. "If any of these people are homosexual and the Bureau thinks it can use them, either now or in the future, it will let them keep their jobs."

Fletcher frowned over this for a moment, then exclaimed, "Blackmail? Albert, it's not in your interests, or mine, for you to make me dislike the FBI anymore than I already do."

"You must have encountered similar situations in the past, working for the Bureau."

"I guess I've been lucky, because nothing's touched me quite this personally before."

"It seems more likely that they've kept you away from moral dilemmas."

Fletcher was about to dispute this, but then thought of Caroline. She had faced exactly the dilemma he'd described, and had proposed a compromise she could live with. But Fletcher found it harder to live with half–truths and white lies, and she knew it. Had she avoided placing him in difficult situations before now? And, if so, wasn't she taking a great risk by not passing her suspicions on to the Special Agent in Charge? Fletcher sighed deeply. "I feel like eliminating the middle man and quitting anyway. Save everyone the trouble. It's not just that, or the serial killer, it's the boring old financial cases as well, infinitely boring. All the bureaucracy and the paperwork. I don't feel I'm doing good anymore."

"What would you do instead?"

A silence. Albert had asked the question easily enough, perhaps intending to make the point there are few good career options for retired law enforcement officers. But Fletcher's unwillingness to respond prompted the answer.

"Let me guess," Albert said, dripping sarcasm. "Personal assistant to your pet politician."

"Is that so ridiculous?"

"Yes!" Furious.

"Why? I want to do good. This seems like a better way for me to do something useful."

"Obviously you have not only taken leave of your instincts, you've abandoned all common sense as well."

Fletcher took a breath. "Is this tirade motivated by jealousy?"

"No, you imbecile. Not everything relates to Councilor Lachance, except from your perspective."

"That's untrue and unfair, Albert."

A heavy silence. Then, "As McIntyre so quaintly puts it, you're people–smart. Look at these people without the influence of your –" He seemed to struggle for the right word. "Your lust for Lachance. What do you see? Anything noble or worthy? Anything at all other than self–interest? They're politicians, Ash."

"Xavier is ambitious for his own sake but he also wants to do good with the power he's seeking. Equality for gays, for instance – you won't argue with that, surely. Equality of opportunity for everyone."

"You're missing the point again. Look at how these people operate, Ash. If you're finding you can't compromise your ideals for the sake of working for the FBI, then how do you expect to work for a politician?"

"I don't accept what you're saying, Albert. Politicians aren't all corrupt and they aren't all in it for their own egos."

"And now you are being naïve. The whole political system is based on favors and bribes. You ask Lachance how he got this far and what he'll have to do to get to Washington."

"Perhaps I will. And perhaps the answer won't horrify me as much as you anticipate."

"You're too honest and idealistic, Ash. You wouldn't last five minutes."

"I seem to have survived ten days, anyway. One of the things I like about him is how he translates ideals into reality. And so what if I'm honest and naïve? He finds that attractive and interesting."

"You mean, he finds that unusual."

"At least that's an improvement on you – you just get impatient with me."

"Really."

"Really." Fletcher let the silence stretch, let his annoyance ease, before offering, "There's no point in talking about it further. Is there? We're not going to agree right now. We probably can't even agree to disagree." No reply. "Albert, this call will cost you a fortune."

"That is of no consequence. If you wish to end the call, then say so directly."

"Yes, it's getting late. I'm exhausted." He eased off the bench and checked on his second load of washing; it was about to enter the spin cycle.

"Consider one thing, Ash, for your own sake. Think about the consequences of letting this killer remain free. No one else will catch him for you."

"I'll think about it, Albert, that's all I'm promising."

"You're uncomfortable with the part of you that understands the serial killer –"

"You don't believe in that."

"But *you* do. If you turn away from it, if you ignore or suppress that part of you, then that will have a far worse effect on you in the long term. If you live with it and use it for good, that will be healthier than if you shut it away and let it fester."

Strange for Albert to be that smart about Fletcher, but be unable to apply the principle to himself. "I'll think about it," Fletch repeated, frowning.

"I'll let you know when I'm due to arrive."

Fletcher sighed, prevented himself from groaning. "I was serious about needing a little time, Albert. If I agree to do this, can we make it next weekend or the weekend after, instead of this one? Let me mull a few things over, all right?"

"Procrastination, Ash?"

"Give me a break, will you? You never know, I might come around to your way of thinking."

"All right," was the brusque reply.

"I'll call you soon, love. And thanks for spending half the night talking. I appreciate it."

"Do you," Albert said flatly.

"Yes. Goodnight, love." And Fletch hung up, knowing it was pointless to wait for a farewell from Albert. He had just enough energy to throw his washing into the drier with the first lot before climbing the stairs to his apartment and his bed.

CHAPTER TWENTY-SIX
COLORADO
APRIL 1985

"Xavier," Fletch murmured into the dimness of the bedroom.

The man stirred, tugging the sheets out of the way as he moved to take Fletcher into his arms, grinning beautifully. "What, lover man? You want to talk some more? Or fuck some more?"

"Both, of course," Fletch said with a laugh. "But this time I was thinking of talking. If you don't mind missing a little more sleep."

"What would I need sleep for? We're on the last leg of the campaign, the election's in three days." Lazy puzzlement. The pause was filled by slow exploration of Fletcher's face with Xavier's, in a skin-to-skin kiss. "Did I apologize for not being able to see you this week? Other than tonight, of course."

"You did, very graciously. I understand you have other priorities."

"You've been more than understanding, sweet lover man. More fair than smart."

"No – what did you call me before? More honest than smart. They're going to carve that on my tombstone."

"You don't have to think about epitaphs and eulogies yet, Fletcher. Plenty of life left in you." Xavier leaned closer to kiss him on the mouth, a nice unhurried loving kiss. When they were done, Xavier settled himself comfortably beside Fletch, facing him, an arm companionable around his waist. "Now, what did you want to talk about? I'll tell you, it's rare for me to find someone who enjoys conversing as much as I do. Though these last couple of weeks have taken their toll." It was true: the rich brocade voice had grown noticeably hoarser, which added a not unattractive rough note.

Fletcher let a silence grow, doubting again how he should approach this. But he had always tackled personal matters head on, and this should ideally be no different. "I've been doing a lot of thinking lately," he began. "I'm due for a change – I *need* a massive change in my life. I've been trying to look into the future, trying to work out what I want to do. Every aspect of my life – work, relationships – is troubled right now."

A pause, into which Xavier said, "Go on."

"Well, in the middle of all this hard thinking, I had a day dream. *I have a dream,*" Fletcher quoted whimsically.

"What's your dream?"

"I don't know if it's even possible, but I was day dreaming about you being mayor and me staying around. On a long term basis. As your lover."

"Were you, sugar man?" Xavier murmured, smiling lazily. "That's nice. So tempting to imagine such a delightful thing." Then the smile quirked. "Do you always propose to your lovers so soon in a relationship?"

"Soon? We've been together for over two weeks now. That's almost a record for me. I'm so good at falling in love with the most impossible women, sometimes we don't last through the first date. The number of desserts I've missed out on is tragic."

Xavier laughed. "You're one of a kind, Fletcher."

"Let me tell you about this day dream, lover, and then I'll let you think it over in peace." Fletcher took a breath and continued, "There's no way we could keep it secret, which is as it should be, so I'd have to leave the FBI, which I'm not overly sad about because the Bureau and I don't see eye to eye on a lot of things. I thought I could work for you instead, as political staff or a personal assistant or whatever. If you can't pay me at first, I'll volunteer. I have some money that would last a while."

"Maybe you could do that, maybe that is possible. There's certainly work you could do, or learn, and a smart guy like you could wing it in the meantime." A pause for reflection. "We might be able to present you as my long term lover, my partner, package it nicely. You're so cute, that helps, with your lovely cream skin and thick dark hair and those beautiful hot blue eyes. I bet the camera loves you. A fine upstanding honest intelligent gay ex–FBI agent, forced to resign his noble career in order to openly be with his lover. Oh yes, the queer black and the straight–as–an–arrow white liberal romantic, in love and unashamed of it … Beautiful copy. We'll appeal to people across so many demographics, it's ridiculous. And you'll make a suitable First Lady if ever there was one."

"You make it sound prettier than I'd expected. Do we get to live happy ever after as well?"

"I doubt it, lover man, other than in the media releases – but we can try." A pause before Lachance warned, "You'd have to give up your man."

That hurt like a blow to the stomach, even though Fletcher had half expected it, half prepared for it. "I know."

"*Can* you give him up?" Xavier pursued.

"Like you said, I'd have to." Though the prospect of leaving Albert behind was far bleaker than the idea of turning his back on the Bureau. And Albert wouldn't even believe Fletcher's heart was breaking, too. "But he and I could remain friends."

"I don't think so, lover man. If he values his job, and if you value your reputation as my faithful partner, then you'll never see him again."

Worst case scenario, damn it. "I take your point."

"If you can do that, and if you'll do one other thing for me, this day dream might translate into reality."

"What one other thing?"

"I'd like to take you on, Fletcher, but I'd need a serious commitment from you. I need you to burn your bridges and tie yourself to my bandwagon. Because I can't afford to be seen as fickle. If we do this, then it's a political marriage, based on convenience as well as romance, and we can't divorce."

Fletcher frowned at the wording, though he'd anticipated the intent behind it. "What would you want me to do?" he asked again.

"One favor, while you're still with the Bureau. I need information on a certain entrepreneur. I took a rather generous campaign donation from him and, once I'm in, he'll expect me to give him the go–ahead for some pretty risky land development. I want something to hold over him, to cancel the favor."

"You don't want the land developed?"

Xavier shrugged. "I'll probably give him the go–ahead anyway, but then he'll owe me again."

"Why do you want him to owe you?"

"You understand this already, Special Agent. He's the one with the money, and therefore the power. I need him aligned to me."

"Aren't you the one who's going to be in power?"

"Yeah, I'll have my share of it, but the reality is that he has a bigger share and he's here for the long haul."

Fletcher moved to lie on his back, and he stared at the ceiling, mind numb except for one thought: *Albert, you bastard, why did you have to be right?* He said lightly, "You really want me to do that, Xavier?"

"Sure, lover man, if you want to deal into this game."

"And you think I'm the sort of person who could do it?"

"Yeah. You're honest but you believe in the same things I do, as passionately as I do. And we both know that the ends justify the means."

"Do we?" Fletch whispered to the distant ceiling.

"You're an idealist, sweet man, but you have to come down from that ivory tower to actually do anything about your dreams and principles. You've learned that already – you work with the FBI, for Christ's sake."

"Again, I take your point." Because that was, in another person's words, a fair summary of why he'd fallen out of love with the Bureau. Fletcher shifted uncomfortably, and sat up cross-legged.

Xavier, turning to lie on his front but leaning up on his elbows to talk to Fletcher face to face, continued, "Revolution from within. Taking the system and then using it to progress what you believe in. That's the only feasible way."

"But if the process of *taking* the power corrupts you, then you disqualify yourself from holding it. You can't ever be clean again."

"But if you don't take the power, then the next bastard will – and I'll lay bets he'll be a right wing, reactionary, homophobic racist."

"Sexist, too," Fletch added faintly.

"Within this system, Fletcher, I'm the best you'll get. And I'm more than good enough for you to accept – no, for you to be happy about."

"You're dangerous, Xavier."

"How so?"

"You're too damned seductive for my peace of mind. Quit talking for a moment." He held his hand up, palm out, mind racing. "The central issue is ends and means. You really care about certain ends, you passionately care – and you'll do anything it takes to reach those ends. But I disagree with that approach, I entirely disagree with it. I think you blight any good you achieve, you undermine any success, you sow the seeds of failure, if your means are suspect." Fletcher paused, then said, "The peripheral issue is that part of me wants to believe in you, to be seduced by your rhetoric, because our ends, our goals happen to coincide.

But if I wouldn't approve of your means and tactics in the hands of a right wing reactionary, then I can't in all conscience approve of you."

"Ah, lover man, so serious," Xavier murmured with some regret. "Why did I seduce the one FBI agent with morals?"

Ignoring that last sortie, Fletcher said, "Yes, I am serious. I fear you, and I fear for you. And that makes me so damned sad because you're a wonderful person, so smart, and working to such an admirable agenda. But you're flawed."

"You're talking of complicated problems, and expecting simple answers."

"Simplicity is unrealistic, is it?"

"Yes, sweet man." Xavier leaned a little closer. "Are you still going to vote for me?"

The unexpectedness of that winded Fletcher. "All political debate comes down to that, does it?"

A broad smile. "Are you?"

"I don't know. I don't know that I want to vote for anyone right now."

"You don't have enough nerve, Fletcher; you just need that extra nerve to go that extra distance. You're building barricades for yourself that needn't be there."

"Maybe I have too many doubts about too many things. If I'm sure of something, I'll do what I have to do, within the rules – I respect the fact that society is nothing without limits – but there are so few things I'm sure of."

"That's not true. You know what's right and you judge people accordingly."

Fletcher grinned without humor. "I envy your certainty, your commitment to your beliefs. At the same time, it scares me – do you ever stop to question yourself?"

"Do you ever stop questioning yourself, and take action?" Xavier shook his head. "You think too much, Fletcher. It un–mans you."

"I think," Fletch murmured, "therefore I'm terminally confused."

"Let's start with the basics, lover man: 'We hold these truths to be self–evident, that all men are created equal, that they are endowed by their Creator with certain unalienable Rights, that among these are Life, Liberty and the pursuit of Happiness –'"

"Yes, all right. Putative creators aside, I suppose there are a handful of bedrock truths and equality is the first of them – but what if I'm wrong about even that? You see, if I insist that my bedrock truths are applicable to everyone, that makes me as much a dictator as the Klansman who insists that blacks are little more than animals."

"The difference being that your truths don't impose on anyone else's rights and freedoms – in fact, your truths support human rights, and how can you doubt the worthiness of that?"

"I don't, not really. I doubt myself instead."

Xavier was finally exasperated. "For Christ's sake, Fletcher, how do you get out of bed in the morning? And how on earth do you work for the FBI?"

Fletch said quietly, "I'm currently asking myself that very question."

"Which leads us back to my request for a favor. Will you give me some information on this guy? His file must be twelve inches thick."

"Xavier, you're … disenchanting me."

The man murmured, "I enchanted you, lover man? You're sweet."

"This day dream of mine is impossible, isn't it?" Fletch suddenly demanded. "That's what this whole conversation has been about: you explaining why it wouldn't work for you and me to be lovers. You knew all along that it wouldn't work, but you've been humoring me."

Shrugging in easy agreement, Xavier said, "But these couple of weeks have been nice, sugar man."

Rather than being affronted by this final manipulation, Fletcher felt appreciative. "You're letting me down gently," he said with a tiny smile. "You're taking care of my interests, seeing as I'm more enchanted than smart right now."

"Call it gentle if you like, lover man, but you shouldn't always think the best of people."

Fletcher grimaced. "My boss said something similar to me recently."

"Then she's a smart lady and you should learn from her. You're so keen on honesty, Agent Ash: do you want the truth about you and me?"

A long pause, while Fletcher wondered whether he could cope with this. But, inevitably, he said, "Go on."

"You were a low risk fuck, a safe way to get my rocks off, and it's been far too long since I was last able to afford to do that."

"Really," Fletcher said flatly.

"I saw you; you wanted me; you're damned cute for a white boy; and you were safe because you have far more to lose than I do."

"Everything comes down to cold–hearted calculation with you, doesn't it?"

"Does that surprise you?"

"I suppose it shouldn't." Fletcher sat there, deliberately not touching Xavier; feeling so distant from this man who, not an hour ago, had been so intimately in possession of Fletcher; beginning to wish he wasn't in the same bed, the same house with him. "I'm naïve about politics. Or I was. I think you're unscrupulous enough to go far."

"I'm willing to do what I have to do to solve the problems you agree need a solution."

"Fine. But I couldn't work like that."

"Sure, go solve your own problems, Special Agent. And try to remember that the end never justifies the means." A pause. "You know, you should read up about your hero and his big brother. There are plenty of lessons in the Kennedy story about public image and private truth, ideals and compromise, dreams and reality. You and I probably admire them for very different reasons."

"Probably. Which is your hero? Jack, I suppose."

"Sure, he got to the White House, didn't he? And he was the youngest man, and the first Catholic, to be President. Whereas you like Bobby, who seems to you like more of a white knight."

Silence. Fletcher slowly became aware of how late it was, of how every fiber of his body ached with exhaustion. "All right, I've been fooling myself about you, and about us. So let's just call it quits. That's what you want, isn't it? I've become a liability, with all this talk of day dreams."

"Is that the truth? It sounds ugly sometimes."

"Maybe it does, but it's necessary to speak and hear it."

"We found a lot of joy together, lover man; that's a truth, too. I don't want you to leave like this, so unhappy."

"No, you want me in love and ready to vote. Well, let me go now without anymore garbage, and we'll see."

Xavier reached out a hand, but Fletcher steadfastly refused to respond. Instead he climbed out of bed, and began gathering his clothes together.

"Goodbye, Mr. Lachance."

"Goodbye, sweet man. Later, when you're not so pissed off with me, remember the joy we had, won't you?"

"I'm not angry with you," Fletcher said, tired and quiet.

"You are. I've let you down, I've rained on your parade, I've confronted you with realities you didn't want to know about."

Fletcher sighed. "Never mind."

"You care too much, sugar man. One day, you're going to have to let go of all these things that are troubling you."

"But not today."

"One day when you're old," Xavier predicted, "and there's nothing left of you."

"Maybe then." Fletcher smiled a little. "Yeah, maybe then." He was dressed now, and it was more than time to go. He didn't say anything more, just looked once at this beautiful, corrupt, seductive man and walked out.

Sweating hard, pushing himself to the limit and beyond, felt so damned – not good, but necessary. The ball bounced where he'd anticipated, Fletcher lifted his racket and slammed the ball back against the wall. Caroline chased after the rebound, expression as fierce as Fletcher's. She hit it at a good angle and Fletcher scrambled to return it.

"Congratulations," she said afterwards. "That was the longest, most furious game of squash I've ever played." She arched an eyebrow. "That's the only way you can beat me, right?"

"Yeah." Fletcher buried his face in his towel, scrubbed at his damp hair and wet face. The discontent was still simmering away within him but the ferocious exertion had at least quieted it for a while. He wondered whether that was why Caroline always played to win.

"Are you feeling better now?"

Fletch looked across at her, considering the teasing but concerned tone, and he slowly smiled at her for the first time in days. "Yeah, I believe I am."

She returned the smile in full measure. "Good. Go have a shower, Fletch, and I'll meet you at the cafe. I might even buy you lunch. Then we've got work to do."

CHAPTER TWENTY-SEVEN
COLORADO
APRIL 1985

They barely spoke during the drive from the airport to Fletcher's apartment, even with a stop for grocery shopping.

Fletch reflected that, while Albert would never be a happy or open sort of person, the older man had made some advances over the years since he and Fletch had been friends – at least, he wasn't quite as stony and uncommunicative when it was just the two of them. Until recently, of course, though Fletcher hoped to begin making up lost ground this weekend. There were surely ways of being lovers without making each other thoroughly miserable. The problem was convincing Albert that the ways Fletcher had in mind were logical and beneficial. The other problem was convincing Albert to trust him again.

At the apartment building, they climbed the stairs, disdaining the elevator as usual, and Fletcher let them in. The briefest surprise crossed Albert's face. Fletch laughed and said, "Looks pretty organized, doesn't it?" Down the further end of the long room, the dining table and two chairs were cleared and waiting; boxes of files and papers were lined along the wall nearby; the few other pieces of furniture and junk were tidied away into a corner; the kitchen was clean. Fletch wandered over to the files, indicated a single box: "This is Wyoming, 1978." Then a row of five overflowing boxes: "This is our case. Colorado, 1980." Then two groups of two boxes each: "Georgia, 1982 and Oregon, 1984."

Albert nodded, placed his briefcase by the table and then took his compact suitcase into the bedroom.

Having hoped for a compliment, or even a comment, Fletcher shrugged. It didn't matter. Albert had said once before, years ago, that he was glad Fletcher's general carelessness wasn't evident in his work – and Albert was not in the habit of repeating himself.

Fletcher went to put the coffee on, soon joined by Albert who quickly unpacked the groceries he'd bought, putting most away for later. They probably wouldn't have to leave the apartment all weekend, except that Albert would no doubt go buy a newspaper each day.

"While I prepare dinner, you can fill me in on how you've been checking your list of suspects."

"All right." Fletcher poured himself a mug of coffee then leaned back against the kitchen bench. Albert was a flurry of organized activity beside him. Nice, this domesticated comfort with each other.

"I assume you're working from the Colorado list," Albert prompted him.

"Yes. It's been taking some time, so I haven't gotten very far."

"As long as you haven't been checking them in alphabetic order."

"No, in order of suspicion. Though, in this case, that doesn't mean very much. We eliminated the known sex offenders at the time and the few likeliest suspects. There's no one else on the list who has more than two points against his name." Fletcher continued, "I've been trying to do this by the book. My instincts tell me no one I've interviewed so far is a killer, though I did solve two separate spates of burglaries and one heavy duty tax evasion in the process. But I've been feeling pretty weary lately. I can't afford to trust myself to pick up the nuances."

"I see."

"All right," Fletch said, having thought Albert would approve his approach. "If they're still living in Colorado, I talk with them as long as I can, going back a few times if I have to. Most have been fairly cooperative. I ask them what they were doing in the fall of 1978, 80, 82 and 84. I corroborate that with two other people outside of immediate family, if possible, and their employer. I ask if there were any absences around those times or trips to other states. Once we have what they assume is the business out of the way, I talk to them about football – I've developed quite a patter on that, you should hear me. There's all this jargon about tight ends and scoring and penetration, which sounds like sublimated homoeroticism to me." Fletcher grinned. "And I have you to blame for that perspective."

No response.

"I talk to them about cars, ask what they drive, what they were driving back in fall 1980 – remember Drew Harmer was picked up by a man in a black car, who appeared rich. I try to find out whether they'd have been able to take Drew and the others home for the evening, somewhere they could work undisturbed, without arousing the suspicion of family or friends or neighbors. I try to form an opinion whether Drew would have seen him as Prince Charming. Most of this is difficult because it was four and a half years ago."

"And if they've moved away from Colorado?" Albert asked.

"Much the same. Trying to establish where they were at the relevant times. One guy had moved to Oregon in 1981, but I can't place him in Georgia at all. Three of them have had jobs that entailed traveling but again, they weren't in the right states at the right times."

"All right."

"Meanwhile, of course, Mac is keeping an eye on the newspapers and incoming police reports. I also have Celia keeping an ear to the medical examiners' network across a few states down south. She says most of the work they get down there is gunshot wounds or domestic violence, so anything out of the ordinary like this, she'll make sure she hears about." And Fletcher asked, "How about you?"

"I've run the fingerprint from Doherty's shoe against the computer records every month, with no results."

Fletcher shook his head. "I'd have anticipated a criminal record showing up for this guy. Some young man he's gone too far with, assault or a sodomy charge or even statutory rape, though I think he's particular about them being of age. It's odd that he doesn't pick the most liberal states to live in."

"So, what sort of person can commit sodomy with impunity? Or have an assault charge against him dropped? Or buy his way out of trouble?"

"Exactly, Albert, I'm one step ahead of you there. It seems that most serial killers have a working class or lower middle class background. But, to get away with this over the years, I think our man has money or prestige within whichever community he lives in. He can also afford to move to a new state every two years."

Albert nodded.

"Anything further on this DNA business?" Fletcher asked.

"No. I told you they applied for a patent for the identification process. That could take years to approve and then make available. Meanwhile, they're not describing enough detail of the process for me to be able to recreate it. I've kept samples of semen from different victims, just in case."

Fletcher was grinning. "You tried to recreate the process, for me?"

"For the case. And I failed."

"I really appreciate you putting in that much effort. You must have spent weeks on it."

"It wouldn't have been admissible evidence," Albert said flatly. "I shouldn't have told you, because of the patent pending on the process. In any case, I failed."

"Love you anyway," Fletcher said.

Of course there was no response. Albert, busy serving dinner onto two of Fletcher's mismatched plates, might not even have heard him. As they carried their plates and cutlery over to the table, Albert said, "I believe it would be useful for us to review the current status of the case this weekend, determine what evidence we do and do not have, then plan our next few months accordingly."

"All right."

As they began eating, Albert continued, "Better use might be made of McIntyre and Mortimer."

"Really? I never thought I'd hear you say that."

"At this juncture, they are better than no resources at all."

Fletcher smiled at the man. "Thanks, Albert."

A pointed stare. "There is no cause to thank me."

"Yes, there is. Apart from you being fairer to our friends, your phone call from Seattle made me realize a few things. I didn't believe at first but once I began hauling all these boxes of files around, I found some motivation again. I actually began looking forward to doing this."

The man seemed indifferent. His attention remained on his meal and once Fletcher had grown silent, Albert began to talk about the serial killer again. Surely friendship was behind that long, late night phone call and also behind this weekend – Fletcher still relied on that friendship but Albert seemed determined not to allow Fletch to take any joy from it.

Midnight, after four solid hours poring over files and reports, pushing his brain to distil the essential facts of these cases. But Fletcher was glad of the challenge, enjoying the process, even beginning to believe again that they might solve this. There was so much information, too much for them to realistically deal with – though surely the answer was amongst it all, camouflaged and innocuous until the right facts were linked together.

But there were also other things on Fletcher's mind tonight. "It's late. Let's go to bed, love."

Albert took a moment to finish the page he was reading and make a neat notation, but then he obediently stood and headed for the bedroom. Silence while they undressed, took turns in the bathroom, switched off the lights, and climbed into bed. Albert was lying on his back, not touching Fletcher, eyes closed as if already prepared for sleep.

"I have something to tell you," Fletch said. He was on his side, propped up on an elbow.

It was difficult to see Albert's face in the darkness, but he seemed impassive. "What?" he prompted after a while.

"I'm all yours again, if you'll have me."

A long uninterested silence, with no visible reaction from the man. At last Albert said, "I take it you've decided to make do with second best."

Fletch could hardly read resentment or jealousy into the words when they were pronounced so flatly. "You were never second best and you know it."

"Don't patronize me."

"You were right – about politics, I mean. Xavier made it abundantly clear to me that I wouldn't fit in. He was quite cruel about it but I think that was deliberate, I think he was trying to do the best thing for me."

"I'm not interested in the detail."

"So I've called it quits with him."

"Am I supposed to care?"

"Of course you care," Fletcher muttered. Then he continued, "Albert, I was wrong about politics, about working with Xavier, I admit that. But I wasn't wrong to have an affair. I love you, I really do love you and you're my best friend, but there are things missing between us. Can't we work that out? I don't want to have to go elsewhere to fill in the gaps."

Albert opened his eyes and glared at Fletch, before staring up at the ceiling. "Don't waste your breath on threats. I am not interested in your fidelity or lack thereof."

"But you are, Albert. You were hurt by my lack thereof."

"There is no point in discussing this further."

"There *is* a point, a very important point. I don't regret Xavier but if you and I could work things out between us, I reckon we'd have something pretty wonderful. Something far more wonderful than I could have had with him. I need more from you, Albert. I need your passion."

"I have none to give you."

"Don't be ridiculous, of course you have passion. Bucket–loads of passion."

Albert's stare become even more fixed and cold. "If I did, I wouldn't trust *you* with it. There is no point in discussing this further."

Fletcher took a long breath and sighed it out, briefly wondering at his own dogged certainty of this man. "We obviously have our share of troubles, Albert. But you were really starting to make an effort to strengthen the connection between us that weekend we spent up in the mountains, before I told you about Xavier. You were trying to make things work between us, not just to maintain our connection but improve it. You came here to Colorado for a start, you were trying to communicate with me, you were sharing the things I like to do. Even now you're making an effort: you were concerned enough with my sanity to come here again, to help me with the case, to plan for us to work together on it –"

"I'm ineligible for sainthood, Ash."

"Listen to me, this is important."

The man grimaced, impatient, and closed his eyes again.

"If we both try a little harder, surely – If you were willing to make that much effort, won't you keep trying now?"

"You have obviously misread me. I certainly don't intend to pretend this relationship is something it's not."

"Something it's not? I don't understand."

"I do not consider you worthy of any further effort, Ash, if in fact that's what I was doing. And this weekend's work is a result of my concern with the serial killer rather than with you."

"You say you're unwilling to trust me. But, as long as we begin making progress again, I'm perfectly prepared to promise that I won't be unfaithful again. I'll promise you anything within reason."

"I've already told you I'm not interested. And it would be a worthless promise anyway."

Fletcher almost growled in frustration. He sat up cross–legged, and buried his face in his hands. "Does this have to be so damned difficult?"

And in a very small but decisive voice, Albert said, "Yes."

An admission of sorts. After a moment of consideration, Fletcher said, "I know you have to swallow your pride, Albert, to take me back on the same understanding that we had."

"I don't recall that we had any understanding."

Fletcher did growl then. When he had words again, he continued, "Of course we did. You can't have it both ways, Albert – either this is a marriage and you can't forgive me for being unfaithful, which is certainly how you're acting, or there's no requirement for fidelity, in which case you should let us get on with our relationship instead of putting us through this."

No reply, though the expression was disturbed and bitter.

"All right, you have every right to put me through the emotional wringer. But what we have is worth it. Let's get through all the trouble. Let's cut through it all now."

"You can't manipulate me like that."

"I'm not –"

"Yes, you are, and I'm sure it would work on anyone else. You're saying, in so many words, let's rise above the petty jealousy, how noble it would be for me to welcome you back and pretend nothing happened. But I'm not the hero in one of your romance novels, so it won't work on me."

This man is impossible! The thought was fuelled by frustrated anger but then Fletcher almost laughed. Surely it meant something that, while Albert was the most unfeasible in a long line of impossible relationships, they had lasted together far longer than anyone else Fletcher had had an affair with. He said, "The core of all this is that we're important to each other, we value each other, we're friends. We're still not calling it quits, are we? So we may as well try to make it work."

"It is working," Albert said.

"Don't be ridiculous."

Albert was moving, sitting up, kneeling in front of Fletcher, bending to kiss him. The fingers wove through his hair, tilting his head back, and the tongue sought entry, which Fletcher surrendered with a moan. He swayed for a moment, caught his balance with his hands at Albert's waist.

But when one of Albert's hands drifted to Fletcher's chest, began to tease a nipple, Fletch broke the kiss. "How can you do this? How can the sex mean so little to you?"

"What should it mean?"

"Between us, something wonderful. You're so cold–blooded, trying to seduce me like this when I'm talking to you. Like when we were up in the mountains."

The man was, surprisingly enough, persevering. His hands were gently stroking the inside of Fletcher's thighs, drawing nearer to his genitals with each sweep. And they were so low, it was almost as if Albert was promising to touch him … *there*. Fletcher shivered.

"You've made your point," Fletcher said, grabbing both of Albert's hands in his own. "You know all my buttons and which ones to push in what sequence. What else are you trying to tell me? That our relationship is nothing but sex and therefore it doesn't matter if I'm unfaithful?" He added wistfully, "Am I just a convenient way for you to get your rocks off?"

"*Convenient* is hardly the word I would use."

Fletcher looked at him, and sighed. "Not tonight, all right? Give me some time, Albert."

And Albert, even though Fletcher could see that he had an eager erection, drew away immediately.

"We could have everything, if you were willing to try," Fletcher said, resentful. "If you were willing to give me a little more of your true self."

No reply. Albert settled himself on the other side of the bed, back to Fletcher.

"How do you repress that much of yourself?"

"Go to sleep, Ash."

"Am I ever going to get through to you?"

"No. Go to sleep."

"So this is all we'll ever have." Fletcher sighed, neglected to say goodnight. They lay there, not touching, both wide awake. Fletcher closed his eyes, hopeless …

And was spinning into blue nothingness; weightless, lost, terrified.

He blinked awake with a soft protest. Maybe only a moment had passed, maybe hours. Albert was turning towards him, barely hinting at an offer of their usual embrace, but Fletcher could read him. And he tried to put his fear and frustration and annoyance aside, and he let Albert hold him. Fletcher figured that if he could put aside all their disagreements and impossible prospects for happiness, lying back in Albert's arms might feel like coming home.

Though somehow that made it worse, because Albert was sure enough and determined enough to allow Fletcher this much and this much only. It all seemed so damned futile, with only the comfort of an embrace to set against the bleak future.

With the minimum of words exchanged, Fletcher and Albert began work again in the morning. The motivation Fletcher had found over the last few days now evaporated, the moments of euphoria proved as insubstantial as mist, and he simply didn't have the energy or inclination to manufacture more. But this case was important, and if there was one lesson he could learn from Albert, it was the value of deciding on a priority, then grimly putting the time in to meet it, no matter what. It would be worse than counterproductive to let his personal disappointments get in the way of catching this killer.

The phone rang, and for once, Fletcher didn't have to search for it – he'd made a couple of calls relating to the case and the phone was perched precariously on a pile of papers in front of him. Expecting this to be work, he said in a formal but distracted voice, "Hello, Fletcher Ash here."

"Happy birthday, Fletcher."

He grimaced, wholly unprepared for a civilized personal conversation. "Thanks, Dad. I'd forgotten what day it was."

"Forgotten your own birthday?"

"Yes, forgotten my own birthday," Fletch repeated with a touch of impatience. Trying harder, he asked, "How are you?"

"We're all fine up here and business is good. Harley and Beth said to tell you they'd call this evening, once the dinner crowd have gone, if you're going to be home."

"Yes, that's fine, I'll look forward to it."

"What are you doing to celebrate?"

"Nothing much. Albert is up for the weekend but we're just working on a case."

"Working at home? That must be the old murder case you're spending your spare time on. Don't you have better things to do on your birthday?"

"Not really." Fletcher sighed. Peter wouldn't understand because he didn't know anything about the case, about Fletcher missing the 1982 and 1984 deadlines that the killer had set. He wasn't going to miss 1986. Peter also didn't know about the mess of his son's personal life. Instead of an explanation, Fletch offered, "Albert will no doubt cook me yet another delicious meal tonight."

"That's good. Any presents? That shirt he sent at Christmas was beautiful."

"No," Fletch replied, looking directly at his lover, "no more blue silk shirts." Albert, perfectly able to hear at least this side of the conversation, did not react. Fletcher, though he didn't really feel like being fair, continued, "However, Albert did try to recreate the DNA identification process for me."

A brief pause. "That means something to you, does it?"

"Yeah, actually it means a lot."

A longer pause. "Fletcher, you're sounding unhappier than ever."

"I'm all right, Dad." Though they both knew that was a lie, and that there was nothing Peter could do anyway. Staring pointedly at Albert again, Fletcher said to his father, "Go on – do it with *impossible*."

"Impossible, inconceivable, insuperable. Unimaginable, unattainable, unworkable."

"You've still got it, old man," Fletch said, though his laugh was bitter. "I'd better get on with it, all right?"

"All right. I hope your thirty–fourth year is happier and even more productive than your thirty–third."

"Thanks, Dad, I hope so, too. Talk to you next week." And Fletch hung up the phone.

A silence stretched until it became clear that Albert did not intend to provide any good wishes for Fletcher's birthday. And he must have known all along what day it was, anyway, without the prompt of Peter's call. *So be it*, Fletcher thought, *if that's the way you want it, you cold–blooded bastard.*

"LIFE BEING WHAT IT IS ..."
ILLINOIS
SEPTEMBER 1965

No one came to tell John Garrett that they'd put his mother in the hospital. He'd walked home after school to find the living room empty; after checking the bathroom and bedroom just in case, he'd headed over to the shop where she worked five hours during the day to try to find her. Surely the right thing to do would have been for someone to come to the school and tell him?

"Your mother was drunk again," the old man said, hostile. He ran the shop, but John's mother had said he didn't really own it, even though he'd like everyone to think so.

John shrugged at this statement. When wasn't his mother drunk? He asked, "Where is she?"

"She fell over and hit her head."

The old man pointed, and John turned to look: a whole lot of scrubbing and water and detergent foam couldn't hide the fact there was a blood stain on the floor. The boy stepped closer, peering intently, fascinated. The stain was a dark color, sort of black rather than red, and it had soaked in really well. He wondered what color it would be once all the water was gone and the wooden floorboards had dried.

"We had to close the shop and take her to the hospital."

Surely the right thing would be for the old man to express some concern or sympathy or something? Instead, all John could see in him was impatience and anger. What with that and the uncertainty of this situation, John began feeling angry, too. Scowling, he asked the proper thing: "Is she all right?"

"They said she'll be fine, other than losing the blood. Other than being a drunk," the old man added spitefully. "But she won't be coming back here. Tell her she's fired."

That was it. John stepped to the counter, reached one arm over to grab the man's lapels, hauled him closer. "The right thing to do," he ground out menacingly, "would be to go over there, and take her some flowers or something, and tell her yourself."

It was pathetic, really, how scared the man was of a fifteen–year–old boy; pathetic even though John was big and strong for his age, even though this anger and this action released a flood of vivid and violent images through his mind. Maybe the old man saw the fate John's day-dreams decreed for him, maybe he realized there was nothing John would like better than to beat the man senseless and leave him for dead.

But, no, the right thing was to push the old man away, stalk out of the stupid little shop, and go visit his mother in the hospital.

Despite the fact that the images replayed for him all the way up the street, adding the abject fear in the old man's eyes to John's favorite day-dream, and adding the dark blood stain, too.

His mother looked just the same as she ever did, except for the thick bandage around her head, and the neatness of the bed she lay in, the cleanliness of the room. She was curled up on her side, deeply asleep, obviously having drunk enough to send her far under.

John supposed the right thing to do was to sit here with her, even though she wouldn't be waking any time soon. There were two other women in the ward, each surrounded by family and friends and flowers. He would wait at her side, like a dutiful son, and ask the nurses what she needed – a nightdress at least, he figured.

First, he had to find a decent chair. The one by the bed had arms, which he didn't like. He was never comfortable in a chair with arms. It was all right at school, because they sat on stools and benches most of the time. But here, there weren't any without. John stood for a while, but soon the other visitors were casting glances at him, so he finally sank to perch on the chair by the bed, and he stared at his mother.

She used to tie him by the wrist to a chair, and turn the television on, and leave him, sometimes so she could go out, but more often so she could get drunk in peace. To think of that was bad enough, and aggravated the anger inside of him; let alone remembering the fact he was still wearing diapers at age six, when he wasn't in school, because his mother wanted to be left alone. Until his father had come home unexpectedly, and flew into a rage at this negligence – and taken it out on John's tender backside. Unfair but, as Father said, it was wrong to hit women.

Closing his eyes, John turned it all around: his father tied to the chair, unable to get away, cowering as John took his time visiting all his anger on the man. The fear in his father's eyes, the shame as he realized he'd just filled his diaper, the bruises already welling dark and swollen.

The clatter of metal on tile, and John snapped to the here and now. His mother slept undisturbed, a nurse was picking up a couple of pans that had fallen, and John was aware of an intense arousal.

It seemed strange that he should be so excited by these day–dreams, it didn't seem to be quite the right thing. But it was better that than chasing girls, which Father said was wrong until you met the right woman who would be your wife. Mother said Father chased girls anyway. *He screws anything in a skirt*, she'd say, the disgust evident despite the slurring. John felt the disgust, too.

Once, before his father had known John's place was tied to the chair in the front room, he'd come home late at night, and there was Mother lying curled up on the sofa – and Father had lifted her skirt and dropped his trousers and screwed her, and she was in such a stupor she didn't even know. Of course, John had only known enough to keep quiet back then. Once he learned to associate sex with that brutal, long ago image, he better understood his mother's distaste.

There was a book in the art room at school, that had all these paintings of brown–skinned women with their breasts exposed. The other boys hauled it out to look at the pictures whenever the teacher wasn't around. John wasn't interested in such things, but had once found some words in the book that he could understand: *Life being what it is, one dreams of revenge.* Some French painter had said that, which was smart, but he'd also painted naked ladies, which was wrong.

Surely it was better for John to think of the words rather than the pictures when he jerked off.

The irresistible urge was on him even as he thought this, so he stood and headed down the corridor until he found a restroom, locked the door, and unzipped his pants. That image – of a boy terrified, crawling along the floor on his knees and one hand, the other arm dragging the chair with him, trying to hide behind the thing, as John followed, letting the boy creep away for now, but anticipating the thud of his fist against flesh, the bruises flowering, the skin cut and bleeding so much the whole floor was stained dark. And now the boy was naked, too, and utterly defenseless – and for no particular reason John was coming, muffling a groan.

It was best jerking off back home, when the house was empty, or when Mother was in too drunken a sleep to hear, because then John could yell to his heart's content. He could even scream, high and thin and scared, like the boy in the day–dream screamed.

Now that he thought of it, he was glad that this dream hadn't featured Father tied to the chair, even though that's what he'd been imagining when he got hard. His father had been a good man, after all, and he'd taught John about the right things. He'd taught John that maintaining the family was the most important thing, and Father had tried so hard to always do the right thing for John and Mother, before he'd gone away for good.

That sounded like heaven on earth to John – Father had gone away for good. And staying here was for bad, but John had to do the right thing by Mother.

No one back in the ward seemed to have noticed John's absence. He perched himself on the chair again, and waited. Another half hour would be right and proper, and then he could go home.

Just as he was finally thinking of leaving, Mother stirred. "John?" she whispered. Then she put a hand to her head and moaned.

"I'm here, Mother. You're in the hospital." Wasn't that the right thing to say? "You're going to be fine."

"I know," she said, impatient. "Did you bring me a bottle, John?"

He glanced around, expecting a nurse to overhear such a request, no matter how quietly spoken. "No."

"Get me something to drink. Sneak it in for me."

He thought about this for a moment, but doing as his mother asked, and fooling the nurses at the same time, sounded like the right thing and the fun thing to do. "Okay. I'll go home, and come back in an hour or so."

"Be careful. If they find out, they'll watch me like hawks."

"Yes, Mother." John stood, leaned over the bed; Mother suffered him to press his dry lips to her cheek; he turned and left the hospital.

There was a bottle of vodka at home, only half empty, which John figured was the best bet: it wouldn't be obvious on his mother's breath;

also, it was strong and she wouldn't need as much, so he could transfer some to a smaller bottle and sneak it in all the easier. He was looking for something innocent, like a perfume bottle, when there was a knock on the door. Startled, he waited for a second knock. No one ever came visiting the Garrett place.

When he finally opened the front door, John found a kid from his class standing there, pie dish steaming, wrapped in a towel and his hands. The kid said, "Let me in, this is hot!" and pushed past him, locating the kitchen by trial and error.

John let the door close, and followed warily.

The kid was chattering away, unfazed by the lack of response. "You remember me, Geoff from school; I know we've never really talked or anything, but my mom knows your mom from down the shop, and she said to bring this over for your dinner, and I can stay and help you eat it if you'd like the company, but if you'd rather not just say so; my mom says your mom is a real sweetie, but very quiet –"

Frowning, John watched as Geoff found a couple of plates and knives and forks from various cupboards, and dusted them off, all without missing a beat in his one–sided conversation. Mother was a real sweetie? It seemed odd that anyone would describe her that way, would call her anything but a drunk, would know her at all. He'd never considered that Mother, who'd never worked a day in her life before Father left, might enjoy her job, even though it was nothing but serving in the stupid shop with that cranky old man. How strange. And now she'd been fired, and she didn't even know.

But John had enough to cope with right now, like figuring out how to shut this kid up. Or maybe it was easier just to let him talk, because that way John could just ignore him and eat, which was standard procedure for meals around here, not that Mother often ate much.

The pie was good, with chunks of meat and potato and rich gravy. Even the pastry tasted nice. John hadn't had anything like it since Mother had stolen a chicken pie from the shop. He ate over half of it because Geoff, who was smaller, couldn't quite finish his share, no matter how hard he tried.

Then they watched TV, Geoff providing endless commentary. Only Geoff didn't know anything smart, because he was sitting in John's place, and his hands were on the arms of the chair, and John was sweating with all those images until he couldn't bear it any more. He stood, and went to collect the pie plate and the dish–towel.

The kid broke into his own monologue, and said, "You want me to go already? That's fine, but I just want to stay until this episode finishes, I want to know who did it, and it doesn't look like the butler this time, does it? What are you doing?"

"Cowboys and Indians," John mumbled. He'd tied one end of the towel around the chair arm, and now began tying the other around Geoff's wrist. He knew how to tie a knot that would hold.

"Yeah, we play that at home, but we get to chase each other around the yard first, though Brad always wins because he's bigger than me, but he can't climb the tree, so I try to get up there first –"

"Shut up," John whispered when the boy was secure.

"Mom always says I talk too much, but there's no grown–ups around here, with your mom in hospital, so we can talk all we like, can't we, and –"

John stood, towered over the stupid brat. "I said to shut up. Aren't you scared? I have you tied up, and you can't get away."

"Scared? Right, I'm the Indian, I guess, Brad always gets to be the cowboy, which isn't fair, but he's bigger –"

A slap across his cheek, hard enough to knock his head back, and really sting.

"Hey!" the boy cried out, more confused than anything. He brought his free hand up to his face, gingerly felt for damage. "No need to get rough."

"Yes, there is," John whispered. Then he carefully spelled it out for the kid: "There is a need for me to get rough. Scared now?"

Silence at last. The boy nodded.

"Try to get away. Go on, just try. If you can get away, I'll let you go."

The boy's free hand wandered over to the towel, began to pry at the knot on his wrist.

John slapped him, harder this time. "No. You're too much of a baby to know you can get away like that."

Wide eyes never leaving John's face. After long moments, the boy pushed against the floor with both feet, managed to shift the chair back a little, did it again. And then he was far enough away to quickly stand and turn. He grabbed the chair arm in both hands and, with a great deal of effort, swung it around between them.

"That's better," John said.

"Don't like this game," the kid muttered.

"But I do. Come on, try to get away."

The boy backed away slowly, dragging the chair with him, eyes still watching John like a trapped animal.

Long delicious minutes before he reached the other side of the room, and then John strode after him. The kid fell to his knees, almost sobbing with an abrupt increase in fear, tried to crawl around behind the back of the chair – but John was on him, landing one blow to the boy's belly, then another, and losing his balance so he fell sprawling across the kid's quaking body – and John was coming in great hot waves, letting a triumphant yell echo through the house.

Quiet, broken only by the boy's snuffling tears. "I want to go home," he pleaded.

John eventually moved off him, let the kid pick at the knots until both were loose. Then John stood, still glowing from the orgasm, and went to pick up the pie plate. He broke it cleanly in two with a giant crack against the chair arm. "Here, take this. Tell your mom you're crying because you broke it. And if you tell them anything about me hitting you, I'll come around and kill you."

"All right," the boy whispered, still kneeling on the floor.

"And don't think I won't," John added menacingly.

"I know you would," Geoff agreed, nodding.

"Go on home, then, you sniveling little brat. You disgust me."

The boy stood, one arm wrapped protectively around his stomach, and took the pieces of pie plate from John without touching him.

John watched him out the door, then wandered dazedly down to his own room, lay across the bed, and fell into the deepest sleep.

He was barely through the back door on his way to school the next morning, when hands grabbed him and he was on the dirt. A fist cracked against his face, and John fought to hang onto consciousness. His arms were hauled back over his head, and sudden weight held them down, prevented him struggling. Painful.

"What did you do to my little brother?" a voice demanded.

Brad, of course, looming over him. Another fist in the face. John tried to sit up, then remembered he was pinned down. One of Brad's friends from the football team was kneeling on John's arms, so heavy that they were going to sleep already.

"Come on, what happened? Geoff wouldn't get that upset over a stupid plate. You hurt him."

"Did not," John said.

"Tell me what happened." Punctuated by another fist flying.

"No." God, he hated this, and it went on for what seemed like hours. "No," he kept saying through broken lips. "No."

"That's enough," the friend finally said. "He ain't gonna talk." The guy stood up, but John couldn't move his arms – they felt like dead weights. He lay there in the dirt, vulnerable.

"You keep trying out for the football team, don't you, Garrett?" Brad said. "You tried out for the new season. Well, you play okay, but coach says you can't keep your grades up."

Warily, John nodded. That was one of his dreams, to play football, but the school wouldn't let anyone play unless they passed all their other courses, and John could never concentrate long enough to do that. Which he hated, because he was plenty smart.

"Well, you can kiss that goodbye. I'm telling coach you're not a team player, I'm telling him you're worthless, I'm telling him none of us would play on the same side as you."

John closed his eyes, weary anger washing through him. When he looked again, the two boys had gone, and the sun had swung a little further overhead. He got onto his elbows and knees, and crawled back inside, and just lay on the cold floor for a while, figuring that if the pins and needles in his arms didn't kill him, nothing ever would.

Scrubbed up that afternoon, he didn't look so bad, though the crack in his bottom lip wouldn't stop oozing blood. A black eye and a swelling along his jaw were the only other obvious injuries. To compensate, he washed and combed his hair, and found an old shirt and tie of Father's.

Despite all this effort, the head nurse at the hospital stopped him as he walked in. "Been in the wars, John?"

"I tripped and fell."

"And the ground fought back, right?" she asked sarcastically.

"Caught my face on the corner of the back step," he retorted. "Lucky I didn't lose my eye."

"Sure, John." She folded her arms, as if she was about to lay down the law. The teachers used the same stance. "You can't see your mother, she needs her rest."

"I'm the only family she has."

"I'm not letting you go in looking like that. You'll only worry her."

"She'll want to see me, black eye or not."

"I'm sure she will," the nurse said heavily, "because you're trying to smuggle her some alcohol."

John tried his best, but failed to hide his guilty reaction.

"She needs a rest from that as well, John. You're not helping her by bringing it in."

"If she wants it –"

"If you love her, then help her give it up. I know it will be hard, but I'm keeping her in here for a few days to give her a chance. The head injury isn't so bad, not much worse than yours actually, though she lost some blood. Mainly, I just want her to rest."

"Great. Meanwhile, she's lost her job. If she could have gone back to the shop today maybe the old man would have –"

"Her health is more important."

John grimaced. There was no arguing with grown-ups. The right thing was to respect them, and do what they said, which would be easier if only they would quit telling him so many different things. If only they didn't confuse everything by breaking their own rules. He wanted to ask his father why hitting John was the right thing to do, because now he remembered it had happened more than once.

"You go on home now," the nurse was saying, "and look after yourself. But I expect you to go back to school tomorrow. Don't go using this as an excuse to cut classes."

"Yes, ma'am," John muttered, and he turned and left the hospital.

At a loose end, he went home as ordered, and watched the television, even though it was only kid's stuff in the afternoons.

He tried not to look at the chair still askew over by the far wall, tried not to think of the boy cowering in fear with his eyes wide, tried not to remember how powerful the unexpected orgasm had been. Tried not to be scared at what he had done. It was wrong, very wrong, and he was lucky Geoff hadn't said anything, lucky he'd gotten away with nothing more than a beating. And losing any chance of joining the football team.

He couldn't let himself do it again. Mother would come home soon, and there would never be the chance, anyway, there would never be another time when he would be alone with some boy, and let the day-dreams loose.

It wouldn't hurt to think about it, but he couldn't risk actually doing it again, no matter how wonderful the arousal. So John masturbated, there in the front room, and in his mind instead of Geoff it was Brad tied to the chair and trying to get away, Brad pleading for mercy, Brad's body under his as the older boy wrestled to get free. So vivid, so beautiful an image. John yelled his joy. It was enough.

The head nurse drove Mother home two days later, after school had finished so John could be there, and walked her into the front room. Mother seemed weak and pale, but she looked fine otherwise. The nurse said, "You remember what we talked about, John."

"Yes, ma'am," he replied politely.

"And remember you promised me, Mrs. Garrett."

Mother smiled gracefully and, as soon as the nurse was gone, John fetched her a glass of vodka. She gulped a few mouthfuls, and sighed. "John, come here and talk to me."

It was an unusual request. Avoiding the chair, John sat on the floor in front of her, and leaned back against the wall.

"I've been fired. I can't go back to the shop."

He nodded. "I know. The old man told me."

"I can't get another job, I can't be the breadwinner anymore." A pause. "You're going to have to drop out of school and go to work, John."

"No," he said quietly, dismayed.

"Where else will the money come from?"

Shrugging helplessly, he asked, "What about that money Father left behind?"

"It's gone."

"But that was going to send me to college!" he protested, scrambling to his feet.

She smiled a little and shook her head. "It's gone, I drank it, and it wouldn't have been enough anyway. You're a smart boy, John, but you only see what you want to see, don't you?"

He began pacing backwards and forwards. He wanted to go to college, succeed where his parents hadn't. Well, if the money wasn't there, he could get a football scholarship – only they would never let him play. And his grades weren't good enough, anyway, even though he was intelligent, because his teachers could never keep him interested. All his options cutting off one by one, all his chances being taken away.

"Listen to me, John, I'll only say this once. You can leave if you want to."

"What?" he muttered, confused at this unexpected statement.

And she said, very calmly, "Your father wanted a real wife, and you want a real mother, you want apple pie and love. Well, I never wanted a husband or a child. People like your father think they have a right to reproduce. People like me, we realize not everyone is cut out to be a parent. I would have had an abortion, but I didn't know I was pregnant until it was too late."

John stared at her, unable to take much of this in, his world threatening to shatter.

"You see what you want to see, don't you? Just like your father, you pretend everything is fine and we're all happy. But everything is not fine, John."

"We'll work it out," he said faintly.

"I'm saying we don't have to, you don't have to work it out. I'm not a real mother, so you don't have to be a real son and do the right thing by me. Your father tried to do what he thought was the right thing, and look where we are now. When he finally woke up to what was going on, he left. Now it's your chance. What he told you was the right thing? It was all a load of garbage, and he knew it. He hit me, even when he'd just finished telling you it was wrong to hit a woman."

He hit me, too. But surely Mother knew that already.

"I never cared for him, John, and I never cared for you. So you don't have to care for me."

"That's the drink talking."

She laughed. "John, I've never been more sober in my life." And she took a generous mouthful of the vodka.

Slowly, John walked back to face her, and sat down. He waited until she had another mouthful. "We'll work it out. I'll get a job. A good job." After all, he could learn things at work, too, he could build a career rather than just work in a stupid shop. "I'll look after you."

"Will you?" she asked, swallowing some more.

"Yes, Mother."

She was looking at him strangely, but after a while she nodded, and said, "Get me the bottle, John."

Wordlessly, he did so. Mother settled back comfortably, and life began to continue just as it always had: Mother was home and drunk, and John was a good son, and surely he hadn't really hit Geoff over there by the wall, it had just been a particularly vivid day–dream.

She wasn't done talking yet, though, she hadn't settled in to the old ways that far. "This is all your father's fault, you know. I never had a drink before I met him, but he used to drink beer all day, and I began to, too, only I graduated to the hard stuff. When he knew I was pregnant, he insisted we get married. He should never have done that, but he only saw the idea of having his own perfect family. That's what we were, you know, a perfect nuclear family. Nuclear, like the bomb." She laughed at that. "He said so, and therefore we were, like he could change the world. Crazy. His sister's in a mental home, you know. I would be, too, if you didn't look after me, or the hospital anyway."

"I'll look after you, Mother," he said, hoping all she wanted was reassurance.

"Yes, because you want to be the perfect son for the perfect mother. Well, you had your chance, John, and you didn't take it, so I guess you're better at this family thing than I am."

"It's all right, Mother, you don't have to worry anymore."

"No, I don't." And finally she lay her head back, and swallowed some more of the drink, and she went under again – she wasn't unconscious yet, but she could drink all day and stay in this quiet reverie. It was easy that way.

John watched her until he was sure she was back to normal, and then he turned the television on and watched that instead.

CHAPTER TWENTY-EIGHT
WASHINGTON DC
AUGUST 1985

Albert was waiting outside Jefferson's office, ready to submit his weekly report of tasks on hand, when he heard something heavy fall to the floor inside and then a second, lighter crash. Jefferson's secretary apparently heard it, too, for she glanced at the door and then fearfully at Albert, as if wondering whether she had the nerve to investigate.

Having already decided to do so in the absence of anyone more appropriate, Albert stood and opened the door. He'd interpreted the noises correctly: Jefferson was on the floor behind the desk, one hand clutching the telephone receiver, the other knotted at his chest, mouth open as if gasping for air; his chair had rolled back into the bookcase. Albert said to the secretary, even as he was walking to Jefferson and kneeling beside him, "Call an ambulance; suspected heart attack. Then clear it with security and get rid of this call."

The secretary, who hadn't ventured further than the doorway, withdrew to hopefully carry out the brusque instructions.

Establishing that there was a rapid and arrhythmic heartbeat but no breathing, Albert rolled Jefferson onto his back, checked his airway was clear, and began administering artificial respiration.

The secretary returned to hover in the open doorway just as Jefferson began breathing for himself again. "What's wrong with him?" she asked, apparently unwilling to come closer. "Is he all right?"

"He's alive," Albert said curtly, not taking his gaze off this unexpected and unwanted patient he'd acquired. He waited for a moment to ensure respiration would continue before rolling Jefferson onto his side and into the recovery position. The man seemed to be in a great deal of pain but there was nothing more to be done for him right now. Albert remained crouched, fingers on the pulse in Jefferson's neck, and said, "I'll monitor his condition. You keep the curious out of the way and make sure the medics can get through."

"Okay," she said, and backed away.

Albert waited there, watching Jefferson carefully. This seemed to be a major heart attack but the man would live if they got him to an intensive care unit quickly. It would, however, no doubt mean the long–anticipated end of Jefferson's career.

At last the medics arrived, equipment on a stretcher between them, led by one of the security guards. Albert stood out of the way, answered their terse questions about the situation with equally terse facts, and then left.

A crowd had already gathered outside the office but, fortunately, they seemed more interested in Jefferson and the medics.

Albert dropped his weekly report in the secretary's tray and returned to the forensics labs, where he washed and scrubbed his hands and face as if preparing for an autopsy procedure. And then he returned to work, attempting with mixed success to ignore the unusually high numbers of staff who seemed to find it necessary to visit the labs this morning.

Thirty minutes later, the phone rang. Albert picked it up and said, "Sterne."

"What's this about you being a hero?" Fletcher.

"I see no need for any fuss," Albert bit out.

"People are making a fuss over you?" Fletcher seemed amazed, even charmed, by the idea.

"People are staring at me. I suppose McIntyre relayed the gossip."

Ash chuckled. "I can neither confirm nor deny that rumor. Seriously, though, is Jefferson going to be all right?"

"I assume so, unless there are further complications."

"And you saved his life."

"Apparently." Albert sighed, and rubbed at his face with his free hand. "Is this really of any consequence? I have work to do, Ash."

"Of course it's of consequence."

"Only to Jefferson," Albert replied.

"All right, point taken." There was a strained stretch of silence, familiar these days. "Shall I call you at home tonight?"

"If you must."

Ash apparently heard the grudging note in Albert's voice because he said a quick goodbye and hung up the phone.

Determined, Albert put any consideration of Ash or Jefferson aside, and recommended study of a police report regarding a murder.

◆

There were fewer distractions that evening. Albert didn't feel like eating, so didn't even have any cooking to occupy him. Instead, because he felt unusually unclean, he had a hot shower, using the soap to good effect. Then, because the weather was humid, he adjusted the temperature and let the shower run cool for a while, before dressing in his more casual clothes, and heading for the backyard.

Though he'd installed an automatic sprinkler system some years ago, Albert occasionally watered the garden beds by hand, especially on long hot summer evenings such as this. He carried a bucket and trowel with him, in order to deal with any new weeds.

The garden was pleasant, despite the neighbors, both adults and children, who were also enjoying their patches of civilized nature, though with somewhat more noise and abandon than Albert. The shrubs Albert had planted around the three boundaries and the decades–old trees provided some privacy and a far more attractive appearance than the alternative of ugly, minimally–attired humanity.

Fletcher liked the garden and often said so. Liked the endless varieties of green foliage, forming subtle and complex and asymmetrical patterns; liked the simple beauty of the few flowers, all white, cream and yellow; appreciated the peaceful atmosphere, fragile though that peace was given that it could be disturbed any moment at the whim of the neighbors. Fletcher had compared the garden, due to the apparent informality of the arrangements, to the perfection of a forest glade. That was hardly surprising, as the man's imagination often led him to overstatement and inappropriate imagery.

Albert sighed. He had no wish to think about Fletcher right now because Albert suspected Ash was so miserable that he was finally considering ending the sexual component of their relationship. And Albert had no idea whether he wanted that to continue, but he suspected not.

It seemed impossible to continue any component of their relationship under current circumstances, and neither of them had the power to change the situation. Fletcher had tried every way he could think of to – as Ash put it – get through to Albert and Albert would not, or perhaps could not, let Fletcher succeed.

Albert knew he wasn't punishing Ash for the affair with Xavier Lachance. Surely he wasn't. It was more about the fact that they'd been miserable enough before the affair and had no hope after. Albert had known for most of his life that there would be no one to love him as Miles and Rebecca had loved each other. If he'd ever dared to dream that Fletcher Ash could love him, then Albert was a fool and he was wrong. And he hated being one let alone both of those things.

Fletcher never seemed to mind appearing foolish. For a while he had continually protested his love for Albert, in tantrums and sanity, in reasoned statements and heartfelt pleas, in melodrama and poetry, even once in a physical assault that owed more to frustration than passion – which was all plainly ridiculous. The man was honest but, in this instance, deluded. Or perhaps the word *love* meant radically different things to each of them. For Albert, love meant what Miles and Rebecca had. And that was impossible for him and Fletcher – surely they had made that patently clear to each other by now.

When Fletcher hadn't managed to get through to Albert with his protests, then Ash had pleaded with him to talk about things Albert had no intention of discussing. Fletcher would talk, endlessly, about himself, trying to elicit confidences in return. Fletcher would beg Albert to trust him. How the younger man could stand the humiliation of it, Albert had no idea.

Fletcher seemed to think the sex should be something it wasn't and couldn't be. He tried to trick or surprise Albert into feeling more, doing more –

Albert didn't want to be thinking about any of this. Damn Fletcher Ash and his manipulations! Damn the man's selfish needs.

Spying a weed amidst the flowers, Albert turned off the hose, put it aside and crouched at the edge of the lawn. Once he'd carefully pushed away the surrounding foliage, he dug the thing out, roots and all. The weed was then placed in the bucket and the soil was tidied. Albert rearranged the plant's runners – and then realized it was the damned blue–flowered groundcover that had been running wild in his garden for years. He should never have let the thing grow.

He did something then that he never did – Albert sank his fingers deep into the soil, let the dirt push beneath his nails, clenched his fists around the damp rough texture, imagined the dirt ingrained in the whorls of his fingerprints.

Surprised at himself, Albert stood and dusted his hands off, then rinsed them under the hose. Dismissed the impulse as meaningless.

Continuing with the watering, even methodically allowing the groundcover its quota, Albert endeavored to recollect and review the details of the latest murder case to cross his desk.

But thoughts of Fletcher intruded again.

When Fletcher failed to reach Albert, by means more foul than fair, Ash instead tried to draw Albert out, to make him over–commit himself. Fletcher would pretend a wounded vulnerability, apparently expecting Albert to take greater care of him. Or Fletcher would fall back on his old trick of taunting Albert with some false accusation, hoping that Albert would retort with some truth, some secret.

And then Fletcher would ask, with the heat of those blue eyes now dispirited, "Is this all we'll ever have?" Would assert, "We're capable of more."

Are we? Albert would ask himself, but would say flatly, "I don't think so."

And then that ghastly conversation on the phone two days ago, and Fletcher's accusation: "Albert, you're trying to make me the same as you. You're forcing me to withdraw, to care less, to distance myself, to build barriers. But I don't *care* that I'm vulnerable where you're concerned, do you hear me? It doesn't matter that you *can* hurt me – it only matters that you choose to do so. I love you but I don't want to live like that, behind walls. You're going to have to stop driving me to it. I don't want to change that much."

"Yet you expect me to change," Albert had said.

"No. I want you to be more true to yourself, I want you to be all that you can be. I want you to be honest about what we mean to each other."

Dangerous and irresponsible words if they had been overheard, but Albert had been calling from a hotel in North Carolina and Fletcher had been in his laundry.

"You used to help me, Albert, you used to be the only thing keeping me sane. Now you're one of the things driving me crazy. And you know me too well, you know just how to really hurt me."

Silence. How was Albert supposed to respond when he didn't even credit these wild statements? All he could do was be thankful he couldn't see Fletcher, that he wasn't in the same room as the man who looked his most beautiful when intense, focused, half–crazed.

"Please let us get over this. Do whatever it is that you have to do, forgive me all my damned indiscretions if that's the problem, and stop putting us through this hell."

But this hell was all Albert knew. He managed to say, "You expect too much."

Fletcher replied, as he had before, "No more than you're capable of." Though his tone now was despairing.

And even if Fletcher had been there, the fire of him all but irresistible, Albert would still have been wholly unsure how to respond. All he could do was watch that relentless happy optimism of Fletcher's die. All Albert could do was hope this wasn't revenge.

"You have no idea how much I love you, do you, Albert? You don't see it as possible." A return to Fletcher's protestations. "Why? Do you consider yourself so unworthy?"

It was more about the fact that Fletcher considered Albert unworthy, surely. Second best. And Fletcher would therefore never be content, never stop regretting, never fully entrust himself –

That sounded like disappointment. There was too much to this, these trivialities had gained too much importance. Because Albert expected too much, as well, and neither could meet the other's needs.

These days, Fletcher was dissatisfied with even the sex. During the early months of their relationship, Fletcher had always called the sex 'perfect', had always been hungry for it, always seemed overly impressed with the results. It had been their one constant, their one infallibility. These later months, Ash seemed full of sad yearning, even in the warmth after his completion, perhaps especially then. Memories of his affair with Lachance, Albert assumed. He was at a loss to explain it, otherwise, because Albert approached the act the same way he'd always done: he worked hard to inspire Fletcher's beautiful intensity, to capture and hone the man's focus, to thoroughly satisfy him, to adapt his own skills to the situation, to expand his knowledge of Fletcher and Fletcher's responses. Obviously, that wasn't enough anymore. Equally obvious, there was nothing else Albert could do for the man.

Nevertheless, Fletcher seemed to think there was. He'd approach Albert at unexpected times or in unexpected places, whispering something supposed to be shocking while they were in public, running his hands around Albert's waist while Albert was working in his study, stealing a kiss while Albert was cooking. Apparently his intent was to inspire Albert. Instead, Albert would indulge him, as soon as it was safe and appropriate and convenient, in the same manner he always did. If perfectionism and hard work weren't enough for Fletcher, then Fletcher would simply have to manage as best he could.

Damn the man. Albert did not need his peace disturbed by all these thoughts of Fletcher, did not want to match Fletcher's tendency to mull over all the whys and wherefores of inconsequential matters. It was a complete waste of time and energy.

He was almost glad to be interrupted, even though it was by a child's multi–colored ball landing on his lawn. Albert turned off the hose, set it down and walked over to the ball. He picked it up with the intention of tossing it back in the direction it had arrived from – and then came to a halt. Contemplating the garish reds and yellows covering the sphere in his hands, Albert recalled that he'd never once thrown a ball in his entire life. This would be the point where Fletcher began to feel pity for him.

Albert frowned. Rather than attempt this thing for the first time now, and risk great embarrassment if his aim was wrong or he misjudged the strength needed, Albert walked over to the boundary of his garden.

A small child waited on the other side of the shrubs, about two yards away. Her posture indicated an urgent desire to flee but her eyes lit up when she saw the ball. Rather than toss it to her, Albert reached out, and let it fall onto his neighbor's shabby grass. Then he turned away, not bothering to acknowledge her timid, "Thank you, Mr. Sterne."

How ghastly that the child knew his name. Albert grimaced then headed for the house as he heard the phone ring. He took a moment to wipe his hands before walking to the study and lifting the receiver. "Sterne."

"It's me." Fletcher, sounding curiously subdued.

Despite the lack of enthusiasm – though, secretly, Albert was inclined to find Fletcher's enthusiasms rather alarming – Albert felt something within him sink. "Ash," Albert said in greeting.

A long silence, which was odd. Fletcher usually talked incessantly on the phone, unless Albert had given him something to think about.

Eventually Albert said, "Did you call for a reason? If so, perhaps you might tell me what it is."

Another pause and then, very quietly, "I've found him. I know who he is."

"You know who whom is?"

"The serial killer."

It was Albert's turn to pause for a moment of contemplation. He wondered if he'd expected Fletcher to be happy at this juncture. "Who?" Albert asked at last.

"His name is John Garrett. I know –" A deep intake of breath that sounded perilously shaky. "I have his name. I shouldn't say I've *found* him. I don't know where he is right now."

"How do you have his name?"

"Do you remember that he was on the list of suspects in Oregon? He was Tony Shields' boss at the building site. He'd disappeared before the police found the bodies, which made me suspicious but there was nothing more to go on. I just found his name on the list of suspects in Colorado. Same social security number, same date of birth. Drove a black four–wheel–drive here in Colorado, which fits with how Andrew Harmer described the man to his friend. His general physical description fits, too. Something that bothered me back in Oregon was that Philip Rohan, in Georgia, also worked as a construction worker, though John Garrett can't have been a suspect because Alanna said there were no matches on the two lists."

Albert considered this with a frown. "That's not much to go on, Ash."

"It's enough. It's by far the best connection I've found." A pause. "Anyway, it *feels* right."

"Your instincts?"

"Yes." The tone was flat, resolute.

"I see." Albert didn't bother arguing. "Well, I suppose it's worth investigating. What do you plan to do?"

"I've left messages for Gordon Tomelty in Wyoming, Alanna Roberts in Georgia and Owen Ross in Oregon. They can chase him up as a suspect for their cases, while I chase up all I can here. If I give you his details, will you check him through the national database?"

"Running the fingerprint hasn't located any criminal record."

"This might. Albert, please –"

"Of course." Albert's frown deepened. "I'll go to headquarters now."

"The next problem is trying to locate him. I have no idea where he might be."

"There are similarities in the climate and terrain of where he's lived so far. We could begin with Washington State, Idaho and Montana; Tennessee, Kentucky and the Carolinas; then work out from there."

Fletcher sighed. "I'm not sure. I don't even know if we should rule out the states he's already lived in – he's capable of that kind of double–think. Anyway, I thought I'd ask Mac to start hassling the states through vehicle registration. This man would definitely own a car, for the sake of mobility if nothing else."

"All right."

Another silence. Then, even more unexpectedly, Fletcher changed the subject. "How's Jefferson? Have you heard?"

"No. He'll live, though I doubt he'll be able to return to work."

"So you'll have a new boss soon."

"That's the conclusion I drew." Albert frowned. "Is this of any relevance?"

Fletcher said, "You have to tell him or her that I'll need you over the next few weeks. Or months."

"Of course." Albert reached for pen and paper. "Give me Garrett's details." Once he'd jotted them down, he told Fletcher he'd call back by midnight, whether he had any news or not. Then Albert found himself wanting to offer this strangely quiet man something, though he had no idea what. He started, "I hope –" but didn't know how to continue.

Before he hung up, Fletcher said, "Me, too, Albert. I hope, too."

That wasn't at all what he meant.

Six days later, Albert was reading Fletcher's first report on John Garrett while eating a late dinner. Ash sat across from him at the walnut dining table, picking at his food. "This is very thorough," Albert commented as he reached the last page.

"It had to be, to convince Caroline."

"How far was she convinced?"

"Still no taskforce," Fletcher said. They both knew this lack of support made success virtually impossible. "But I have all my time, and reasonable travel and expenses, for a while. I guess I'm here in

Washington for the duration, until we find him. It'll be easier to coordinate from HQ. Is that all right?" When Albert nodded, Ash asked, "What about you? Can you spare me your time?"

Albert shrugged. "The first thing Jefferson's replacement asked me was why I had a year's accumulation of leave credits. I may as well use those."

"If you could get official support –"

"She agreed I could have full access to facilities on your case, on my own time, subject to review of progress in a month."

"She?" Fletcher queried. It was the closest he'd come to smiling since he'd arrived earlier that night. "Your new boss is a woman?"

"Yes. Is that of any relevance? She seems competent enough."

"How grudging of you. I suppose that translates to, *She's wonderful.*"

Another shrug. "That remains to be seen."

"How fascinating." Fletcher was leaning back, considering him. "Imagine you working for a woman."

"I fail to see what has piqued your interest."

"You don't come into as much contact with them as some, especially here at HQ."

"It's not as if women are a different species, Ash," Albert said flatly. "I anticipate that the difficulties will not be related to gender."

"All right." Fletcher apparently decided to let the topic go, despite the fact he was obviously itching with further questions and comments.

"What next?" Albert asked.

A pause, and then Ash said in distracted tones, "We need to find this man."

"Yes." When Fletcher wasn't forthcoming, Albert said, "Why still refer to him as 'this man' now you know his name?"

"Would you prefer 'this monster'?"

"Why would I prefer melodrama?"

Fletcher sighed, and pushed his food around the plate some more. "I suppose I don't feel like dignifying him with a name. I know that's ridiculous. I know I shouldn't be emotional. But at least I try to keep such ridiculous reactions between you and me."

"I'm glad," Albert said very flatly.

That almost won a smile for some reason. "You'd have been proud of me with Caroline. I was so damned professional and eloquent, she couldn't say no. On the other hand, it's make or break for my career. If I fail, or if I'm wrong, I get the distinct impression I'll be confined to a desk job at best, if not fired. Depends whether I manage to embarrass the Bureau in the process."

"That's a risk. But you feel it's worth it, I assume."

"Hell, I don't care about my damned career, Albert, not anymore. I thought you understood. What's important is that if I fail, this man's on the loose and more young men are killed. *That's* all that matters."

Albert nodded. "All right." Then he asked, "Are you finished?"

"Yes, sorry." Fletcher looked across at him. "It was a great meal – I just don't have much of an appetite right now."

Collecting up the plates, Albert headed for the kitchen. As usual, Fletcher drifted in to help with the washing up. They spent fifteen minutes in busy silence.

"I might head for bed," Fletcher said once they were done. "I'm tired already and the case isn't going to let up from here on in."

Having already locked up, Albert walked down the hall after him. Fletcher, however, turned into the guest bedroom.

"Goodnight, Albert," he said, with no more than a glance behind him.

Without breaking pace, or acknowledging the man, Albert went to his own room.

Albert had only dozed for half an hour when he was woken by a mewling sound. It didn't seem to be from outside, which ruled out the neighbor's cat. He frowned and decided Fletcher must be having yet another bad dream, though those usually resulted in a terrified yell. For a few long minutes, until the clock's hands reached three–thirty, Albert lay still. But the noise was too damned pitiful and insistent to be ignored. With a sigh, he climbed out of his bed and headed for the guest room. The door had been left open, which explained why the noise had carried.

Rather than disturb or startle Ash, Albert left the light off. He walked over to the bed, saw that the man was curled up, listened again to the whimpering. It was almost as if Ash were crying in his sleep, his breath no more than ragged gulps. "Fletcher," Albert said quietly. No response. Albert reached for the man's shoulder, rubbed rather than shook it. "Ash, wake up."

Still the noise went on, the man oblivious to all. Albert sighed again, and got into the bed, scrambling over Fletcher to do so. When he was lying behind Ash, under the quilt, Albert eased him into his arms, began rocking him reassuringly. "Fletcher, wake up," he said again. "It's all right. Wake up."

Gradually the whimpering ceased and the breathing slowed and evened. Ash stretched out, shifted back against Albert, moving instinctively deeper into his embrace. Nevertheless, he remained asleep.

Of course, just as Albert was beginning to doze again, Fletcher finally woke. He turned his head a little, taut for a moment as he registered that he had company. "Albert," he murmured. Then Ash turned within Albert's arms, and kissed him.

It was their first kiss that night, Albert now realized. How strange that Ash hadn't bestowed one as soon as they reached the safety of home, as had been his habit. Still, this seemed intended to make up for any lack: it was warm and affectionate, involved rather than intense.

When the kiss ended, Fletcher remained nose to nose with Albert. "I'm glad you're here," he whispered.

"You had a bad dream again," Albert said.

"Do you really need a reason to come hold me?" Ash didn't wait for an answer. "I'm sorry I woke you. Did I yell the house down?"

"No, you were very quiet. Almost crying."

Ash frowned, pulled back a little to examine Albert's expression as if he suspected Albert of misrepresenting the situation. "That's odd. It doesn't feel –" He sighed, and settled close again. "Never mind. What I need is this." He tightened his arm around Albert's waist.

"What I need is sleep," Albert said flatly.

"Sorry, love, but I'm going to impose on your better nature for a few minutes."

Albert shot him a withering stare. *Better nature, indeed.*

"I wanted to say something to you, resolve something. We've been going through all kinds of trouble over the past few months. And I've been trying to demand all kinds of things from you." A brief silence, as if daring Albert to comment or contradict, then Fletcher continued, "This might not be perfect, what we have. It might be fraught with difficulties. You might not be willing to call it love. I might have lost my faith. But, Albert, I've come to realize that it's *necessary*. You and me together, it's *necessary*. That's all. Very simple, really. And I'm willing to proceed on that basis."

"I see," said Albert.

"What about you?"

Fletcher obviously expected an agreement, apparently thinking this was a compromise they could both live with. Well, Albert reluctantly admitted, maybe Ash was right. Albert had spent the past days and weeks and months either deliberately *not* thinking about Fletcher, or considering how utterly impossible their relationship was – and Fletcher now managed to completely undermine all that with two simple words. *It's necessary*.

It might not even hurt to concede the point. After all, Fletcher had already ascertained that Albert could not find the strength or the will to call an end to the damned thing. Fletcher already relied on that, and acted accordingly. In fact, perhaps it would be wise to agree. It might serve to quiet Fletcher's unrest, it might bring them both some peace.

At last Albert said hoarsely, "Yes. It's necessary."

"Good," Fletcher said, though he sounded more satisfied than happy. He kissed Albert again, with the same warmth as before.

That was pleasant enough. Suspecting that Ash would want sex to properly seal this unexpected agreement, Albert began to work his hands down Fletcher's back, massaging the tense muscles. Sex between them was becoming quite a rarity. But Fletcher turned away once he'd ended the kiss, and settled into his usual place in Albert's arms.

"That was nice," he murmured. "Goodnight, Albert. I hope I don't disturb you again."

Albert glared at the back of the man's head, then tried to settle as well. Surprisingly enough, he got two hours of decent sleep that night.

He didn't know what made him halt in the open doorway to the room Fletcher was using at headquarters. Perhaps Albert heard his name mentioned by either McIntyre or Ash, or perhaps he'd become so unused to seeing Fletcher smile that it gave him pause.

Casting a look around the room, Albert heaved a silent sigh, glad he didn't have to share an office with this pair. Ash had been allocated floor space, McIntyre, computer terminals, and sundry office equipment – which was relatively generous for headquarters. In lieu of windows, Ash had tacked a few posters up, all of mountains and trees and lakes and such. None of them hung straight, which made Albert itch to set them right. One wall bore photos of many of the victims, prior to death – which contrasted with the usual practice of pasting up a range of crime scene pictures, the grislier the better. Fletcher's precious boxes of reports from the four existing cases were lined up against one wall. Every other horizontal surface, including much of the floor, was covered with papers and files and print–outs. It was amazing how much chaos could be generated by two men in nine days.

"Have you heard about what happened to Jefferson?" Mac was saying in hushed and amused tones.

"What?" Fletcher asked, smiling away. The pair were sitting at one of the computer terminals, heads bent together as if in conspiracy, their backs to the door. Albert wondered at Ash's response, given that Mac had ensured Fletcher knew all about Jefferson, within half an hour of the man's heart attack.

"He was clinically dead, you know, and he had one of those afterlife experiences. Yeah, he saw a beautiful bright white light, and he followed it, thinking he was heading for heaven. Jefferson's a happy man, in the company of angels. Then he looked up and saw Albert bending over him. That was when he figured he must be heading for hell – so he up and turned around as quick as he could, and came back to life instead."

Fletcher snorted, a quite undignified noise, and burst out laughing. Mac was watching him with a grin, apparently pleased at this reception of his story.

Albert let them have their fun, at the risk of Ash falling out of his chair due to his mirth. Then, when he judged the timing to be right, Albert said very dryly, "I give good mouth–to–mouth; Jefferson wanted more. That's all."

"Can't blame the man for that," Fletcher said firmly. "But I trust you'll disappoint him."

Mac had started, looked around to see Albert standing in the doorway, and now turned back to the computer, absolutely mortified. Even the nape of his neck was blushing pink.

Still laughing, Fletcher reached out a hand towards Albert, as if expecting him to take it in his. "Come on, quit skulking around out there. One day you'll overhear us being really rude about you."

"You don't have the wit to be really offensive," Albert said. He walked over to stand behind them, frowned at the computer screen for a moment to see what they were doing. The system appeared to be searching through vehicle registrations.

"That sounds like a challenge, Mac."

"No way," McIntyre muttered as he tapped a few more instructions into the computer, refining his search. "I value my health and my sanity far too much to get into a slanging match with him."

Fletcher smiled up at Albert. "How's your day been? More productive than ours, I hope."

"Inevitably," Albert replied.

"So you've come to ask me out for a late dinner, haven't you?"

"No. In fact, I was planning –"

"Fletch," Mac said.

But Ash was continuing, "Well, I could take you out for dinner instead. You still haven't been to the Hard Rock Cafe, have you? And there it's been, just across the road, all this time."

"Fletcher!" This time, Mac grabbed the man's arm. He was staring fixedly at the computer screen. "That's him."

"What?" Fletcher and Albert both leaned forward to see the data.

"We've got him," Mac said. "New Orleans, Louisiana."

"How strange." Fletcher was frowning in consternation. "I can't quite picture him down there."

"It's him, though. Social security number and date of birth both match. We've got him, Fletch. And, oh Christ, he's down there in the same damned city as Celia."

"She's all right," Fletcher muttered. "She's safe." Having read through the screen of information, he sat back, apparently beginning to accept this unexpected location. "Hell," he said to himself, then he looked up at Albert. "This scares me. We're getting close."

"I know," Albert offered, though he found himself inadvertently mirroring Ash's frown. Fletcher was finally on the trail of this man he'd been obsessed with for over four years, and Albert had expected those blue eyes of Fletcher's to catch fire again, had thought the man's intensity and focus would return in full measure. Instead, Fletcher seemed as dejected as ever. The most Albert could see was a new edge of worry and fear.

A long moment, as Fletcher Ash grew used to the idea of progress made. He rubbed at his face with his hands, deliberately rough. Then he stood, and said, "Go home and pack your bags, both of you. Mac, make the bookings and feel free to give Celia a call and warn her. The three of us are catching the first plane tomorrow to New Orleans."

Mac was all fired up at this news. He stood, headed for a phone and was soon talking into it at a hundred words a minute, even as he began shoving paperwork into boxes.

Albert lingered. Fletcher seemed oblivious to all. Albert said, "How perfect. You even get to indulge your penchant for melodrama. *Pack your bags, gentlemen, we're going to New Orleans.*"

Nothing more than a tired smile in response, and even that was forced. Ash shouldn't be acting this way. Still, Albert had little interest in solving that particular puzzle right now.

CHAPTER TWENTY-NINE
NEW ORLEANS
AUGUST 1985

The prosecuting attorney hadn't believed Fletcher anymore than anyone else had. Nevertheless, he couldn't fault her: she had presented his case to the judge with as much conviction as he could have wanted. They were in the judge's chambers, rather than the courtroom, with Fletcher and Prosecuting Attorney Atwell standing before the desk and Judge Beaufort sitting impassively behind it. The silence stretched, and Fletcher anxiously tried to read Beaufort's face, in vain.

"Special Agent Ash," the judge said at last. He was as slow and massive and imposing as a mountain, with a deep ponderous voice to match, and as black as midnight. "If I grant you this search warrant, what do you intend to do with it?"

It was the first time Fletcher had been required or allowed to speak. "Your Honor, I'd ask the suspect to come to the police station for questioning. While I conducted the interview, my colleague, Dr. Sterne, would secure the suspect's house. Dr. Sterne is more than qualified to do so, he is a forensics expert with Bureau headquarters. Once I'd completed the interview, I'd leave the suspect in custody and join Dr. Sterne at the house. I'm willing for a crime scene officer from the NOPD to accompany me in a thorough search. I'm sure that we would gather enough evidence to arrest the suspect, through both the interview and the search."

"How can you be sure? That is the issue." The judge held up one enormous hand as Fletcher opened his mouth. "No doubt you and Ms. Atwell have already told me everything you're sure of. Well, Agent Ash, it is not enough. I cannot issue a warrant based on these circumstantial connections, you have no grounds to arrest the man, and a grand jury would not indict him if you did."

"But I can place the suspect in all four states at the times of the murders," Fletcher said, knowing that his tone betrayed his frustration and desperation. "And he's on two separate lists of suspects."

"How many other men are on those lists?"

Fletcher said, "Almost three thousand in total, Your Honor."

"That's a lot of innocent men."

"But the suspect is the only name common to all four – that has to indicate something."

"Something or nothing. Perhaps that's the only substance in your case against Mr. Garrett, and it is not enough. I cannot issue this warrant, Special Agent, because you cannot demonstrate probable cause."

Atwell took a breath, and tried again. "What harm does a search warrant do, Your Honor? If Agent Ash and his colleagues find nothing, then Mr. Garrett is cleared of suspicion, and the matter is over. If Agent Ash does find evidence of these crimes, then justice is served."

The judge turned sharp eyes on Fletcher. "*Would* you be satisfied if you found nothing at Mr. Garrett's house?"

Fletcher returned Beaufort's stare, and admitted the truth. "No, Your Honor."

"As I thought." The judge set both hands palm down on his desk in a gesture of finality. "Neither of you can persuade me at this time. And I'll tell you what harm it does, Ms. Atwell, as you asked. I'm doing you both a favor, in fact. If I grant this search warrant and you discover nothing, then you'll find it next to impossible to be granted a second search warrant. As Mr. Ash intends to pursue this case as vigorously as he can, I believe it to be in no one's interest to issue a warrant prematurely."

"Yes, Your Honor," Atwell murmured.

The judge continued, "You have obviously devoted a great deal to this case, Agent Ash. I admire you for having the courage and resources to do so. However, I will not risk one man's liberty for the sake of another's crusade."

A silence. Fletcher wondered if he'd expected any other outcome.

Then Beaufort said, "You interview Mr. Garrett tomorrow, Special Agent, as planned. If you obtain any results, anything at all, then find Ms. Atwell and come down to my court. There's nothing going on that can't be interrupted. Bring me something solid and I'll give you your warrants, both search and arrest."

"Thank you, Your Honor," Atwell and Fletcher said, verbally stumbling over each other.

"You'll be available to assist in this matter, Ms. Atwell?"

"Yes, Your Honor, of course." She threw Fletcher a glance as if to say, *I'll fit this crazy crusade in somewhere.*

"Then get out of here, the pair of you, and go about your business."

Fletcher stood in the doorway of the interview room and watched John Garrett walk across the room, weaving between the desks. There was plenty of time to observe him because his progress was impeded by various police officers who stood to greet him and pass the time of day. The young uniformed officer who'd gone to collect him, and the lieutenant in charge of homicide, were at Garrett's shoulders, behaving more like groupies than an escort. This was Fletcher's first sight of the serial killer who'd haunted his days and nights for too many years – but it was more like watching someone campaign for mayor, with all this glad–handing, all these sincere smiles, all this chit–chat with everyone who approached.

Albert was standing a few feet away, arms crossed and expression stony, dividing his attention between Fletch's reactions and Garrett himself.

But Fletcher believed he didn't betray his reactions, not even to this man who knew him better than anyone. There was disgust and fear, a rise of the dogged determination. There was also some objective part of him noting that Garrett was handsome, in a suave kind of way. And so at ease, so friendly with these men, his smile broad. Yes, this man could be Drew Harmer's Prince Charming; this man could seduce and trap unsuspecting young men. This man had the strength and the bulk to subdue them. This monster.

Ash had never actually pictured Garrett, hadn't filled in the shadowy details of his nightmares and imaginings. Nevertheless, this must be the serial killer. This must be the monster that Fletcher had to battle. This big hungry angry bear that he knew too well.

But after all these years, events were abruptly moving too fast. The whole case had never seemed so hopeless as now, when Fletcher had the man literally in his sight. This interview was premature, Fletcher's hand had been forced. After all, these friends of Garrett's had probably tipped him off already. Then there was Judge Beaufort: Fletch was desperate to take something solid to him while the man was still prepared to listen.

At last, John Garrett was there, approaching Fletcher. Being introduced by Lieutenant Halligan. Rather than shake hands, Fletcher invited Garrett into the interview room with a smooth gesture. Ash shared a glance with the uncommunicative Albert, then Albert turned and entered the observation room, and Fletcher joined Garrett and the lieutenant, closing the door behind him.

Garrett had paused a moment, then smiled broadly. "You want me to sit here, right, Halligan?"

"Sure, John," the man replied with a shrug. Halligan stood by the door, leaning his shoulders against the wall, as if relaxed and certain this wouldn't take long.

"Pity about all the movies, isn't it?" Garrett continued. He turned his smile to the one–way mirror that allowed Albert and the others in the next room to witness this, then sat facing it. "You can't fool anyone with that anymore."

Fletcher sat at the table opposite him, his back to the mirror, and pressed the record button on the tape player. "Tape one, side one. This is Special Agent Fletcher Ash, Federal Bureau of Investigation, interviewing Mr. John Garrett, in the presence of Lieutenant Harold Halligan, New Orleans Police Department. It is two–fifteen on the afternoon of August twenty–second, 1985." He waited a moment, lifted his gaze to Garrett's. Ice blue eyes, calm and confident. "Have you been told why you're here?"

"Bill, the kid who picked me up, he said it was in connection with murder. What's that phrase? You believe I can assist you in your inquiries."

"You don't seem terribly upset at being questioned regarding murder."

Garrett's smile returned, easy and open. "It's so ridiculous, this has nothing to do with me. I'm sure we can quickly clear it up, whatever it is you think you have."

"If you want a lawyer present during my questioning, you're entitled to one."

"I don't need a lawyer."

"You understand that you can have a lawyer here but you're refusing? Whether you're guilty or innocent, that could be seen as rather naïve."

The man nodded, all good humor. "I understand, Special Agent, both the advice and the warning."

"All right. I've been investigating the murders of fourteen young men across four states. I believe they're all linked and that they've been committed by one man. Given that you were in each of those four states at the relevant times, I was hoping you could help me."

A shrug. "If I know anything about these murders, it would only be what I've read in the newspapers."

"It seems suspicious in itself that you happened to be living in those particular states at those particular times."

"I move around a lot. I see a business opportunity, or a good job with some responsibility, I take it no matter where it is. When the job's over, or when I've built the business up, I sell for a profit, and move on again. There's nothing sinister in that."

"The odds against this being a coincidence are enormous."

"But it *is* a coincidence, Special Agent." So self–assured.

Fletcher considered the man. "Again, you don't seem upset at being accused of a number of murders."

"It only happens in the movies, you know," Garrett replied, "that an innocent man is convicted of the sorts of crimes you're investigating."

"What sorts of crimes are those?"

"Murder, you said it yourself, on quite a grand scale." Garrett paused, and smiled confidingly. "Bill told me some of it. Ask him if I was shocked at first, being accused of these things. I'm sorry if you feel the shock's worn off too quickly, but it's really nothing to do with me." The eyes were cold and assessing, though the expression remained relaxed and sincere as he leaned forward. "Let's sort this thing out, Special Agent."

Fletcher looked down at his notes, more to provide a beat of silence than because he needed to. He'd had some time to consider how he'd handle this. "Oregon," Fletcher began. "You worked on a construction site, building offices."

"I was project manager for the site."

"One of the young men who worked for you is now dead."

"Yes. I read about that in the paper, I had a colleague send a wreath to the funeral."

"What was the young man's name?"

Garrett seemed to have no qualms about meeting Fletcher's direct gaze. "Tony." After a moment, he added, "Tony Shields."

"You found Tony attractive."

Shrugging, Garrett said, "Yes. Is that a crime? It's not something I make a secret of." He looked over at Halligan, who echoed his shrug, as if to say, *It's no big deal.*

"I am not concerned with your homosexuality per se. I am, however, concerned about your violence."

"I am not a violent man, Special Agent."

"Did you ever proposition Tony Shields?"

Garrett said dismissively, "The kid was straight."

Without reacting to this, Fletcher repeated, "Did you ever proposition Tony Shields?"

"No." Though the man glanced away.

"Why is that the first question to make you uncomfortable?"

"Only because ... I'd have liked to, sure, Tony was quite a guy and he knew it. But if I'd put the word on him, he would have belted me. Hell, he might have dropped a bag of cement on me from the seventeenth storey." Garrett paused, glanced around at Halligan again. "Makes me sick, what happened to him. Fine young man like that."

Halligan nodded. "Some crazy," he said. "Some nutcase."

Again, Fletcher didn't react. If Halligan was going to run a good guy/bad guy routine, deliberately or not, at least Garrett would recognize the ploy from the movies and dismiss it accordingly. Fletch asked, "How well did you know Tony Shields? Did you ever socialize with him? Have a drink after work?"

They filled forty minutes of tape dealing with Oregon, Fletcher asking a variety of questions either directly related to Tony and the other victims, or adding detail to Fletcher's notion of who this man was. Garrett, while apparently willing to answer everything he could, didn't offer anything he didn't have to. Neither did he say anything that would incriminate him. Fletcher had always known this man was clever.

"Georgia," Fletcher eventually said. And was interrupted by a knock on the door. Halligan opened it, and there was young Bill with a tray of steaming coffee mugs. Well, Fletch wasn't going to get angry over this, or let it faze him. In fact, he welcomed the coffee itself. He took the mug handed to him, though he couldn't bring himself to smile or thank the man, then waited through Garrett's pleasantries. Halligan at last sat down once Bill had left, though he remained over by the door rather than joining Fletcher and Garrett at the table. Fletcher repeated, "Georgia. What do you remember about GTK Builders?"

"I remember the name. That was a while ago."

"But you had business dealings with them."

"During a couple of large projects, I think I sub–contracted some construction work to them. Yeah, nothing major."

"Who do you recall from the company?"

Garrett shrugged. "I dealt with a guy named Kowalski, he's the K in GTK. Why?" The barest hint of impatience. "Is Kowalski dead, too?"

"Not that I'm aware of. Do you recall anyone else?"

"It's too long ago to remember names."

"Philip Rohan."

The man looked blank. "Doesn't mean anything. Was he with GTK?"

"Yes."

"And he's the one who's dead, right?"

"Yes."

Another shrug. "I don't remember the kid."

"Maybe Philip Rohan was middle–aged. Why call him a kid?"

Garrett stared at Fletcher, unflinching. "You said at the start of this that you're investigating the deaths of several young men. Why else would you mention this Rohan guy?"

"What happened to Stacey Dixon? Why was she shot?"

"I don't know. I don't know who Stacey Dixon is." And, after another thirty minutes of tape was devoted to questions relating to Garrett's time in Georgia, Garrett asked, "How much longer is this likely to take, Special Agent?"

"I'd like to talk to you about Colorado as well, but of course you're free to go at any time."

Garrett considered him for a long moment, tired but shrewd. "No," he said. "Let's get this over with. Maybe then you'll be satisfied. Otherwise you'll be hounding me, won't you?"

Ignoring this, Fletcher said, "Colorado. You drove a black four–wheel–drive vehicle, top of the line, very expensive."

"Yes. Is *that* a crime?"

"Did you use it to pick up boys?"

The expressions passing over Garrett's face encompassed amusement, frustration, vexation. "Believe it or not, Special Agent, there are young men – consenting adults – who are prepared to have sex with me. Ready, willing and able, I assure you. I don't have to cruise the streets for the kind of boys who'll be impressed by a shiny new car."

"You might not have to," Fletcher conceded. "But have you done so?"

There was a long silence. At last Garrett said, "Perhaps. Once or twice. In the past."

"Did you pick up Andrew Harmer on the street, in your four–wheel–drive?"

"I don't recall the name."

"Drew Harmer was a college student in Denver."

Garrett shook his head, slowly, apparently searching his memory. "I don't recall."

"He told a friend that a man of your description, in the type of car you drove, propositioned him in the street."

"It's remotely possible," Garrett said, shrugging. It seemed he couldn't be less interested. "But I doubt it was me."

"Later that evening, Drew planned to meet with you. He was never seen again."

"I certainly had nothing to do with him disappearing," Garrett said.

"Drew's friend is prepared to testify in court." It was more an overstatement than a lie. Fletcher said it smoothly, relieved when Halligan didn't contradict him, or react in surprise. Fletch added, with slightly more truth, "The description Drew gave him is uncannily accurate."

Garrett retorted, "Hearsay is inadmissible. You're bluffing."

"It's not inadmissible in these circumstances. Don't believe everything you see on TV. You're the one who's bluffing."

A brief silence, then Garrett said, "You have the wrong man, Special Agent."

"I don't think so," Fletcher said firmly. He leaned forward a little for the first time, staring hard at Garrett and letting the man see how driven this FBI agent was. "I have you in all four states at the right times. I have links between you and at least one of the victims in three of those states. What are the odds against that, if you're not the killer? So remote that it's statistically impossible."

"Whatever the hell the odds are, it's still a possibility. Obviously. Because I am not the man you want, Special Agent."

"How did it feel, Mr. Garrett?" Fletcher asked in the same tone of voice. "This was Drew's first date. There he was, infatuated, full of hope, all yours. How did it feel to see the fear in his eyes when he realized what you are?"

"I don't know what you're talking about," Garrett said flatly.

"How did it feel to have him helpless, begging for your mercy? This pitiful boy–child crying and sobbing, screaming and bleeding."

The man hadn't moved, hadn't flinched – but Fletcher had seen those cold eyes flare. Garrett said flatly, "Sounds like you know better than I do, Special Agent."

"How did it feel to hit him, to hurt him?"

"Is this really necessary?"

Fletcher didn't miss a beat. "How did it feel to watch him die? Did you look into Drew's eyes as you strangled him? Or were you raping him while you killed him?"

"Enough!" At last Garrett stood. "I don't have to listen to this. Halligan?"

The lieutenant said, "That's enough, Special Agent."

Having already fallen silent, Fletcher was staring at Garrett, noting the fixed expression of distaste. It were almost as if the man was in shock, his breathing hard but shallow, his face pale and that distaste plastered over the top. There had been a reaction to the horror Fletch had thrown at him, a truer reaction than this discomfort: Garrett had understood all that Fletcher described. This was the serial killer. If Fletcher had been in any doubt, he had none now.

"Mr. Garrett," Fletcher said, also standing, "perhaps you'd wait here for a moment. I need to talk to Lieutenant Halligan."

The man briefly lifted his hands in exasperation, then sat down again. "Sure. One moment, for the sake of clearing this up. Then I'm leaving."

Fletcher ushered Halligan out into the main office, bent his head close and whispered urgently, "That's him, Lieutenant. I want you to hold him in custody while I go talk to Judge Beaufort."

Halligan also whispered, presumably for the sake of privacy. "He's not your killer, Ash."

"He damn well is. Weren't you watching him? Didn't you see how he reacted? He knew exactly what I was talking about."

Halligan looked even more annoyed than Garrett, though he didn't raise his voice. "I was looking, all right. I saw an innocent man trying to clear his name and being damned patient about it. Of course he was shocked at what you said, you went way too far, Special Agent. If he wants to complain about how you conducted that interview – and it was a preliminary interview, remember, not an interrogation – then I'll support him."

Fletcher gazed at the man, hard and bitter. "Are you telling me you won't support me in this investigation, even though I have the jurisdiction and the authority?"

"I wouldn't tell you that, Special Agent."

"Only because you know it would be your career if you did."

Halligan had the sense to look ill at ease, but he asked, "Why the hell did you go that far? 'Were you raping him while you killed him?' How would you feel if someone threw that at you, Ash?"

"Like dirt, whether it was true or not. But he understood me, Halligan. He understood me because that's exactly what he did."

"Now you're throwing it at me."

"How else can I get you to take this seriously?"

"The way I see it," the lieutenant said, face still two inches from Fletcher's, "you have no grounds to hold this man. If he wants to walk, he's free to walk, and I'm not about to stop him."

"I'm going to talk to the judge."

"John Garrett won't be here when you get back, Ash."

Fletcher looked at the man. "I know." Albert had joined them, but Fletcher ignored him. Turning his back on Halligan, and not even glancing at the interview room where Garrett waited, Fletch headed out of the police station.

Judge Beaufort demanded, "What have you brought me, Agent Ash? And where is the prosecuting attorney?"

"I saw no reason to bother Ms. Atwell, Your Honor, because I've brought you nothing. I'm afraid the interview was inconclusive." Fletcher wondered if he sounded as weary and hopeless as he felt. The courtroom was large and empty and echoing. He tilted his head to look up at the judge. "I'm here to ask you for your help."

"What can you expect me to do?"

"The suspect is aware of who I am now, Your Honor, he didn't know anyone was onto him before this afternoon. But I couldn't hold him at the station, he gave me nothing." *The ugly truth, Fletcher*, he admonished himself. "I failed. I failed, and he's free right now and no doubt on his way home. If there's any evidence there, it will be gone by tomorrow. At least, I'm sure Dr. Sterne would be able to find things, if there's been any crime committed at the house, but he'll dump any material relating to the previous crimes –"

"Such as? What exactly would you expect to find, Special Agent?"

"As Ms. Atwell detailed yesterday, anything to do with the victims. Serial killers often keep trophies, items they've taken from the victims, clothing or jewelry or driver's licenses. None of them were mutilated in ways to suggest he keeps body parts. But he might have press clippings about the cases. Even photographs, or audio or video tapes of the actual murders."

"I cannot give you your warrant, Agent Ash. Mr. Garrett is a respected man in our community –"

Fletcher turned an imploring and frustrated stare on the judge, unable to stop himself. "Your Honor, *that's* how he gets away with this time and time again. He works hard to be the kind of man who's above suspicion – "

"No, you listen to me, Special Agent. No one is above suspicion in this courtroom. No one. Don't you imply that I would treat Mr. Garrett any differently than I would a homeless man or a senator."

"I'm sorry, Your Honor, I didn't mean to imply that."

The mountain appeared somewhat appeased. "Now, what I was going to say was that Mr. Garrett has ties to New Orleans, he has a business to run. He's unlikely to move on without any warning."

"But he has before. He completely disappeared from Oregon, and not many people could do that so thoroughly."

"He had time to plan in that instance. I don't consider him a high flight risk."

"Yes, Your Honor." Fletcher knew his tone conveyed his disagreement.

"The rules of evidence are there for a reason, Special Agent. *Innocent until proven guilty* – they're strong words, it's a strong principle. And sometimes we fallible human beings need strong rules to follow in order to live up to our principles." A pause, and then in a more reasonable voice, "Look at it from this perspective, Mr. Ash. You could be the only one who's seen the truth in this case. If so, I admire you and I pity you. On the other hand, you could be fixated, obsessed with nothing more than a phantom. I have to protect Mr. Garrett from that fixation. *You* hold the power in this, Special Agent, even if you feel powerless right now. You're the one with the badge and the gun."

Fletcher sighed. "Look at it from my perspective, Mr. Beaufort. The courts seem to be more about law than justice, more about procedure than results."

"Maybe you're right. The law certainly isn't perfect. But human beings have high ideals and we try to apply them. You can't ask for more than that."

"Can't I?"

Judge Beaufort considered Fletcher, gazing down at him from his bench. "When this is over, you and I will share a bottle or two of burgundy, and discuss justice and law, ideals and realities. These are fascinating areas to debate. But not now, Special Agent; I have work to do, and I believe you do, too."

"Yes, Your Honor. Thank you for your time and your patience."

The man nodded, and left through the door behind the dais, moving slowly and steadily and inevitably. Fletcher watched him go, then headed out of the court. If Fletcher did have work to do right now, he had no idea what the hell it was.

Fletcher had been planning to walk over to the FBI offices but he'd been distracted almost immediately. There was a park occupying the block between the federal building and the courthouse, and the green of it beckoned.

So now Fletcher was lying on his back on the grass, his jacket spread under his head and shoulders, heedless of what this might do to his suit, staring up through the branches of spreading oaks. The leaves were so abundant that they provided total shade, a welcome darkness and an illusion of coolness – at least when compared to the direct bleaching sunlight a few yards away.

"It's me, Fletch," someone said above him.

Tilting his head back, Fletcher found McIntyre standing over him. "Hello, Mac."

"Albert sent me to find you." The man was sitting down on a park bench a few feet away. Obviously nothing urgent.

"Did he?" Fletch murmured.

Mac asked, "How are you doing?"

"I've been better." The silence stretched, then Fletcher complained, dull and weary, "This damned heat. It's even worse than Washington."

Mac looked over at him, and offered, "I'm afraid it's always like this. A long summer, with no relief, and then a long winter. It's the humidity that gets you."

"You lived here for a while, didn't you? Where's the romance of New Orleans? It's all office buildings and hotel chains around here."

"You're in between the best of it. The French Quarter is a few blocks to the north–east; that's the oldest part, with lots of the history, and all of the nightlife. The Garden District is behind us to the south–west; that's where all the beautiful big houses are." Mac pointed across the park. "Look, that's the trolley car that takes you up Saint Charles Avenue through the Garden District. Sometime, when we have an hour to spare, we'll take a ride."

Fletcher obediently lifted his head to see the trolley car go by, then sank back down again. "This damned humidity," Fletcher repeated. It was thoroughly draining, and he'd been tired enough when he came here.

"You want to head inside?" Mac suggested.

"You go, if you want." Fletch summoned a chuckle from somewhere. "It takes a lot to make me appreciate a closed air–conditioned office, believe me, but I think this climate might do it."

Another silence began to stretch between them. At last McIntyre asked, "What's wrong, Fletch? You're not giving up, are you?"

Fletcher let out a sigh. "No, I'm not giving up. I just don't know what to do next."

"It's only been five days since we got here. Give it time."

"If I had time, I'd be happy to give it, but he's forcing my hand." Fletch tilted his head again to look at his companion. Mac was too loyal to really question Fletcher's methods and motivations, and therefore deserved an explanation. "The police here don't believe me. You and Albert are still the only people who give any credence to my theory that these crimes are connected. Halligan's first reaction was, 'that crosses too many states and too many years'. I'm beginning to suspect you and Albert of humoring me."

"Albert wouldn't humor anybody, not even you." After a moment, Mac amended, "Especially not you."

Fletch squinted up at him, wondering if Mac were becoming more astute, or if they'd all been guilty of underestimating the man. "That's true. Cold comfort, perhaps, but true." He continued, "The prosecuting attorney didn't believe me, though she did her best. It wasn't her fault that the judge didn't believe me either. Though the judge was actually listening to me for a while."

"So, why do you say Garrett's forcing your hand?"

"He has friends everywhere. In fact, I'm impressed at how thoroughly this man has become part of the community; he only arrived here last October or November. It reminds me of how well he disappeared from Oregon, actually. He's very clever at this, infiltrating and camouflaging, then extricating himself. The way he did it this time was by buying a failing renovation business and turning it around so it's become the most popular one in town. He worked on a senator's house in the Garden District, and some businessman's house at Metairie, and made all the right friends doing it. He employs the sons and nephews and cousins of almost everyone I talk to. He's assistant coach of the high school football team – the Cherubs, I think they're called." Fletcher shrugged as well as he was able. "Everyone thinks he's wonderful. Then along comes an interfering fed with this tall tale of how everyone's favorite guy is a serial killer. Of course they're not going to listen to me."

Mac was sitting there, apparently waiting for Fletcher to make his point.

"I had to make my move quickly because even if they didn't take me seriously, all Garrett's friends on the police force were going to warn him about me. There was no point in giving him the opportunity to leave town before I'd even interviewed him."

After a moment, Mac said, "I understand the interview hasn't helped your case."

"It helped me. He talked a lot, I feel I know him better than ever. But he didn't say anything that will convince anyone else that he's the killer."

"You're still convinced?"

Fletch sighed. "Halligan didn't see what I saw, and I guess the observers didn't, either. When John Garrett looked at me, he recognized me as his enemy. He was shrewd, he was cold, he was wary. He heard everything I was saying – I mean he *heard* it in his heart, he understood it because it was the truth."

"Even if Lieutenant Halligan saw some of that, he'd hardly blame Garrett for being wary of you."

"Yes. Especially as Garrett created the impression that he's innocent and I'm paranoid. That idea fits too well with our behavior." Another silence, as Fletcher once again reviewed all he'd done in the last five days. "No matter how I add it up, Mac, I've tried everything legal and it's not working. I've run out of options."

"It takes time."

"We don't have time, especially now he knows I'm onto him. We need to take him as quickly as we can, otherwise he's going to take advantage of the fact that no one believes me."

"So what do we do next?"

"Like I said, I have no idea." Fletcher slowly sat up, and turned to face Mac. "Where's Albert? At the Bureau offices?"

"No, he phoned me from the police station. Told me to come and find you. Said he was performing damage control."

"What?" Fletcher stared at the man, confused. After all, Albert was the one who caused damage when it came to dealing with the police and suspects and witnesses, and Fletcher was the one who worked to minimize the effects.

Mac frowned. No doubt he also found this whole thing strange. "From what Albert said, I think he was going to follow Garrett, and see what he did next."

Stranger and stranger. "Oh, hell," Fletch muttered. He couldn't decide whether he was fearful or excited or impressed at what Albert was allegedly doing. "Why didn't you tell me?"

"Well, he said not to, not right away. I think he's worried about you." The frown deepened. "I'm worried, too. Both of you are acting kind of crazy at the moment."

"Can't blame me for that," Fletch said absently. "Goes with the investigation. Not to mention the humidity." Curious, he asked, "What exactly did Albert say?"

Deadpan, Mac recited, "Fletcher spat the dummy. Find him, hose him down, tell him I'm doing his job for him."

Fletcher laughed hard at this ludicrous interpretation, finally managed to say, "The truth, Mac."

"He was in a hurry, I guess he didn't want to lose Garrett. He said something like, 'The interview wasn't successful. Ash is heading for court though it's useless. Find him, give him some time if he needs it, then tell him I'm following Garrett for him.'"

"I see." After a moment, Fletcher said, "I hope Albert took a car with a radio. Let's go find him." They headed for the car Mac had been allocated. Setting the radio to the open channel the police used, Fletch picked up the handset. "Albert, are you out there?"

A pause, and then, "Yes."

"What the hell are you doing?"

Another pause, slightly longer. "Sightseeing."

"Sure," Fletcher replied, trying not to laugh.

"Perhaps you should join me." And Albert named the street he was on.

Though Albert hadn't given him a number, Fletcher knew immediately where the man was: outside the shopfront of Garrett's renovation business. "All right, I'll see you soon." He hung up the handset, and turned to Mac. "You know where that is?"

Mac was already starting the car. "Have you there in ten minutes."

Fletcher sat in the passenger seat, Albert beside him, both of them gazing at the shopfront, thirty feet away on the opposite side of the street. They had been silent since Fletch had sent Mac back to work, mostly because Fletcher found he had too many things to think about, and too many questions to ask. Eventually he decided on the simplest and most relevant of the questions: "Did Garrett go back to his house?"

"No," Albert replied, "he came straight here. It appears he's attempting to act as an innocent person would. His only apparent concern at present is the work hours he's lost."

"Does he know you followed him?"

"He might. Halligan had the uniformed officer drive him back here and either of them could have seen me. I didn't have time to be subtle about it."

Fletch turned to consider this man, his friend. "Why are you doing this, Albert?"

The silence returned. Albert was expressionless behind his dark glasses. At last he said, "When you left the police station, Garrett spoke with a few of the officers. While he did, I told Halligan you'd expect to have Garrett's immediate movements tracked, but Halligan refused beyond offering him a lift."

"I really appreciate this, Albert. I wasn't thinking very clearly at the time. But Halligan wasn't cooperating, either." No response. Fletcher mused, "I'd assumed he'd go home. Start to destroy the evidence."

"He's intelligent enough to realize that and act accordingly."

"You're right, of course." Almost afraid of the answer, Fletch asked, "What did you think of the interview?"

"You did what you could, Ash. Don't blame yourself for not achieving a result."

"I don't know what to do next, Albert."

"What do you have McIntyre doing?"

"More of the same: going through the police reports of unsolved crimes back to last October and trying to find anything that might have been Garrett. What have you been up to?"

"A couple of similar investigations," Albert said distantly.

Fletcher studied him for a moment, then smiled as something occurred to him. "You're the only person I know who remains unruffled in this humidity. How do you do it?" It seemed impossible that Albert should appear so cool, especially as he inevitably wore a suit and tie every waking moment. "What's your secret?"

"There is no secret, Ash," the man said, as if bored.

"Well, I know you're perfectly capable of sweating, lover."

Albert didn't react to that. He stared at Garrett's shopfront, his dark glasses and immobile expression giving nothing away.

"Sorry," Fletch muttered. "I don't know what the hell I'm doing right now. I say all the wrong things, I can't convince anyone of anything, I annoy people. I'm absolutely lost."

Always impatient with Fletcher's lapses into self–pity, Albert didn't turn to him. He did, however, say, "You need some evidence."

"I know that, damn it! But how the hell do we get it?"

"You tell me, Ash." The voice distant, quiet.

"I'm at the stage of considering breaking into Garrett's house while he's out one evening. Getting in there, and seeing what there is to see."

"What would be the point? The evidence would be inadmissible, and such an action would jeopardize your whole case, not to mention your career."

"*Damn* my career, stop throwing that in my face. All right, so it would be inadmissible but at least it would give us something to work on. Hell, if Hoover was still around, it would be called a black bag job. Standard operating procedure."

"But J. Edgar Hoover is dead."

"Yes, and I'm almost sorry for it. Because we could tap Garrett's phone, we could lift his fingerprints without his permission, we could do all kinds of underhand things."

"Are you telling me that you now believe the end justifies the means? That's the way your pet serial killer thinks and that's the way your pet politician thinks. You used to be above that, Ash."

Fletcher glared at the man but after a moment, turned away and rubbed wearily at his face. "Maybe Xavier had a point. At least, maybe when you're dealing with people like John Garrett, dealing with those few people who are beyond the pale, a hundred miles beyond the pale – then maybe you can only do it on their terms. Otherwise they win. They win because they have no limits to their behavior."

"You wouldn't have believed, a few years or even a few months ago, that you would say that, let alone consider it to be true."

"I'm too close to Garrett now and I won't let him go. I've tried all the legal ways and I've gotten nowhere."

"But your evidence wouldn't be admissible in a court of law, Ash, and your conduct would throw your case into disrepute. No judge would give you any leeway or any benefit of the doubt. All Garrett would need is a good defense lawyer and the whole thing would be dismissed."

"I know that, I haven't taken complete leave of all my senses. I wouldn't be gathering evidence, I'd be gathering information and an understanding of who this man is."

"All right," Albert said.

"What do you mean, 'all right'?" Fletch burst out.

"As long as you are absolutely clear about the reasons why, and the possible ramifications, then tell me what you intend to do."

Fletcher stared at him. "You're supposed to be talking me out of this, Albert."

"Am I?" Albert still wouldn't turn to him. "You tried your best within the law enforcement system. I believe you did your best to resolve this legally, Ash, remember that. While you are certain that John Garrett is the serial killer, however, you've made it equally obvious that you no longer have any faith in the law enforcement system as a method of dealing with him. The people you've been working with can see your lack of faith, and your doubt, and they are no longer inclined to assist you. It appears to them as if you're merely going through the motions. You are used to convincing people with your charm, your passionate belief, your honesty. Now that force is working against you because people don't trust it anymore."

Fletcher didn't know whether to be more amazed at Albert taking the time and trouble to observe all this, or at Albert talking to him about such difficult ideas, or at what Albert was actually saying. It was shocking. "You're telling me we need a new rule. And the new rule is that there are no rules."

"I believe that's the conclusion you'd inevitably reach, given time. You've already begun talking along these lines. It seems clear, however, that you don't have any time to waste."

A long silence. "I don't know what to say to you, Albert."

"I don't require you to say anything; I require you to consider your priorities and the related issues. Consider how you felt about McIntyre locating Garrett in New Orleans for you. Did you even think about how he was doing that? He was calling in favors across the country and performing illegal searches of data, for the sake of progressing this investigation. He has a network of acquaintances and colleagues, low level staff who have access to all kinds of databases. Within their own convoluted system of ethics and loyalties, these people have no problems with the concept that the end justifies the means."

Fletcher closed his eyes for a moment. "I suppose I knew that, to be honest, and found it convenient to ignore the matter."

"There he is," Albert broke in. "It appears Garrett has finished work for the day." They both watched as Garrett walked out to his car, which was parked on the street. "Do you care if he sees us?"

"No," Fletch said faintly. Then, with more conviction, "No, I don't care. And let's follow him."

"Yes." Albert started the ignition, let out the handbrake, and turned on the blinker.

Garrett pulled his car out onto the road and headed towards them. Perhaps he sensed these two men watching him or perhaps something caught his eye: he fixed his gaze on Fletcher, full of disbelief. They had a long moment to stare at each other as Garrett slowly drove past. Garrett's expression turned cynical and then he was gone.

Albert pulled out and turned the car around, cutting traffic off in both directions. He was only one vehicle behind Garrett's once they were traveling.

"Xavier would laugh if he saw me now," Fletch muttered. "He asked how I could work in the Bureau if I don't believe the end justifies the means. He asked how I can take any action, how I can even get out of bed in the morning, burdened with all my self-doubt."

"You don't doubt that John Garrett is a serial killer," Albert said.

"No. If I did before the interview, I can't doubt it now. Did you see it in his eyes, Albert? It was there: all the perversion, all the strength. The coldest heart and the hottest need."

"There is no need to wax lyrical, Ash. But I wasn't in a position to see it in his eyes."

The car they were following pulled into a space on the side of a one–way street. Albert pulled in at the next corner, parking illegally to do so. They shifted in their seats to see Garrett cross the road and enter a bar. He glanced over as if checking the FBI men were there but didn't acknowledge them.

"This is the French Quarter," Albert said. "Perhaps he is having a drink, or meeting someone."

"Yes," Fletcher agreed. He cast a look around but felt little interest in the old buildings with their lovely colors and ferns and cast iron balconies – though he noted them as beautiful. "You know, I told Xavier I doubt everything in my life, everything except for your love and the serial killer. But I still can't doubt either. Maybe I should. The serial killer, I mean, not you – maybe I should doubt that it's John Garrett, seeing as everyone else does. Maybe I am wrong."

"You question yourself often enough, Fletcher. There's no need to do so now."

Fletch looked at his companion, who must be serious indeed to use his first name.

"Perhaps," Albert continued, "you learned something from Mayor Lachance. If you learned something, then now is the time to use it."

Silence. A motorcycle cop stopped by the car, bent to look in Albert's open window, and advised them to move on. Albert quickly got rid of him by showing his Bureau credentials.

"It is possible to break the rules in one instance, Ash, with justification, and then continue to abide by them from then on."

"I thought you valued consistency."

"There can be valid exceptions to a rule. It follows that there can be consistent ways of assessing when to make an exception, of deciding when a situation warrants the rule being broken."

"I should go in and check that he is having a drink," Fletcher said. "He might have left by another door."

Albert nodded once. "If he drives off, and you're not here, I'll follow him anyway. The Quarter's police station is a block up that road on Royal, a large white building. Call me on the radio from there."

"All right." Fletch reached to grasp the man's shoulder for a moment. "Thank you, Albert." Then he got out of the car and jogged over to the bar.

The place wasn't a dump but it wasn't quaint or classy enough to attract the tourists, either. Fletch felt it almost an anticlimax to find Garrett sitting there quietly, at a table near the open door, sipping at a glass of what might have been whisky or bourbon. Fletcher stood in the doorway and let his presence be felt. The man met his gaze, steadily, though it seemed he was mildly irritated.

"Special Agent Ash," Garrett said, in a low voice that carried to Fletcher. It didn't draw attention, mostly because there wasn't anyone sitting close by. "Why don't you join me?"

"I don't care to drink with you."

"Then let's talk instead."

Fletcher deliberately walked closer, though he didn't sit down. "What would we have to talk about, Mr. Garrett?"

"You're using my name now, that's good. It was a cheap tactic, don't you think, to refuse to name me when we were at the station, whenever you could get away with it?"

"It wasn't a tactic, it was simple revulsion."

"There's no need for that." Garrett smiled, an easy smile. Fletch might have found the expression pleasant, if only the smile had reached those ice blue eyes. Garrett continued, "No hard feelings, Agent Ash. You have a difficult job to do, and sometimes it involves treating people like garbage. We can put that behind us, can't we?"

"No."

"But I tell you, you're up against the wrong man."

"And I tell you, Mr. Garrett, I know who you are and what you are, and I'm going to bring you to justice no matter what it takes."

"Is that a threat, Special Agent?"

Fletcher considered the man. "Yes, and not an empty one."

"Then I'm going to have to talk to Lieutenant Halligan about this. Sounds like harassment to me."

"You do that, Mr. Garrett. But I don't think your friends on the police force are going to be able to help you this time." And Fletcher turned and headed out the door.

Albert was there in the car, waiting for him. Of course. Fletcher slid into the passenger seat, and looked at his lover. "He's there, having a drink by himself. He's not upset yet, but he will be, he's already talking harassment." Fletcher took a breath. "No rules and no hostages, Albert. You were right."

"It has to be your decision, Ash, not mine."

"It is my decision, don't worry, this is too important for any other approach. I won't blame you if it goes wrong. Hell, I've already lost my self–respect, so why should I still fear compromise? I might lose my career but that's all right, I've lived with that idea for a long time now." Fletch shook his head. This was all happening so fast. "I might lose your respect, love, which isn't all right. But if I can bring this man to justice, it might be worth even that."

Albert was watching the bar where Garrett sat, but he glanced at Fletcher occasionally, watching him just as carefully. It sounded like no more than a token protest when Albert murmured, "A return of the melodrama. Wonderful."

Ignoring this, Fletcher continued, "What's the worst that could happen? I end up alone and empty, back in Idaho, waiting tables at the family diner."

"And arresting Garrett would be worth that?" Albert asked, apparently wanting a last confirmation. "You'd be miserable."

"It's not about getting Garrett, Albert, it's about stopping the pain and the fear and the death. It's about saving the lives of all those young men Garrett would prey on if he were free."

"All right."

"Albert, I know I can't ask you to approve of this –"

"If you're clear about why you're doing it, then I'll help you."

"Thank you." Fletcher dearly wanted to ask whether Albert was clear about his own reasons for doing this, but decided that now was not the time. He said, "I should cut Mac loose."

"Don't be more naïve than you have to be, Ash. He's already broken the rules for you. Talk to him about it, for the sake of your conscience, but he'll give you the same answer I did."

Fletcher looked at him, amused. Strange to hear Albert putting himself in the same boat as Mac.

Then Albert surprised him even more by saying, "You're doing the right thing."

"Why? Why do you say that?"

"Because you have finally regained your certainty and your motivation. You have been reacting in ways that demonstrated your doubts and your lack of faith, until now. You are therefore doing the right thing, for your own sake, at least." Albert started the car as he said this, and Fletcher turned to see Garrett stride out of the bar.

Garrett drove past them with barely a glance. He appeared angry. Again, Albert cut off a few cars in order to pull out after him and then he had to break the speed limit to keep up, even within the narrow crowded streets of the French Quarter.

"He'd just love us to bust him for a traffic violation," Fletcher said.

Albert cast a glance at him. "Maybe you should look into his financial records. You might be able to send him to jail for tax evasion. It has been an effective strategy in other cases."

Fletcher looked at this man, this best of men, and began to laugh. It felt good. Humor, especially shared, had been all too infrequent lately. After a while, he said, "I don't ever want to have to manage without you, Albert."

"No rules and no hostages, Ash, remember."

"Maybe there are no rules except not losing you," Fletch said quietly.

"I don't believe that's an issue," Albert said.

He was concentrating on driving through the evening traffic. Fletcher wondered if that concentration on other matters had made it easier for Albert to make what amounted to a declaration of commitment. "You and me together. It's necessary," Fletcher murmured, because Albert would accept that.

There was no further response, and Fletcher hadn't expected any. A few minutes later, Garrett pulled into the driveway of his house. It was a relatively modest place and not in a fashionable suburb, though it was built of brick rather than wood, and was a decent size for a man living alone. Garrett walked in through the front door, and shut it firmly behind him.

"If he tries to dump anything in the trash or take anything away, we have to find a way to search it."

Albert seemed unenthusiastic about this idea, though he nodded once in agreement. Perhaps he found the idea of ferreting through someone's trashcan distasteful.

"Tell you what," Fletcher said, changing the subject to an equally urgent one. "I am starving to death."

A pained and then a resigned expression quickly masked the relief on Albert's face. "Of course you are," he said, distant.

Fletcher briefly wondered, for the millionth time, where Albert went when he was that withdrawn. "There was a phone booth back around the corner. I'm going to call Mac, get him to bring us something."

"Why don't you use the radio?"

Fletcher looked at it. "No, not yet. Halligan will find out what we're doing soon enough." He smiled at Albert, and climbed out of the car. "I'll be back in a minute, love."

Within forty–five minutes, Mac drove up behind them, then walked up to the car. Celia followed, with a flat cardboard carton balanced precariously on each hand. Mac was grinning. "One large vegetarian pizza, as requested."

"You're miracle workers," Fletch declared, taking the box Celia passed him through the window and setting it on the seat between him and Albert.

"And if you don't mind, we carnivores will eat ours in the back seat."

"Be our guests," Fletcher said, already munching on a slice of pizza. "Hello, Celia."

"Hello, Fletch. Albert." She slid in behind the driver's seat, apparently not noticing that Albert didn't acknowledge her greeting.

"Come on, Albert, have a slice," Fletcher said. "Why do you think I ordered vegetarian?"

After a moment, Albert deigned to select a small piece and began to eat it very carefully.

Fletcher grinned. Albert was probably the only one of the four of them who could eat pizza in a car without making a mess of himself or his clothes or his surroundings. "This is great." Fletch added, "Actually, it's almost as good as Albert's," which earned him an angry glower.

"I have my contacts," Mac explained. "I know who to ask to find the best pizza in town."

Celia said, "I should have guessed before. Cops are a mine of information about these things. The best pizza, the best donuts, the best hamburgers, the best beer."

"I told you, they spend a week every month doing comparisons across the city. They investigate taste, cost, convenience, service, cooperation. It's a vital piece of detecting work."

They were silent, then, as they ate and darkness fell. Albert wouldn't have more than two slices, so Fletcher happily munched through the rest of their pizza. Then Mac returned to his car to retrieve the bottled water and coffee he'd bought.

A light was turned on in one of Garrett's front rooms, and then the changing muted colors of the television glowed through the blinds. The four of them had all turned to watch.

Mac said, "So you're really doing this, Fletcher?"

"Yes. The new rule is that there are no rules and no hostages."

"Good," was the response. "We'll take the graveyard shift tonight."

Fletcher swung around in his seat to look at Mac and Celia. "What? This isn't exactly acceptable operating procedure, you know. And once the Bureau hierarchy finds out, we'll be in all kinds of trouble."

"We'll help," Mac said. "You've got to get this guy, Fletch, that's the bottom line."

Celia nodded. "That's got to be the priority."

Fletch said, "At least we have the excuse that it's related to our jobs, Celia. You don't."

She shrugged. "I'll deal with the trouble when I have to, though I think they'll treat me as a citizen, an innocent bystander. Meanwhile, this friend of mine takes me parking in suburban streets. I guess he doesn't want to compete with the distraction of an interesting view for my attention."

Though he smiled at this cover story, Fletcher opened his mouth to protest some more.

Celia didn't let him speak. "You're not used to accepting loyalty, are you, Fletcher?"

He glanced around at Mac, and an oblivious Albert, then back to Celia. "No, I suppose I'm not. And, to be honest, I don't like the responsibility."

"It's our decision to help you," Mac said.

And Albert quietly reminded him, "No rules, Ash."

"No prisoners!" Mac cried. *"No prisoners!"*

"You've been watching too many late night movies, Mac," Fletch said with a laugh. After a moment, he nodded. "All right. I'll accept your help, with thanks."

Mac offered, "How about we relieve you at midnight? Give you until eight to get some rest."

"We'll be back around six," Fletch said. "You'll have to be careful, though, he might try something in the small hours. I'd bet anything you like that he has evidence in there and he'll try to hide it, or dump it, or destroy it at some stage."

"We'll be careful," Mac said.

"Any light or noise or movement," Celia added.

Fletcher said, "But don't do anything you don't have to."

"Relax, Fletch, we know what we're doing."

"I'm glad someone does." He grinned at them, then Mac and Celia were leaving. "See you at twelve. And thank you both."

All was quiet once they'd driven away. Albert, who'd talked more that evening than he had in the couple of weeks since Fletcher left Colorado, was now silent. Fletch occupied himself with thoughts of how he'd present this case in court; there was nothing like continually reviewing the material and being prepared. Added to which, mulling matters over like this had often brought him connections, inspired him with insights.

The object of his thoughts walked out his front door and approached their car. Fletcher sat up straighter, watched the man carefully.

"Thought you might want a beer," Garrett said, holding out two cans, slick with moisture, grasped in one large hand. He already had an open can in his other hand, from which he now took a swig.

"We're on duty," Fletcher replied.

"Really?" Garrett looked away, laughed to himself. "This sort of harassment couldn't be official, surely."

Fletcher decided to ignore that. "We don't want the beer, Mr. Garrett."

"You have some crazy notions about me, Special Agent. You go ahead and run with them. But we can act civilized in the meantime, can't we?"

"I don't know," Fletcher said slowly. "I've never met a civilized serial killer before."

Another laugh. It took an obvious effort for the laugh to sound easy. "Sleep well, boys." And he headed back inside. Moments later, the light in the front room was turned out, and Garrett apparently moved towards the rear of the house.

Fletcher frowned, trying to slot Garrett's behavior into what he already knew about the man. This was what he felt to be an important weakness in himself: Fletcher needed time to think and to consider. He saw himself as being on input most of the time and therefore needing time to assimilate all he'd learned. That wasn't bad in and of itself, but he thought it left him slow on his feet. Apart from which, it forced him to seek time alone and quiet each day, which could often be a luxury in this job.

"You've tried to tell me that you have an understanding of John Garrett," Albert said into the silence. "That your instincts enable you to empathize with him."

"Yeah," Fletcher said, wary.

"I believe that you do have one trait in common."

Albert left a pause, which Fletcher was unwilling to break. This was scary, his lover proposing such an idea.

"He is used to convincing people with charm and certainty, with apparent openness and the power of his own will. He manipulates people through knowledge of who they are and what they want. People rarely remain unmoved by him, particularly when he's trying to influence them."

"Ah," Fletcher managed. He would have loved to say, with all the sarcasm he could muster, *Thank you so much for sharing.* But that would have been no more than a crude defense mechanism, and its cruelty would only dissuade Albert from ever talking to him again.

It hurt, though, applying this character sketch to himself. To Fletcher, charm was almost synonymous with artifice and artifice meant lies, and honesty was far too important to him. He didn't want to manipulate people, either, or influence them, which implied that he was forcing them to act or think differently than they would have otherwise. More lies, as well as unwanted responsibility for others.

But he reminded himself that the instinctive hurt wasn't important. Pushing it aside, Fletcher began applying all this to Garrett instead, and considering what there was of truth in what Albert had said. And, of course, there was quite a lot.

Albert and Fletcher were back at their hotel by twelve–fifteen. It was a functional, anonymous building, one of the chains convenient to the federal building. They had rooms on the same floor, though they were located forty feet apart.

Undaunted by a glare from Albert, Fletcher tagged along behind him until they'd reached Albert's door. They'd been silent since Albert had told him what he thought Garrett and Fletch had in common. It appeared that, if Albert had his way, they would remain so.

Fletcher stood close to the man, and murmured, "I appreciate everything you've done for me."

Of course, Albert didn't respond to this.

"It's been one hell of a day," Fletch continued. "Would you do one last thing for me? Just hold me, like a friend would."

Albert whispered, "May I remind you we are in the Bureau's designated hotel? No doubt our rooms are bugged."

"That's why I asked you in the corridor," Fletch retorted with a smile.

"The corridor is probably bugged, too."

"But they'd only be watching or listening if they thought there was something going on."

Albert let out a breath. "You want me to treat you like a friend," he asked, "when *anyone* could walk by?"

Fletcher's smile grew. "Ruin your reputation, I know, the thought of you having a friend."

A full wattage glower blazed into him, but then Albert was reaching his arms around Fletcher's shoulders in a brief but strong hug. "Is that how it's done?" Albert asked, sour. "Apart from the backslapping, of course."

And then he was gone, and his door was shut behind him. Fletcher was grinning. No matter how the man tried to deny it, Albert was so damned vulnerable where Fletch was concerned. And Fletcher was determined to treat him as finely as he deserved.

They were back at Garrett's as the sun rose, and the heat rose with it. Mac and Celia climbed out of their car to greet them and to stretch their legs. Fletcher joined them, asking, "Anything happen?"

"Good morning, Fletch," Mac said politely. He shared a laugh with Celia at Fletcher's chagrined expression, then said, "Nothing happened. He didn't stir all night."

"You're sure?"

"As sure as I can be. A couple of times, I walked around the block – you can get a good view of his back windows if you know where to stop – otherwise, we were both out here and wide awake all night. I don't think he'd be able to get away across the back fence without making a ruckus. So he's still in there and still in bed, as far as I can tell."

"Good," Fletcher said, nodding. "Good work, both of you."

"So what's next?"

"Get some sleep, whatever you need, but then get back to it. I'm still interested in the unsolved cases on the police records but seeing as there are no rules, I want you to start gathering any information on this guy, any way you can. Where he's lived, what work he's done, who his friends are, what his finances are like. You probably know better than me what to look for and how to get it."

"Sure," Mac said. "Celia, you can work on the stuff that's public record, can't you?"

"Yes, I can, but not right away. Fletch, I'm due some leave, so I thought I'd take a week or two off, just while we're doing this. The catch is that there are a few things I need to clear up first."

"That's fine, Celia. If you're happy to take some time off, of course that's fine with me." He smiled at them both. "I really appreciate this. If I was hesitant last night, it wasn't because I don't want you on the team. I'm just worried about the fallout, that's all."

They returned his smile. "We'll be in touch," Mac said, and the pair of them got back into Mac's car and drove off.

Fletcher returned to his car, where Albert waited. "Nothing to report," Fletcher told him. Then he added, "I'd expected you to bring some reading material, or even some work. Do you realize I've never once seen you sit around and do nothing?"

"But we are not doing nothing. We are on surveillance."

"Well, I can watch and you can do your work, if that's what you want."

Albert said dryly, "That would be fine, if you didn't keep losing yourself in your thoughts. Convince me that you can pay adequate attention and I'll be glad to do other work as well."

Fletcher smiled self–consciously. "All right. I'll try harder."

Not bothering to reply directly, Albert indicated Garrett's house. Fletcher turned his head to see Garrett again strolling towards them. The man appeared tired and pale, as if he hadn't slept much, and his expression of good humor was forced. He stopped by Fletcher's open window and looked at them both. Then he nodded his head towards Albert and said, "Who's the goon, Agent Ash?"

The description was so incongruous that Fletcher glanced around to ensure it was Albert in the car with him. "This is Dr. Albert Sterne, of the FBI. The best forensic pathologist in the country. He's going to be my leading expert witness at your trial."

"Really." Garrett seemed unimpressed. "What's he doing out of the morgue? No dead bodies here to get his thrills from."

Fletcher stared at the man. "What a strange notion. I've never heard the like before, have you, Albert? Mr. Garrett, why is it that the first thing you think of in relation to forensics is the thrill of dealing with dead bodies?"

Garrett returned his stare, furious, those blue eyes frozen. "Don't get too cute, Agent Ash. Don't go drawing inferences that you can't support."

"I don't have to draw inferences, or speculate, or make conclusions. I know you're a killer, Mr. Garrett, and I will prove it in a court of law."

"More day dreams." Garrett leaned closer. "You might not listen to that clown Halligan, and I don't blame you, but I have friends who the Director of the FBI listens to. And when the Director hears what's going on, marginalized grunts like you and your goon here are going to find yourselves in it up to your eyeballs."

Nodding genially, Fletcher said, "You take it as high as you like, Mr. Garrett. You have far more to lose than we do." The man turned his back and walked to his car. Fletcher had planned to say something about trying Garrett's case in whichever of the four states had the death penalty, but he lost his nerve. There was time for that kind of threat later.

As they drove off, following Garrett, Albert said quietly, "Don't misinterpret his comment about forensic pathologists. It is a popular myth that we're all necrophiliacs."

Fletcher, already feeling somewhat shaken, had no idea how to reply to that.

The previous night, Fletcher had slept soundly and deeply. He'd taken this as another indication that he'd made the right decision. The return of his humor and his energy and his appetite all seemed to support the notion that, in this case, there were no rules.

Tonight, however, he was restless. He'd allotted himself and Albert six hours of rest, and he'd been determined to make the most of it, to sleep well and wake refreshed. It seemed that was not to be. Knowing that Albert, and Albert's arms around him, would help him settle only added to his dissatisfaction.

Too keen, that was his trouble. Too eager to go pester Garrett again, to progress the case. Too pumped full of adrenalin. Fletcher had always been the sort who, once he knew what he wanted, would jump in with both feet. He found control and patience to be a trial. Right now, he could keep working, use all this restless energy, that was definitely the option he'd prefer – but he knew it was only a short term option. And Garrett was a long term problem. At least, Fletcher couldn't afford to burn out; he had to be prepared to deal with this for however long it took. Even though, now that all rules were off, events would surely speed up. That was what he needed to do – provoke Garrett into doing or saying something rash.

Somehow, as his thoughts churned through this for the tenth time, Fletcher slipped into sleep, into dreams.

The nightmare was different this time. At first, he didn't even recognize it. He wasn't hanging on, he wasn't scrambling up, he wasn't in danger. He was simply walking in the mountains, in the Rockies south of Denver, high above the timber–line. The sky was limitless blue, the air thin and pure. He was alone.

He walked, happy and confident. This was a good dream. The air was cool with that brisk sparkling clear coolness he loved. He'd left the damp heavy heat of New Orleans behind, along with the stale conditioned air of the hotel room. This was his idea of perfection.

When he came to the edge of the mountain, a cliff abruptly giving way to the valley below, Fletcher thought, *No rules and no hostages*. And he kept walking.

At first it felt like flying, soaring in the endless champagne air, the pale blue surrounding him. But too soon he was tumbling. There were grey jagged rocks, thousands of feet below, rapidly drawing closer. *I'm flying*, he told himself. *No rules and no gravity*.

The sharp hard rocks disagreed. The valley floor beckoned. *Let us bear your broken body*. Fletcher saw himself down there already, on his back, limbs gangling unnatural, a shattered wretch in this barren place two miles above sea level. The rocks exposed him, displayed him to the cool air, the merciless mountain peaks, the pale sun.

It wasn't Fletcher down there – someone waited, arms outstretched in welcome. Someone with ice blue eyes. Garrett. "You're like me now," the man said, with that charming smile. "No rules, right?"

"No!" Fletch protested.

"You understand me so well."

The tumble became a hundred–mile–an–hour rush. Fletcher struggled, trying to reach the mountainside. Tried to imagine himself clinging there, safe. Hopeless. Where the hell was Albert when Fletch needed him?

"Once you've made the decision, there's no turning back, no regrets. You'll learn to love it."

"No!"

"Welcome," Garrett said to him.

So close: Garrett almost touched him but Fletcher sat up in the bed, gulping conditioned air down a raw throat. His scream still seemed to echo amongst the mountains.

Not mountains. Walls. Gradually the room settled into dim familiar shapes. Slowly he lay back down again – then curled up on his side rather than mirror that wretch broken by the rocks.

Symptom of a troubled conscience, he told himself. Perhaps the nightmare would never leave him: perhaps it would only get worse. Perhaps it was more than time to actually examine the thing, to consider it rather than ignore it. But that seemed too brave a notion here, alone and in the dark.

If Albert were sharing his bed, the fear would once again be dispelled with a few blunt words and a solid embrace. But that wasn't possible; Fletcher couldn't even go knock on Albert's door and ask for his comfort.

Fletcher sighed, turned on the light and got out of bed. If he wasn't going to sleep, he might as well get some work done.

"Come and have a drink with me, Agent Ash."

Fletcher had been gazing nowhere, deep in his thoughts, Albert silent beside him. A little startled, Fletch looked up through the car window at Garrett. They were in the French Quarter again, where Garrett often stopped after work. "I'm on duty, Mr. Garrett."

The man sighed, impatient. His humor and his reasonableness had dwindled to nothing over the past few days. "Agent Ash, we need to end this investigation of yours, one way or the other. Come and talk with me, and let's see if we can sort something out."

"If you want to talk, why don't you get in the back seat? We could go do this properly, in a police station."

"Don't you have a life, Ash? Is that the problem? You don't have anything better to be doing with your time than bothering me."

"There's nothing I'd rather be doing right now, Garrett."

"Well, I have a business to run. This is ridiculous. People are beginning to ask me what's going on."

Fletcher remained silent.

"I thought you'd welcome the offer to talk with me."

"Why? Are you going to make a full confession?"

"Come on, get out of the damned car and talk."

After a moment, Fletcher climbed out and leaned his arms on the open door. In turn, Garrett propped his rear against the car hood, arms crossed, expression open. It made a casual, friendly tableau. Fletch asked, "You want to confess to murder, right here in the street?"

Garrett almost laughed at that, though he was obviously exasperated. "If I did, this would be just the city for it."

"Is that why you came here? It's a lot different to Oregon."

"I came here looking for business opportunities, Ash, and I found them. Everyone's crazy to renovate these old houses before they rot away."

"Lots of good–looking young men, too."

Garrett sketched a smile. "You noticed that?"

Fletch shrugged, ostensibly uninterested. "What did you want to talk about, Mr. Garrett? Were you going to tell me how it felt to rape Mitch Brown? He would have gone down fighting, that's what they told me. Did you like it when they fought back?"

Silence for a moment. Garrett shifted his weight, re–crossed his arms. Then, heedless of the couples sauntering by choosing restaurants and bars for the evening, he said, "So you think you've linked me to three victims out of – how many? Fourteen?"

"Fifteen," Fletcher amended. "Don't forget Stacey Dixon."

"And you can't link me to the other eleven – twelve, sorry."

"Not yet, but there's plenty of time to get the details once I have you in jail. The trial won't be for months. Years."

Shaking his head, as if all this was not only ridiculous but insignificant as well, Garrett said, "If you had anything on me, you'd have arrested me already."

"I'm waiting for more, that's all. The MO links the victims together, and you're linked to at least three of them. That's plenty to be getting on with."

"The MO. You mean they were all killed in the same way."

"Similar ways," Fletcher said.

"Similar? That's enough to link them, is it, across four states?"

"Yes."

"Then how come you're the only one investigating me, Special Agent?"

"You know I'm right and I know I'm right. That's enough for now." Fletch considered the man. "You only wanted to talk to see how much I know."

"You never give up, do you?" Garrett sounded as if he'd be impressed with this persistence if he wasn't so angry about it.

"No, I'm not giving up on you," Fletch said lightly.

Garrett declared, "This has to end, Special Agent." He reinforced the statement with a glare and then Garrett turned away, headed for his usual bar. It was obvious he'd been drinking more and more since Fletcher had begun tailing him.

Fletch watched him go then got into the car again. "This *will* end," he murmured.

"He keeps suggesting you talk with him," Albert said. "Perhaps he wants to tell you something."

"He'll get the chance soon enough."

"You should be encouraging him."

"Not yet. I'm working on annoying him right now." Fletcher turned to his companion, and grinned. "How do you think I'm doing?"

"Quite well," Albert said from behind his dark glasses.

"I know you could do better," Fletcher assured him. "But I've spent all these years annoying you, and I figure that has to count for something."

Albert didn't reply, though he let out a quiet breath. Almost like a laugh. Fletcher chuckled for both of them.

Halligan shut his office door behind them and got right down to business. "John Garrett's going to put in an official complaint about you, Ash. My captain's getting nervous. I'm telling you to back off, and I'm not going to tell you again."

Fletcher sat down in the visitor's chair, and looked at Halligan calmly. "I'm not going to back off, Lieutenant, and you can let the captain know that, too. This man is a killer and I intend to bring him to justice. If he were innocent, he would have lodged a complaint the first day I began pestering him."

Halligan shook his head. "It was difficult to take you seriously when you first arrived because it was so obvious that the FBI didn't. Sending three people to investigate a serial killer? No chance. Especially when only one of those three is a special agent. Though I have to admit that bastard Sterne has a reputation in forensics. He adds clout to your little team."

"I'm sure Albert will be glad to know that."

"Sure he will," Halligan said with a humorless smile. "It was difficult at first, but you're making it impossible now. If you kept within the law –"

"I have tried for years, Lieutenant, to keep this within the law. I honestly gave it my best shot when I came here. It cost me a lot to realize that wasn't going to work."

"So it's cost you some scruples already, big deal. What's it *going* to cost you?"

"What do you honestly recommend I do? Let him go? He'll move on, and begin killing again. But that's all right, because when I see the corpses of his next three young men, I'll think, 'Yes, I had him in my sights, but I was too decent to pull the trigger.' What a comfort that decency of mine will be. The families of those young men are sure to understand."

"You are running so damned close to the line, Special Agent. Personally, I think you're already over it. And now you're talking violence."

Fletcher said, "It's worth stepping over the line."

"Maybe I'd agree, if you were sure it's the right guy."

"But he is the right man." Fletcher sighed. "You said he employed your cousin, didn't you?"

"Yes, over the Christmas break. And now he's employed Andy again, promised him a couple of months' work."

"Andy?" Fear crawled through Fletch. He hadn't expected Garrett to be that provoking. Hiring a boy named Andrew right now was surely equivalent to waving a red flag in Fletch's face. "How old is your cousin, Halligan? What does he look like?"

"The kid's only nineteen. A good–looking sort, and smart, too. Real popular with the college girls."

Fletcher rubbed at his face, leaned forward, said, "Andy sounds just his type, Halligan. You watch he doesn't rape and torture and murder your Andy, too."

The lieutenant's expression was at first sickened but then righteous anger took over. "Yeah, you keep throwing your shit around, Special Agent. You threw it at him during that mockery of an interview, and it didn't stick. So now you're throwing it at me again."

"It's the damned *truth*, Lieutenant." That was the closest Fletcher had got to shouting.

"Yeah, well, he might file a complaint about your conduct. He might sue you for libel. He might tell the world you're prejudiced against him because he's queer. And good luck to him, I reckon. About the only thing you haven't done is call the press in."

"They'd love all this dirt, wouldn't they? What a great idea, Halligan. They'd blow the whole thing wide open."

"Don't be ridiculous, Ash. They'd get the waters so muddy you'd never get an indictment."

"You admit there's a possibility I'm right?"

"There's always a possibility, isn't there? I'm warning you, that's all. The press won't help your case. They love scandal and they'll ruin John, but they won't help your case against him."

After a long moment, during which Halligan sweated, Fletcher nodded. "That was my conclusion, as well."

Halligan was still looking disgruntled. "One more thing," he said. "Next time you have something to say to me about how I run this outfit, or how my men behave, you tell me to my face. Don't go setting Sterne onto me. He has the rudest mouth I've ever heard, which is good for a man who never damn well swears."

Fletcher didn't know whether to laugh or frown. "When was this? What did he say?"

"After your interview with John Garrett. Said young Bill had undermined your authority and I shouldn't have let that happen, or words to that effect. Well, maybe I shouldn't have, but I won't be spoken to like that in front of my own men."

"All Albert told me was that he'd asked you to conduct surveillance for a while and that you refused. But I can imagine how he phrased the request." Fletcher decided to laugh. Albert was certainly looking out for Fletcher's interests at present. "I'm not going to apologize, Lieutenant. I wasn't going to make an issue of it, but I should have had more support from you and your people. On the other hand, Albert no doubt said some things he shouldn't have. Let's call it even, all right?"

Eventually Halligan nodded, but he also said, "I still think you're after the wrong man."

"Support me and we'll get to the truth of it. That's my best offer." And it seemed reasonably acceptable. A temporary truce was declared.

CHAPTER THIRTY
NEW ORLEANS
SEPTEMBER 1985

Albert ate the room service meal without any appreciation. Rather than detail and categorize all the meal's failings, however, he considered the man sitting across the table from him. While it had been Fletcher's idea to have a late dinner in Albert's room, for the sake of quiet and the illusion of privacy, he seemed as dissatisfied as Albert was. He made little attempt to eat. In Albert's dispassionate opinion, Fletcher looked terrible.

The pale face and bruised eyes and fatigued expression were presumably the result of a combination of factors: coping for an extended period with little sleep; working hard, with little obvious result, on a case Fletcher had always found emotionally draining; waiting through a situation he was not fully in control of; hating the fact he was working outside both the law enforcement system and his own system of ethics, even though Fletcher realized that it was the only course of action he could take; spending hours crammed with activity, followed by hours of monotonous surveillance. Once this case was finally resolved, whether successfully or not, Fletcher would be a ravaged wreck. A melodramatic description but given that this was Fletcher Ash, a true enough one. How Albert was then going to deal with the man was another question entirely.

The silence continued unbroken while Albert ate. Once Albert had set aside his plate and cutlery, however, and before he could reach for some reading material, Fletcher said, "I know you'll disapprove but I think I'll take the night off. And you can, too, of course." He continued in hurried explanation, "Mac and Celia said they'd take a longer shift, if we give them some time off tomorrow night."

"All right," Albert said.

"You're supposed to be talking me out of this."

"Am I? I agree that you would benefit from time off duty but I'd be surprised if you were able to sleep well or even relax."

"Well, it's no use asking you for tips on how to relax," Fletcher commented with a faint smile. Then he said, "Sorry. No doubt you're right but I intend to try. Meanwhile, you'll have plenty to catch up with, I assume."

"Yes, I have work to progress. If you require me and I'm not here, I'll probably be at the Bureau offices."

Fletcher nodded. "I think I'll turn in. Would you do me a favor? Don't disturb me unless it's really urgent. I'll ask reception to put any calls through here, if that's okay with you."

"Of course."

The man stood and walked around the table to where Albert sat. A long moment, as Fletcher gazed down at him. Then he gripped Albert's shoulder, and said, "Goodnight, Albert," in meaningful tones.

"Goodnight," Albert curtly replied, frowning up at him. This sort of behavior usually signified that Fletcher wanted to say something personal but was managing to restrain himself. Given that the behavior was so easy to interpret, it didn't serve to hide anything. Annoyed at the man, Albert was surprised to find himself reacting to the subtext. He lifted a hand to Fletcher's, grasped it briefly, and said, "Get some rest."

Fletcher nodded. "Necessary," he said. "Absolutely necessary." An observer might have assumed he was commenting on his need for sleep. And then Fletcher was gone, and Albert was alone.

This was almost too convenient. Albert decided to work in the hotel room for an hour, so that he was available in case Fletcher changed his mind. If he remained undisturbed until ten o'clock, then Albert would leave. He had plans, and he would put off both sleep and the bulk of his work for a few hours until he could see those plans through.

Albert cast a glance around the diner and chose a booth as far away as possible from the few other patrons. Not bothering to take off his jacket, he sat down and watched the two waiters sharing a joke with the cook. The atmosphere here was definitely slow and casual.

Within a few minutes, however, one of the waiters approached this new customer. Albert had the chance to observe him: a man in his early thirties; dressed in torn blue jeans, a faded green T-shirt, and an open shirt patterned in darker greens and blues, with a small apron around his hips that might once have been white; long dark brown hair caught back in a tail; deep brown eyes that were warm if not friendly. When he spoke, it was all on a breath: "Hello, what can I get you?"

"Bottled water," Albert said. "And then, if possible, Ricardo, a few minutes of your time."

The waiter grimaced and fell back a step. "Hey, man, I'm clean. Have been for years."

Albert just looked at him, resisting the urge to draw out his dark glasses.

"All right, months," Rick amended. "Don't you cops ever give up and leave a guy alone? I'm a law–abiding citizen these days, mostly."

"We've been through this before," Albert informed him. "You are outside my jurisdiction and I am, in any case, off–duty."

"Before? Do I know you?"

"Sit down, Ricardo." When the younger man reluctantly slid onto the seat opposite, Albert said, "I don't expect you to remember me. My name is Albert. We met one evening some years ago. October 1971, to be exact. We spent a few hours together."

"You were one of my clients?"

"Yes."

"Albert. That was a long time ago, you know." Rick frowned at him, and reached into his apron pocket for his cigarettes and a lighter. Then recognition dawned. Grinning he said, "I remember, all right, G–man. You were so damned rude! I mean, no one treats a hooker well, but you had a hard line in insults. But then you said – Well, you remember what you said."

I love you. "Yes."

"That was weird enough." The grin returned, turned into genuine amusement. "And I'll tell you what else I remember. You were a virgin."

"Yes," Albert said again, the syllable clipped short.

"Despite which, you were good." Rick considered him, lit a cigarette. "We had some fun together, right? Before you started insulting me again."

"Yes."

"Yeah, I remember. You were so rude, you really pissed me off, but I liked you, too. It's usually one or the other, but you managed both." A long moment. "So what are you doing here, Albert? And how did you find me?"

"I have access to various forms of information."

Rick shrugged. "Well, that don't surprise me. Big brother, and all that. The cops here have everyone in their books."

"On their databases," Albert corrected him.

"So why are you here, if you're not going to bust me?"

"What time do you finish work?"

"I could probably get away by twelve, if it stays this quiet. Why? Do you want to wait for me?"

Albert nodded once.

Rick smiled. "Sure, all right." He stood. "Bottled water, you want? Anything else? Anything to eat? It'll be a while."

"Water will be fine." Refusing to return the young man's smile, Albert settled in to wait. He hadn't brought any work with him, so he took the newspaper that had been left on the next table and read that, tawdry though it was, rather than think about the question of Rick's that Albert hadn't answered. *What are you doing here?*

Apparently checking about leaving early, Ricardo was also glancing back at Albert rather more than necessary. The cook and the other waiter were developing speculative expressions. Albert attempted to ignore the lot of them.

Ricardo had been born only a year after Fletcher, Albert reflected, but Rick seemed much younger. Albert was walking down the midnight-quiet streets, with Rick beside him chattering away about New Orleans as if Albert were a tourist. Not long ago, Fletcher had been this irrepressible, this full of good-humored energy. The serial killer case had worn Ash down – while Rick's circumstances, surely difficult, had left their mark but hadn't seemed to harm him irretrievably.

Having spent some time framing a question about Ricardo's life now, Albert found he needn't ask. Rick soon began telling him, unfazed by Albert's silence. "I got in off the streets about nine years ago. I had a couple of regulars, which was fine, but other than that I was losing business to the young kids. Tough little things, these days. Bitter, you know."

Albert asked, "How did you escape bitterness, Ricardo?"

"I don't know. It doesn't have to be like that. Maybe that's all it is – realizing you don't have to be unhappy about the things life does to you.

Does that seem simple to you?" Not earning a response, Rick continued, "Anyway, I've survived this long. I'm thirty–two now, for God's sake. Old age."

'Don't be ridiculous," Albert said. "This should be the prime of your life."

Rick laughed, shifted his backpack to the other shoulder. "So here I am, in the prime of my life, waiting tables at a diner. It's all right, though. I like the people there, I've made friends, and the boss is pretty cool. He treats us well, pays us a bit over the award rate. He helped me quit the hard stuff, too, though I still smoke some grass every now and then. But you're not going to bust me for that, are you, Albert?"

"No."

"I'll show you what I really love doing." Rick was watching him with a mischievous smile. "Is that all right? Do you have the time?"

Albert nodded, and did not deign to ask what the mystery was.

They walked a further two blocks, turned onto a smaller street, and Rick came to a halt. "Well," he said, "what do you think?"

Following Ricardo's grand gesture, Albert cast his gaze over the side of a brick wall that was covered with a busy mural. "I assume you painted that."

"Yeah." Rick was grinning. "Do you like it?"

Frowning, Albert considered the abstract shapes. At first they appeared bold and simple but on further inspection, there were subtleties and patterns capable of different and surprising interpretations. Faces and leaves appeared out of randomness. Words scattered throughout in different styles declared 'Things are seldom what they seem'. Albert said, "It is cleverly done. Perhaps it is best seen in daylight, to receive the full benefit of the colors."

"You're right, you know. The colors are my favorite part, I mix them back at home to get them right and use brushes. I only bring two or three paints at a time, so it's a long process. Sometimes I don't get a mural finished before someone defaces it, either the owner or some kid. The worst was when the local council covered one up in grey. Mostly people who do this use spray cans, which is quicker and easier, but you only get a limited number of shades that way. Do you like colors, too?"

"I have noticed that you do. Both times we've met, your clothes have been harmonious in color and texture. Not many people would have managed to successfully combine the blues and greens you are currently wearing."

Rick's grin broadened. "You'll do anything to avoid answering a question, won't you? You'll even pay me a compliment."

Albert sighed. "What is the question I am supposedly avoiding?"

"Do you like colors, too?"

"I believe I have answered that, at least indirectly."

"Yeah, okay, I guess," Rick said, nodding. "Hey, would you mind if I worked some more on this? I'm almost done, you see, and I like to make a little progress each night. Do you have the spare time?"

"Yes."

"Thanks." Rick began taking jars out of his backpack, and lining them up on the sidewalk. Then his mischievous expression returned in full measure. "You could stand look–out for me. The cops don't like this sort of thing. Neither do the good citizens. Defacing public property, or whatever. You must know the law better than me."

"That is not an area of the criminal code I have any dealings with," Albert said. He took a couple of paces back to the street corner, in order to watch for passers–by. "It seems unlikely there will be any witnesses," Albert commented. He hadn't seen anyone else since they'd left the diner behind.

"That's partly why I chose this place. Plenty of people during the day to see this, but not much disturbance at night. The crowds are mostly over on Bourbon Street."

Albert watched Rick more than he did the street. The young man was still too slim, though he wasn't as gaunt and undernourished as he had been fourteen years ago. It now seemed far more likely that Ricardo would survive for at least the foreseeable future.

"There's enough light to work by," Ricardo was continuing, concentrating on adding a bright yellow to various shapes. A tangle of flowers was revealed; they were vibrant one moment and about to decay the next. "This place has been abandoned for years, so it's not gonna annoy the owner or any tenants."

"A logical choice," Albert said.

"There's three of my paintings still around." Rick glanced at him. "It'd be great to show them to you."

"I doubt that will be possible."

Rick nodded. He seemed a little disappointed – but Albert dismissed this notion as improbable. Rick said, "How come you're here? In New Orleans, I mean. Are you working on a case?"

"Yes." Albert left a pause, then walked closer. "Do you know a man named John Garrett? I have a photograph of him."

Rick stood, looked at the photo, returned to his paints, began working with a lighter shade of yellow. "Don't think so. What do you want him for?"

"We believe he's a murderer. His victims are all young men."

"And you're concerned for my safety? I'm flattered."

"You may consider yourself warned," Albert said flatly, "though you are somewhat older than his victims. Are you aware of any assaults or rapes, missing persons or murders that have gone unreported? From the police records, it seems that this man hasn't committed any crimes while he's lived in New Orleans, but I find that unlikely."

Rick sighed. "Of course I've heard stories of violence. Happens every day to the street kids. If it's not the clients, it's the pimps or the cops. I can't help you there."

"If you think of anything, you could contact me through the FBI state office. They are in the phone book."

"You know all about me, don't you, from your databases. And I don't even know your last name."

A long moment, and then Albert took one of his business cards out of his wallet. "Albert Sterne," he said. "That's my phone number at headquarters in Washington."

Taking the card, Rick frowned at him. "Is that why you went to the trouble of finding me? To ask me about this murderer?"

"It took little trouble. I knew your first name, your racial background, an approximate age, and what type of criminal record you might have. That was more than enough to enable a search of the databases. Details of your hair and eye color, and estimations of your height and weight confirmed your identity."

"Answer my question, Albert. Was this just about your murder case?"

Again, Albert resisted sliding on his dark glasses. At last he said, "No."

"Good." Rick began packing up his paints and brushes. "Come on. Walk me home."

Apparently assuming Albert would agree to this, Rick headed back down the street. After only the smallest hesitation, Albert followed him.

They walked in silence for a few blocks, before Rick asked, "Do you have someone now, or do you still pay for it?"

"I have someone," Albert said flatly. He added, "I no longer pay for it in cash."

Rick shouted a laugh, apparently both surprised and amused. "So what does he cost you? Freedom? Or something more expensive?"

Albert didn't bother to argue with the assumption that the someone was male. "I pay for it in peace of mind. He creates a constant state of disruption."

Apparently this was amusing as well. "But you love him anyway, right?"

"That is not a word I would use."

"It's an emotion you feel, Albert."

"Really."

Rick shook his head. "You've changed in some ways but you're still stubborn, aren't you? Frustrating, too."

Not deigning to reply, Albert walked on beside the young man. He was relieved when Rick again lapsed into silence.

They soon reached their destination, an old wooden house that had been divided up into apartments. Rick jogged up the three steps to the front door and began searching his pockets for his keys. He cast a glance down at Albert, who remained at street level, and said, "Come on up. I have a couple of canvases I've been working on, a whole new direction for me. Maybe you can be rude about them. Relive old times, right?"

Albert felt infinitely wary of this situation, but he hadn't yet achieved what he'd set out to do, so he nodded once, and followed Rick through the door and up to the second floor. The house would have been rich and attractive in its prime. Now, though battered and neglected, it retained a certain dignity. Rick led Albert into his apartment, which was one of the old rooms, converted by the simple expedient of placing a sink and a hot plate in one corner.

"This place isn't much," Rick was saying, "but I like it and it's cheap." He was dumping his bag, returning his jars of paint and his brushes to his other supplies.

"It is pleasant," Albert said. The room was well proportioned, with a high ceiling, and was square, which Albert preferred to rectangles or less regular shapes. Double glass doors appeared to lead out onto the shared rear balcony.

Rick said, "Here," and backed away from two canvases that he'd propped against a wall. "What do you think?" He was frowning down at them, apparently critical of these efforts. "I love doing walls, you know? Walls are big and sort of … common, home–grown. By the people, for the people. This is new for me, and I don't know if it works."

Both canvases were covered in vital color, and both were as full of surprises as the mural, though on a smaller scale. One appeared to be an African–American man dancing and the other was lush jungle. Each canvas was square, which added to the illusion of seeing into a different self–contained world that wanted to burst into this one. "They are very effective," Albert said.

"You know, I've always loved painting, but at school they told me I had no talent. I gave it up for years because of that. Now I think maybe I was just doing things that they thought were too simple, or they didn't understand what the complexities were, or something. One of them told me this was no better than graffiti. But even graffiti is still art, you know, or the best of it, anyway. What do you think? About my stuff, I mean."

"I believe it has merit," Albert offered. "Your work is full of energy. Your teachers were wrong to discourage you."

"Really? I don't show this to everyone, you know. I mean, I haven't showed these canvases to anyone, and I've only shown the wall paintings to my boss and my friends at the diner."

"I appreciate that you are willing to show them to me."

"Good," Rick nodded, dividing his attention between his work and his companion.

After a moment's consideration, Albert said, "I purchase compact discs of classical music. Most of the covers feature a work of art. Maybe there are varieties of music that your work would suit. In fact, it would even suit some classical music."

"Album covers?" Rick asked, staring wholly at Albert now. "You really think these are good enough?"

"Yes."

"Jesus. That's wonderful."

"This one," Albert added, nodding towards the canvas of the dancer, "reminds me of the zydeco music I have heard."

Apparently Rick was spoilt for reactions. At last he asked, "You like zydeco?"

"No; a friend of mine does. I believe he would like that painting, too."

"Really?" Then Rick frowned. "You think this might sell. But where do I start?"

"I don't know, I have no experience in these matters. But I have noticed a number of street stalls in the French Quarter, where art is sold to the tourists."

"Yeah, of course. If you think this is good enough. Maybe I could put them up at the diner, too. The tourists would want something with a New Orleans flavor, that's fine, I can do that. I could do walls, still, like in a restaurant or a club or something." Rick surfaced from his thoughts, looked at Albert, and the frown turned into a smile. "You're wonderful, you know that?"

"I'm merely telling you the obvious. I'm surprised this person you work for hasn't done the same."

Albert was watching Rick but didn't feel alarmed when the younger man drew near – probably because he hadn't expected Rick to move in smoothly and kiss Albert on the mouth.

At first Albert was too startled to respond. And then he welcomed the gesture. After all, other than Fletcher, this was the only time anyone had ever voluntarily kissed him. Memories of their previous physical interaction returned; Rick was naked and moving under him again, exclaiming, 'Man, that's sexy.' But Albert found that the memories had lost their vivid immediacy. Thoughts of Fletcher intruded, along with the yearning realization of how long it had been since he and Ash had had sex.

Rick's arms were around Albert's waist. For a moment, Albert returned the embrace, but then he gently and firmly put Rick away from him. He said, "That's not why I came here, Ricardo."

"No?" the younger man murmured. "But maybe it's why you're going to stay the night."

"I don't think so."

"It'd be good."

"It would," Albert agreed. "But I have no intention of accepting your offer."

Rick turned away. "You *are* still stubborn, aren't you?" he said over his shoulder.

There was a silence. Knowing he was handling this badly, when he'd assumed it would be easy, Albert reached for his wallet. "I brought money, in case you need it."

"You wouldn't have to pay me this time."

Albert sighed, glad Rick's back was the only witness. He felt ridiculous, with the bundle of fifty–dollar bills in his hand, so he slid them into his pocket. "I would pay," he explained, "in other ways."

"Guilt? Trouble?" Rick let out a humorless laugh. "You wouldn't have to tell him, this friend of yours. Are you worried he'd leave you?"

"I doubt that he'd leave me. But, yes, I would feel something akin to guilt and remorse."

"Hasn't anyone ever offered it to you for free?"

Wondering again why he came here, Albert left a long silence before saying, "He thinks he has."

"Well, everyone needs a little disruption in their life, Albert." Rick turned to face him again, his expression and tone indicating he'd accepted defeat. "I'm sure the good outweighs the cost of having him around. And did you ever really have any peace of mind in the first place?"

"I didn't come here for homilies about my personal life," Albert informed him.

"Why, then? I thought you wanted to relive old times."

"I came to see if you were dead yet."

"No, you didn't." Rick was watching him carefully, the defeat forgotten. "You wanted to see if you'd changed. Well, you have."

"I don't think so," Albert said flatly, responding to both suggestions.

"You're more interested in me, as a person, my own person. Last time you said you were, but you wanted me to fit in with your ideas of good and bad. Now, it's like you'll let me have my own ideas, but you're still willing to help."

"Is that why you refused to let me help last time?"

"Come on, you didn't offer in a way I could accept. You weren't even trying, it was impossible." And he explained, "You didn't know me, but you decided I had a bad life, I'd made all the wrong decisions, I couldn't take care of myself."

"You're saying I was arrogant and judgmental."

Rick was brought to a halt by this bald statement. He grinned, drew close again. "Yeah, you were," he said softly. "But you've changed. You've already helped me tonight. So stay with me, Albert. Come to bed with me."

The bed in question was a pile of two single mattresses in the corner, haphazardly covered with sheets and a quilt and a variety of pillows. Albert deliberately returned his gaze to Rick's, and said, "No."

A smile reflecting both regret and amusement. "Blunt, but not rude anymore."

Albert reached into his pocket, and handed over the bundle of cash. "Take this if you need it."

Rick gaped, riffled through the bills. "Must be more than a grand here."

"Yes."

"A whole heap more than a grand. Jesus, Albert, when you do something, you do it thoroughly, don't you?" Rick looked at him. "If you're serious, I'm not going to refuse. I'm not so proud anymore."

"Then keep it," Albert said with a trace of impatience.

"Is *this* why you came?" Rick asked, and then shook his head in answer. "No. It wasn't to warn me about that man, or ask for information, or give me money because you didn't last time. Those are your excuses, Albert – but you came to see if you'd changed."

"Why would I want to do that?"

Shrugging, Ricardo said, "I can't read your mind, man. But I bet it has something to do with your friend."

"Really," Albert said shortly.

"You're not even going to ask me what I'm going to do with the money, are you? You have changed, see? Last time, you would have told me to go get a haircut and some decent clothes with it, so I could find a better job. You would have told me to get in off the streets."

"I obviously don't need to advise you anymore, Ricardo. You have begun to achieve something with your life, without my help or hindrance."

"Hey, you really like my painting? You think it's good enough to sell?"

"Yes," Albert said, the impatience obvious now.

Rick laughed, and darted in close for another kiss.

This time, Albert didn't respond, and immediately pulled away. "Don't flatter me with your persistence, Ricardo."

"I bet your friend has a thick skin, being with you." A pause, and then Rick said, "I'd give you that painting for him, if you think he'd like it. If you wouldn't be too embarrassed explaining where you got it."

Albert frowned at the painting again. "I believe he would like it. And I'm not ashamed of knowing you."

"Really?" Rick's grin was broader than ever. "Then take it."

But Albert shook his head. "It would be wisest for you to sell it through the diner, as you suggested. The theme is one that should prove commercial."

After a moment, Rick nodded. "All right, I understand. Thanks, Albert."

"Goodbye, Ricardo," Albert said. He turned away, and headed for the door, glad that Rick didn't follow him.

"Goodbye, princess," Rick murmured, his tone wistful.

Albert closed the door behind him, jogged down the stairs, and began walking away at a reasonable pace. Very glad that Rick didn't follow him. He had never expected to feel temptation. He wondered if Miles or Rebecca ever had.

CHAPTER THIRTY-ONE
NEW ORLEANS
SEPTEMBER 1985

John Garrett held himself very, very still, otherwise he might kill the young man lying on the sofa. His hands stirred restlessly. He could feel the boy's skin under his palms, feel his fingers digging into the boy's throat leaving a chain of bruises, feel the heart pounding blood through the jugular in panic; it was far more physical sensation than mere imagination. It took all he had to stop himself from actually doing it, so much strength to deny the hunger, but Garrett was sure murder would be a mistake right now and the control was the important thing, the one thing he couldn't lose.

What the hell was the guy's name? He frowned in difficult thought. Ridiculous, to let it slip his mind when Garrett saw the man every day.

All the guys at work were being ridiculous – trust it hadn't rubbed off – behaving as blind and devoted as a fan club. There were rumors, of course, with this damned FBI agent tailing him and not bothering to hide the fact. Those of his employees who had fathers and uncles and cousins on the police force soon heard the story or a version of it. But they misguidedly decided on loyalty, rebelling against the very people who wanted to save them. Pathetic that Garrett had them so thoroughly fooled, that he'd achieved this blameless cover so easily. They didn't mind that he was drinking or hungover most times, and he had a temper when hungover; didn't even mind that he was working them twice as hard. Except for one of the guys, who'd heard enough of viciousness in the rumors, who'd resigned and gone home. The only sensible one of the lot, and all he achieved was encouraging solidarity in the others, stupid idiot.

Steve here was an even bigger idiot – of course, the young man on the sofa was Steve. He'd let Garrett fuck him a couple of times, before the FBI showed up and changed everything, and now Steve assumed a familiarity, a defiant trust that Garrett found laughable, acting like he was Garrett's boyfriend. Steve obviously didn't realize he'd be dead right now if he hadn't fallen asleep.

The football had been on, the start of the new season, and Garrett had somehow divided his attention between the boy and the play. He'd been rough and demanding, and Steve loved it – every now and then Garrett was distracted from the increasingly vehement clinches by touchdowns, and Steve laughed indulgently. Seemed like Garrett would be half way through killing the guy before Steve even realized the danger he was in. Fascinating idea, to see how long it would take Steve to feel afraid if Garrett didn't make his intentions clear beforehand. When he would realize this time it was all the way, Garrett would take him to hell and leave him there, Garrett would call on the darkness and let it claim the boy.

Garrett gripped the arms of the chair, willing himself to stay still. Surely it wouldn't be smart to kill Steve. Half out of his mind on dope now, anyway, what was the point right now when the kid would be numb to the pain? When Steve woke up, maybe then – but it wouldn't be clever.

Hell, there were times when giving in to the impulse seemed to make as much sense as anything else. Amusing, to turn up at work tomorrow as if nothing had changed, and the others might take a couple of days before they began to worry about where Steve was, and maybe a few more of them would begin to suspect there was some truth to the rumors: their beloved boss got his kicks from killing young men.

Smarter, surely, to track down the one who'd resigned. Couldn't remember his name but he was a good strong lad from the country, a homely face begging to be terrified out of the few wits he had. No one would miss the kid, he was already gone.

No, Garrett wanted to do it now. If Steve hadn't fallen asleep, under the influence of the damned weed, maybe he'd have done it and to hell with the consequences. He would definitely have done the deed … How foolish. Where had the control gone?

He'd once had this spaced–out image of the deaths spanning time with all the reverberation of beats of his heart – slow deep beats, two years between each, no one else could see the perfect pattern. There was something of beauty in it, these long and elegant arches, and no one but he would know where the next column would fall, who it would destroy.

Frowning, Garrett let his eyes rove. Couldn't move the rest of him, didn't know what he'd do next if he didn't hold himself still. There was a can of beer in his hand and he remembered sharing a few already with Steve, no wonder the kid had fallen asleep on him, what with the beer and the dope. No wonder Garrett was getting poetic with this stupid weird image of the arches. It hardly applied now, with his heartbeat racing demanding.

And the football season had started, so why was he sitting here worrying over the inconsequential when he should be having fun?

Fun. The word hardly described the power and the beauty of dealing in death, the finesse of creating comprehensive terror, the joy of letting a boy's pain loose to buffet the walls the city the unknowing world.

Steve wouldn't fight him, though, wouldn't struggle. If Garrett wanted to fuck a corpse, he wouldn't have cared that Steve was lazy sleepy numb with the weed, he'd be doing it now. But, even fully conscious aware, Steve would let him take it so far – Steve wouldn't protest until way too late, would think this was just another damned game. No good.

Not like Tony back in Oregon. Only a year ago and still so vivid, those furious cursing eyes of his, the uninhibited strength of him that couldn't fight death. Glorious. Garrett adored them when they had the spunk to refuse surrender.

Only a year ago. What the hell was wrong with him, what the hell was going on in his head? It was a cardinal rule that the deaths were every two years, no more and no less. Yet here he was barely restraining himself from strangling Steve where he lay, from searching for that country boy who'd resigned, from finding his next victim and ...

The control was the important thing. He was nothing, this meant nothing, without the control.

Garrett sat in the chair, holding himself very, very still; sweating with the heat, with the effort not to move.

He stared at Steve, both confrontation and distraction. The boy lying stretched out on his back, one arm flung carelessly over his head. Sprawling abandoned. Long blond hair straggling across the cushion. A disorienting moment of, what did they call it, déjà vu, only something wasn't right.

Light brown hair instead of blond, and both arms dangling back, broken. Concentrating on the image, the face resolved into that of the corpse Garrett had found in his cellar back in Oregon, and that was one mystery solved.

He'd killed a boy, without planning to, and then forgotten all about it, even when he'd discovered and disposed of the body. Just how crazy had he been?

Garrett fumbled for the pack of cigarettes in his pocket, mind racing as fast as his heart. A mistake, a self–indulgent greedy meaningless death, and he was having great trouble stopping himself from repeating it. This was madness, surely this was madness.

Perhaps he'd made other mistakes – even as he considered the notion Garrett felt it was true, feared it was true, knew it was true. Perhaps that was how Special Agent Fletcher Ash managed to find him. Maybe all Ash's harassment, his contrary unsubtle hounding of Garrett, was Garrett's own fault. Had to be.

It was getting harder and harder to pretend that life was proceeding as normal, to maintain any kind of composure with these people tailing him everywhere, waiting for the slightest slip. That was surely what they intended. Harassing, annoying, never letting him alone. It was an obvious method but effective. The question became who would tire first. Four against one in a war of attrition – well, Garrett had beaten longer odds.

All right, Garrett thought, another attempt to figure it out. Ash said he was investigating fifteen murders in four states. He'd named three of those states, which meant Ash knew about Wyoming as well, but not Washington State or Minnesota or Illinois. Fine. But Garrett couldn't make the numbers add up to fifteen – four states, three boys in each, was only twelve.

So the kid he'd killed this time last year, dumped in the cellar and then forgotten about – he made thirteen. Sam, that was his name, he'd worked at the gas station. Garrett couldn't think who this Stacey Dixon was that Ash mentioned; a girl, for God's sake, that made no sense at all. From Ash's point of view, that was fourteen. So who the hell was the fifteenth?

Mistakes, that was the only damned answer. A vague recollection of terror, back when he first moved to New Orleans, suffering through the fear that he'd begun making mistakes, breaking his own rules, and not even realizing it at the time. Blank spots in his memory. He'd finally dismissed it as ridiculous back then, but it was his confidence that seemed ridiculous now.

That damned FBI agent had probably been onto him for years, and fool Garrett never even guessed. Ash was determined, had resolve enough to make up for a whole precinct even though he was on his own. And he had decided that this was the end for John Garrett.

Who the hell was Ash to decide such a thing? – Garrett almost cried it out loud.

Cold calculation abruptly replaced the righteous fury. Yes, Fletcher Ash was acting on his own. His ragtag friends from Washington hardly counted for much. Garrett's fool buddy Halligan was probably hindering Ash as much as helping him. But, even if no one in the FBI or the police force was taking Ash seriously, Garrett was too smart not to.

And what that all added up to was that Ash was alone, and Ash was therefore vulnerable.

Garrett smiled. He'd been more than clever over the years. Few men got away with what Garrett had. He was definitely clever enough to deal with Fletcher Ash. There were always options for a man as clever and as ruthless as John Garrett.

Maybe he'd feel better about this if he took it all the way with Steve. Maybe he should get away with murder yet again, satisfy the old hunger, feel the return of the control for all the hunger of the years to come. Prove to himself, and to Ash if he were paying enough attention, that John Garrett was going all the way to the Super Bowl. Maybe that was the best idea right now.

There was a knock at the front door.

Ridiculous how something so trivial could set his heart pounding again, just because it was unexpected. Garrett remained in the chair, hands clutching cramping, willing the stupid panic away. He dragged his gaze away from Steve, who hadn't stirred. Had to deal with this, so it was all right if he moved now, it was safe. Garrett lit the cigarette he'd been holding, stood stiff after this tense hour, this muscle–taut evening, went to investigate.

Special Agent Fletcher Ash standing outside, arms folded, posture weary. He could hardly look less threatening if he tried, so it was probably an act. "Mr. Garrett," the man said, as if this was nothing out of the ordinary. "May I come in?"

Fumbling to regain the attitude necessary to deal with this man, Garrett snapped, "Why?" He thought to glance down at the street, but Garrett could see no sign of the man's friends, and Ash's car seemed empty.

"You've said a few times that you want to talk, Mr. Garrett. So let's talk."

"It's after ten, Special Agent." He said it shortly, checking his watch, as if he'd been asleep.

Ash held his right hand up, palm out, to show it was empty. "I didn't bring my credentials. This isn't official."

"It's after ten, Mr. Ash." Garrett sighed his impatience. His mind was clearing, the confidence beginning to return. It was only now, when he needed to make sense, that he realized how incoherent his thoughts had been. He grabbed for the shit–eating attitude, tried to make it his own again, and said, "It's late for a social call."

The man replied with a shrug. "You said you wanted to talk, I thought this might be a good time, in your home, without the distractions of work. You suggested we could sort this out, Mr. Garrett, so let's try."

None of that could be true, Ash couldn't possibly want to deal with Garrett one on one, outside the law: the special agent, credentials or not, must have some other agenda. Frowning, Garrett asked, "Where's your motley crew? Where's that goon you always have tagging along beside you?"

"I gave them the night off, which they richly deserved. So it's just you and me, Mr. Garrett, like you wanted. Let's sort this out."

Of course it was too good an opportunity for Garrett to let pass, which only increased his mistrust of Ash. What in hell did the man expect to accomplish? But what did Garrett have to lose? If things didn't go well, Garrett could always heap on the righteous indignation, and throw Ash out – meanwhile, Ash was not only alone and vulnerable, but alone and vulnerable in Garrett's house. Garrett's lair. The man was a bigger idiot than Steve.

After a long moment, Garrett nodded in agreement, stepped back to let Ash through, then closed the door behind him. How best to bypass the living room and the complication of Steve's presence? "Do you want a beer?" Garrett asked, expecting a refusal but planning on getting one for himself.

But Ash said, "Yeah."

They ended up in the kitchen, sitting opposite each other at the table, sipping at their cans of beer. Mind racing, Garrett forced half his attention to watch the man, trying to figure him out, and the other half to deciding how to approach this. He guessed he had to show Ash the same face he presented to the rest of the world. Consistency was important vital. Every other man in America was fooled by Garrett's friendly I'm–just–one–of–the–boys routine. Hell, Garrett enjoyed it so much that he even fooled himself sometimes. It hadn't appealed to Ash but it was worth one more try.

"You look exhausted," Garrett observed at last, with a good pretence of sympathy. And it was true enough. There was nothing more than nervous energy in Ash.

"No worse than you," Ash said, not denying this vulnerability. Must be an act, wanting to draw Garrett out. The FBI agent added, "It's been a long four years."

"What has been? This case?"

"I found the bodies in Colorado four and a half years ago and I've been on your trail ever since. Amongst dealing with other things. However, if you're hoping I'll collapse in an exhausted heap now, Mr. Garrett, when I've finally found you, you're in for a surprise or two."

Garrett shook his head, as if he didn't understand Ash's meaning. Playing dumb innocent uncomprehending.

A silence. Ash prompted, "You wanted to talk."

"Sure." It had been a bluff, of course. Garrett almost grimaced, very inappropriate. What would the reasonable intelligent man say at this stage? "I wanted to know why you're doing this, Special Agent, why you're accusing me." Garrett took a moment to swallow some more beer, offered an apologetic shrug. "I wanted to ask you to stop. You're not good for business. I already lost one of my staff, it's a wonder I haven't lost them all."

"I'm doing this because you're guilty, Mr. Garrett, it's that simple. Therefore I will not stop until I've brought you to justice."

The man's tone had been flat, but still with that edge of determination. Seemed like Ash would carry that edge until his dying day. If Garrett didn't deal with the man one way or another, this would be the end, like Ash wanted.

A mild panic as Garrett feared he'd left too long a pause in the conversation, his sense of time failing him. He smiled a little, hoping to cover himself. "Tell me about your case," Garrett suggested. "Tell me why you think I'm guilty."

Ash sat back. He was watching Garrett carefully, but trying to appear casual. "There's no point in discussing the evidence because it's all circumstantial. Otherwise I'd have arrested you already, as you said. But I saw the truth in your eyes, Mr. Garrett. You're a serial killer."

Garrett laughed in surprise at this bold bald statement. Was Ash trying sincerity, or was this a bluff as well? The laugh turned confident, as Garrett's wits returned. "I'm not surprised no one else believes you, Ash," he confided. "There isn't a jury in the world who'd convict me because of something you thought you saw in my eyes."

"But I will make sure you are convicted."

Garrett gestured expansively, the most genuine and reasonable of men. "What can I say to convince you that I'm innocent?"

Ash was refusing to buy, though Garrett was hardly surprised at this stage. The FBI agent said, "There's nothing you can say. But, if you're serious about proving your innocence, there's one thing you can do: come down to the police station and let me take your fingerprints. It's a simple procedure; it would only take a few minutes."

A long moment, while Garrett's mind sped up again. Surely he'd been cleverer than that. "Why?" he asked at last. "You have the man's fingerprints?"

"I have a partial print from a boy's shoe. If your prints don't match, I don't have any case at all."

Garrett couldn't believe this intense man would let the case go for something as mundane as a lack of evidence. But how to call that bluff? Garrett eventually said, "A partial print? As in, just part of one fingerprint? You and your forensics goon could make anything match that." He shook his head, and sat back, confidently matching Ash's posture. "No. I won't do it. I'm not guilty but I don't trust you that much."

Ash said, "Then I will continue to work on this case until I get enough evidence to convict you."

Humorless bastard, Garrett thought. What did Ash hope to accomplish? That interview at the police station, Ash seemed like he was going through the motions. The harassment since had been dogged. Tonight, Ash was dispirited. So what had driven the man through four years of investigation? Garrett suspected feared he was missing something here.

Giving himself a moment, Garrett took a long swig of the beer. Specifics, had to deal with the detail. He'd left all his boys naked, so where did this shoe come from? It might be safe even wise to volunteer his fingerprints, if the shoe was from some unrelated case Ash had mistakenly attributed to Garrett. Unless Ash was lying and this was a trick. No doubt the FBI agent was more than capable of that kind of double–think, which was fine because Garrett was, too.

And then Garrett remembered Sam. That body in the cellar in Oregon, fully dressed, except his sneakers tossed loose beside him. Garrett had pushed them back on, unlaced. But obviously he hadn't been careful enough. *No*, he concluded. *No deal.* This bastard had more than he thought.

Garrett returned his attention to the man sitting opposite him, and smiled again, despite the flicker of fear in his gut. He said, "Sounds like checkmate. You won't believe I'm innocent, and you sure as hell won't convince me I'm guilty. What happens next?"

"You tell me," Ash said.

"I'll tell you," Garrett said. What the hell did Ash want out of this? "All I want is for you to get out of my life." He was frustrated with this and he let it show. Ash had suggested they talk, and all he'd done was threaten Garrett with a fingerprint. A partial fingerprint. What else did he have? Garrett said, "I'm going to file a complaint, like Halligan suggests, and the damned courts will tell you to leave me alone."

"But I won't leave you alone. You're a murderer, Mr. Garrett."

Maybe Ash was here to let Garrett know how serious he was. *All right.* That was a game two could play. Deliberately keeping his tone conversational, Garrett said, "If all this were true, I could kill you now, Mr. Ash. Why come here and put yourself at risk?"

Ash didn't betray the slightest surprise. "I took the risk because bringing you to justice is my only priority. I'm not going to let you kill me."

Garrett lit a cigarette, frowning as if he were considering a few things. "But the man you're after has no limits. If you've cornered him, he's desperate. How would you stop him?"

"I didn't bring my credentials, but I did bring my gun."

Shrugging as if all this were new to him, Garrett said, "Let me warn you, Special Agent: New Orleans is a crazy dangerous city. No one would think twice if you were found dead on a street corner, mugged and beaten." Who cared about reasonable? At this point, Garrett just wanted to convince. "No one would pay any notice if your body was hauled up out of Lake Pontchartrain in a fishing net early one morning."

Still no reaction. "I know someone who'd notice. And you would be the obvious suspect."

"What? Your friends would pick up where you left off?"

"They would. Dr. Sterne would make sure you were arrested, tried and convicted."

"Sterne? The goon who has his hands on – and in – dead bodies all day. Imagine getting *paid* for that, what a great job." Garrett grinned, but Ash refused to react. Insinuating now: "What did he do to those dead boys you found, after the killer finished with them?"

"If you're trying to discomfort me, that's not the way to do it, Mr. Garrett."

Serious advice, one man to another: "He's nothing but a forensic pathologist, Ash. If he hasn't provided you with the evidence you need with all these other murders – *fifteen* of them – then how far would he get with just one?"

Ash considered him across the table, apparently unmoved. He took a last sip of his beer, and put the can down, then commented, "You must be scared, Garrett, to threaten me like this."

Garrett shrugged, endeavoring to appear as relaxed as the other man. Difficult, when all he wanted to do was throttle this guy – slowly, so Ash had plenty of time to realize he had lost. How would the fear look in Ash's eyes when he saw the darkness coming to claim him? Garrett shrugged off the lovely image, said, "I'm simply warning you to be careful who you're dealing with."

"You're scared, all right," Ash repeated. His voice was quiet, but full of confidence. There was the smallest damned smile on his face. "I guess you know who you're dealing with, too."

The crazy thing was for that moment he didn't know how to respond. Garrett watched the man, waiting, almost as if mesmerized. The lull in the conversation became full of suspense. Garrett wanted to shake himself out of it, but couldn't. He wanted to push the table out of the way and feel Ash's throat under his palms, but didn't.

And Ash abruptly leaned forward, slammed his hand down on the table – the sharp noise cracked the silence apart – "You're scared because *this* is the end of the line, Garrett. *I* am the end of the line." Ash didn't raise his voice, but the sudden focus to his intensity had the same effect. "Don't make the mistake of underestimating me because I'm on the side of law and order. Don't think there's anything I won't do, don't imagine I'll draw the line anywhere. I am prepared to do anything it takes to bring you to justice."

Impressed despite himself, Garrett protested, "There's no need for all this drama, Mr. Ash."

"It's not drama, Mr. Garrett, this is real. You're not the only one acting without limits."

About to retort, unsure of what to say, Garrett was interrupted saved by a younger voice: "What's all the racket?"

It was Steve, of course, standing in the doorway to the living room in nothing but his jeans. The kid was stretching, sleepily provocative but Garrett found far more of interest in the sight of Special Agent Fletcher Ash: there were *shock horror* headlines written all over him. He glanced at Garrett, back at the boy, and then fixed his gaze on Garrett again. Accusing. Afraid.

Garrett could hardly stop laughing. He managed to ask, "Didn't your friends tell you he was here? Didn't they put out a red alert?" He beckoned the kid over, slipped an arm around his waist. "Steve, this is Fletcher. He's looking like that because he thought we were alone." Garrett chuckled some more. "Fletcher, this is Steve. He works for me."

"Hey." Steve murmured a lazy greeting, propping himself on Garrett's shoulder as if he were still too stoned to stand.

Ash nodded once. If Garrett's laughter was getting in the way of speech, Ash's fear was having the same effect. He finally said, "Hello, Steve."

"Actually, your friends didn't miss him," Garrett explained to the FBI agent, in a reassuring tone he knew would only add annoyance. *Too clever for you.* "I gave Steve my keys, told him to let himself in this afternoon. Didn't want you all leaping to the wrong conclusion."

"I see," Ash said with great disapproval.

"That's a cool name," Steve was saying, somehow not picking up on all this tension. Idiot. "Fletcher, like Fletcher Christian in that movie, right?"

A brief silence, and then Ash smiled with a great deal of effort. "My father was a writer," he said to the boy. The words were halting, this was unexpected. "He has a writer's imagination. My brother's called Harley, but our names have nothing to do with motorbikes or *Mutiny on the Bounty.*"

"It's still cool." Steve leaned in even closer to Garrett. "Hey, John, I've got the munchies real bad. Can I raid your fridge?"

"Help yourself. And get me another beer, kid, all right?" Garrett turned to Ash, almost laughed again – Ash was still looking surprised. "How about you?"

"No."

Garrett waited until he had the beer and the kid's attention was solely on the contents of the fridge. It had been amusing enough to get Steve here behind Ash's back but the special agent's reactions were even funnier. Garrett leaned across the table to share the joke, said, "Gave you a scare, didn't I?"

Ash leaned in close, too – odd because he'd physically avoided Garrett at the interview, hadn't loosened up since. He said, very low, "If you think I'm going to let you hurt even one more young man, you are gravely mistaken."

"Gravely," Garrett echoed. "That's very good, under the circumstances." He laughed again, defying Ash's taut expression, which demanded silence.

Steve soon wandered over with a plate of haphazard sandwiches, and sat down at the table. Garrett hauled his chair closer to the boy, sliding his arms around the slender waist. The kid began eating – but Garrett, in a merry mood, nuzzled into Steve's neck, mouthing and biting the flesh, threatening to tear at the skin with his teeth. The boy rolled his head back, still chewing away while happily accepting these advances. "Hey, John," he murmured, "let me finish this first, okay?"

"Sure, kid," Garrett replied. "Then we'll have some fun." Plans for this boy rapidly unfolded in his imagination; beautiful, thoroughly cruel plans. Blood surged at the power of it, amusement fading to nothing. Heedless of Ash, Garrett almost groaned in need. This time would be even better than all the others. Experience counted for so much.

The coldest of tones, the FBI agent said, "We have business to discuss, Mr. Garrett. Why don't you leave Steve alone?"

Garrett looked over at Ash, about to protest, but was instead distracted by the man's expression. The shock and the fear had been joined by fascination. Ash was sickened but he knew what Garrett was wanting to do with this boy. Yes, Ash knew, and in glorious detail. Garrett murmured, "You told me what you saw in my eyes, Ash, now I'll tell you what I see in yours."

Silence. Steve continued eating, oblivious to all. Ash seemed to be holding himself very, very still.

"During that interview, describing all those terrible things. And right now. You understand, don't you, Ash?" Garrett laughed at the thought of it. Of course, Ash had managed to track Garrett down because he had an idea of what sort of man the killer was. "Interesting. That's why you've been so obsessed with this case, isn't it? Because you know how it feels to do those things. Tell me."

"No," Ash said flatly. He was tense, as if still but wanting to leap into action. Did he imagine Garrett would rape Steve here and now, on the kitchen table? Surely he knew Garrett had more finesse than that. The question became whether he would leap in to protect Steve, or to join Garrett.

"No," Garrett echoed, considering the man. "No, you're right, you don't exactly understand. Because you've never actually done it. So why don't you try?" Without facing the boy, Garrett said, "Steve, can you handle two of us tonight?"

"Sure," was the immediate reply, with a wolfish grin.

Fierce, Ash said, "Tell him what you mean, Garrett. You're not just after sex, are you? You want more, far more than Steve would be willing to give."

Garrett glared fury at the man, and sat back. *Don't spoil our chance, Ash.* He let Steve go, just a hand on his waist. "No need to scare the kid," he protested. "Anyway, he likes it rough, don't you, Steve? Don't get prudish on me, Fletcher."

"There *is* a need to scare him," Ash contradicted. He reached into a pocket, placed a twenty–dollar bill on the table. "Steve, here's some money. Call a cab from the phone booth round the corner and go home. Mr. Garrett and I have some things to discuss."

The kid frowned, turned to Garrett. Once he'd swallowed his mouthful of sandwich, Steve said, "You want me to leave? I thought we were gonna have a good time. I don't mind if it's both of you."

Garrett thought hungry about what the good time would have involved. Ash better make this worth his while. "I thought so, too, kid. In fact," Garrett turned to Ash, "perhaps Fletcher should be the one to leave."

"You know very well that I won't," Ash said with his flat determination.

"All you want to do is discuss business. That's not half as much fun as Steve staying here."

Ash stared at Garrett, anger fierceness adding fire to the direct gaze. That had provoked him, sure enough. "You're right," Ash said at last. "I understand. I'll talk about that with you if you want, but Steve doesn't have to know. There's more than business for us to discuss, Garrett. Let him go."

That was the offer he wanted. Always the urge to get away with all this pain and death, and then tell the world about it once he was done. Enough in itself to achieve so much through his charm and wits – but Garrett also wanted people to realize what he'd accomplished. To be in awe of it all. And here was someone who could understand, who could see the perfection of it. Someone who knew how clever Garrett was to avoid getting caught. Garrett could leave his story to this man. If Ash survived he would tell the world. For that, Garrett could do without the boy. For now. "Steve, take Fletcher's money, and go home."

Shrugging, though he was disappointed, the boy said, "Well, all right." He stood, collected the last of the sandwiches in one hand, and stuffed the money into a hip pocket with the other. "I'll see you at work tomorrow, John."

"Sure." Garrett managed a smile when the boy leaned in to press a kiss to his forehead, then waited impatiently until Steve had located his shirt and shoes, and the front door closed behind him.

"You're a clever man, Garrett," Ash said once they were alone. "You like the fact you've gotten away with fifteen murders. You'd love to get away with one more, right under my nose, wouldn't you? That would have been quite something for you, killing a boy, with an FBI agent sitting outside the house."

Silence. Time for confession, time for truth. Garrett said slowly deliberately, "Yes. That would have been something."

Ash nodded. "You've been clever – but you're losing control, Garrett. You're making mistakes and have been for years. You can't afford to be that daring. It's hardly smart to prey on a boy I could link to you through your business here, when I'm watching you so closely." And he leaned forward again to make his point: "The control was important to you, wasn't it? But it's gone now. You've lost it."

Not bothering to reply, Garrett considered the man for a while. Ash should be glad they finally had the truth between them. Instead he just accepted it with the same matter–of–fact manner he'd used with Garrett since the interview. Eventually, Garrett prompted, "Tell me, Ash. Tell me what you think this is, if you understand it so well."

Barely hesitating, and with the direct gaze never faltering, Ash murmured, "I understand what it means to you. That their death be slow, that their terror be great. That their fear and your joy, their pain and your life, be one and the same. That your control over them be absolute. That they suffer like you've suffered."

"Sounds like poetry, Fletcher. You're a writer, like your father."

"No."

Garrett suddenly leaned forward, too. "How can you understand it that well, and not *do* it?"

"I understand, but I want you to tell me about it. I want to know all you've done."

"Better to show, not tell," Garrett suggested, sly but serious. "I'll go call the kid back." He remembered the boy's name with an effort. "Steve, I'll get Steve back here."

"No," Ash said again. "Tonight it's just you and me."

"Then I'll show you, Fletcher, I'll show *you*." Garrett grinned. "You're older than I like them, but you'll do fine. And you'll put up a fight, won't you? You were right about Mitch: he went down fighting, and I loved that." The words came so smooth, words he'd never spoken to anyone, had a power all their own. "Tony was the same, fought me every inch of the way, cursed me with his dying breath. It's best like that, but it's never been perfect, it's never quite perfect. Maybe it will be when I show you, and you'll understand everything I do to you, how will that be?"

"You're not going to show me," Ash said easily, as if he felt quite safe. If Ash had drawn away, or been afraid, Garrett knew the impulse to go for the man would have been too strong to resist. Unaware of how close he was to danger, Ash continued, "I told you, this is the end of the line."

Garrett stared at him for a moment. Perhaps he could have it both ways, have everything, of course he could – they could talk, Ash would be amazed, would be truly afraid – and when the words stopped flowing, then maybe a demonstration. Garrett nodded, and said, "All right. I'll tell you, tell it all. Because you'll understand, won't you?" And then he saw the difference between them, should have realized from the first. "You don't *like* that you understand. You hate that about yourself."

"Yes."

"You hate that you're capable of murder, that you were tempted to join me with the boy tonight."

Ash just stared at him, not bothering to voice any denials.

"It's been a long four years, you said. And you're never going to leave it behind, are you? This will be with you all your life, what I've done and what you've understood. But you still want to know." Garrett nodded again. "I'll tell you all of it. But when I'm finished talking, then one of us dies."

Ash still seemed unafraid of the threat, damn the man to hell. He said, "Mr. Garrett, when you're finished telling me, then I'm going to arrest you."

"No, you won't," Garrett said firmly. He'd decided years ago he'd never go through jail, and psychiatric evaluations, and a trial, and the newspapers telling lies uncomprehending, and still more jail until blind society finally decided to execute him. John Garrett deserved better than that. He said to Ash, "If I die, then you tell the world all I achieved. You carry on with the burden of knowing everything that I did. Will that ruin your life, Ash?" There was no reply. Garrett continued, "If you're the one who dies, well, we've had a fascinating conversation. That's the deal."

"You call murder an achievement, Mr. Garrett?"

"You know it is, Ash. Fifteen deaths – more than fifteen, if you want to hear about it – and I'm still free." A pause, when Ash should have jumped at the chance. "Come on," Garrett said. "You found me, so I know you're not stupid. This is the best offer you'll ever get."

Ash said, "If we're going to do this, I need to tape it."

Garrett smiled. "You think you're gonna survive tonight?"

"Oh yes," Ash said easily. "We both are. And this will be invaluable evidence."

A long moment, and then Garrett agreed with a shrug. What could it matter, whichever way this ended? If Garrett was the one to survive, these tapes could join his collection of memorabilia, in amongst the chains and earrings of the dead boys. He could add to them later, maybe even tape Ash's death as well, and leave the lot to someone in his will. Someone appropriate like the Director of the FBI.

If Ash lived, then he would have all the detail, in Garrett's own words, to publicize. And to haunt him at night.

Garrett stood and went to fetch the cassette player from on top of the fridge.

CHAPTER THIRTY-TWO
NEW ORLEANS
SEPTEMBER 1985

Fletcher sat there at the rickety old kitchen table, across from John Garrett, with nothing to do but watch him. The man's mood was almost contemplative now, a distinct contrast from the euphoria of half an hour ago, and different again from the dull confusion when Fletch had first appeared on his doorstep. Garrett had grabbed up a handful of music cassettes, saying with a laugh that he'd buy replacements the next day, and was now carefully fixing a piece of tape over the end of each so that they could be recorded over. He was engrossed in the simple task and in his own thoughts, and seemed not to notice the silence. He might have forgotten Fletcher's presence.

Considering the man with as much objectivity as he could muster, Fletch decided his first impressions weren't far wrong. He could still see how Drew Harmer might have found John Garrett attractive. Garrett was a couple of inches taller than Fletch, built on a more generous scale, and smoothly handsome with his grey hair and blue eyes. Right now, while Garrett was quiet, it didn't take too large a leap of imagination to see how Drew had thought the man good for cuddling. And no doubt the boy had been taken in by the man's friendly all-charm and no-nonsense attitude.

The silence stretched. Fletcher remained outwardly calm, although internally he was afraid and so tense it was as if someone was squeezing his gut in two mammoth fists. He was also in dire need of something to focus on other than his own thoughts and emotions. To his surprise, for it seemed the most inappropriate of situations, he was considering the nature of love.

He was in danger, Fletch knew that all too well, and he kept a very wary eye on Garrett. As far as he could see, though, Garrett had no weapons to hand – and Fletcher's gun was a reassuring and worrying weight between his ribs and his arm – but Fletch didn't even begin to trust the man. Fletch was in danger and, right now, he was free to reflect on all the causes and possible consequences of the situation.

The fact that Garrett was willing to talk, and on tape, meant that he was intending to kill Fletcher. Garrett surely didn't want Fletch to be able to use this knowledge or these tapes to convict him. At least, that was the logical conclusion – but Garrett wasn't behaving consistently or logically. He was acting on impulse, reckless in all he said and did. The friendly innocent act of his was coming apart at the seams and even though he'd now decided to tell the truth to Fletcher, Garrett had already spent the evening revealing far more of himself than he'd intended.

There was one definition of love Fletcher had heard, about a readiness to put the other before yourself. Well, Fletch was sadder for Albert's sake than for his own right now. Fletch wouldn't mind losing his life if it meant Garrett lost his as well.

Of course the best result, the one Fletcher grimly reminded himself he must work towards, was surviving and arresting Garrett, with ample evidence at hand of all the man's crimes. And these tapes that Garrett was still fiddling with would provide that.

But if Fletcher died, it would hurt Albert. Fletch knew that the loss would hurt Albert so damned much. In fact, Fletcher's death would hurt Albert even more than the death of his parents had. Their deaths had at least left the boy capable of love. Fletcher's would destroy the one chance the man ever had. Fletcher considered this notion with a great deal of grief, and only the smallest sense of triumph.

Albert loved, even if he'd never admit it, but he'd never believed Fletch loved him. *Why not?* Fletch silently cried out. He preferred his own definition of love, vague though it was. Something about being true to yourself, and offering yourself openly and honestly to the other. Letting them challenge who you really are, and challenging in turn. *Didn't I do that, Albert? Did I fail, or did you fail to see?* Fletcher had played a part in so many other doomed relationships, he now wondered why he'd expected this one to work.

The important point was that Albert would continue, Albert would forever endure. The hurt would not be fatal. But if John Garrett remained free, the hurt he inflicted would be deadly, and there would be more victims – many more victims, and so much more hurt than that relating to the broken heart of a solitary forensics expert.

Just in case, Fletcher had tried to say goodbye. Tried to write something, though he'd soon given up. He'd read the words he committed to paper with Albert's critical eye, and dismissed them as melodramatic. Anyway, why would Albert believe a posthumous written declaration of love, when he'd refused to be swayed by Fletcher's verbal protestations?

His own life and Albert's miserable repression were worth ending Garrett's freedom. Albert would probably have agreed, if Fletch had asked.

Fletcher distracted himself with the observation that Albert would deplore Garrett's taste in music, which appeared to be mostly country and western, with some Elvis thrown in for good measure. From the number of cassettes, Garrett planned a long and detailed confession. What might happen after that was, at this stage, anyone's guess – though Fletcher was absolutely determined that, one way or the other, this was the end of the line for John Garrett.

Finished with his task at last, Garrett was turning a cassette over and over in his hands, quite distracted by it. Eventually he looked up and said, "One of the guys left this, back in Oregon. Metallica isn't my thing. Don't know why I kept it."

"What happened to him?"

After a moment, Garrett looked up at Fletch, an amused glint in his eye. "Don't worry, Fletcher, I let that one go. He was just a runaway. Fed him, gave him some money, told him to go home. I guess he forgot his tape, though. He'd play the damned thing twenty–four hours a day because he didn't have a cassette player of his own."

Fletcher nodded, feeling unwilling gratitude for this small example of – surely it was self–preservation rather than compassion, to let the boy go, even though letting him listen to his music was the act of a friend.

"See," Garrett said, "I can be a nice guy, too. What did you say? You've never met a civilized serial killer before." He grinned. *Well, you have now.*

Barely restraining himself from reacting with at least skepticism, wishing Albert were here to cut the guy down to size with some choice sarcasm, Fletcher said, "Let's do this." When Garrett nodded, Fletcher put one of the other cassettes in the player, and pressed the record button. "Tape one, side one. This is Fletcher Ash talking with John

Garrett. It is eleven–forty on the night of September first, 1985." A slow breath, and then Fletcher began. "John, you said you'd tell me all about these matters I'm investigating. Would you confirm for the record that you're doing this voluntarily?"

"Sure," Garrett said, sounding amused at these niceties. "I'm not under any duress."

"Thank you. Where would you like to start?"

"Where do you want me to start?"

Garrett still expected Fletcher to take the lead in this conversation, seemed surprised that Fletcher mostly refused to take the initiative. He hadn't yet realized this confession had to be Garrett's choice, Garrett's words, without Fletcher prompting. After a moment, Fletcher said, "Tell me about the last time you killed someone."

"Tony, back in Oregon, right?"

"You haven't committed murder here in New Orleans?"

"Not yet," Garrett said with a broad grin, looking directly at Fletch. But then Garrett's expression degenerated into puzzlement. "Don't think so. There was a guy, last year, I thought about it."

"What was his name?"

"Zac. Hooked on coffee. Street kid, lived in a place falling apart down in the French Quarter, probably squatting. I picked him up for sex. Maybe I went back and killed him and his nosy friend."

"Who was the friend?"

"Idiot of a girl. Self–righteous just because I got a bit rough with the guy." Garrett shrugged. "It was no big deal. I paid them to shut up. She took the money but she didn't like it."

"You thought of killing them to shut them up?"

"Thought about it," Garrett repeated. "Don't know if I did."

"How does that make you feel, that you can't remember?"

Silence for a while. Then Garrett said, "Tony was magnificent. Thrill's in the hunt as well as the kill, you know. He was as straight as they come, knew I had my eye on him, but he trusted me enough to have a drink with me, to come home with me. Had to do some smooth talking for that one. Fought once he realized, almost got away, determined to be free, but not as determined as I was to have him. Would have beaten the life out of me. Sweet to take him lower than he ever thought possible. Be in control of someone who never lets anyone get the better of him."

"Where did you meet him? Where did you take him for a drink?" And Fletcher worked on getting all the detail from Garrett, much of which could be verified. There might be witnesses at the bar Garrett mentioned, even after all this time. The very existence of the bar would add substance to Garrett's story, with the pool tables he and Tony played at, and the decor he described. There had been mirrors on the wall, which provided the chance to watch not only Tony but a half–dozen reflections of him – and also to let Tony catch Garrett at it. Shared glances through the slightly unreal medium of the mirrors, Garrett of course getting turned on and Tony merely amused, too confident to feel the danger.

And then, of course, there was all the detail of what Garrett had done with the young man once they'd reached Garrett's house. Fletcher listened as Garrett described what caused each of the injuries Albert had so meticulously listed in his report. Worse than his imaginings of it, to know the hot and brutal truth; somehow worse to know the truth, even in the few instances where his imaginings had been crazier, crueler. Fletch did not want to be here, did not want to be listening to this, did not want to be seeing this so damned vivid in his mind's eye, breathing in the night's heavy humidity.

"You really do understand, don't you, Fletcher?" Garrett said after he'd described Tony's death. "It's wound so deep inside that you'll never be free of it."

"Perhaps."

Garrett began rambling again. "The other two in Oregon, I suggested they try this sexual asphyxia thing. You know about that, Ash? Tony wouldn't have been into it, though, not as keen or queer as the others. Half–strangled, could do what I liked with them." He frowned, losing some enthusiasm. "Wasn't as exciting as it should have been, have to admit. Mistake – no, misjudgment. Used a silk scarf. Soft, shouldn't have been any sign of it. Did your goon find any trace?"

Fletcher started, stirred from the troubling images. "No," he said. "Dr. Sterne knew the cause of death and suggested the use of a scarf, but he couldn't say for sure."

"He's not stupid. Neither are you, Fletcher. Wouldn't have got this far otherwise. But wasn't smart to come here tonight."

Fletch asked, "How did you dispose of Tony's body?"

"You want all that boring stuff as well?"

"You don't find it boring," Fletcher said. "That part of it is almost as significant to you as the violence. And just as necessary, in its own way."

Garrett considered him for too long a moment. But, apparently willing to explore his own deeds and motivations rather than Fletcher's – apparently too self-centered to really take an interest in this other man – Garrett continued, describing the care he took and how clever he was. There were plenty of details that the public didn't know. This was exactly the kind of evidence Fletch needed.

The story of Tony Shield's death took almost a full tape. Fletcher stopped the player, and put a fresh cassette in, thinking for a moment about the young man as he must have been in life. The images were so vivid, it felt as if Fletch had known him. But the combination of grief and fear was almost enough to undo him, so Fletch put the thoughts aside and pressed the record button. "Tape two, side one. Tell me about the first time you killed, John. What happened?"

"Why do you want to know? It doesn't really count."

"Tell me why it doesn't count."

Shrugging, Garrett said, "It was beautiful, sure. But it was an accident. It wasn't planned. I hardly knew how to enjoy it. What I've done since is more significant."

"I'm no psychologist, John," Fletcher said, "but I'd have thought that the first time and the last time are the most significant of all. Do you disagree?"

"It's all significant," Garrett insisted.

"Yes." A moment to gather himself, then Fletcher offered, "You said yourself that getting away with murder is an achievement in itself. Humor me. Tell me about the first time. How did you get away with it if you didn't have any plans?"

The flattery seemed to work. After a moment, Garrett said, "Took me a while to figure out I was queer. When I did, I always liked it rough, and once it went too far. A kid called Mark, back in Illinois. I was twenty-four. Didn't know what to do, figured I may as well just enjoy it. Took him three hours to die. Glorious."

"What was Mark's last name?"

"Only remember their first names. When I'm in the middle of it, Ash, they're nothing more than flesh and blood, they don't have names. But I try to remember, it's only fair. Like them with spunk, like them to be real, you know?"

"Where did you meet Mark?"

"Cruising. He was just a whore." Garrett must have read Fletcher's fleeting protest, for he laughed and said, "Expendable. They're *all* expendable, Ash. That why you don't like understanding this? You don't like thinking all these guys are nothing more than flesh and blood? They're there to be used, you know. You can let some of them go, give them some food and money to shut them up. The ones you don't let go, you give them to the ground afterwards, that's all right. But don't let the rules and regulations get in the way, don't let society make you impotent."

Fletch nodded as if he understood all this, even agreed with it. *No rules, you cruel bastard. That was your beginning, and it will be your end.* Fletcher nodded some more, swallowed hard, feared and suspected he wasn't behaving as consistently as he should. Had to fool this man, continue to fool him. Finally he said, with a firmer voice than he would have thought possible, "What caused this first death? I would think there was some event in your life that triggered the act."

"It was a mistake, I wasn't prepared. Had no idea. Would have happened sooner or later, though. Always liked it rough." Garrett's interest abruptly focused. "It's a shock, finding out who you really are. What you are. Makes sense, all adds up, sure – but still a shock. Tried to end it then. Does that surprise you?"

Garrett was unbuttoning his left shirtsleeve, pushing it up to his elbow, laying his arm on the table, palm up. There was a long scar down Garrett's forearm, unswerving, so that Fletch could imagine the force behind it driving the knife deep through the flesh. Fletch knew that some serial killers became suicidal, just as he knew that the first and the last deaths were the most significant, but he also guessed that John Garrett would not take kindly to comparisons to other people, favorable to Garrett or not. Fletch decided to say, "It does surprise me, John. Tell me why you did that."

"It was a shock, like I said. To realize that's what it was all about. The death. The pain and the terror and the death." The man paused for reflection. "Guess I thought I wasn't up to it. Wasn't clever enough to take it all the way, to invite the darkness back again and again. You can see the darkness coming, you can see it in their eyes. It's incredible. Terrifying. But the darkness didn't take me. This is what I became. Of course I'm clever enough, brave enough. I guess not everyone is, right, Ash?"

"No, not everyone." As Garrett talked more about those first days, about the neighbor who'd called an ambulance in time, Fletcher's mind cried, *Why didn't the damned darkness take you, too?* A death for a death, Garrett carrying out his own justice, that was surely fairer than the man surviving to kill at least fifteen more. But, if that was so, why should that long–ago boy Mark be sacrificed to save the other lives, to save Fletcher's sanity? Fletch might as well ask why Garrett even existed. No point in getting into all that now, probably no point in getting into it ever.

Fletch didn't want to be here, didn't want to be doing this. But, seeing as he was, he might as well do it the best he could. When Garrett had quieted again, Fletcher said, "Let's talk about the other victims. You said there were more than fifteen in total."

"Can't even figure how you got fifteen."

"Let's run through those," Fletch suggested, "and then you can tell me about the others."

"You know about Wyoming, Colorado, Georgia and Oregon. Three boys in each state, that's all I allow myself, gets dangerous otherwise. Except there was this kid, Sam, in Oregon. Didn't mean for that to happen. That's thirteen, Ash, not fifteen. And there was blood in my cellar, too, but you wouldn't know about that. I mean, you didn't get in there, right? I sealed it up."

"No, I didn't know about that. Tell me."

Garrett almost laughed. "Don't know, either, Ash. I'd dumped Sam down there, but it wasn't his blood. Perhaps this tramp I picked up for sex, when I first arrived, thought about it then, cutting a cross into his arm like I cut mine. But I think I let him go. Maybe I got him later, maybe it was someone else."

"I see," Fletcher said. "Are you having trouble remembering some of the deaths?"

A fierce, shrewd look. Silence, and then a quiet admission: "Guess I am."

There had almost been a question in the tone of voice. Fletch nodded a little, said carefully, "I think you are, too." He continued, "I'd like to know what happened to Stacey Dixon. Do you remember her?"

The only response was an irritable glare.

"She was Philip Rohan's girlfriend, in Oregon. We found her in a river, downstream from where Philip had been buried. She'd been killed around the same time as Philip."

"I remember Philip. Shaggy short blond hair, mischievous. Knew what I wanted, knew I wanted to jump him, he was high on the idea, and scared. Brought his girlfriend along to save him –" Garrett stopped, stared at Fletcher for a moment, then let his eyes rove around the room as he apparently searched his memory. "Hell," Garrett muttered after a time. "You're right, Fletcher. Forgotten her. But I didn't make a mistake, did I? Didn't leave you any clues, didn't even leave you the bullet."

"What happened?"

Garrett suddenly grinned. "Didn't expect her, had to change plans. Have to be clever, to factor in something like that. Seduced them both, would have done anything for me, got them upstairs." He left a pause, then leaned forward as if grabbing at Fletch's attention: "I made her watch."

Fletcher almost shuddered, but somehow prevented it. "You made her watch while you killed her boyfriend?" It was bad enough imagining how Philip had died – the victims in Georgia had suffered massive injuries, their deaths would have been long and painful – let alone imagining Stacey having to watch it all. Didn't want to be listening to this, enough to make him believe in hell.

"Wanted a witness, someone to know. You're my witness now, Ash. Don't turn on me."

"What do you mean?"

"Didn't work. She gave him strength, can you believe it? She should have humiliated him." A return of the grin. "So I shot her. That brought him lower than he'd ever thought possible. That was good."

Fletcher said, "Tell me about Sam Doherty."

"Forgotten him, too, until tonight. Thinking of that boy, what's his name, Steve." Garrett smiled. "Sam. Dry humping on the sofa like a pair of teenagers. Sweet, but killing him was sweeter. Just a hand over his mouth, that's all it took. Never done it like that before." The smile grew confiding. "Intimate. Should have done it again." Then Garrett asked, "Who was the fifteenth?"

"There were four young men killed in Wyoming, not three."

"Yeah?" Garrett sounded disbelieving, even uninterested. "What happened there?"

"I don't know, John. It seemed like you carried out your plans with all four. In Colorado, where one went wrong, you didn't seek a fourth to make up for it."

"That's right, had to kill one before I was finished. Not in Wyoming. What were their names?"

"You tell me."

Garrett rubbed at his face with both hands, remained silent.

"You said there were more than fifteen, John. Who am I missing?"

"Enough questions," he said gruffly.

Fletcher stared at the man. "You wanted to talk, John. You wanted to tell me all you've achieved." He waited a few minutes, but Garrett remained still and silent, elbows propped on the table, head fallen forward. "What happened after the first one in Illinois, John?"

"Moved to Minnesota. Tried not to do it again. But I got carried away, few months later." The voice was dull. "And then a third one, went kind of crazy for a while. Gave them both to the ground, Mark I dumped in a river. Moved to Washington State."

"When did you begin planning it?"

"Washington. Realized the cops didn't have much of a chance if I wasn't still in the same state. Decided I was going to do this smart, and get away with it."

"How many young men did you kill there?"

"Washington? Three. That was the rule. Three every two years. After Washington, I went to Wyoming."

"Waiting two years between the deaths must require a lot of restraint."

"Control," Garrett said, bleak. "Doesn't mean anything without control."

Fletcher left a beat of silence, then leaned forward. "I know, John, it's all right. This is the end of the line."

Garrett stared at him, intent, almost mesmerized, with the faintest glow of what looked like relief in his eyes. Then the glow turned angry. "The hell it is, Ash, I'm not finished yet, not even halfway through the season. Plenty more deaths to arrange, pain to plan. Going to reach the Super Bowl. Magnificent." He drew a deep breath, and asked, "Ever heard a boy scream, Ash, because of something you did? Ever created that perfect pitch, made him hit it time and time again? Ever create sheer utter terror, they can't remember their own name? Ever see the fear in their eyes as the darkness comes near?" Brief wait for an answer that Fletch didn't provide. "Of course you haven't, coward. Don't tell me it's the end, when I've barely begun. What the hell have you ever created?"

It's destruction, how can you call it creation? Fletcher almost screamed it out. *All right*, he thought, willing himself to remain calm and outwardly unmoved, *he acknowledges he's out of control and that it's meaningless to continue without control.* Where to from there? Another appeal to Garrett's vanity, perhaps. "Explain it to me, John. Tell me what you created with Drew Harmer."

"Yeah," Garrett said. "Yeah, it was the first time for him, like you said. You know, I can have sex like any other man. Better than any man. Don't need the pain, not all the time. Did it with Drew, real gentle like he wanted, real sweet. Then showed him who I am, that was sweeter. Created the most perfect betrayal. Most incredible surprise. Took him so high, then so damned low. You couldn't do either." A pause, then, "If his friend could testify, you would have used it by now, Ash. You didn't have any evidence when you came here. Except the partial fingerprint."

"The evidence was mostly circumstantial, that's true. But it added up to be statistically impossible that it was anyone else."

"You couldn't arrest me on that basis."

"But I knew it was you. And now I have these tapes."

"You won't be in a position to use them, Ash."

"Yes, I will." And Fletcher smoothly changed the subject. There was no point in returning to the threats. Not yet. "Tell me about how you camouflaged yourself in each new state."

"People see what they want to see, bunch of idiots. Self–deluded, right? I'm this nice friendly guy, I employ their sons and friends and nephews, I buy them beer. That's what they want to see, they don't look beyond it. It's easy, all you have to do is charm them." He grinned for a moment. "You know what works? Tell them enough of the truth, they won't look for more. Tell them you're queer, but still be a friendly regular guy, they won't go looking for anymore dirt."

"You've always been open about being gay?"

"Sure. It's no big deal. Or it wasn't, times are changing again. Just buy people off, with charm and money. Donate the right amounts to the right political campaigns. Do some volunteer work for them, putting up signs, handing out pamphlets, applauding speeches, whatever. Then they work for you. I usually follow the Democrats, they'll hate that when they know what I am. If you get through this, tell them all about me, Fletcher." He laughed at this joke he'd been playing on an entire political party. "You know how the system works, Ash. Money and deals."

"Yeah," Fletch murmured, "I know." 'Favors and bribes' was how Albert had described it. Not a nice idea, Xavier being friends with a man like this for the sake of his money and support. At first Fletcher felt relieved that it was years since Garrett was in Denver because that meant he'd missed the beginning of Xavier's career – and then Fletch wondered what sort of people Xavier was mixed up with now instead.

"It's easy," Garrett was continuing. "Never enrolled to vote, though, no one ever realized that. Never gave anyone my name and address I didn't have to."

This was exhausting. Not only the late hour and that they had just begun on the fifth tape, but the very nature of the interview was draining Fletcher. And then there was all the tension of fearing what the outcome would be. Nevertheless, he had a few more questions to ask. His first priority, of seeking enough verifiable evidence to arrest and convict the man, had been fairly well covered. The second priority, of discovering what crimes Garrett had committed that Fletch didn't already know about, was broadly met – though Fletcher needed names and more detail. His third priority, of discovering something of who Garrett was, required some further answers. Fletcher asked, "What's the link between the victims?"

Garrett didn't reply, again seemed to have lost interest.

"What are the similarities? What are you looking for?"

"What do you think?"

"For a start, they're all attractive. Is that vanity on your part, or is there some reason?"

"You understand, Ash. You find them attractive." Garrett smiled a little. "Are you queer, too?"

Fletcher said, very easily, "No."

There was a silence, as Garrett returned to his own thoughts. *At least*, Fletcher took the time to reflect, *I'm a better liar than an honest man should be.* Discovering this fact was merely one more of a million reasons he didn't want to be here, to be doing this.

From the first, when he'd resolved on this confrontation, Fletcher had little faith he would survive the night. Though he seemed to have Garrett fooled with his mock confidence, Fletcher took the man's threats seriously. But Fletcher remained certain of one thing: if he was going to die tonight then he would take Garrett with him. *This is the end of the line.*

And the latest lie was easy, too, though with it he denied his love for Albert. *Don't believe me, Albert, just like you never believe me.* It was easy to lie because some day half the people in America would be listening to this tape. Fletcher had never really known whether he'd be able to lie if Caroline asked him directly. He couldn't quite imagine how she'd word it. Probably something like, 'Fletcher, please tell me my suspicious mind has been working overtime. You're not having sex with Albert Sterne, are you? I don't know how I could ever have even thought such a ghastly thing.'

But he should be able to lie to Caroline – he'd lied to Albert, Mac and Celia that night, after all. And they had accepted the stories necessary to ensure Fletcher could do this on his own, they had trusted him enough to not even question him. He'd lied because he had to do this, and they would have stopped him. Because they shouldn't be a part of this horrible thing, or no more a part of it than they already were.

Strange that he and John Garrett should be sitting here silently, each immersed in their own thoughts, almost like companions. *How can this be possible? And what the hell is going through Garrett's mind right now?* Fletcher let out a quiet breath, recalled his last topic. "Your victims," he said, and Garrett lifted his head, looking almost as dull as when Fletch had arrived that night. "You said something about wanting them to be real. What does that mean?"

"Important to know them, know who they are." He shrugged, asked heavily, "What does it matter?"

"It matters," Fletcher said. "Most of them were young men who had a future, who were doing things with their life, who had potential. Why?"

"Important they didn't surrender." The words almost listless. "They had spunk, they fought me, that was the best. They had further to fall."

Fletch abruptly asked, "What made you this way?"

That seemed to generate a little more interest. Garrett looked across at Fletcher. "Wanted to play football, they never let me on the team. Didn't do well at school, grades were poor, wanted to go to college, had to work instead. Things might have been different."

"It can't be that simple, John."

"If I'd known I was queer," Garrett said, apparently appealing to Fletch. "Might have been different. If I'd had a friend, a boyfriend."

"Maybe. But there's a lot of other men out there who never got to play football, who never had a boyfriend or a girlfriend. Why didn't they become killers?"

"They weren't as smart as me."

"Tell me about your parents, John."

This obviously annoyed the man. He shrugged and looked away. "My father left us when I was a kid, left us for good. My mother – hell, she never did anything in her life but get pregnant and drink herself to death. Why?" Garrett asked with great sarcasm. "Think I'm their fault?"

"There are no easy answers for any of us. I don't know what made me the way I am, either."

"Then don't practice your psychology on me. Amateur hour. Who are you to tell me it wasn't because I didn't go to college? What do you want to hear?" The tirade grew louder: "You want to hear my father hit me? My mother tied me to a chair because she was too drunk to look out for me? Child abuse, sure it's in all the newspapers now. Real fashionable. Didn't know what it was then. No one to help. No one to tell. No friends. Just had to deal with it and do the right thing. Tried to do the right thing, never understood why it was so damned important."

Fletcher said quietly, "I'm sorry, John." Strange that he could feel grief for the boy John Garrett used to be. But grief for the boy didn't forgive the crimes the man had committed.

"Fuck you, Ash. You're twenty years too late with *sorry*. Don't want your pity. Obvious no one was going to give me a damned thing, I did the right thing or not. So I took what I wanted. You're all cowards, living by the rules. Have to be brave enough and smart enough to stop taking all the damned shit."

"You're aware that you've broken the rules?"

"Of course I damned well know."

"You realize that murder is wrong? Yet you choose to commit murder."

Garrett was glaring at him, furious. "Don't give me this shit, Ash. If I know right from wrong I'm sane, I can stand trial. Crazy. Right and wrong has nothing to do with it. Right and wrong has nothing to do with laws or what my father told me or any damned thing. Nothing to do with a boy's pain, nothing to do with the heat when the darkness comes. Said you understood. Said – their death be slow, their terror be great. Right and wrong is nothing compared with that."

"John, listen to me," Fletcher said, very calmly. "Listen to me now. There was a point to it, there was meaning in what you did, when you had control. But you don't have control over it anymore."

"Who the hell are you to tell me that?"

"You said it yourself. You said it doesn't mean anything without control."

"No," Garrett said.

Unsure whether that was agreement or denial, Fletcher continued, "I'm arresting you, Mr. Garrett, for the murders of Andrew Harmer, Philip Rohan, Stacey Dixon, Sam Doherty and Tony Shields. I'll also charge you with the other murders we've talked about." It was almost frightening, how little effort it took for Fletch to list all of the deaths from memory. "One in Illinois, two in Minnesota, three in Washington State, four in Wyoming, three in Colorado, four in Georgia, five in Oregon. Twenty–two murders, Mr. Garrett. This is the end of the line."

"No."

Garrett had both hands on the edge of the table, gripping hard. If he pushed now, Fletcher would be temporarily pinned in his chair. Fletch kept a very wary eye on the man, ready to move.

"This isn't the end," Garrett said, colder now. "Can't be. Stupid to come here, Ash. Going to kill you. Planned it out for Steve, how it would be, you'll do instead. Better. You'll know exactly what I'm doing. How long I can make the pain last."

"I'm not going to let that happen, Mr. Garrett."

"You'll do fine. Then whatever boys I want. Maybe Steve. Maybe Andy Halligan. Maybe I'm too smart for that. I'll move on, another state. Find three boys. Another three after that."

"Listen to yourself. You used to be in control. You used to wait for two years. You've lost the whole point."

"No."

"You used to be so clever, but you're making mistakes, John. You're making mistakes and then deliberately forgetting about them. You've got yourself fooled but you can't fool me."

"Who the hell do you think you are, Ash?" The man was almost roaring. "When this ends, it's on *my* terms. Long way to go yet. Plenty of deaths along the way."

"No, John, this is the end now."

"You're not arresting me, I told you that. Deal is you die or I die. That was the deal. Maybe we both die, Ash."

"I don't think so."

"You die, then. Long and slow. Beautiful. Could make it last for days. Tell me which was your favorite? Which was the one that really turned you on? Maybe Georgia. So brutal, no finesse to those deaths. Mass of pain until the darkness came."

Fletcher stared across at the man, unable to respond.

"You die, and I keep killing. No one else knows what I am. They'll let me go. Nowhere near finished killing, Ash. So many boys out there. So many lovely boys with the spunk to fight me. Glorious."

"I won't let you go, Garrett. I won't let you hurt anymore young men."

"You'll let me go. You'll be a beaten bloody mess. Won't lift a finger to stop me – your fingers will all be broken." And the man laughed.

"I'm arresting you," Fletch repeated. "Your threats are worthless."

"If you're so damned determined this is the end of the line, Ash, kill me. You die or I die." Garrett paused, breathing heavily. "What? You'd rather society did it for you. Gas chamber, electric chair, hanging, injection, bloody firing squad. All care, no responsibility. Coward. You want to end this, *you* end it."

"Don't think I won't, if you force me to."

"Coward, can't even say it."

"Don't think I won't kill you, Mr. Garrett, if you force me to." Fletcher explained, "There are a handful of people who have to be fought on their own terms. You're one of them. And I choose to fight you."

"You'd better do it, Ash."

Garrett was standing, pushing at the table.

Fletcher was standing, too, left arm hooking the chair out from behind him, swinging it away, all in one smooth motion, taking one step back – right arm aimed straight at Garrett's chest, gun steady in his hand. But the table had only shifted an inch. Left arm came up to support the right.

"Better do it now," Garrett said. Voice seemed full of adrenalin, full of crazed humor like this was fun, full of serious intent. "Once I get my hands on you, Ash, it's over. Except for the pain. Days of unbelievable pain. You'll wonder how it's possible to survive. Eventually you won't."

"I'm arresting you, John. Step back from the table and put your hands on your head."

"I'm taking you with me," the man was saying, voice full of promise, "whether you live or die."

"Step back from the table, John."

"You live, you live with me inside you, every day, every hour."

"Last chance, John. Step back and put your hands on your head."

The man was still for a moment, staring at Fletcher. The air was thick with the possible consequences of whatever happened next.

Garrett abruptly leaned forward, hands shoving the table to one side out of the way, his whole body behind the push. A roar grew, his mouth opening letting the sound free from his chest. Hands reaching, his fingers talons. One more moment and this powerful man would be upon his next victim.

Fletch took one step to the side, towards where the table stood askew, gun tracking the centre of Garrett's chest. *I know what I'm doing*, Fletcher Ash silently announced, and he pulled the trigger once. Twice.

CHAPTER THIRTY-THREE
NEW ORLEANS
SEPTEMBER 1985

Death wasn't a peaceful closing of the eyes like in the movies. Fletcher stood watching Garrett for a few moments, sick at heart. The man, face-down and shaking as if having a fit, was surely dying if not already dead. Less blood than in the movies, which was a more acceptable state of affairs, and the one exit wound Fletcher could see was simply a mess – none of the detail that the special effects provided these days in gruesome glorifying Technicolor.

Once the body quieted – must have been minutes or even seconds, not hours – Fletch knelt and tried to find a pulse in the closest wrist. Arm out-flung, as if reaching. Yes, he'd been reaching for Fletcher. Putting the thought away, Fletch carefully searched, but there was nothing: warmth but nothing else, no movement. Warmth bleeding away: not literally yet, but in his imagination the body was already cooling.

Fletch recovered his chair, sat at the table, carefully placed his gun down. Saw that the cassette player had fallen over, set it upright. It was still recording. Fletcher sighed and said, "I've shot him, he's dead. It's three-ten on the morning of September second, 1985." A dull moment passed, though Fletcher knew what he had to do. "I'll attempt to call Lieutenant Halligan of the NOPD."

He let his eyes rove, located the phone over on a kitchen bench. When he went to pick it up, he saw it was on a long lead, so he brought it back to the table. Garrett lay on the floor maybe three feet away. After a few minutes' search through his wallet, Fletch found the card listing Halligan's phone numbers, and dialed the man's home.

After only two rings, Halligan answered with a barely conscious grunt.

"Lieutenant, this is Fletcher Ash."

"God damn it," the man said. He sounded more awake when he continued, "Ash, this better be real important."

"Yes. I am at John Garrett's house." And he gave Halligan the address, just in case the man didn't know it.

"What the hell – ?" Another pause. "It's three in the morning. What's going on?"

"I have shot him. He's dead." Fletcher waited through an ominous silence. "Lieutenant? Perhaps you'd better come here."

Grim, Halligan asked, "What happened?"

"Mr. Garrett made a confession on tape. We've been talking for hours. He is the serial killer. He *was* the –" Fletcher broke off.

"And then you executed him."

"Self–defense, Lieutenant. He was about to attack me. I'm not happy about it but he's dead."

"All right. I'll be there in twenty. I'll call the crime scene boys, you know the procedure, Ash."

"Yes. Of course I am willing to follow procedure. But can you call Albert Sterne, too. I want him here." Had to be clear about this. "I want him to assist. The Bureau will want him involved."

"Right," Halligan said, abrupt. "Don't move, don't touch anything." And he hung up.

Fletcher put the phone down, and remained seated. He was about to stop the tape, but thought better of it. Halligan would want to hear for himself that Fletch hadn't been rearranging the evidence.

He wondered how he would feel when this numbness wore off. Terrible, he supposed. Fletcher had never wanted to kill anyone. In fact, he'd wanted to never kill anyone. Never figured he would. Feared he might.

If any one person in the world deserved to die, Fletcher thought, that one was John Garrett, and Fletch of all people knew exactly why. But, even so, who was Fletcher Ash to make that decision, to carry out that judgment?

Was he going to be able to live with this? Other people did, he reminded himself. But that didn't mean anything to him. Live with Garrett's words in his ears and Garrett's blood on his hands. Live with twenty–two deaths in his imagination and in his memory. Twenty–two of Garrett's, and one of his own.

His gun lay there on the table. It had only been used on a firing range until tonight. Fletcher stared at the thing and considered the nature of justice. Why not use the gun again now, while he felt nothing? Because when he began to feel again, Fletcher suspected he'd never be free of the blood–guilt and the sick terror. He'd killed a man. Where was the justice in that? How could he have taken that responsibility on himself?

The tape was still running, he could even leave a message, an explanation. A farewell.

Dull and slow, he remembered that he'd moved the cassette player, and Halligan had told him not to touch anything. He allowed himself a sigh, and said, "For the record, I picked this chair up from the floor. I'd been sitting on it but when he began pushing at the table, I stood and slid the chair out of the way. It was on its side a few feet away." Would Albert appreciate this pedantic detail? "I also righted the cassette player, which had fallen on its face. I brought the phone over to the table." Damn this. "I checked his right wrist for a pulse. I haven't touched anything else."

The silence returned. Fletcher closed his eyes rather than look at the gun. Time stretched impossibly. *Let this be over.* Stillness like a dead weight bearing down on him.

And then at last the clatter of the front door opening, footsteps approaching, some heading into the living room. Fletcher opened his eyes. A uniformed officer was gazing at him from just inside the doorway, a strange mix of wariness and curiosity in his expression. The cop called back over his shoulder, "He's in here."

Halligan walked in, more of them pushed by – a motley surge of uniforms and plain clothes – some crouching over Garrett's body checking for signs of life, others looking around for anything else of interest. "Ash," Halligan said in terse greeting.

"Lieutenant," Fletcher acknowledged.

"Is that your gun?" The man tilted his head towards the table.

"Yes. It's the gun I shot Garrett with."

"I see. Self–defense, you said."

"Yes. This cassette player has been recording the whole time. Since before midnight, anyway. You can hear what happened." As if on cue, the tape ran out, and the player clicked off. Fletcher and Halligan looked at it for a moment, but the sharp sound barely drew glances from the others.

The place was swarming with activity, with Fletcher and Garrett and Halligan at the heart of it. But then, for Fletch at least, the stillness gained a different focus: Albert had walked in, metal case in hand. Dark eyes searching, quickly finding him, sweeping intense across Fletcher as if to see for himself that Fletch was still whole and breathing. If there was relief, Fletcher couldn't make it out. Perhaps there was anger, perhaps outrage, but Fletcher didn't have time to fathom it. With barely a nod of greeting, Albert headed over to stand by the body, watching as the crime scene officers took photographs and outlined Garrett in white adhesive tape.

Already, they were rolling Garrett over to lie on his back. Fletcher made himself glance once at the man's face – *I know what I've done* – then turned away.

Albert finally looked up at Fletcher again, and said, "You want me to assist with this procedure."

"Yes, Albert. The Bureau will want you involved, they'll want their own reports."

The briefest of pauses, as if Albert wanted to say something despite all these people hovering around. Fletcher waited, needing whatever reassurance he could get. But it was silly to expect Albert to ask Fletch if he was all right, pointless to want Albert to be polite as if he were any ordinary person.

Halligan spoke first. "I hope you don't want Sterne here to muddy the waters. Arguing jurisdiction is only going to mess this up even more."

Fletch said very calmly, "It's a Bureau matter, Lieutenant, because I'm directly involved. But I'm asking you to take part for the sake of clearing this up. I want everyone to be satisfied with the result."

"Don't expect me to let Sterne get you off the hook, Ash. I'm playing this one strictly by the book."

"Of course you are. And Dr. Sterne will behave as scrupulously as always." Such a damned effort to maintain this carefully balanced truth and politeness and reason, when all Fletch wanted to do was go hide in a corner somewhere and cry his heart out. "It's best that both the Bureau and the police are involved, Lieutenant, that's the bottom line. Both agencies have an interest in knowing what happened. Let's work together on this one."

At last Halligan gave him a grudging nod, even seemed to relax. Perhaps the toughness had been partly an act in order to sound Fletcher out. "All right," the man said. "Come over here, Ash, and let them get on with it."

A glance at Albert, but his expression was even more unreadable now that Albert was on the job. Surprisingly enough, the man seemed to be cooperating well with the crime scene officer, though there were minimal words exchanged. And then Albert glanced up at Fletch, and the younger man could feel the anger. Of course. Albert was unique, but he was still human. His reactions at being lied to, and to his lover putting himself in a dangerous situation, were going to be much the same as anyone else's when faced with betrayal and a loss narrowly averted.

Fletcher nodded in acknowledgment of this, picked up the cassette player and a fresh tape, and headed over to where Halligan stood by the kitchen benches. It was a relatively small room but at least the table now blocked the view of Garrett's body.

"Tell me what happened, Ash," Halligan said. When Fletcher plugged the player into a nearby electrical outlet, moving a toaster to do so, Halligan asked, "Why do you need that?"

"By the book, Lieutenant, remember? It's best that we're all clear about everything that's said and done tonight." The man was watching him, almost suspicious, but with no reason to prevent this. Fletcher pressed the record button. "Tape six, side one. This is Fletcher Ash talking with Lieutenant Harry Halligan. It's three–fifty in the morning, the previous tape ran out some minutes ago. We are still in John Garrett's kitchen." Then he waited for Halligan to start again.

"All right. Tell me what happened."

And Fletcher went through it all, beginning with the decision to confront Garrett alone. He detailed as much of his early conversation with Garrett as he could remember, describing how that led to Garrett's confession and his agreement to tape an informal interview. Halligan, naturally, was interested in the fact that some of the earlier conversation had been witnessed. "The young man's name was Steve," Fletcher repeated. "I don't know his last name but he worked for Garrett so he won't be hard to find. Early twenties, long blond hair, very slim. They appeared to have a sexual relationship, they were very comfortable with each other."

"I'll tread carefully," Halligan said.

"Steve appeared to be mildly stoned, Lieutenant, and both of them had been drinking. The boy didn't even pick up on the seriousness of what was going on. Don't expect him to verify everything I've told you, except the obvious."

Apparently Halligan was satisfied with this. "Anything else for now, Special Agent?"

Fletcher prevented himself from protesting at the title – he had not been acting officially tonight, he did not feel as if he were still an agent of the FBI – but he was smart enough and cynical enough to let the lieutenant treat him as one. Very evenly, he said, "For the record, Lieutenant Halligan, I came here with the aim of breaking the deadlock in my investigation and arresting Mr. Garrett. I did not intend to kill him, though I realized it was possible that either he or I, or both of us, might die as a result of me coming here. When it happened, it was a situation he forced. He wouldn't let me arrest him, he didn't want to go to jail. So he was determined either to kill me or to be killed. I'm not happy about it, Halligan, but that's what happened and I don't think I'd do anything differently if I had it to do over."

After a moment, Halligan nodded. "All right. I'm going to turn this tape off now and listen to the other tapes." He waited a moment but, when Fletch didn't argue, he pressed the stop button.

Grimacing at the thought of reliving it all, Fletcher said, "Tape five, if you want the end of it. This one."

With the volume down, so that only Fletch and Halligan could clearly hear it, the lieutenant played the tape. There was the last of Garrett describing how he used the political system as part of his cover, and then Fletch asking about the victims. Garrett asking whether Fletcher was queer. A long silence, but then Garrett's words made it clear, if Halligan had doubts, that he was the serial killer Fletch had known him to be. The recorded voice became louder in response to Fletcher's questions as they briefly discussed his family. Fletcher didn't want to be here, didn't want to be listening to this.

One of the uniformed officers came in to the kitchen with a large cardboard box in his arms. "Look at this, Lieutenant."

Halligan, intent on the tape, said, "In a minute." But Fletcher, seeking any distraction, wandered over to the table where the man dumped his burden.

The box was full of silver chains and crucifix earrings, watches and wallets. There were a couple of folders containing neatly cut newspaper clippings, many of which Fletcher recognized from his own files. There was Drew's college ID card, the notice of Sam's funeral, a gold chain that might have been Mitch's, a bracelet of woven turquoise beads that might have been Tony's.

Fletcher had known, of course, that Garrett killed these young men. But to be faced with what little remained of their lives brought all his sorrow cascading back like the deluge of a New Orleans rainstorm. He grabbed up two handfuls of the dead jewelry and sat down, bowing his head, grieving over it if only he weren't so numb. He should be crying right now, he should be crying his heart out for the twenty–two boys and for himself. Even for John Garrett.

Time passed. Dimly aware of the murmur of his own voice on the tape and Garrett yelling; cops all over the house searching for further evidence; Albert and another man dealing with the body, preparing to bundle it up and take it to the morgue. Time stretched, though it could only have been minutes until a gunshot blasted from the cassette player. Once. Twice.

Standard operating procedure. In his broadest Irish accent, Mac had always described it as *To be sure, to be sure.* Fletcher used to smile at that.

Halligan at last wandered over, cast an uninterested eye over the box and its contents. Eventually he said, "You were right about John Garrett."

"Yes," said Fletcher, lifting his head, hands still heavy with cold metal.

"And you're not going to say you told me so?"

Fletcher shrugged a little. "No."

A brief silence. "Guess we should have been more willing to believe you."

"No. You did what you thought was right. Can't ask for more than that."

Apparently that was as much of an apology and an acceptance as Halligan was prepared for. He continued, all business now, "There'll be an internal investigation. Maybe a grand jury, but I doubt it, they're not going to indict you for murder."

"Perhaps a grand jury should consider the matter as an abuse of civil rights."

"You tell me, you're the fed. Anyway, you're free to go for now."

"Thank you, Lieutenant." Fletcher sighed. "Perhaps I'll take a look around here. I won't touch anything," he quickly promised. "But I want to get a better feel for who he was."

Halligan nodded. "That's fine."

Alone again amidst the bustle, Fletcher began putting the jewelry back into the box, examining each piece as he did. What with the wallets and the newspaper clippings, he should be able to identify all twenty–two of the boys, which would at least close the books on some missing person cases. Allow some grieving parents to at last know the truth, terrible though it was. 'It was the not knowing that was the worst,' Tony's sister, Jane Shields, had said. 'It was the hoping he'd walk in the door one day, though he never did.'

When he was done, Fletcher stood and found Albert waiting for him. The man said, "I'll take a swab of your hands."

It would have been funny under any other circumstances. Not that there were any other circumstances it could have happened in, with Fletcher admitting to shooting a man and Albert seeking the evidence of gunpowder residue. "You're so damned thorough," Fletch complained, but he sat again for the procedure. Albert, deft in rubber gloves, moistened a cotton ball from a small bottle, swiped it over the back of Fletcher's right hand, and placed it in a plastic bag. He repeated the procedure for the palm of the right hand, and then the same for the left.

"All done?" Fletcher asked. When Albert nodded, Fletcher turned away, wandered out to the living room. He didn't want to see Garrett's body being carried out. Knowing he should be curious about this house, Fletcher spent a few minutes in each room, trying not to get in the way of the cops who were looking through everything. It was just a house, and strangely empty now as if it knew its sole occupant was dead. Fletcher remained unmoved.

Once the ambulance had taken Garrett away and while Albert was too busy gathering evidence in the kitchen to notice his absence, Fletcher walked out the front door, climbed into his car, and drove away.

The sun rose behind him, glaring gold in the rear vision mirror, as he left New Orleans.

◆

Mid–morning. Fletcher was parked off the road, looking down over a small and uninspiring beach. Must have driven into Texas, must have only recently stopped given how far that was, though he had no memory of any of it. There was no traffic, no one else around.

The ocean shifted under the sunlight, restless shimmers. The most minimal of waves broke a few feet out, surged onto the sand only to listlessly fall back again.

Fletcher rubbed at his face but he really didn't want to wake up, didn't want to get to the other side of this numbness. He was tired and aching and afraid of the despair he was going to start feeling soon. He felt grubby all over and thoroughly confused. Battered and used.

The ocean waited. *Let me wash you clean.*

He was heading down the dunes to the beach, stripping off his clothes and empty holster, letting them fall to the sand, walking naked into the water. Fresh and invigorating, not cold. Welcoming. Fletcher strode out until he was waist deep, enjoying the water's resistance to each step, and then he began swimming.

Good to feel his body work, all of it in splendid coordination, strong and able. Traveling through the water as if it were his home. The tiredness and the aches, the sweat and the grubbiness sloughed off him, dissolved in the salt water.

Amazing how far he'd reached. He floated on his back for a while, having glanced back to see the land distant. It was good out here, away from all the trouble and confusion. Away from the guilt and despair. The ocean bore him gently as if he were its child, rocking him in the sunlight, lapping at him.

Maybe he should just stay out here. Maybe he should keep swimming. Maybe this was the only peace he would ever know.

Albert could never follow him here, though, Albert would never share this peace. Albert would be left alone and grieving, would repress all that love and passion in him so deep that it would never see the light again.

Poor Albert, left behind to endure. Poor Fletcher –

He shouted. It was so unexpected and so full a shout, that Fletch promptly lost his balance and submerged, trying not to let the shout grow into a laugh. If he was going to drown, it wasn't going to be because he couldn't stop laughing. When he surfaced, Fletch began treading water. The burst of self–mockery, the joyous uncompromising thrust of truth, had faded already – but the revelation it brought hadn't. *Who am I trying to fool?* Fletcher asked. *I'm considering suicide.*

If that was what he was going to do, then it would have to be a conscious decision. None of this swimming off south, conveniently ignoring the fact that he wouldn't be able to reach land again. How romantic and melodramatic an end, with his clothes a sad trail on the shore. How lonely and pointless and stupid a death. What a ghastly thing to do to Albert.

No. If he'd survived the night, if he'd lived through the confrontation with Garrett, then Fletcher could survive the aftermath. He'd been prepared to die in return for something of the utmost importance – but that didn't mean he *had* to die now that he'd achieved that goal. Ludicrous notion.

He'd killed a man, but he would manage somehow to live with that. Fletcher would give the blood–guilt its due, would make some kind of reparation. He'd probably never be quite the same again but he'd get beyond the pain of it. He owed it to Albert and he owed it to himself. Fletcher almost laughed again. He'd been prepared to die to ensure Garrett killed no more, and yet here he was considering whether to become Garrett's posthumous twenty–third victim. Ridiculous, truly ridiculous.

For a moment, joy threatened. This case, this horrible case was over now. Fletcher needed to tie up all the loose ends, he needed to talk to the families of those young men who'd died, but it was over. All those years of unrecognized work were over. And he'd won.

Fletcher began swimming, heading for what he thought must be the beach he'd started from.

Leaving the ocean, he felt the clarity and the cleanliness falling away from him again. But he was alive, and he was determined to stay that way. Without bothering to dry himself, Fletcher pulled on his clothes, and walked up to the car. Luckily, no one had stolen it, though he'd left the keys in the ignition. He climbed in, and turned the car around, drove down the road.

Now, if only he could find some signposts, he'd get back to New Orleans.

CHAPTER THIRTY-FOUR
NEW ORLEANS
SEPTEMBER 1985

Albert once again found himself pacing the length and breadth of Ash's hotel room. He was furious. It was two in the afternoon, Ash had left John Garrett's house at some time between five and five–thirty that morning, and nothing had been seen or heard of him since. This was absolutely typical of the self–indulgent, melodramatic, thoughtless idiot.

McIntyre and Mortimer were afraid, even Halligan was worried. More to the point, Halligan's suspicions of Ash's motives had been re–awoken. McIntyre wouldn't express his concerns directly but it was obvious he thought Ash might try to destroy himself in one way or another. If Ash didn't return, Halligan was planning to issue an APB as soon as the twenty–four hours were up; he'd already told the patrol cops to keep a watch for Ash in the bars.

Furious. What possessed Ash to create this mess? It hardly helped his case of self–defense to run as if he'd committed murder. There was no rationality behind this disappearance, no logic, no consideration.

Except for an hour late that morning, Albert had remained at the hotel, waiting for Ash. Had remained in Ash's room, with strict instructions to the hotel staff to put any calls through to him there – had stood next to the phone, but for brief mindless wanderings around the room, restless due to this mental and physical inactivity. Having conducted his own examination of the body at the scene, Albert hadn't even attended Garrett's autopsy, delegating Mortimer to assist instead. And if Ash didn't like that, given he had told Albert to be involved in the procedure, Ash was in no position to argue.

Furious.

This waiting was pointless, really. It achieved nothing. In fact, Albert's only useful activity since six that morning was during the hour he was absent from the hotel, which left seven very empty hours in his day filled with nothing but impatient fury. Though, if Ash didn't return, the arrangements Albert had made during that solitary hour would become pointless, too. He wasn't used to wasting time, wasn't comfortable with it, couldn't remember ever just doing nothing like this. But, after a few attempts, he'd found he couldn't settle to any task, couldn't even settle to any productive thoughts.

If Ash didn't return.

There had to be a time when Albert could stop waiting. At some logical moment, he would forget this uselessly melodramatic gesture of Ash's and stop waiting, get on with his work.

The fury, however, was another matter. Albert didn't think he'd ever leave the fury behind. He had lived with anger and bitterness, but this pure white nauseous fury was something else. Felt like it would blaze out of him, blaze out of his chest and face in all–consuming devastation. That was as melodramatic an image as Ash had ever managed.

Damn Ash and all he brought Albert to.

Albert had barely returned to his hotel room early that morning after meeting Ricardo, when he received Halligan's call. A uniformed officer had driven him to Garrett's house, where he'd found Ash sitting next to the man he'd just killed. Ash's mental and emotional condition appeared worse than Albert had ever witnessed before, and Albert had seen Ash in many difficult situations. There had been a sense that the composed, reasonable facade would break apart as soon as it was no longer required.

So where had Ash gone, in order to be as raw and vulnerable and utterly miserable as he'd ever been? What was he doing? It didn't seem likely that he was seeking comfort: he hadn't wanted Albert's company, or that of McIntyre or Mortimer, and surely Ash hadn't had the chance to make any new friends here in New Orleans. For a moment, Albert pondered calling either Peter Ash or Caroline Thornton to ascertain whether they'd heard from Ash, but it didn't seem a wise or even a feasible idea.

Someone at the door was attempting to fit a key into the lock. Either a confused neighbor, or – Albert reached the door in three strides, opened it to find Fletcher Ash in the corridor, looking distinctly bedraggled.

"Ah," the younger man said, his whole manner drab and disheveled. "Albert."

"Where the hell have you been?" Amazing that he could say it so coldly, so calmly, when this fury in him was reaching awesome new heights.

Ash wandered in, apparently too dazed to respond. He was frowning, as if being kept from a goal by something he couldn't quite understand.

Closing the door firmly behind him, Albert asked, "What have you been doing?"

The frown was turned on Albert, who revised his first impressions. Ash wasn't so much dazed as very narrowly focused, and unaware of much else, although it wasn't clear what the man might be focused on. At least Ash was alive. There was the same sense of hurting rawness Albert had sensed that morning but Ash had a protective layer or two firmly in place now.

Because Ash seemed to be waiting for something, Albert repeated, "Where have you been?"

"I needed to get clean."

"Clean?" Ash's hair was damp and tangled, and his clothes were in much the same state; there were also traces of sand, especially around his trouser legs and shoes. "You've been in the sea," Albert concluded.

"Yes, I – I'll have a shower." And Ash was heading for the bathroom, already unbuttoning his shirt.

"No," Albert said. When the man didn't even falter, Albert caught up with him and grabbed Ash's arm. "Not yet. We're moving to a different hotel."

The physical restraint was the only thing making an impression. Ash's focus appeared to be on getting clean, in a shower this time, and Albert was in the way.

"I've already packed your clothes and other possessions, Ash. We can be there in ten minutes and you can have your shower then."

When Ash didn't even nod, Albert simply turned the man around and began walking him toward the door. He kept a hand at Ash's elbow, as if Ash were blind, until they were in the hotel's underground garage. Luckily, there was no one in the corridors and only one person in the elevator, so this proximity drew little attention.

"Where's the car?" Albert asked, though he spotted it before Ash roused himself to reply.

The drive into the French Quarter was completed in silence with Ash sitting docile in the passenger seat, staring unseeing through the windshield. Albert located the small hotel he'd already checked them into, parked the car on the premises, walked Ash past reception with a nod to the owner, then up to the room he'd booked on the second floor.

Once safely inside, Ash glanced at Albert. "Yes, have a shower," Albert said. Barely pausing, even for this permission, the man absently shed his clothes as he headed for the bathroom. Albert cast a critical eye over the scattering of sand, glad it wasn't his own carpet. And then, hearing the water running, Albert walked over to the phone, and dialed the Bureau offices. After some minutes, he was put through to McIntyre. "This is Albert Sterne."

"Any news?" was the immediate question.

"Yes, Ash has returned."

"Thank God for that," McIntyre said fervently. "Is he all right? Where was he?"

"He hasn't yet told me where he was. I believe he will be all right." Albert continued before McIntyre could ask anything more: "Would you inform Halligan and Dr. Mortimer that he has returned. I'll give you the phone number of the hotel where we are staying in case you need to contact him, but he'd appreciate it if you didn't disturb him at least until tomorrow."

"Of course, I understand." McIntyre took the number down, then as Albert was preparing to end the conversation, said, "Hang on, can I speak to him now? Is Fletch there with you?"

"He is taking a shower."

McIntyre made a noise that was apparently supposed to convey sympathy. "Did you hear the autopsy supported Fletch's story? Celia's down there again seeing to the last of the tests and finishing her report."

"Dr. Mortimer phoned to inform me of the results as soon as the procedure was complete. And, McIntyre, if you call yourself Ash's friend then it isn't appropriate for you to characterize his statements of fact as a story."

"It's not going to be an issue, though, is it?"

"Perhaps not." A moment of silence. "I will tell Ash you were concerned about him. I am sure he appreciates Dr. Mortimer's work."

"Good. He's really all right?"

Albert left a pause, impatient with this meaningless conversation. "I said that I believe he will be."

"Make sure he knows Celia and I are thinking about him."

"Yes," Albert said. "Either Ash or I will talk to you tomorrow." And he put the phone down, then sat in the nearest chair to wait for Ash.

Some while later, Albert frowned, and again consulted his watch. Ash had been in the shower for almost twenty minutes, which seemed excessive. Deciding to investigate, Albert walked over to the bathroom and knocked on the door. No response, but for the fact that the water was still running. It sounded as if Ash had the taps on full.

A moment of something as potent and as physical as the fury, though it was merely apprehension. Could Ash be in a self–destructive mood? Albert opened the door, and was relieved to see Ash obviously alive and in one piece. Through the steam, it appeared that the man was washing himself, reaching behind his back, then working across his chest.

He would have closed the door and left Ash to it, but Albert's attention was caught. There was a noise, almost as if Ash were whimpering. Albert had heard that once before, back in Washington when Ash was in the throes of yet another bad dream.

And, apart from this pathetic noise barely audible over the tumult of water, Ash's movements appeared random and compulsive, almost violent. There was no logic to this act of cleaning, if that's what it was. Ash could have thoroughly soaped and rinsed himself within a few minutes. As Albert watched, the man leaned down to scrub at a thigh, then his calf, the sole of his foot. Ash straightened to again work at his shoulders, apparently trying in vain to get at the middle of his back, when Albert knew very well the man was usually flexible enough to have no trouble reaching the skin between his shoulder–blades. The man was using the loofah that the hotel supplied, which wasn't in itself a matter to draw Albert's attention – until Ash used it to scrub at his face, rubbing two–handed, the muscles in his arms taut, then even ran it back over his head, as if trying to clean his scalp through his hair.

This behavior was surely crazed. Albert stepped forward, said, "Ash. What do you think you're doing?"

No reply, not even a reaction, as if Ash had no idea he wasn't alone.

Albert walked up to the glass door of the shower, spoke louder: "Ash! Stop this." Unthinking, he blurted out, "What the hell is the matter with you?"

Still no response.

There seemed no other option. Albert began stripping off his clothes, hanging his jacket and trousers on the hook on the back of the door, quickly folding the rest and piling it on a nearby shelf. Then he stepped into the shower.

He faltered for a moment under the torrent of hot water. Ash, left with little space in which to move, began scrubbing at his stomach. "Stop it," Albert repeated. He managed to prise the loofah out of Ash's claw–like fingers, then took the man into his arms, endeavoring to contain him. The mewling noise continued. Even now Ash wasn't responding to Albert's presence. "Fletcher," Albert murmured. "Fletcher, listen to me. It's over now, it's all over. Stop this."

Ash's movements became struggles, then slowed, though he remained unyielding within Albert's embrace. For a couple of minutes, Albert simply held him, stroking the thick tangles of dark hair. Gradually, Ash's head tilted to rest against Albert's. Freeing one arm, Albert reached behind him to turn off the water, sparing a moment to wonder what heating system the hotel used as it was obviously efficient. Then he led Ash out of the shower.

It was immediately apparent that Ash's skin had suffered: it was bright red not only from the heat of the water, but raw from the scrubbing. Albert alternated between briskly drying himself and patting the towel over Ash, careful not to exacerbate a condition that would surely cause Ash a great deal of discomfort.

Collecting the hand cream from his bathroom gear, Albert led Ash out into the main room and sat him on the side of the bed. Soothing the cream into Ash's abused skin, beginning with each arm, Albert tried to find something to talk about, tried to establish some kind of communication between them. Risking total inanity, he said, "Water is an abrasive substance, Ash, and is often used as such industrially. Perhaps you are aware of that, given your actions during this current mania for cleanliness. I own this cream because of my work. I am constantly required to wash my hands, which guards against me inadvertently contaminating evidence, and also helps protect me from catching or transmitting infections. I use this cream to prevent the skin of my hands from drying out, which would not only be painful but would eventually result in a lessening of function."

He had worked from the arms down Ash's torso and now began on the man's legs. What else could he talk about? He had no interest and no talent in making conversation, particularly when it was this one–sided. "I moved us to this hotel because I assumed you would appreciate some privacy during this time, and more comfort than the Bureau's designated hotel provided. We will probably need to stay here in New Orleans for a week or more until the current situation is satisfactorily resolved. This place has benefits, as you have already discovered: the bathroom is fully equipped with every convenience; in fact, every luxury. What you may not have noticed is that there is an alcove that contains a basic kitchen. I will be able to cook simple meals for us as necessary. I believe you may enjoy exploring the environs, as well. No doubt you will find the French Quarter both attractive and interesting."

This last was said as Albert worked on Ash's feet, propping each in his lap in turn. When he was done, he lifted his head, only to find Ash looking back at him, aware and focused on Albert. Despite that awareness, however, the man's expression was almost blank, enlivened by nothing more than the faintest hint of bemusement. A long moment passed, Albert searching for something more to say. His impulse was to murmur, 'Hello, Fletcher,' which was plainly ridiculous and would also draw attention to the fact that Ash had not been mentally present for some while. Instead Albert said, "If you lie down, I will take care of your back."

The suggestion was acted on. Ash slowly turned and slid down onto the bedcovers, lying on his front with his arms folded under his head. Albert worked in silence now, his touch remaining appropriately business–like even as he smoothed cream into Ash's reddened buttocks. As he finished, and capped the tube, he was rewarded with a quiet, "Thank you."

A response was surely required. "You're welcome." Unsure about what to do next, Albert returned the hand cream to the bathroom and brought his clothes back out, intending to put them away. And then, of course, there were Ash's damp and sandy clothes to deal with.

But Ash was leaning up on his elbows, watching Albert closely. After a moment, he said, "Come and hold me."

Albert put his clothes down on the nearest available surface, and walked around to the other side of the bed. Drawing the covers and quilt down, he encouraged Ash to join him lying on the sheets alone, which would surely be more comfortable for Ash's skin. Settling back into their usual embrace, Ash seemed almost eager for this contact. They lay quietly for a while, undisturbed by the hum of the air conditioner and the muted traffic noise. Albert eventually said, "You should sleep, if you can."

"No," was the immediate reply.

Deciding he may as well state the obvious, Albert said, "I am sure you had no sleep last night, and you were already tired."

"I'm afraid I'll have another nightmare." Silence again, until Ash explained, "I'm afraid that next time I fall, I'll hit the ground."

"I see," Albert said, though he didn't really. Ash had never described these nightmares to him. "Would it help if I stay awake, and rouse you if necessary? I believe I am familiar with the external symptoms of your dreams by now."

Ash shifted so that he could look back at Albert over his shoulder. Surprisingly, Ash was smiling, though the expression seemed more painful than amused. "You can arouse me any damned time you want, Albert," the man said, though it was obviously intended as a joke rather than a declaration of interest.

"I am fully aware of that," Albert offered in flat response to the tentative humor. "Do you think you can sleep on the condition that I don't?"

"That's hardly fair, is it?" Ash murmured. He turned away again, and settled. "But I'm good at taking advantage of you."

"It is an ability that has improved with repeated practice."

"Huh," Ash said, but it was almost a laugh. "Goodnight, Albert." Sooner than either of them could have expected, Ash was gently snoring.

All people dream, Albert knew. The dream state occurred approximately every ninety minutes throughout a night's sleep and lasted at least ten minutes. Albert, however, neither experienced nor remembered his dreams, and was content that it be so.

I do not dream, he declared to himself, even as he knew that he was. Strange – even repugnant – to be perfectly aware that he was lying asleep in bed, and yet be unable to prevent a dream occurring. *I do not dream*, he repeated. *I will wake up now.*

But he didn't wake. And the dream itself seemed harmless: he was simply scrubbing up, preparing for an autopsy. He was alone, and the labs stretched large and empty and echoing around him. When his dream–self was ready, he walked through into the morgue, heading for the wall of drawers that each contained a body. He went to a particular drawer, and pulled it out.

When he lifted the sheet aside, he saw that the body was Fletcher's.

Albert stared down at it, noting the dull pale skin, the traces of blue around the lips, the hair neatly combed back from the forehead, the cold rigidity of the posture. It wasn't immediately apparent how Fletcher had died and Albert supposed he must now find that out – though the thought of cutting into that chest and cracking the rib–cage open was terrible.

In life, Fletcher had been warm and unpredictable, those blue eyes hot behind the unruly tumble of thick hair, his body enthusiastically joyfully sensual. Some unique combination of qualities had enabled him to see so much more than was apparent to anyone else. The hair at the centre of his chest was shaped like a flame; before they became lovers, Albert had longed to cool that flame with the flat of his tongue but once he had the chance, he'd felt the impulse was too foolish to indulge.

His dream–self simply stood there, staring down at the body as if mesmerized, hardly reacting at all, as if he must forever maintain the pretence that he and Ash were no more than colleagues.

But, to add to the confusion and the sense of dislocation, his dream–self was imagining a truer reaction. In his dream–self's mind, Albert Sterne was crying.

He was still simply standing there, looking down at Fletcher, but this imagined–self was crying as if his whole life had shattered. He wasn't sobbing, Albert noted, he wasn't tearing his clothes and throwing a tantrum as he had at his parents' funeral. He was simply crying, and his face was wet with tears and mucus, and his mouth shaped the sounds of grief. Inside of this shattered self, inside of him was nothing but a great empty yearning that couldn't yet grasp the entirety of what he'd lost.

I will wake up now, Albert decided. Perhaps because he felt he had truly acknowledged the grief, he did wake. For a moment, he stared up at the ceiling, glad to be leaving the dream behind even though the vividness stayed with him. And then Albert realized that he was alone.

Another moment of that potent and physical apprehension. Easier to recognize the sensation for what it was now – fear for Ash's sake, and fear for his own – though the revelation was hardly welcome. Where the hell was Ash now?

Twilight had invaded the room. No sign of Ash. The bathroom door stood open, revealing nothing more than darkness. Albert got out of the bed, pulled his robe on, and walked over to look through the nearer of the glass doors that opened onto the balcony. While the sky still held a glow fading from gold in the west through the deepest of blues to charcoal overhead, the balcony itself was sheltered by the dense foliage of a tree that grew immediately beside the hotel. And there in the shadows, of course, was Fletcher, standing at the railing, surrounded by leaves and branches.

When he heard the door slide open, Ash turned around and leaned back against the railing, still in contact with this small piece of nature. He was wearing an old pair of track pants and a T–shirt, and seemed comfortable enough, though his arms were folded. "Hello, Albert."

Nodding once in reply to the greeting, having stepped just outside the door, Albert wondered how to voice his concern. "I should have stayed awake," he eventually said.

"It's all right, I didn't dream," Ash reassured him. "And you needed your rest as much as I did."

Nevertheless, I wish I hadn't fallen asleep, Albert thought, but he wasn't about to tell Ash why, so he let the matter go.

Ash was, however, continuing. "You know, I had the best sleep I've had in years. Feels like it, anyway." He smiled, both easy and self–conscious. "I was just thinking that maybe I can relax now, I know that sounds weird, but maybe I can finally let myself relax, because John Garrett isn't out there anymore. Does that sound crazy?"

"Not at all," Albert said, despite the fact that this calm and peaceful Ash was such a contrast to the man focused only on cleaning something that could not be scrubbed away.

"Don't lie to me, Albert." The smile broadened for a moment, then faded away. "I've been acting crazy, I know. I killed a man, you see, and I can rationalize it all I want because of what he was, but that doesn't help. I did what I had to do but it's hard to live with the fact I killed him. I think the blood–guilt will weigh on me all my life." Ash nodded, seemed to still be examining this notion. "At first I thought I was contradicting myself, but it's easy to live with the knowledge that he's gone."

"Good." Albert walked over to sit in one of the wickerwork chairs. The darkness was complete now, and the night's heat was leavened by a breeze that rustled the leaves around Ash.

"This is a nice place," Ash said, indicating the hotel with a lift of his chin. "Thanks for arranging it. You were right: I appreciate both the privacy and the comfort." He looked around at the little to be seen in the darkness. "It must be one of the older places, done up, right?"

"I assume so." Everything indicated this to be the case, from the cast iron railings Ash was leaning against to the inconvenient layouts of the rooms. Often in these situations, for instance, the bathroom used to be a dressing room.

"It's great." But Ash could not be distracted for long from what was on his mind. "I'm sorry about how I've been, it can't have been easy for you to deal with." He left a pause, as if to allow Albert the chance to accept this apology. "I feel sort of clear now. Empty and clear. And light – I might just float away."

"You haven't eaten in twenty–four hours," Albert observed.

A noise emanated from Ash that might have been a snort of amusement. "You are so damned practical," the man said. And then, very gravely, "Yes, I think I could eat something."

It was a matter of one phone call, and thirty minutes' wait, to have one of the local restaurants deliver a meal. Wanting to tempt Ash to eat while suspecting the man wasn't really hungry for once, Albert ordered a variety of small servings. He took advantage of the wait to dress in a shirt and trousers, and to locate the cutlery and crockery in the kitchen, and set it out on the table on the balcony. Ash had fallen silent and didn't talk much through the meal, but he was in a contemplative mood rather than a crazed or depressed one, so Albert willingly left him to it.

Whether it was due to Albert's strategy or because Ash would always be hungry no matter what, the food was devoured in a short space of time. Then Ash sat back and offered Albert another smile. "I love it out here," he said. "This tree is magnificent. But I think I also need to be in your arms right now. In fact, I definitely need to be in your arms. Any chance?"

Albert glanced around, which was superfluous. He'd already ascertained that they were enclosed on two sides by the tree and that not even the nearby streetlight could illuminate them through the foliage. The third side of the balcony was overlooked by nothing more than a tall brick building that had no windows above the first floor and was in total darkness. The only other balcony on this side of the hotel was directly above them. Feeling safe enough, Albert got up to turn off the light they'd eaten under, and to take one of the cushions from the chairs. He sat on the floor of the balcony, with the cushion between his back and the iron railings. "Come here," he invited.

Ash responded with alacrity, walking over to sit between Albert's legs, leaning back against his chest, settling in comfortably. "Thanks, love." He sighed, though it sounded happy enough, or at least satisfied. "Do you have any idea how therapeutic your hugs are?"

Rather than replying, Albert asked, "Is your skin causing you discomfort?"

"No." Ash shifted a shoulder in a lazy shrug. "Not really. No more than anything else." He reached a hand to where the tree had invaded beyond the railings – Albert reflected that he would have cut back the new season's growth before now – Ash gently rubbed the leaves in his fingers. And, finally, Ash began asking questions and talking, not about hugging and other nonsense, but about the matters that were concerning him.

Easing his arms around Ash's waist, Albert pressed a kiss to the man's temple, very casually, as if it were an insignificant gesture.

"You know," Ash was saying, "John Garrett made himself a popular man. I mean, even though I knew what he was, I could still see how he attracted people. Young men, in particular. It was like he was everyone's favorite uncle. If that had all been genuine, if he really was the person he pretended to be, he would have been a great guy. But he wasn't, I know very well he wasn't." A moment, and then, "How did the men who worked for him take the news? I'm sure it was hard, finding out what he'd done and how he died. Who went to tell them?"

"Halligan," Albert replied. "I believe he took two officers who also had friends or relations working there. He wanted to question the boy you met at Garrett's house."

"Steve? Poor kid, he had no idea. I hope Halligan handled it all right."

"He would have dealt with them appropriately." Albert offered the truth: "Perhaps not as sympathetically as you would have."

"Hell," said Ash, "I can't handle this myself, let alone help them through it. Much as I'd like to."

"If you can admit that you are in no condition to help anyone else, then stop worrying about them."

But Ash continued, "When I think about how many victims there are. Not just the twenty–two deaths, terrible deaths, but the families who lost sons and brothers. Even the people who knew Garrett, his acquaintances will be hurt, betrayed by their own judgment. They won't trust so easily next time. I figure no one will ever be the same again."

"Give yourself time to work through it. Don't let fear of what you feel hinder your healing."

A brief silence. "I hate it when you're wise about me but you won't apply it to yourself as well."

It was easy to ignore this petulant statement. Albert said, "I understand that the boy Steve was resentful, of course, and scared. But he corroborated the facts of what happened last night, as far as he was able. You underestimated his powers of observation, Ash. He'd realized there was tension between you and Garrett."

"They gave me one thing, Steve and John Garrett."

"What was that?" Albert prompted after a time.

When he finally spoke, Ash asked, "Did you listen to the tapes?"

"I heard some of it."

"He knew I understood him. That was one of the reasons he decided to talk to me about it. He could see there's a part of me that understands what it is to kill."

"Ash –"

"Let me finish, Albert. He knew that was why I've been obsessed with this case."

"It was hardly the only reason," Albert said.

"But it was a reason." Ash drew a deep breath. "Garrett suggested that he should demonstrate what he did on Steve. He suggested that I witness it, or even participate. Albert, I had the perfect chance then and there,

I could have done it, could have done anything I wanted with the boy. Then killed Garrett, too, like I did – and blamed Steve's death on him."

"No, you couldn't." Albert frowned. "And obviously you didn't."

A relieved moan, and Ash twisted deeper into Albert's embrace. "That's still the first thing you say, that I couldn't do it? Even when it's obvious I've thought about it?"

"Of course. You're no murderer, Ash."

"I know that now. That's what they gave me, you see. At the time, the only thing on my mind was getting Steve safely out of there. I didn't even consider taking the opportunity, didn't even think about it. It was only afterwards I started thinking, and my imagination did it all for me, even to the point of tidying it up afterwards and blaming it on Garrett. Though you would have found me out, wouldn't you? I couldn't have hidden all the forensic evidence."

"I doubt that you could have, unless the investigators were incompetent or didn't look beyond the obvious."

"Last night, I also discovered I can lie. Maybe I could even have lied about Steve's death."

Surely, after all these years, it was time to end this line of speculation. "You are no murderer," Albert repeated. "The empathy that allows you to understand John Garrett also allows you to have pity for his victims, their families, and even the people who knew him. If you were ever in a position to victimize someone – and you are probably in that position every day – your empathy would make it impossible for you to inflict pain. You would show nothing but compassion, mercy and understanding."

"Got *you* fooled, haven't I?" Ash said weakly.

"John Garrett only saw the understanding. While I am sure you showed him compassion, I doubt that he was capable of recognizing or responding to it."

"Really." Usually, when either of them reacted with that word, it carried a bite of sarcasm or challenge. This time, Ash was unable to even attempt the right tone.

"I am not paying you a compliment, Ash, there is no need to be shy of accepting it as such. I am simply telling you the truth."

The man sat quietly in Albert's arms, subdued. Finally he said, "Love you, Albert. Haven't told you that lately, have I?"

Unwise, Albert blurted out, "Your compassion obviously extends even to me."

"But you so rarely require compassion." Ash's tone was light, and Albert was relieved when the younger man didn't pursue the topic. Instead, Ash said, "You're right, I did feel sorry for Garrett. Not for who he became but for the boy he used to be. If someone could have helped him twenty years ago, he might never have become a whole or happy person, but he could at least have avoided the violence and the death."

A timeless while of silence again, until Albert said, "Your compassion, in fact, extends to everyone except yourself. You said that you can't handle this situation but then you talk of everything peripheral to yourself."

"It's no good talking about it, Albert. You probably expect me to rationalize it away, but I can't do that. I killed a man. If anyone deserved death, he did, but that doesn't make me feel any better about the fact that there's one less life now because of me."

Albert said, "Of course you are going to react to that emotionally rather than intellectually."

"That's what you don't understand, right? You'd be able to deal with the whole thing on a purely intellectual level."

"Perhaps," Albert replied, trying not to withdraw from the man in his embrace. If Ash thought Albert only ever reacted intellectually, then Ash was wrong – but it might be as well not to disabuse him of the notion. "I am unlikely to ever find myself in such a situation."

"Count your blessings," Ash said dryly. "To go there on my own, knowing what the outcomes might be, that was the most difficult thing I've ever had to do. Leaving you behind, knowing I might not see you again, that was ghastly. And I had to listen to a whole lot of stuff I really didn't want to know about. It's going to take a while to sort through all that." A moment, and another change of tone, before Ash continued, "But, beyond all that, the worst thing by far – he deliberately goaded me into killing him, you know. His death was suicide and murder and self–defense all at once. He was goading me into it but the worst thing is that I goaded him into it, too."

"Explain that."

"I was provoking him the whole time. I wanted to get behind his defenses, to get him to admit the truth to me, to make a confession, to let me arrest him. But, by provoking him, I put him in a situation where he only had two options: to kill me or to be killed. He didn't see there were other options."

"It is not your fault that Garrett refused to be arrested."

"I should have guessed that might be the case. So many of them get suicidal towards the end. He even – He showed me this terrible scar on his arm. You would have seen it."

"Yes, his left forearm. It was some years old."

"He told me he did that after his first murder. He didn't understand why but he'd tried to suicide afterwards. Maybe he didn't understand why he was showing me, either, but now I think he was trying to tell me that he was prepared to die. That he'd tried to carry out his own justice once before but I must do it for him this time. What do you think?"

"That is all possible but I really cannot say. You are in the best position to judge."

Something that sounded like breathless disbelieving laughter. "You have a lot of faith in me, Albert."

"If so, it is not undeserved." Silence again, long enough this time to indicate that Ash might have talked all he wanted for now. Albert said, "Your hair is still tangled with salt and sand. Rather than take another shower, perhaps you'd like me to help you wash it in the sink before we retire for the night."

"You're kind. No, don't tell me –" Ash almost laughed again. "You're only thinking of the pillows."

"Of course."

"It's a wonder you've allowed me to rest my head on your shirt." But when Ash moved, it was only to turn within Albert's arms, to cling to Albert as if he might leave. "I have to tell you something," Ash said quietly, his face at Albert's throat.

"Yes?"

"I almost killed myself twice today."

Impossible to prevent a physical reaction to such bluntness: Albert's whole body tightened its hold on the man convulsively.

"After I'd called Halligan, sitting there at Garrett's house, I almost fired my gun again. And then when I tried to get clean in the ocean, I almost kept swimming. And I wouldn't have reached South America."

"I see," Albert managed to say.

"But I didn't, Albert, I decided to live. I have to figure out how to live with the fact that I killed a man, but I will live."

A pause, which Albert didn't attempt to fill.

"If I didn't commit suicide today, then I never will. I had to tell you that. I know I scared you but you don't have to worry anymore, you can trust me. I promise."

"You did not scare me, Ash," Albert said flatly.

"Yes, I did. You were terrified you'd never be with me again." The man lifted his head and locked his gaze with Albert's, with only an inch between them so there was no escape. A moment that felt like agony, and then Ash apparently decided to show some mercy. "I would love you to wash my hair for me," he said simply, as if neither of them had talked of anything else since Albert's offer. His mouth quirked into a genuine smile. "And then you can do that thing with the hand cream again, if you like."

Once he thought he could rely on his voice, Albert said, "All right." But first they just sat there for a while, holding each other close. And eventually Albert found it in him to kiss the man again, simply to press another kiss to his temple, lightly as if the gesture had no significance.

CHAPTER THIRTY-FIVE
WASHINGTON DC
SEPTEMBER 1985

Fletcher felt as if he were in some kind of limbo, felt as if he were waiting for something, waiting for something he didn't even know the nature of. Here he was, alone and bored and rattling around Albert's home most days, while Albert went in to his labs at headquarters. Thankfully, the man was only working standard hours, rather than the ten- or fifteen-hour days he used to put in. Though it seemed pitiful, even to Fletcher, that the only thing Fletch found himself thankful for was Albert's company each evening.

The physical exertion of spending a day working in Albert's garden didn't seem to be helping, either. It didn't make him *feel*, or stop his mind racing back over recent events. Disappointing, really, to be busy mowing the grass, and still be fretting.

Limbo. In the immediate aftermath of killing Garrett, Fletch had feared what would happen when he began feeling again – now he was impatient for it. He wanted out of this numbness, this neutrality, this going through the motions. The only distraction from this nothingness was poor Albert. The only interruption from loitering was the discomfort of occasionally being called in to headquarters.

During those last days in New Orleans, and while here in Washington, Fletch had written up a dozen lengthy reports, including an annotated transcript of his interview with Garrett. He'd discussed it all a hundred times, with the Bureau's investigators in New Orleans, with the Behavioral Science Unit at Quantico, with the public relations people, and with damned well everyone else who wanted to know. He'd relived that last night of John Garrett's life a thousand times. It had been ghastly. The only thing he was thankful for, other than Albert's ever-present company, was that the Bureau respected his wish for privacy – which meant he didn't have to deal with the media. The Bureau, usually adamant in ensuring that special agents remained anonymous but always keen for good publicity, had really pushed Fletch on that one. *I'm no hero*, became his standard refrain. With which too many people disagreed.

The period post–Garrett – which he mentally labeled PG – hadn't been without its high points. The problem was that Fletcher had been in no condition to really appreciate them.

Albert, who'd been surprisingly supportive throughout the last days of Fletcher's investigation, had been even more amazingly wonderful during the first day of PG. Exactly what a wounded man needed, all the quiet loving care Albert provided.

Things had changed since then, of course. During those first twenty–four hours PG, both Fletch and Albert had been so reduced by all that happened, so raw and stunned and vulnerable. Now they were returning to themselves, and all the old tensions and difficulties and disappointments were also returning. Though nothing, for Fletcher at least, could diminish the fact that Albert had cared so well for him, so much for him – and Fletch suspected that Albert wouldn't forget that fact, either.

Another high point had been sharing a couple of bottles of burgundy with the ponderous mountain that was Judge Beaufort. The man hadn't seemed surprised to see Fletcher sitting up the back of his court one afternoon, with Albert in tow. Fletch and Albert were virtually inseparable PG, which Fletcher assumed must soon drive the older man quite mad.

Beaufort had invited them home for dinner, over which he and his wife and Fletcher talked about the nature of justice. Albert provided minimal comments – though as all his observations cut right to the heart of whichever issue was being explored, this participation was both amusing and annoying, and tended to put a damper on the conversation.

Fletcher had at last said to the judge, "You've heard how my case ended."

"Yes," Beaufort replied, as slow and deliberate as ever. "The man is dead."

"I never intended that – at least, I knew it was one possible outcome when I went to his house. I didn't want it, but he forced the situation."

The judge said, "What is it that you want to ask me, Special Agent?"

Fletcher looked at the grave faces of his three companions. "Your opinion matters to me, Your Honor."

"It is no use asking me to sanction your actions, Fletcher: I wasn't there, I don't know what happened between you and Mr. Garrett. It seems that you acted properly. Though approaching him alone was unorthodox, I do not believe you went there with murder in your heart."

This was close to what Fletcher wanted to hear. But, once heard, it didn't seem enough. He nodded, unhappy.

"You can't deal with this on a rational level," Beaufort continued after examining Fletch's expression. "It is an emotional issue for you, not an intellectual one. It doesn't matter to you whether your friends support you, or what my opinion is, or whether you were cleared by the Bureau's investigation – what matters is whether you can forgive yourself."

"All of that matters," Fletch said, though he felt dismal. "It matters that I was cleared by the field office this afternoon."

"It doesn't matter as much." Beaufort shifted a little in his seat, leaned forward. "Your own conscience matters most to you, and you have fine principles: that is partly why I trust you. If you want my opinion, then, if the matter came before me, and there was nothing more to know, I would dismiss any charges. Of course, no one can tell the whole story – not even you, now that Mr. Garrett is dead. But you should consider dismissing the charges you've laid against yourself. You should move on to other things."

And Fletcher had taken heed of this advice, though he felt he was still missing the vital parts of the puzzle. There had to be a way of dealing with this blood–guilt. There had to be something more than the time needed to heal. Because otherwise his whole life might not be enough time.

As he finished mowing the lawn and began weeding the garden beds, Fletcher reflected that he'd been disappointed in the Bureau's investigation. It was over so quickly that he felt there couldn't possibly have been suitable consideration given to the issues. But everyone involved had been relentlessly supportive, which was such a complete turnaround from the previous lack of belief in him it was absurd. Fletcher suspected that all the evidence proving Garrett was the serial killer might be overriding people's other concerns.

It was too easy from this side of it to wonder if there were anything else he could have done.

Albert seemed to be the only one treating this seriously. He had insisted on taking Fletcher to talk with a defense lawyer, and from what Fletch could make out, the best and most expensive defense lawyer in town. Uncomfortable with this, believing that the truth should be enough, Fletcher nevertheless acquiesced for Albert's sake.

After ten minutes of conversation in her subtle but rich offices, the lawyer had fastened Fletch with a sharp gaze and said, "I'm beginning to understand Mr. Sterne's concern. I trust you wouldn't plead guilty if they charged you with murder, Mr. Ash."

And Fletcher had been forced to find the answer, which was, "No." Even though he thought someone, somewhere should at least make that accusation.

When he and Albert returned to their hotel that evening, Fletcher immediately headed for the balcony and leaned forward, arms outstretched, into the living wall of green that surrounded and infiltrated the railings. If the closer branches had been stronger, he probably would have climbed right in.

"Communing with nature, Ash?" Albert had commented, sardonic, when he joined Fletch outside.

"This is wonderful," Fletcher replied. He turned around to see his lover, though he remained in contact with the tree. "You chose this place for me, didn't you?"

"You may think it's wonderful but it also makes us vulnerable to burglary. I trust you'll ensure the balcony windows remain locked when you're not out here."

Fletcher considered the man for a moment. "Just think of all that energy you waste being a wet blanket twenty–four hours a day."

"I am being practical."

"It's really illogical, you know," Fletch mused. "Being gloomy is such a waste of time." But he relented, and said, "This place is wonderful and you chose it for me, and I love you for it."

"Platitudes and sentiment," Albert observed.

The phone rang at that moment, saving Fletch from having to retort. He headed inside and picked up the receiver. "Hello, Fletcher Ash speaking."

"It's Caroline. How are you, Fletch?"

"I'm getting there." He wasn't going to lie to her, but when he'd tried confessing all he felt, in a long painful difficult phone call the second day after he'd killed Garrett, Caroline Thornton hadn't managed to empathize with the depth of Fletch's angst.

"You did what you had to do, Fletcher," she said now. "Don't beat yourself up over it. The man was a monster."

"I know." Grimacing, Fletch added, "I'll be all right." He turned to lean against the wall, wondering how often he and Caroline had to do this. It seemed impossible to really communicate with her these days. Hoping to change the topic of conversation, Fletch asked, "What's new?"

"Oh, you're still flavor of the month and so am I." Her nonchalant tone couldn't really hide her genuine satisfaction. "And so is your friend McIntyre, if you haven't picked up on that yet."

"That's good." Fletcher could only find the enthusiasm to match Caroline's for this last piece of news. "Perhaps Mac can be promoted as a special agent now."

"Perhaps."

"And maybe I can be his supervisor."

"Maybe. No promises, but I'll work on it, if that's what you want." She paused, then said, "I called to see if you'd decided what you're going to do. Right now, I mean."

"I need some time off, Caroline."

"Understood. How long?"

"I don't know how long; I need to just get away and not worry about when I'm due back." He sighed. "I might spend a while up in Idaho, I really can't say yet."

"That's fine, Fletcher. Actually, I think that's really good. You feeling able to go away and leave all the loose ends in other people's hands is a good sign."

Fletch gave a non–committal grunt.

"There's one condition. You take all the time you need and let us know when you're ready to come back. But I'm setting one condition, for the sake of your career: tell us what you want to do when you're ready to work again. For your own sake, you should take the opportunities you're being offered while you can. Have you thought about it?"

"Yeah, I've thought about it. All I ever wanted to be was a special agent, Caroline, I'm not ambitious like you. And I don't want to join the Behavioral Science Unit, I don't want to be doing this kind of work all my life. But I was thinking maybe I could act as the BSU's criminal profile coordinator in one of the field offices."

"That's a good idea. I'll raise it with them. You know they'll give you anything you want right now."

"Fine, thanks for that." Fletch asked, "What about you?"

"Onwards and upwards: New York City field office."

Fletcher grinned. "Well done."

"I owe you, Fletch. If you weren't flavor of the month, it wouldn't be rubbing off on the rest of us."

"You believed enough to support me, Caroline. And you damned well know you deserve a promotion anyway."

"Yeah," she said, the satisfaction now obvious. "Take care and call me again before you leave, all right?"

"Goodbye, Caroline." Fletcher barely waited for her farewell before hanging up. His grin quickly faded, and he rubbed at his face with both hands.

Albert had apparently been listening in. He walked over, took Fletcher's shoulders in his hands and said very seriously, "I know this has cost you."

Fletch sighed. "I needed to hear someone say that."

"But don't lapse into self–pity."

Yes, Fletcher reflected, Albert was back to his merciless self. Despite that, Fletch took the opportunity for a hug.

He'd met Mac and Celia for dinner that night – with Albert still in tow, surprisingly enough. They ate at a French restaurant, the four of them sitting around a U–shaped booth. Fletcher had passed on the news that Mac's career might also benefit from his involvement in this case. "If they don't make you a special agent," Fletch had promised, "it won't be for lack of Caroline trying." And he'd done his own lobbying on Mac's behalf, of course, since he'd come to Washington.

"That's terrific," Celia had said warmly, clasping Mac's hand in hers on the table.

"Thank you," Mac said to both of them. "I appreciate it. Don't quite see what I did to deserve it but that's not the point, is it? You're in the limelight, and so are we."

Fletcher replied, "You deserve it, don't forget that. Just sit back and let Caroline do her bit. She's got the hang of all this political stuff."

Much to everyone's amazement, Albert said coldly, "Don't waste time with false modesty, McIntyre. Your work has been significant in progressing this case."

Mac was almost gaping. "Who are you, and what have you done with the real Albert Sterne?"

"Don't be any more ridiculous than you have to be."

"When you realize that added up to a compliment, I know you'll take it back." But there was no reply, no retort. More seriously, Mac asked, "What about you, Albert? What dizzy heights is your career going to reach now?"

"I have no interest in performing any job other than the one I occupy."

Fletcher frowned, unhappy that this was the first time any of them had thought of Albert and the rewards the Bureau should be offering him. It wasn't comfortable, wondering whether his own lack of concern was simply because he knew Albert well enough to guess he wouldn't welcome a promotion or, indeed, any other form of recognition.

Mac was frowning, too. In fact, he was looking almost indignant. "After Fletcher, you deserve the most out of this. I know all the work you put in, or I can guess, and you supported Fletch the whole time. Make the most of the opportunity."

"I am not interested in taking advantage of any putative opportunity."

Taking pity on Albert finding himself at the centre of attention, Fletch re-directed the topic by saying, "Where do you want to work, Mac? Do you want to stay in Washington? Because if we're in the same field office, I'd love to be your supervisor. I told Caroline that already."

The frown was replaced in an instant with a broad smile. "That would be great! Do you think they'll agree?"

"Of course they will," Albert said distantly. "The Bureau always teams the staff it perceives as potential problems. Thornton and Ash are a classic example. If things go wrong, there are plenty of people to blame."

"Ignore him, Mac," Fletch said. "Albert is the biggest cynic I've ever met."

"Hell, he's probably right. But we've already proved them wrong once, haven't we?"

"Yeah, we have," Fletch agreed with a smile.

"You're not staying in Denver, Fletcher?" Celia asked the question lightly, but there was an unusual tone in her voice: pensive; unsure. Both Mac and Fletch turned to look at her. "Seems ridiculous, I know," she continued, "but I've become used to having you here with me in New Orleans, Mac."

"That's not ridiculous," he said, almost in a whisper.

"It is, seeing as it's only been a few weeks. Shouldn't be able to form a habit that quickly. Especially one I've been resisting for so long. Fiercely independent, that's my trouble."

Fletcher found himself smiling inanely. He'd always had the impression that Mac and Celia's relationship was far more casual than Mac would have liked it.

As for Mac, he'd obviously decided words wouldn't do. He slid closer to Celia, took her in his arms, and kissed her as if he were auditioning for the role of Clark Gable. Fletch let out a cheer.

And then there had been all the rigmarole of Fletcher's good wishes for the pair, and Mac and Celia making it quite clear that they could each move to wherever the other was based, and Fletch admitting he didn't have the first idea where he might end up, but it would be a field office somewhere closer to Washington than Denver was. And Albert silent and uninterested through it all, not even reacting to this last piece of information and all it implied. Having decided that was enough of a hint, Fletcher restrained himself from commenting on the horrors of long distance relationships – instead, he bought a couple of bottles of champagne with which to celebrate and drank far more than his share.

Three days after that dinner – a week ago now – Fletcher had flown back to Washington with both Albert and Mac in tow. And here Fletch was, in limbo, pruning and trimming the plants in Albert's garden, which he supposed was an improvement on rattling around Albert's beautiful house wondering what on earth to do with himself.

The answer, at least immediately, was obvious. Albert was due home soon, so Fletcher would clean up and wait for him on the front steps as usual. It was a lovely day, with the first hints of that crisp fall flavor to the air that reached all the way up to the pale blue sky, with most trees still richly green and others beginning to stain their leaves gold. Fletcher sat there, wishing he could appreciate it like he used to, wishing he could appreciate even the rusty ache in his limbs from all this manual work.

Limbo. He hoped he wasn't becoming the kind of person who could observe but not feel.

As soon as the Saab turned into the street, Fletch headed for the garage and opened the doors so that Albert could drive right in.

"Pathetic," was the man's first comment once he joined Fletcher outside. "I thought you now had more productive tasks to accomplish."

"Done them," Fletch informed him.

This obviously surprised the man. After much begging and convincing on Fletcher's part, the list of garden chores had been handed over that morning, along with detailed verbal instructions and much barely suppressed trepidation. It was now evident Albert believed that, if Fletch had managed to complete all the chores, the quality of the job must be lacking. Fletcher accompanied the man on a tour of inspection. His work was eventually pronounced, "Adequate."

"Is that all?"

"This is satisfactory, Ash. What more do you wish me to say?"

Fletch replied, "Nothing." He began smiling. Given the man's high standards, it was quite a compliment for Albert to describe something as satisfactory – for a moment, Fletcher had forgotten that.

"Perhaps tomorrow you can buy two new shrubs for the border on the left there, and plant them."

"All right." He added with a grin, "I'm sure you'll tell me exactly what sort."

"Yes."

"Albert," Fletcher said, while they were still wandering the backyard, amidst the peace of myriad greens. "Would it be all right if I stayed here while I'm on leave?"

"What would be the purpose of that?"

Fletcher sighed, looked around at the nearest flower bed. "Guess I've formed a habit, too." But Albert wouldn't appreciate recycled words. "I want to be with you. It helps. It's really helped me to be with you."

"I see."

"I don't mind that you'll be working. In fact, I could be your assistant – at work, I mean."

"You're suggesting that you tag along on my cases, both at headquarters and in the field offices, like a lost child? It wouldn't be appropriate."

"I don't want to be a burden, I just thought I could help you in turn. But if not, can I stay here, in your home? Next time you have to travel, I could go up to Idaho for a few days, or something."

Silence for a while. Presumably Albert was weighing the positives and negatives of having Fletcher live with him for a time. At last the man said, "It was my intention to take a period of leave to coincide with yours. I thought we might drive somewhere and you could sightsee."

"Yeah?" Fletcher found he was grinning broadly at this unexpected offer. "That would be wonderful. Why didn't you say before?"

Albert seemed impatient. "I assumed it was obvious. I am finishing a variety of tasks at work, I'm in the process of closing up the house, and you have just assisted me with the garden."

"You should have said," Fletcher insisted. "You can be such an idiot."

"Compared to what?" the man asked, distant. Then, more directly, "I have made some unwarranted assumptions."

"No, you haven't. At least, I have, too. I never thought you'd want to come with me. Hell, the last time we took a few days off together – remember?"

"Yes, I recall."

It had been when they'd first become lovers, and they'd headed to New England for a crazed long weekend of driving and sightseeing and sex. In fact, Fletcher now realized their first anniversary had passed him by while they were in New Orleans, and he'd entirely forgotten it. "That was a year ago, love, a year and a few days," Fletch said. "Seems appropriate we're going to take some time off again."

Albert seemed uninterested. Fletcher reflected that the bastard had no doubt remembered the exact date, and hadn't bothered to remind Fletcher of it. Though he supposed they'd both had other things on their minds at the time.

Rather than accuse him of this dereliction, Fletch continued, "Let's just get out on the road and see where it takes us. In fact, how about we aim for Idaho but take a couple of weeks or more to get there?"

"You wish to visit your family."

"Yeah, I do. And if you'd come with me, that would be perfect."

"Perfect," Albert repeated, as if he were unsure of the word in this context. The silence threatened to return.

"Please, love. It won't be too painful. If it is, just let me know and we'll keep driving, won't stop until we hit the Oregon state line. Well, Nevada, maybe – too many memories in Oregon for now. But I want to see Dad and Harley and Beth and the kids again."

A nod, which might have been acknowledgment but that Fletch chose to interpret as agreement.

Before he could have second thoughts, Fletcher blurted out, "And you can ask Dad for my hand in marriage."

Silence again. Albert was apparently trying to decide whether the lawn had been mowed evenly. But eventually he said, "Such an alliance would require a substantial dowry to make it attractive. I doubt that your father could afford it."

Fletcher grinned. "I've missed your insults, you know that?" But that wasn't enough. He felt like hugging the man, so managed to shepherd him inside despite a lack of cooperation. Once behind closed doors, however, Albert drew Fletch into his arms with only the smallest display of unwillingness. They held each other close for a while, they even kissed – during which Fletch could sense that Albert was holding back, was restraining an eagerness.

It had been so long since they'd made love. And Fletcher felt he could do it now, if he wanted. If he wanted to bring himself to the act, to give himself to Albert. But he couldn't quite want that. Limbo. That was crazy, when Albert was here and ready and eager. Imagine Albert being the one missing out, Fletcher reflected – that was a turnaround from the usual.

Fletch let the man go, and offered a smile. "I'll call Dad." Then he quickly amended, "I'll call Dad tomorrow."

Albert didn't seem to notice the change in plan. He headed for the kitchen, and began to prepare a meal. Sitting at the kitchen table with a mug of coffee, Fletcher considered this man. Albert was so reliable, yet so full of surprises, and as Fletch felt that both these traits were essential in a lover, he figured it was really no wonder that he loved Albert so much.

Within half an hour, Albert brought dinner over, and they ate in silence. Until at last Fletcher said, "Thanks for trusting me with the garden."

Albert merely nodded once in reply.

As soon as Albert left for work the next morning, Fletcher collected Albert's bike from the garage, rode to a phone booth some distance away, and called Peter Ash. "Dad, it's Fletch."

"Hello," Peter said, apparently both surprised and relieved. "I missed talking with you, it's been two Sundays. Your boss said you were in the middle of a case."

"Yeah, sorry. Things have been a little crazy lately." Before his father could ask for details, Fletch continued, "Actually, the reason I'm calling is that I have some leave and I thought I'd come visit for a while."

"You know you're always welcome, as long as you can put up with us working the diner most of the day. How long can you stay?"

"I don't know, my plans are pretty open–ended."

"When do they expect you back at work? Don't worry," Peter added with a laugh, "it's safe to tell me. I won't expect you to spend *all* your leave with us."

"I just have some time off," Fletch said, knowing he sounded uncomfortable. "Whatever time I need."

Silence for a moment as Peter realized the ramifications. "What's happened?"

"It's all right, they haven't fired me." Sighing, Fletcher asked, "Remember that old murder case I was working on in my spare time? Well, I solved it. I'm getting time off for good behavior."

It was soon evident that Peter realized there was more going on than Fletch was prepared to tell. "All right, that's fine, Fletcher," he said, reassuring. "You're welcome, of course, for as long as you need. In fact, I'm flattered you thought of coming to us."

Before his father could go as far as rolling out the red carpet, Fletch said, "There's one other thing. Remember Albert? I want to bring him with me."

The slightest hesitation before Peter replied, "That's fine. He can come up here and be 'vastly bitter and rude' to his heart's content."

"Yeah, I hope so. I have to warn you about something, though." Fletcher took a moment to feed more coins into the phone.

"What is it?"

"Me and Albert, Dad. We've been more than friends for a year now. Not that there's anything more valuable than friendship. I mean, we're lovers. More than that, even. This is it for me, Dad."

"I see," Peter said. "You're telling me Albert is your ... spouse."

Fletcher closed his eyes. He'd love to be able to agree with that statement, especially as Peter was being so good about this. Instead he continued, "So I thought I should warn you. And ask if we're still welcome."

"Of course you're still welcome." The tone was hearty, betrayed by only a hint of uncertainty. "You're very welcome here, both of you. We'll be glad to finally meet him."

Something like a laugh escaped Fletcher. "I also want you to give him a chance before you decide you don't like him."

"We're not going to like him?" Peter asked, at last beginning to sound a little dazed.

"You'd better warn Harley he's a vegetarian, too."

And Peter did laugh then, though it seemed born of surprise. "I *think* we'll cope with that as well."

"All right."

There was a silence, perhaps thoughtful, perhaps simply reeling. Eventually Peter said, "This must be difficult for you. I mean, difficult in all sorts of ways – but especially working in the FBI."

"Yeah. Albert's kind of paranoid about it. That's why I'm at a phone booth."

"I understand. Well, I understand as well as I can from this distance." Another pause. "Fletcher. Are you happy?"

"Happy with Albert, yeah. You probably won't see why, but I am."

"So what is it that's wrong? Why is the FBI giving you all this time off? Or don't I want to know?"

"You don't want to know," Fletch said. He sighed, and added, "Except that it's over now, it's all over, and I just have to find the pieces and pick them up."

"Maybe," Peter Ash said, "maybe we can help you with that."

"Maybe you can," Fletcher agreed, though he knew he could never share the blood–guilt with anyone but Albert, because no one but Albert would ever quite understand. Fletch said goodbye, and hung up the phone.

Imagine that – he'd just come out to his father, and Peter Ash had been as accepting of that as of all the other things Fletcher had thrown at him over the years. They weren't close, he and his father, but Fletch knew Peter would always be there for him. Still, Fletch knew this phone call was only the beginning. Peter would have to think it through, Beth and Harley would need to be told, and then they'd all have to deal with Albert himself. *Oh joy*, Fletch thought with bleak humor. He had no idea how Albert would, in turn, deal with the Ash family.

Fletcher had another phone call to make but, before he did so, he climbed onto the bike and rode it around the block, legs pumping furiously. There were some things he didn't want to have on his mind when he rang headquarters. When he finally called, he located Mac, and asked the man out to lunch.

"So I guess I wanted to apologize," Fletcher said to Mac over their usual meal of steak and chips. "I need some time away from all this, I need to deal with what I've done."

"You had no choice −" Mac began in standard reassurance.

Fletcher waved that topic away. "Caroline will look after you for me while I'm gone. If she can't kick−start our careers for us, no one can."

"That's fine, Fletch. You didn't have to take me out to lunch to explain."

"Well, I might not be back for a while, I just don't know. I need to figure out where all this leaves me."

To his credit, Mac didn't comment on that last statement. "Where are you heading?"

"We're going to get in the Saab and see where the road takes us, but we're sort of heading for Idaho."

"Who's *we*?" Mac looked askance at him. "You're not taking Albert."

"Yeah, I am. He offered before I thought to ask, believe it or not."

Mac said lightly, "Figured it was time he met the family, did you?"

Fletcher looked up at his friend, and tried to match the bland expression − the trouble being, Mac was betrayed by curiosity, and Fletch by amusement. "Exactly what are you implying, Mac?"

"I'm not going to say it," the man protested.

"You think *I'm* crazy enough to say it?" Fletch retorted.

A taut moment, before Mac began laughing. "What a ludicrous notion, I don't know how I could even have imagined it in the first place." He put his cutlery down. "I've lost my appetite. If it's true, you *are* crazy."

"I don't know what you're talking about."

"Fine, we can play it like that." The man leaned forward. "But I'm your friend, Fletcher, you can tell me what's going on."

"No, I can't. Albert would kill me if he knew you'd figured it out."

"God preserve me, it *is* true, isn't it?"

Fletcher grinned. It was only lunchtime, and here he was coming out for the second time that day. "It's true. I'm as nuts about him as you are about Celia, if you won't get offended by the comparison."

"Of course not." A delicate pause. "And what about him?"

"Oh, he returns the favor, even if he won't admit it."

"You're a braver man than I," Mac said fervently. "Don't tell me: you found the pony behind all the shit." They were silent for a moment, until Mac offered Fletch his hand across the table, and they shook on it. "Are congratulations in order?"

"Yeah, and I'm grateful. Tell Celia if you like, if you think she'll be okay about it – but no one else, Mac, not even Caroline. We'd lose our jobs if the Bureau found out, and you know what Albert's work means to him."

"Yeah, your secret's safe, and all that." Mac shook his head. "I have a million questions."

Fletcher's grin grew broad. One of the traits he and Mac shared was a devilish curiosity. "When I get back," he promised. "You can buy me a few drinks, somewhere we won't be overheard, and I'll tell you all the gory details. Though, if Albert finds out you know *anything*, he'll kill you."

"I guess I'll take the risk to hear the story." Mac nodded, and returned to his meal.

The silence settled while they finished eating, then Mac began to talk about more mundane topics over another beer. Not contributing much – and apparently not being expected to – Fletcher reflected how good it was to be able to share the fact of his love with his fellow creatures. He hadn't realized what a burden the secrecy had been until some of it lifted. Hopefully, sharing Albert with his family, and with Mac and Celia, would be enough to lighten that load.

Fletcher smiled, and swallowed some more beer. He was looking forward to some long conversations with Peter Ash. And then he realized that he wasn't really in limbo anymore. When it came to his lover, and to his father and friends, Fletcher was at last beginning to feel and to respond as if he were still alive.

Albert, of course, had the house and the packing fully organized within a suitable timeframe prior to their date of departure. The last item to be placed in the Saab was Albert's briefcase. "You're going to be working?" Fletch asked, unsurprised. What else did Albert ever do with his time?

"I would like to write a paper on a particular area of forensic chemistry I have been researching – I doubt that you'd want to know the details, Ash – but my caseload and my other responsibilities haven't allowed me the necessary time. This journey seems the ideal opportunity to consider my findings and to write them up."

There was a pause, and Fletcher belatedly realized that Albert was waiting for a reaction. It would have seemed impossible, not so long ago, that Albert would get even this close to asking Fletcher's permission regarding anything relating to work. "That's fine," Fletch said, stumbling over the words in his haste. "I mean, I was wondering what you were planning on doing with yourself."

Amidst the momentary bustle of settling the luggage, Albert said, "It will not require my undivided attention."

Fletcher smiled at this unexpected but very welcome information. And then his face fell as Albert slid a comprehensive map out of the briefcase and took it around to the driver's door. "I thought," said Fletcher, "we were going to see where the road took us. But I suppose you have our itinerary all planned."

"No, I don't. The map is to assist when your impulses get us lost. And also to demonstrate that it would not be logical to drive through Florida on the way to Idaho."

The smile, of course, returned. "You are an idiot," Fletcher declared, "and I love you for it."

Looking somewhat pained, Albert slid into the car with a last glance at his home. When Fletcher joined him, Albert asked, "Where do you wish to head for today?"

"I don't know. What's in Kentucky?"

Albert nodded, and backed out onto the road. As he shifted into first gear and pulled away, he said, quietly yet very clearly, "You're an idiot, too."

Fletcher found himself too busy glowing to be surprised at this declaration.

"You're proving my assertion," Albert continued after a moment. "You obviously lack the mental capacity to realize when you've been insulted. Either you're idiotically ingenuous, or you're too ingenious in inferring things that I have neither stated nor implied."

"Sure, Albert," Fletch said easily, the glow continuing unabated. He settled down into the seat, comfortable now, and in some small measure content.

THE BEST PRESENT EVER
IDAHO
OCTOBER 1985

It had been easy to ignore the discomfort in the initial fuss of their arrival. Fletch and Albert had reached Fletcher's old home a little after three o'clock one afternoon, and were greeted by a bustle of Ashes. Peter, Harley, Beth and the two children all wanted to share exuberant hugs with Fletcher – between which, Fletch managed to introduce Albert, who solemnly shook hands with each member of the family. The children, Frances and Patrick, obviously hadn't forgotten their love for their uncle, despite the length of time since his last visit. Fletcher found it overwhelming to be plunged into such energy and noise; it was a dramatic contrast to the undemanding thoughtful quietness he'd shared with Albert during the past two weeks.

Then there was the fuss of retrieving their luggage from the car, finding bags small enough for the kids to help carry, and taking it all inside. The discomfort became obvious when Peter led everyone to Fletcher and Harley's old room, where the two single beds had been replaced by a double. "Will this suit you both?" Peter asked Fletcher.

"Sure," he replied. Though Fletch wasn't game to look at Albert or any of his family, he became keenly aware that the adults were all feeling varying degrees of uncertainty and embarrassment. The luggage was dumped on the bed, with Albert quickly righting and rearranging his, and then everyone headed back out to the kitchen, the kids dancing around Fletcher like he was a walking carnival.

Peter put the kettle on and made a round of coffee – and a herbal tea for Albert – while the Ashes passed on family news and asked about Fletch and Albert's trip. Things became quieter once the children ran through to the other end of the house, having been asked to clean up: they were only persuaded to do so by the suggestion that they could then bring their latest drawings and toys out to show Fletch.

As the adults settled around the kitchen table, with steaming cups and a plate of cookies before them, the discomfort could no longer be ignored. Fletcher looked around at his family, noting the silence: it seemed born of confusion, as if none of them knew quite what to say; which was perhaps inevitable, given that he'd brought his lover home, his lover who happened to be a man. Albert, of course, seemed oblivious: he was staring at the wall opposite him, over the heads of Beth and Harley, no doubt considering nothing more than the next point he wanted to develop in his forensic chemistry paper. The drinks were still too hot for any of them to sip at, and no one seemed to want to eat. The silence stretched.

Fletcher let out a laugh. Everyone turned to him – even, after a long moment, Albert. "It's all right, Albert," Fletch began. "It's fine. They just don't know what to say to you. Because I already phoned Dad and warned him – I had to warn him, you see." The atmosphere had become fraught. "I warned him that you're a vegetarian."

And Fletch cracked up, laughing so hard that he had tears in his eyes within moments. He could sense everyone's gaze on him, felt the confusion thicken.

Which was when Albert said, very smoothly, "I trust that won't be a problem for you, Mr. Ash."

Lifting his head, Fletch saw his father looking bemused. "Well, no, it's not a problem, Albert. You know, the one thing we can rely on with Fletcher is that he always has a surprise for us. The only real surprise is that we still get surprised. I should be expecting this kind of thing. But I must say that when Fletcher phoned me and said he was involved … he'd become involved with a vegetarian …"

Beth was chuckling at this conclusion. "We're not used to it here in Idaho," she explained. "If we have vegetarians, they're all in the closet."

"In the pantry," Fletch countered. He glanced back at Peter, and burst out laughing again. Peter began chuckling, too. It seemed Harley didn't appreciate the joke: his expression betrayed a touch of distaste. Albert, however, simply appeared neutral, unconcerned – which was so far from his habitual stony face, he could almost have been smiling.

"It seems," said Fletcher's father to Albert, "you'd better start by calling me Peter."

Which was when the kids descended on Fletcher again. "What's funny?" Patrick demanded as he climbed onto Fletch's lap. The boy had inherited his mother's blond hair and cheerfulness: he was all sunshine.

"I was just telling your grandpa that Albert's a vegetarian."

"Fletcher," Harley pleaded. "Don't get too clever."

"What's that?" asked the boy.

"He doesn't eat meat, not even chicken or fish."

"Why?" Which had apparently become Patrick's standard response: Fletch remembered Frances forever asking the same at Patrick's age.

"He doesn't eat meat: that is pretty funny," Frances declared with the utmost seriousness. She was kneeling on the chair beside Fletcher, arranging a sheaf of paper and her tin of colored pencils on the table. It seemed Frances took after her father and grandfather, with her hazel hair, and the big hazel eyes that she opened wide when emphasizing something. She asked her uncle, "Is Albert your new brother?"

Fletcher grinned, and reached out a hand to ruffle her hair – being four now, she was almost too old to put up with that. "No, he's my best friend."

"Why?" asked Patrick.

"Because he's the best person I've ever met."

Harley let out a breath that sounded like relief: apparently he could deal with this description of his brother's lover. He began passing the plate of cookies around: everyone but Albert took one.

"Dad," Patrick asked, "who's your best friend?"

"Your mother is," Harley replied easily. And then he realized the implications of claiming that his marriage had any similarity to Fletch and Albert's relationship.

Dead silence for a long moment as the adults waited for the children to add this up.

But they didn't – at least, not for now. Frances simply announced, "I'll draw you a picture," and Patrick began describing the party he'd like for his third birthday. Fletcher offered Harley a smile, and bent to kiss the top of Patrick's head.

It seemed Harley was prepared to warily accept the situation. Until Beth asked, with a straight face, "Is it true what they say about decadent old Washington? You know, vegetarian bars on every corner?" Which was when Fletch, Peter and Beth cracked up all over again.

The family's diner was a dim and comfortable place, with a steady stream of customers. Fletcher had elected to help for the afternoon, given that the Ashes had taken the previous day off for his sake, leaving the diner in the hands of the two casual staff they employed. Unexpectedly, Fletch found he was enjoying himself – despite explaining a dozen times that yes, he was young Fletcher – and even while they told him my hadn't he grown and could he really be thirty–three already. He had helped out in the diner twice before, during his visits since the Ashes had bought the place; and he was observant enough to know what waiters were generally expected to do for the customers: however, Harley was having great difficulty deciphering Fletcher's cryptic orders, and had occasionally prepared the wrong meal.

Albert had brought his work with him, and settled in the booth at the back near the kitchen, where the Ashes usually based themselves. Concentrating on the paper he was writing, Albert seemed completely oblivious to his surroundings, only acknowledging Fletcher when he went over to refill Albert's glass of water.

Late in the afternoon, in the quiet time before the dinner crowd began arriving, Fletcher propped himself by the cash register, and contemplated his lover. The man was being remarkably restrained. Wholly withdrawn. Which, while it meant Fletcher's family wouldn't be mortally offended by Albert's scathing insults, wasn't good. Fletch felt that he and Albert needed to return to themselves, after all that happened in New Orleans. They had begun to get back to what they'd been, later in Washington, but Albert's withdrawal into utterly polite privacy wasn't going to help either of them. At least, it wouldn't help Fletcher and it wouldn't help their relationship; whether it would help Albert was another matter.

"Taking a break?" Peter asked from just behind him.

Fletch started. "Sorry, what should I be doing?" He looked around, but didn't see any of the customers needing one of the hundred little attentions that added up to good and smooth service.

"Relax," Peter said with a laugh. "You're entitled to a break, you've been doing a terrific job, other than annoying poor Harley. Here –" and Peter handed over the cup of coffee he'd just poured.

"Thanks." There was a silence, before Fletcher said, "Spit it out, Dad. What do you want to ask me? Something about Albert, right?" Albert, who continued working obliviously, even though he was only fifteen feet away.

Peter's laugh returned. "It *is* love, isn't it? Not everything revolves around Albert, Fletcher: at least, not for everyone else."

"What, then?"

"Don't worry, we'll talk about Albert later," Peter reassured him. "For now, I wanted to ask again what's happened to you. Why the FBI let you have all this time off. Why you're ..." Peter seemed unable to find the right word. "Why you're so sad," he eventually said. "It seems to me that you've been rather troubled. I can see that you're coping with it, but maybe you need to do more than cope."

Fletch shrugged. "I'll be all right."

"You've been hurt, Fletcher. Maybe I can't help you heal, but I'd like to try. If you want to talk about it –"

"No." Then he softened the rejection with a smile. "I know you're there for me. But there are some things you wouldn't want to help me with." Fletch continued, overriding Peter's instinctive protest: "I'll be all right, Dad, as much as I can be. Albert – Albert's been wonderful. Very supportive."

"Yeah?" Peter, of course, seemed skeptical.

"Yes," Fletcher said firmly.

The two of them stared at Albert, who was industriously covering a page with his neat writing. Peter said quietly, "It's been in all the papers. The serial killer caught in New Orleans. That's the old murder case you were working on, wasn't it?"

Fletcher closed his eyes. He should have known Peter would add it all up.

"You've done a fine thing, son. Once I'd guessed enough to read between the lines, I received the distinct impression that your persistence was the only thing that caught the man."

Forcing the words out, Fletch said, "There was nothing fine about it."

"Was it you who killed him, Fletcher?"

"Persistence runs in the family, doesn't it? I don't want to talk about it, Dad."

"All right, I understand. At least, I understand enough to leave you alone, if that's what you want." Peter's hand dropped onto Fletch's shoulder. "What I want is for you to know that I still love you, Fletcher."

Keeping his eyes closed, and wishing he could cry, Fletcher whispered, "Thanks, Dad. But you wouldn't, if you knew."

"I think I would." There was a silence. Then Peter offered, "You tell me Albert loves you. And he knows all the worst of it, doesn't he?"

"Yeah, he loves me." Fletch smiled a little, looked across at Albert again. "You probably won't see any evidence of it," he said to his father. "I saw it right away, and I've never doubted it since, but I think I know him better than anyone."

"He's here, isn't he?" Peter shrugged as Fletch turned to query him: "I can see it's difficult for him, meeting us, being with us. He must be a very private person. If he's here, then he loves you."

Fletch's smile grew to a grin. "Yeah, you're right."

"Good," Peter said, gripping Fletcher's shoulder tight. "Now, table five needs their order taken." The bell out in the kitchen rang twice. "And Harley's getting impatient."

Fletcher reached to clasp Peter's hand in his for a moment, then headed over to their latest customers.

Beth and the children arrived about half an hour later, in time for Beth to help Harley with dinner. Patrick was content to set up his collection of little plastic farm animals on the floor, fencing them into haphazard paddocks and pens. Every now and then he'd take a particularly interesting one over to a customer, and show it off. Frances wanted to sit in her usual seat and draw: Albert made room on the table for her, and they both sat there in the family's booth, concentrating on their work, totally ignoring each other – and apparently oblivious to the great, if quiet, amusement of Fletch, Beth and Peter.

Lying back in the grass a few days later, letting the sunlight warm his face and relax his aching leg muscles, Fletcher felt somewhat closer to peace. He and Albert had hiked up to one of Fletch's favorite places from his teenage years, with backpacks full of food and other necessities that Albert and Harley had prepared with a small measure of cooperation. The climb had been more of an effort than Fletch remembered. But his exercise regime, which was irregular at best, had been neglected during all those weeks since he discovered John Garrett's name – which was definitely something he needed to rectify. Hell, he hadn't even had sex with Albert since he couldn't remember when.

Albert was now sitting beside Fletch, cross-legged on a folded blanket, distant behind his dark glasses. The poor fellow looked a little ridiculous in a hat he'd bought for the sake of protection from the elements – a little ridiculous and very self–conscious. Still, Albert was here, half way up a mountain in Idaho, and his work had been left behind at the Ashes' home, and all of that meant he loved Fletcher. Peace definitely seemed within reach right now – or, at least, as much peace as Fletch felt he deserved.

Smiling, Fletcher considered this man. From the neck down, Fletch decided, ignoring the hat, Albert looked anything but ridiculous. He liked the tailored trousers Albert was wearing, made of yet another subtle shade of green, smoothly woven. But Fletch decided he had to get Albert into a pair of blue jeans – expensive and stylish if need be – at least once in his life. For now, though, Fletcher felt he should concentrate on other impossible but more immediate goals.

He'd like to, for instance, run his hands over that neat butt and around those narrow hips. He'd really like to do that, but it wouldn't be permitted, even out here, miles from any witnesses.

All this idle speculation was simply postponing the inevitable, Fletcher knew that. Enough time had passed, surely. And Fletch was safe here, with Albert forever at his side. Perhaps now he could work his way further through the effect of Garrett's death on Fletcher's life. "Albert," he said, shifting again to gaze up into the endless blue of the sky.

"Yes."

"Let me talk this through, will you? I need to talk about John Garrett."

"Yes," Albert repeated, with the neutral patience that was exactly what Fletch needed.

"I know you won't agree with most of this, but it's true for me, okay?" Fletcher took a deep breath, and began. "I'm guilty of Garrett's death, no matter what the Bureau or the police or Judge Beaufort or you think. I feel guilty and I probably always will, so I have to find a way to accept that, and learn to live with it. When I was swimming in the ocean, the first day after I shot him, the idea of making some kind of reparation occurred to me. Reparation for a life. Reparation for the death of the boy that Garrett used to be. Does that make any sense to you?"

"Yes, of course it makes sense, Ash."

Fletch squinted up at the man. "Aren't you going to tell me I'm being melodramatic, and I should just put it behind me and get on with life?"

"Such advice in these circumstances would be inadequate to the point of irrelevance."

"Yeah." Fletcher pondered the message behind all the three–syllable words, and decided he liked it: it seemed that Albert was willing to let Fletcher be Fletcher. "I assumed you'd tell me I was being too sensitive. Plenty of other people have."

"Many other people become desensitized when dealing with this type of crime for any length of time. The people in the Behavioral Science Unit, for instance, wouldn't share your compassion for Garrett."

"I suppose that's why I couldn't stand to always be doing this sort of work." Fletcher continued thoughtfully, "You know what else bothers me? I was in the situation where it was either him or me. I chose me; I decided to put my life ahead of Garrett's. And that's one hell of a cruel judgment to make."

Rather than reply, Albert asked, "How do you propose making reparation?"

This in itself was promising: Albert asking for information. Fletcher smiled for a moment, before explaining. "That night I talked with him, Garrett told me why he thought he'd become a killer. He didn't really admit there was a complete lack of love in his life, no meaningful connections or relationships with anyone, though he did mention that he'd been abused as a child. Both his parents abused him, from what I could make out. He also said he'd never had the chance to play on the football team, or to go to college. He said he'd never had a friend, he didn't know he was gay – he called himself queer, not gay – he'd never had a boyfriend. I guess that if he'd had those things, he might never have been a whole or happy person, but he could at least have avoided becoming a killer." Fletcher frowned. "Anyway, I have all these advantages compared to that. Privileges. So I was thinking how can I help the kind of boy Garrett used to be – how can I help him not become another Garrett?"

"What were your conclusions?"

"I thought I could take part in the Big Brother program, be some kid's friend, give him a connection, maybe even some love. I could help coach a football team, I could do it for free, for one of the poorer schools. Work would get in the way sometimes, but I can get around that. Spend quality time with them, whenever I can."

"Do you think that playing football will help these boys?"

"It can," Fletch said. "It's about teamwork, and winning, and those sorts of things. But me being involved is about showing them I care enough, that they're valuable enough for me to help." After a moment, Fletcher added, "Then I had this other idea that maybe you can help me with."

"Yes?" Albert prompted when Fletcher didn't continue.

"Well, you know I have some money put aside. I don't spend all my salary, though the trips to Washington this year haven't helped. And I know you must have some money, too." Fletch left a brief pause, hoping in vain for confirmation. "I was thinking maybe we could go halves in setting up a scholarship for an underprivileged kid to go to college."

"I see."

"What do you think?"

A brief silence before Albert said, "I have money, but not an unlimited amount. Your idea is a suitable one, but we must ensure we'd have enough to live on if we're required to leave the FBI."

Fletcher twisted around to look at the man; he was absolutely spoiled for reactions to this statement. "Leave the FBI? You mean, because we're gay?" He shook his head, amazed that Albert had brought the topic up. "I didn't know you'd even thought about that. What would we do instead?"

"Under the circumstances, it is unlikely that we could work for the government at federal, state or local levels. I could perhaps work with a private research organization, though that has never been my ambition." Albert, staring off at the scenery and avoiding Fletcher's gaze, nevertheless needed a pause before he could continue. "If we wanted to begin our own business, that would require capital."

"What kind of business?" Fletcher asked, fascinated by all this. He'd never thought he and Albert might find a different life together, a different life in which there need be no secrets. An answer to his own question occurred to him: "I know, we could run a garden center, a plant nursery. You have all the knowledge; I could help you with the work, and deal with the customers. Or a restaurant. Oh yeah, that would be perfect – you cook, and I'll be the head waiter." He leaned closer to Albert, grinning and wanting to grab the man. "I've got it: a vegetarian Cajun restaurant; vegetarian Cajun and Creole. You can't say it wouldn't be unique."

Albert nodded, apparently not sharing any of Fletcher's enthusiasm. "It's a possibility. Perhaps Virginia would be a good location, within reasonable driving distance of Washington."

"The country is so pretty out there. You really have thought about this, haven't you, love?" It seemed wonderful. Fletch had only ever wanted to be a special agent, but since he'd fallen out of love with the Bureau, and since he'd suffered through the Garrett investigation, the future seemed gray and depressing and endless. Now it seemed there was a colorful life out there that he could share with Albert: a colorful happy honest life. "What about your work, though?" Fletch asked. "You couldn't leave that behind. I know it means everything to you."

"Being a special agent used to mean everything to you."

"Things change, you mean? I don't see that you've become disenchanted with forensics, though, like I have with my work."

Albert let out an impatient sigh. "This may never become an issue, Ash: I don't intend to let the Bureau discover the nature of our relationship. It is simply wise to consider the situation, and plan accordingly."

"All right," Fletch said, nodding. For a moment, he felt like he was almost–three–year–old Patrick and someone had taken his teddy bear away. And then he remembered that Albert had made more than one admission. "So, did you inherit your money from your parents?"

The expression became stony before Albert turned his face away. After a long moment, Albert said coldly, "Ash. You are no doubt aware that my birthday is approaching."

Another topic Fletch had never thought Albert would voluntarily broach. "Yes, of course."

"If you tell your family, or arrange any kind of celebration," Albert informed him, "I will never forgive you."

"Now who's being melodramatic?" Fletcher retorted lightly. Still, the idea of an implacably unforgiving Albert was a scary one.

Albert swung his head around to glare at Fletch from behind the dark glasses: he obviously feared the worst. "Have you already told them?"

"No. No, and I won't." Fletch frowned. "I mean, I'd like to, but I can see there wouldn't be any point, it wouldn't be fair to you." The image of an implacably unforgiving Albert became even more frightening with the addition of a garish party hat. Frightening, bizarre, and rather amusing: Fletcher put the idea away to enjoy some other time, when he was alone.

"Fair?" Albert repeated. "It wasn't fair of you to not tell me you'd informed your father of the reason we would be prepared to share a double bed."

Fletcher shrank inside. "I'm sorry," he said weakly. "I thought it was right to warn him, I told him we're lovers. Then I suppose I wasn't quite game enough to let you know I'd told him, and the whole thing slipped my mind. Call it avoidance. I didn't mean to dump you in it like that." He just hadn't wanted to face the man. *Call it cowardice.* Fletch groaned and rubbed at his face with both hands. "And then I began that stupid joke about you being a vegetarian. I'm really sorry."

"I believe that will be enough self–castigation for now."

After a while, Fletcher tentatively returned to the previous topic. "Look, about your birthday. Just between you and me, surely we can … not celebrate. Surely you can do what you want for the day. Indulge yourself, just a little. You could even let me love you a bit more."

Very distantly, Albert said, "I am not interested in such a changeable emotion."

"What?"

"One that fluctuates according to occasion."

"That's not what I meant." What had he ever done, Fletch wondered, to deserve such a difficult lover? *By being so difficult yourself,* was the obvious reply. "I guess, if I'm in the mood by then, I meant you could let me express my love more than you usually do. You could let me take care of you. You know. I don't even mean sexually."

"No, I don't know." And it seemed Albert wasn't interested in finding out, either.

"Damn you, Albert." But Fletch couldn't find much heat to put in the words. He sighed, and lay back in the grass. Albert was Albert, and Fletch must find the grace to let him be so. Another sigh, before he closed his eyes and let himself doze. Halfway between sleep and awareness, Fletch wondered if this was peace, if this was all the peace he'd ever have.

Which was when something occurred to him. Fletch opened his eyes, startled out of his doze. "Albert. Albert, I'm not juggling anymore."

There was no reply, but Fletch relied on the fact that the man was listening to him. "I'm not on that tightrope, and I'm not juggling all the parts of me."

"Where are you, then, and what are you doing?"

"I don't know." Fletch let his gaze rest in the blue sky, and searched for another image. "I guess I'm walking. On the grass, and the sun's shining. Barefoot on the grass," he added, smiling. "I've let everything fall for now. I can pick up the pieces I want to keep. I do that, and I hold them to me, to my chest, and they melt into me. And all the rest, I can just leave behind. Leave them and let them fade away in the sunlight, melt away into the grass and the earth."

After a pause, Albert asked quietly, "What about the darkness?"

"Good question." Fletch smiled. "I always forget that you do actually pay attention to me." A moment to gather his thoughts, and then Fletcher continued, "It's not as heavy anymore, the darkness. Not as sharp or thorny. It's not going to cut my hands now. I don't know, Albert: is it a part of me, like I always thought? Maybe it isn't part of me anymore, because I didn't even think about killing that boy Steve, not at the time. Though I sure as hell thought about it afterwards."

"I can't answer that for you, Ash."

"I know, but I'm asking for your opinion. You always said I was no murderer."

"Then, in my opinion, you have many characteristics within you, and you are open to others; both of these contribute to your gift of empathy. You share many traits with Garrett, and that enabled you to understand him. It does not mean you have to be Garrett." Another pause before Albert continued, "If knowledge of this is any assistance, I also share certain traits with Garrett. But I am no murderer."

Fletch found he had tears in his eyes, but he still couldn't quite cry, even in gratitude. "Thanks, Albert," he said. "Thank you for sharing that with me." And Fletch considered all this for a while, and contemplated the darkness he held in his hands. Eventually he said, "I didn't kill my darkness when I killed him. It's part of me," and he lifted it to his heart, and he let it in.

Peace after that. Fletcher would have liked to kiss Albert, to seek physical reassurance and to share his love, but such a thing wouldn't be allowed. At least once in his life, Fletch would like to kiss his lover in the beneficent sunlight. But, if that was ever going to happen, it would not be now. Instead, Fletcher smiled at the man, curled up on his side, and fell asleep.

"Morning, Dad," Fletcher said, making his way to the kettle and the jar of coffee.

"Good morning," Peter replied. He let out a laugh: "You're walking like an old man. Or should I say hobbling?"

"That mountain we climbed yesterday – it's gotten higher since I left."

"Incredible. And I always thought continental drift was a slow process."

Fletch grimaced, and pushed his tangled hair back out of his face. "Leave me alone, Dad; I haven't even begun to wake up yet." And then something occurred to him as he brought his mug of coffee over to the table: "Albert hasn't woken up either, actually. That's about the first time he's slept later than me. And I mean the first time ever."

"He was talking with me last night, we stayed up through the small hours. I'm not surprised he's sleeping in."

"I'm dreaming, aren't I?" Fletch said flatly.

Shaking his head, Peter smiled. "No, he was here. In fact, he was sitting where you are now. Why do you think you're dreaming?"

Fletch sank his face into his hands. "I knew he was gone, I assumed he was working on that paper of his. But he was talking to you? That's so bizarre."

The smile grew. "Why is it bizarre?"

"Because it took me years to get through to him, Dad. And you damned well do it in a few days."

"You sound like you want me to apologize."

"No, of course not." Fletcher sighed, and swallowed a mouthful of coffee. And then he fixed Peter with a sharp stare. "So, what did you talk about?"

"This and that. The meaning and the mundanity of life. He's a very interesting man."

"I know." Fletcher felt the familiar tugs of curiosity leading him in all directions. He commented, "Not many people see behind all that attitude he throws at them."

"Then your perceptions have served you well."

Fletch smiled. "You like him."

"I'm more interested in how you feel about him, Fletcher."

"Me? Where do I start?" Fletch drank down the rest of his coffee, made himself and Peter a fresh cup each. When he was seated again, he said, "If you want to know, I love him. And, like I told the kids, Albert's my best friend. He challenges me. I trust him more than I trust myself. How's that to start with?"

"Those are powerful feelings," Peter commented.

"I know he's not the most obvious person to fall in love with. I mean, apart from him being a man; he's not handsome in a conventional way." Crazy to talk about Albert like this: Fletch adored it. "I reckon he could be handsome if he wanted to be, but he's just not that sort of person."

"It's all right," Peter said. He sounded amused. "It's all right, Fletcher: you can find him handsome if you want to."

"I guess I can." Feeling foolish, Fletcher admitted, "I think he's wonderful."

"Then explain this to me. You're in touch with all your emotions, all your abilities and qualities." Peter lifted a hand to halt Fletcher's protest. "You may not be in control of them, son, but you're as true to who you are as you can be. On the other hand, Albert denies a great deal of himself. That makes him fragile. Explain to me how you can trust him so much."

"Well, sure, parts of him are fragile. But the parts of him that are strong are the strongest I've ever seen." Fletcher searched for an image. "Like diamond: so valuable, and so damned hard, too. And those strengths include his love for me, and his passion for his work, and his love for humanity – though I suppose that's in the abstract – and his determination to do good."

"Why do you say he loves humanity?"

"Because he expects so much of them. The trouble is, the individuals he meets never live up to those high standards. Not even me, not even the one person he really loves. You should be asking how he can trust me." Fletcher dug his fingers into his temples, his scalp, trying to find the words for matters he'd barely thought about, let alone voiced. "You're right: parts of him are fragile. His strengths aren't just the good parts of him, and his weaknesses aren't just the bad things. But if any of the fragile parts break, his strengths will still be there. They'll endure. I'll still be there." Fletch paused to finish his coffee. "I help him with the bad things, and the fragile things, Dad. Maybe no one else can see the changes in him since I've been his friend, but I can. And I love that."

"You love to be needed, Fletcher. And I can see that he needs you."

"No one else ever has," Fletch admitted. "You know that, don't you? But that's not the only reason I'm with him. I mean, there are a hundred reasons." He looked across at his father, wondering what would best convince the man. "Try this one. From experience, I'd always assumed love was conditional, temporary. Romantic love, I'm talking about; though I guess I hadn't found any other kind of love, either. One word, or one look, or the absence of a word or a look, would change it. Change it for the worse. One moment love would be there in all its glory, and the next it would wither and die."

"That's sad, Fletcher," Peter said.

Fletch nodded. "Yes, but Albert's love for me has been unconditional, no matter what I did, with or without him."

Peter took his turn to make them a fresh round of coffee. "I can see that Albert would be loyal," he said after some consideration, "but I can't see him as forgiving."

"I've been unfaithful to him," Fletcher confessed before he could change his mind. "I had an affair. Brief, but very intense. And I told him about it, and he's still here with me."

A few moments before Peter asked, "Was it a man or a woman?"

Grinning, Fletcher said, "I'm glad you thought to ask. It was a man, Dad. Does that bother you?"

"No," Peter said slowly. "No. All this – I can't deny it's been a surprise. But only because it's outside my experience. It takes a while for theories and beliefs to catch up with initial reactions, a short while, that's all."

"Would you rather not know any more?"

"No, that would be unfair. And cowardly. Anyway, who do you think you inherited your curiosity from?"

Fletch's grin returned in full measure. Incredible, to talk to someone about this. "All right. I've definitely developed a taste for men – and I was curious, even before I saw that Albert loved me – but I haven't lost the taste for women. In fact, I've become a real equal opportunity fuck, if you'll excuse the French."

"Such a short, pithy vulgarity is probably Anglo–Saxon, and I will excuse it."

"The man I had an affair with," Fletcher informed his father with a waggle of the eyebrows, "was black. And gorgeous. So, what do you think of me now? I'll sleep with anyone: man or woman; black, Jewish, you name it."

"I'm in no position to pass judgment on you, Fletcher: I was born in a different world. But I am interested to know what that means for your relationship with Albert."

"Don't worry, I doubt I'll be unfaithful to him again. He'd never admit it, but I hurt him. We survived that time, under those circumstances. I don't think we'd do so well again – things have changed." The smile this time was wry. "We've still got some changing to do. Some growing."

"But has he forgiven you, Fletcher, or has he simply buried his resentment and his jealousy so far down that it won't see the light of day?"

A troubling notion. Frowning, Fletch said, "It was obvious he resented it, at first. Though he refused to call our relationship off, even while I was still seeing this other guy. For months afterwards, we weren't happy together, we kind of didn't do anything but endure. Then, once we began focusing on the murder investigation again, everything shifted."

"What shifted exactly?"

"Maybe the investigation gave him a reason to be supportive, to care for me, because I was in the thick of this terrible thing. Maybe he thought it was safe, because it was work, it wasn't personal – though that was wrong, of course it was personal. He was my lifeline, Dad, he was –"

"Wonderful. You've said."

"Only a thousand times," Fletch retorted with a smile. Then, serious again, "He accepts who I am, Dad. He argues with me about the things he disagrees with because he cares, about me and about so much else. He insists I always do my best. He tries to make me see his point of view, but he doesn't try to change me."

After a while, Peter nodded. "If all this is true, you've found yourself something very precious. Someone very precious."

"But you don't believe me? Or you think I'm wrong about him?"

"I don't know. Something's bothering me – and I don't mean I'm bothered that you're both men."

"Aren't you? Honestly?"

Peter grimaced. "Honestly, then: it's outside my experience, like I said, and I'd find it easier to accept if you were marrying a woman, easier to understand. I'm sorry you won't have children, Fletcher, sorry for your sake. But none of that means more than you'll have to give me time. I was right to assume you consider Albert as your spouse, wasn't I?"

Letting his head sink to the table, Fletch groaned. "Honestly? I wish I could say yes, but I can't. I mean, that's the way I see this working, but he doesn't see it that way or won't admit it if he does, though he sure reacts that way sometimes – I can't really let you assume that."

"All right," Peter said. Then he asked, "Let me get to know him better, Fletcher. I don't imagine it would be very important to you, whether we approved or not, but if you genuinely want my opinion about Albert, and about your relationship with him, you're going to have to give me some time."

"I'd value your opinion. I'd even like your blessing, if that's possible. Call me old-fashioned."

Smiling, Peter reached across the table to grasp Fletcher's hand in his. "That's one of the last descriptions I'd use."

And they were silent then, while Fletch made them another coffee, and they each considered their own thoughts. Silent, that is, until Harley and the two children tumbled in through the door, fresh from their early morning amble. Frances and Patrick were carrying paper bags filled with bread rolls still warm from the oven. Fletch breathed in deeply: "I can never get enough of that smell."

"Morning," Harley said to his father and brother, before beginning to discuss the day's menu for the diner with Peter.

Frances clambered up onto Fletcher's lap, reached for the tub of butter and a knife, and literally tore into the first bread roll. "Breakfast," she announced once the roll was haphazardly and generously buttered, and she held it up for her uncle to take.

"Thanks," Fletch said, belatedly remembering how hungry he was. He began munching happily, while Frances buttered another roll for her grandfather. Already there were crumbs everywhere. And then Fletcher realized something. "You sneaky old man," he said to Peter: "you completely avoided answering my question. What did you two talk about last night?"

"That's confidential," Peter informed him, "and it will have to stay that way."

"Don't hold out on me," Fletch warned. "You know how sorry I can make you."

"Settle down," was Harley's advice, as he sat at the table and took the bread roll Frances offered him. "What are you upset about now?"

"Dad and Albert were up all night talking, and he won't tell me what they said."

Patrick clambered onto Harley's lap and began loudly insisting on having the next bread roll. Peter was laughing and shaking his head at his younger son's reaction. Harley muttered, "You'd think Dad would be the one to get upset, having to talk to the guy for hours."

"Why?" asked Patrick.

"Harley!" Fletcher cried with some outrage. "It's a privilege talking with Albert, you know. Not everyone gets to do it. Not even me, most of the time. I just want to know what they talked about, I don't see what's so unreasonable about that."

This plea for understanding was greeted with nothing more than a shrug.

"I'm jealous," Fletch explained to Peter. "I want in." But then he smiled at the thought of Albert actually valuing Fletcher's father enough to hold a conversation with him. "I'm jealous, and I'm hopelessly curious, and I'm delighted."

"Good," Peter said. "And, if you want to know the truth, I'm fascinated."

Fletcher's smile grew broad. "Fascinated, fixated –"

"Engrossed, enthralled, enchanted."

"Oh, not you, too," Harley groaned. "I hope you're exaggerating."

Then Albert himself arrived, already showered, shaved and neatly dressed. "Morning," Fletch said, beaming up at him.

Albert nodded to him, and offered Peter, "Good morning, Mr. Ash."

"Morning, Albert," Peter replied.

After pouring himself a fruit juice, Albert joined the others at the table. Silence, apparently born of discomfort, for a moment or two. Everyone began watching Frances, because she was the only one doing anything. Which was when they all realized something strange was happening. Frances had cut a bread roll neatly in half, rather than tear it in two, and was now buttering it with precision, covering the surface with a minimal amount of butter. Once she'd finished, she reached to hand it to Albert, leaning so far that Fletch had to hold onto her hips to keep her balanced.

"Thank you, Frances," Albert said as he took it.

"You're welcome," she said politely. And then she tore into the next roll with her usual gusto.

The silence now seemed the result of surprise. Beth wandered in, blond hair spilling and robe trailing – Fletcher couldn't help but smile in fond memory of his years–long crush on the woman. "What's going on?" Beth asked, suspicious of the quiet.

"Nothing," Harley said. He opened his arms, and she walked into his hug; Patrick, caught between them, began giggling and squirming.

Fletcher watched them, not daring to look at Albert. This was the thing he missed in his relationship with Albert – one of the many things, he amended. He missed the simple joys of displaying affection. Albert wouldn't often sit still for it when they were alone, and of course it was impossible when other people were around. But seeing Harley now, kissing Beth's mouth and tickling Patrick's belly, Fletch felt happy for his brother and sad for himself.

And then everyone was on the move again, as Harley made a round of coffee, and Beth and Peter began talking, and Patrick started setting his farm animals out on the table amidst the breadcrumbs. Fletch wound his arms around Frances, who was on his lap munching her own breakfast, and he gave her bear hugs until she squealed. His lover sat, contained and silent, on the other side of the table.

Another late afternoon at the diner, having coped with lunch and the afternoon teas, and waiting for the dinner crowd. Albert was working through that paper on some obscure but useful aspect of forensic chemistry, which Fletch had to assume was terribly erudite: he'd asked Albert to explain it to him the other day, and hardly understood a word. The man had a number of autopsy reports spread before him, two weighty books, and a carefully annotated list of notes. Fletcher had taken a few minutes off from helping with the customers and was sprawled back on the seat opposite Albert's in the family booth.

Harley came over with two plates, and set one down in front of Albert. "A cheese and mushroom omelet for the vegetarian," he said, in pointed tones.

Albert glanced up at the man, stony expression firmly in place.

"Hey, is the other omelet for me?" Fletch asked, not bothering to sit up. "I'm a vegetarian, too, these days."

"Though your brother still likes meat," Albert informed Harley. "I believe the term for his preferences is bi–gastronomical."

Fletcher burst out laughing. "Yeah, Albert still lets me have a good thick steak every now and then, as long as I don't bring it home with me. He's very broad–minded."

Grimacing unhappily, Harley put the plate down and headed back for the kitchen.

"I'm sorry," Fletcher said once he was alone with Albert again. "That vegetarian joke is wearing a bit thin, isn't it?"

"Your sense of humor has always been an inconvenient one, but at least it has been some while since you inflicted me with puns."

Ignoring the opportunity for low humor, Fletcher said tentatively, "I guess we're both pretty new at this coming out thing."

Albert raised both eyebrows. "Indeed." He picked up his cutlery, pulled his plate closer, and took a neat bite of the omelet. After a moment, he continued, "The only people who I've made aware of my sexual preferences are the men I've had sex with."

Fletcher's mouth dropped open as he tried to ask a hundred questions at once. What was it with Albert's confessional mood lately? He'd learned more facts about Albert's history in the last few days than he had in years. And, wondered Fletcher, how could he make the most of the situation. "So, what men?" he managed to ask. "I mean, who?" And he mentally scrambled through the where, when and how.

"That is not something I intend to discuss," Albert informed him with finality.

Some day you will, Fletcher promised. He tried a different line of interrogation: "Well, have there been women?"

"Do you consider that to be any of your business?"

"Absolutely not," Fletcher replied with no hesitation.

A moment passed as Albert cut and ate another piece of omelet. "Yes, there have been women." The man glanced across at Fletcher, expression becoming impatient. "Ash, close your mouth: you look ridiculous."

Fletcher couldn't help himself: "I love you."

Albert somehow managed to silently convey that this was a state of affairs he could grudgingly cope with, but only because he had an unusual store of fortitude.

"Thanks for sharing that with me," Fletcher said. "In fact, I'm so glad you did, I'm going to repay you in a way you're going to appreciate far more than me: I won't ask you any more questions. Well," he amended after some reflection, "no more questions about your other lovers. For now."

"How many times do I have to remind you that this isn't a romance novel, Ash?" Albert said sourly. "They were not my lovers."

Before he could think twice, Fletch blurted out, "Am I your lover?"

Silence. Albert put his cutlery down and pushed the plate away; he had barely eaten half of the omelet. Fletcher waited the man out. Finally, Albert said, very distantly, "If you wish to delude yourself."

Fletch grinned. "I do. You know, sometimes I think that loving you is plenty of reparation to make to the world."

For the briefest of moments, Albert actually looked offended. But then he said, "In that case, I'll endeavor to make the task as difficult as possible. I imagine you'd be as enthusiastic about martyrdom as about anything else in your misdirected life."

The grin grew into a laugh. "If you don't watch out, I'll kiss you, and then you'll be sorry."

"You obviously lack the common sense to realize that wouldn't be a wise thing to try. Luckily, you also lack the bravado to carry it off."

"You're tempting me," Fletcher warned him; "provoking me badly."

"The temptation is being provided by nothing more than your hyperactive imagination: being kissed by you in an Idaho diner is not amongst my ambitions; particularly not with your brother as a witness."

"Harley? Don't be afraid of him. He just doesn't have the first idea what we are to each other." Fletcher leaned forward over the table to confide, "Actually, he does: he knows what love is; he even said Beth was his best friend, like you're mine. We should just show him what we are, Albert, and let him accept it."

Albert was staring hard at him, having drawn back against the wall of the booth. His expression was fixed, and rebellious.

It took Fletcher a moment to interpret: Albert was terrified, assuming that Fletch wanted to attempt a physical demonstration right now. Fletch drew back as well, to give him room, and smiled gently. "Trust me, lover. Just give him time, that's all I meant. Just give Harley time to see that I love you." Letting out a sigh, Fletcher's gaze fell to the table. "I'm sure he'll see it," Fletch said, allowing himself a trace of resentment. "Harley will probably see it better than you can. You still have no idea how damned much I love you, do you, Albert?"

"If that is true," Albert replied, his voice strained, "then an extravagance of protestations will not assist your case."

"All right." Fletcher nodded. "I'll do you a favor, and leave you alone for a while." He offered Albert a smile, which was not accepted. "I'm sure you'd rather be getting on with your paper."

Silence, as if such a conclusion was self-evident. Fletcher sighed again, and headed for the latest customers. It was an hour before he realized he hadn't eaten even a bite of his dinner. Which only gave Harley an extra reason to glare at him.

Fletcher knew he was dreaming, and that worried him because he was sure that the next time he fell he would hit the ground. And that would mean his death, one way or another; if not literally, then metaphorically. Though this time there seemed little danger: he was strolling down a city street, and there was someone walking beside him he couldn't quite focus on, but Fletch knew his companion was a friend. It all seemed very ordinary. A small plane flew far overhead.

Rounding a corner, Fletch found a park covering one of the city blocks. There were a few people dotted around amongst the trees, standing or sitting on the grass, looking up into the sky. Following their gaze, Fletcher saw sky-divers, tiny human shapes spread-eagled against the clean spring blue.

It all seemed like fun – but fear slammed through Fletcher's heart. The sky-divers were growing so rapidly in size that he could already make out their faces, and the details of their white and blue overalls. Fletch frowned: it seemed he knew one of the sky-divers, even though he didn't recognize the man's face. A few seconds passed while the divers loomed closer. They looked like they were having the time of their lives, even though the ground must be speeding up and surely it was too late to open the parachutes they didn't even have.

And then something on the ground caught Fletcher's eye: there was a cluster of white ten–feet–tall inflatable pillows, and it seemed the sky–divers were aiming for these. Despite everything that might go wrong, despite the buildings and the streets and the trees they could crash into, they acted as if they were quite safe.

Fletch watched as the sky–diver he seemed to know landed in one of the pillows, and bounced up again, yelling with a rush of joy. Relief almost obliterated Fletcher's fear; he smiled as the sky–diver bounced up and down as if he were on a trampoline. Someone, somewhere, was laughing. Fletch's smile grew, and he drifted away from the dream into dim awareness.

Alone in the bed he shared with Albert, in the room he'd shared with Harley throughout childhood; everything dark but familiar around him. Fletch wasn't used to being alone these days. He missed the comfort Albert might have provided, but Fletcher also appreciated the solitude: he'd always needed time alone each day, to allow himself to work through everything he'd been exposed to. He'd once explained it to Mac using a computer metaphor: he was forever on input when he was with people so he needed time by himself to process the data, to integrate the bits he wanted to keep, and to dump the rest.

But Fletcher soon became restless, because he thought he could hear a quiet murmur of voices, and that meant his father was talking to Albert again. And that roused Fletcher's curiosity and jealousy.

The murmur of voices paused, and there was a sound Fletch couldn't quite identify, a sound that echoed something in the dream, something both familiar and unexpected. A sound that hadn't been used for a long time, like an old gate rusted in place for years that was now creaking open under great pressure. Albert, there was some tone that meant it was Albert – but could he be laughing? Crying, maybe, for it sounded painful, and there were odd pauses.

Fletch clambered out of the bed as silence fell, and padded barefoot through the hall and into the kitchen. Albert was there, sitting opposite Peter, hands wrapped around a steaming mug, with the dregs of a smile on his face. Staring at the man, Fletcher rounded the table, carefully approached him. "What's going on?" Fletch asked. And, just as urgently, "Are you all right?"

"Of course I'm all right." Though the words lacked the usual snap, there was still impatience.

"Fletcher," said his father, "I'll make you some tea."

Too bemused to protest and ask for coffee, Fletch sat down next to Albert, unable to tear his gaze away: his lover's face was somehow subtly different. Fletch wanted to take that face, frame it in his hands, and examine it closely with sight and touch – but he restrained himself. They were in company, after all. "Did I just hear that? Don't tell me I was dreaming. You laughed!"

Silence for a moment, and no reaction from Albert. "So he laughed," Peter said as he plugged in the kettle. "What's the drama?"

The smallest smile lingered on Albert's mouth, quirking now at Fletcher's expression which must be betraying both anxiety and outrage.

"Why?" Fletch demanded. No reply. "What did you say to him?" he asked his father, suspicious and bereft.

"That would be telling."

Peter's back was turned, so Fletch figured Albert might forgive him one small hug – he leaned in and wrapped his arms around the man, fitting his head as neatly as ever into Albert's shoulder. "Are you all right?" he murmured. An arm slipped around Fletcher's waist, and Albert let him stay there, close, even when Peter returned with Fletch's mug of tea.

They hadn't been at all demonstrative before now, especially physically, but no one seemed uncomfortable, so Fletcher settled in. Sweet to be like this with his lover, with his father there, too. Silence for a time: it seemed Peter and Albert had done with talking for now.

"What's going on?" Fletch asked his father. "I've been trying to make this guy laugh for years. And you've taken to drinking Albert's tea! I don't get it."

Peter, under his son's gaze, shrugged and looked away. Albert remained quiet.

"Were you laughing at me? That's fine, I'm not going to take offense, I just want to know."

Albert let out a breath that might have been an amused snort. Peter said, "Your paranoia is growing, Fletcher. Not everything in this world revolves around you, not even for me and Albert."

"Oh, this isn't fair," Fletch protested, knowing he'd lost. He complained to Albert, "You didn't even laugh at my Three Bits of String joke."

"Drink your tea," Albert advised.

Letting out a sigh, Fletcher sat up, pleased that Albert's arm didn't leave his waist. He reached for the cookie jar that was always on the table, and plunged a hand in.

"I believe it's chocolate pecan tonight," Albert said. "Harley is striving to impress."

"Yeah? I told him how good a cook you are."

Peter was laughing at his son. "It's been a while since your eyes lit up like that. If all it took was a chocolate cookie …"

Albert patted Fletcher, reassuring and amused – but his hand was resting on Fletch's hip, so it felt sexual. Again, no one seemed to notice except for Fletcher. He smiled at his lover's strange but welcome behavior, and drank his tea, ate another cookie, then settled in close to Albert again. Peter and Albert were talking now, but only about the pros and cons of living in Washington DC. Fletcher soon began dozing, resting his head on Albert's shoulder.

"Go to bed, Ash," Albert said at last.

"I want to hear you laugh again."

"There is no point in waiting for such an unlikely occurrence."

"I want to stay here with you."

Albert sighed. "You didn't warn me that you revert to childhood whenever you return home."

"And you could at least call me Fletcher when there's a whole heap of other people around named Ash."

"I believe it was perfectly clear whom I was addressing."

Tightening his hold on the man, Fletch said, "I don't want to let you go."

"Then perhaps we should both go to bed," Albert suggested heavily.

Fletcher asked, "Don't you two want to talk some more? Or have you sorted out the meaning of life already?"

"You're making it impossible." Albert stood, and Fletcher followed him up. "Goodnight, Mr. Ash. Thank you for the tea."

"You let him make you laugh, then you're polite to him?" Fletch giggled, undignified and too sleepy to care. "Who are you, and what have you done with the real Albert Sterne?"

"Goodnight, Albert," Peter said; "take care. Night, Fletcher."

"Night, Dad." And, within moments, Fletch was content in the haven of cool sheets, heavy blankets, and firm embrace. "Night, love," he murmured.

But he didn't fall asleep right away, as he'd expected to. Instead he basked in the sensual pleasure of having Albert hold him. Every now and then Fletch shifted, easing closer and deeper, enjoying the simplicity of another's skin against his own; and Albert moved to accommodate him, to answer his wordless requests.

And at some stage Fletcher realized they'd left the easy sensuality behind, and were both feeling the golden tug of sexual need. "Albert," he said, grinning for all he was worth; "are we gonna make love?"

"It's not making love," Albert said, impatient but dazed: it seemed Albert had been hungering for this for some while. The man leaned up on an elbow, and initiated a driving kiss, holding Fletcher's head still with one hand, and exploring the closest hip and thigh with the other.

Fletcher responded in kind, meeting the initiative with his own energy, wondering how long either of them could possibly last at this intensity. It had been months, surely, since they'd last done this. It felt like years.

The mutual desperation was understandable, then, but Albert seemed to also be getting annoyed. Perhaps because Fletch just wouldn't stay still; for once Fletcher wouldn't lie there and do Albert's bidding, no matter the pleasure to be had from doing no more and no less than that. Every time Albert secured a hold on him, Fletcher would shift and answer it with a hold on Albert, forcing the man to try a different strategy. At last Albert snapped, "You will make me lose my balance."

"So what if I do?" Fletch retorted. But then he smiled, and ran a hand down Albert's back. "What if I do?" he asked again, soft. "The world won't end."

A pause, and then Albert began again: he bent his head to bite at one of Fletcher's nipples, while his hand stroked from a buttock down the back of Fletch's thigh.

Fletcher stayed still this time, and enjoyed the attention. But, when Albert was preparing to move on, Fletch stopped him. "My turn," he said. And he returned the favor, finding Albert's nipple hard and his thigh sensitive to the lightest caress. The man started to protest verbally, but it was obvious that he appreciated it physically. "Your turn again," Fletcher invited.

Apparently unnerved, all Albert did was kiss him, concentrating on his collarbone and shoulder. But that was fine: Fletcher enjoyed it, and then happily did the same to Albert. In fact, he found what appeared to be a tender spot at the juncture of Albert's shoulder and throat, and he explored it with tongue and lips and teeth. "Ash, what do you think you're doing?" His tone too weak to be more than a token protest.

"You're the scientist. Never heard of an equal and opposite reaction?" He lifted one of Albert's hands in his own, drew it close to kiss the palm. "Do this to me," Fletch suggested, and then proceeded to demonstrate exactly what he liked: a trail of kisses from his palm along his forearm, down the triceps and then across the underarm, finishing again at his nipple.

Albert was frowning. Perhaps he didn't find this particular play terribly erotic himself, but he seemed willing enough to repeat the process with Fletcher, precisely how Fletch had showed him.

And then it was time to do something Fletcher knew Albert did like: he pushed the man onto his back, and liberally applied his mouth to Albert's belly and hips and balls. This sensitivity must be one of the reasons Albert got such a kick out of frottage, Fletcher assumed: for this erogenous zone extended far beyond the obvious focus.

A verbal protest, of course, and Albert's hands trying to push Fletcher away.

"Let me do this for you," Fletcher said in between bestowing kisses. "Let me overwhelm you for once." He spoke against tender skin, hoping even the vibrations of his vocal cords would have an effect. "You're strong, lover, you're the strongest person I know. So you won't lose anything if you give some of yourself to me." Another kiss or two. "Trust me with yourself."

"What have you been reading lately?" Albert said. His flatly uninterested tone couldn't hide his need. "Romance novels or self–help books? This dialogue –"

"Hush," Fletcher said, continuing regardless. "Let me at you. Share this with me. Let me do for you all the things you've done for me."

A sigh, as if Albert felt he was being sorely abused. Fletch almost laughed: he knew, he had ample evidence, that Albert was in great need of sex right now; and Fletcher was not above using that fact to help make this happen. Perhaps Albert had reached that very conclusion, for he said, "If you had something planned, or if there was something in particular you wanted tonight, you might have warned me. I believe I've met your stated requirements before now."

"I didn't have it planned," Fletcher said easily. He lifted himself a little, still supported on his elbows, so he could talk more directly to the man. "I wasn't even interested in having sex, until we just inspired each other. Now I'm very interested, and we have a lot of time to make up for. I don't know about you, but abstinence holds no appeal for me."

Albert looked merely dazed and distant, despite this opportunity to pass on another fact of his life pre–Fletcher.

"So let's share this, lover," Fletch continued. "Let's really do this together for once. Because I think that's how it should be, don't you?" Fletch was used to not waiting for an answer: he bent to his task again, trusting that the pleasure of it would give Albert's hunger adequate cause to crash through the last of those defenses.

And it soon seemed that Fletcher was having an effect: Albert's breathing, despite obvious efforts at control, was deep and ragged. As he discovered another tender spot – this time just at the top of Albert's right thigh – Fletcher wondered whether anyone had ever explored Albert like this before. He suspected not. In fact, knowing the man as well as he did, Fletcher guessed Albert had never explored himself in any great detail, either. Fletcher himself was guilty of letting Albert focus more on Fletch's pleasure than his own. Which was all rather sad. *We both have a lot of time to make up for,* Fletcher decided.

A hand pushed at his shoulder, and Fletch looked up, about to tell Albert to just lie back and enjoy it. But it was obvious that Albert was enjoying it all too much – he seemed dazed and withdrawn in the way that meant Albert was dealing with his own pleasure. Fletcher wondered how many other people had seen him like this.

Within moments, Albert had Fletcher on his back, and was scrupulously returning the attentions that Fletch had just shown him. Which was fine, but Fletcher was rapidly wanting more. "Albert," he whispered, and he reached for the man when Albert looked up. "My arms are empty," Fletch said. "Come here and share this with me."

It hadn't even been really pleasurable until then – Fletcher had been trying to prove a point – but now pleasurable became an understatement. So many times Albert had moved over him like this, and yet Fletch felt he could never tire of it. For once, there was no pattern, nothing but the clumsiest of harmonies: Albert was too needy to choreograph anything; and Fletcher was busy adding his own arrhythmic inspirations. Albert stayed close; they were close enough to kiss each other without pause, close enough for Albert's nipples to graze Fletcher's chest with every thrust. Far too intense to last.

"Are you ready?" Fletch asked on a breath. "I sure as hell am."

"Yes," said Albert.

"You first," Fletcher demanded. He was grinning wildly, barely holding himself back, but this was something he had to insist on. "You first, lover."

Apparently Albert was in no state to argue: he buried his face in the pillow beside Fletcher's, and let his orgasm take him. Both sad and incredible, all the energy Albert contained within himself like this, all the energy that for Fletcher was joy to be released and shared. And Albert shuddering in his arms, with the proof of his satisfaction spreading between their bellies – those sensations were enough to trigger Fletch's climax.

"Why did we wait so long?" Fletch asked whimsically as they settled into their usual embrace. There were a million reasons they'd waited, of course, none of which Fletcher wanted to think about right now. "You're not going to tell me the one about anticipation heightening the experience, are you?"

"Go to sleep," Albert said.

"Sure, love." Fletcher twisted around for a last kiss. "Sweet dreams." And he settled back into Albert's arms, and let the last of his troubles go.

◆

Basketball in the morning's fresh sunlight, one on one with Harley. Years since they last did this. Fletcher wasn't sure whether Harley was testing him or bonding with him; couldn't be sure whether Harley needed to win, or wanted Fletch to prove himself. The hell of it, for Harley's sake at least, was that Fletcher was in too good a mood to care. It was the morning after the first sex he'd had in months, and Fletch's spirits were soaring, which only served to increase Harley's irritation.

The same old hoop was still crookedly fixed to the shed wall opposite the kitchen door. Fletcher jogged and danced around on the bare dirt; Harley was stronger and larger, but Fletch was irrepressible and energetic and unpredictable.

They had an audience of sorts: Beth and Peter were lazily swaying to and fro in the swing chair, chatting away, with Frances and Patrick climbing over them or sitting on the ground; none of them were paying much attention to the game. Even Albert was there, in his hat and dark glasses, sitting up straight on the kitchen chair he'd brought outside with him, and reading through the mail he'd had forwarded.

Fletcher was winning, nine to eight, and Harley was beginning to get mad. "Better watch your blood pressure, big brother," Fletch advised, dodging around, dribbling the ball just out of reach. "Might drop dead, the way you're going."

"Only way you're going to win," Harley retorted.

"Yeah, and then Albert can finally get his hands on you. We'll both be winners."

Harley paused, stalled by anger and revulsion and maybe sheer terror.

Fletcher skipped around him, and shot at the hoop. "Ten – eight, old man. Get his hands and his scalpel into you. And what's that little circular saw thing you use, Albert?" The rhetorical question was, of course, ignored: Albert was frowning over a medical journal. "Buzz buzz," Fletch taunted his brother in passable imitation of the saw.

Growling, Harley grabbed the ball and began dribbling it in place. Dust rose around their feet from the repeated impacts. "Doesn't that worry you, that your boyfriend likes corpses?"

"Only when he wants me to roll over and play dead," Fletch said cheerfully.

A glare that was worthy of Albert himself – and Fletcher knocked the ball out of Harley's hands. But before he could aim for the hoop, he found himself on the ground and tussling with his big brother, who more than half meant it.

They finally rolled to a halt just in front of where Peter and Beth sat. Peace for a moment, until Patrick leaped into the fray and began happily wrestling about.

Trying to contain his son, but tickling him as well, Harley muttered, "You weren't playing dead last night. Making too much noise for that."

Albert said, quietly but very distinctly, "Fletcher has never been known to follow instructions."

Fletch picked himself up out of the dirt, and brushed himself down, wincing at places that felt bruised. He considered his brother, who now lay at his feet. "Is that what this is about? Did we wake you up?"

Silence. Harley was looking somewhere else entirely. Frances had clambered onto Beth's lap, and was industriously drawing a picture.

"You weren't happy about it before, but this is something else. What's the problem, Harley? Can't you pretend to yourself that me and Albert are just friends now you've heard us? Well, I'm not apologizing for any of it."

Beth said, "No one's asking you to apologize, Fletch." Peter agreed with her.

"What does he want, then? I'm not going to lie about loving Albert."

"What do I want?" Harley asked, climbing to his feet, with Patrick clinging on to his shoulders and laughing at this upheaval. "Does it matter?"

"Yes," Fletcher said. "It matters. But I might not do anything about it."

"Dad, can't you talk some sense into him?"

"No, Harley," Peter replied, "I can't, and I won't."

Frances suddenly asked, in the voice of great impatient reason, "What are you all so cross for?"

Harley reached a hand to ruffle her hair. "It's all right, sweetheart, we're not cross with you." He looked around at Beth and Peter and Fletcher. "What I want ... is to know what you'd all like for breakfast."

"Waffles!" Patrick cried, almost deafening his father.

"Waffles," echoed Frances.

"Don't run away, Harley," his wife advised, "even if it is to make breakfast."

"Yes, wait a few minutes," Peter said. "I want to talk to you all." Once Fletcher sat on the ground cross–legged, and Harley squashed in next to Beth and Frances, Peter continued, "My father–in–law, your mother's father –"

"Albert," Fletch said, interrupting in an effort to involve the man in this. "That's the Irish grandfather I've told you about."

"Yes," Peter agreed. "He was a difficult man. Aggressive, quite overbearing, though he had plenty of good qualities. He did, however, know that your mother could do far better than me. But she'd made her choice, and I was prepared to do anything for her if she wanted me. My Aunt Kit, who you probably all remember, was very supportive."

"I remember her," said Beth. "She was the coolest person I knew when I was growing up."

"Yes, she was cool," Peter said with a smile. "She was also a very direct person; though it was never what she said, it was what she did. She let her actions speak for her. Kit made your mother – your mother–in–law, Beth – very welcome in our family." Peter paused for a moment. "I suppose I was a gentle kind of man, compared to your grandfather. He didn't see writing as a useful occupation."

"Is that why you gave it up?" Fletch asked. "That's terrible."

"That's not the reason."

"How could mom even let you?"

"It was my choice, Fletcher, as I've always told you." Peter said, "Why I'm talking about your grandfather is that ever since the time I was courting your mother, I swore I'd never stand in the way of the choices my own children made. And I won't, even if I do find those choices hard to understand. Your mother wasn't wrong to love me."

"And I'm not wrong to love Albert."

Peter nodded. "Now, Harley, if you're waiting for my disapproval of this, then you'll be disappointed. If you have some sense you want to talk into your brother, you'd better try to do it yourself."

A long silence, until Harley finally muttered, "Since when did he ever listen to either of us, anyway?" And then he offered, "Sounds like he doesn't even listen to Albert."

Fletch couldn't help but chuckle. "Depends what he's saying. Last night –"

"Don't you get clever again," Harley warned.

"Unfortunately," Albert said, "your sons seem to both have regressive genes, Mr. Ash. Neither is clever enough to realize that neither is clever."

"There are plenty of big brothers around here," Harley informed Albert, "who would have punched your lights out by now."

"Am I supposed to assume that none of them share your rudimentary verbal skills?"

"Forget it, Harley," Fletch quickly interrupted. "If anyone's going to hit Albert, it'll be me. Unfortunately, he's not going to play one on one basketball with you, either."

"All right, all right." Harley sighed.

Beth said, "Just tell them what's bothering you, sweetheart."

A pause before Harley said, "The thing is, Fletch, how can he make you happy, when he's such a miserable bastard himself?"

There was a silence as Fletcher considered this. To Fletch's surprise, Albert said, "It's a reasonable question: happiness has never been my goal. If Harley is astute enough to realize that, are you astute enough to answer?"

"I don't know. I don't know that I have an answer, except that I wouldn't be happy without him, not anymore. And he doesn't stop me from doing what I want, even if it is just having fun, or laughing, or whatever. He expects a lot of me, but it begins and ends with expecting me to be me, the best I can be. And I'm a happy, optimistic person, even if Albert isn't." Fletcher looked around at his family, which for him at least encompassed Albert. "How's that?"

"Well fielded," Beth acknowledged, and the others nodded.

"I finished my drawing," Frances announced. "It's for Fletcher and Albert to take home with them."

She handed it over to Fletch, and he looked at it: there was the family's house, and everyone lined up out the front. Though they were stick figures, they were clearly Peter, Harley, Beth, Frances and Patrick, with Fletcher and Albert standing next to what appeared to be the Saab. "That's lovely, Frances," Fletch said. He looked again at the figure of Albert, with his close–cropped hair. "But you know what? Every time I look at it I'll have a hard time deciding whether Albert looks more like a porcupine or a toilet brush." And he burst out laughing, falling back onto the dirt again when Patrick gleefully landed on him.

There was a silence, in which Beth was heard to be guiltily chuckling. When he could, Fletch looked up and found himself the target of twin glares: one from the artist, and one from her subject; each appeared more offended than the other. Which only made him laugh the more. It felt good; it had been far too long since he'd had cause or peace of mind enough to laugh so hard his belly and his jaw ached. Frances, with encouragement from her parents, jumped on Fletch and began pummeling him.

When things finally quietened, Harley and Beth took the kids inside to begin making waffles. Peter and Fletcher were left alone on the swing chair, gently rocking back and forth, while Albert ignored them.

"I am happy, Dad," Fletch murmured. "I know it must be difficult for you all to see why. But, you know, even the insults are a good sign. I've known him over nine years, and he only stopped insulting me once we became lovers. And I reckon that's because he's been so unsettled, he had no idea how to behave with me, or even what he wanted from me. Now he's getting back to himself, and he finally feels comfortable enough to hassle me. Of course," Fletcher added with a grin, "every time he insults me these days, he's really telling me he loves me."

Peter shared an amused glance with his younger son. "No wonder you take it so well."

"Yeah. The closest he ever came to really saying it was when he told me I was an idiot. But if you tell Harley that, you'd better explain that he shouldn't get worried: when Albert insults him, I'm sure it's genuine dislike."

"He'll be relieved." Peter let a beat go by, then said, "I can't pretend that I've ever really understood you, Fletcher; but I do love you, and I've always wanted the best for you. I've been sorry, because I've never thought of you as a happy person. So I'm not surprised it takes a job and a lover, neither of which I understand, to help you find happiness. And I can see that you are happy, with Albert at least, so you have my blessing. I always knew there was nothing else I could do for you."

"You're doing everything I need right now," Fletch told him, grasping his father's hand for a moment. "Thank you. Yes, I'm happy with Albert. I'm not sure about work anymore; that's why I asked for this time off. I fell out of love with the Bureau, and that murder investigation scarred me, Dad. I don't think that's ever going to fully heal."

"What about the pain? You are an ethical creature, Fletcher. Has the pain of dealing with that man died?"

"It's faded."

"And you don't want to talk about it."

"No, I don't, Dad. There are parts of me you've never felt easy with, and the investigation was all bound up with them. I'm dealing with it; I'm dealing with myself."

"I can see you're more at peace now than when you arrived. Albert helps, doesn't he?"

"Yes. And I've had a few ideas about how I can make up for what I did. I'll be all right." Fletcher brightened. "The best thing is that if I leave the Bureau, I've realized I have options and I'll still have Albert. He's even thought about what we might do if we get fired for being gay. When we were talking about it, I almost started wishing we could get fired, so we could start a new life together, something different, something honest; though of course he sees it as a last resort."

A brief silence, before Peter said, "You never talk of Albert as a happy person, but he seems quite content to me."

"Does he?" Fletcher grimaced in surprise, first at his father, then at the oblivious Albert. "Content. How odd. Are you sure?"

"Yes, I think he's content. Content, composed, comfortable. I'll tell you a secret," Peter added in a whisper: "he even almost said as much last night while we were talking; though I don't think he's very conscious of the feeling."

"No, he'd utterly deny it." Fletcher felt like he'd cry with joy, if only his tear ducts hadn't atrophied over the years. "You know, Dad, that would have to be the best present you've ever given me." And he held Peter's hand in his again, and watched his lover carefully for any signs of this unexpected development, until Frances called from the back door: "Waffles!"

SOMETHING YOU DO
IDAHO
OCTOBER 1985

Albert had long ago realized he could never have the kind of relationship that Miles and Rebecca had; he'd long ago accepted that as fact. But he had to admit that, on occasion, he and Fletcher Ash managed to approximate a reasonable facsimile of the next best thing. Today, for instance, Ash was radiating a thorough contentment and satisfaction: it seemed similar to the solid core of unquestioning unquestionable love that Albert's parents had for each other. Albert wondered whether Ash, as someone who doubted everything, appreciated these brief moments of certainty.

Miles and Rebecca couldn't have reached their deep level of understanding without plenty of hard work in the years before he was born, Albert was aware of that; even though their understanding had seemed as natural a part of them as respiration. Albert was also well aware that he had never shirked hard work before. This was, however, the first time Albert found himself wondering why he wasn't prepared to make any further effort with Ash.

It was never going to be an easy relationship, and it would never be perfect – if there could even be such a thing as perfection in a relationship. Every now and then, though, something essential and fundamental seemed within their grasp. The issue became what, if anything, Albert should do about it.

Meanwhile, another mundane day passed in Ash's family home, with the dull variation of an afternoon and evening at the diner in town. Albert attempted to progress his forensic chemistry paper, but found he lacked his usual discipline. This was something he despised: interference of the personal in the serious business of life. Too many people indulged themselves like this. The mediocre McIntyre used his feelings for Mortimer as an excuse for under–achievement. Ash, who of all people should know better, had let his relationship with Albert get in the way of his investigation of the serial killer. Not to mention his relationship with Xavier Lachance.

The trouble was that Albert was brimming with sexual hunger. Overflowing, so that it became more than a physical need – there was an undeniable and unwanted emotional need as well. Albert finally admitted all this to himself late in the evening, as he sat in silence at the Ashes' kitchen table with Fletcher and his father. He reflected that he'd managed to abstain from sex for a full eleven years before he had surrendered to Fletcher's demands, so it now seemed ridiculous that he had become subject to all the distractions of frustration before eleven hours had passed. Ridiculous and highly inconvenient – and embarrassing as well, given that Ash had made it quite plain to his family that Albert had indulged him the previous night. Albert simply wasn't accustomed to people being aware of him as a sexual creature. It was extremely uncomfortable, this vulnerability. And yet the hunger continued unabated.

Fletcher, of course, was feeling something similar, but apparently saw no point in hiding the fact. He finished eating another cookie, and drank the last of his coffee, before asking, "Are you two going to be talking tonight?"

Albert didn't reply. Peter said, "I don't know. I'd be happy if we did, and if we don't that's fine, too."

"Because I think there's something else Albert should be doing."

"And what would that be?" Peter asked, pretending innocence.

"Gonna have to let you use your imagination on that one, Dad." Fletcher was staring intently at Albert, even while speaking to his father. "Is your imagination up to it, do you think?" And then he asked, "Ready for bed, Albert? I sure as hell am."

It took a ridiculous amount of courage simply to let this happen before a witness. Albert said, "If you haven't showered since you rolled around in the dirt with your brother this morning, Ash, perhaps now is a good time."

Silence for a moment, Fletcher still staring at him, apparently not daring to hope this was anything other than wishful thinking.

"I will join you in a few minutes," Albert continued. Which was as much as he could offer.

Quite startling, the joy that suffused Fletcher's face once he realized Albert was serious. The man's beauty had returned, with all its old focus and intensity. Albert found that he had been mourning it, and could only hope that Peter Ash – and, indeed, Fletcher – were unable to read or decipher his appreciation.

As for Fletcher himself, it was obvious he wanted to kiss Albert right now: Albert could read the impulse in every move of the man's body. Settling for something less demonstrative, Fletcher grasped Albert's hand in his own. "See you soon, love." And he as good as skipped out of the room, calling a cheerful, "Night, Dad," over his shoulder.

Difficult, then, to sit there alone with Peter Ash, while considering what he needed to do with Fletcher. Albert found himself, for the first time in his life, wishing for something inane to say. He managed to wait those few minutes without looking at the man, and then said, "Goodnight, Mr. Ash."

"Night, Albert," Peter Ash replied. When Albert summoned the determination to glance at him, he saw Peter was gently smiling. "Take care."

Albert nodded an acknowledgment, and escaped to the darkness of the bedroom he shared with Fletcher. There was some peace to be found in the ritual of undressing, and folding or hanging his clothes. Then, hearing the shower still running, Albert pulled on his robe and headed for the bathroom.

Ash hadn't been expecting him, and didn't realize Albert was there until he'd discarded the robe and stepped into the shower. "Damn!" Fletcher exclaimed. "Where did you appear from?"

No point in replying. Ash had apparently been standing under the hot torrent of water, doing nothing more than revel in the sensation; Albert picked up the soap, quickly cleaned himself, and then cleaned Fletcher as well, using exactly the same brisk patterns. Ash, for some unfathomable reason, was laughing, and wriggling so much he impeded progress.

When he was done, Albert lathered up his hands, put the soap down, and drew Ash closer into his arms. Initiated an intense kiss to distract the man, before locating the man's anus and pressing a finger inside.

Breaking the kiss, Ash moaned softly and stretched, letting his weight lean into Albert's embrace. And then, with a return of consciousness, Fletcher lifted his head to stare at Albert. "What are you –" But, apparently fearing Albert would have second thoughts, the words halted and Fletcher dropped his head to Albert's shoulder. "Do you have any idea what that does to me?" the man mumbled. "Just please don't stop."

"It is obvious what this does to you," Albert informed him. The man's skin was flushed, and not only from the heat of the shower; his body was flexing slightly, instinctively reveling in this penetration; his voice was roughened; and, when Albert lifted his free hand to Fletcher's throat, he found the man's heart was beating with impetuous strength.

Ash straightened to throw a confused and troubled glare at Albert: *So why make me do without it?* But all he said, in an anxious whisper, was, "Please don't stop."

"I have no intention of stopping." And Albert stood there, letting a sensually stupefied Fletcher lean on him, continuing his invasion of the man's body until the water began to cool. "We should go to bed."

"Yes," Fletcher murmured. "Damn it, Albert, I could come right now if I didn't want to make this last."

That was obvious as well: even as Albert withdrew and soaped his hand again, even as he rinsed both himself and Fletcher, then toweled them both dry, the man remained dazed with excitement. Pre–ejaculate welled from the tip of his penis. "I suggest," Albert said, "that you attempt to make this last."

A smile. "If I can." And then the expression fell into something that held both fear and need. "Please don't stop, Albert."

"I won't stop." But, even after the repeated reassurance, it seemed Fletcher could not trust that Albert knew what Ash was asking for, let alone rely on Albert providing it. And Albert knew all too well that he deserved this lack of faith. "Come to bed," he suggested.

They each donned their robes, and walked hand in hand to the bedroom. It was warm enough – or they were hot enough – to push the blankets away, and meet each other's embrace on the sheets. Fletcher was unsettled with need and mistrust, so, with few preliminaries, Albert lay behind Ash, and pushed his penis into the man, pushed until he was fully engulfed. Because they were both so close to completion, he fitted Ash closer into his embrace, and then lay still.

Albert had only performed anal intercourse once in his life – just over a year ago, with Fletcher Ash – so, now that he let himself fully remember it, every unique sensation was vivid. The memory, combined with all the immediacy of the act, was almost enough to send him … Albert quickly decided to concentrate on the details.

Fletcher was no longer a virgin.

Last time, the grip of Fletcher's body on his was so tight as to mix equal parts pain and pleasure; this time, the feel was comfortable though firm, pleasure alone.

None of which detracted from the fact this act was ultimate.

Another man had been in this place, had taken from Fletcher what he had to give, what he loved to give. Amazing, that the physical results of such a brief relationship – which surely lasted only a few weeks, and happened some months ago – were still apparent. Perhaps not so amazing when Albert considered Ash's appetite for this act.

But that was in the past, and Albert could not regret anything of the past that led to this incredible sensation, this promising present, this hint of future.

Fletcher moaned, and stretched, and that was so close to bringing Albert to full satisfaction ... Albert had no wish to own Fletcher Ash, but he could not deny that this act brought with it all the joy of possession, an ignoble glorious victory.

Ultimate, even while holding perfectly still, poised in this ownership. Not the slightest move.

"It's all right," Fletcher said, his breath ragged; "you won't hurt me." Another timeless moment before he said with a laugh or a sob, "It doesn't hurt anymore."

"I know." And, because Fletcher needed to hear it, Albert continued, "I understand. The only reason I won't forgive you is that there is nothing to forgive."

"Thank you." A torn sigh, something of peace or relief in this fraught ultimate moment. "I thought maybe you didn't do it –" A pause for a shaky breath. "Because you couldn't bring yourself to hurt me. Physically, I mean. But he's done that for you, he did the hurting for you."

Albert took a moment to wonder how Fletcher developed these ridiculous convoluted ideas, but soon concentrated again on the here and now. The other man – Xavier Lachance was with them, but Albert could not consider him a threat, and felt no need to lay that presence to rest. After all, Rick was with them, too. And Albert knew the young man had been wrong: *Love isn't an emotion you feel, Ricardo,* he thought: *it is something you do. At its best, the word is a verb, not a noun.*

"Albert, please." Begging; a hand reaching back, trembling, to encourage progress.

"If I move now," Albert informed the man, "this will be over very quickly."

Genuine laughter. "Then move, Albert." A breath. "Don't make us wait any longer. Enjoy yourself. Rejoice in this. Let me hear how much you enjoy it!"

Impossible to do otherwise. Fletcher was looking back over his shoulder, those blue eyes hot and potent. Albert captured the man's mouth in a kiss, and as their lips and tongues meshed, Albert's body moved of its own accord, undulated in gentle primitive dance.

Infinitesimal, the movements, yet the orgasm that built within him, gathering momentum so that ripple grew to tidal wave in a moment – gentle, yet the orgasm was devastating. Dimly aware he'd freed Fletcher's mouth, Albert obeyed and let the sound of it roll and crash out of him – a long agonized wordless cry, as painful as releasing as laughter.

Aftermath of overwhelmed nerve endings readjusting to normality. Peace. And then somehow he relived it all without wishing to; the pleasure of it in retrospect clearer than the original tumult, if not as involving.

Fletcher was laughing, quietly and happily. "Love, that is the most beautiful sound I've ever heard."

Albert kissed him for a while, not withdrawing from the embrace, the penetration. He was still erect, the waves of pleasure refusing to fade.

"You've always been quiet when we've made love," Ash was saying. "I hope you start making some noise. Only if you want to, of course."

Time to satisfy Fletcher. Albert withdrew and moved to kneel between Ash's legs, took the man's penis into his mouth and sucked gently; he was rewarded with a groan, the inflection demanding more. Controlling Fletcher's attempts to push up by weighing one hand heavily on the man's hip, Albert carefully slipped the forefinger of his other hand into Fletcher's anus. The groan this time echoed the agony of his own cry. Albert slowly began a rhythm of thrusts, sliding his finger almost out and then fully in again.

"Just do that," Fletcher panted within moments. "Don't make me come yet."

Obediently withdrawing his mouth from Fletcher's genitals, Albert continued the rhythm for a while, watching the man buffeted by conflicting impulses – he bucked and tossed, wanting to thrust into the air in reaction – and he tried to hold himself still enough to allow this to continue.

"Damn you," Fletcher cried out. "That's too damned good."

Albert responded by pressing his finger in deeply, and exploring the rectal wall with his fingertip. He soon located his goal, and rubbed gently. Amusing to watch Ash's expression shift from surprise to great internal concentration to a bemused kind of pleasure.

"What the hell are you doing? Feels incredible."

"I am touching your prostate gland," Albert said very dryly.

"Really? What's that?"

"It is part of your reproductive organs, and contributes secretions to your semen. I understand that some men also use its sensitivity for sexual purposes." Albert left a pause before commenting, "I am surprised that Lachance didn't explore the notion with you."

"No, he missed that, missed out on that." Fletcher sounded distracted, which was perhaps understandable. "This one's all yours." After a moment, he continued, "Pleasure with Xavier was all over the place. What do you call it, diffuse. Pleasure with you can be the most precise, the most perfect experience."

Rather than reply directly, Albert bent his head and began to suck at Fletcher's penis, maintaining the careful internal caress.

"Yeah, make me come now, love, make me come now …"

It took the briefest of assaults to meet this demand. Within the space of a few beats, Ash's seed was spurting into his mouth, and the man was crying out. If Harley was awake, he'd be miserable.

"Devastation," Fletcher murmured once he'd quietened. "Absolute devastation." He reached to pull Albert up into a hug, and they held each other for a while. The night was country–dark and country–quiet. "That was incredible."

"I intended it to be."

"Idiot," Ash said fondly.

They began something new then; something that was familiar and safe, because this was Fletcher Ash, and Albert knew the man better than he knew himself; yet somehow different. They were crazed, forever moving, finding the closest possible embrace, and then shifting to discover something closer. Apparently Fletcher wanted to touch as much of Albert with as much of himself as possible – not just mouth and arms, but all of him. Luxury to take equal part in such an energetic embrace. No chance to control this maddened dance, and no wish to, even though at times they rolled to the edge of the bed. Somehow, between them, they transcended perfection and left it far behind.

"Love you," Fletcher was murmuring between kisses, "love you." For a moment they were on their sides face to face, then Fletcher pushed them over so that he sprawled across Albert, still moving. The hunger continued, though it seemed to encompass all of them both. Albert wondered if this sensation was what Ash meant by diffuse. They shifted, and shifted again, and now Albert gained ascendancy. "Love you. Fuck me again, Albert. Fuck me."

And the pleasure abruptly focused. "Yes." Refusing to be alarmed by how much he wanted this, Albert tried to get free of Fletcher's embrace, intent only on getting behind the man and seeking the ultimate.

"No, like this, Albert. Let's do it like this." Fletcher on his back looking up at Albert with those burning blue eyes, now lifting his legs so the tender skin inside his thighs caressed either side of Albert's waist.

Do you know how to do this? Albert couldn't voice the question, but it was apparently interpreted correctly. *Because I don't.*

"I'll show you, let me show you," Fletcher said. He smiled, completely shameless. "Hell, maybe you can find that gland again. And not with your finger."

Too provocative. "Do you require a pillow under your hips?" Albert asked, his tone too even to hide his excitement.

"Good thinking. You know, I love watching you learning on the job." Within moments they were both suitably arranged, and Albert was ready to enter the man. "Albert, love," Fletcher said, that smile lingering, "don't be gentle with me."

Albert found he had groaned at that. It was easy to decide, under the circumstances, to obey Ash, just this once. But before he indulged Ash, he decided to indulge himself: he bent his head and ran the flat of his tongue up the flame of hair in the middle of Fletcher's chest.

Indescribable, how it felt then, creating love like this with Fletcher Ash. Except that Ash tried to put it into words. At the height of it he cried out, for Peter and Harley and Beth and all the world to hear, "This is the truth! This is the truth."

◆

Albert woke to sunlight after a sleep so long and heavy he felt stunned. Ash was lying there, so deep in Albert's arms it seemed they would never part. But of course, after a lazy time of what Ash called cuddling, they did separate for a few minutes to each visit the bathroom. Ash said, "Come back to bed." And, when they were lying together, he said, "Let's do it again, love. Fuck me."

"I would have thought you'd be too uncomfortable."

"I'm all right. A little sore, but I'll be fine."

Absently stroking Ash's hair back from his forehead, Albert commented, "I believe that sex between men is illegal in Idaho."

"It's illegal in Virginia, too, but that never stopped us, did it?"

"We weren't annoying your brother when we were at my home."

Ash frowned at him. "Harley wouldn't turn us in."

"It's a possibility. Or he might inform the Bureau of our relationship; an anonymous letter would be enough to start an internal investigation."

"He wouldn't, Albert, I know he wouldn't. Sure, he's unhappy that I love you, but he won't do anything, let alone go outside the family about it. He's not the sort, and you should have figured that out by now." Silence for a long moment. "What's really bothering you, love?"

"Your propensity to use endearments." Albert suffered Ash's scrutiny as long as he could, and then said, "I do not intend to perform anal intercourse with you on a frequent basis."

"Why not?"

"There could be unfortunate medical consequences for you."

"You are so damned clinical, aren't you?" Ash grimaced. "Thank you for caring," he said with some sarcasm, "and for making the decision for me."

"I do not wish to cause you physical harm, as you have already pointed out."

"You can't tell me you don't enjoy it. You sure as hell enjoyed yourself last night."

"I did," Albert admitted, "and I know you did; and that is why I do intend to indulge you occasionally. But not frequently."

Ash was looking resentful and mutinous. "Then you'd better damned well do it again now, if you're going to make me wait for the next time."

A difficult silence stretched. Finally Albert said, "Fletcher."

That gained a little interest. "What?" Ash asked.

Impossible to say it: *I cannot have sex with you in this mood.* Albert settled in closer to the man, offered a gentle caress of his arm and shoulder, pressed a kiss to his throat.

Eventually the atmosphere eased, and Ash let out a chuckle. "How often?" he asked. "I know you, Albert, remember. How long are you going to make us wait for it? I bet you've got a schedule all figured out."

"I do, but I suspect that the anticipation and the surprise will add to your enjoyment, so I do not intend to tell you."

Ash was smiling now. "You rotten, conniving – No, insults are too good for you. I'll call you darling instead. You're despicable, sweetheart, and you don't deserve me loving you so much." The man pushed closer into Albert's embrace. Serious now, and intense: "Fuck me, lover. Fuck me because that's the truth, and we both adore it."

"Yes," said Albert, and he brought all his concentration to bear on the task.

The usual chaos over breakfast: noise and breadcrumbs and high spirits. Still, with all that going on, the Ashes rarely noticed Albert sitting quietly at the table, especially now the novelty had worn off of Frances providing him with a bread roll cut and buttered to his own specifications. Harley had finished making another round of hot drinks, and took a seat at the table with the children, Peter, Beth and Albert; only Fletcher remained standing, leaning a hip against one of the benches on the far side of the kitchen.

A rare moment of relative peace as everyone tried to decipher a story that Patrick was telling. And then Harley said, "Sit down, Fletch, and stop hovering. You're making me nervous."

"Don't know that I want to, actually," Fletcher said, adding a self–conscious chuckle. What with that, and the noise they had made the previous night and that morning, Ash could hardly have been more obvious if he tried. The adults all turned to look at Fletcher, who smiled with great embarrassed satisfaction. He explained, "I was just attempting to make the most of the situation. Albert's a tiger when he gets going. Unfortunately that means I really don't want to sit down just yet."

Peter, Beth and Harley – as one – turned to look at Albert.

"He's not a tiger!" Patrick exclaimed, smiling uncertainly as if he suspected someone was playing a joke on him.

Under this scrutiny of Ashes, Albert had no recourse but to slide on his dark glasses. "I suppose I should be grateful," he commented distantly, "that you are not likening me to a rabbit."

"A tiger …" Beth tried to stifle a giggle. "Harley, perhaps you should ask him what his secret is."

"Yeah, right," Harley said, dismissive and angry. He muttered in his brother's direction, "I can't believe you let him do that."

"Oh, I encourage it," Fletcher said airily. Then he added, "Albert, if you don't stop being so reasonable, all hell will break loose, because I will not be able to resist hugging you in front of Harley and the kids."

The issue of the children. The family had discussed the situation on the first evening the visitors arrived, once the children were safely in bed, and had stated that they had few reservations about Frances and Patrick knowing the nature of Fletcher and Albert's relationship. Seeing as that relationship must remain a secret, however, it was decided that the children shouldn't be told, as they would inevitably feel free to talk to any of their friends and acquaintances about it. Despite which, the family's jokes and Harley's snide remarks were becoming more and more transparent.

"Frances," Albert said, "may I have another bread roll?" And he suggested, "Don't pay any attention to your uncle Fletcher; he is playing word games. At times, as your father says, Fletcher tries to be too clever."

"Don't you like him playing word games?" the child asked.

"Sometimes it can be tiresome."

Peter said, very quietly, "Tiresome, troublesome, tormenting."

"Is he still your best friend even if he's tiresome?"

"I am afraid that he is," Albert told her. It seemed only fair to be as clear as possible with the child.

"You are begging for a hug," Fletcher warned him. Albert spared him a glance: Fletcher was beaming happily; an expression that Albert tried in vain to quell.

Peter was laughing. "Obviously it's not just chocolate cookies that make your eyes light up, Fletcher."

"No, Dad, there's a few other things, too."

"But you're going to have to get fit again, son: the other day you couldn't walk because of climbing mountains …"

"Yeah, and today I can't sit because I've been climbing molehills." And Ash promptly burst into laughter; after a surprised moment, Beth and Peter joined him.

Apparently still resenting Beth's advice to him in relation to tigers, Harley said sourly, "Well, it might be a molehill, but apparently he knows what to do with it."

"Thank you, Harley," Albert said urbanely.

The man seemed horrified by the realization that he had just complimented Albert: he dropped his head into his hands with an unhappy groan. Everyone else simply laughed even louder.

Albert decided it was more than time to extricate himself from the situation: he nodded a general farewell, headed out the back door, and walked down to the road.

Over the last few days, Albert had formed the habit of walking down to the town post office to collect the family's mail, and his own mail that he'd arranged to have forwarded. He welcomed the exercise and the solitude. Though he would never admit as much to Fletcher, Albert was even beginning to enjoy the attractive countryside that surrounded the Ashes' home, and took different routes each day in order to explore it. Of course, another reason for him to collect the mail was that he was expecting a letter from Elliott Meyer soon, and he wanted to avoid Fletcher's curiosity being reawakened.

"Albert!" It was Beth's voice, from some distance behind him. "Wait for me." Albert stopped by the side of the road, and examined the scenery. As she finally caught up with him, Beth commented, "You walk so fast, I thought I'd lost you."

"What did you want?"

"Well, I wanted to walk into town with you."

Not moving from where he stood, Albert offered, "If there is something you need to purchase, or a task you have to perform, perhaps I could do that for you."

"I wanted to talk with you, Albert. Spend some time with you." She tried unsuccessfully to meet his gaze. "You'd rather not, I suppose, but maybe you'll be a gentleman and let me insist?"

It seemed that he would have to, if he didn't want to mortally offend a member of Ash's precious family. Albert nodded once, and began walking again, slowing his pace a little.

It was some while before Beth began by saying, "If the object of your visit was for us to get to know you, Albert, I'm afraid we're failing to do that. Except for Peter, of course."

Albert said, very distantly, "The object was for Fletcher to have some time away from work."

"Time to heal?" Beth paused before continuing, "You really do care for him, don't you? Because you didn't make him choose between coming here and being with you. I realize that staying with us is difficult for you, because you're such a private person; Peter helped me see that." Another pause. "If Fletch hadn't needed to come here, would we ever have met you?"

"Fletcher being who he is, I suppose it was inevitable that you would eventually meet me."

"Yes," she said with a laugh, "he does know how to get his own way, doesn't he?" They turned from the side road onto the dirt path that ran beside the main road. Serious now, Beth said, "Something terrible happened, didn't it? Something terrible has happened to Fletch through his work."

"Yes," Albert said.

"But he won't talk about it, not even to Peter; and he's a talker like the rest of us, of course you know that. That's one of the reasons I fell in love with the Ashes, actually. Don't you think Fletch should talk about it?"

"Not if he chooses not to."

Beth sighed. "He always was very independent, even as a boy. And, frankly, most of the problems he's tried to talk to me about over the years, I haven't been able to help him with much; there's far more to Fletch than any of us really understand. But I hate to think of him dealing with whatever this was on his own."

In order to avoid Beth raising this with Fletcher directly, Albert said, "I believe he has discussed the situation with the people he feels might help. And he is capable of working through issues within himself."

"Yes." They reached the top of a rise, and saw the town spread in the valley below. Beth said, very casually, "You certainly seem like a permanent fixture in Fletch's life."

"We met nine years ago," Albert said.

"And you're planning to be around for all the years to come, right?" She seemed to have left her worry for Fletcher behind, because of or despite Albert's reassurance; perhaps she found that the easiest way of dealing with it. It seemed that Fletcher had been right: his family tended to be comfortable with him, with the obvious exception of Harley's unease about Fletcher's relationship with Albert; but there were certain topics that were avoided. Even their concern for what had happened to Fletcher wasn't enough to generate more than the most basic questions about Fletcher's work. Instead of Beth's worry now, there was this warm personal interest that Albert could happily do without. "The two of you are married, aren't you? So to speak."

Wishing he could simply deny this accusation, Albert searched for an acceptable answer. Eventually he said, "We haven't spoken."

"You mean you haven't made any promises? You haven't –"

"No."

"Not even talked it over?" Apparently Beth found this difficult to fathom. "It hardly matters, I guess. I mean, you're still a permanent fixture, aren't you, whether you've made a promise or not?"

Albert acquiesced with a nod, wanting to avoid any further questions.

"I hope so, because I can tell Fletcher's heart would break if he lost you."

The family seemed to share a penchant for curiosity and melodrama, Albert reflected, while maintaining a blank expression.

"I wanted to say," Beth was continuing, "if we haven't exactly made you welcome, I'm sorry. I mean me and Harley, of course; I know you and Peter are getting along fine. But Harley hasn't been very fair. We were talking about this last night. You know, Frances and Patrick are very comfortable around you, and they have good taste in people. Harley's just going to have to bow to their judgment."

"He is unlikely to do so, as the children are making a judgment based on a false idea of my relationship with Fletcher."

"Oh, I don't think it would make any difference to them if they knew. If anything, they'd like you even more. I wish we could tell them, actually, but I understand why you need to keep it a secret."

"At times Fletcher does not share that understanding."

Beth chuckled. "I bet he doesn't. He was always impatient with what he saw as lies and deceptions." They were drawing close to the first buildings in the town, and there would soon be people within earshot. Beth said, "I wanted to welcome you, Albert, and to tell you I look forward to all the difficult times ahead."

Albert nodded in acceptance of this.

"Fletch thrives on difficulties, you know," Beth said with some mischievousness, "and he's hit the jackpot with you, hasn't he?" She added, soberly, "I'm glad for you both: not everyone could put up with Fletch. I was beginning to worry that no one would."

And they turned into the post office with what Albert assumed were Beth's unspoken words between them: *Not everyone could put up with you, either.*

"Will you still love me," Fletcher asked, busily munching, "when I've put on twenty pounds due to Harley's cookies?"

"I have no idea why you assume I feel that way now," Albert informed him. "Or why, if I did, it would have anything to do with your weight." He was trying to concentrate on the forensic chemistry paper, with his work neatly arranged on the kitchen table, but Ash was making it difficult. He had put the children to bed over an hour ago, which Albert had assumed would result in peace and quiet: the assumption was wrong, however, because now Fletcher had no distractions.

"Harley's really out–doing himself, isn't he? What are these?"

"They appear to be cherries and macadamia nuts in a shortbread dough."

"Delicious. You know –" There was a pause, as if Fletcher had suddenly remembered something. Albert glanced up at him, but couldn't decipher the man's expression. "I had a dream last night," Ash eventually said.

As far as Albert was aware, Fletcher hadn't had a bad dream since John Garrett's death, so this development was disappointing. Albert also felt a little guilty, because he had not been aware of Ash dreaming, and had therefore not offered him any comfort. "You have never described these dreams to me," Albert said, though he would hardly be able to provide any useful analysis of them.

"I'll tell you this one," Fletcher offered with a laugh.

Albert looked up again, surprised. Apparently the dream had been good, or at least amusing, for Ash was soon laughing too much to stand up: he tottered over to land on one of the chairs, and propped his head in his hands and his elbows on the table. By the time he was able to talk – perhaps ten minutes later – Ash was so weak his head was on the table, and it was a wonder he hadn't fallen off the chair.

"It's the silliest dream," he said at last.

"That much is obvious."

Another giggle before Ash began a halting explanation, frequently interrupted by laughter. "I dreamed that you and Harley had a bake–off. There's Harley, all slapdash and covered in flour, asking, *How can Albert be creative, when all he does is follow a recipe?* And you're asking, *How can Harley achieve anything amidst all that chaos?* You tell him he shouldn't need to use every utensil in the kitchen just to make a simple pie. So all this threatening and boasting is going on, but the whole point is that if Harley wins, then he's going to tell you to never darken our doorstep again, and to keep your hands off his little brother. And you say, *I don't care about Fletcher; I just want to prove that I can bake a better pie than you.*"

"This amuses you, does it?" Albert asked.

Apparently it did, because Fletcher broke out into further paroxysms of laughter. Luckily, Peter, Harley and Beth walked in a few minutes later, having worked all evening at the diner. "What's the joke?" Beth asked.

Fletcher waved a weak hand at her in reply, and remained giggling on the table.

The family turned with puzzled frowns to Albert for an explanation: he raised his eyebrows, trying to convey the uselessness of attempting to understand Fletcher Ash. This was not wise, however, as Fletcher saw his expression, and laughed even harder.

Peter had made a round of tea before Fletcher calmed down enough to talk. Even then, he shook his head when any of the Ashes asked him to explain. All he said was, "Harley, I love this man, and you're just going to have to get used to the idea."

"Why?" Harley responded dryly. "Are you gonna giggle yourself to death if I don't?"

"Maybe." Fletcher sipped at his tea, occasionally smiling vaguely at Albert, while the others began to discuss the day's business. And finally Fletcher announced, "I'm exhausted. I'm going to bed."

Much to Albert's chagrin, the man planted a kiss on top of Albert's head on the way out. When Albert saw Harley looking unhappy, though, he recalled that defiance was a far better reaction than embarrassment, and he stared the man down.

A hopeless task, attempting to avoid Ash's curiosity.

Elliott's annual letter had finally arrived at the post office that morning; on his return to the house, Albert found himself alone, so took the letter into the living room. This in itself should have enabled him to read it undisturbed, as life here revolved around the kitchen. Before he had finished the third of five closely–written pages, however, Albert looked up to find that Fletcher had quietly entered the room. "How long have you been there?" Albert asked wearily.

"Long enough," Ash replied. "Who's the letter from?"

"Is that any of your business?"

Last time Albert had asked that question, Fletcher had immediately and honestly replied, *No.* This time, the silence indicated he thought otherwise. Fletcher drew closer, and said, "It's from the mysterious Elliott Meyer, isn't it? I remember he wrote to you this time last year. Does he write for your birthday?"

Anger roiled through Albert. If he spoke now it would be venomous.

"You don't share very much with me, Albert. You won't share anything of who you were before I met you, or anything outside of work and our relationship. Why not?" A brief silence in case Albert felt like replying, before Fletcher continued, "This Elliott Meyer; he must mean something personal to you. Otherwise you wouldn't be hiding him from me. I bet you haven't told him about me, either, have you? Is he family? Or a friend? Or –" Apparently a fresh idea occurred to Ash: "Was he your lover? Is that why you won't tell me about him?"

Albert grimaced at this. "Pay attention, Ash," he said bitterly; "I told you a few days ago that I have not had any lovers."

"Are you worried that I'll be jealous? Because I won't, or I'll try not to be. I'll understand, like you did."

"Sexual jealousy has nothing to do with this." The anger and the defensiveness were like acid inside of him, acid that had to be spat out. How to hurt this man? "Those men and women you were so curious about, those men and women who were not my lovers."

"Yes?" Ash prompted, eager to learn more, coming to kneel on the floor close by Albert's feet.

"They were prostitutes," Albert said. Pain lanced through him at this revelation: but an echoing pain pierced Ash, as well. "A series of one–off transactions, and nothing more. They were not lovers, and they would not be writing to me years later."

"I'm sorry," Fletcher whispered.

"What do you have to be sorry about?"

"I've hurt you."

"You should be used to doing that by now," Albert informed him. There was silence for a while. Grateful that Ash hadn't attempted to touch him, Albert sought to calm at least his exterior. He was aware that he had just lied to Ash: one–off transactions and nothing more did not cover the fact that Albert had found Ricardo again, and given him money, and responded to the young man's kiss. He was acutely aware that, if he had succumbed to the temptation of Rick's offer of sex, Albert would not have returned to the hotel room in time to assist Ash in dealing with John Garrett's body. None of this should be anything to feel guilty about, but that only added to his discomfort.

"This Elliott Meyer," Fletcher said gently. Albert glared, but that did not dissuade the man. "He must be one of your family or friends, then. Why won't you share him with me? Why won't you let me into the rest of your life, Albert?"

How to end this now, once and for all? "Because I left him behind over twenty years ago. Elliott is no longer a part of my life; he deludes himself in thinking otherwise. You will have to accept that, Ash."

The man appeared very reluctant.

"Fletcher," Albert tried. "You share my life as it currently is. That is more than I ever anticipated happening. It will have to be enough for you."

Reluctant and miserable. "I'm not really close with my family," Fletcher said. "We all love each other, but they don't understand me. Plenty of times, I unnerve them and they frustrate me. I only see them once a year, and I even put that off – or I used to before they had the kids, I try to see them more often now. But my family are there for me, and I'm there for them." The man looked at Albert very directly. "What

I'm trying to say is that I don't understand you completely breaking off ties to your family or your old friends, even if those ties were difficult."

"It doesn't matter whether you understand it. It only matters that you accept it."

"You are such a hard man," Ash murmured. He shivered a little, though it wasn't cold, and wrapped his arms around himself. "If you stopped loving me – or stopped wanting to love me, which is more to the point – would you be that implacable in breaking our relationship off?"

Apparently the man didn't require an answer, because after he searched Albert's face for a long moment, Ash stood and left the room.

It was a long while before Albert could return to Elliott's letter with even the pretense of composure.

Peter was obviously aware that Fletcher was unhappy with Albert at present; even so, Albert had found it easiest to sit up talking most of the night with Peter, sleeping for only a couple of hours, and getting out of bed again before Fletcher woke up. Fletcher finally joined them in the kitchen before Harley and the children returned from their walk. He said, "Morning, Dad. Albert," and headed for the coffee.

"Morning, Fletcher," Peter said. The silence lengthened, until Peter offered, "I've been thinking about why you two get along so well together."

Fletcher's reaction to this was an inelegant snort.

"I've really enjoyed my discussions with you, Albert. And, Fletcher, I know how much you love talking. The two of you must have some fascinating conversations."

That appeared to be Peter's advice: talk the unhappiness through; but both Fletcher and Albert knew that was unlikely to happen. Albert expected Fletcher to now inform his father of exactly why this was impossible, and perhaps to complain that Albert talked more to Peter than he ever had to Fletcher. Instead, Fletcher shared an ironic glance with Albert. "Yeah, we do, Dad," was all he said. "Fascinating."

Which did not mean that Albert was forgiven, or that Fletcher would let the issue of Elliott Meyer go.

Once Fletcher had finished his first cup of coffee, he stood and headed out of the room. When he came back in, he was carrying what appeared to be a photo. "I've got something for you, Dad," he said, and handed it over.

It was indeed a photo: a copy of the only one in existence of Fletcher and Albert. "That's lovely," Peter said. "Thank you."

After looking at it carefully, Peter lay the photo down on the table, and he and Fletcher examined it together. "This was a year ago, up in New England," Fletcher was explaining. "Sort of our honeymoon, I guess."

No, Albert reflected; he had not been forgiven.

"It was Fall, and of course the trees were magnificent, though it was early in the season. Really beautiful. Don't know why I spent so much time looking at Albert, come to think of it." This barb earned a guilty chuckle from Peter. "Anyway," Fletcher continued, "I got a tourist to take this with my camera, and Albert only stood still for it because he would have had to make a scene in front of all those strangers to get away."

"Is that why you're looking so mischievous?" Peter asked his son.

"Yeah, it's always been my life's ambition to look like that."

Albert did not have to look at the photo: he knew it by heart. Fletcher wasn't aware of this, but Albert kept a copy of it in his study, in the drawer with the photos of his parents. Right now, he felt like driving home – alone – and ripping the thing into pieces.

In it, Fletcher did indeed look mischievous; his expression was almost hidden by his wind–blown hair, but the gleam in his eyes and the manic grin could be clearly seen. His shoulders were hunched up; which meant that his hands had been stuffed into the front pockets of his jeans, though this could not be seen as the shot was only of their chests and faces. Albert was looking somewhere else entirely, and was patently annoyed. The blue sky behind them brought the viewer's attention back to Fletcher's bright eyes. Fletcher was in an off–white T–shirt and a denim jacket, and Albert was wearing a sage green knitted sweater over a white cotton shirt: the colors in the shot were harmonious. And it did seem a true representation of some essential part of each of the subjects. Perhaps, Albert admitted to himself, it was an adequate photograph; though that didn't mean he liked it.

"I'll have to buy a frame for it," Peter was saying. One of the kitchen shelves contained a few family photos, in different frames and haphazard arrangement: Peter was there now, propping this new one by a shot that appeared to be Fletcher as a teenager. "We'll treasure this, thank you both."

Fletcher wandered over there, too, and put an arm around his father. It seemed that Fletcher was looking at a shot of a woman whom Albert assumed was his mother. The woman exhibited both strength and humor, and while she wasn't pretty there was something unusual about her that might have been beautiful in life. "I still miss her," Fletcher said.

"Yes, son; I do, too." Peter asked, "What do you think she'd have made of Albert?"

They both turned to look at Albert, and Fletcher said, very confidently, "Oh, she'd have adored him." Peter and Fletcher laughed at this idea.

Albert rolled his eyes in exasperation, and went to collect the mail.

He was lucky enough not to be chased by Beth, or to meet Harley and the children on the way – but on his return, as he left the road, Albert was ambushed by Fletcher. "Come walk with me for a minute," the man asked. Seeing no reason not to that was worth the effort of arguing, Albert followed him around under the trees behind the house. "I'm sorry," Fletcher eventually said. "I shouldn't have made a fuss over your letter. I should learn to mind my own business."

"Yes," Albert said.

"I can't stop being curious, mind you; I'll probably keep asking questions. But I'll try to stop badgering you into replying. I'll try not to hurt you so much. All right?"

"If that is all you can offer."

Fletcher sighed. "For now, I guess that's the best I can do."

"All right."

"I want to kiss you," Fletcher said, "so I can feel whether you've forgiven me. But I won't impose. It's not exactly private here, I guess."

Albert glanced around: they were almost out of sight of the house, and the nearest neighbors were acres away. It required some courage, but perhaps Ash was worth it: Albert murmured, "Fletcher," and then, when he had the man's attention, Albert stepped closer and kissed him lightly on the mouth.

The reaction was beyond all proportion to the act: Fletcher seemed dazed and happy and quite beautiful. "Thank you," he said with quiet sincerity once Albert was done. "You have no idea how much that means to me."

Nodding once in acknowledgment, Albert led the way back to the house. They were only a few paces from the backyard, where Peter and Beth were sitting in the swing chair, and Harley was bouncing the basketball around.

"Harley, run and fetch Frances and Patrick," Peter cried with some excitement: "it seems we have fairies at the bottom of the garden."

More insane laughter from Beth, Peter and Fletcher. This was really getting monotonous.

Harley was looking disgusted. "Oh, please," he said.

Albert attempted not to wonder whether Peter had seen him kissing Fletcher: he had to work on the assumption that it didn't matter even if Peter had, though Albert felt his face burning at the thought. He went inside to fetch his hat and a kitchen chair, then held the door as Frances rushed out with a tray full of bread rolls, Patrick dancing along in her wake. It seemed the children had simply acted on the assumption that he would see the need to hold the door open, and that he would do so, which indicated a fair amount of trust in the world. Sooner or later, they would have to learn otherwise, though Albert did not feel it was his business to teach them. Distributing the mail, Albert tried not to meet anyone's gaze.

Even Patrick had two items of mail today: he ripped the envelopes open to reveal riotous cards. "When's my birthday?" he asked with a frown.

"Tomorrow, sweetheart," Beth said.

Albert carefully did not react, especially when Fletcher winked at him. It seemed that he shared a birthday with this child.

Luckily, Fletcher seemed willing to keep his promise of not mentioning the situation. Albert did not want to imagine the disaster of a double birthday party – though he was sure the idea would have occurred to Ash. For now, however, Fletcher was saying something that Albert was definitely pleased about: "I'm thinking of heading off soon, Dad. Albert and I were planning on doing some traveling, and then we have to get back to work."

"You're sure you're ready for work again, son?"

"Yeah, I will be. I've got a lot of tidying up to do on that case I was working on, and all sorts of other things to be getting on with. I'll be ready. You've all been wonderful." Fletcher smiled around at his family. "But, Harley, I'm not going until you give me a hug like you used to. A cuddle like you mean it. Because I have to know that you still love me."

A silence, with Harley uncomfortable in the middle of it.

"Doesn't have to be right now," Fletcher offered. "Just sometime soon. If you can."

"Guess I can," Harley muttered. "Might as well be now."

"Good." And Fletcher stood while Harley drew reluctantly near, and then the two brothers had their arms around each other. Even Albert could see when Harley finally relaxed into the embrace, and caught Fletcher up close. It appeared that everyone but Albert was moved by the spectacle. Fletcher murmured, "Love you, Harley."

"Love you, too," his brother replied. "Even if you are a fairy."

Fletcher chuckled. Patrick exclaimed, "He's not a fairy!"

Beth tickled the boy. "No, he's not. More word games, chicken."

Amidst the giggling, the declaration, "I'm not a chicken!" could be distinctly heard.

"Welcome to the family, tiger," Harley said to Albert, who did not deign to reply.

"Okay, now we've sorted that out, I guess I'll head off in a couple of days," said Fletcher. "But, Harley, I won't take Albert with me unless you hug him, too."

Judging from the man's expression, Albert suspected that Harley was as horrified by this idea as Albert himself was.

Fletcher, however, was laughing so hard he had to cling to his brother in order to stand up. "Only kidding!" he managed to say.

"Frances and Patrick," Harley said very solemnly, "come here and help me tickle your uncle, would you?"

Mayhem, as the four children of the family rolled to and fro in the dirt shrieking. Albert sighed, and concentrated on his mail.

"Happy birthday, love," Fletcher murmured once he was half awake. He tried for a sleepy kiss and then, because Fletcher seemed to expect it, Albert initiated some undemanding sex. It was a pleasant enough way to begin what would no doubt prove to be a difficult day.

Breakfast was even more chaotic than usual, with shreds of wrapping paper amidst the breadcrumbs: Patrick was given a number of presents from the family. On behalf of Albert and himself, Fletcher had bought the child a range of colorful toys for the bath, which he seemed happy with. Patrick thanked Fletcher with a hug and a kiss, and shook hands very solemnly with Albert.

On his return from the post office, Albert discovered that Fletcher was in the shower, so he sat down to wait for him in their bedroom. There was something he had been planning to do for a few weeks now, and even though he was still annoyed with Fletcher, Albert intended to see it through. The annoyance, tinged with self–righteousness, at least helped to quell any residual fear.

"Escaping from the mayhem?" Ash asked when he arrived, wrapped only in a towel which he soon dropped. Fletcher didn't seem to expect an answer to his question: he simply began dressing, disrupting all his clothes before finding those he wanted. "Can't say as I blame you. Did you know they're having a few of Patrick's friends over to the diner this afternoon for a party? What do you say to the two of us skipping that and driving somewhere, doing some sightseeing? Even I'm not keen on the thought of coping with ten screaming three–year–olds."

"That would be fine." When the man seemed as organized as he ever was in the mornings, Albert said, "Come here, Ash."

"What is it?" Ash sat beside Albert on the bed. "I'd better confess right now that I don't have your birthday present yet. I know exactly what I want to get you, but they don't sell the damned things here in town. Maybe we can find one this afternoon, if we combine some shopping in the city with some sightseeing."

"That doesn't matter," Albert said. "There is something I wanted to show you. Share with you," he amended. "I've been planning to do this since we were last in Washington, Ash, so don't assume your tantrum the other day had any useful result."

Fletcher frowned at him. "I'm not to hassle you about Elliott Meyer again: I've got the message already. Go on."

Albert drew a photograph out of his briefcase, and held it for the other man to see. "Fletcher," he said very formally, "these are my parents, Miles and Rebecca." Not that he wanted this to sound like an introduction, but Albert hadn't been able to think of any better way of saying it.

Ash was gaping in surprise; staring at the photo with incomprehension. "Albert, love," he finally whispered.

More difficult than he'd feared, to share this precious fragile memory. "That, of course, is me as a child. I understand this was taken in 1949, when I was two years old."

Stunned silence for a further moment. "Albert, I can't believe you're showing me this. Thank you." Attention finally focusing on the photo, Ash continued, "They were beautiful, love. Did they feel they had to look solemn for the camera? Or were they serious people? They seem kind of strong and decent. How old would they have been?"

"Rebecca was thirty–four and Miles was thirty–three when this photo was taken, and they died three years later. They were Jews born in Europe who survived the Second World War, Fletcher, and who helped others survive: they were rarely happy, but I believe they were content."

"I understand," Ash said. "They must have seen some terrible things, probably lost a lot of people they loved." Then he added, "They died in 1952? That's the year I was born."

"Irrelevant," Albert declared before Ash could say anything more. It would be just like the man to see something of significance in that coincidence.

"What sort of work did they do?"

Rather than answer, Albert passed over the newspaper article that had been published only days before they died. It described, fairly succinctly, the uses to which Miles and Rebecca had put their time, energy and wealth while he had known them.

Fletcher read it through twice. "They were fine people, Albert." He was nodding, mulling over all this information. "Sounds like the reporter didn't know what to make of them, do you think? He doesn't sound overly impressed. But they must have been fine, strong, generous people to do these things."

"Yes." Albert passed the other photo over, beginning to feel that this may not have been such a disastrous idea.

"This was the soup kitchen, right? And that's you, reading a book – you even look like you. Were you about five then?"

"Yes."

"I didn't start looking like me until I was twelve." Fletcher paused. "They were wonderful people, love; and you're wonderful, too. They must have given you a great start in life. I'm sure they'd be proud of you now."

Albert shrugged this off as needlessly sentimental.

"I still can't quite believe – Why are you doing this, Albert? You were so angry at me for prying about Elliott Meyer, you're still angry, and despite that you share this with me."

"I'm not doing this because you deserve it," Albert told him; "I'm doing this because it seemed the right thing to do. I trust you won't make me regret it."

"But I don't understand."

"I do not require you to understand."

"Just to accept it, right?" Fletcher offered, "I really appreciate it, far more than I can ever tell you. You can trust me – I won't hurt you because I know more about you."

"But you will hurt me, Fletcher," Albert said flatly. "It is inevitable."

"Never maliciously. I love you, Albert. I think you're as fine as Rebecca and Miles were."

"All right, Ash," Albert said impatiently.

A few minutes of welcome silence as Fletcher took in every detail of the photos and the article, as if he suspected that he'd never see them again. Feeling something that might be contentment – letting himself feel it, though it required an inordinate amount of trust – Albert slid an arm around Ash's waist. "Love you," the younger man said absently, reaching an arm to hug Albert's shoulders.

"Fletcher," Albert said. And, when the man looked up, Albert kissed him.

"That was beautiful," Ash whispered afterwards. "That was a beautiful kiss, and do you have any damned idea what all this means to me?"

"I am afraid that I do."

"Miles and Rebecca – would they have liked me? I wish I could have met them. Would they have approved of us being together?"

"Perhaps," said Albert. Other than the significance of this act, to both Ash and himself, there was something else that Albert feared: his understanding of who his parents were was fragile after the decades without them; and any speculation, any interpretation that Ash offered, any of Albert's memories being reduced to words, might be terribly wrong; even the photos on fresh examination might reveal something different to what he knew. But the truth was that he had asked himself the same question that Fletcher asked now. Albert relented, and said, "I have no reason to think they wouldn't have approved. I believe one of their close friends in Europe was homosexual."

"I'm glad. Because I love you, and I know that you love me, and you're absolutely stuck with me now, till death do us part."

"There is no need for melodrama, Fletcher." Albert put the photos and the newspaper clipping safely on the bedside table, then wove his fingers into the damp wilderness of Fletcher's dark hair; and he kissed the man again, merely as a way of keeping him quiet. But the kiss was indeed beautiful, and Albert soon decided to initiate something more that he wanted. Fletcher seemed rather amenable to the idea.

EPILOGUE
IDAHO
OCTOBER 1985

Albert stood on the bare dirt out the back of the Ash family home. He was alone; everyone else was at the diner in town. Everything was very quiet, except for a breeze rustling through the trees that surrounded the place. Even the sunshine felt mild. Albert stood with the basketball in his hands, contemplating the hoop attached askew to the wall of the shed.

He had never thrown a ball before but figured that it all came down to physics. In his mind he plotted vectors of force, and various trajectories. Surely it couldn't be too hard to do this thing; hopefully he wouldn't humiliate himself in the attempt. He could visualize a dotted line making a perfect curve from his hands, across blue sky and wood weathered grey, to the metal hoop. He could see that but for some illogical reason, there were no guarantees the ball would follow it.

Finally Albert asked himself what Fletcher's advice would be. Perhaps something like, *Trust yourself, trust your instincts, and just throw the damned thing.* That, Albert had to admit, made some sense under the circumstances.

Albert took a deep breath and glanced around to reassure himself there were no witnesses. He lifted the ball to just in front of his chest, as he'd seen Fletcher and Harley do, and closed his eyes for a moment to help clear any extraneous thoughts.

When he opened his eyes again, Albert focused on the hoop, took another breath – and he threw the damned thing.

ABOUT JULIE BOZZA

I was born in England and lived most of my life in Australia before returning to the UK a few years ago; my dual nationality means that I am often a bit too cheeky, but will always apologize for it.

I have been writing fiction for almost thirty years, mostly for the enjoyment of myself and my friends, but writing is my love and my vocation so of course that's where my dreams and ambitions are. In the meantime, technical writing helps to pay the mortgage, while I also have fun with web design, reading, watching movies and television, knitting, and imbibing espresso.

If you would like to know more, please come and join the conversation at juliebozza.com

CPSIA information can be obtained at www.ICGtesting.com
Printed in the USA
LVOW04s1014040215

425517LV00043B/1638/P